PAVEL'S

GIFT

Pavel's Gift

Spiderwize
Remus House
Coltsfoot Drive
Woodston
Peterborough
PE2 9BF

www.spiderwize.com

A CIP catalogue record for this book is available from the British Library.

ISBN: 978-1-911596-39-4

PAVEL'S GIFT

LAWRENCE BELL

For my Sister

With special thanks to Collin McMorris and Annie Crook for their valuable time and assistance.

CHAPTER 1

It was a cool, bright April morning and John Lawton stretched in his bed and yawned. It was another day and it had all the possibilities of being a good one.

He slowly glanced over to the bedroom window and saw the yellow tinge from the sun as it seeped through his bedroom curtains and that was always a good sign.

John always woke around six o'clock. Always, give or take a minute or two, it was his habit.

It had been daylight for about an hour and as he lay there he listened intently above his wife's steady sleeping breath for the questionable sound of the rain, and there was none. And that pleased him, because John Lawton was a builder and for all of his working life the weather had been crucial to each and every day. It was either an enemy, a friend, or just a plain nuisance. And for all of his working life he'd worked every job around the weather, in reality so did a lot of other people in a lot of other jobs, but that's the price of living in England.

John gave a final yawn as he slid out of bed. He turned and gave his wife a discerning look and then went into the bathroom to shower and start his day.

Half an hour later he was downstairs drinking a good cup of tea and eating his usual two slices of toast and marmalade. He did this most mornings as he sat there contemplating the day ahead and he considered why his own brew always tasted better than any cup of tea anyone else made for him and that included his wife.

He kept his eye on the time and when the tea and the toast were finally consumed he went over to the fridge and took out the sandwiches which were his lunch. His wife made him the same sandwiches every day, they would be either ham salad or cheese salad and John smiled. 'Nice one love,' he thought to himself, as he did most mornings.

Then he went to check the house as usual to make sure that everything was in its place.

The vacuum cleaner had to be put under the stairs, the cups and saucers and plates at the side of the sink and the toaster and kettle placed side by side, always side by side.

Then once again John went back upstairs to the bathroom to make sure that there were no towels on the floor and that there was toilet paper in the holder. The soap and the shower gel were in the right place and the tooth brushes were correctly in the holder with the toothpaste placed right at the side of them. John's toothbrush was as ever on the left and his wife's on the right. Everything was where it was supposed to be, his wife liked it like that, of course she did.

He very quietly looked into their bedroom again, she was still asleep and John was glad of that. If she'd stirred or had been awake he would have made her a cup of tea and then brought the cup of tea up to her in bed. But he knew that she didn't really didn't care for that, for her it was more fuss than it was worth. And some mornings he wondered if she really was asleep and sometimes he wondered if she was just pretending, waiting for him to leave the house.

But there was nothing he could do about that.

He looked around the house and it was immaculate. Neat and tidy and everything perfectly in its place as usual, and he knew that she would be pleased. That was the way John and Sarah Lawton lived their life and they liked to think that they were organised.

Well you had to be, didn't you?

If things weren't in their right place his wife got upset and it was rather distressing for her. So John made sure that everything was just perfect, it simply made his life easier if she was happy. And John loved his wife, so every morning he made sure that everything was just as she liked it and then he could go off to work knowing there would be no problems back at home.

It wasn't that his wife was awkward in any way or that she was especially 'fussy' that made him do all of these things every morning, although she could definitely have her moments.

No, the simple reason why John Lawton had to be so organised every day was that his wife, Sarah, was blind.

The problem had originally started ten years earlier. Sarah Lawton began to suffer from bad eyesight and was having difficulty with her vision. Naturally, like everyone else, she considered that she probably needed glasses. She'd just turned fifty and that was something else that she wasn't really happy about either. And now 'glasses' which for her was another admission of her age and an aggravating reminder that the 'clock' was forever ticking.

The 'fifty' thing had got to her slightly. She'd discussed it with her friends and they'd not been very happy at turning fifty either as they too realised that they were now what was termed as 'on the other side of the fence'. And there was also the unfairness of it all. A fifty year old man was still in his prime and had promise, but for a woman it seemed to be all about trying to retain your looks and having to 'watch your back' in case a younger model came along. And so, Sarah and her friends would meet up once or twice a week and they would all sit together and talk about holidays and restaurants and dieting as they passed around the chocolate cake and the creamy cappuccino coffees.

The other topic of conversation was of course their children. And it was always something that Sarah felt slightly excluded from. In Sarah's life, there were no children. And when she and her friends used to meet up, the other women would continually and singularly promote the importance of their own particular child or children and they would give regular updates of how well young Jimmy or Johnny or Suzy were doing at school or at cricket or acting, or whatever.

It was almost a 'pecking order' sort of thing. The success of the child was obviously a reflection of the mother's never ending care and hard work. And that accomplishment alone would let you climb another 'rung' on your own personal ladder. But there was no such ladder for Sarah. During those conversations she would just sit there with her friends and feign interest and nod inanely with wide eyed agreement as the women chattered away about the continuing achievements of their offspring. Sarah had always felt left out and at the back of her mind she felt bitter at being excluded from those particular conversations. She almost considered it a personal cruelty, surely they all realised her position and her history.

She and John once did have a child, a beautiful child. It was after two dreadful miscarriages that Sarah finally became pregnant once again and this time she went full term.

But seven months into the pregnancy and after tests, the doctors realised that there was something disturbingly wrong. Once this was discovered, the doctors had sat with John and Sarah and warned them that all was not well with the baby and then finally they were told that they should expect the worst.

Two months later their baby, a little girl, was finally born and she was straightaway put into an incubator.

Their little girl never came out of the hospital and for three months, three months of heartbreaking agony and desperation, she hung onto her precious little life. John and Sarah named her Louise and they stood and watched her every day for the three short months that she lived. And they waited, readying themselves in silence for the inevitable crushing blow.

In the final hours of their precious child's life, Sarah held little Louise in her arms and she and John watched as their baby daughter just faded away.

There was a small grave in the corner of the local cemetery that John and Sarah visited every week. They always took with them a small posy of fresh flowers and sometimes a toy. And they laid them at the side of the small white marble cross that carried the simple engraved inscription...'Our Louise'.

There would be no more children.

It was just one of life's nasty little tricks.

And then there was another, and that was Sarah's vision.

After a trip to the optician, she started to wear glasses, which were soon to be replaced by different pairs with stronger lenses. At one point she gave contact lenses a try but they turned out to be quite useless. So from there she and John discussed some kind of Laser surgery, it was supposed to be a tried and tested procedure. And it was during her initial examination at the Laser surgery clinic that she was informed that there was a problem with her eyesight, a problem that was beyond the clinic's facilities. She was recommended to go and see her doctor, which she did and he in turn referred her to a specialist. However, Sarah's declining vision turned out to be something beyond that specialist's particular knowledge and it was certainly beyond the usual antibiotics and painkillers that he regularly administered to his patients. There were trips to different specialists and then repeated visits to a private clinic. Finally they were given a result, or at least a diagnosis. It seemed that Sarah was suffering from a rare form of something called 'Severe Macular Degeneration'.

It was an aggravated form of the complaint, very aggravated and one of those things that only 'one in three million people' suffer from and Sarah was the one in those three million.

The specialist, a 'Dr Ramos', sat with them both in his office and explained to them that within a year or at the most two years, Sarah would lose her sight. Total blindness.

There was no treatment in her case and there would be no remedies.

After several questions and quite a bit of upset, John and Sarah thanked the doctor for his time and his help and then they both went home to discuss their future.

Dr Ramos had been right and within twelve months Sarah's vision had deteriorated badly.

Another year passed and by then she was totally blind.

Fortunately, John and Sarah were a strong and loving couple and they'd discussed everything and talked about how they were going to handle things.

And yes, they would manage.

But Sarah began to feel vulnerable. She was offered tuition on how to get around using a white walking stick, but she fell badly a couple of times and it affected her confidence. In the end she would only go with John or with her close friends, but that too became another matter.

The one thing that hurt Sarah more than anything else was that her circle of 'social' friends started to slowly and steadily disappear. The phone began to ring less and less as her vision declined and the invites to the regular coffee mornings seemed to wane as her circle of so called friends became somewhat smaller. In the end she was regularly visited by just two of her lifelong friends and it was at that point she realised that the ladies who she had once considered as 'her group', were really no more than just a set of acquaintances. Sarah knew of course that her two remaining friends still met up with the others for their regular coffee mornings, but she retained her dignity and made the decision never to ask.

So, that morning John Lawton quietly left his house. He carefully closed the front door and got into his car and then set off for work. It would take him around an hour to get there. John was originally a bricklayer by trade, or used to be a bricklayer by trade. Times had changed in the building trade and John wasn't building anymore, he was demolishing. House building in general had come to a difficult end around four years before as yet another recession had kicked in. There was as usual a shortage of money and with it and with the same tedious regularity, the banks and building societies had decided to stop handing out mortgages to all but the wealthy. House building had screeched to a dramatic halt and had left thousands of tradesmen scratching their heads and wondering what on earth to do next.

John had been lucky, he'd been in the building business a long time and he knew the game. Over the years he'd made a lot of contacts and was generally very well thought of. In the past he'd known and had dealings with a man called Peter Ainsworth and Peter Ainsworth was now the site manager of Connell Construction and Civil Engineers, a huge company.

John had made a phone call to Peter Ainsworth and had laid his cards plainly on the table. Peter Ainsworth had remembered John Lawton of course, and he knew that John was a good and very reliable worker. It was also a fact that on one disastrous occasion, it had been John Lawton who had helped him solve a major problem and had saved Peter Ainsworth a lot of embarrassment and quite possibly his job.

John Lawton was a good man to have around and Peter Ainsworth was, to a point, more than slightly in his debt.

So thankfully, it was Peter Ainsworth who had found him work. There was no construction work at that particular moment, in fact there was no house building at all. Peter Ainsworth had explained that to John, but Connells had just won a huge civil contract to build a brand new road. The road was going to be named the 'A 800' and would be a twenty mile stretch of 'A' road that would completely circumnavigate the City of Manchester. The A 800 would alleviate traffic chaos and would also give direct access to all the main motorways. Millions of pounds were involved and huge areas of land had to be cleared. And not only open land, there were also all the houses, those many houses that were 'in the way' and in the way of so-called 'progress'. Those same houses would be acquired by the government under the 'compulsory purchase scheme', which in effect meant that the government had the right to buy them from the owners, whether those owners wanted to sell them or not. Those same houses would then of course be demolished, but that in itself threw up another set of problems. Ecology ruled and it wasn't just a matter of just driving a bulldozer through them. These were different times and different days. The power sources, the gas and electricity, all had to be individually shut down, it was a legal requirement. There was also the matter of the water supply and the drains, the new environmental laws required that each and every property would have to be individually switched off and sealed. Everything would have to be inspected and reports would have to be written and filed. It was a huge enterprise and an enterprise that Peter Ainsworth and Connell Construction certainly didn't want tying up with 'red tape'. If all these properties had to be closed down, and to a definite system, it would have to be a system that ran smoothly and efficiently. In any new project there would always be hiccups of course, and there would be many inconveniencies and minor problems, because there always were.

And it had struck Peter Ainsworth that John Lawton with his vast experience of the building trade could possibly be the right man for the job. John Lawton was a man with a level head who could solve those little problems and all those little hiccups.

So John was given the position of 'demolition manager' on one of the first of many sites.

The job suited him and he was grateful for the work, very grateful. John had to 'cut his teeth' on his first site and he soon understood and recognized how to get the job done quickly and efficiently. By his own admission, John was also a 'hands on' sort of man and he liked to be physically involved with the job. However, he also appreciated that he was rapidly heading for his sixtieth year and was no longer capable of taking on heavy labouring, not all day and every day, not anymore. And though the job did involve some physical work, John had management skills to hone and a great deal of paper work to do, but he'd gotten to grips with the system and had quickly taken onboard exactly what needed doing. From that first site, John had been moved on a few times, usually to take charge of some failing project, which he'd returned to schedule.

The closure of each individual house required the disconnection of all power sources and the stopping and sealing up of the water supply, sewers and drainage. Once he'd personally inspected the work, he would produce a written report and then call in the Inspectors, both Council and Environmental. They in turn would inspect the designated property or properties and then usually give the 'O.K' and sign the appropriate paperwork.

Then, and only then, could the properties be demolished, and in reality even after that the dwellings were not just flattened. The new Ecology and Reclamation Laws meant that nothing was to be wasted. The houses had to be taken down in stages, bit by bit and section by section and all the materials reclaimed, to be used again wherever necessary.

First of all they would take down the roofs. The tiles or slates would all be stacked separately and taken away, along with the wooden rafters and the beams. In fact anything at all made out of wood had to be systematically removed, all was re-usable or recyclable in one way or another. Even the waste wood could be ground down and sent off in huge containers to be burned at the nearest power stations.

No wastage at all, that was the new rule.

Eventually the bulldozers would be called in and the empty shells of the remaining houses would be knocked down. Then one of the brick reclamation companies would take away the old bricks for cleaning. When all that was done there would be nothing left, nothing more than a piece of bare land and the remaining thin skeletons of the old foundations.

And so, on that same morning and approximately one hour after leaving his home, John turned his car into an empty and deserted housing estate, which was at that moment John's place of work. It was quite a small estate really, only about fifty or sixty houses and as estates go it wasn't really that old. Built in the early nineties, the 'Meadows Estate' was hardly showing any signs of urban decay at all. The brickwork on the properties was excellent and most of the houses had modern windows and doors, all of good quality. Even the gardens were in good order, in fact most of them only needed a good mowing and a bit of weeding and they would have been back to normal. In fact, anyone at all could have moved right back into almost any house on the estate without much of an issue because most of the properties were pristine.

The only problem was...that those houses were in the wrong place.

Slap bang in the middle of the proposed route for the new 'A 800', the Meadows Estate was unfortunately a 'rock in a hard place'.

The residents had only become aware of the government's decision for the new road when they each received a letter from the Council telling them about the planned proposal and the result of that decision was they would all have to move out. They would be given further notification from the Council, who would liaise with the appropriate government department in regard to the compulsory purchase of their properties and in particular, further information regarding the calculation of 'adequate and fair' compensation.

The residents of the Meadows estate were of course stunned and to a great extent astounded. Then they were angry and then they got together and formed a resident's association and then of course, a committee. They called on their local councillors for help and then lobbied an M.P. But it was a waste of time, just a complete waste of everybody's time. Officialdom, in the form of their Councillors and their local M.P actually wanted the road. Not through their own home or their back garden of course, but then again, it wasn't was it?

So the plans were formally agreed, passed and stamped. It turned out that the 'The Meadows Estate' was actually going to become a huge roundabout.

There was great disappointment and highly charged emotion on the estate, some of the residents talked about barricades and even sabotage was considered. But, being British, nothing much happened and when the dust finally settled, everybody just moaned despondently, took their compensation and eventually shuffled off.

John was the first to arrive that morning. He was always the first to arrive. He'd taken this job onboard and was totally committed to it because he had to be. This was his fifth project and his fifth clearance for Connells Ltd. His first had been a row of old terraced cottages and on that first clearance he'd recognised and understood the system of 'close down' and the demolition process, and he'd understood the procedure and also the paperwork involved. It had been a personal success for him and a learning curve. John realised that all he had to do was repeat that same process wherever they sent him and everyone would be happy, especially his boss Mr Peter Ainsworth. And if everyone was happy, John knew that his job at Connells would be secure. Happy bosses meant continuance and for John, who was now fifty nine years old, it meant that he could continue to work on this huge project and for Connells all the way until retirement. And it wasn't heavy physical work, he had younger men working for him who could do all the heavy stuff and that suited John Lawton down to the ground.

So John arrived that morning and it looked as though it was going to be a nice day. The sun was shining and the birds were chirping away merrily. Well they would be, they had an estate full of empty gardens all to themselves. John parked at the side of his mobile office, got out of his car and stretched, then he went to unlock the office door and once inside he filled the kettle with water. It was his daily routine, he'd make a brew and then survey the work for the day ahead. This was his favourite time of the day and it would be about an hour before his 'lads' would arrive. With a mug of tea in his hand, he wandered around the site and inspected the work in hand. He also made sure just where 'his team' were up to as he checked out which properties were next in line for closure and demolition.

Some mornings he would take a chair from his office and go and sit in one of the back gardens. If the sun was shining it was very pleasant, almost therapeutic. He would sit there on his own and look at the empty house and the garden and wonder about its history and who had actually lived there. And he wondered about the people, the owners of these houses and how they'd lived their lives. Each house must have its own story to tell, the happy times and the bad. And he wondered how those people must have felt when they found out that they had to leave their cherished homes. John was sorry about that and it left him feeling a little guilty.

The 'Meadows' was a lovely little estate and John could have easily lived there himself, the houses were well cared for and so were the gardens and John would begin think about his own home and then his thoughts would eventually turn to Sarah, poor Sarah, his darling wife and he wondered about their future and about the subject that both of them had never discussed. What was going to happen to her, if and when John died. And he wondered and he worried about how she would cope and he knew that at some time they would both have to sit down and they would have to talk about it.

But that was for another day and this was another morning and so after his inspection John went back into his office and refilled his mug of tea and then went to sit outside in the early morning sunshine to read his files and check more of his paperwork.

Within the hour the rest of his team had turned up. They were four younger men and they ranged in age from nineteen to forty and John called them 'his lads'. He knew the importance of teamwork and he looked after them. They too slotted into the equation, his team of men were the tools that made the job work. He knew the strengths and the weaknesses of the four men who worked for him, he knew their likes and dislikes and more importantly he recognised their preferences. They were all big strong lads and John organized them by using a constantly repeated system. Everybody played their part and everybody knew what they had to do, but more importantly, everyone knew what the others were doing.

One of the men would start on the roof work and the rafters. Another would remove all the timber from inside the properties as the other two men worked on the electrics and the pipe work. One man sorted out the gas and the electricity and the removal of all the cables and wire along with the gas piping. The other was in charge of water, the sealing of the drains and the removal of all water bound pipe work. Everything was for reclamation, those were the new rules. Once all that was done, the whole team would work together on the final demolition and the brick clearance, then they could start on the next property. Everybody was happy with what they did because it was an efficient and repetitive process and it didn't tax the brain. And in truth, John didn't want 'his lads' to have to think, he just wanted them to get on with the job. He would do all of the thinking. John would oversee the project and step in whenever he was needed. Everything ran like clockwork and the system worked well, really well. And Peter Ainsworth and the bosses at Connells Ltd had realised that and appreciated it.

So the 'lads' finally arrived and parked their cars and straightaway went into the office to make their early morning brews. They came out of the office and into the morning sunshine with four mugs of tea and started their usual banter. They were 'easy' with the job and they were happy because it was good, steady work. John had his usual chit chat with them, the weather, the traffic, their wives and their lives and eventually things turned to the day's work. Things were going well. Yes, nice and steady.

That morning, John's roofer was ready to start working on the next house, he was always the first man to start on the demolition of the following property. After the roof was taken off everybody else could take over from there. The roofer would start his work as the other lads were finishing off the previous property.

As they stood there drinking their tea and talking, John looked at his roofer and studied him for a moment. There was the incessant yawning and John noticed the slightly red eyes, and as he watched him closely John noticed that the roofer's mug of tea was shaking slightly in his hand.

John knew that he had to speak to him.

'On the beer last night were we?' John asked.

The other lads laughed. They all knew, they could all smell the alcohol on the man's breath.

'God help us,' continued John light heartedly, 'look at the state of you man.'

'Sorry Boss,' said the roofer, 'I met up with my brother for a pint and things got a bit carried away, I'm sorry,' he said and was more than little embarrassed.

John quickly summed up the situation 'Right then, well I'd better give you hand on starting that new roof. Or you'll be falling off the bloody ladder.'

The other lads laughed and they appreciated it. John was a good boss and a good man to work for and because of that reason alone they worked hard for him. It was all about respect. John Lawton wasn't like some of the other fools that they'd had to suffer.

'Cheers Boss,' the roofer replied and he smiled and tried to brighten himself up a bit.

They finished the mugs of tea and started their work. John sorted out some paperwork and made a few phone calls and within half an hour he came out of his office and as promised, he climbed up the ladder onto the roof to give his man a welcome hand. The roofer was suffering. A hangover and bright sunshine do not mix, especially if you have to work at the same time.

John looked at him and shook his head 'You don't look well' he said.

'Never again,' replied the roofer.

'Yeah...right,' said John. He'd heard it all before, of course he had.

So together they set to work on the roof.

Once they'd removed some of the roof tiles and stripped back the roofing felt, John had his roofer start on the beams and the rafters. John carried on stripping the tiles and the remaining felt from the roof. It was the more precarious job and John wasn't entirely wrong when he'd joked about his roofer possibly 'falling off' the ladder.

They'd worked steadily all morning and at ten o' clock they stopped for a well earned break.

'How's he doing Boss?' asked one of the other lads and they all smiled, except for the roofer.

'I could get more work out of his wife,' said John. He laughed and so did the rest of the men.

The roofer shrugged his shoulders and grinned back at them all 'I know... I know...' he said.

It wasn't an issue, alcohol wasn't generally a problem with his team and John knew that and so he would let it go, this time. After their short break, they all went back to work.

At a quarter to twelve, John looked across at his long suffering roofer.

'Go and get your lunch,' he said to the man, 'I'll finish off here.'

The roofer looked back obligingly 'Thanks Boss,' he said and he scuttled off down the ladder. He would have an early lunch and possibly a quick half hour in his car to 'sleep it all off'.

John carried on, he had the last of the roof tiles to take off and there was another hour's work to do. He decided that he'd carry on whilst the lads had their lunch and let them talk amongst themselves. After that, the roofer could come back and finish his own work off.

John had done enough.

So he carried on and as he worked he looked down and watched his men as they finished their own work and then went to sit at the table outside the office and start their lunch. They appreciated the sunshine and the good weather. They were a good team.

John was just starting to lift the last three rows of tiles. Taking a claw hammer, he pulled out the nails which held the tiles onto the rafters. Once the tiles were freed he would take them down the steps and stack them in piles on the main beams below, ready to be taken away and recycled. He was on the third set of tiles when he took his hammer and again pulled out the fixing nails. As he lifted the first tile he suddenly stopped and looked down and there on the rafter in front of him was a small parcel, it was actually nailed to the rafter, nailed there and tied tightly with a length green string or some sort of coarse green twine. John looked down at the parcel and frowned, he was puzzled by it. He looked at the parcel and studied it for a moment. Somebody had nailed it there and for what purpose, and what was it? It could be something or nothing, something trivial or something silly and stupid. It could have been be some rubbish, maybe it was a kiddie's toy, a toy that a child had hidden.

Then John considered the fact that someone had climbed into the loft space and had nailed it there, so it definitely wasn't some kid. Maybe it was a teenager's cigarettes, or drugs? Maybe it was a secret stash?

So John down put his hammer and slowly reached for the parcel and slid it off the nail.

There was something solid in there, he could feel it. It was something hard and small and solid and definitely not cigarettes. He sat there on the roof and looked down at the parcel in his hand and he realised that it was actually made out of an envelope, a large brown envelope that had been sealed and then folded over three or four times and then tied with the green twine. He took hold of the twine and started to undo the knot that tied it. Apart from a little dust, the envelope was totally intact, as intact as the day that it had been put there. The loft space it was in was dry and clean, so the little parcel had just remained there until its discovery today.

John undid the knot and then unwound the twine and slowly unfolded the sealed brown envelope and then he suddenly stopped and looked.

Written on the inside of the envelope in bold black letters were the words...

'To the finder...To whom it may concern'

John stopped and stared at the writing and he looked down at the envelope and he thought for a second. A moment before he was going to rip the envelope open, expecting to find something vaguely interesting or something funny. If there had been some vintage and very aging cigarettes, he was going to go down the ladder and he would have given them to the lads. Most of them smoked and they would have laughed. Whatever had been in the parcel, he would have taken it down to show them, but now... now, suddenly, no.

John looked at the writing on the envelope and he had to think. This was personal somehow, the message on the envelope...'To the finder...To whom it may concern'.

It intrigued John and he suddenly felt that whatever was inside the envelope, he didn't want to share it with anyone. He glanced over his shoulder and looked down at his men, they were busy with their lunch and their usual small talk. None of them had seen him find the parcel and nobody was taking any notice at all of what he was doing up there. So he folded the envelope back into its original shape and slid it into his inside jacket pocket. He'd suddenly had enough of working up there and so he stood up and came down the ladder. John then walked back over to his office and went inside. He opened one of the drawers in his desk, took out his lunch and then slid his hand into his jacket pocket and took out the parcel, put it into the drawer and closed it. After that, he went back outside to have his lunch with the men.

They all sat there talking as John opened up his sandwiches. And yes, today it was ham salad and he smiled at that. As they all sat there, John's roofer got up and went into the office and came back out with a mug of tea.

'Cheers Boss,' he said as he put the mug down on the table in front of John.

It was a way of saying 'thank you', without any fuss.

John just nodded. 'Thanks buddy,' he replied, again without any fuss.

A pleasant half hour in the sun passed and the men finally finished their lunch and their mugs of tea and they got up to go back to work. John issued them a few instructions and the men strolled away.

He sat there for five minutes, contemplating and he thought about Sarah as he ate his sandwiches. He also thought about the parcel that he'd just found and he began to wonder just what was in it and that thought somewhat niggled him. He knew really that he wanted to go back into his office and open it, but somehow he felt that his curiosity was a weakness.

In the end though, that same curiosity got the better of him, forever a human trait. John finally stood up and with his mug of tea in his hand he went back into his office.

He sat down once again at his desk and put his mug down. Then he reached over and slid open the drawer. Inside was the parcel, the folded brown envelope. He took it out of the drawer and placed it on the desk in front of him.

'Now then, what's it going to be?' he thought to himself and once again he slowly unfolded the little parcel and re-examined the writing on the envelope.

'To the finder...to whom it may concern'

He could feel something solid inside the envelope and so he ripped the end open and awkwardly felt inside. There was some sort of small box and John slid it out of the envelope and put it on the desk in front of him. He looked down at it. It was a square black box made from leather and it had a thin gold embossed decoration around the top and was obviously made to hold some sort of jewellery.

John stared down at the little box, his curiosity now bristling. He knew that the box had to contain something, obviously, but what?

'Anticipation' is another human trait, an emotion, and that anticipation suddenly made John's pulse beat a little bit faster, like the gambler who reaches for another card.

What would be in the box? Hopefully something valuable and then again it could just be some rubbish. It could be 'fool's gold'.

So he turned the box around and then he slowly opened it. The first thing he saw inside was a folded piece of paper, it was a small piece of writing paper and it was a note, not a tissue or any sort of packaging. No, it was definitely writing paper. John knew that there had to be a message or something similar written on it, he realised that straightaway and again it intrigued him. But when he picked up the note, he wasn't ready for what lay underneath.

It was midday and the sun shone brightly into John's office and across his desk and as he moved the note, the sun's rays shone down and reflected onto the most beautiful ring that John had ever seen in his life, and the sight of it actually made him gasp. There in front of him was an opal ring, a large oval cut opal ring in a diamond surround that was so striking that it made John stop breathing for a couple of seconds.

He just sat there, awestruck at the sight of it and its utter beauty. He was absolutely mesmerized. He stared down at the large bright oval turquoise stone, it was the colour of the Caribbean Sea and he suddenly couldn't stop himself from touching it with his forefinger, the stone felt so cool against his skin. John slowly eased the ring out of the box and he held it up in the bright sunlight so that he could see it properly. The sun shone directly onto face of the opal and John was captivated as he looked into the translucent turquoise and blue. And as he gazed at it, he stared into its centre and there deep within the stone he saw a line of red fire, an explosion of red iridescence from within the centre of the opal. It was absolutely spectacular.

John held up the ring and he turned it slowly and deliberately in the sunlight and as he did he saw the tiny gold and dark blue flecks of colour that almost floated across the surface of that precious opal. Then the sun caught the stone again and the inner red fire blazed from inside the turquoise, like red flashes of lightening. The opal itself was set on a bed of cut diamonds, they were slivers of clear crystal that dazzled as the sunlight lit them up. They made the opal look as though it was floating on a glistening pool of water on a summer's day.

John was absolutely enthralled by the sheer beauty of it. For the next fifteen minutes he just sat there and studied the opal and the diamonds and how the light flooded through the stone, and then suddenly, he understood it. He understood it all.

He understood the simple physical mechanics of how the ring 'worked' and the cleverness and the skill in its design and construction. It was the diamonds, the diamonds in the setting. The opal had been cut into a large oval shape and all around it were the slivers of diamonds, they were set like small pointing fingers all around the stone and were slightly inclined towards its centre. The diamonds somehow picked up the sunlight and reflected the sun's rays back into the centre of the opal.

It was ingenious.

The diamonds shone the beams of bright sunlight back into the centre of the opal and lit up the turquoise and the blue and the gold and the spectacular red fire within its centre.

John gazed intently at the ring and it made him smile, the feeling was almost hypnotic.

He sat there for several more minutes, just turning the ring in the light and at every angle there was a different pattern of dazzling colours. John had never known about or understood the nature of fine opals and suddenly he was captivated.

Eventually he realised the time and when he looked at his watch he was slightly surprised to see that nearly half an hour had quickly passed by. John was just about to return the ring to its box when he realised that the note that he had taken out with the ring still lay on his desk. He'd very quickly forgotten all about it, but not now, not after seeing the ring, and his curiosity rose as he unfolded the small piece of paper.

The first thing he saw was some writing, so he flattened the note out on his desk before he attempted to read it. He stared down at the small sheet of paper and written there in scrawling black ink, it read...

'You've found this ring and now it's yours. You can have it'

It was signed by somebody called 'T. McCall' and underneath the signature it read...

'And now I've lost everything...'

John stared down at the writing and wondered just what on earth he had uncovered.

The ring was beautiful, but the message accompanying it was disturbing. He re-folded the note and put it back into the box along with the ring. Then he put the box back into his desk drawer, but this time he locked the drawer and then he went back to work.

It was past five o' clock when the last of the men had finished for the day and finally headed off home. John, as usual, went around the site. It was his site and he checked that everything was all right and that everything had been closed down properly. No tools were to be left hanging around and all the machinery had to be closed up and made vandal proof. Vandalism had always been a problem on building sites and the wanton destruction by bored local teenagers could be costly and time consuming. John finally went back into his office to finish off and while he was there he unlocked his desk drawer and once again took out the box. He was tempted to look at the ring again and if truth be known he'd not stopped thinking about it all afternoon, and of course there was the note. But after a moment's consideration, he tucked the box into his inside pocket and then he put his files and some important papers back into the drawer and locked it again for safekeeping. He switched off the lights and finally locked up his office for the night. John got into his car and drove through the site gates and then stopped. He got out of his car and went back to close and lock the large steel mesh gates so that the site was now hopefully secure. Then he got back into his car and made his way home. As he drove, his thoughts once again returned to the ring and the strange note that accompanied it and the words...'And now I've lost everything'.

Well, how curious was that?

He wondered what Sarah would make of it all and he couldn't wait to tell her. It would be something to brighten up her day and their day of course, because sometimes there was precious little to talk about anymore. And that saddened him, because he knew that most of their conversations these days were about his job and that there was very little else.

Poor Sarah, she was left alone in the house most of the time and John had known long ago that many of her so called 'friends' had quietly disappeared.

Then suddenly, the realization of it all struck him. What on earth was he thinking of?

Sarah couldn't see. She wouldn't be able see the ring, let alone understand its beauty. And suddenly John felt very guilty and very stupid as he drove his car home. He considered his dilemma and he wondered if he should simply take the ring down to the local jewellers and get it valued and then sell it. Maybe that would be the easier and the best thing to do.

John arrived home half an hour later and he and Sarah met with their usual greeting. They both went into the kitchen and John sorted out their evening meal. Tonight it was chicken with roast potatoes and vegetables, everything had already been cooked of course, Sarah had seen to that.

During the day she was quite capable of getting a chicken into the roasting dish, along with the potatoes, and she'd also prepared the vegetables and had put them into a separate dish. Everything went into the oven to cook and when John arrived home he would take over. He would take the hot food out of the oven and then he would make the gravy.

It was a division of labour. It was still a partnership.

They would usually both chat over the evening meal and then turn on the radio, sometimes the television, but usually the radio. The television wasn't much use to Sarah, whereas they could both sit and listen to the radio and it nicely filled the occasional but obvious silences.

There was only one day in the year that they both spoke in complete earnest and that was on the thirteenth of March. The date was the birthday of little Louise, their baby daughter and the daughter that they'd both lost. And every year, it was the one day that they could speak openly about her and of what could have been, or should have been. And every year of course, she would have been a year older and it was their homage to her. She was never to be forgotten, not to them anyway.

But that evening as they sat there talking John decided to open a bottle of wine, not his usual habit, not on weekdays anyway.

Sarah was a little surprised and she smiled, because for her any sort change was a pleasure.

Deep in her heart, she understood that John was almost naively unaware of how unhappy she was and that the mind numbing monotony and boredom of each and every day was slowly and inevitably draining the life out of her. And so along with the wine, their conversation flowed. The wine relaxed them both and John wondered why they didn't do this more often.

They talked and laughed together, it was good and it was those precious moments of almost relaxed intimacy with his wife that made John suddenly decide to tell Sarah about the ring.

He explained the events of the day and she was intrigued, and then because of Sarah's insistence he went into the hallway and took the box out of his jacket pocket and brought it back to show her.

He was still wary.

'I didn't know whether or not to tell you about it,' he said quietly.

Sarah shrugged 'Why not?'

'Because it's so beautiful,' and then he paused for a moment, 'and because you wouldn't be able to see it'.

There...he'd said it.

Sarah smiled 'Pass me the ring John,' she said, 'and you can describe it to me. Tell me all about it.'

John opened the box and then he gently took hold of Sarah's hand and placed the spectacular opal ring onto her outstretched palm.

She picked up the ring and ran her fingers over the large, smooth oval stone and her forefingers quickly touched the diamonds that surrounded it.

'John...it feels so beautiful,' she said.

'It is Sarah, it's the most beautiful ring I've ever seen.' and again, just for a moment, he felt a short pang of guilt.

'Go on, describe it to me,' she said enthusiastically, 'Tell me all about the colours.'

John started to tell her all about the opal and he described the translucence of the turquoise and the blue and the brilliant red fire in its centre that cast tiny specks of gold out across the face of the stone. Then he explained how the diamonds cast their light back into the opal and made it shimmer and sparkle in the light.

Sarah sat there and listened in awe and she and ran her thumb gently over the opal and she smiled.

John watched her every movement as he spoke and when she finally put the ring on her finger, he smiled too.

'What are you going to do with it John?' she said at last.

'Do with it? What do you mean?' he said.

'Well, it's not ours.'

'Hang on a minute, just let me read you the note that was in the box with it,' he replied.

John took out the folded note and then he straightened it and read it out to her.

'You've found this ring and now it's yours. You can have it. And it's signed by someone called 'T. McCall', and then he looked across at her, 'There you go,' he said.

'So, it could be ours?' Sarah asked.

'It is ours. It is as far as I'm concerned anyway,' said John.

'And the man who owned it, the "McCall" man, who was he?' she asked again.

'Well I think it's a man,' said John, 'I don't think that a woman would have managed to climb into those rafters. But who he is, I have no idea. He's was obviously somebody who lived in that house at some time, it could have been years ago. That ring could have been hidden away in the roof for ages when you think about it.'

'How old are the houses John?'

'Well, they were built in the early nineties. So presumably, what, twenty to thirty years old? Those houses could have changed hands several times in between and they probably did.'

Sarah smiled 'So you think we can keep it?'

John looked across at his wife. She was happy and that made him feel good.

'Of course we can love, it's ours now.' and then he stopped for a moment.

'In fact, no, it's now 'your' ring Mrs Lawson. I give you this beautiful opal ring because I love you so very, very much.'

Sarah clapped her hands with delight and she laughed at him and then she stretched out her arms and John went over to her and kissed her.

'So I can wear it whenever I want?' she asked him.

'Yes, whenever you want,' he replied.

Sarah sat back in her comfy chair and grinned as she slowly stroked the opal ring. It was suddenly 'her' opal ring.

'I'm going to have some fun with this John.' she said and it was almost a declaration.

John looked across at her, curiously 'Oh yes and how's that?' he asked.

'Can I ask you one honest question John and please be truthful?'

He was a bit struck by this, but 'Yes,' he replied and then, 'Why, what's wrong?'

'Is the ring really as beautiful as you say it is John, honestly? You know that you already make me happy and a ring won't change that, but I just need to know.'

John smiled at her 'Yes Sarah, it is 'that' beautiful. It really is, it's the most beautiful ring I've ever seen,' and he laughed, 'And just let me tell you something, like most men I don't know a thing about jewellery. We're all the same, most men never actually look at jewellery. It's something that we leave you women to sort out.'

It was now Sarah's turn to smile.

'And I have to admit,' he continued, 'even when I bought your engagement ring and your wedding ring, it was you who picked them. To tell you the truth, most of us blokes think that diamonds are just little shiny pieces of glass. In all honesty, we haven't a clue.'

Sarah leant back in her comfy chair and pretended to look at her opal as she slowly ran her finger over it again and she gave a short laugh, to herself really.

John asked her again 'So what's all this fun you're going to have?'

'Oh, my circle of so called 'friends'...' she replied casually.

'And what about them?' asked John.

'Well, word does get around,' she again replied, almost innocently.

'I don't understand.' He wasn't getting this at all.

'It's like this my love,' and as she sat there she grinned at him, 'When that circle of bitches find out about this ring, they'll all want to see it, I know they will. I know how they all think. They live in their own little world and they're all full of their own little jealousies.'

'And?' again John asked her.

'And suddenly, I'll be 'flavour of the month' again, only for a month and then they'll all drop me again.'

'How do you know that?' John asked.

'Because I know.'

'So why bother?' he said.

'Because I want to drop 'them' this time, just like they dropped me. I want them to know that I don't need any of them anymore. I don't need them at all. I've got other things in my life, like 'my pride'...'

And at that point Sarah started to get upset and John suddenly realised that his wife was on the verge of tears.

So he leant over and took hold of her arm 'Well, you're right there love, they definitely are a set of bitches. Even I know that and I'm a bloke.'

The moment was diffused and Sarah smiled again and they both began to laugh.

Sarah turned to him 'I'm going to wait until my two friends turn up and I'll show them the ring and of course they'll report back to the others and then 'ha-ha', I can't wait. And when they all want to come around and see it, I shall be 'unavailable'...'

'What will you tell your two friends about the ring?' asked John.

'Oh, I shall tell them that we've had a 'windfall' and that my darling husband bought this ring for me as a 'treat' because he loves and adores me,' Sarah giggled, '...'Oh yes', he just went out and bought it, the money was simply no object.'

'Well the first parts true. I do love and adore you,' John said to her.

'Yes, I know that,' she replied and she giggled again, 'They'll all be intrigued because they 'love' money and they'll all want to know how we've got it. But they never will know and it will drive them mad, they'll all be as jealous as hell.'

John suddenly came up with a thought 'Actually you know, we do need to take it to the jewellers.'

Sarah stopped smiling for a moment 'What for?'

'A valuation, we'll need a valuation for the insurance. We'll have to put the ring on the house insurance?'

'Oh yes, right.' she said.

"Well it's valuable Sarah and it makes sense to get it insured. People do get burgled and things get stolen.'

She nodded in agreement.

John continued 'We'll go down to Lancaster's Jewellers on Saturday and leave it with them.'

They both decided that this was the right course of action and that it would be interesting to find out about the ring and what it was possibly worth.

Come Saturday, they would be a little bit wiser.

Set in the centre of town, 'Lancaster's' had long been established as the town's principal jewellers. They proudly declared that 'They had been in business for over one hundred years'. And if truth be known, Lancaster's Jewellers had probably at one time or another supplied most of the townsfolk with the engagement rings and wedding rings that were an open endorsement of people's love and eventual marriage. In fact, Lancaster's Jewellers had probably supplied most of the town with the trinkets, baubles and other shiny little things that draw women into the wonder and mysticism that is the world of jewellery.

It's something that women love and it makes men sigh and simply give up.

John and Sarah walked through the impressive chrome and glass doors of Lancaster's Jewellers on Saturday morning at eleven o' clock on the dot.

John stared around in wonder at the place, everything was encased in glass. From top to bottom and along every wall there were glass cabinets containing seamless glass shelving on which were displayed the most beautiful arrays of rings and beautiful jewellery. There were countless numbers of rings on display, all of different shapes and colours. Set on silver or black velvet trays, there were rows and rows of them. Some were in gold, others in silver or even platinum. There were rings with plain bands and others mounted with precious stones, and each type of stone had its own section. There were cabinets dedicated to emeralds and another full of blood red rubies and next to that sapphires, and of course there was a huge display of diamond rings, all with cut stones of different shapes and sizes. There were stones of every type and colour. Another cabinet displayed nothing but pearls and another was full of turquoise and dark blue Lapis Lazuli. There were necklaces and brooches and other pieces of jewellery and all were brightly illuminated by tiny halogen lights that shone down onto each and every piece of jewellery. And it seemed to give them a life of their own. It was simply spectacular.

John led Sarah over to the large central glass counter which contained the fabulous watches of Switzerland. Inside, there were crisp looking Omega and Rolex watches, along with large Breitling chronometers that were brimming with dials. And the Tag Heuer watches and the Cartiers, all looking as sharp as blades and crafted from surgical steel. John looked down at them with envy and awe. Some of those watches would cost more than a decent car, and it was strange, but for some reason John found them hypnotically beautiful. He'd once heard somebody say that 'the only jewellery a man could wear was a good watch'. And for once, he had to agree.

There were several customers already in the shop who were being attended to by the various assistants, so John guided Sarah over to the main counter and they waited their turn. A young lady assistant suddenly appeared out of a door at the rear of the shop and straightaway noticed John and Sarah. She immediately made her way over to them as she quickly finished munching her 'elevenses'. Wearing a black pencil skirt and a white blouse, she was dark haired and was wearing 'professional' makeup with the obligatory deep red lipstick. She could have just as easily been selling expensive perfume at a top department store. It was the professional look and as John looked at her and at the other similarly attired assistants, he smiled to himself. They could have all been sisters.

The young lady approached them both with her best smile in place.

'Can I help you?' she very pleasantly asked.

'Yes,' replied John, 'we have a ring, an opal and diamond ring and we'd like to have it valued. It's for insurance purposes,' he added quickly.

'Oh right, okay,' she said helpfully and she smiled at Sarah and then was a bit disconcerted when she thought that Sarah was completely ignoring her.

John picked up on this 'My wife is visually impaired, she doesn't see very well.'

He had of course been put in the same position many times before and for him and Sarah it was a standard reply and almost an excuse.

'Oh, I'm sorry,' replied the assistant, but Sarah immediately put her at ease by giving the girl her best smile. It was also Sarah's standard reply and it worked.

'Right,' said the young lady, she was trying to be efficient, 'Can I see the ring please?' she said and she reached down and from somewhere found a form on which she would enter John's details.

John took out the fairly unassuming plain black box and slid it across the counter. The assistant almost ignored the box and concentrated more on writing down John's name and address correctly. Names, addresses, home telephone, works telephone, contact numbers. At one point John wondered if she was going to ask for the name of their family doctor.

Then she finally glanced down at the box and picked it up.

'Right,' she said again, 'We'll just have a quick look.' and with that she opened the box and looked down at the ring.

For a moment, the assistant just stood there and stared down, and she found that she couldn't look away. Finally she glanced up at John, and then back at the ring. Then she let out a deep sigh.

'Oh my lord,' she said, 'I've never seen anything like it. It's so beautiful.'

She looked back at John, who was smiling at her.

'You didn't expect that, did you?' he said.

'No,' she replied, almost breathless, 'I certainly did not.'

Sarah suddenly spoke to her 'Is it so beautiful?' she asked the girl.

The assistant looked across at Sarah 'Have you never seen it?' she asked and then bit her lip at her careless question.

'No I haven't,' Sarah replied easily, 'John has described it to me of course, but I've never been able to see it.'

The girl looked back down at the ring, which now shone brilliantly in the strong white lights inside the jewellers shop.

'It's the most beautiful thing I think I've ever seen.' the assistant said, she was almost speaking to herself.

And then as though she'd suddenly come out of a trance, the assistant picked up the telephone. She looked up at John as she pressed one of the buttons on the phone.

'I think I'll call Mr Lancaster, he needs have a look at this. I don't think this ring fits in with our normal valuation service and we may need someone who specializes in this sort of jewellery. It's better that we check first.'

And with that the phone began to buzz and she spoke to someone.

'Hello Paul, its Julie downstairs. I've got a customer here with an opal ring that's come in for valuation. It's...err, a little bit special and I just wondered if you could come down and take a quick look at it please. It's not our everyday stuff, so I wonder if you could give it a quick appraisal. It really is a bit special,' and with that she gave John a quick smile of approval, 'Yes okay' she said again and then she put the phone down.

She looked back at John 'Mr Lancaster is going to come down to have a quick look at it.'

'The owner?' remarked Sarah.

'Yes,' replied the girl, 'I'd feel better if he looked at the ring first.'

John and Sarah waited in anticipation for the couple of minutes that it took for Mr Lancaster to appear. As they stood there, two of the other assistants came over to look at what was causing all the interest. Both girls gazed at the ring in admiration and the first assistant turned the box into the bright light and they watched it sparkle.

Suddenly a door on the first floor opened and Mr Paul Lancaster walked across the top lobby and then came down the stairs to meet them. A tall slim man, he was around six feet tall and in his late fifties. He had very short grey hair and beard which was also closely cut. Wearing a dark blue suit with an accompanying dark red tie, he approached the counter with an expectant smile.

'Hello,' he said to everyone.

Then he turned to John and Sarah and introduced himself and they shook hands. John in turn introduced himself and Sarah.

'So what have we got Julie?' said Paul Lancaster to his assistant.

'Mr Lawton here has brought in a ring for valuation purposes and I just thought that you should see it.' And with that she turned the box containing the ring around for Mr Lancaster to see. As she did, the full glare of the internal lights hit the ring and Paul Lancaster almost went rigid.

'My God,' he said out loud.

'Yes,' continued Julie, 'As soon s I saw the ring I thought it was a bit special, I knew you would want to see it.'

Paul Lancaster just stared down at the ring. Still he said nothing.

'We thought we should get it insured,' said John, trying to make some sort of conversation.

But Paul Lancaster just reached down and picked up the box containing the ring and he lifted it up for closer inspection. He just stood there in silence and even the assistants were looking quizzical.

Paul Lancaster suddenly spoke, almost to himself.

'I've never seen anything like it...' he said slowly, 'this ring is absolutely incredible.'

He continued to stare at the ring as he turned it in the light.

'How did you come by it?' he asked nonchalantly.

John slowly reached for Sarah's hand, for some strange reason he felt slightly threatened.

'We just acquired it,' said John.

'Have you really,' Paul Lancaster replied and he raised an eyebrow. And John Lawton saw it.

John had always been ready for this possibility and he gently squeezed Sarah's hand.

'It was a gift Mr Lancaster,' he said firmly.

Paul Lancaster glanced across at John and realised that the subject was not for public discussion. He turned to his assistants and informed them that...'he would sort everything from here.' The girls looked at one another and knew that they were no longer needed. Assistant Julie nodded to her boss as she and her friends tactfully disappeared.

Paul Lancaster finally put the ring back down on the counter. Then he turned to John and Sarah.

'This is an incredible piece of jewellery. Those stunningly cut diamonds that surround the opal make this a fabulous ring. From a jeweller's point of view, it's the diamonds that I find fascinating. Whoever made this ring had an outstanding ability. For a start, I don't understand how he managed to cut the diamonds into that particular contour. They're a different shape from any traditional cut that I've ever seen. And it makes me wonder, how did the maker know how to make the diamonds throw their light back into the centre of the opal. Whoever he was, he was a true genius. I think that if we want to obtain an accurate valuation, we're going to have to trace the maker.'

He took out his jeweller's eyeglass and then carefully took the ring out of its box. Then he examined it closely.

'There are hallmarks here, so it is traceable.' he said. Then he returned the ring to its box.

'I have to tell you, I think that this ring has some history. I don't know how or why, I just have a feeling about it. It's a masterpiece and its construction is quite unique.'

John was still holding Sarah's hand tightly 'We never knew,' he said and then he felt slightly stupid.

'This is one of the joys of our business,' said Paul Lancaster, 'Every so often something special like this comes along.' Then he spoke to Sarah 'what do you think about it Mrs Lawton?'

Sarah just smiled at him.

'My wife is visually impaired Mr Lancaster,' explained John, again, 'Sarah can't actually see the ring.' and again he squeezed her hand.

Sarah smiled 'Yes, I seem to be missing out on all the fun.'

For a moment Paul Lancaster paused and then 'Oh, I'm so sorry Mrs Lawton, I never realised. Well I have to tell you, it is a beauty. And by the way, will both of you please call me Paul.'

The awkward moment passed and John and Sarah relaxed a little.

'Right then,' Paul Lancaster continued, 'We will endeavour to get a valuation on the ring once we find out a little more about it. But first of all, I want to show the ring to my father. He's retired now, but his hobby is studying rare and antique jewellery. He may be able to shed a little more light on its history. I'll also check our records, there may be something there. I also think that we may have to send it down to London. We have a specialist down there that we deal with. We'll send it there by special courier.'

'Good heavens,' said Sarah, 'This is more complicated than we thought.'

'I know it may seem it,' said Paul Lancaster, 'but leave it with us and we'll sort it out for you. If you could give us a week or two and then we'll contact you.'

And that was it. John and Sarah thanked Paul Lancaster for his help.

John and Sarah then went home, after that, all they could do was wait.

On the way home they both spoke excitedly about their visit to Lancaster's Jewellers.

'There's something about that ring,' said Sarah, 'I don't know what it is and obviously I can't see it. But everyone who can seems to be in awe of it.'

'I know,' replied John, 'it's obviously quite valuable, but I just keep wondering why it was hidden in the roof space of that house and what on earth that note meant.'

That evening, Paul Lancaster finished work earlier than usual and he hurriedly went around to the rear of the shop to where his car was parked in their private car park. Before leaving, he'd put the box containing the ring securely into his inside pocket and then he'd telephoned his father, explaining that he was going to call in and see him on his way home. Twenty minutes later Paul Lancaster turned into the drive at his father's house.

'Old Harry' Lancaster lived on the outskirts of town in a large private detached property which looked out across the surrounding moors. Harry Lancaster, now a widower, lived in one of the better houses in a prestigious part of the town, the jewellery business had been good to Harry.

Harry Lancaster was a 'canny' sort of man. Though now well into his eighties, he'd certainly never lost touch with the jewellery trade. He was a great exponent of the internet and through his computer he still bought the jewellery and the various valuable 'cut' stones that could be sold in their shop. His other hobby was to research antique jewellery. Retirement for Harry Lancaster had been just a brief consideration. Though his son

Paul now totally ran the shop, old Harry still liked to keep his 'hand in' and his historic knowledge of the jewellery trade was invaluable.

Paul parked his car and walked straight inside his father's house through the large double fronted doors, it wasn't locked and he called out to his father to let him know he'd arrived. It was their usual practice, his father wasn't too good on his legs anymore and Paul walked through the house and into his father's study where he knew Harry would be, either on the computer or watching the television. The newspaper was always a third option.

Harry Lancaster smiled when he saw his son, it was always a pleasure.

That evening, his father was sitting at the table with his computer. Paul, through habit, went to the drinks cabinet and as they exchanged a few pleasantries he poured them both a glass of Port. Harry only stocked the best. He sat down with his father and they both took an appreciative sip of the dark red vintage Ruby Port. Paul sat back and then he took the jewellery box out of his inside pocket and placed it on the table in front of his father.

'I have something for you to look at dad.' he said.

Harry reached over and picked up the box and then he leant back in his chair with a slight feeling of anticipation. This was what the jewellery trade had always meant to him, all the little surprises hidden away in simple black boxes. He knew that it must be something special if his son Paul had called in with it, and he smiled to himself as he opened the small black leather box with the gold decoration. He looked inside and he gasped. For a moment he was speechless, and then he looked across at his son.

'My God,' he said, 'I never thought that I would ever see this ring.'

Paul stared at his father, this didn't happen often. The 'old man' was taken aback and even a little shocked.

'You recognize it Dad?' Paul Lancaster asked.

'Yes Paul, I recognize it. I saw it many years ago in a trade catalogue. You never forget a ring like this, not if you're in our trade. It's as beautiful as the first day I saw it. It looks even more beautiful in real life. The photograph could never do it justice.'

Harry Lancaster gently prised the ring out of its box and he held it up to the light to inspect it.

'My God...Paul, look at that opal. Have you seen the fire inside it, and look at the purity of the turquoise in the stone, it's absolutely fabulous.'

Paul agreed with his father. 'Look at the diamonds dad. I've never seen anything like them.'

Harry turned the ring in the light and he watched the diamonds shine tiny beams of light back into the centre of the opal. And then he saw the flashes of gold and dark blue floating above the crimson of its centre and it made him breathless.

'Those diamonds dad,' said Paul, 'I've never seen cuts like that. They work like small torches that direct the light back into the stone. They're shaped slivers of diamonds, but cut with angles within them to somehow refract the light. They're fantastic.'

His father just nodded in the appreciation of what his son was telling him. He stared down at the diamonds, they were like tiny spearheads, but they'd been cut with absolute precision.

'Whoever made that ring dad, he must have been an absolute genius.'

Harry Lancaster continued to gaze at the ring and then he spoke to his son.

'Yes he was Paul. He was a "genius". He was one of best cutters in the business and yet very few people even know his name.'

Paul looked across the table at his father.

'And you do?' he asked

'Yes. I think so.'

'Who was he dad?'

'He was Russian. And he was one of the best. His name was "Vasily Orlof Bratz".'

Harry Lancaster held the ring up to the light and then he said the name again.

'Vasily Orlof Bratz'

CHAPTER 2

It was September the 4th in the year 1860 in the small and almost unknown town of Zhumyov. Although virtually unheard of, Zhumyov was a small and shabby backwater that lay approximately one hundred and fifty kilometres south of Smolensk in the great and vast nation that was Russia. On that day in the cold early hours of the morning, Ivan Bratz's wife Martha gave birth to their third child. A boy 'Pavel', he was to be their third son in a family that would eventually consist of three brothers and one sister. Ivan Bratz was a carpenter, as was his father and his grandfather before him. But the years passed and by the time young Pavel was twelve years old, his father Ivan had slowly managed to extricate himself from the established family business of building and house repairs and he had gone into the production of household furniture. Ivan Bratz had long before realised that the construction industry in Russia during those long winter months was a hard task, and it was a hard task that could shorten your life expectancy. It was extremely difficult to make a living in that unforgiving country's harsh and desolate climate. It had been several years before when Ivan Bratz had started to make simple chairs out of the spare bits of timber that were left over from his construction business. They were just basic chairs and he would stack them outside his small house every morning before he went off to work. Using a piece of white chalk, he would write the price of his chairs on a square piece of wood and then would leave his wife Martha to sell them on. To his delight and slight amazement, every day when he came home some of his chairs had usually been sold. Ivan then decided to make tables to go with the chairs. They were slightly crude at first, but they were well constructed, solid and strong and typically Russian. They were also very cheap and of a decent quality and the good folk of Zhumyov soon realised a bargain when they saw one. Before long Ivan Bratz was not only making tables and chairs. He realised that there was a demand for his cheap but functional furniture and he started to make beds and cupboards and small sideboards. All were simply made, but again they were of a decent quality and they were not overpriced. Ivan Bratz finally stopped working on buildings and construction altogether when it became clear that there was better money to be made by making furniture, and once he went into full time production there was eventually a waiting list for his goods. Within a couple of years the local people took it for granted that you bought your household furniture from 'Bratz' and before long there weren't many houses in Zhumyov that didn't have at least one or two pieces of Mr Bratz's manufacture.

Ivan Bratz's small business started to show some success and he moved the family into a larger house that had land and some outbuildings that could be used as workshops. From there the family business also went into cabinet making and they started to improve the quality and design of their furniture. Along with this, Bratz also had a lucrative sideline with the local undertaker and some of the surplus timber was also used to make coffins.

It made sense. Ivan Bratz hated wastage, another Russian trait.

Ivan Bratz had three sons and those three teenage boys were soon enlisted into the family business, whether they liked it or not. The boys however did realise that working in the family workshop was definitely preferable to working anywhere else. In those days Russia was a hard country to live in and it was all about the survival of the fittest, or the cleverest.

The three boys inherited their father's skills at carpentry and under his stern instruction and tutelage they quickly became adept at their craft. But it was Pavel, his youngest son who had the 'gift' of carpentry. From an early age the young boy had quite naturally taken to whittling spare bits of wood with a little penknife that he had somehow procured. Bratz would watch his youngest son as the family sat by the open fire after their evening meal. Everyone would be in conversation, but Pavel would quietly sit there, comfortable and warm and skilfully producing little wooden figurines, usually of small animals.

And the one night Ivan Bratz had a moment of inspiration. And a week later he managed to procure a set of small fine wood chisels. Pavel was fifteen by then and Bratz sat the boy down and explained to him how he would like his son to carve some designs into the tables and cabinets that they made. He showed Pavel an old carpentry book that had belonged to his father and in it there were some rudimentary designs. Bratz gave the young lad a pile of used timber and let him use the chisels to create the designs. Two weeks passed and by then Pavel was beginning to show some credible results. Within another month, Ivan Bratz stood there and watched his youngest son meticulously carve a border around the edge of a table top and then the next day cut a matching design on the arms and legs of the accompanying chairs. The results were excellent and those pieces of furniture were no longer just the usual box carpentry, the intricate carving gave a look of quality. The design looked good, it was good and Bratz quickly realised that they could charge more for it. That was the start of young Pavel's 'carving period' and before long every piece of furniture that they produced had a carved finish. Bratz then instructed Pavel to teach his two brothers how to carve, so that they too could produce the same type of quality furniture.

Ivan Bratz had also started to supply the furniture shops in the surrounding towns and his furniture was beginning to sell. He had a quality product at a good price and those shop owners were interested.

Ivan Bratz was busy. And Ivan Bratz was beginning to make money. Before long he was employing a couple of local men to work in his workshop.

Once a week Bratz and a driver would deliver their goods by horse and cart to some shop or other in one of the local towns and then travel to the next town to hopefully receive another order.

It was on one of these trips and after dropping off a delivery that they then went onto the town of Sevska to take an order for some furniture from 'Lavrov Furnishings and Fittings'. After speaking to the owner, Mr Lavrov himself, and successfully sorting out a deal for some beds and a couple of wardrobes, Bratz instructed his driver to go back home to Zhumyov without him. He then made his way to Sevska train station and caught the train to the city of Smolensk. When he arrived there he walked around the city, looking through the windows of the various furniture stores. Some he even went into, under the guise of 'possibly' purchasing something. But what he was looking for of course, were the ideas for different designs that he could copy back at his own workshop in Zhumyov. His other task that day was to visit the premises of 'Shefner Machine and Tool Supply' and it was there that he would spend a great deal of his hard earned money in purchasing an industrial wood lathe. The lathe was a woodcutting machine that could quickly and efficiently produce chair and table legs. It would also give purpose to his latest endeavour. Ivan Bratz was going to produce staircases. This machine could produce beautifully turned balustrades, banisters and circular finials. Bratz decided once again that he would leave the workings of the lathe to his youngest son. He knew that Pavel would soon master the machine and then pass his knowledge and skills onto his brothers. Pavel could then hand carve the finials and the heads of the banisters. It was Pavel's intricate carving that would make the staircases beautiful.

Ivan Bratz was slightly in awe of his youngest son. In fact he had always been fascinated by him, back from the early days when he would sit and watch Pavel whittle away at a piece of random wood and finally produce something special. He'd always known that his son had a talent. Yes, it was a gift.

Whilst Bratz was away in Smolensk buying the lathe, he'd also wandered around the quality furniture stores and examined the beauty and the skill of the carpentry there. And the one thing he did notice was one particular brand name on many of the most pieces of beautiful furniture. The name of the manufacturer was 'Schwabs of Smolensk'.

Bratz knew that he was capable of making furniture of a similar quality and also that there would be a large market for his goods here in Smolensk, especially when he saw the prices that were being charged. Bratz knew exactly how much it cost to make a table and some chairs and the prices being charged here were astronomical.

However, there was one problem. A lot of the finer furniture was inlaid and it seemed that marquetry was highly fashionable. Marquetry, parquetry and the inlaying of wood was a very specialized technique in furniture decoration. It was achieved by cutting out fine sections of the original wood and then inserting an exact match made from different types of coloured woods to form an intricate pattern or design. It was a very skilful and specialised procedure. However, Ivan Bratz had given it some thought, and Bratz knew that his youngest son Pavel, if educated and trained, would be capable of the task. In fact he would excel at it. Pavel had the 'gift'.

Bratz went back home to Zhumyov and within a couple of weeks the new lathe arrived. It was a spectacular machine which totally transformed their workshop. They could suddenly turn out chair legs by the dozen as opposed to the laborious method of sawing and hand cutting. Pavel was utterly fascinated by the lathe and he mastered the machine in a less than two weeks, he then went on to show his brothers how to use it.

And Ivan Bratz was a happy man. He could suddenly foresee a possible future. His workshop could be turned into a small factory if they continued to flourish. And in his mind he kept remembering Smolensk. There were many furniture shops there that he could supply and at the 'right price'. He knew that he could make money in Smolensk but he had to get his product right and getting the product right meant getting the design right and that meant knowing how to make 'inlaid' furniture. That was the mark of quality. But Ivan Bratz was nobody's fool and he knew that the best growth for his business was slow and steady growth and that was what he was achieving at the moment. But he also had to look to the future, one way or another the business would have to continue to grow.

Two weeks later Bratz once again took the train to Smolensk. He arrived early in the morning and by lunch time he had asked around and learned the location of the furniture factory belonging to 'Schwabs of Smolensk'. Just over an hour later he walked through the factory gates of the famous furniture manufacturer, which was conveniently situated on the outskirts of the city. He then quickly found the whereabouts of the company office, and he knocked on the door and straightaway walked in and enquired if he could speak to the owner, 'Mr Schwab'. An attractive young secretary, who was slightly annoyed at his rude intrusion, asked him what his business was. But Bratz just replied that it was 'family business'. The young secretary shrugged and then went to knock on the door to the right of her desk. She put her head around the door and spoke to someone and then turned back to Bratz and nodded to him to come forward and enter. After ushering him in, she closed the door. At the other end of the long office sat the owner of the company, Ernst Schwab. A tall thin man and probably in his sixties, he looked directly at Bratz and decided quite rightly that he was dealing with a peasant. He also wondered 'what on earth' this man wanted after he'd been informed by his secretary that this was 'family business'.

Ivan Bratz was certainly nothing to do with Ernst Schwab's family.

Bratz removed his hat and nodded at Mr Schwab.

Mr Schwab just stared back at him and then bid him come forward and sit down.

'And you are?' asked Ernst Schwab.

'My name is Bratz, Mr Schwab. Ivan Bratz.'

'And what do you want Mr Bratz?' again asked Mr Schwab.

'I want you to give my son a job Mr Schwab. I want you to give him an apprenticeship at your company and teach him how to become a carpenter.'

Mr Schwab was not at all impressed with this peasant who he considered was wasting his time, and he straightaway told Bratz that they didn't need anyone. However, Bratz had expected this and he was ready to be turned down, and so he told Mr Schwab that his son Pavel would be willing to work for nothing, simply because his son needed a trade.

Ernst Schwab saw the look of desperation on Bratz's face, but there was also something else there too. Schwab was a shrewd man and somehow he 'smelled a rat'. So he took the opportunity to tell Bratz that there may be a possibility of giving the boy an apprenticeship, but that Bratz would have to pay for the boy's training. It would take five years to train young Pavel to obtain the skills to become a master carpenter and for that Schwab wanted to be paid twelve hundred roubles a year.

Ivan Bratz nearly fell off his chair.

And so the wheeling and dealing began, between the two very wily opponents. There was a lot of dramatics, mostly by Bratz, who exclaimed quite loudly that he could only afford four hundred roubles a year, after all, he was a poor man. That amount was immediately met by distain from Mr Schwab. He had the upper hand and he knew it. Twenty minutes later and after a lot of dealing and heartache, especially for Bratz, they both agreed on nine hundred roubles a year. This was a huge amount of money for Ivan Bratz to part with. However, for the nine hundred roubles it was also agreed that Pavel could live at the factory, and rather resentfully, Schwab also agreed to feed the boy. It was arranged that Pavel would start in three months time. Bratz lied and told old man Schwab that his son would have to finish his schooling. In reality Bratz wanted three months of frantic manufacture from his son and he also needed to know that his other two sons would have mastered the lathe by then.

Both men then shook hands on the deal, and it was only then that Mr Schwab asked Ivan Bratz what he did for a living.

'I do a bit of building and construction,' Bratz lied again.

Mr Schwab nodded. But somehow he didn't believe it.

In July of that year, Ivan Bratz along with his son Pavel, once more got onto to train for Smolensk. They arrived at the Schwab Furniture Factory in the early afternoon and Bratz took his son straight to Mr Schwab's office. The same young secretary once again ushered them through to Mr Schwab where Bratz introduced his son. Schwab eyed the boy with a slight look of distain.

'You will have to work hard to become a skilled carpenter,' said Schwab to young Pavel, 'It will take you at least five years to become a fully trained craftsman, and that's only if you have the skills of course. And one other thing, any laziness or stupidity and you're out. Okay?'

Pavel silently nodded.

Schwab then turned his attention to Ivan Bratz.

'Go and see my secretary, tell her to take the boy over to Mr Koenig, he's my foreman and manager. And Mr Bratz, also give her the money that we discussed.'

Bratz grimaced and then nodded back at Schwab as he was dismissed. He and Pavel then left the office. He gave an envelope containing the money to Mr Schwab's secretary along with his instructions and then he went to stand outside with Pavel as the secretary counted the money and put it into the company safe.

As they stood there waiting, Ivan Bratz turned to his son.

'You will have to work hard Pavel.'

Pavel nodded to his father 'Yes father, I will,' he replied.

Bratz looked down at his son, the son he admired, only because of the boy's natural ability.

He was the son with the 'gift'.

'Work hard,' he said to Pavel, 'You have four years to complete your training. I'm not paying that old bastard nine hundred roubles a year, not for five years.'

Pavel agreed. He knew it was too much. More than his family could afford.

Ivan Bratz shook his son's hand and wished him well and then he walked out through the open gates of the Schwab factory. Bratz wouldn't return there for four years, but when he eventually did, it would be for an entirely different reason.

He then made his way back to the train station, but instead of returning home to Zhumyov, Bratz bought another train ticket for another destination.

Half an hour later he was on a train heading for Moscow. Ivan Bratz had a plan.

Young Pavel Bratz stood there and watched his father walk out of the factory gates. Ivan Bratz didn't look back to wave to his son. Pavel knew he wouldn't.

The secretary eventually came out of the office and in silence she took Pavel into the main factory building to where the men were working with lathes and saws and drills. Long lengths of timber were being cut down into useable sizes and were then cut and shaped again and made ready to be sent to other parts of the factory to be turned into the different pieces of furniture. At the end of the long factory building, a stout balding man sat at an open desk. This was Mr Koenig. He was the factory foreman and manager and he was Mr Schwab's right hand man. He was only ever known as 'Mr Koenig'. Nobody ever used or even knew his first name and he ran the Schwab factory as though it was his own.

The young secretary just nodded at Koenig, she didn't feel comfortable in the factory where it was always noisy and dusty and full of men's staring eyes. She knew what they were thinking and she knew what was on their minds as they stared and leered and looked her up and down.

'This is the new boy.' she said quickly to Mr Koenig, and without waiting for any sort of reply she about turned and made her way back to the relative safety of her office.

Koenig glanced up at Pavel and then continued to scribble some notes onto a sheet of paper with his sharp dark pencil. Koenig rarely used a pen, it was always a pencil. Finally he stopped writing and he put down the pencil and then leant back in his chair.

'So boy,' he said, 'So you want to be a carpenter. And why is that?'

Pavel, unfazed, thought about the question for a moment.

'Because I love the beauty of wood sir,' he replied.

Koenig stared back at Pavel. It was an astute answer and probably not the one he was expecting.

'Well, you may not love the beauty of wood by the time I've finished with you boy,' he said.

'I'm here to work sir and learn my craft,' said Pavel. He could only tell the truth as he saw it.

Koenig took notice of that statement. This boy was slightly different from the usual bumbling and uncouth youths that he was used to dealing with, dealing with and also rapidly dismissing. This boy had an air of the educated about him and almost a quiet confidence. Maybe he could do something with this young man, it would be a change, instead of trying to glean some enthusiasm from those lazy, idle youths who wanted to do nothing all day and then dash off home for their food, a warm fire and their bed. Hope would spring eternal. However Koenig was used to seeing young men quickly lose their enthusiasm when it came to hard work. And hard work it would be.

Mr Koenig gave Pavel a cursory nod and then he turned to look over his shoulder as he shouted out a name.

'Kibbel..!'

From behind a stack of piled long planking, a thin, stooped man emerged. He was probably fifty but looked sixty with his greying unkempt hair and moustache. He wore frail metal glasses and had all the appearance of someone who had suffered ill health for most of his life. He was carrying a yard brush in one hand and a long saw in the other, a strange combination.

'Kibbel,' said Mr Koenig, 'this is...what's your name again boy?'

'My name is Pavel Bratz,' answered Pavel dutifully.

Mr Koenig raised an eyebrow.

'This is Bratz," he continued, 'He'll be working here...and living here. Show him where he sleeps and start him tomorrow.'

Kibble looked down at Pavel and said 'right' to no one in particular and then walked away. Pavel thought for a moment, then nodded quickly at Mr Koenig and followed Kibble down the long walkway that angled awkwardly between the various stacks of wood.

Kibble took Pavel outside and across the yard to a single storey building that was tucked away in a corner and away from the main buildings. Pavel looked up and noticed the grey smoke slowly rising out of a squat blackened chimney pot on the end of the roof. As they approached the building Kibbel turned to Pavel.

'This is where you'll be living. There's about ten of us in here. It's okay, it's always warm.'

Kibbel swung open the faded whitewashed front door and led Pavel inside. They both blinked to get accustomed to the darker interior and Pavel immediately felt the warmth. There was a long room that contained a dozen bunks. At the far wall there was a large cast iron stove which was lit and burned fiercely. There was a large pile of wood stacked at the side of it. In front of the stove was a long and much used stoutly built table that had about a dozen similarly used chairs lined up around it. And at the other end of the building was another door which led to the washrooms.

'Right,' said Kibbel, 'Pick yourself an empty bunk, there's one over there' and he nodded to his right. Then he continued 'We eat, live and sleep in here. The washrooms are there at the rear and the toilet shed is around the back of the building. We're lucky, there's always plenty of spare used wood in the factory and Mr Schwab lets us use it. So we're always warm in here and we can always cook or make something hot to drink. The winters are damn cold here in Smolensk.'

Pavel nodded. The winters were cold in Zhumyov too. He knew all about being cold.

That evening, Pavel sat at the long table with ten other men and quietly ate the stew that Kibbel had made for them all. It turned out that Kibbel was in charge of the cooking and he doled out the plates of stew accompanied with large wooden platters of Russian black bread.

The stew was good and that was not a bad thing, because it was the only dish that Kibbel ever prepared. It was made from any kind of meat, be it beef or bacon or pork, and it contained an array of vegetables and always plenty of cabbage. The stew was cooked in a large iron pot on top of the stove and Kibbel had a strange but efficient way of cooking it. He simply added more meat, vegetables and cabbage to the pot every day, day after day, so it was a 'never ending' concoction. The stove never went out and the pot of stew was always warm and the men would dip their bowls into it for breakfast and again at lunch and then Kibbel would again serve it out on plates with the large lumps of black bread for their evening meal.

Nobody ever complained. The stew was good.

On that first evening Pavel sat there at the table with the other men and he listened to the conversations. He would soon realise their repetition.

They talked about the everyday politics of the factory and the things that affected them personally. And if their job, or anyone else's job had changed in any way and it made their life easier, then all was well and for a short time they or that particular individual would be happy. But conversely, if the work or the workload had become harder and more difficult, then there were mutterings from the men, who moaned, groaned and cursed as they ate their food. The other topics of daily conversation were of course the weather, which was either too hot or too cold, usually the latter. There was also the question of 'what sort of mood' Mr Koenig was in on that particular day and finally, as ever, the debate regarding Mr Schwab's young secretary. She was the constant topic of interest between the men. They were always ready to discuss her anatomy and there was huge interest in the shape of her legs and her buttocks and also the size of her breasts, along with her pretty face and her lovely hair. And of course, with deep breaths and a faraway look in their eyes, they considered what they all would like to do with her between the sheets. There were also the constant and unvarying rumours that either Mr Koenig or 'old man' Schwab was definitely having regular sex with her. And with that vision in their minds, the men would go quiet for a brief moment as they considered their lustful thoughts.

It was rude and it was wrong, but that was the character of Russian men and that alas was the nature of things.

That first night as he lay in his bunk Pavel mulled over his future. He was determined to do well, he knew he could, all he needed was a chance. After all, everyone said he had the 'gift'.

He also considered his present situation. He was warm and he was well fed and he reckoned that he could get on well enough with the other men as long as he kept his 'head down' and his mouth shut. He closed his eyes that night, wondering what the following day would bring. But whatever it was, he was determined that he would do it well.

It was the sound of the bowls and wooden spoons being noisily stacked on the long table that awoke Pavel that first morning. Kibbel was up and about and getting on with the breakfasts and he whistled to himself as he collected up the tin mugs that would eventually be filled with the dark tea that was already bubbling away quietly in a large urn on top of the hot iron stove.

Some of the men were also up and awake and were parading into the washroom. Pavel quickly got out of bed and followed them in and stood his turn, dutifully waiting for the first empty sink. He would have to do this every day, he realized that and he knew he would have to get used to it.

After washing and a quick visit to the toilet shed outside, he went back inside and followed the other men to the long table. They would each pick up a bowl and go over to the stove and ladle some of last night's stew out of the hot iron pot. Kibbel would hover over them and serve out the mugs of hot tea. Some of the men lit their pipes and the calming smell of tobacco permeated the room. Pavel took a bowl of stew and sat down with the men. A mug of tea was thrust onto the table in front of him and he sat there and ate quietly.

A man who was sitting directly opposite Pavel looked over at him.

'Where are you from boy?' he asked.

'Zhumyov,' replied Pavel, and he was immediately alert.

'Never heard of it,' said the man with disinterest and he turned away to talk to his other comrades. Within twenty minutes the men had all finished eating and smoking and they stood up and proceeded to get ready to go to work.

Pavel approached Kibbel.

'What do you want me to do Mr Kibbel?' he asked.

Kibbel looked down at the boy. This was the first time anyone had called him 'Mr Kibbel'.

Kibbel liked that, he liked that a lot.

It wasn't that he was disrespected within the factory, he wasn't. Everyone in the factory actually needed Kibble for something or other, but nobody ever called him 'Mr Kibbel', not even the secretary, although he wished she would.

'Right,' said Kibbel, 'Wash out all the bowls and the mugs and stack them on top of the cupboard over there in the corner.'

'Right sir,' said Pavel.

Kibbel liked that too.

'And tomorrow morning you can pour out the tea out for the men,' he said.

Pavel nodded.

Kibbel helped himself to a second bowl of warm stew and then went to sit down.

'When you've finished you can mop the floor while I go and speak to Mr Koenig. We'll see where he wants you to start.'

Pavel again nodded.

Kibbel finished his extended breakfast and then ambled off to the factory to find Mr Koenig, who was sitting at his desk as usual, amid the piles of paperwork.

'Morning Mr Koenig,' said Kibbel as he repeated the greeting he gave to Mr Koenig every single morning.

'Yes Kibbel.' was the ever recurring reply.

Kibbel put on his 'helpful face'.

'It's the new boy, young Pavel Bratz. Where do you want to start him Mr Koenig?'

Mr Koenig looked up from his papers and he stopped writing for a moment. He'd forgotten all about the new boy. At that particular moment he had bigger problems to sort out. Production targets were not being met and there was the risk of cancelled orders.

Mr Koenig sighed. These young lads were usually quite hopeless, and he gave this new dilemma a moment's thought.

'Right,' he said, 'There's some wide planking stacked against the wall in 'B' shed. It'll make decent tops for the small tables. They'll need cutting down to a basic size before the final cutting and shaping. You'll have to measure and mark them out for him Kibbel, these young lads haven't a clue on measurement. Mark out the sizes for him, do about fifteen tops and then give him a saw and have him hand cut them. We'll see if there's any work in him and we'll also see if he's capable of sawing wood in a straight line. Mark them out generously Kibbel. We can always straighten them up later on the circular saw in the main factory. No doubt the boy will make the usual hash of things.'

Mr Koenig shook his head 'They're all idiots and they're all bone idle. There's not a day's work in any of them. I keep telling Mr Schwab that they're all a waste of time, all they want to do is run home to their mothers.'

Kibble nodded in agreement, as he always did.

'I'll get him started Mr Koenig,' he said unquestioningly. Kibble knew of course that there was no need to cut the table tops by hand. The wood could be cut to an exact size in the main factory on an industrial circular saw. But he supposed that the lad would have to learn and he would have to learn the hard way. After all, if the boy was going to be a master carpenter, he'd have to learn the skills and as a carpenter he'd definitely have to know how to use a saw properly.

'And keep an eye on him Kibbel,' growled Mr Koenig, 'we've enough wasted timber in this factory.'

It was a timely reminder and Kibbel retreated hastily.

As he went off to get Pavel, Kibbel shrugged his shoulders.

'Whatever happens,' he thought to himself, 'the boy was not his problem.'

Pavel was taken around to 'B' shed where he had to lay the long planks of timber flat as Kibbel measured and marked out the wood with a thick black graphite pencil. Kibbel then disappeared and returned shortly carrying an old and very used saw.

'Here, use this,' he said to Pavel and he handed him the saw.

Kibbel then pointed to an old joiner's bench and he then instructed Pavel to cut the timber planking down to size.

'Use the saw carefully,' he said, 'and make a good job, you've plenty to do. I'll be back to check up on you later' and with that he walked away, leaving the boy to get on with it.

Pavel smiled to himself once he was left alone. This suited him. He liked to work on his own because he always had. He picked up the first length of timber and laid it on the bench. He instinctively felt the grain of the wood, he knew all about wood. It was like an old friend. He then picked up the saw and started to cut the timber down to size. For Pavel, it was almost a joy. The saw was actually fairly decent when compared to the saws back home and the timber was good, very good really. It had been carefully stored and dried and therefore wasn't warped and it didn't have a lot of 'knots' in the grain either. So he started to saw, effortlessly.

Back in the factory Kibble, Koenig and not even Mr Schwab, none of them, not even the other men were aware that working in their midst was a young man who had a 'gift'.

Pavel started to saw, straight and true. It was the only way that he knew how to saw, it was almost impossible for him to falter and cut a wavering line. He'd been sawing up pieces of timber since he'd been five years old, when his father had given him a small tenon saw to cut up the random bits of wood, the wood that he would later whittle into the small animal shapes as his family sat by the evening fire.

Two hours later, and he'd finished.

Kibbel had gone off to do his own work, which basically involved following Mr Koenig's instructions. He would distribute the timber around the factory so that all the men were constantly working. In his spare moments he would call back to the kitchen in their living quarters and start to prepare the food for the next meal.

Mr Koenig supplied the roubles to Kibble, who would buy in the food for the kitchen. Kibble shopped around and acquired the food from various sources, and he also managed to make himself a reasonable profit.

He'd re-stoked the cooking stove with more wood and he'd put the pot of stew back onto the heat to warm. He'd bulked up the stew with more cabbage and beetroot and after the men had eaten their lunch he'd replenish the pot again. Today it would be a large lump of bacon and some potatoes and more cabbage of course.

It was as he walked back into the factory that he was met by Pavel. His heart sank for a fleeting moment. He'd quite forgotten about the boy and he immediately wondered what had gone wrong. Had Pavel broken the saw or had he just stopped through his own laziness? Well at least there was no sign of blood, so that was one problem less.

'What's wrong?' asked Kibble tersely. It was almost a threat.

Pavel looked up at him. 'Nothing's wrong,' he said in reply.

'So what are you doing?' again asked Kibble.

'I've finished,' replied Pavel.

'Finished what?'

'Finished cutting the table tops,' said Pavel.

Kibbles heart sank. Yet another disaster was in the offing and he immediately conjured up the image of a ranting and raving Mr Koenig. And of course it would all be Kibble's fault for not keeping an eye on the boy. More wastage and more grief...

'What do you mean 'you've finished'..?' said Kibble, his voice rising.

'The table tops. They're all done,' said Pavel.

Kibbel sighed and his shoulders began to sag. The inevitable, it would be another disaster.

'Right,' he almost moaned out loud, 'let's go and see what you've been up to.'

They both walked around the back of the factory and into 'B' shed.

Pavel took Kibble over to the old work bench.

'There,' he said as he pointed, 'Is that alright Mr Kibble?'

Stacked by the side of the bench were fifteen perfectly cut table tops. They were all uniformly cut and each one was identical and absolutely square.

Kibble was slightly dumbstruck. These table tops were good, so good that they wouldn't need finishing off on any factory saw.

'Have you done these?' Kibble asked, almost wondering if some of the other men were playing a hoax on him.

'Yes Mr Kibble,' answered Pavel.

'Right,' said Kibble, still taken aback, 'Well then, go to the kitchen and start getting things ready for the men's lunch.'

As Pavel walked back to the kitchen, Kibble once again checked the fifteen table tops. They were absolutely perfect. He took a deep breath, turned around and went off to find Mr Koenig.

Koenig was as usual, sitting at his desk behind a mass of paperwork when Kibbel suddenly arrived. He gave his underling a resigned look.

'What is it Kibble?' he asked.

'It's the new boy sir.'

Koenig began to grind his teeth.

'What the hell's happened now?' he asked again.

'Oh no, it's nothing like that Mr Koenig. It's just that I'd like to show you something.'

Koenig leant back in his chair and took a deep breath, and then he pulled out his silver pocket watch and checked the time. Lunch was fast approaching and so he considered that he may as well stop what he was doing and find out what Kibble was blithering on about. So he stood up slowly and followed Kibble's slightly shuffling figure out through the factory door and over to' B' shed. Once they were there Kibbel directed Mr Koenig over to the workbench to show him Pavel's work.

Mr Koenig looked and he frowned, and then he raised an eyebrow. Then he took a closer look. He then picked up one of the table tops and ran his hand around the slightly rounded edges.

'These tops have been smoothed around the edges, have you done this Kibbel?' he asked.

'No Mr Koenig, I just told the boy to cut the wood to size. I didn't notice that he'd smoothed down the edges too.'

And with that, Kibble picked up one of the table tops and ran his hand appreciatively over the wood. Both men stared at each other for a moment.

'What saw did he use?' asked Koenig.

'Just one of the old factory handsaws.' and Kibbel looked around for a moment and spotted the old saw on top of a stack of wooden blocks. Beside it was an old and ancient wood plane.

'That's the saw,' he said, 'and he must have used that old plane too.'

Mr Koenig put down the table top and then went over to inspect the tools. Then he went back to the stack of table tops and checked every one of them. They were all identical.

'So you're telling me that with those old tools, the boy produced work of this quality?'

'Yes, Mr Koenig.'

'How long did it take him?'

'Err...two, maybe three hours.' Kibble had to think about that one.

Mr Koenig raised his eyebrows, again.

'Where's the boy now?'

'He's back in the kitchen cleaning up.'

Mr Koenig looked directly at Kibble.

'Let him eat...and then after lunch send him over to me.'

An hour later, after the men had eaten and gone back to work and the kitchen had been cleaned. Kibble turned to Pavel.

'Mr Koenig wants to speak to you.'

Pavel's insides immediately tightened.

'Have I done something wrong Mr Kibbel?'

Kibbel looked down at Pavel and he suddenly realised that he liked the boy. And why not.

'No, I don't think you have anything to worry about. Mr Koenig wants to talk to you about the work you did this morning.'

'Was it not right Mr Kibbel?' again asked Pavel.

'No it was good Pavel, very good. So go and speak to Mr Koenig. Go right now.'

Pavel turned and quickly headed for the door.

'Just one thing,' added Kibbel.

Pavel looked back at him.

'Keep your wits about you boy. Mr Koenig isn't a man to be messed about...or lied to.'

Pavel nodded, and left.

As he walked back into the factory Pavel wondered just what Mr Koenig wanted to see him about. He decided to take heed of Kibble's advice and be on his guard. Pavel knew he had to do well here at the Schwab's factory. His father had told him to work hard and he couldn't go back home in disgrace. And also his father's business depended on him learning the furniture business. Yes, he would have to keep his wits about him.

So he entered the factory with some trepidation and made his way to Mr Koenig's desk.

As Pavel approached, Koenig looked up from his unending pile of paperwork and files and then returned to his notes and carried on scribbling for the next two or three minutes.

Pavel stood there in front of the desk in respectful silence.

Eventually, Koenig sighed to himself and put down his pencil. Then he leant back in his chair and looked directly at Pavel.

'Hmmm' said Mr Koenig

Pavel just stood there, rigid and silent.

'What's your name again, boy?'

'Bratz Sir, Pavel Bratz. I'm from Zhumyov, Sir'

'Are you really Bratz?'

'Yes Sir.'

'And were exactly is...'Zhumyov', Bratz?'

Pavel had to think for a moment.

'Err...South, I think Sir. But I don't know how far south, Sir.'

'Hmmm' said Mr Koenig, again.

'And how old are you, Bratz?'

'Sixteen, but I'll soon be seventeen, in September sir.'

'And what do you do, Bratz?' asked Mr Koenig calmly.

'Beg your pardon sir?' asked Pavel.

'What do you 'do'...Mr Bratz?' Mr Koenig asked again.

Pavel was now confused. He didn't understand the question and he was becoming a little flustered, and then he started to blush.

'I...I don't understand you sir.'

Mr Koenig stared at Pavel, unremittingly. Then he continued.

'What have you been doing with the first fifteen years of your life?' he asked.

'I've been to school, sir,' replied Pavel, hopefully.

'And what else have been doing Mr Bratz?'

'Sir?' asked Pavel.

'Do you work at all?' asked Koenig.

Pavel had to think about that for a moment.

'I help my father, sir,' he replied.

'And what does your father do, Bratz?'

'Err...building work sir,' lied Pavel.

'And does he let you work with wood at all?'

'Yes, sometimes sir.'

'And what does he let you do?'

'Err...sometimes he lets me saw up some of the beams sir.'

'Hmmm' said Mr Koenig.

Pavel was beginning to feel hot under Mr Koenig's steady gaze, uncomfortably hot.

Koenig picked up his pencil and began to tap it repeatedly on his desktop. Then he stopped.

'Well then Mr Pavel Bratz of 'Zhumyov', which is apparently 'somewhere south' of here. Could you tell me please, how it is that a sixteen year old schoolboy who pretends to know 'nothing about nothing', can suddenly walk into this factory and in two or three hours produce fifteen quality table tops to a standard that only a couple of my top finishing carpenters could equal? I am slightly mystified by it all. And so, would you like to enlighten me please, Mr Bratz?'

There was a silence, a few moments of intense silence in which Mr Koenig expected an answer, and Pavel was expected to give an explanation.

Pavel just stood there. He knew he would have to 'come clean' and give a relevant answer, or at least give a fairly honest answer. His brain suddenly began to work and he decided that he would tell the truth. Well his version of the truth anyway.

'I have the 'gift' sir,' he suddenly blurted it out.

Mr Koenig just sat there and looked at Pavel. 'I beg your pardon?' he said. He was a little astonished by the boy's outburst.

'I've been told I've got 'the gift' sir. Well, what I mean is I've got 'some sort' of gift, sir.'

'And what is this 'gift' that you apparently have?' asked the still quizzical Mr Koenig.

'It's with wood sir. I have the gift with wood.'

'Oh really.' said Mr Koenig, who was still slightly taken aback with the young man's explanation.

'And who told you that you've got this 'gift'..?'

'My father, sir,' said Pavel.

'Oh really,' said Mr Koenig again.

Pavel tried to explain.

'From being a small boy, I've always worked with wood sir. When I was five years old I used to cut up pieces of spare timber with a little saw and then whittle them into animal shapes and from there and working along with my father, I've just kept on learning, sir.'

'And you've learned all of this from whittling bits of wood and cutting up the odd beam or two for your father?' asked Mr Koenig.

Pavel suddenly stopped looking at Mr Koenig and he stared down at the floor. He was caught. He'd tripped himself up and he knew it.

There was a silence.

'What does your father actually do boy, and this time I want the truth?' said Mr Koenig.

Pavel looked up at Mr Koenig.

'We make furniture sir.'

Mr Koenig looked down at the boy and he had to put his hand over his mouth to stop himself from laughing out loud.

'Of course you do,' he said to Pavel, 'Of course you do.'

It was then all so obvious.

Pavel coughed 'It's not like the furniture here sir,' he spouted, 'it's just simple everyday furniture, for the people in our town.'

'And your father would like you to learn how to make the quality furniture that we at Schwab's manufacture?'

'Err, yes I suppose so sir.'

'And then he wants to steal our business does he, eh?' Koenig smiled.

'Oh no sir, I don't think we could ever do that. We're from Zhumyov. It's only a small town.'

'So you keep telling me,' said Koenig as he eyed young Pavel.

Pavel, quite wisely decided not to mention that his father now owned a lathe.

'Well Pavel Bratz,' said Mr Koenig seriously, 'you may have a talent, and you may not. Your work on those table tops was quite good. However, you will now have the chance to spend the next five years in this factory and if you have any talent at all, we will find it. You will have to work very hard and once you have gained one skill, then you can move onto another department and learn another. After five years you may make a reasonable carpenter. We'll see. It's up to you to put in the work.'

Pavel nodded.

'Right,' said Mr Koenig, 'Go and find Kibbel, I'm sure he can find you something to do.'

'Yes sir,' replied Pavel and he turned and quickly left.

Mr Koenig once more tapped his pencil on the top of his desk as he watched Pavel walk away. There was something about that boy, just 'something'.

And he sat there for a moment, thinking, and then he smiled to himself.

'With my luck, I'll probably end up working for him one day' and with that thought he turned back to his paperwork.

As Pavel walked through the stacks of uncut timber on his way back to the kitchen, he considered just what Mr Koenig had said to him, and he shook his head angrily.

'Five years be damned,' Pavel cursed, 'I'll learn it all in three years.'

It would actually take four.

CHAPTER 3

On the day that Ivan Bratz left his youngest son at the Schwab furniture factory in Smolensk, it had been his full intention to return home straight away and get back to the creature comforts of his nice warm house, back in his home town of Zhumyov.

But for some reason, no.

When he'd arrived at the grand old railway station in Smolensk he'd looked for the daily train timetables, which he finally found bolted to a steel pillar inside a green metal case for all to see. He looked for his destination, which was Sevska; it was the nearest town to Zhumyov that any train actually ran to. But his gaze fell elsewhere. And it was the city of Moscow that kept drawing Bratz's attention.

He'd never been to Moscow. He'd never even considered it. But now the thought of that city seemed to hold some sort of fascination for him. He suddenly really wanted to go there and now of course, he was free to go where and wherever took his favour.

Bratz would never know why he decided to change his plans on that particular day. Maybe it was the sense of freedom. Now that he was earning a reasonable amount of money he suddenly realised that he was able to travel freely. His business could run well enough without him for a few days, so that wouldn't be a problem either.

Ivan Bratz suddenly smiled to himself. Yes, he was a free man and he could go anywhere he wanted. And he wanted to go to Moscow.

He went to the ticket office inside the station and pulled out some roubles to pay for his fare. Twenty minutes later he was sitting in a window seat in the carriage of the train that was taking him north, towards Russia's capital city.

Moscow was a revelation and a complete shock to Ivan Bratz. The train had taken several hours to travel through the hills and valleys and the never ending plains that was Russia. When he finally arrived at Rijskiy train station in central Moscow the sky was beginning to darken. He initially walked around the streets of the busy Meshchansky District for a couple of hours and then he found himself a small cheap hotel where he could spend the night and also eat. After his meal he immediately went to his bedroom and slept. He wanted to get an early start the next morning. From his slightly bleak hotel in the Meshchansky District it was only half an hour's walk into central Moscow

The next day and after his breakfast, Bratz paid his bill and then set off to discover the city. He was astounded by Moscow, he'd never been anywhere like it in his life. The city was huge and seemingly never ending and so very busy. He'd never seen such a mass of people in one place.

Compared to Moscow, Smolensk was almost a small town. All the buildings in Moscow were so large and so tall. As Bratz wandered around the city he looked at the furniture shops and stores and he was absolutely astounded by the prices that were being charged there. He very quickly realized that there was money in Moscow and that there was money to be made, and suddenly Bratz saw another future, and another possibility.

The high quality furniture that he'd seen in Moscow was something that 'Bratz Factory' could one day eventually produce. There was one problem though, and it was a problem that Ivan Bratz had already almost unwittingly made inroads to solve. The furniture of the highest class, and price, was undoubtedly the inlaid furniture. Beautiful tables and chairs and cabinets all inlaid with intricate designs made from various exotic woods and all in different colours and textures. Bratz looked through the shop windows at that furniture and it actually made him jealous with frustration.

And then he thought about his son Pavel, and he knew what his son was capable of, and Ivan Bratz suddenly understood what the future could hold.

Bratz smiled. His time would come.

It was late morning and Ivan Bratz had decided to make his way back to Rijskiy train station. He'd already realized that the City of Moscow was too vast for him to see in one go. He'd also taken the decision that he could now get on a train and travel back to Moscow whenever he liked. And that thought also made him feel good.

On his way back to the station he stopped at a small cafe for some lunch. He'd sat down at a table outside the cafe and decided to have a glass of dark beer and some bread and cheese. As he sat there watching the never ending crowds of people pass by, two men appeared. They were both heading in his direction and they were carrying a large wooden ladder. It turned out that they were there to do some repair work to the gutters on the shop adjacent to the cafe where Bratz was having his meal. He turned to watch the men. Bratz at one time had worked on buildings and in construction and he felt rather at ease watching other men doing the same work that he'd had to do for years. The men propped their long ladder against the building and Bratz remembered the days when he'd had to take on the same sort of work. Even the ladder that they were using reminded Bratz of his own old ladder. It was made from two long lengths of timber with flat wooden slats crudely nailed across the two timbers to form rungs.

Yes, a basic ladder and simply made. Back in those days everyone made their own ladders out of the spare bits of timber that they'd acquired.

One of the men went off to collect his tools and the other man went into the shop, which was a hat shop, and he went in to speak to the owners. The first man returned and both of them had some sort of discussion. Apparently some of the old guttering was leaking and needed replacing. One of them then climbed up the ladder to inspect the work. The building was quite high but the ladder was long enough and once he was up there, and with a bit of effort, the man started to grapple with the length of guttering. But for some reason, he couldn't seem to get it free. So he came back down the ladder for a wood saw, and then he stopped for a while to have a chat with his partner. Bratz smiled to himself as he watched the two men. Workmen were always the same, more talk than work. The man then went back up the ladder with his saw and he began to cut through the long length of wooden guttering. His partner held firmly onto the bottom of the ladder to keep it rigid and to stop it from slipping. Finally the man managed to cut the guttering free and he quickly grabbed hold of it to stop it from falling onto the pedestrians below. It was quite a long piece, probably five or six feet long, and the man had some difficulty coming back down the ladder whilst carrying the length guttering and the saw.

Bratz watched as the man started to descend.

Very carefully, the man slowly made his way back down, but at that moment one of the rungs on the ladder snapped in half. The wood cracked as it broke and the man screamed as he fell backwards and somersaulted through the air.

Bratz sat there in horror as he watched the man arch and then fall backwards.

Within seconds the man hit the floor, head first. There was a sickening thump followed by a woman's screams. The man's head had split open and his bloodied brains had splattered onto the pavement like some spilt food. There was a collective groan as everyone instinctively turned away.

Bratz jumped to his feet as the man's partner cried out in shock. He ran over to the dead man and as he did he grabbed a tablecloth off a nearby table. It was an act of mercy and the only thing that he could to do was to cover the poor man. The dead man's partner was visibly shocked and Bratz took hold of his arm as a crowd slowly gathered, suddenly inquisitive at the sight of blood.

One of the owners from the hat shop and some of the staff from the cafe ran over and there was a panicked discussion. The owner of the hat shop ran back to his premises and returned with a large blanket which covered the man's body completely. In the end there was nothing that could be done. Somebody acquired a man with a horse and a flat cart and then several men got together and lifted the dead man's broken body onto the back of the cart. The dead man's partner was helped onto the cart and he sat there silently at the side of the driver as instructions were given as to the whereabouts of the local morgue. The staff from the cafe washed away the blood and mess with mops and shovels and buckets of water and Bratz and two other men took hold of the broken ladder and dragged it down by the side of the hat shop and then returned to move the workmen's discarded tools.

Within ten minutes the crowd had moved away and life went on as though nothing had ever happened.

Bratz observed all of this with some uncertainty, and then he realized that this was city life. A far cry from small town Zhumyov where a tragic death would affect the whole community.

He then turned around and decided to go and examine the offending ladder. On inspection he noticed that the ladder was fairly old and very used, and in places the timber was beginning to show signs of rot. The broken rung was mouldy and decayed and it had simply snapped under the man's weight. Bratz looked more closely at the ladder. It was shoddily made from cheap timber, the rungs were no more than flat nailed slats and the whole design was weak and flawed. Unfortunately, it was typical of every ladder that Bratz had ever seen, even those that he himself had used. And though it had never happened to him personally, he had seen other ladders fail and had seen other men fall. But he'd never seen anyone killed before and he wondered how many people must have suffered serious injury or been killed because they'd fallen from faulty old ladders.

With that thought in his mind he made his way back to the Rijskiy train station and he went to the ticket office to purchase a ticket that would take him back to Sevska. Once he was on the train he slept for half an hour but his sleep was troubled and he awoke repeatedly. Eventually he gave up and just stared vacantly out of the window. The city had been left long behind as the train travelled onwards through the vast Russian countryside.

It was the new age of communication and Bratz's mind began to wander as he watched the newly installed wooden telegraph poles flash by the side of his carriage window as the train headed south. There were hundreds, if not thousands of those same telegraph poles and Bratz began to think about the amount of timber that must be being used. Dark brown, and almost black, those telegraph poles would stand the test of time in the hot summers and the freezing cold winters of the bleak Russian climate and those same poles would still be happily standing there fifty years hence. Bratz considered this and he realized that those telegraph poles were actually going to outlive him. And his inquisitive mind began to work as he wondered how it was that they could last so long after years of heat and cold and damp.

He'd worked in construction for years and had dealt with a lifetime of rotten wood and timber and again he thought about the broken ladder and the other ladders that he'd owned which had rotted and broke and that he'd had to throw away or burned. And he wondered what sort of timber the telegraph poles were made from, and again, why was it that they lasted so long.

With that thought in mind, he leant forward and looked through the window and down the track, only to see those same telegraph poles disappear into the distance.

He stared intently at them, pole after pole, all tall and round and strong.

And suddenly, like a burst of light, the answer lit up in Ivan Bratz's brain. The poles, and their strength, it was because of their shape. They were round. It was so obvious. If the telegraph poles had been cut squarely like the timber beams in roofs they would perish and warp and break. But no, being round gave them their remarkable strength. He saw it for what it was, so damn obvious, and yes, that same strength could and should be incorporated into the design of ladders. Of course it should.

And Bratz knew that he could design and make those ladders. Ladders with stronger rounded rungs. Because back in Zhumyov he had a lathe that could make those rungs, and not only make them, he could churn them out by the hundreds, all day long. No more nailed and weak wooden slats, these 'new' rungs could be inserted into holes drilled into the ladder's legs and they would be incredibly strong.

Bratz's mind was now moving considerably quicker than the train that was carrying him. Suddenly there was another future, and yet another possibility. He sat back and closed his eyes and in his mind he began to design his 'new ladders', and then he set in motion a possible business plan.

Finally he drifted off to sleep and an hour quickly slipped by. When he awoke he pulled out his old pocket watch and checked the time. It had turned three o' clock and there was still a long way to go. He once again turned his attention to the telegraph poles and he gazed intently as they still flashed by. Then something suddenly happened which made Bratz turn and look again. The train had just gone past a group of men who were working on the telegraph poles. Bratz immediately realized that these were the men who were fitting the all important telegraph wires to the poles, the wires that would allow people to contact one another from all over the vast expanses of Russia. Bratz once more sat back and considered their task. There must be thousands of miles of telegraph wire which then had to be attached to the thousands of those tough wooden poles. How many wooden poles would they have to put into the ground? Once again Bratz wondered where all that timber came from.

The train travelled another couple of miles and then out of the blue it went past another group of men, and this time Ivan Bratz did take notice.

There were a gang of about fifteen men with three large carts that were being pulled by more than a dozen horses. Two of the carts were stacked high with long dark telegraph poles and the men were digging the large holes in the ground in which the poles would be erected. Some of the men were unloading the poles and others were setting the poles into the ground and making them ready for the following gang who would fit the connecting wires. There was a third cart which contained the workers provisions, their food, water and supplies.

At that moment Ivan Bratz made a decision.

Half an hour later the train pulled into the tiny station at 'Raevka'.

Raevka itself had been a small village that through sheer chance had been in the 'right place' when the railway tracks were being laid. Since then it had continued to grow steadily and eventually Raevka would become a small town.

Bratz got off the train there. He stepped down off the train and onto the railway track and without delay he started to walk back in the direction he had just travelled from, and he kept on walking.

Three hours later the skies had just begun to turn a darker grey as Bratz finally approached the camp where he'd seen the men working. The digging was done and the poles had been set in the ground and for the workmen the day was over. The men were sitting around a large campfire, eating stew and telling tales. Tomorrow would be another day.

As they all sat there one of the men saw Ivan Bratz walking down the line towards them. He quickly alerted his workmates and they all turned around to stare at the stranger who was walking into their camp, apparently from 'nowhere'.

'Who was he?'

As he approached the men Bratz hailed to them.

'Hello there, how are you?' he called out as he approached.

They were astounded. They asked him 'where on earth' had he come from, to which Bratz replied, 'Raevka train station. It's been a long walk.'

They then gave him some hot stew and a tin mug full of strong dark tea which he readily accepted. Then they asked what he was doing out there.

'I've come to speak to you,' he replied.

This slightly baffled the men, who wondered 'What on earth did he want?' Bratz turned to them.

'Tell me, where do all those telegraph poles come from and what sort of wood are they?'

The men looked around to a tall man who was wearing a long woollen coat and had thick grey hair poking out from the worn homburg hat that he was wearing. He was smoking tobacco from an equally worn brown pipe. It turned out that this man was the foreman.

He looked at Bratz strangely as he wondered about this oddly curious man had wandered into their camp from nowhere, and was now was asking questions about telegraph poles.

The foreman took a long draw on his pipe and then he spoke to Bratz.

'My friend, the wood is Baltic Pine and it comes in from two regions. Most of it is from Karelia, which is a large timber region up in northern Russia, next to Finland. The rest comes from eastern Siberia, but that's a long way to transport it and makes it expensive.'

Bratz thought about that for a moment.

'And what stops the wood from rotting away?' he then asked.

The foreman took another draw on his pipe and glanced at his men. They all just stood around listening and it struck the foreman that though his men worked day after day with these poles, none of them actually knew the history or geography of the timber that they were handling.

'Baltic Pine is a very tough wood,' the foreman continued, 'first of all the trees are cut down and then stripped and left to dry out. After that they're taken and boiled in large vats of creosote. That's why the poles are a dark brown colour. After being coated in creosote the wood never rots. It's tougher than steel. Steel goes rusty and will eventually perish. These telegraph poles will still be here in fifty years, probably a lot longer.'

And then he turned to his men and smiled.

'These poles will still be here when all you bastards are dead.'

Some of the men laughed as somebody muttered 'and you...'

The foreman took another draw on his pipe and nodded to himself.

They all just stood there, and then it was Bratz who broke the silence.

'Thank you my friend,' he said, 'that's all I needed to know.'

And with that he turned and walked away from the camp.

The men were slightly flabbergasted and they stood there amazed as they watched Bratz walk away into the darkness.

One of them called after him 'Where are you going?'

'Back to Raevka,' Bratz shouted in reply.

The man again called to Bratz to warn him that he would get lost.

'I'll follow the railway line,' Bratz shouted again as he disappeared into the night.

The foreman relit his pipe and shook his head as he tried to understand what exactly had just happened.

The next morning Bratz got on the first train that drew into Raevka train station and from there he made his way home. When he finally arrived back at Zhumyov he ate a hearty meal and then went to bed and slept for nearly twenty four hours.

The next day he awoke refreshed and with his mind full of plans.

He spent the next two days scribbling and drawing on pieces of paper and when he'd made sure that his business was still running efficiently, he set off back to Sevska. Once there he called into see his timber supplier, a Mr Ertel, who had premises on the edge of town.

Mr Ertel smiled when he saw Ivan Bratz walk into his office. Bratz had become rather a 'decent' customer and Mr Ertel was now making rather decent money from him. They shook hands, as was customary and then they sat down as Bratz told Mr Ertel that he wanted some 'Baltic Pine' from Karelia. Bratz went on to explain to Ertel that Karelia was a region up north, next to Finland.

Ertel knew exactly were Karelia was. He'd been in the timber business long enough to know precisely where every type of wood used in Russia came from.

'What do you want the timber for?' he asked.

But Bratz was giving nothing away.

'I have some new ideas Ertel,' he replied, 'but if it comes off we may need quite a bit of this 'Baltic Pine'...'

Ertel smiled. There was a lot of Baltic Pine about. In fact, Karelia was full of the stuff.

So Bratz gave him a basic order and Ertel gave him a basic price, which of course would be negotiable depending on quantity.

They then shook hands again and the deal was done.

Bratz left Ertel's office and once again headed for the train station. He bought a ticket and within half an hour he was on his way back to Smolensk. Not to visit his son, Bratz was far too busy for that.

Once he was in Smolensk, Bratz made his way to the premises of 'Shefner Machine and Tool Supply' where he spoke to the owner, Mr Shefner, about a special order. It was to be a simple enough project really. Bratz gave a description of a steel tank of quite large proportions that he wanted to be constructed. The tank would be approximately twenty foot long, and around five foot in width and the same in depth. He wanted it to be built on steel legs so that it would stand roughly three foot off the ground. Bratz then described the series of lids that would fit on top of the tank and that one of those lids would need to be fitted with a small funnel. He then went on to order two hundred and fifty gallons of refined creosote.

Once again Bratz shook hands as the order was acknowledged, and he was promised that the tank would be delivered in three to four weeks. That suited Bratz, it would hopefully be around the same date that his Baltic Pine would arrive.

It took just over a month and the timber, the steel tank and the creosote all arrived within three days of one another. The tank and the creosote were carefully placed in the corner of Bratz's yard and the timber was stacked outside the 'cutting shed'.

During the month Bratz had spoken about his plans at length with his two other sons, Yakov and Nikolai. He'd told them both all about his idea to start manufacturing ladders, a new type of ladder, a ladder that would be solid and strong and safe.

He'd then told them about the second part of his plan.

Once the ladders were manufactured he was going to boil them in creosote, just like the telegraph poles that he'd seen. And that was what the tank was for. They would put a small lit brazier under the steel tank and let the ladders slowly simmer away. Then after cooling he would let them dry out. Those ladders would then be virtually indestructible. They would be the best ladders in Russia. Surely they would sell. After all, everybody needed a ladder at some time or another. Bratz considered that the demand in Moscow alone would be huge, because nobody else was making anything like them.

So they started. His men cut the wood to size and his sons took turns on the lathe producing the rungs. From the start their first ladder was good, it was very good. Bratz had worked out the exact the sizes and dimensions required. The circular rungs were stronger than anything Ivan Bratz had ever seen. His design had worked.

They placed that first ladder in the tank to give it a 'trial run' in the boiling creosote. It simmered away for a few hours and then they left it to cool down overnight. Finally they took the lid off the tank and retrieved their shiny new 'offspring'. They propped their new ladder up by the side of the tank and let it dry off in the sun. The result, an hour later, was superb. The pale timber had turned the deep brown colour of strong tobacco. Their ladder was tough and durable and unyielding.

Bratz looked on and he smiled. It was a success.

And so they went into production. They had to give their product a name, it was simple enough really, and with that 'The Baltic Ladder Company' was born.

Bratz had a branding iron made and each and every ladder that they produced would bear 'The Baltic Ladder Company' brand. It was just like branding cattle, and it worked. The deep black lettering stood out proud on every one of their ladders.

Two weeks later Bratz sent a driver with his horse and cart all the way to Smolensk. On the back of the cart were twenty of their 'Baltic Ladders'. Bratz went to Smolensk on the train where he met up with the driver and they then made their way to the premises of 'Shefner Machine and Tool Supply'. Bratz showed the owner Mr Shefner his new tough industrial ladders and it turned out that Mr Shefner was more than just interested. A deal was struck and a discussion as to a possible distribution agreement took place. Bratz then sent his driver back to Zhumyov and he returned there on the train. As he travelled he considered all the possibilities. He also decided that he might have to employ more men.

It's strange, the way things happen. Sometimes a word or a simple action can often alter the whole perception of someone's plans. And so it was with Bratz.

Once he'd starting to make his ladders he continued with his old habit of putting his goods 'on show'. It was just the same as in the early days when he first produced his basic furniture. Bratz leant several of his 'Baltic ladders' against the main gate of his yard with a sign advertising their price. There was plenty of local interest and the ladders started to sell, although in small town Zhumyov trade was a lot slower than Bratz had hoped.

About a month had passed by when one day a local woman, a widow by the name of Mrs Kasslik, ventured into Bratz's yard. Mrs Kasslik was in her late fifties and had lost her husband to pneumonia several years prior, she was sadly childless. She had also unfortunately never remarried. The widow Kasslik lived alone and in Mother Russia back in those days a single woman living on her own would lead a regrettably hard life.

Mrs Kasslik took in sewing and stitching and she repaired people's ripped, torn and worn clothing. She lived in a small house on the edge of town from where she eked out a meagre living. Living alone meant that she also had to constantly maintain and repair her own small property. She certainly couldn't afford to pay a tradesman. But after being widowed for several years she had become accustomed to carrying out some of the regular maintenance work herself. She could paint and clean the windows and whitewash the walls and she had taught herself how to clear and even repair the guttering. On more than one occasion she had even ventured onto the roof of her small house to replace a slipped or broken tile.

As she entered Bratz's yard on that particular day Mrs Kasslik had a problem. She owned an old ladder which she stored in her back yard and it was now rotting away. The ladder had been kindly given to her by a neighbour a few years before, but the constant weathering had taken its toll and the ladder had become unsafe. Mrs Kasslik had never been too fond of heights but had been forced to climb up and down the ladder through necessity. But now that same ladder was rotten and worn and to continue to use it was to possibly risk serious injury.

She had mentioned this to a neighbour earlier in the week and the neighbour had told her about Mr Bratz's new venture. Mrs Kasslik had bought some of her furniture from Bratz's in the past and had been quite impressed by the quality and definitely impressed by the price.

So on that day she'd gone to Bratz's factory where she inspected the ladders that were propped up outside the factory wall on display. She tried to move one of the ladders but realized straightaway that she had a problem. The ladders were just that bit too heavy and she struggled when she tried to lift them. So Mrs Kasslik quietly ventured into Bratz' yard to find Mr Bratz himself. One of the workmen had directed her to the office and Mrs Kasslik walked in there to find Mr Bratz at his desk, eating a sausage and drinking a mug of tea.

'Good morning Mr Bratz,' she said pleasantly.

'Oh hello Mrs Kasslik,' Bratz replied. Of course he recognized her immediately, in Zhumyov everybody knew everybody.

'How are you and your family Mr Bratz?' she enquired.

'We are well thank you Mrs Kasslik, very well.'

'Mr Bratz,' she continued, 'I need a ladder.'

'Ah,' replied Bratz, 'there I can help you Mrs Kasslik.'

'Well, maybe,' she said to him, 'but it seems that I have a slight problem with your ladders Mr Bratz.'

Bratz frowned.

'And what's the problem Mrs Kasslik?' he asked her.

'They're a bit too heavy for me Mr Bratz. You see, I need a new ladder and I need one that's safe. You're ladders are very well made and I've just looked at the ones outside, but I'd struggle to lift them. I'm not getting any younger Mr Bratz and I need something a little lighter in weight. Do you have anything?'

Bratz considered her request and yes, he could make something lighter for her. She had always been a likeable woman. He remembered her husband and he was a decent man too.

'Leave it with me Mrs Kasslik,' he said to her, 'We'll make you something a bit narrower and lighter for you, you'll be able to lift it and it will still be very well made, I can promise you that.'

'Oh thank you Mr Bratz,' she said, 'and how much will it cost me, please.'

Bratz smiled.

'Don't worry Mrs Kasslik, we'll sort something out.'

Then he thought for a moment.

'I'll tell you what Mrs Kasslik. I'll charge you half of the price of a normal ladder, just as long as you don't tell anyone.'

'Oh thank you Mr Bratz,' she said, 'that's very, very kind of you.'

'We'll make the ladder for you Mrs Kasslik and then I'll have it delivered to your house.'

'Thank you very much Mr Bratz. You're a very kind man,' she said. And with that she turned and left Bratz's office and went off and about her business.

Bratz again smiled. He knew that Mrs Kasslik would of course tell everybody.

But that would be a good enough recommendation.

Bratz took his two sons on one side and explained to them that he wanted a 'special order' making for the widow Kasslik. Both of the lads sighed, but Bratz took no notice.

He instructed them to make the ladder two thirds the width of normal and to cut the rungs slightly narrower and make the legs of the ladder a little thinner, again about two thirds of the original thickness.

His sons went back to their work and by the end of the week they had somehow found the time to produce the widow's ladder. On the Saturday morning, Yakov and Nikolai Bratz loaded all the ladders that they'd made during the week, into the creosote tank and then left them to simmer in the boiling creosote for a couple of hours before removing the hot brazier and leaving the ladders to cool over the weekend. The following Monday they returned to work and before they went into the workshops to finish off a furniture order, they took all the ladders out of the tank and stacked them flat on the ground. The last ladder out of the tank was the widow's smaller ladder and they placed it on top of the others.

At lunch time Yakov and Nikolai came out of the workshop to eat their lunch. The sun for once was shining and they decided to eat their usual bread and sausage outside in the sunshine. It certainly made a nice change.

They walked over to the corner of the yard to the creosote tank where the sun was at its best and they leant against the stack of newly dried ladders and as they ate they discussed the different girls in the village. Yakov, who knew that his brother had taken a fancy to one particular young lady jokingly started to talk about her physical attributes and how he was thinking of pursuing her himself. He inwardly smiled as he saw his younger brother start to fidget at that announcement. He loved to aggravate Nikolai. He did it all the time.

It was simply a 'brother' thing.

Nikolai just stood there, slightly red in the face, and to hide his unease he took hold of the top ladder on the stack and started to push it back and forth as he tried to steer the conversation onto another topic. Yakov watched in glee as his brother began to squirm and twitch. He'd seen this many times before and he knew his brothers habits. When embarrassed or uneasy Nikolai would always try to deflect his emotions by doing something with his hands. It was his body language and Yakov could spot it, always.

As Nikolai gabbled on about absolutely nothing, he kept repetitively pushing the top ladder back and forth, and something suddenly caught Yakov's attention. He looked at the top ladder, it was the narrow ladder that they'd made for Mrs Kasslik, and he noticed that it slotted exactly into the legs of the ladder underneath it. It was as though it had been purpose built to do so. But of course, it hadn't. Their father had given them the rough dimensions to work to and they'd done just that.

Yakov suddenly changed the conversation, much to his brother's relief, and he then showed Nikolai how the top ladder slotted into the lower one and both brothers started to push the ladder along the lower one until they pushed it too far and it tippled over. They slotted the ladder back in place and then pushed it the other way, till again they pushed it too far and it tipped over once more. Nikolai looked on and a thought occurred to him.

'You know something,' he said, 'We could make the ladders longer.'

'What do you mean?' asked Yakov.

'Well, if you somehow tied both the ladders together, you could sort of extend its length.'

Yakov looked at the ladders for a moment and suddenly realized what Nikolai meant.

'Go and get some rope,' he said to his brother.

Nikolai returned five minutes later with a length of rope and a sharp knife.

He and Yakov laid both ladders on the floor and they lashed them together near to the ends. But when they stood this now 'double' set of ladders up against one of the buildings the ladder sagged in the middle.

'We'll have to make it shorter,' said Yakov.

After a bit of trial and error and around twenty minutes later, they realized that the magic formula was actually the same as their father's original dimensions for the ladder's construction. It was the two thirds 'rule'. If they extended the ladders up to two thirds of their length and then lashed several rungs together, the double ladder was stable and strong and could easily carry a man's weight.

Though Yakov was the more practical of the two brothers, it was Nikolai who had the inventive mind. And it was Nikolai who then tried to simplify the system.

'If we put a couple of metal brackets at the top of the 'first' ladder, they would act as runners for the smaller ladder and would hold it in place,' he said, 'Then we would only have to lash one set of rungs together".

Yakov nodded to his brother.

'You're right,' he said and he immediately saw the possibilities.

'Go and get father,' he said to Nikolai.

Ivan Bratz sighed heavily as his son burst into his office. He too had just finished his lunch and was ready for a ten minute nap, but his son's insistence that they had something to show him dragged Bratz out of his office. When he got to the corner of the yard Yakov was waiting for him and at his feet, laid on the floor were the two ladders lashed together.

Bratz was unimpressed until the boys lifted the ladder and propped it against the wall and then Yakov, who was the bigger and heavier of the two, climbed up the ladder. He climbed right to the top and then bounced up and down vigorously on the high rungs.

Yakov laughed as he looked down at his wide eyed father.

'Look father,' he shouted, 'this is how strong our ladders are and now we can go even higher.'

Bratz stood there open mouthed as his son almost skipped back down to earth.

Nikolai intervened. He wanted some of the glory too.

'We can extent the ladders by two thirds by joining them together. You see Mrs Kasslick's narrower ladder slots right into our own ladder. If we could make some metal brackets we could attach them to the larger ladder and they would hold the smaller ladder in place and make it more stable. Then we would only have to lash one set of rungs together.'

The boys then took down the ladders and untied them and showed their father how both ladders slotted into each other.

Bratz looked on with some amazement.

'Tell me again about the brackets,' he said.

Nikolai explained, 'The brackets could be fitted at the top of the ladder and they would hold the smaller extending ladder firmly in place. They would also act as guides, so that you could move the ladder up or down easily.'

'And you say that the brackets would have to be made from some sort of metal?' enquired Bratz.

'Yes father, the brackets would have to be made from iron, something strong, stronger than wood.'

Bratz stood there, looking down at the ladders on the ground in front of him.

His mind was working too, and suddenly he was thinking of 'all' the possibilities.

'Right,' he said, as he snapped back to reality.

He looked over at his two sons.

'Pick up those ladders and follow me, now,' he said to them both as abruptly as ever.

'Where are we going?' asked Yakov.

'To see Kogan,' replied Bratz.

Both brothers nodded at their father.

Kogan was the town's blacksmith.

The three of them marched across the town, the two brothers carrying the ladders. The blacksmith's premises were on the other side of town, but since Zhumyov was a relatively small town it was only a distance of roughly three quarters a mile. As they approached they began hear the rhythmic sound of harsh metallic clanging. It was the sound of the blacksmith Kogan, mercilessly beating hot metal into shape.

They finally reached the forge, it was an old red brick building that was worn and had seen better days. Not unlike a lot of things in Russia back then. On the right hand side of the building was a covered 'lean to', a sort of open shed that was stacked high with the dark black charcoal that would be burned in the furnace and used to heat the iron bars that would be beaten, pounded and pummelled and eventually shaped into useful everyday implements. The building itself seemed to be built around the actual forge, which was a large stone affair whose chimney rose out through the roof, belching out black smoke like a small volcano.

As the three of them approached the entrance they were hit by the obvious heat and the almost indescribable smell of red hot iron. Inside, in the darkness, the pounding continued. The two Bratz boys put their ladder down on the ground and followed their father into the forge. As they entered they all stood there for a moment to let their eyes become accustomed to the dark interior, they also had to adapt their hearing to the terrific pounding of tempered steel on hot raw iron.

Standing there, illuminated in the bright red light from the furnace was a giant of a man. He was stripped to the waist except for the huge leather apron that he wore and he was methodically beating a thick length of red hot iron into shape.

It was Kogan. A huge bearded man with silver grey hair that hung down his broad neck and muscled arms that were nearly as wide as a man's leg.

The three of them stood there and watched as the town's blacksmith continued to hammer rhythmically on his anvil. It was almost as though he was beating a drum.

Bratz called out to Kogan, but the blacksmith was so intent on his work that he didn't hear Bratz's voice over the noise. In the end Bratz had to walk around the anvil to face Kogan and he had to wave his arms and shout to him before he finally got the blacksmith's attention.

Kogan stopped working and he looked across at his old friend.

'Ah Ivan,' he said and Kogan smiled as he spoke. He was one of the only people in Zhumyov who called Bratz by his first name. The only other person was probably Bratz's wife.

He and Bratz had grown up together. They went to school together. And they'd hunted and fished and even pursued the young women of Zhumyov together. It was more than just a friendship. They'd known each other from being young boys and they too were almost brothers.

Kogan was simply known locally as 'Kogan'. Most people didn't know whether it was actually his first or his last name, but Ivan Bratz did, of course he did.

'How are you...you old dog,' replied Bratz.

Kogan chuckled, and his huge body rippled. He grinned back at Bratz

'What do you want you bastard...I'm busy,' returned Kogan, he was still smiling.

And that was how they spoke to one another. It was the customary banter of their long friendship.

Bratz laughed, and then it was straight back to business.

'Come outside,' he said, 'I want to show you something.'

Kogan put down his large steel hammer and followed Bratz outside. As he passed them he acknowledged the two brothers, who nodded back at him like a couple of puppies.

Bratz showed Kogan the two ladders and explained their idea of how to turn them into one 'extending ladder' and how they wanted him to make the two brackets that would hold the ladders together.

Kogan rubbed his grey beard. He immediately understood. He went back into the forge and returned with a pair of callipers and a steel measure. Then he knelt on the ground and took various measurements and then he looked up at Bratz.

'We'll pin the brackets to the ladder with rivets, for strength.'

Bratz agreed with him, it made sense.

Kogan stood up and he and Bratz went back into the forge. The two brothers followed closely.

Kogan took a flat length of medium iron bar and threw it into the hot forge. It was about the width of a man's hand. Once the metal started to glow red he took it out of the flame and cut a short measured length with a huge pair of pincers, then he threw the remaining length back into the forge to keep it hot. He then took the short piece of hot iron to his anvil and punched two small round holes in either end with a short steel punch and then, with a hammer, he bent the ends over to form a 'u'-shaped bracket. Kogan briefly inspected his work and then tossed the newly made bracket into a bucket of water. Ivan Bratz looked on as the metal crackled and hissed and steamed in the cold water.

The whole procedure had only taken a few minutes, it was that simple.

Kogan then returned to the forge and with the remaining length of hot iron produced an identical bracket. It too was tossed into the bucket of water, along with its partner.

As the brackets cooled Kogan placed eight iron rivets into a steel cup which he then placed in the forge to heat up. The ladders were then brought inside as the four of them decided exactly where the brackets should be fixed.

Kogan marked the bottom ladder with a piece of charcoal and then when the rivets were almost white hot and gleaming he took each one and flattened down the end to give it a sharp, chiselled edge. Using these he then riveted the brackets to the ladder. The hot rivets buried themselves into the hard Baltic pine and settled there, immovable.

They then put the ladders back together, feeding the top narrower ladder through the brackets. And it worked, the whole idea had worked and Kogan laughed as his friend Bratz slapped him on the back.

But it was going to be Yakov's day, because at that moment he came up with the idea that would perfect the design of their new 'extending' ladder.

Whilst Kogan had been heating the lengths of iron in the forge and his father and brother had been watching the blacksmith at work, Yakov had begun to look around Kogan's workshop. The boy was inquisitive by nature and could never concentrate on any one thing for long. He gazed around the walls at the different steel implements that were all hung on large iron hooks. Every tool had its own purpose and was readily at hand for Kogan to use. There were also rows and rows of horseshoes, all of a variety of sizes. Yakov realized that shoeing horses was probably the mainstay of Kogan's business. In those days, most things in Russia were transported by horse and cart.

Yakov continued to stare at all the different blacksmiths tools that were hanging on the walls when suddenly he noticed a gun. It was an old single barrelled shotgun that had seen a lifetime of use, its wooden stock was blackened with age and it was marked and chipped. It was presumably one of the guns that Kogan used for hunting. It may even have been the gun that his father and Kogan had used to hunt when they were both young men.

Yakov looked up at the gun. It was hanging across the wall between two large hooks. The barrel was thick and round and dangerous and Yakov could only imagine what the blast would be like from a shot emitted from a barrel that wide.

He considered the gun's construction and for a moment he wondered about the possibility of being able to construct and produce the wooden stocks for guns. But no, the cutting and shaping would be far too complex for them, they wouldn't be able to do it. Then Yakov thought about his youngest brother for a moment. Yes, Pavel would be able to do it. Pavel had the 'gift'.

And thinking about Pavel made Yakov smile. He missed his little brother.

Yakov continued to look at the gun and he wondered how the barrel had been made. Probably on a lathe similar to the one they had back at the yard. And he wondered about a lathe that could cut steel as opposed to wood. The barrel was thick and solid and Yakov realized that it was about the same diameter as the rungs that they produced in their factory.

Yakov stood there for a moment and looked at the gun's barrel, suspended from the hooks on the wall. And a thought suddenly struck him. He looked again at the gun's barrel and then again at the hooks. Yes, the gun's barrel was the same thickness as the rungs on their ladder.

There was something there, but at that moment Yakov didn't see it.

It was only when they propped their 'new' ladder against a wall and extended it to a length and began to lash the rungs together that Yakov suddenly understood what he'd been thinking. He was about to solve the problem.

Yakov suddenly turned to his father.

'We need some hooks,' he said to Bratz, 'All we need is some hooks to hold the smaller ladder in place.'

Bratz frowned, for a moment he didn't understand what his son was telling him.

So Yakov started to explain his idea.

It was the hooks. It was those same hooks that held the gun on the wall that had been his insight. A couple of hooks could easily hold the top ladder in place and then there would be no need to lash the ladders together with lengths of rope. Fit two hooks to the bottom of the smaller ladder and they would lock onto the rungs of the larger ladder. From there the ladder could be adjusted to any length required. It was that simple.

Nikolai looked at his father, but it was Kogan who chuckled with glee. The blacksmith had immediately seen what was so obvious and the simplicity of it all made him laugh out loud.

'I've got the hooks you need,' he said and he turned and walked back into the forge and began to heat up some more rivets.

The two brothers carried the ladders back into the workshop and Kogan took two iron hooks and riveted them both securely to the ladder. Once again they carried the ladder outside and then propped it against the wall and they watched as Yakov extended the ladder to various lengths and to different heights with ease, the hooks would simply lock onto any given rung. Once the ladder was at its full extension, Yakov climbed right to the top and jumped up and down on the uppermost rungs. The ladder took this treatment in its stride. The ladder remained rigid and safe.

Bratz watched his eldest son in awe and his mind began to work quickly. There was nothing on the market like this. They had a winner.

After a brief conversation with Kogan, Bratz had his sons pick up the ladder and they took it back home again.

As they left the forge, Bratz called back to Kogan.

'I'll come over on Friday night with some Vodka.'

'Bring the good stuff,' replied Kogan, 'Not that shit that's made from potatoes.'

Ivan Bratz laughed and shook his head.

Once they got back to the factory the brothers carried the ladder into the workshop and then followed their father into the office.

Bratz sat down at his desk as Nikolai and Yakov, both fresh faced, smiled at their father.

'What do we do now father?' asked Nikolai.

Bratz looked up at his two sons

'You can both go and make the widow Kasslik a new ladder,' he said. And then with a dismissive nod, he returned to his paperwork.

Three weeks later, they loaded twenty five sets of ladders onto a cart which was destined for the 'Shefner Machine and Tool Supply' in Smolensk. Fifteen of those sets were their Standard Ladders. These were a re-order from Shefners, the first lot of ladders had sold well. The other ten sets of ladders were their new Extending Ladders, a 'new' innovation from the 'Baltic Ladder Company'.

The next day Bratz took the train to Smolensk. He couldn't waste time travelling overland with his goods. When he arrived in Smolensk he stood around for most of the day waiting to meet up with his delivery.

They finally arrived at Shefners late in the afternoon and Bratz went into the offices to meet up with Mr Shefner himself. Bratz then took Mr Shefner outside to inspect the ladders, which were then being unloaded. But the real reason was that he wanted to show Mr Shefner their new product. Bratz leant one of his extending ladders against a wall and explained it's workings to Mr Shefner. Then he extended and climbed up the ladder and jumped up and down on the upper rungs to demonstrate the solid construction and the safety attributes. Bratz then came back down the ladder and let Mr Shefner have a go.

Mr Shefner was impressed.

He then raised and lowered the ladder for Mr Shefner, who quickly realised how easily the ladder could be extended. It was so simple. Why had nobody ever thought of this before? For years people had lashed hopelessly inadequate ladders together with rope. Ladders that had often failed and had cost lives and caused injury.

Yes, Mr Shefner was impressed.

With a firm handshake another deal was done and Shefner's took delivery of all of the ladders and another re-order was given.

Bratz paid and dismissed his driver after being dropped off at the train station. He watched as the horse and cart slowly and painfully plodded away, all the way back to Zhumyov.

Bratz shook his head 'this was no use anymore'. Then he turned and walked into the train station, he had to find someone who knew about transporting freight by rail.

It was time to move on.

Two hours later he was sitting in a warm compartment on the train and he was heading home, a wiser man.

CHAPTER 4

The next three years were some of Pavel Bratz's finest.

He was in a world that he loved and understood, and working in the Schwab Factory was akin to being in a second heaven for him.

Pavel had just turned nineteen years old and had grown somewhat, not only in stature but also in reputation. He had risen to be one of the finest carpenters in the Schwab factory and during the past three years of his training he had slowly earned the quiet respect of the other men. None more than Mr Koenig, who had from a distance watched 'the boy' attain his skills. He had seen Pavel Bratz embrace carpentry with an almost religious passion and had been amazed by the boy's understanding and absolute skill with wood. Then, finally, Pavel got his wish. He was moved to the Marquetry section of the factory. After two years of constant questioning about both Marquetry and Parquetry, Koenig had finally capitulated and put the lad to work there and have him learn the skills of inlaying fine wood. It had not gone unnoticed to Koenig that for a long time Pavel had spent his every free hour in the Marquetry section, talking to the highly skilled craftsmen and watching them cut and slice fine strips of teak and mahogany to form delicate and beautiful patterns with the many various types of light and dark timbers. Marquetry was the ultimate skill, the skill that made furniture beautiful and also very expensive. It was an art to be able to work with those different types of wood and form the intricate designs that was a requirement on the most beautiful tables and cabinets. Pavel had immediately embraced that art, it was a skill that had taken other men years to perfect and Koenig had watched, fascinated, as young Pavel eventually started to produce his own designs, some of which were quite astounding.

Koenig now understood, as he remembered Pavel's original outburst and that boyhood proclamation.

'I have the 'gift' sir.'

Yes, Koenig now understood.

One of the highlights of Koenig's week was on Friday afternoons. At around five o' clock every Friday he would gather up his paperwork, together with any other relevant documents and he would go see Mr Schwab.

Their weekend meeting had almost become a ritual.

Koenig would go round to Mr Schwab's office and would always have a couple of minutes of pleasant conversation with Mr Schwab's attractive young secretary, Anna.

Anna was always pleased to see Koenig. He had always treated her with a fair respect, unlike most of the other men in the factory who leered and stared at her silently. She didn't like that, not one bit. However she did like working at the factory for Mr Schwab. He was a kind man who treated her well, very well in fact. Mr Schwab had always paid her quite decent wages and if she had ever been short of money or needed for whatever reason, to take time off, Mr Schwab had always helped her out. No questions asked. In fact, they had never had a cross word. Anna considered her kindly boss as some sort of 'second uncle' and she looked upon Mr Koenig in much the same way. She was drawn to the Schwab factory for some strange reason. She had no family of her own, her parents had died tragically in a house fire when she was sixteen and she had been left a letter of introduction which had allowed her to go and work at Mr Schwab's furniture factory. Anna lived on her own, she had an apartment. During the four or so years that she had worked for Schwabs of Smolensk she had grown to appreciate the feeling of security there. Anna had friends who worked elsewhere and she inwardly shuddered when they told her about the low wages and the sexual coercion, along with all the bullying. Anna had quickly realised just how fortunate she was in working for Mr Schwab.

That kindness and respect earned loyalty and Anna, just like Koenig, thought of the Schwab Company almost as though it was 'family'.

Anna worked hard and long hours for Mr Schwab and he was both grateful and aware that she did.

So, once the Friday afternoon pleasantries were out of the way, Anna would show Koenig through into Mr Schwab's office and then would discreetly disappear to go and make them both a pot of hot, strong, freshly brewed coffee.

Mr Schwab and Koenig were easy in each other's company. They would sit there in Mr Schwab's office, in his comfortable chairs, with the fire burning nicely in the huge old fireplace.

After an hour's conversation, Anna would bring in another pot of coffee and Mr Schwab would go over to his mahogany drinks cabinet and produce a bottle of his expensive French brandy. Schwab and Koenig would sit there and sip the brandy with their coffee, quietly appreciative and both talking at ease. They discussed the business in general, the work in hand and the number of future orders.

And of course they would discuss their workforce...the men.

Koenig knew them all, and their strengths and their weaknesses and he kept Mr Schwab well informed. Between them they knew who were the workers and who were the shirkers. They also recognised the thieves and the liars and the lazy. But they were also aware of those who were honest and upstanding and worked very hard every day for their wages.

The one person whose name was always regularly mentioned was Pavel Bratz.

Koenig was quite amazed by the boy's skill. Mr Schwab would listen intently to his manager's weekly appraisal of Pavel Brat and yes, the 'boy's' progress had fascinated him too.

Mr Schwab would nod as he listened to Koenig talk about young Bratz. They would discuss Pavel's advancement and also 'when' would be the appropriate time to move him onwards and into another department. Then when Koenig finally decided to move Pavel into the Marquetry section, it was with Mr Schwab's full blessing.

The two men would sit there and talk as the afternoon turned to evening. In truth, both men were really quite similar. Both were no longer married, but for entirely different reasons, and both men lived alone. They led singular lives which revolved totally around the Schwab furniture factory, they dealt with very little else.

Their conversation would continue, usually until the early evening and at the same time they would carry on drinking another glass or two of Mr Schwab's excellent French brandy.

Then at the appropriate moment, Mr Schwab would change the conversation and would take out his pocket watch to check the time.

That was always the sign that the evening, and their meeting, had come to a close.

The one thing that Koenig realised and accepted was that he was and always would be the manager and that Mr Schwab was the owner. That was the protocol and it was a protocol that must never be broken. Friendship in any other form would be out of the question. Mr Schwab knew that and Koenig knew that too. It was a balance that had to be maintained, always.

It was on one particular Friday evening as their regular meeting had just finished, Koenig stood up to bid his boss 'good night'. And as he left the outer office, he smiled at Anna and wished her 'a nice weekend'. Koenig would of course be back into work the following day and probably on Sunday too.

Ernst Schwab went to refill his brandy glass. Then he walked over to his office window and looked down into the yard as he watched Koenig stroll out through the factory gates. Both men lived a similar life, both were alone and they spent most of their time working in the factory and had no other real interests. As he watched Koenig make his way out of the factory, Schwab considered his manager and all his years of loyalty.

Koenig lived in the Severnaya district of Smolensk. It was a quiet area where Koenig owned a small but adequate two storey house which was spotlessly clean and filled with quality furniture. The furniture had all been legitimately purchased from the Schwab factory. Mr Schwab had allowed Koenig to buy the furniture from Schwabs at a 'token' price. In fact the price had been lower than the cost of the actual timber the furniture was made from, but that was never going to be a problem.

It was of course a perk of the job and Koenig had been grateful for it. Back in earlier times when he and his wife Ingrid had bought the house and had spent most of their hard earned money, it had been Mr Schwab's kindness that had helped them through those tougher times.

Yes, kindness earned loyalty and Koenig had never forgotten that.

He and Ingrid had moved into the house. It had been their first and only house and they had lived there happily and very much in love for the best part of ten years. Childless they might have been, but they had each other and that had been enough. Then, during a cold Russian winter, Ingrid had caught a chill. She had been peeling and washing some potatoes in a bowl of freezing cold water, it was as simple as that. But that chill turned into a cold and that cold turned into influenza, which then developed into pneumonia. Back in those days the medicines were useless and pneumonia was a killer, and it was a killer that wiped out thousands and thousands of tough Russian people every year. Bowls of hot soup and a warm fire would never be a match for pneumonia.

In the end, the pneumonia killed Koenig's beloved wife too. The loss of Ingrid completely devastated Koenig's life. Mr Schwab gave him as much time away from the factory as he needed, but for Koenig the factory was the only thing he had left.

So it was that Schwab's Furnishings of Smolensk soon became Koenig's life and breath. He realised that sitting alone at home, inconsolably depressed and despairing over the death of his beautiful wife was going to be a never ending tragedy that he just couldn't endure. He also realised that the only way he would survive all the heartbreak and retain his sanity would be to work. And work hard.

Schwab's became his home. His house was just somewhere he slept.

Koenig would usually be in the factory seven days a week. Truth be known, he was comfortable there. He would sit at ease at his desk, it was always warm in the factory and Kibble was always there on hand to bring him his meals and a hot mug of coffee whenever he wanted.

Koenig knew of course that Kibble fiddled the money he was given for the men's food and supplies. But Koenig let it go. Kibble deserved his 'perks' too.

Mr Schwab had always given Koenig a pretty free hand in running the factory. There was never any pressure from the 'Boss'. It was probably nearer the truth that Koenig was almost running the business single handed and Mr Schwab let him. Schwab knew how committed Koenig was, and following their meetings every Friday afternoon, Schwab was aware of absolutely all and everything that was happening within his company.

You couldn't put a price on a man like Koenig. Without him Ernst Schwab would have had to retire years ago.

That evening, as Schwab stood there looking out of the window, there was a knock on his office door, which then opened. It was his secretary Anna. She was about to leave, and as usual she wished her boss a 'goodnight' and he in turn bid her 'goodnight' and wished her 'a good weekend'.

Schwab stood there and gazed out of his window, and as he looked down he watched Anna walking out of the factory, and he remembered.

He remembered everything.

Ernst Schwab had a good life and was very comfortable in his role as the proprietor of the prestigious Schwab's of Smolensk Furniture Company. He was very well known throughout Smolensk and he had many friends there and contacts in Moscow. Life on the whole had been a little easier for Schwab. His father had started the business as a young man and by the time Schwab Jnr. came along the family furniture business was already thriving. There was never going to be any 'competition' either, Schwab Jnr. was the only child of his loving mother and his very strong willed and bullish father.

From the moment he was born until the moment she took her last breath, Schwab Jnr. was absolutely doted on by his adoring mother.

His father however was a different 'cup of tea'. Schwab Senior was a hard and brutish man who did nothing more than bully everyone, including his wife and child, all the way through his loveless life.

Schwab Jnr. eventually inherited the company, but not before his father had forced him into a disastrous marriage with one of the most awful of women.

Irina Klepsky was the daughter and only child of Igor Klepsky, who was the owner of Klepsky Wholesale Timber Ltd.

Klepsky Timber was a Moscow based company who supplied Schwab Furnishings with a huge range of domestic woods from all over Russia, together with the more exotic woods from other areas of Europe. Igor Klepsky, like Schwab Senior, was of a generation of hard men and both of them had been brought up in the same mould. Poverty from birth had made them both hungry and fierce. To get to the top in their respective fields they had crushed everyone around them. To cheat, lie and steal came naturally to both men, who considered it simple business practice. And both men had left in their wake a host of bankrupt suppliers and a trail of broken men whose families had been physically and financially destroyed by both their unscrupulous wheeling's and dealings.

Miss Irina Klepsky was her father's daughter in every way. She too had been spoiled, but that dotage had turned her into a self-centred, greedy and jealous child, who understandably grew up into a self-centred, greedy and jealous woman who was blessed with a devious charm.

She was a dangerous and overbearing young woman and after a couple of embarrassing romantic entanglements, word had gotten out and the young and well heeled young men of Moscow had soon learned to avoid Miss Klepsky at all cost.

Igor Klepsky had done his best to try and 'buy' his daughter into Moscow's social elite, but one brush with Irina was usually enough for most people and the invites to the various parties and evening soirées soon dried up.

Then along came Ernst Schwab, the young and innocent and very naive son of his old business acquaintance, Schwab Senior.

The two men got together and discussed the obvious. That their children should definitely marry. It would be the joining of their two companies, a joint bond with shared profits.

Of course each man was looking at the others profits but it didn't matter. They could both try to rob each other at a later date.

Igor Klepsky discussed all of this with his only child. Schwab Senior certainly did not.

And Irina Klepsky immediately jumped at the idea. She was smart enough to realise what was happening around her. Socially, her doors had closed and Irina unquestionably did not want to be left on the shelf. She was never going to marry a poor man and neither was she bothered about marrying for love. In truth, she didn't actually know what love was. Suddenly the thought of marrying anyone at all with money really appealed to Miss Klepsky.

She had never met the young Mr Schwab, but that didn't matter. All she wanted was a huge wedding that would impress everyone. From there on she would continue to lie to her friends about her new husband's exaggerated wealth.

It was perfect. And the deal was struck.

Schwab Senior dealt with his only child in a completely different manner.

With his characteristic tact, he simply informed his astonished son that he had arranged for him to be married to Irina Klepsky in the spring, which was three months hence. When his wife tried to intervene, Schwab Senior started to scream abuse at her and when the threat of violence became apparent, Schwab Jnr. relented and voluntarily agreed to the union.

The next day Schwab took his son to Moscow to meet his bride.

Klepsky Senior and Schwab Senior left their children alone in the Klepsky family's expansive drawing room to let them get to know one another. Both fathers went off to discuss the marital expenses and then shook hands on what they both looked upon as their new business venture. They also decided that within a twelve month period, both of their companies should join forces. They had a vision. Together they would grow in strength and become even more powerful, and then they would completely crush the opposition. They also had plans to eventually turn their joint companies into a conglomerate. These were heady and controversial plans, but Russia was huge and cash rich companies such as theirs could easily buy out any competition.

Back in the family drawing room the young couple eyed each other hesitantly. Young Ernst Schwab was twenty five years old. However, his bride-to-be had just turned twenty seven and those extra couple of years somehow gave her the edge. She was far more experienced than Schwab and would readily give her opinion on everything. Irina knew that Schwab Jnr. had always lived in Smolensk 'of all places' and Irina quickly recognised her fiancées weaknesses. She also realised that she was marrying a country bumpkin, but a country bumpkin who had money. So she took control. She would rule him. And it was the path they would follow and which would haunt them for most of their wretched married life.

Three months later they were married. It was an elaborate affair which cost quite a lot of money, mainly because Igor Klepsky had to 'buy in' most of the guests. The groom's mother wept all day in despair for her only son, and there were times during that day when her son felt like crying too.

The marriage started badly. Irina was utterly horrified when it was announced that the happy couple were to live in Smolensk. She had screamed and shouted at her father, but he was unrelenting. The wedding had cost him enough and he certainly wasn't going to pay for the newlyweds to live in a new house in Moscow. So Smolensk it was, and together both fathers paid equal shares for a simpler and rather plain house that was only a short walk from the Schwab factory. Irina was incensed. She felt she'd been duped, and in all fairness, she had.

It had simply been another business deal that their fathers had agreed and shaken hands on.

Irina, now Schwab, wasn't happy. And when Irina wasn't happy, her husband quickly realized that he would bear the brunt of her unhappiness, and that became another path to his despair.

Their wedding night had been an unmitigated disaster. At the time of their marriage the couple had actually only met each other four times. They had nothing at all in common and so Irina naturally took control and did all the talking and Schwab Jnr. would just listen and agree.

In later years he would just agree.

On their first 'night of bliss', Schwab, who had never been near a woman in his life, just fumbled about because he felt that he had to. Irina didn't like him touching her at all, not one bit. In fact, he made her feel physically sick.

In her past relationships, a few of the strong young men of Moscow had ravished her. She was actually quite an attractive woman in a dark sort of way and so she was quite aware of what real passion was. However, being under the sheets with young Mr Schwab was like being bedded by a sheep. In the end she lay back and examined the ceiling as he groped and gasped.

Afterwards she decided that it was never going to happen again. If Schwab had been aware of her thoughts he would have gladly agreed.

It was over a year later, when Irina had been put under increased pressure to produce an heir, that they both decided to try again.

Their second attempt was fuelled by vodka. Yes vodka, the national tipple, whose use and consumption was the reason that half the women in Russia got pregnant.

For the Schwabs however, it failed miserably. Under the influence of drink Schwab Jnr. felt dizzy and eventually vomited all over the bed. But his wife unfortunately, had drunk far too much and subsequently turned violent. The whole fiasco ended when she dragged him across the floor and then threw him out of the room.

In the end, and by joint agreement, they decided to remain childless.

Since his home life was so absolutely terrible, Schwab Jnr quickly and rightly decided to spend most of his time at the factory. Before long he was quite happy to work a seven day week and work late. In the evening he would return home to a barely warm meal that had been left for hours in a barely warm oven. To compensate for the poor food, Schwab started to regularly call into the local baker's shop which was just around the corner from the factory. There was always warm bread and pies and pastries for him to choose from and before long he was calling in every day for his breakfast. Then he started to have his lunch delivered directly to the office. The food was always nice and hot and straight from the baker's oven.

The evenings were long and lonely for Ernst Schwab. After his evening meal he would go into the drawing room to read. If Irina was still in there when he entered, they would have their usual short and perfunctory conversation. She would then promptly leave and go to her own bedroom, also to read.

They had both mutually agreed that separate bedrooms would be the more suitable way, considering the manner in which they lived.

The business partnership between their fathers, Schwab and Klepsky, also failed.

Well it certainly failed for Klepsky. Little was he to know that eighteen months after paying a small fortune for his daughter's wedding, he would be dead.

It happened in his timber yard in Moscow. Klepsky had been cursing and swearing at his long suffering workers for most of the day when he suddenly grasped his chest and his eyes glazed over. He then toppled over backwards and smashed his head violently on the floor of the stone cobbled yard.

He'd suffered a heart attack, but whether it was the heart attack that had killed him or his badly crushed skull, nobody would ever know.

It did however leave that business in the grasping hands of Schwab Senior, who silently rubbed those same grasping hands with delight as he considered his apparent good luck.

Schwab Senior quickly moved to Moscow to take charge of the Klepsky Timber Yard. He left his son in control of the family factory in Smolensk with strict instructions on how to run things. Production was to be maintained and Schwab Jnr. was left with the threat of Schwab Senior returning to Smolensk at least once a month to make sure that everything was being done properly.

Life though, has its way of turning out slightly differently than what you expect.

Schwab Senior did go to Moscow, where he soon realised that he was totally out of his depth.

He knew little or nothing about the wholesale timber trade. And because of the secretive and singular way in which Igor Klepsky had run his business, there wasn't much written information at all about how the operation had been run, or the suppliers that he used, or the customers that he supplied.

The other problem had been the money, or to be more precise, the apparent lack of it.

In Klepsky's office at the timber yard there was a large safe. However, Schwab couldn't find the key. Eventually he had to go around to Klepsky's home where he met up with Mrs Klepsky, the widow. She turned out to be a nervous and simplistic woman who had lived all her married life in fear of her husband. She was also totally clueless as to his business dealings. She did however take Schwab into her husband's office at their home and show him the small safe that they kept there. After a lot of rummaging through an old desk, Schwab finally found a key hidden at the back of a drawer. He inserted the key into the safe's lock and turned it. The safe opened, but inside there was very little. A small amount of money which Schwab felt duty bound to pass over to the ever watchful widow, though had she not been present it could have been a different story. There was also some paperwork that appertained to the property, but that was of little use to Schwab. Then in a small metal drawer he found another key. He had to hope that it would fit the large safe in the office, back at the yard.

Within the hour he had returned to the yard with only one thought in his mind. Whatever money he found in that safe, he was going to have and he was going keep it.

He had reconciled himself to the idea that he would need the money for cash flow which would keep the business running. With that thought in mind he suddenly felt totally justified.

When he put the key into the safe's lock it turned with a satisfying clunk, and that immediately made Schwab Senior smile.

Unfortunately, he wasn't going to smile for long.

He swung open the large steel door, only to find a safe so empty that it almost echoed. There was no money at all in there, in fact there was very little of anything, just some bills that had been paid to a supplier in Northern Russia and a new order for timber which had been made out to the same supplier.

Schwab went to sit down on a chair. He had to think.

'Where on earth was all the money?'

It had to be somewhere. Klepsky was a wealthy man, a very wealthy man, but he was also extremely devious. Igor Klepsky would not want to pay taxes, not if he could avoid it.

Schwab could appreciate that, he didn't pay any taxes himself and he too kept large amounts of cash hidden away. So what was he going to do? The money of course had to be somewhere, but where?

Schwab spent the next week at the timber yard. He'd gathered together all the men who worked there and informed them that if they weren't willing to help him out, then the yard would close and they would all be out of a job. So rather begrudgingly, they all sat down in the office and together with Schwab they compiled a list of customers who possibly owed Klepsky Timber some money.

Schwab then visited those same customers and demanded payment or part payment of their accounts. Schwab quite cleverly gave receipts to anyone who paid or part paid him, and by doing so, the customers produced their own original bills. That ploy allowed Schwab to look at those bills and from there he could deduce the exact amount of money that was owed. By the end of the week he'd managed to amass quite a substantial amount of return. After checking the figures he also got a better feel of where the business stood financially. The timber yard itself still continued to trade briskly as customers continually arrived to pick up their timber, resulting in a certain amount of cash flow coming in from that side of the business too.

The following three or four weeks passed by quickly and Schwab finally began to get to grips with Klepsky's business. He had also noted that about a quarter of the stock of timber that was in the yard had been sold, timber that would ultimately need replacing. So with that in mind, Schwab decided that he would have to travel north to try and find Klepsky's timber supplier. It was the same supplier whose paperwork had been in the safe at the office. There was an order already there for the timber he would need so he decided he would take it with him.

Barzak Timber and Forestry was the company that Igor Klepsky seemed to buy most of his timber from. Unfortunately, it was also the only supplier that Schwab Senior knew about because Igor Klepsky never wrote anything down. It seemed that all and everything appertaining to Klepsky Timber was secretly stored inside Klepsky's head. At least that's how it seemed to Schwab Senior.

Barzak Timber was situated high in the vast timber forests of Karelia in Northern Russia.

It was a physically huge area and it would take Schwab the best part of a week to get there. The trip itself would require two or three trains followed with a long trek by horse and cart up to Barzak's camp, which was located high up in the forests.

Schwab also had to consider that since the owner of Barzak Timber had never met him, he was hardly likely to send a valuable load of timber all the way to Moscow on the strength of a smile and a handshake. There was also the real possibility that Igor Klepsky may have owed money to Barzak Timber and there could be some outstanding bills, which would also need to be paid. So with all those thoughts running through his mind Schwab made an uncharacteristic decision, he decided that he would have to take seven or eight thousand roubles with him, just in case.

Two days later he was on a train heading north out of Moscow Central Train Station.

He travelled for a futher two days to get to St Petersburg, where he then boarded another train which took a further two days to get him to the grand old lumber town of Borovov. When he arrived there he discovered that there was an old steam train which hauled timber down from the lumber camps up in the mountains. So he climbed onto it and sat there in a cold rickety carriage along with several bearded lumberjacks who were making their way back up to the timber fields.

On the train he struck up a conversation with two brothers who actually worked for Barzak Timber. They introduced themselves as the Kamisky brothers and they gave him an interesting description of their boss, Zill Barzak. It turned out that the brothers also remembered Igor Klepsky, who it seemed took the long hard trip to Borovov to see Mr Barzak three or four times a year. However, what they didn't tell Schwab was that when Igor Klepsky did arrive in Borovov, he was usually accompanied by two very large and vicious looking Cossack men who acted as his personal bodyguards.

That fact alone put several thoughts into both of the Kamisky brothers scheming minds.

The train finally arrived at the timber station and Schwab hitched a further ride with them on a horse drawn cart that was taking some of the men up to the high camp.

They finally arrived at their destination after three arduous and very lengthy hours spent in the back of the cart. By then Schwab was desperately feeling the chill. It was late afternoon and the thin rays of sunshine that had struggled to keep the cold at bay were all but disappearing.

The camp itself was busy. The lumberjacks were coming in from the forest and along with them were the teams of large horses that struggled in the mud as they pulled the huge carts which were stacked high with the freshly felled timber.

Most of the men seemed to be heading for what was known as the 'canteen'. It was a large, well lit wooden building which contained the kitchens that provided the men with their meals and their drink.

The Kamisky brothers pointed Schwab Senior in the direction of th company's office and then they both sloped off to the canteen for their rations.

Schwab walked into the office. It was a large one roomed affair containing a huge rough cut table which stood in the centre of the room and was used as a desk. There were various cupboards lining the walls and in one corner was a huge burgundy coloured steel safe that stood the height of a man.

Sitting behind the desk, smoking a pipe and examining some paperwork was Zill Barzak, the sole owner and proprietor of Barzak Timber and Forestry. He was a big man with thick black hair and the matching beard that most Russian men grew to keep out the cold.

Schwab immediately introduced himself and then informed Zill Barzak that he was Klepsky's partner.

Barzak glanced at him. It was a look of surprise and suspicion.

'I didn't know Klepsky had a partner, I always thought the business had only 'one' owner.'

'It does now,' replied Schwab, 'Klepskys dead.'

Barzak raised his thick black eyebrows.

'What happened to him, did somebody shoot the bastard?'

Schwab almost smiled. Barzak had obviously dealt with Igor Klepsky's ruthlessness and clearly knew all about the man's shortcomings.

'Believe it or not,' replied Schwab, 'he died from a heart attack.'

Barzak shrugged 'I didn't know he had a heart either.'

Schwab then openly grinned. He saw a possibility. Barzak had no loyalty to Klepsky other than business. That was a start.

'Well the man's dead,' said Schwab, 'and I want to carry on the business. And I'm assuming that you want to carry on supplying us with timber?'

Barzak leant back in his chair and took a draw on his pipe. Yes he wanted the business, he certainly did. And yes, Igor Klespky had been a hard man to deal with, however he had always bought substantial amounts of timber from Barzak's company and the market for timber in Moscow was huge. Igor Klepsky had been a very successful trader.

Schwab produced the sheet of paper from his inside pocket.

'This was the order that Klepsky prepared just before he died.'

He slid the sheet of paper across the desk for Barzak to inspect.

Barzak examined the order. It was consistent with Klepsky's usual instructions. The timber trade was usually a fairly stable industry.

Barzak considered the position he was in. He didn't know this man, didn't know him at all, and for all he knew this could be an elaborate scam. He even considered that this could be an elaborate scam run by Klepsky himself. After all, it was only this man, this stranger's word, that Klepsky was dead. Klepsky could still be alive, the man was capable of anything and Barzak wasn't going to ship a huge cargo of timber off to Moscow and watch it disappear into the wilderness.

'So...how are you going to pay me for all this timber?' Barzak asked.

Schwab stood there for a moment. Two things had registered in his mind. Firstly and most importantly was that Zill Barzak had not at any point asked for any money that was owed to him. So there were no unpaid bills. Klepsky must have paid up front for everything. So that suddenly made Klepsky Wholesale Timber Ltd and Schwab Senior totally debt free.

And that fact alone gave Schwab room to manoeuvre.

'How much do you want?' Schwab asked.

It was a question that Schwab already knew the answer to. Back in Moscow, back in the office safe there were the previous bills relating to the earlier timber orders from Barzak Timber and Forestry.

Yes, Schwab knew exactly how much money Zill Barzak would be asking for.

'I'll want six thousand roubles,' said Barzak casually.

This was the moment Schwab had been waiting for, and he had planned it almost perfectly.

He knew all along that he needed Barzak as a supplier. Barzak was tried and tested and obviously reliable. That's why Klepsky had used him and continued to use him.

However Schwab also realised the position he was in. In Barzak's eyes he was a stranger. He had arrived from nowhere, and unannounced. Schwab had just strolled into Barzak's office and informed him that he was now the new owner of Klepsky Timber. Barzak hadn't even known about Klepsky's untimely death.

Schwab knew he had to seal the deal. He had to command Zill Barzak's respect and show him that not only was he upfront, he was also a businessman.

Schwab unbuttoned the front of his large coat and took it off. He did the same with his jacket underneath. He then reached underneath his woollen top and yanked on a length of cord. Slowly but surely he drew out the cord and along with it slid the large money belt which had been tied around his middle.

He dropped the money belt onto the desk, right in front of Barzak.

'Right...okay,' said Schwab, 'It would be better if I paid you now,' and he smiled.

Barzak stared at the money belt for a moment and then looked up at Schwab.

'Schwab, I think you and I can do business,' he said with a slight grin and a nod of his head.

'How much is there in the belt?' he asked.

'Around eight thousand roubles,' replied Schwab, 'Count out your six thousand and then return the rest to me.'

Barzak again smiled. This was all about trust. Schwab had come prepared and that was good, because getting money out of Igor Klepsky had always been difficult, to say the least.

Barzak was just in the process of counting out the money into thousand rouble stacks when the office door swung open and in walked one of his men carrying a tray full of food.

'Your dinner Mr Barzak,' said the young man carrying the tray.

Barzak looked up.

'Ah Mallik,' he said to the young man.

Mallik put the tray down on the table as he suddenly eyed the money. On the tray was a large bowl of venison stew, accompanied by several chunks of rough wheat bread.

Barzak spoke again. 'Bring Mr Schwab here some dinner Mallik and bring us something to drink.'

Young Mallik, who was still rather taken aback by the sight of all that money, turned and went quickly back to the kitchen. He quickly returned with a second plate of venison stew and two tin mugs full of ale. As he walked back into the office he overheard his boss speaking to Schwab.

'That's my six thousand and here's your two thousand back,' Barzak was saying to Schwab.

Schwab started to put the remaining two thousand roubles back into his money belt as Mallik tactfully placed the stew down in front of him.

Both men had continued to conduct their business as though Mallik wasn't even there.

And that was a mistake.

Mallik then left Barzak's office and returned to the canteen to help in the kitchens. He would only get to eat his evening meal once the rest of the men had finally been fed.

So later that evening, and after retrieving a plate of stew for himself, Mallik went back into the canteen to eat. He sat down at one of the long wooden tables with a couple of the other youths who also worked in the kitchen. With them was also one of the older men who helped to cook the food.

A conversation began between them, which was mostly all the kitchen gossip. It was during this conversation that Mallik told his workmates about all the money he had seen in Mr Barzak's office.

'That Mr Schwab,' blurted out Mallik, 'He was carrying eight thousand roubles in a money belt, all the way from Moscow. That's where he's come from. He gave Mr Barzak six thousand roubles. Phew, I've never seen so much money.'

Wide eyed with all that information, Mallik's three workmates then went on to discuss the merits of being rich and what they would do with all that money.

Sitting back to back with Mallik and his friends were the Kamisky brothers. They had finished eating their meal an hour before and were just sitting there silently and were smoking a shared pipe. As they heard Mallik's tale, the brothers looked at each other with an air of frustration and anger.

Later, as the canteen emptied, they quietly discussed the infuriating reality of it all. The reality that they had travelled hundreds of miles with a man, a lone man, who was secretly carrying a small fortune about his person.

Later the two brothers made their way to their sleeping quarters and they both lay awake for some time, considering what could have been.

That night, Schwab slept at Barzak's house. It was an obvious but welcome gesture. Both men had spent several hours discussing the positive and the negative aspects of their businesses. They had also talked about the future and the possibilities. Schwab told Barzak about his plans for expansion and that the expansion could certainly involve Barzak Timber and Forestry .

By the end of the evening, and with the help of the bottle of vodka they had consumed, both men had decided that they could form some sort of alliance.

Schwab had chosen to leave the very next day. He was a businessman, not a lover of forests. Barzak would have one of his drivers take Schwab back down to the timber station in the late afternoon where he could pick up the evening freight train which would be the start of his long and tedious trek back to Moscow.

As was agreed, Barzak would promptly oversee Schwab's order for the timber and he would get it delivered to Klepsky's yard in Moscow as soon as possible.

The sunlight was rapidly fading as Schwab shook hands with Zill Barzak. He climbed onto the back of the supply cart that would take him down to the station where he could pick up the late train. They set off slowly, as was usual when driving through the dark forests. Schwab made himself as comfortable as possible in the back of the cart and he covered his legs with some spare sacking to try to keep warm. The night would turn cold and could chill a man's bones, and so he got himself as snug as possible for the journey ahead. Schwab had deliberately sat in the back of the cart. The last thing he wanted to do was to sit next to the driver, where he would not only be open to the elements, he would also be open to having a conversation with a man who in all probability was just another uneducated idiot.

That's why he was a driver.

Anyway, Schwab had other things on his mind. Business plans, his company's plans and his expansion into the timber business. For once, Schwab Furnishings of Smolensk would not be his only goal. He was going to take Klepsky Timber to a national level. There was also the export market in Europe to consder. The possibilities were endless.

He gave a little more thought to Schwab Furnishings and decided that he would hand it over to his idiot son to run. However before he did that, he would have to speak to his daughter-in-law. Schwab had always known that it was the 'lovely' Irina who wore the pants in that family. He would talk to her about his plans for Moscow and for Klepsky Timber, because she needed to know exactly what direction Schwab Furnishings must take. He would discuss it all with Irina and then they could leave the everyday running of the furniture factory to Schwab Jnr.

About an hour had passed by which time it was dark. The driver had lit an old oil lamp which he hung from a pole that was attached to the side of the cart. Schwab was still sitting in the back of the cart and was facing forwards. He was watching the lamp sway in the darkness as the cart slowly trundled along.

He had again been thinking about Moscow and Klepsky Wholesale Timber Ltd. It was possibly time to bury Igor Klepsky's name. It was time for a change. Schwab had been mulling over a new name for the company, it had to be something more dynamic and something that would appeal to a wider audience of customers. Then an idea suddenly came to him, he would call the company 'Moscow State Timber'.

It was so simple, 'Moscow State Timber'. It said it all, short and sweet. Schwab thought about it again 'Moscow State Timber'. Yes, it sounded good, and he smiled as he said it once more, this time out loud...'Moscow State Timber.'

At that same moment the dark figure of a man leapt onto the cart directly in front of Schwab. The man smashed the driver over the head with an iron bar and the driver gave a short groan as he keeled over.

It would be the last thing that Schwab Senior would ever see. Another assailant grabbed Schwab roughly from behind and dragged him backwards over the edge of the cart. The assailant, who was also armed with an iron bar, then proceeded to steadily club Schwab Senior to death.

The cart came to an abrupt stop as the horse felt the reigns slacken. The two remaining figures stood there silently at the back of the cart, their hot breaths sending short draughts of steaming air into the night.

The Kamisky brothers took a moment to check their surroundings. They were safe of course. There was nobody else anywhere near for miles. They had planned it well.

The previous evening in the canteen they had listened intently as they heard young Mallik talking about the piles of money that he'd seen on the table in Barzak's office.

It had been simple arithmetic to figure it out. If Schwab had been carrying eight thousand roubles and had given six thousand of those roubles to Barzak, well he still had to be carrying two thousand roubles on him in that damn money belt.

One of the brothers dragged Schwab's lifeless body off the back of the cart and dumped it onto the ground. He ripped open Schwab's coat and jacket then reached down under the woollen vest in order to grasp hold of the still warm money belt that was tied around Schwab's waist. He ripped the money belt from Schwab's body and laughed out loud as he waved it at his brother.

They both climbed onto the cart and lifted the unconscious driver off his seat and put him in the back of the cart and laid him there. Then they put some sacking over him to keep him warm. The Kamisky brothers didn't want the driver to die because they knew him well.

He was a friend.

They tied the horse's reigns to the handrail and gave the horse a smack to send it on its way. It would keep going all the way down to the timber station because it had walked up and down that same track for years

The Kamisky brothers then took hold of Schwab's body and carried it a short distance through some trees to a sloping bank were the ground dropped sharply away to form a small ravine.

Yes, they had planned it well.

They simply swung the body into the air and threw it down the ravine. It landed on a pile of rocks and lay there in a twisted heap.

During the next three days Schwab's body would be discovered by a passing brown bear. The bear would do most of the damage to the body. It would rip and tear at Schwab's clothing to get to the meat. Two days later the wolves would find the remains and devour most of what was left. After that were a couple of foxes, and then the crows, until finally it was down to the grubs and the insects.

Years later, bits of Schwab Senior would possibly be found by somebody passing by, but by then all that remained would be the odd bone or bones spread over quite a large area. Whoever came across the remains would probably think that they were just the old yellow bones of some animal.

Unless of course, they found the skull.

After murdering Schwab, the Kamisky brothers headed back to the camp. They went to the canteen to eat, and they entering separately, ten minutes apart, so as not to draw attention to themselves. They needn't have worried. The canteen was full of hungry men with other things on their minds. The next day the brothers would leave for work as usual, back into the vast forests of Karelia. Along with the other gangs of lumberjacks, their time would be spent with axes and saws, taking down the trees and cutting and preparing the endless supply of logs. The previous day's events would be nothing more than a memory.

The driver finally woke up in the back of his cart, disorientated and with a throbbing and bruised head. His faithful old horse had taken him all the way down to the timber station and had then stopped and waited. The driver lay there for a while, trying to clear his head as he wondered what had happened to him. Finally he managed to sit up and he had to steady himself as he tried to piece together the events. But he couldn't remember. He remembered driving slowly through the forest with Schwab in the back of the cart. Then he recalled being attacked and knocked out. Since there was no-one else there, the driver could only conclude that it had been Schwab himself who had attacked him.

But why? The driver only had a few roubles in his pocket and they were still there, so he hadn't been robbed. The driver rubbed his sore head as he wondered what had happened to Schwab. Had Schwab driven the cart to the station and then caught the train and left?

Perhaps, or had the driver said something to Schwab that had upset the man?

Then he remembered that they hadn't spoken. They'd never exchanged a single word. Schwab had sat silently in the back of the cart trying to keep warm.

So why had Schwab attacked him? Maybe the man was drunk, but he hadn't seemed that way. The driver pondered the questions and came to the conclusion that it would be 'one of those things' that he would never understand.

He took a deep breath and slowly got down from his cart, and then he managed to get his bearings as he realised just where he was. He walked around to the front of the cart and took hold of the horse's bridle. Then he slowly walked the horse away in the direction of the stables that he regularly used when he stayed overnight.

Later he would sleep in the barn along with the other horses, but only after he had found somewhere to eat and had consumed enough vodka.

The next morning when he awoke, his head was still throbbing from the bruising and also from the effects of the alcohol consumed the previous evening. After hitching the horse to the cart he slowly set off back to the camp. On the way back he decided not to tell anyone about the attack, what would be the use, it could get him into trouble with Mr Barzak and he certainly didn't want that.

He would tell the Kamisky brothers of course, they were his friends.

They at least would believe him. But nobody else would. After all, he was only the driver.

Several weeks passed by, and back in Smolensk Schwab Junior was becoming slightly concerned. During the week he had been contacted by the foreman at Klepsky's Timber in Moscow. The foreman had sent a letter asking if Schwab Senior was planning to return to Moscow because someone needed to take charge of the company as soon as possible. It seemed that a huge delivery of timber had arrived back at the yard, but Schwab Senior hadn't.

Apparently Schwab Senior had gone off to the forests of Karelia during the previous month and hadn't been seen since. The foreman presumed that Schwab Senior had returned home to Smolensk. However he was now struggling at the yard, struggling with unpaid orders and therefore struggling to pay everyone's wages. He needed help and instruction and the letter was more than just a subtle hint.

Klepsky's timber yard was in disarray.

Schwab Jnr. had given all this some serious thought. He was more than a little concerned and he wonder where on earth his father had gotten too. He certainly wasn't in Smolensk.

So on the Friday night after he had come home and had eaten a bowl of tepid stew, Schwab went into the drawing room and approached his wife. He sat her down and told her about the letter and about his father's disappearance, and he also told her about the problems back in Moscow.

Irina listened to him with a divisive fascination. Her mind was working, and working in two directions.

Firstly, there was the timber yard. She knew all about the timber yard. She had grown up there and she knew how the business ran and how to run it. Igor Klepsky had brought up his daughter as though she was his only son. He'd taught her the timber business and he'd taught her to be ruthless, although that was already an inbred trait, some things just come naturally.

Irina Schwab listened intently to her husband because she already had an alternative plan, and that was the second line of thought that had been racing through her calculating brain.

Suddenly and incredibly she had been thrown a life line. This was her big chance, her big opportunity. If she played this right she could be out of there and out for good.

For Irina Schwab, living her life as she was and being locked away in Smolensk was akin to being imprisoned. She hated it, and had hated it from the moment she'd married Ernst Schwab, who she considered to be possibly the most boring and tedious man in the world.

Never in her life had she expected to live like this, being locked away in this awful backwater. Moscow, it most certainly was not. Those few short years of marriage had been a disaster for her and Irina felt like a caged animal. She was miserable and depressed and lonely. But the worst of all for Irina was that she was bored...bored so much that she could scream and scream out loud. And every single time she looked at her disaster of a husband she felt like leaping on him and throttling the life out of the wretchedly dreary bastard.

But now this...and her stomach began to churn with excitement as she suddenly felt giddy.

Irina suddenly took a deep breath. She had to hold the moment and take control of herself.

She had to contain the urge to smile, and she had to curb her enthusiasm, and she had to play this one game just right.

So she sat there wearing a mask of sincerity as she played out her part as the 'concerned wife', and she listened intently to the serious nature of what her husband was telling her.

When Schwab had finished talking, Irina sat there for a moment and pretended to mull things over. Yes, she had to play this one right. She had to manoeuvre her husband without blatantly taking control. For once, she had to forge a partnership with him.

She looked at Schwab with serious concern, and for the first time ever she agreed with him.

Yes, she acknowledged that they had a problem.

She began to talk to her husband earnestly, and that was also a 'first'.

What were they going to do? What did he think? Where did he think Schwab Senior could be? Then once again 'What on earth were they going to do?'

She agreed with him that their timber yard in Moscow sounded as though it was in trouble and could end up being an enormous problem for both of them.

She asked him about the furniture factory there in Smolensk. Could he continue to run it without his father's assistance?

Schwab was slightly resentful of that question. Of course he could run the factory. He had been successfully running the factory for nearly a year and with no problems at all. Running the factory was the one thing he could do.

Irina just sat there, thoughtful and caring. Yes, she agreed with him, of course she did. She had to carefully feed him the answers to her questions. And then she gave him all the obvious replies, to let him think that he was making the decisions. It was like training a puppy.

'Ernst...what do you actually know about the wholesale timber industry?' she finally asked him, whilst already knowing the answer.

Schwab was silent for a moment. So Irina continued.

'Do you know anything about timber location or the areas that produce the specific woods?'

Schwab shook his head. No, he didn't have a clue. The different types of timber that he used had just always arrived at the factory. He hadn't a clue as to their origin.

Irina put on her 'troubled' expression. She had to continue to make it all sound very complicated.

'Do you know any of our suppliers in Moscow?' she asked, again knowing the answer.

'No, I don't,' replied her husband sullenly. These problems were beginning to pile up and he suddenly felt out of his depth. He had actually only ever been to the Klepsky timber yard once, and that had been with his father. He remembered having to stand there feeling foolish and out of place as his father and old man Klepsky discussed business. All around him there had been massive stacks of logs and timber, and men rushing about loading up the heavy carts that were pulled by teams of horses. To young Ernst Schwab it had all seemed like absolute mayhem.

Sitting there in their drawing room, talking to Irina, he shuddered at the thought of it all.

And sitting there, watching the expression change on her husband's face, Irina saw the nervousness and the fear. Now was the moment.

She just sat there and let the silence hang over them like a threat. Schwab said nothing.

'I have an idea Ernst,' she said, and Schwab looked up at her.

'What if I went to Moscow?' she said slowly.

Schwab's eyes widened.

'What?'

For a moment Irina said nothing at all. She just let the question hang there.

Then again, 'What if I went to Moscow, to try and sort things out?'

'You..?' replied Schwab. It was almost an insult.

Irina had to bite her lip because at that moment she felt like smashing him in the face.

She took a deep breath.

'There's something I've never told you Ernst,' she said.

Schwab just looked at her. There were actually a lot of things that Irina had never told him. In fact she'd never told him anything at all, other than what to do.

'There's something I've never told you,' she repeated herself.

'And what's that?' asked Schwab.

"Well, I actually do know about the timber business. And I know all and everything about the wholesale timber business, and I do mean absolutely everything.'

Schwab just stared at his wife and Irina looked at his stupid face and realised that he would need an explanation. But she was ready for that.

'My father brought me into his timber yard when I was eight years old. By the time I was ten I knew every type of wood there was. My father saw to that. I knew where the timber came from and as I got older he took me with him and introduced me to our suppliers. I have travelled through the vast forests of Russia up in the north and I've been all the way east to Siberia. My father wanted me to fully understand the business. I have worked for years in our timber yard, working with the men and meeting and dealing with all of our customers.'

Schwab just sat there. He was slightly astounded. His wife had never mentioned any of this.

She continued. 'I know everything that there is to know about the timber business Ernst.'

'You never said,' remarked Schwab.

'It wasn't my place to,' she lied, 'When I married you it was my duty to come here to Smolensk to support you" she lied again.

Even Schwab looked a little sceptical at that statement, but Irina was quick to reply.

'I know we've had a difficult marriage.' she said, 'and I'll admit that things have been far from easy.'

Schwab found himself nodding and Irina gave a silent sigh of relief.

That had been a close one.

She continued. 'No matter what, I am your wife and together we must support the business or we'll be ruined.'

Schwab was still nodding.

Irina chose her moment.

'Do you want me to go to Moscow? If you want me to go, I will. I have the experience, I know what to do and I know how to sort out all of this mess.'

Schwab started to agree, he could see the logic.

Seeing this, Irina again continued with her plan.

'I'll need to get back there as soon as possible, the sooner the better. Once I get there I can make a start. I'll travel back here to Smolensk every month or so, if possible, and I'll be able to let you know how we're progressing. Once your father returns, I shall hand everything over to him and then return home.'

The mention of his father's name broke Schwab's silence.

'You may be right Irina,' he said, 'We'll have to do something, otherwise when he does turn up there'll be hell to play.'

It was Irina's turn to nod. Then she came up with the words that would seal the deal.

'You see Ernst, if 'you' were to go to Moscow, who would look after the factory here in Smolensk? I don't know a thing about the furniture business and I just couldn't cope.'

Once again Schwab heard the logic of his wife's words. And if truth be known, deep in his heart the last place on earth that he wanted to end up at was Klepsky's timber yard in Moscow. Schwab hated the damn place. He knew he would be out of his depth there, and he knew that he would be unable to solve the problems there either. He had visions of the men at the yard, laughing at him as he stumbled from one disaster to another. He knew that they wouldn't help him. Then he considered his position at his own furniture factory, here in Smolensk. He was respected and very well thought of by his workforce.

His job here was quite easy, it was repetitive and safe and it was comfortable.

So Schwab made the decision. If and only if Irina wanted to go to Moscow, he would allow it. The only stipulation was that she would keep him informed and send him regular updates of what was happening. Irina agreed of course, and anyway, she would be back every three or four weeks and would bring with her a detailed report of events.

Schwab was quite satisfied with that, even more so when he realised that he could stay at home in Smolensk. He was quite taken aback when Irina then leant over and gave him a peck on the cheek.

'Leave it to me,' she said confidently, and with that she stood up and went off to her bedroom.

Schwab watched her go, and then began to wonder what had actually just happened.

Irina Schwab left her husband in the drawing room then sedately climbed the stairs and made her way down the corridor to her own room. Once she had entered her bedroom she turned and carefully locked the door behind her.

She then clenched both of her fists as she leant her head backwards and then she laughed out loud. She skipped across the bedroom and threw herself onto the bed giving a squeal of delight as she kicked off her slippers in hysterical abandonment. Her legs thrashed with excitement as she bounced up and down on the bed and it took great strength and commitment to stop herself from screaming out in delight at the top of her voice.

'I'm free, I'm free'.

Eventually she calmed herself down and just lay there on the bed looking at the ceiling, dreaming a different dream. She decided that the very next day she would pack everything that she would ever need into trunks, and then get away from this awful house. On the following day she would start the long journey back. Back to her beloved Moscow.

Irina had made a decision. She would leave the house, she would leave Smolensk, and she would leave her husband. And she would never ever return.

Six months passed by and it became quite obvious that Schwab Senior was never going to return. Irina sent a man to Karelia to speak to Barzak, but of course they knew nothing. Schwab Senior had left the camp after paying for a large order of timber and hadn't been seen since.

Irina did actually write to her husband informing him that they didn't know the whereabouts of his father. In the letter she also informed him that she was making headway at the timber yard. However, she would not be returning home for some considerable time as she needed to stay on in Moscow to look after the business. There was also the hint that this might become a permanent arrangement.

Irina had decided that sending a letter would set her husband's mind at rest. The last thing she wanted was for Schwab to come charging over to Moscow, expecting her to go back home with him.

But if truth be known, Schwab Jnr. wasn't thinking of charging anywhere. He was quite relieved when he received Irina's letter, and for two reasons.

The first was his missing father. His father could remain missing as far as Schwab Jnr. was concerned. He had never got on with the man. In truth, his father had never been anything more than a bully and a tyrant to both him and his long suffering mother. There was also the fact that Schwab Jnr. had become used to running the furniture factory single handedly and was slightly loathe to give back the reins.

The other reason for his relief was his wife Irina, or really, the lack of her.

Since she'd returned to Moscow, Schwab's life had become decidedly easier. Yes, life was now a whole lot pleasanter without the unremitting tension, the never ending criticism and the eternal nagging that he'd had to constantly endure.

The loss of his father and his wife had brought about a significant change in Schwab's life.

He was on the verge of becoming euphoric.

However, there was more to come.

The moment Irina Schwab arrived back in Moscow she went straight to the Klepsky timber yard, even before she had been to see her mother. The place was in disarray. Half the men were sitting in a cabin playing cards, the other half weren't even at the yard. Customers were wandering around helping themselves to timber and were obviously paying the men a few roubles to look the other way.

There was a huge delivery of timber which had arrived from Barzak's Lumberup in Karelia.

It hadn't even been unloaded and remained untouched and stacked high on huge wooden carts.

Irina roared in. She cleared the yard of customers and then set about the men. If those same men had been wary of old Igor Klepsky, they were now in for a shock. The daughter was an even more formidable adversary. She set about them and screamed insults until they were virtually standing to attention. She then sent them to go and find the rest of the workforce. When they all returned she made them clean up the yard and re-stack all the wood, then she had them unload the carts of timber from Barzaks. Irina then sacked the foreman and replaced him with one of the 'brighter idiots' who she considered was probably the best of a bad bunch. Finally, she had all the men line up in the yard and then she proceeded to give them their new instructions. Irina explained the new rules to her workforce, it was quite simple.

She demanded total commitment, and she stipulated that her orders were to be followed to the letter, and no questions asked.

When later, she finally arrived at the family home, Irina scoured the house for any cash or financial documents, but found none. Eventually she sat her mother down and tried to glean some information out of the old woman. The poor old dear didn't know much and in truth she never had. When Irina asked her mother where was she getting the money she had been living off, the old woman told her daughter that whenever she needed cash, she simply went to the bank.

That bank turned out to be the Moscow Principal Bank, a well known and long established local bank used by many of the wiser and thriftier citizens of Moscow.

The next day, Irina marched into the bank and demanded to see the manager, a Mr Smitt.

After a bit of a fuss she was quickly shown into Smitt's office and introduced to the slightly wary bank manager. He shook her hand agreeably and then asked her to take a seat and he ordered them both some coffee. This seemed to calm Irina down somewhat because she was finally being shown some respect. She introduced herself to the manager and immediately informed him that she was now running the Klepsky timber yard. After a few pleasantries, Mr Smitt cautiously, but in a committed manner, began to discuss her father's business. He was aware that all was not well at the timber yard, a common occurrence following the demise of the owner, especially when the owner ran the business in a totally 'hands on fashion', as Igor Klepsky undeniably had. They carried on their conversation for a while, until Irina finally manoeuvred Mr Smitt onto the question of money and cash. Basically, she wanted to know what monies were in what accounts and how much could she get her hands on. The timber yard was in dire need of some cash flow and Irina desperately needed some funds.

Mr Smitt raised his eyebrows at these questions, which rather intimidated Irina.

He then proceeded to inform Irina about the bank's financial situation regarding Klepsky Timber.

'Your father, Mr Klepsky, decided to transfer his funds away from us and deposit them with another bank Mrs Schwab. We were quite disappointed with your father's decision, he had been a longstanding customer at this bank for many years and the loss of his business, well... losing a long established customer is never good.'

That news worried Irina and she almost squirmed in her seat.

'Where is his money now then?' she asked, trying not to sound too desperate.

Smitt stood up and excused himself for a moment and then left the office.

Irina sat there alone, tapping on the desk impatiently.

A few minutes later Smitt returned carrying a green file. He sat down again and then sifted through the paperwork contained within the file.

'Ah,' he said as he looked up and smiled at Irina Schwab, 'I thought so, but just wanted to check to make sure that my information was correct.

Your father transferred most of his funds to the National...The National Bank of Russia, here in Moscow.'

'Oh right,' said Irina, suddenly a little more relieved now that she had finally found the money.

'I have a copy of the transfer papers here,' Smitt continued, 'Your father transferred half a million roubles from his account here last year.'

Irina gave a sigh of relief as Mr Smitt pushed the transfer papers across the desk for her to check.

'You should retain that copy,' he said, 'You must present it to the National. It will notify them as to your authority as head of Klepsky Timber. You will probably need identification too, but to ease things along Mrs Schwab, I am prepared to give you a personal letter of introduction, which when presented to the bank manager at National Bank will certify that you are recognised by our bank. It is a form of guarantee and will allow you access to the Klepsky account there.'

Smitt then took a sheet of headed paper and began to write his letter. Once done and signed, he folded it and put it into an envelope. He then addressed it to the manager of the National Bank of Russia, Moscow. Then he passed it over to Irina Schwab.

Irina was relieved and curtly thanked him.

'Can I ask you something Mr Smitt?' she enquired.

'Yes, what is it Mrs Schwab?' he asked.

'Why did my father transfer his funds Mr Smitt, why did he move the money?'

Smitt sat back in his chair and reflected.

'Your father was unhappy with our rates of interest Mrs Schwab. Put quite simply, we are a small local bank and when the National Bank of Russia approached him with an offer of higher interest, we just couldn't compete. We explained that to your father, an explanation which he accepted. It was by mutual agreement that he would transfer his funds, after all business is business. We did agree however, that if we could at any time reverse the situation, then your father would return his funds to invest with us. With that agreement in place, he actually did leave one remaining account open.'

'I take it that's the account that my mother has been living off?' said Irina.

'Yes it is,' replied Smitt, 'Your father had a separate account that he used solely for living expenses.'

'And how much is there in that account Mr Smitt?' asked Irina.

'The last time I looked, I think there was approximately ten thousand roubles,' he replied.

'I'll take that money right now Mr Smitt. All of it,' said Irina quickly.

Smitt once again raised his eyebrows.

'And you want the money right now?'

'Right away if you will. And Mr Smitt, I'm in a hurry,' said Irina, now taking command of the situation. It was now her turn to give the orders.

Smitt stood up and silently walked out of his office.

Fifteen minutes later he returned with a cashier who was carrying the money. The cashier placed the bundles of money on the desk in front of Irina and then left immediately.

Smitt produced two sheets of paper and asked Irina to sign them both.

'You will retain one of these as a receipt,' he said as he picked up the other.

Smitt then opened one of the drawers in his desk and produced a blue canvas moneybag. He stuffed the bundles of roubles into the moneybag then passed it to Irina, who put the money into the shoulder bag that she had with her.

'What do you want me do with the account, now that it's empty Mrs Schwab?' asked Smitt.

'You can close it Mr Smitt. I don't need your bank anymore,' she replied and with that she turned and walked out of Smitt's office.

Smitt stood there and watched her go. Then he took a deep breath.

'Arrogant bitch,' he said quietly.

But as he stood there looking across his office, Smitt's expression slowly changed.

Then suddenly, Mr Smitt, the manager of the Moscow Principal Bank burst out laughing.

'You stupid, stupid, arrogant bloody bitch,' he said out loud and he walked around his desk and sat himself down. Smiling, he opened the bottom drawer and took out a bottle of good vodka. He then reached into the opposite drawer and lifted out a small wooden box which contained several cigars. After lighting one, he poured some vodka into the cup he had just used to drink his coffee. Then he leant back in his chair and considered his present situation. He'd done it, he had actually done it. And what's more, he'd got away with it.

'Stupid bitch,' he said again, 'You bloody stupid bitch,' and he laughed out loud.

As bank manager of the Moscow Principal Bank, Mr Smitt...Mr Arno Smitt had put up with Igor Klepsky for years. He'd not only had to put up with the man's ranting and raving, but had been bullied and coerced by Klepsky until he had finally become complicit in Igor Klepsky's utterly corrupt business world. He'd had to stand by and watch Igor Klepsky break up businesses and destroy families, simply because of the man's utter greed. And Smitt, by association, had somehow become implicated in some of Klepsky's seedier deals and from then on Klepsky had felt free to use him at will. In the earlier days, when Klepsky needed money to fund a deal, Smitt had somehow found him the cash and covered it. As a reward for his services, Klepsky had paid Smitt good money, but these payments had been traceable and it wasn't long before Smitt realised he'd been hooked like a fish.

In the end Klepsky had built up a considerable fortune. And it had been Smitt's job to hide the money in different accounts so that it couldn't be found and therefore couldn't be taxed.

Things had actually been going fairly well for the last couple of years. Klepsky was almost trading honestly because his timber business had become quite successful, and Smitt had been quite good at covering things at the bank. He was the manager, he had always kept things shipshape and head office had appreciated that and so too had the directors.

Then suddenly, Klepsky had dropped the bombshell. Klepsky wanted to transfer all of his money to another bank. Smitt couldn't believe it.

But it was true. The National Bank of Russia had approached Klepsky, or should we say, one of its directors had. That director had offered Klepsky an extraordinary deal, a deal so good that Klepsky couldn't refuse.

Corrupt it was of course, but that was Klepsky.

When Klepsky informed Smitt that he wanted to transfer everything to the National, the nervous bank manager nearly keeled over. He pleaded and begged Klepsky to think again, but Igor Klepsky would have none of it. Smitt then promised to double the rate of interest that Klepsky was already getting. He didn't know how to, but he vowed to find the money from somewhere. However Klepsky was still not overly impressed. Smitt then warned him that the movement of all that money from all the different bank accounts over to the National would look as if there was a run on their bank. Questions would be asked and the money may even be blocked. Whatever happened the result could end up being a catastrophe. It would also end up being very public.

For once, Klepsky saw sense. He certainly didn't want his finances to become common knowledge. So he sat down with Smitt and together they devised a plan that would make Klepsky's money more accessible.

Over a period of time, Smitt would open two new accounts for Klepsky Timber. An 'A' and a 'B' account. And over a period of time Smitt would transfer all the monies from Klepsky's various accounts and put the cash into either the 'A' or the 'B' account.

Those smaller accounts would then be closed down. The trick was not to make waves.

So that was what they did and it worked. Klepsky ended up with just two bank accounts which together contained over a million roubles. Success indeed.

However, once that was complete, Igor Klepsky instructed a very unhappy Arno Smitt to transfer the half a million roubles that was in the 'A' account over to the National Bank of Russia, just as he had always planned. Smitt was incensed and felt betrayed.

Not long after that transaction had taken place, Smitt was called in before the directors of the bank for an emergency meeting. They wanted to know the details of what was going on and why Smitt had allowed the bank to lose all that money. They were also aware of Smitt's relationship with Klepsky, the rumours had circulated for some time but the directors had decided to turn a blind eye to it all. However, something had now gone seriously wrong and if Smitt could not go some way to rectify the problem, well his position could be on the line.

Would be on the line.

Smitt had two problems, and both related to Igor Klepsky.

First of all, it was quite obvious that Igor Klepsky would eventually move the rest of his money deposited in the remaining 'B' account, over to the National Bank.

Of course he would.

Klepsky was a scheming, merciless bastard and Smitt knew it.

Secondly, was the regrettable decision that Smitt had taken when he had allowed himself to borrow money from Klepsky to pay off an unfortunate gambling debt. Klepsky had freely offered the money to him and stupidly Smitt had accepted it. Klepsky had never asked for the money to be repaid and Smitt had never offered. But then suddenly during a conversation with Klepsky the subject had regrettably come up.

'It's time you paid me back the money, my friend,' Klepsky had said. Then he grinned and smiled at Smitt's complete and utter look of surprise.

'I'll start paying you something every week,' Smitt had stuttered.

'Just make sure you do.' replied Klepsky.

Yes, Klepsky was a bastard, and Smitt realised that Klepsky was going to cut and run.

He was going to dump Smitt with all the financial misdemeanours and start afresh elsewhere.

By the same token, Smitt's immediate answer to this growing calamity was in itself, rather illegal.

One of the bank's oldest clients was Mrs Kapinsky. A reasonably wealthy widow, childless and in her seventies, Mrs Kapinsky had been suffering from dementia for the last four or five years and Smitt had made it his business to handle her accounts personally. He had also forged a letter that made him the sole executor of Mrs Kapinsky's affairs. Along with that he had also managed to forge her will, in which of course, she left absolutely everything to Smitt. However, Smitt had grown impatient whilst waiting for the old lady to die and for the last couple of years he had regularly dipped into her account to fund his comfortable lifestyle and also to ease the burden of his gambling debts. Just small amounts here and there and Smitt had justified these as expenses as part of his fees. However as the habit continued he was starting to borrow heavily from the old woman's account. He found that he had to steal more and more of Mrs Kapinsky's money to bolster the weekly payments that he had promised to Klepsky. And then suddenly, Klepsky had demanded the entire repayment of Smitt's sizeable loan and Smitt didn't have the money. Arno Smitt had always been an unlucky gambler and still was. So whilst owing Klepsky a large gambling debt he'd continued to borrow from Mrs Kapinsky's account in order to fund his habit at the Casino. Now he owed them money too, and Mrs Kapinsky's bank balance was beginning to diminish at an alarming rate.

Over the past few months, Smitt had started to call in and see the old lady quite regularly. He was her only visitor, except for the cleaner who would generally call in once or twice a week to keep the place tidy. Mrs Kapinsky lived in a faded but quite nice old house in a decent suburb of Moscow. Whenever he called round, Smitt always brought the old woman a bottle of the cheapest vodka he could find. It was always his hope that the old bag would finally drink herself to death, but he wasn't having much success. The toothless old woman would open the front door and almost snatch the bottle out of his hand. And even though Mrs Kapinsky didn't know what day it was and couldn't even remember her own name, she somehow did manage to associate Smitt with booze. Whilst she was downstairs drinking vodka straight from the bottle, Smitt would be upstairs stealing her jewellery, which he'd started to pawn on a regular basis.

Arno Smitt was in trouble and he knew it and he was becoming depressed with worry. The constant pressure, along with trying to run the bank was beginning to crush him.

But sometimes, just sometimes, there is a light at the end of the tunnel.

Smitt had been sitting in his office with his head in his hands when the shocking news broke.

His secretary had burst through the door, not even thinking to knock.

'Mr Smitt, Mr Smitt,' she was almost shouting.

Smitt looked up at her in amazement.

'Mr Smitt...Its Igor Klepsky. He's dead.'

Nearly a year had passed by.

It had been an interesting year for Arno Smitt. Interesting and fruitful, and it had been an education.

After Igor Klepsky's death, Smitt had been in a constant state of worry. If anyone found out what he and Klepsky had been up to it would have meant more than just losing his job, it would have meant a prison sentence for the unfortunate bank manager. But then, the month after Klepsky's demise, Smitt had once more been called up in front of the bank's directors. The board realised that chasing Klepsky's money now that he was dead was an impossibility, it was lost forever to the National Bank. They were willing to give Smitt the benefit of the doubt. However, they warned him to clean up his act and when he openly admitted to them that Klepsky had always been a problem for him, they were willing to let it go and give him a second chance. Mr Arno Smitt had in fact always been a very good bank manager.

It was after that meeting, as Smitt was walking back to the bank that he considered how lucky he had been. Thankfully the board knew nothing about Klepsky's 'B' account. They had no knowledge about account 'B' nor did they know about the half a million roubles that Smitt and Klepsky had hidden there. As he walked along he took a sigh of relief.

'Thank god' he thought 'that nobody knows about the money'.

Then suddenly Arno Smitt stopped dead in his tracks.

Nobody knew about the money.

Absolutely nobody.

Smitt started to walk back to the bank again but this time he wasn't walking quite so quickly. In fact, he was mindfully strolling along because his brain had just started to work.

On arriving back at the bank he asked his secretary to make him some coffee and then retreated to his office. As he sat there sipping the hot fresh brew, he scribbled some notes onto a notepad. He needed tangible notes for what he was planning. After about twenty minutes he re-read his plan and he smiled.

The next day, and after a little thought, Smitt began to put his plan into action. It was actually quite simple because most of the groundwork had already been done.

Smitt opened a new account with the bank. It was in the name of North Star Investments. It was a brand new business, very new, in fact it was only twenty four hours old. North Star Investments was a new company that had only one owner and only one director and in truth it had only one employee. And all of those were Arno Smitt.

Once the account was opened, Smitt deposited fifty roubles, just to make it look official. And once the account was open, Smitt just let it sit there for over a month. As he expected, nobody even noticed the new account as it was added to a myriad of others. Like all bank accounts, it was merely a number.

Smitt remembered his own words. 'Don't make waves'.

After a while, Smitt began to make some internal transfers, transfers within the bank. Principally, he moved money from the Klepsky 'B' account into his North Star Investment account. There was nothing substantial at first, just a few thousand roubles here and a few thousand there. Don't make waves.

Of course nobody noticed because nobody knew. Smitt would oversee all the transactions and personally okay them. He was the manager and he could do whatever he wanted. Over the next few months he became bolder and he transferred larger amounts.

Nobody of course had a clue, but why would they?

Eventually and with great diligence he managed to transfer nearly the whole half a million roubles into his North Star account.

Nobody noticed a thing, nobody at the bank and certainly none of the directors. This time there had been no huge withdrawal of money, it wasn't like the fiasco with Klepsky's disastrous 'A' account. This time the money hadn't been moved out of the bank, it had simply been moved sideways.

There were no waves at all, not even a ripple.

Once all of the money had been moved, Smitt almost made the mistake of closing the Klepsky 'B' account. And at the very last moment, it struck him that if he closed the account down, everything became irreversible. If the Klepsky family knew anything at all about the remaining money and 'came a calling', Smitt would suddenly have a lot of explaining to do. This after all was gross embezzlement, and once again he would be facing a hefty prison sentence, and in Russia that wasn't a good idea.

So he let the account run. There wasn't a huge amount of money in there of course, just ten thousand roubles, enough to keep Klepsky's old widow happy. If anything did go wrong he could simply transfer all the money back into the Klepsky 'B' account. Of course he would personally oversee the transaction and therefore no questions would be asked.

After congratulating himself on the ingenuity of his scheme, Smitt did absolutely nothing. He decided that would be the best course of action. Be prudent, be cautious and wait.

If need be he could sit on the money for years. Nobody knew who North Star Investments were and the money certainly wasn't going anywhere. In addition, deep down, Arno Smitt had a feeling that sooner or later there would be some sort of loose ends to tie up.

It finally happened the day that Irina Schwab charged into the bank demanding to see him. Dealing with her was just like dealing with her father. She was rude, arrogant and demanding and in her own way she was just the same bullying person that her father had been.

But Smitt had always had this day planned. Planned and rehearsed.

Smitt very quickly realised that Irina Schwab knew very little about her father's finances. In fact, she hadn't a clue. So it was so very simple to throw her a 'red herring'. So easy to tell her where she could get her greedy little hands on half a million roubles. So easy to steer her away from his bank and over to the National where the money was sitting, ready and waiting for her.

He had seen the expression change on Irina Schwab's face and he'd seen her eyes light up, those dark and greedy eyes. She had wanted everything, even the money that her mother lived off.

When Irina Schwab had first walked into his office she had needed him, but as soon as she got what she wanted, the lovely Irina was ready to discard him, just like her father had.

And of course, her final stinging comment, 'I don't need your bank anymore'.

And then she'd left.

Arno Smitt sat there at his desk with his lit cigar and his good vodka and he smiled to himself.

Later that afternoon he would finally and once and for all close the Klepsky 'B' account completely and with it destroy all of its history.

After that it could never be found, because it would have never existed.

There had also been some good news appertaining to Mrs Kapinsky. She'd died.

A couple of months earlier she had unfortunately fallen down the stairs. Smitt had continued to visit the old lady, but had started calling at her house two or three times a week and always taking with him two or three bottles of the cheap vodka.

Mrs Kapinsky was by then in a constant state of drunkenness and Smitt had started to wonder just how long the old woman could last.

Then one night, after she had been sat on the upstairs toilet for over two hours wondering where she was, she experienced a moment of clarity. As she looked at the bottle of vodka in her hand she realised that it was less than half full and that another couple of swigs would see it just about empty. She wondered if there was another bottle downstairs in the kitchen, but she just couldn't remember. So, completely inebriated, she staggered to the top of the stairs and reached out for the handrail. Unfortunately and due to the effects of the alcohol, she was by then seeing double and the handrail that she reached out for actually wasn't there. She toppled down the stairs from top to bottom, snapping her neck and breaking various arms and legs whilst on the way down. She lay there dead and in a crumpled, broken pile for three days, until the morning the cleaner let herself in and found old Mrs Kapinsky at the bottom of the stairs, deceased.

On the fifth step, just lying there, was the remaining half of a bottle of vodka.

The cleaner stole it.

So with the death of Mrs Kapinsky, Smitt finally inherited.

He had actually considered moving into his benefactor's house. He thought that with a bit of modernising and some painting and decorating it could be made quite presentable. But then he considered the possible consequences of being seen to be associated in any way to Mrs Kapinsky. He had already transferred the money that she had unknowingly left him into his North Star account. He then closed down her account too and again destroyed any of its history. So with a little foresight, he modernised the house, and had it painted and decorated and then he sold it for a very good price.

Smitt had also made some plans. He had been taking French lessons for some time and was doing quite well. It was something that he was really going to need. Smitt had thought long and hard about his future. He didn't really want to spend the rest of his life in cold and dreary Moscow or even cold and dreary Russia. He'd had enough of the bank and having to justify himself to its stuffy directors.

So he decided to give the bank and the French lessons another six months and then he would resign from both. His next destination was going to be Paris, where it was sunny and warm and the women were beautiful and people laughed and enjoyed life.

Once he got there, Smitt would look around for a couple of French banks. He would put his money in one of them and try to get a job at the other. He was quite confident that there must be a bank somewhere in Paris which needed a manager who could speak both French and fluent Russian.

However, now that he was worth three quarters of a million roubles, he really didn't care.

Irina Schwab remained in Moscow.

Several years passed by and thankfully for Ernst Schwab, his wife had decided never to return home to Smolensk. He blissfully assumed that they were now estranged.

Schwab had heard that her timber company was thriving. He had a feeling that it would. Once Irina took charge and ran the business with her iron fist it was bound to be a success.

And good luck to her.

Schwab shuddered when he reflected on the fact that 'if' Klepsky Timber had gone into bankruptcy, his estranged wife would have had no other option than to return home to him.

Yes, good luck to her indeed.

After a couple of years or so of non-correspondence, Schwab decided that it would probably be wiser ethics to slowly but surely change his timber supplier. Irina Schwab too, must have also thought it was a good idea, since there were never any queries regarding the ever dwindling order. There were no questions ever asked, even when Schwab finally stopped dealing with Klepsky Timber all together.

Monday morning arrived and for Schwab it was the start of another week. Once Irina had left Smolensk and was permanently ensconced in

Moscow, Schwab had decided not to work on Sundays anymore and he quickly realised that he enjoyed the free time.

Ernst Schwab was a man of repetition and whatever he felt comfortable with he repeated.

So on that Monday morning as he strolled to work, he did as usual call into the little baker's shop which was just around the corner from the factory.

He loved the smell of the freshly baked bread straight from the oven. The baker also roasted a fresh ham every day. and so every morning Schwab would call in for his breakfast.

It was always the same order. Two sandwiches made from the freshest of bread with some slices of the still warm cooked ham. They were always delicious.

Schwab walked into the open door of the shop and stood at the counter. One of the assistants, a young man, was filling up the shelves with the loaves of fresh bread. The young man had his back to the counter as he busily went about his work and he hadn't heard Schwab enter the shop. Schwab just stood there in an absentminded fashion, he was in no hurry, in fact he was looking at all the different varieties of bread. The young man must have been a new assistant, Schwab had never seen him before, but he took notice that the lad had a cropped haircut of the blondest hair that he had ever seen. The assistant finished stacking the bread and turned around and was quite shocked to see a customer standing there, waiting.

But not as shocked as Ernst Schwab. Schwab just stood there and for a moment and he couldn't speak. He blinked and his eyes widened as he looked back at the assistant. Not a young man, not at all. The assistant was a young woman, strikingly featured and with short blond hair and the darkest hazel brown eyes that he had ever seen.

Schwab actually stopped breathing. He blinked with confusion as the assistant stared back at him. She looked slightly confused by his behaviour and the moment was only broken when she smiled at him and asked for his order.

Schwab stuttered slightly, but then managed to ask for his usual sandwiches, filled with ham.

She quickly prepared the sandwiches, wrapped them in thin paper and then handed them across the counter to Schwab.

"There you go" she said.

"Thank you" he replied as he paid her.

But it was as he handed her the money that he noticed it. There was a small silver band on her third finger. It was a ring. It was a wedding ring.

Schwab gave her a nervous smile as he picked up his sandwiches and left the shop. As he walked away he suddenly felt an emotion that he didn't quite fully understand.

It was a feeling of bitter disappointment.

Schwab walked to the factory and into his office thinking about the encounter he had just had in the baker's shop. It was really quite strange, but then his work took over the day and he busied himself with the never ending manufacture of furniture.

Factory production had always been good, ever since he had taken over the day to day running of the company. His management style had been different from his father's. His father was overbearing and arrogant and the men resented it. But young Schwab's approach had been more communicative. He would talk to the men and take an interest in their work. This in turn promoted a more positive attitude within the workforce and the factory had gradually become a different place to work in. Schwab had set into motion the idea of teamwork. Instead of being blindly ordered about, the men now worked more as a whole team and that had brought about a natural progression to work more efficiently. There was a more relaxed attitude and his workers appreciated it. Gone was the 'do as little as possible' approach to working and over time, and overall production had quite successfully increased. Schwab was also open to suggestions and had listened to and taken on board some of his worker's individual ideas. As a result of this Schwab's company was now producing better quality furniture than ever before.

Things were looking good. The company was successful.

Lunchtime arrived and Schwab was in his office going over some orders when there was a tap on the door. Schwab glanced up at the clock, it was dead on twelve and that tap on the door would mean that his lunch had arrived. At the same time every day the baker's wife would deliver his lunch, and typical of Schwab, it was exactly the same order every day.

A potato pie and a small but delicious custard cake, Schwab's favourite.

He and the baker's wife would always exchange a few pleasantries for a moment or two, and after she had left, Schwab's secretary would enter the office and bring him in a cup of coffee to accompany his meal. It was possibly the highlight of Schwab's day.

So as usual, Schwab called out for the baker's wife to enter, he was glad that it was finally lunchtime because he was feeling quite hungry. But his appetite was about to be put on hold because when the door opened, standing there in the doorway with his lunch in her arms was the young blonde assistant that had served him with his breakfast. This threw Schwab into a sudden perplexity. He had in truth thought about the young lady several times that morning, actually it was probably more. In his mind he had decided to try and make polite conversation with her when he went into the bakers for his breakfast the following day, if she was there of course. But now this. She was here, standing right in front of him. And he hadn't had time to prepare anything at all that would be 'bright and interesting' to say to her.

She just stood there in the doorway then she smiled at him.

'Hello again,' she said, and Schwab's heart flipped a beat.

He just looked at her, she was so beautiful.

'Oh err, come in, come in,' he spluttered.

The girl walked straight up to his desk.

'I've brought you you're lunch,' she said brightly.

'Oh, thank you, thank you,' replied Schwab, and then he realised that he kept repeating himself.

'I didn't know that you were the Mr Schwab who owned the factory.'

'Err, oh yes, yes,' said Schwab, and he suddenly felt like kicking himself.

'Well I'm your new delivery girl,' she said and she laughed, 'The baker's wife has now passed the job onto me.'

'Oh,' said Schwab, 'I've never seen you in the shop before, do you normally work in the back?'

'Oh no,' she replied, 'I've only just started there.'

'Oh good,' said Schwab and then, 'Well, I'm a really boring person and I have the same food every day, even for my breakfast.'

'I believe so,' she said, and then she hesitated, 'Oh no, I don't mean that you're boring, I meant that you always have the same order. The baker's wife has already told me.'

And with that she looked a little flustered.

And that made Schwab laugh.

'I know I always order the same food, but it's very good food.'

'You should try something different.'

'Maybe I will,' said Schwab, 'but you don't know me, it will take a long time. Unfortunately I'm a creature of habit.'

'Okay then,' she said, still smiling, 'I suppose I'll see you tomorrow morning for breakfast.'

'You will,' he replied.

And as she turned to leave him to his lunch, Schwab suddenly had an uncontrollable urge to know her better.

'What's your name?' he asked her.

She turned back to him.

'My name's Rachel. It's Rachel Hartman.'

'Well Rachel Hartman, I will see you tomorrow morning.'

The next morning Schwab walked into the baker's shop. And for once, breakfast was actually the last thing on his mind. He wasn't even hungry.

He strolled rather nervously into what turned out to be an empty shop. At that particular moment, whoever was supposed to be behind the counter wasn't there.

He stood there for a few minutes and just as he was beginning to wonder if there had been some sort of problem, the door to the bake house flung open and in walked a huge tray of bread. Well it was actually a large tray stacked high with bread with somebody hidden behind it, struggling to carry the load. Schwab had been a little startled when the door had just burst open, but then when he looked down and under the tray, he saw a pair of slim legs. Then he smiled, because he knew who those legs belonged to.

Rachel Hartman, trying her best not to drop the tray or the bread, staggered to the shelf. Once again she had her back to Schwab and once again she hadn't a clue that he was watching her.

She wasn't aware that he was looking at her short cropped blonde hair, and at the nape of her neck, her ever so beautiful slim neck, and that he was looking down at her trim figure and supple shape and her slender firm legs. And in that brief moment he was completely spellbound, it was as though time had stood still. Then his commonsense and his own shyness got the better of him, and he had to stop himself from ogling Rachel Hartman, just in case she suddenly turned around and caught him.

And still, she was unaware of his presence.

So he made the mistake of giving a short but noticeable cough, which completely spooked her. She thought there was nobody in the shop and she gave a short scream and launched the tray into the air. Loaves of freshly baked bread flew everywhere. Three or four loaves bounced onto the counter and one of them actually hit Schwab on the top of his head. She spun around just in time to see the offending loaf bounce off the top of Schwab's skull and leave him standing there, mouth wide open and slightly shocked.

They stood there facing one another for an instant and she immediately recognised him.

There was a second's silence and then she smiled, and suddenly they both burst out laughing.

'I didn't know you were there...again,' she laughed.

'I know. I'm sorry. It was just that you were in so much of a hurry and I didn't know that it was you behind that mountain of bread,' he lied.

'Oh it's been madness here this morning, we're short staffed.'

'Why's that?' asked Schwab.

She looked at him, and then back at the bake house door. Then she leant forward to speak to him, somewhat covertly.

'It's the baker and his wife. They've had a argument. I think he's been drinking the vodka again and they've had a big quarrel and now she's refused to come into work. He's in the back nursing a hangover and I'm having to do everything else.'

She shrugged as she started to pick up the scattered loaves

'I could come back later,' he said.

'No, no,' said Rachel, 'I know exactly what you want. I'll get your order for you.'

Schwab stood there while she prepared his breakfast and he smiled to himself.

Rachel Hartman had no idea as to what he did really want.

Actually, he wanted her.

For the first time in his life he had suddenly met a woman that he desired. Not only did he want her emotionally, he also realised that he wanted her physically. He wanted to reach out and touch this woman, he wanted to take hold of her beautiful slim neck and he wanted to be up close to her strikingly attractive face and look into those deep hazel brown eyes. For the first time in his whole life he had met a woman who stirred him. For Schwab it was like turning on a switch, a switch that he had never known existed.

So they talked and laughed and continued to talk for several minutes until the baker shouted something from inside the bake house and Rachel had to go and help him with another chore.

Schwab bid her 'Good morning' and regretfully turned to leave.

She called after him 'I'll see you at lunch with your pie and custard cake,' and she laughed.

And as Schwab looked back into those beautiful hazel eyes, he knew that he was smitten.

'Thank you Rachel,' he replied, 'until lunch then.'

As he walked away from the bakers shop he suddenly experienced the strangest of feelings. He was both happy and sad at exactly the same time. He realised, absolutely, that he was totally besotted by this girl. However, in reality he was still a married man and that silver wedding ring on Rachel's finger meant that she was a married woman. She had a husband who she probably loved and loved very much. The thought of that almost made Schwab feel sick. So much so, that when he finally arrived at his office he threw his breakfast into the bin.

For another half hour Schwab stamped around his office, frustrated and deep in thought. In the end he went down into the factory to talk to the men and oversee the daily production.

Anything at all to clear his mind.

Inevitably lunch time came around and so did Rachel Hartman. Schwab had decided earlier that he would have to calm himself down and forget any hopes, aspirations or even thoughts that he possibly had in her direction.

What on earth was he thinking of?

He had just about talked himself into making a more sensible decision, and that he would try to maintain a distance from her. Yes, common sense it seemed, would rule the day.

That was until Rachel walked into his office and he looked at her and her short blonde hair, and her beautiful elfin face and those deep brown eyes. And with that, Schwab just sighed and realized that all of his so-called plans had just been irreversibly dashed.

He knew he was being an idiot, yes he did, but he just couldn't help his feelings. Not one bit.

Rachel Hartman walked into his office, and for Schwab it was as though the sun had just started to shine.

He was so pleased to see her, and she arrived smiling as usual and carrying a leather bag which contained his lunch.

'Your pie and cake,' she said to him, 'just as you like it,' and she giggled.

'Ah, you think I'm boring,' he said pleasantly.

'No' she replied, 'you're just stuck in a rut. The baker told me that you've had the same breakfast and lunch for years.'

'Not on Sundays,' he said defensively, 'I always have something different on Sundays.'

Rachel Hartman suddenly burst out laughing.

'Yes, only because the bakers shop is closed on Sundays,' she said, still laughing at him.

Schwab shrugged 'Yes Rachel, you're absolutely right. I'm hopeless.'

And he started to laugh to.

All this good humour was infectious and they carried on talking for the next ten or fifteen minutes, until she finally glanced up at his office clock and realized that she was going be in trouble if she didn't get back to the baker's swiftly.

Schwab judged the moment. 'Tell the baker it was my fault. Tell him I might be considering changing my order and we were discussing the options.'

Rachel Hartman shook her head and giggled.

'See you tomorrow,' she said, and then she was gone.

That left Schwab alone. He sat there on his own once again. He was always on his own and a thought suddenly crossed his mind, an awful thought. That really he'd been on his own and had been lonely for most of his life.

Schwab sat there for a while, tapping his pen repeatedly on his desk whilst deep in thought.

In the last fifteen minutes he'd had more enjoyment than he could ever remember. It was the simple joy of conversation with someone that you felt attuned to and someone that you were comfortable with. It was something that had always been missing from his life.

And he wanted more.

So that was how it started.

At first he would see her twice a day. Seeing Rachel every morning for his breakfast would put a smile on Schwab's face that would stay there till lunchtime, when she would again arrive at his office with his food. She would stay for a while and they would happily talk to each other for as long as possible. Then she started to alter his lunch by adding different pastries to his 'historic order'. A thin slice of a different pie or another type of cake, all little treats, but treats that he really enjoyed and moreover, began to look forward to.

Rachel would ask him about his work which he found easy to discuss with her, but when he tried, very subtly, to find out anything about 'her' life she would somehow manage to change the subject. All he did know was that she lived in the Glinka district of Smolensk, which was quite a rundown area. That was a lie of course. Rachel Hartman didn't want him to know where she lived because Rachel Hartman was married and she had a husband. When Schwab had once tried to pursue that particular subject, Rachel had suddenly checked the time and rather awkwardly excused herself and had to leave.

It seemed to Schwab that Rachel Hartman was definitely not comfortable in talking about her home life. He also felt that if he did try to pursue that line of conversation, he would lose her.

Then one lunchtime, after she'd arrived with his food and they had been sitting there chatting as usual, Rachel casually asked him if the factory was busy. It was the month's ending and Schwab had a desk full of paperwork, everything around him was invoices and bills and receipts. It was the usual chaos. Schwab happened to mention that he would definitely be burning the midnight oil that evening and that he would have to work very late.

As she was leaving, Rachel suddenly turned to him.

'I'll bring you some food over. When I've finished at the bakery tonight I'll call in with something for you. You do have to eat you know.'

Schwab nodded and thanked her.

It was all done in complete innocence. It was as simple as that.

As Rachel Hartman walked back to the bakery she wondered just what was going on. Something was happening, and for her it was beginning to get out of hand, and somehow she just didn't fully understand it. Here was a man, a man she had met one morning in the bakery and he had now become a friend, a good friend. She could talk to this man for hours and she loved his company. And now she was feeding him and caring about what he ate, and suddenly she found that she was caring about his well being too. Her feelings for him were becoming emotional and she really looked forward to seeing him every morning and every lunchtime. Seeing Schwab and talking to him every day had become her only pleasure.

Then her mind turned to something else, and she thought about her own life and the problem that would never go away, the problem that burdened her life and would continue to destroy any joy that she could possibly hope for.

Rachel looked down at her left hand and at the wedding ring on her finger. It had been the biggest mistake of her life because she was trapped. She was trapped and she was owned.

She was nothing more than a possession. Unloved and abused.

Yes, Mrs Rachel Hartman was a married woman, she had a husband.

And that man was Yuri Hartman.

If you could call him a man, Yuri Hartman was someone who would without doubt be described as an 'undesirable'. Mother Russia had always been a hard and cruel place to live in and it was in Hartman's nature, as with many other Russian men, to be brutal. However, in Yuri Hartman you had someone who was also a thief and a liar, and more disturbingly a murderer.

At the start of his career Yuri Hartman had been employed simply as a casual worker for the infamous 'Gotz Family' of Moscow. His actual roll was no more than that of a lowly retainer.

The Gotz family lived in Moscow, where they ruled and ran most of the highly illegal activities in that dark and menacing city. Illegal liquor, drugs, prostitution, larceny and fraud were all collectively practised under the 'umbrella' of the Gotz family's business interests.

Once an individual became involved in any way with the Gotz syndicate, they quickly became ensnared. And anyone who decided to extract themselves from that 'relationship' also quickly discovered that they had a problem. Transgressors were quickly taken care of and were simply terminated.

And that was where Yuri Hartman's skills would eventually come into play.

Hartman had elevated himself to the position of 'chief henchman' for the Gotz family, almost by accident. It had simply been a matter of being in the right place at the right time.

Yuri Hartman was also an antagonistic drinker, and after enough vodka he was capable of acts of violence which ranged from aggressive beatings to the most brutal of murders.

For Yuri Hartman, it was a way of life. He just didn't care about anyone at all.

He'd started working for the Gotz family, basically as a messenger and a delivery boy. His job was to deliver cheap vodka or drugs to the illegal network of underground bars located around the city. Occasionally he would be asked to deliver wrapped paper packages of bribery money to the 'right' people. And sometimes he would collect the takings from the various prostitutes who stood around of an evening on dark street corners.

Everything it seemed was controlled one way or another by the infamous Gotz family.

However, wealthy and powerful they may have been, but it seemed that the 'family' had their share of enemies too.

The Gotz family was headed by Manny Gotz, who at sixty years old was robust and intelligent, and a man who had the stature of someone much younger. In the world of illegality, Manny Gotz had seen and done just about everything that could be done.

And Manny Gotz ran his organization with an iron fist. It was the only way.

Unfortunately, there would always be somebody, somewhere trying to steal his crown.

Yes, the Gotz family had their enemies. There were other gangs and there were other crime syndicates in Moscow, but Manny Gotz had beaten them down to a level where he could allow them to have the 'crumbs off his table'.

One evening, Manny Gotz and his accountant had been to a small local restaurant for a business meeting and some very good food. Manny had always enjoyed going to this particular restaurant because they served roast wild boar cooked exactly to Manny's liking. After the food, the wine and some good French brandy, the two men decided to walk the short distance back to the Gotz family residence, a dark regal mansion situated in the upper district of the 'Kirzhach'. The two men strolled along at a leisurely pace, each of them enjoying one of Manny's exceptional cigars, cigars that Manny Gotz had illicitly sourced direct from the island of Cuba. The two men were not alone of course, walking behind them were Manny's two bodyguards, along with Yuri Hartman. The bodyguards were there for obvious reasons, but Yuri Hartman was there because he had a parcel of money with him that he'd collected from a local pimp whose girls had been having a busy night. Yuri was casually strolling along behind the bodyguards. He was carrying the parcel of money in his inside pocket, with the intention of dropping it off at the Gotz residence as instructed. Then he would immediately leave.

Yuri Hartman was just one of the many subordinates in the Gotz Empire. He was nothing more than a lowly messenger.

He'd met up with the two bodyguards earlier at the restaurant. While Manny Gotz and his accountant were dining, one of the bodyguards had stood at the front door of the restaurant, making sure 'who' came in. The other bodyguard was in the kitchen, keeping an eye on the back door and checking the kitchen staff. When Yuri Hartman had turned up at the restaurant, the bodyguard at the front door had told him to go around to the back and wait in the kitchen. So he walked around the building, and down the side street. The street seemed to be deserted, and as he made his way around there he wondered just how much money he was carrying in the parcel. He had actually given a thought to stealing the money and running off with it, but then he remembered the stories that he'd heard about what happened to people who had tried to get the better of Manny Gotz, and he'd quickly changed his mind.

It was at that moment that he heard a tapping sound, and he suddenly looked up. From nowhere at all, a man was suddenly walking towards him. The man was wearing a long dark coat and a matching cap that was pulled firmly forwards so that his face was nearly hidden. And the tapping, a click-clicking noise, was the echoing sound of the man's heels on the hard cobbled surface of the empty street. From the first moment Hartman was alert. This man had just appeared out of the dark and for a split second Hartman wondered if he was going to be attacked and robbed. With one hand he gripped the parcel in his pocket, and his other hand reached for the razor sharp hunting knife that he always carried in a leather sheaf attached to the back of his belt. But the man just walked by. Strangely, he never even looked up. Hartman gave a quick sigh of relief as he relaxed again, and then suddenly an odd thought struck him. The man must have been to a cobbler and had metal caps put on the heels of his boots so as to make them last longer. It was just a passing thought, but it was there. Yuri knocked on the back door of the restaurant and the bodyguard let him in, and for the next hour while Mr Gotz and his accountant were still dining, Yuri Hartman sat with the half bottle of vodka that he'd helped himself to, which he drank as he made himself comfortable.

Finally the meal was over, and Mr Gotz and his accountant were talking, smoking and amiably walking back to the Gotz family residence. The two bodyguards followed closely by and Yuri strolled along some way behind. The vodka was making him feel good. He'd had the first flush of alcohol and it was making him feel exuberant. He felt exhilarated and alert.

And as he ambled onwards, it was then that he suddenly heard something, it was the faint sound, a click-clicking. Nobody else seemed to hear it. The two bodyguards were close up behind their boss and were probably listening in on the conversation. But Yuri Hartman heard it. And Yuri Hartman recognized it for what it was. He looked up, and on the other side of the road and walking towards them was the man who had passed Yuri earlier at the rear of the restaurant. He recognized the man, with the long coat and the cap still pulled down over his face. And suddenly, and for some strange reason, the blood in Yuri Hartman's veins started to pump a little bit faster. Something was wrong. And at that moment he wondered if this could just be a coincidence, the same man wandering around the same streets, and at that hour. And something somewhere hit a nerve in Yuri's senses. He'd lived off his wits for the whole of his life, and he'd always learned to trust his first instincts. And suddenly this didn't feel right and the vodka in his blood urged him on.

Yuri stepped silently off the pavement and crossed over the road. It only took him a matter of seconds and nobody even noticed. Crouching slightly, he continued to move along silently and he watched as the man approached. Then suddenly, the man stopped behind a lamp post, and Yuri realized that the man was going to use the lamp post as cover, he was sure of it.

Yuri figured that the man was going to wait for Mr Gotz and his bodyguards to pass directly opposite him and then something was going to happen. And suddenly the hair on the back of Yuri Hartman's neck started to rise and his natural instincts began to take over. He slowly reached back to the sheaf on his belt and he extracted his knife, his long sharp hunting knife with the seven inch blade that Yuri Hartman had used often, and for the same reason.

Yuri watched as the man reached into his coat, and as Mr Gotz and his accountant and the bodyguards walked directly opposite, the man pulled out a gun and started to shout something. The party of men stopped in horror as the man stepped off the pavement and walked halfway across the open road. With the gun in his hand he could have shot any one of them with ease. He started to shout something, presumably orders, because the four men suddenly got down on their knees and put their hands on the top of their heads.

Yuri immediately realized what was happening. It was an execution.

Yuri made a decision, and he started to slowly and silently creep closer to the gunman. But there was a problem. If any one of the four kneeling men saw him approaching they would naturally turn to look at him, and that would give the gunman a warning. Yuri looked at the four men, and he knew straightaway that it would be the accountant who would be the problem. The man was kneeling there, trembling and completely terrified at what was about to happen.

Yuri Hartman had to think, and think quickly. He reached into his inside pocket for the parcel of money. He considered the moment and the timing, and then he slowly stepped back and threw the parcel high, high and over the gunman's head. He watched the parcel fly through the air and just as it was about to hit the ground, Yuri started running. The parcel thudded loudly onto the road and the gunman turned sharply to see what it was. At that moment, and almost silently, Yuri Hartman leapt forward and wrapped one arm around the gunman's head, expertly bending it sideways, and then he stabbed his long knife down and into the man's neck. Yuri pushed the knife in all the way, deep and into the man's chest cavity.

Yuri knew exactly what to do, because he'd done it before.

The gunman just gurgled blood and died instantly. It was over.

The accountant keeled over sideways and had to prop himself up with one hand. The two bodyguards immediately jumped up to go to Mr Gotz's assistance. But Manny Gotz had already stood up and was brushing himself off. Manny Gotz was angry.

One of the bodyguards went to help the accountant to his feet as Manny Gotz walked over to the gunman's still bleeding corpse. With his foot, Gotz roughly turned the body over. The cap was now gone and Gotz stared down at the gunman's bloodied face.

'One of Zwerner's,' he said out loud and to no one in particular. He stood back for a second, and then he kicked the dead man in the face. Even though the dead man was now a corpse, there was a crunching noise as the man's nose broke and flattened.

'Bastard,' spat out Gotz...'Bastards.'

He then turned to Yuri Hartman. But Yuri was walking across the road to retrieve the parcel. He picked up the money and turned to see Manny Gotz staring at him. Yuri put the parcel back into his inside pocket and walked over to Mr Gotz. No words were spoken, Gotz nodded at him and Yuri just shrugged his shoulders in reply.

Manny Gotz then turned to his two bodyguards.

'And where the fuck where you two? How could you let this happen, you fucking imbeciles?'

Gotz was blazing with anger.

'So this is how the Zwerners want to play it,' he said out loud, 'Okay then...we'll play.'

Manny Gotz then took hold of his accountant's arm.

'Come on my friend, let's get you home. You've had a rough night.'

Gotz's accountant was visibly shaken and when they finally arrived at the Gotz residence, Manny had one of the bodyguards take the accountant directly home.

As the three men walked through the doorway of Gotz's mansion, Gotz turned to Yuri Hartman.

'Come with me into my study.'

He then dismissed his other bodyguard with a cursory glance.

They entered the large study, where there was a fire burning slowly in the hearth, the room was warm and comfortable.

Gotz had Yuri close the double doors to the study. He required some privacy.

Manny Gotz walked over to his desk and sat down in a large burgundy coloured leather chair. Yuri followed him over to the desk and then took the parcel of money out of his pocket and placed it in front of Gotz. Manny Gotz again nodded. Then he opened a side cabinet in his desk as he looked across at Yuri.

'A drink?' he asked.

'Yes,' said Yuri.

'Brandy?'

'Vodka,' replied Yuri.

Gotz took out two glasses and two bottles. One was honey dark Brandy, the other was colourlessly clear Vodka. It was the purest distilled vodka, the liquor that had forever fuelled Russia. Gotz slid the bottle of vodka over to Yuri and told him to pull up a chair and help himself to the bottle.

That suited Yuri Hartman. Manny Gotz stocked only the very best.

The two men sat there for a moment, with drinks that were as different as the men themselves.

'You did well tonight,' said Manny, breaking the silence.

Yuri Hartman just nodded and took another swig of his vodka. Manny Gotz nodded at him to replenish his glass.

Yuri was grateful, as was Manny really.

'I'm no fool,' said Gotz, 'I take it that you've killed before?'

Yuri nodded.

'Often?' asked Gotz.

'Enough,' said Yuri Hartman

It was the reply that Manny Gotz was waiting for.

'I have a problem,' said Gotz 'You may just be the man to solve it for me.'

Yuri looked again at the bottle of vodka, and Manny nodded.

Yuri poured another full glass and then leant back in the chair.

'What do you want me to do Mr Gotz?'

Manny Gotz put his glass of brandy down as he spoke to Yuri Hartman.

'There is a family. They are the 'Zwerners' and they're becoming a problem. They've tried a few times to step into my operations, they keep trying to pinch a bit of my territory and with it a bit of my business, and they keep pushing. In the past they've been an inconvenience. But tonight they've pushed it too far. Tonight I've realized that they want it all. And that won't do. It won't do at all.'

Yuri sat there, listening.

Gotz continued, 'I want them out of Moscow. I want them gone Yuri. Can you do that?'

'Who are these Zwerners?' Yuri asked.

'They're an ignorant bunch of thugs who arrived from 'Kursk' about two years ago. Apparently they caused some commotion over there too, and were finally chased out by a rival gang. There are five or six brothers, they're headed by 'Lev Zwerner', he's the eldest brother. They all live together in a big old house over in the 'Ruza' district, some of them are married and there's a few kids. That's as much as I know.'

Yuri Hartman simply nodded.

The meeting was over and he stood up and turned to leave.

Gotz looked at the parcel of money on the desk in front of him.

'What about the money Yuri?' he asked.

Yuri looked back quickly.

'I haven't touched it Mr Gotz. I don't even know how much there is.'

Manny Gotz smiled.

'But I do,' he said and he leant forward and pushed the parcel back in Yuri's direction.

'It's yours Yuri. Let's call it a payment for tonight's services.'

Yuri Hartman was staggered by the gesture. For him this was real money, more than he had ever earned before.

Gotz suddenly shouted out a name, and the study door opened immediately and a bodyguard entered, he was never far away.

'Give this man the addresses and any details we have on the Zwerners,' instructed Gotz.

After he'd been given that information, Yuri Hartman went to leave Manny Gotz's home. As he was walking out of the front door, the bodyguard took him to one side and spoke to him.
'You've been lucky tonight peasant. But now listen to me. Stay out of our way and be careful peasant, be very careful.'
It was a warning.
But Yuri Hartman let it go. He already had enough enemies.

After counting the money and almost laughing out loud. Yuri went off to buy some vodka. Two hours later he staggered into his apartment, he climbed into bed and reached over and took hold of his young wife. The poor girl was then made to endure the most appalling and brutalizing sex until her husband finally passed out. She'd prayed for him to stop. But he never did. These days, Yuri Hartman only ever made love to his wife when he was drunk. And his idea of lovemaking was nothing more than vicious rape.
Afterwards, she managed to get herself out of the bed and she crawled over to the open fire were she sat with a blanket wrapped around her.
She sat there sobbing, her body aching and abused.
Rachel Hartman looked into the flames, and then she held out her left hand and stared down at her wedding ring, and she wondered why she had ever married this man, this animal.

Her husband hadn't always been like this. When Yuri Hartman had arrived at her village four years earlier, he'd been well mannered and quiet. He'd cast his eye on Rachel and immediately tried to woo her, but her father had disapproved. Rachel's mother had died at an early age, and her father had taken care of her for most of her life. Rachel knew that her father was over protective, but nevertheless she'd stood by his wishes and turned Yuri Hartman's proposal down. Unfortunately, within a month Rachel's life was thrown into turmoil when her father had a heart attack and died. She'd found him one morning, lay in bed. He'd apparently passed away in his sleep.

Yuri Hartman then stepped into her life and promised to take care of her. They married quickly and then Yuri informed her that he wanted to move out of her village. He wanted a better life. After that they drifted from town to town, Yuri never holding down a job, but every so often seeming to obtain an unexpected amount of money, for which he would never give an explanation. They would then move on. Within the first year of marriage his drinking became apparent, and with it the violence. And within the next couple of years Rachel Hartman realized that she was married to a very bad man. It was obvious that he was a thief and that he had no qualms at all about robbing people, she'd quickly understood that. But there was also a darker side, because her husband had one great failing. Yuri Hartman had a flaw in his character that could open up a raw streak of unbelievable violence. And that flaw was fired by his absolutely uncontrollable jealousy.

Rachel Hartman was beautiful, unquestionably beautiful. And men noticed her and were attracted to her. But whenever her husband saw this, he would go into a rage and usually beat the offender to a pulp. In the past he'd had to be dragged off many a poor individual for fear of killing them. And killing someone had never been a problem for Yuri Hartman.

He'd also started to spend more and more time away from home, which would leave Rachel alone and on her own. And that would often arouse the interest of some man or other who would eventually try to befriend her, even though she always informed them that she was a married woman. But men will be men and there was always someone who unfortunately would not take no for an answer.

Yuri would eventually arrive home, always unannounced even to his wife. For a day or two he would spy on her, just to see anyone was calling around, or at least trying to. And if he observed anybody trying to woo his wife, Yuri would track them down and that was the last anybody would ever see of them. That person would simply disappear.

Rachel began to take notice of this repetition, and she tried desperately to dismiss the thought. But eventually, deep in her heart she realized the truth of it. She was married to a murderer, and a man who was capable of anything.

Six months earlier, they had arrived in Moscow and moved into their shoddy apartment in the Drezna District. It was a derelict and run down area of Moscow, full of thieves and undesirables. It suited Yuri Hartman needs and he actually felt quite at home.

From there, Yuri had got involved with the Gotz family and the nature of his work required him being out for most of the night, then he would arrive home in a drunken state and sleep all day. There was a distance between them now as Yuri's brutal demands increased. Rachel had to get out of the house during the day and she eventually found herself a job at a baker's shop in another district. It became her retreat, and she felt safe and comfortable for a few hours every day. The old baker had started to show her how to make bread and pastries. He actually reminded Rachel of her father, and for the first time in a long while she was reasonably happy.

Yuri of course followed her to work one morning and then he spied on her for the next two days before he realized that nothing was happening, and then he left her to it.

He also realized that now she earned her own money, he could spend more of his on 'better' vodka.

That had been six months ago, but now Yuri Hartman had other thoughts on his mind.

And that was the Zwerner family.

After the attack on Manny Gotz, Yuri had gathered all the information he could find about the Zwerners. It turned out that they were a hard, rough bunch, headed by the eldest brother who was known as 'Lev' Zwerner. They'd arrived from Kursk where they'd been beaten and thrown out of the city by a rival gang. So they came to Moscow looking for a fresh territory and the chance of easy money. They pursued that line of thought by dealing out beatings and harsh punishment to anybody who got in their way. Their method was crude, but very effective. Fear after all, is a great persuader.

Within the first year, most of the businesses in their area were paying the Zwerner family 'protection' money. That was to be the beginnings of the Zwerner business empire, and from there they started to expand into other profitable areas. Predictably however, the areas that they were expanding into began to overlap into the Gotz's family interests. Very soon there began an aggravated 'stand off' as the interests of both families began to conflict.

In truth, Manny Gotz had to take some of the blame for it all. He'd been slow to act, and he now realized that he should have stamped on the Zwerners a long time ago. Those 'upstarts' from Kursk had finally begun to flex their muscles and it was time for a show of ultimate strength. Manny Gotz had to prove himself, the personal attack on him was beyond unacceptable and it was now obvious to Manny that he had to make his play.

The 'King' was certainly not dead. So long live the King.

Yuri Hartman soon found the Zwerner's house, it didn't take him long. He'd cautiously turned up there, and then he watched and he waited. From then on, every day, Yuri would carefully watch the Zwerner family going about their business, and from various vantage points he observed the family's routines. Yuri knew that everyone had a routine, and routines were a weakness, routines were dangerous and they could be your downfall.

He spent around ten days watching the Zwerner's house and then after a night of clarity and without any vodka, he initiated his plan.

On the Friday morning Yuri Hartman set off once again for the Zwerner residence. He carried with him a small sharpened axe. Yuri had set off early, and he was standing on the corner of a street, about thirty metres away from the Zwerner house just as Lev Zwerner's wife, 'Yulia' appeared with their youngest son. Every morning at the same time, she would walk the boy to school.

'Every morning', that was her routine.

And for several days Yuri had walked a short distance in front of them or behind them, all the way to the school. And once Yulia Zwerner and her had child entered the school, he would walk all the way back and stop and wait at that same street, just thirty metres from the Zwerner's house. He never had to wait long for Yulia Zwerner to return. He knew he wouldn't, because Yulia Zwerner was a creature of habit.

And on that Friday morning, returning from the school, she once again unknowingly strolled towards him. Yuri had knelt down to re-tie his boot lace, and as she passed by he quickly stood up and smashed in the back of her head with his axe. She groaned just once as she fell to the floor. Whether she was dead or not at that particular moment was of no interest to Yuri Hartman, he simply grasped hold of the collar of her coat and quickly dragged her down the deserted street. He took hold of the woman's hair, and pulled it as hard as he could so as to stretch out her neck, then he took the axe and swung it high and he hacked off her head, completely.

It took four attempts, four sharp chops. He knew it would.

Hartman then lifted Yulia Zwerner's headless body and threw it over a neighbour's fence into some bushes. To Yuri, she was no more than a piece of meat. He then picked up Yulia Zwerner's severed head and went around to the Zwerner house. He walked up their drive and he dumped the bloodied head there on the ground in front of the house for all to see.

Then he turned around and went home.

The next day he returned. With him he had a letter. He walked past the Zwerner house and he noticed that all the curtains were closed. He then wandered around until he saw a young boy, who was merrily skipping along towards him. The young lad was poorly dressed and rather scruffy. He was just the person that Yuri was looking for. He took the boy to one side and offered him enough roubles to get his attention, and then he handed the lad the letter.

Witten on the front of the envelope was the name 'Lev Zwerner', and inside the envelope there was a note. It read 'You have one week to leave Moscow. After that, we will start to kill your children'.

Yuri Hartman watched the boy skip up the drive to the Zwerner house and push the letter into the letterbox.

Then once again, Yuri turned around and went home.

That same evening he returned, this time he came on a horse and cart.

It was now Saturday, a Saturday night, and Yuri had brought with him two small wooden barrels which were both full of turpentine. He unloaded the two barrels onto the side street were he'd previously decapitated Yulia Zwerner, and then he quietly drove away.

Yuri stopped and tied the horse to a tree about three hundred metres up the road, and then he walked back to where he'd left the barrels. He very cautiously carried one of them up the drive and to the rear of the Zwerner house, and then he went back for the other. After liberally emptying the two barrels of turpentine over the front and the back porch and all over the walls, he set fire to the house.

In those days most of the buildings in Russia were built of timber, and the Zwerner house went up like a torch. The blaze was phenomenal.

Some of the wives were burned to death, as were their husbands and also some of the children. Yuri Hartman didn't wait to see. He quietly walked back to his horse and cart and drove back home.

On the Monday morning, Yuri arrived at the Gotz house unannounced. He simply knocked on the door and waited until one of the bodyguards opened it. The big man who opened the door was quite shocked to see Yuri Hartman standing there.

He nodded at Yuri and beckoned him in.

'Is Mr Gotz in?' Yuri asked the bodyguard.

'Yes, I will go and tell him that you're here,' he replied, and he nodded to Yuri.

And Yuri noticed that there was a slightly different tone in the man's voice, and there was a subtle change in the bodyguard's previously callous attitude.

To Yuri's surprise, the man was now showing him some respect.

Yuri was shown into Manny Gotz's study. Manny was sitting behind his desk smiling.

As Yuri entered, Manny Gotz actually stood up and shook his hand.

'Sit down my friend,' he said graciously, and he offered Yuri a chair. Manny then sat down himself and promptly offered Yuri the bottle of vodka.

Respect indeed.

Yuri too nodded as the bottle was handed over.

Manny Gotz sat back as he watched Yuri Hartman pour himself a drink.

'Never too early, eh Yuri?'

'Yes boss, it's never too early.'

Manny sat there for a moment, and Yuri sipped his drink and waited.

'You did well Yuri, very well.'

Yuri just sat there and listened.

'Those Zwerners,' continued Manny, 'Those bastards, they've gone, fled.'

Yuri nodded.

'You did well Yuri, and I appreciate that. And you will of course be rewarded.'

'Thank you Mr Gotz,' Yuri replied.

'And also, I feel it's time that you were, how can I say it...'promoted' Yuri. Yes that's it. It's time that I found you something better to do.'

Yuri raised his eyebrows. This was something he hadn't considered.

'In fact Yuri, I have a special position for you. You have talents that I can use.'

At these words, Yuri leant forward to listen. For the first time in his life he was actually being offered something.

'Yuri...' Manny Gotz continued, 'There are plenty of other people out there who become nuisances and they too need to be taught a lesson. It's a fact of life, and it goes with the business. Most of the time we can take care of it ourselves and it's not a problem. But every so often, I need a 'special job' doing. And I need it doing quickly and I need it doing efficiently. Every so often there seems to be someone who thinks I'm a fool, and I need that someone taking care of, and I need it taking care of so quickly that they don't even see it coming. And that's where you come in Yuri. What you did with the Zwerners. You sorted out the problem immediately, without a lot of people getting involved. They never saw you Yuri, they never saw you coming. You were like a ghost. Yes Yuri, a ghost...and you solved the problem straightaway.'

'Thank you Mr Gotz,' said Yuri again.

Manny Gotz looked at Yuri Hartman.

'At the moment you are invisible Yuri, you are my 'ghost' and I have work for you, but if you stay here in Moscow, you won't remain a ghost for long. People talk Yuri, people talk all the time and rumours spread and so does notoriety. And before long, people would know that you work for me, and eventually someone would be sent to find you and your family too. I believe you have a pretty wife?'

At the mention of his wife, Yuri bristled, and for a brief moment he moved in his chair.

And though it was only a slight movement, Manny Gotz saw it, and he saw the sudden change in Yuri Hartman's face. It was only for an instant, but it was there. And Manny Gotz realized that his 'ghost' had a weakness. And it was something that he could possibly use, if ever his 'ghost' went sour.

Yuri Hartman looked back at his boss 'Okay, yes I have a wife Mr Gotz,' he said.

Manny Gotz smiled to himself. Yes he was getting there, and getting to the point of this conversation, slowly but surely.

'I have a plan for you Yuri, and it's this. You will work for me as my 'ghost'. But I will have to hide you Yuri, I will have to hide you somewhere safe, somewhere no one can find you, both you and your wife. And when I need you I'll get a message to you and you will know what to do'.

'Where will I go Mr Gotz?' Yuri asked.

'I have a place Yuri, I have a place where no one will find you. My enemies will scour the whole of Moscow looking for you, and their associates and their informants will all be looking for you, but they won't find you Yuri, because you won't be there.'

'And where will I be Mr Gotz?'

'In Smolensk Yuri, you'll be in Smolensk.'

Manny Gotz then leant down to reach into his drinks cabinet and he picked out his favourite French brandy. He felt that it was time for him to celebrate too. He'd given this plan much thought.

Manny knew that much of what had happened was his own fault, and that he should have taken care of things earlier. Whether it was his age or that he'd gone soft, he didn't know. But what he did realize was that it had been bad management on his part. When he'd been a younger man he would have never have allowed anything like this to have happened. The Zwerner problem should have been nipped in the bud right from the beginning and he should have never let them get a toe hold into his territory. He'd allowed the Zwerner family to slowly make a name for themselves. He'd shown a weakness, and now there were other individuals within his empire who had become aware of that.

Eventually those loyalties would be tested.

When he'd let loose Yuri Hartman, Manny Gotz was hoping that Yuri could have possibly taken out Lev Zwerner himself, or at least one of his brothers. He was looking for anything that would curb the family's activities and dissuade them from expanding their territory any further.

On reflection, that decision would have been a disaster. It would have roused tensions and there would have undoubtedly been repercussions, violent and irreversible repercussions. There would have been a 'turf' war, and with that there was always the risk that the Gotz family might have lost, and then lost everything.

And then along came Yuri Harman, and in a single weekend he'd smashed the Zwerners. He'd destroyed them completely and restored the balance of power.

For Manny Gotz, it had been a lesson learned. He would never again let it happen, and he would once again run things with an iron fist. Nobody would ever try to steal his crown ever again. Not now that he had 'the Ghost'.

Manny Gotz slowly poured some brandy into one of his favourite crystal brandy glasses.

'I have a place in Smolensk Yuri, an apartment that I own. Nobody at all knows about it and you'll be safe there. Nobody will ever think to look to Smolensk. It's an obscure sort of city and nobody will ever link it with Moscow. It's the last place anyone will ever think of, but its close enough. When I need 'the ghost', I will get a message to you. You will receive money on a regular basis but we must never meet. We will retain an association, but if for any reason I do need to speak to you personally, I will arrange the time and the place. Do you understand Yuri?'

Yuri nodded, 'Yes Mr Gotz...completely.'

Manny Gotz opened the left hand drawer of his desk and took out a parcel. He slid it across the leather bound desktop to where Yuri was sitting.

'This is yours. Don't open the parcel until you get home. In there is enough money to play with and there's also the address and the key to the apartment in Smolensk".

There was a short silence. It was an indication that there was nothing else to be said.

Yuri Hartman drank the last dregs of the vodka in his glass and then stood up. He slipped the parcel into his inside pocket and turned to go.

'We'll be in touch,' said Many Gotz.

'I'll be waiting,' replied Yuri, and he left.

An hour later he arrived back at their flat in the Drezna district. He counted the money, it was another sizeable amount. He'd also taken note of the new address in Smolensk and he'd pocketed the key. Then he uncorked a bottle of vodka.

At that moment there was a rustle at the door. It was Rachel Hartman trying to open the door, a door which was already unlocked. Yuri Hartman let her struggle.

'Stupid bitch,' he cursed to himself.

Rachel finally burst through the door, struggling with the various bags that she was carrying.

'Oh you're in Yuri,' she said, trying her best to sound cheerful.

Other than a grunt, there was no reply from her husband.

She carried the heavy bags through to the kitchen and dropped them on the floor. She dreaded the moment as she wondered what mood Yuri would be in, on that or any other particular day. She could never judge his frame of mind. For a long time Rachel Hartman had lived in fear. She never knew where her husband was and she never knew what he did. And if truth be known, she didn't want to know. All she knew was whatever he did would be illegal and probably harmful to someone. And she also knew never to ask.

In the past, Rachel had seriously considered running away. For a long time she'd wondered if she was actually capable of getting away from Yuri, getting as far away from him as possible. But she couldn't, because she knew that Yuri Hartman would track her to the ends of the earth and he would always find her. She knew that he'd always had a dangerous fixation with her, and Rachel also knew that when he finally found her, he would either kill her, or damage her out of all recognition. And it was that thought that chilled her.

She called through from the kitchen, there was some food for him, she'd brought some pies and pastries from the bakers. It was as she put his meal on the table in front of him that he made the announcement.

'Tonight you can pack up everything, and tomorrow go and tell the baker that you're finishing. And make sure he pays you.'

'Why's that?' Rachel suddenly dared to ask.

'We're leaving,' he replied with yet another grunt.

'Where are we going?'

'To Smolensk.'

Rachel was about to ask another question, but the vodka bottle was now half empty and she saw the perilous look in his eyes. She turned and left him there, she needed to get out of his way and she quietly slipped off to the bedroom where she sat and desperately hoped and prayed that he'd only bought the one bottle.

Two days later, they were travelling to Smolensk on the train. When they arrived there they found a driver with a cart to take them to their new address. Once there, they dragged their belongings up the one flight of stairs to their apartment. It was a sizeable place and Rachel gave a sigh of relief when she saw it, it was twice the size of the old flat in Drezna and in what seemed to her, a better area.

Yuri then left her to sort the place out. When he eventually arrived back, it was after midnight and he was soddenly drunk and incapable. Thankfully for Rachel, he collapsed on the kitchen floor and stayed there.

That first night in Smolensk set a new precedence in their life, and ultimately marked a change in their relationship. It seemed that Yuri didn't have to work anymore. He would wake up in the middle of the day and start drinking again, day after day. He would go off, only to return after midnight in a complete state of drunkenness and collapse either on the floor or in bed. However, he was usually so drunk that Rachel was safe from his demands. This would go on, day after day and week after week. And then suddenly he would disappear. Rachel didn't know where he was, but she knew it had to be something to do with their present existence.

It was the only way that Yuri could be earning any money. She didn't know what he was doing, but she suspected that it would be something bad, appallingly bad.

Within a couple of weeks of moving to Smolensk, Rachel had without doubt had enough of her husband's drunken tantrums and bad temper. Whatever time he woke up, he would still be half drunk. He would then either want sex or food or both and Rachel felt that she was living on a knife's edge. To try and deny Yuri anything at all would send him into an infuriated rage, and then he could be capable of almost anything.

To get out of the house and away from him, she decided to find herself another job. In the past, she'd loved working at the bakers shop back in Moscow, and with that in mind she decided to find herself something similar. She also decided to look somewhere on the other side of Smolensk, so that she would be out of Yuri's easy reach.

And that was how she'd found employment at the bakery, just around the corner from the 'Schwab Furniture' factory. And that was how on her first day, on a Monday morning, she had met Mr Schwab for the first time, and how he'd introduced himself and how they had laughed at each other. Then of course, she'd started taking his lunches to his office, and then they'd started to talk, and talk in earnest. And slowly but surely, a bond had formed between them, and the bond that had started as a friendship was now becoming something more.

It was a closeness that was drawing them both together and was teetering on the edge of becoming something physical. They'd become very comfortable in each other's company, their conversation was easy and flowing and relaxed, but whenever they sat close to one another and inadvertently touched, there were almost sparks flying. It was as though someone had turned up the heating in the office and there was a growing feeling of exhilaration and anticipation that had startled them both

Unfortunately for the love struck pair, each of them didn't realize that the other shared the same feelings of passion, and whenever anything physical happened between them they both fumbled about, feeling awkward and slightly embarrassed. And the truth of it was that they both wanted to embrace and hold one another, and feel the warmth and love and the touch of another human being. It was something that they'd both been denied for the whole of their lives, and now it was becoming a hunger that was leaving them both rather overwhelmed.

And on that evening after work, Rachel was on her way to Schwab's office again. This time she was bringing him his evening meal. He had to work late and Rachel wanted to make sure that he was eating properly, and for some reason she felt the continuing need to take care of this man and she didn't fully understand why. She just wanted to spend more time with him.

The pinnacle of Rachel Hartman's every day was calling into Schwab's office. It had become her solace. And to sit there warm and comfortable, talking to this witty and wonderfully interesting man had become her absolute pleasure. It was for her a short moment of happiness and contentment. And more than anything, and as the weeks had passed by, Schwab had grown to be her friend, and now more than a friend.

Rachel walked through the factory gates and into the factory. She was carrying a woven basket that contained a hot beef and ham pie, with a bowl of small potatoes that had been basted in butter. There was also a lemon tart baked in almond pastry. Rachel had lovingly prepared this meal after her work and the baker had allowed her to because she'd worked late and he thought that she was simply making an evening meal for her husband. Rachel had quietly made enough food for two. She was going to share the meal with Schwab, and why not. Yuri had disappeared once again to god only knew where, and she suddenly shuddered as she thought about him. She lived in permanent fear.

Rachel didn't want to go home that night, she didn't want to go back to that cold apartment and sit on her own. She wanted the friendship and the warmth and comfort that Schwab had shown her. She wanted to be with Schwab. And then, as she approached the steps up to his office, everything suddenly struck her. And she stopped dead in her tracks, as she realized the absolute obviousness of it all. She wanted to be with Schwab because she loved him. Of course she did. And the realization of it all was like being hit by a hammer. Yes, she loved him, and of course she wanted to be with him, she wanted to be with him all the time and all of the time. Having never felt the emotion of true adult love, all those feelings had been lost to her. And for the whole of her life, it was as though she had been tragically blinded as to what real love actually was.

Rachel took a deep breath and started to head up the stairs, and as she cautiously knocked on the large wooden office door, her heart skipped a beat when she heard him call out 'Yes'.

She suddenly felt like a schoolgirl with her first 'crush' and she smiled, she couldn't help herself.

She opened the office door and peered in, and there was Schwab, sitting behind his desk with a mountain of paper, completely oblivious to the time. Rachel knew him so well, and she knew that once he'd buried his head into his paperwork he would work all night.

But not tonight.

Tonight he would eat with her and relax, if only for a short while. She walked into his office with the basket of food and Schwab looked up at her and smiled, and then he glanced across the room to the clock.

'Good grief,' he exclaimed, 'I didn't realize that it was so late.'

'I knew you wouldn't,' Rachel replied, 'that's why I've brought you some food. You are completely hopeless.'

Schwab beamed at her with delight and Rachel giggled as she caught his mood.

She decided to take the initiative.

'You carry on working and I'll set the table and put out the food. Oh, and by the way, you've got company tonight. It seems that someone is going to dine with you.'

For a moment Schwab looked more than a little disconcerted, in truth he didn't want any interruptions, not with his paperwork and definitely not with the brief time he would have with Rachel.

'Who...who's coming?' he asked.

Rachel looked at him and smiled.

'Why...me of course, silly,' she replied.

And for Schwab, it was as though all of his birthdays and Christmas's had been rolled into one.

He looked up at her and he smiled too, she was so damn beautiful, so bright and so, so full of life. And now here she was, and they were going to sit together and eat and talk. And the thought of it, just for a second, made Schwab gasp with pleasure.

Rachel flitted around his office, she knew where the cutlery and crockery were, and she chatted away to him as she laid out the table.

'Tonight, you're having a change,' she informed him, 'I've made a hot beef and ham pie and I've brought a lemon tart baked with my special pastry"

Schwab was in heaven, and her presence along with the smell of the delicious food had completely sunk his plans for continuing with any paperwork. In fact, it could all go to hell.

'Right,' said Rachel, 'I'll go into your secretary's office and brew us both a pot of hot coffee.'

'Yes, that would be nice,' replied Schwab, and then he gave it a moment's thought.

'I have an idea,' he said, 'Since we're both dining, we could have a bottle of wine.'

Rachel turned and smiled in agreement, and Schwab stood up and walked over to a large dark oak cabinet. He opened the cabinet door and peered in.

'I have some red wine in here, it's from Italy. We have a supplier in Tuscany who we get our olive wood from. He sometimes sends us a case of wine with our delivery. Ah, here it is, its 'Chianti', it's supposedly very good.'

Schwab reached for the bottle, along with a corkscrew and two wine glasses, and then he sat himself down at the small square dining table, the table that had remained unused in his office for years. He opened the bottle of wine and poured.

Rachel took charge of the food and filled their plates with the steaming meat pie and sweet buttered potatoes. Then she sat herself down at the table. Curiously, she sat at the side of him and not opposite, and for a moment Schwab had thought it strange. But somehow it felt more intimate, she was sitting right at the side of him and when they spoke, they both had to turn to face one another and it made their faces closer. They could almost touch.

They both raised their wine glasses, and giggled when they realized how good the red wine actually did taste.

Rachel suddenly quipped, 'It's like being in a restaurant.'

And in a sparkle of exuberance Schwab replied, 'I'll take you to a restaurant one evening,'

Then he suddenly stopped and blushed slightly.

But Rachel immediately swept away any embarrassment.

'That would be nice,' she said softly, 'I'd really like that.'

Schwab had always known that he was naive around women, but suddenly he understood. He was aware that his friendship with Rachel was turning into something more.

They ate the good food, and they drank more wine. And as they ate, they both made witty conversation and it made them feel ever closer. They continued to talk, and eventually their discussions turned into a deeper more intimate exchange. It was almost a prelude to affection. And it left them quite breathless.

Rachel leant easily across the table, reaching for her prepared dessert, the lemon tart. And while she served the food out into fresh bowls, Schwab went over to his cabinet and brought back another bottle of the same red wine. They refilled their glasses and continued to eat, the acidity of the lemons made the red wine taste deep and sweet, it was so very drinkable and their mood returned effortlessly. It was easy and uncomplicated conversation, and they were becoming comfortably eager, and they were warm and willing.

As they spoke, their legs finally touched under the table, and both of them felt it and they both knew. They stared at one another for the briefest of seconds, but neither drew away and the wine kept them ambitious.

Schwab looked at Rachel, he looked at her beautiful face and he looked into her deep hazel eyes.

"What are you thinking about?" she asked him softly.

It was the moment. It was the wine, and the food, and for Schwab, it was him being there alone with her. He was so close to her now that he could feel her heat.

And now it would have to be everything, because for him, she was everything.

He gazed quietly at her.

'I'm thinking about you Rachel...and only you.'

There it was. He'd finally said it. He'd finally spoken out, and there was that wrench of agony because he could never relive the moment, and no matter the result and no matter what happened next, there would be no going back.

Rachel sat there, silently overwhelmed. For her it was the moment of understanding. She'd been so unsure, so uneasy at not knowing if her friendship with him was simply just that. Was it just a friendship, or just good manners, or even pity?

But not now, no...not now.

And suddenly there was nothing else to say, she just looked at him and she knew that whatever happened next was up to her. He'd put himself up for her love or rejection.

It was the final angst.

She saw his face and the look in his eyes. This was his own personal quandary too, he'd been living with this predicament every day and he was now a man who needed an answer to his question. Schwab had always resisted pursuing her, it had been his own personal dilemma, and all of his his hopes and fears rolled into one.

And now was the moment.

She moved closer to him, and she stopped just inches away from his face. And then finally, she leant forward and kissed him.

It was the moment, and as Rachel continued to kiss him she sighed. She'd waited so long for this, possibly for the whole of her life.

Schwab was almost delirious at her touch. To finally kiss this woman, to finally be physically intimate with her made him gasp, and he slid his hand around her waist, and the touch of his hand made her gasp too.

Schwab pushed the table out of the way and then pulled her closer to him, so that they now openly embraced. She kissed his face and then he kissed her neck and he took in the intoxicating perfume of her body and it made him stir. He kissed the back of her neck, her short cropped hair left her neck exposed and vulnerable. Her slim neck was so pale and white and so very beautiful. They both began to breathe heavily as their passions rose and Rachel moaned as she felt his hand slide over her stomach. He reached up for her breast and she threw her head back to catch her breath. She looked at him and kissed him again and with her left hand she undid the top buttons of her dress. Once undone, she took hold of his hand and kissed it, and then she led his hand inside her dress and onto her breast. Schwab took hold of her, and she once again moaned with pleasure. She slid her arms out of her dress to expose both of her breasts to him, and then she reached to the back of his neck and pulled him down onto her. He gently took her breasts to suckle them, making her squeal softly with pleasure. The tender intimacy of this act overwhelmed them both, and their infatuation for each other demanded even more. Rachel suddenly reached down and hurriedly unloosed his belt and then unfastened the buttons of his pants. She reached in and down and took hold of him, and Schwab thought that his whole body would explode. He'd never experienced a woman's touch, ever, and his legs quivered at the excitement of it. He slid his hand onto her thigh up to the top her legs and he felt her body move and tremble, and as he touched her she moaned in ecstasy.

For Rachel too, this was a whole new experience, an experience that made her want to cry out with joy. This was real love and tenderness and true affection for the first time in her life, and not the brutality that she'd had to endure from her husband.

For Ernst Schwab and for Rachel, this was the misplaced passion that they'd both craved.

Rachel suddenly stood up and together they almost ripped off her dress and her underwear, and then she stood there in front of him and she let him look at her naked body.

It was a moment without any shame or embarrassment. Schwab looked at her, her exquisitely physical beauty, and Rachel wanted him to look at her, she wanted him to see all of her and enjoy what he saw.

She reached forward to unbutton his shirt and Schwab stepped out of his pants and then stripped off too. They embraced again, now with a greater determination. He was erect and she was hot and eager and then they suddenly realized that there was nowhere to lie down. And so Schwab gently moved her against the wall as he continued to caress her. She reached down and took hold of him again and then parted her legs and guided him into her. They coupled there against the office wall, face to face in an act of pure ecstasy, each looking directly at the other. It was erotic, and it was honest, and it was an open pleasure without any embarrassment or shame. Schwab grasped her buttocks as she undulated with him. Their thrusts becoming ever more vital as their eventual climax made them both buckle and slide to the floor, breathless and spent.

Schwab lay on his back on the cool office floor with Rachel on top of him, both of them still breathing hard and fast. She lifted her head and kissed him and Schwab opened his eyes to look at the most beautiful woman in his world.

As they both lay there, comfortable and warm, Rachel gently poked his chest.

'Mr Schwab,' she almost purred, 'you are a very naughty man.'

'And you Miss Hartman, deserve everything you get,' he replied and they both laughed.

She realized that he'd used the word 'Miss', but at that moment it felt totally appropriate.

She was no longer Yuri Hartman's exclusive property.

He rolled her over and kissed her.

'You really need to get some carpet put down in here.' she giggled.

They played affectionately with each other for a while until the wooden floor boards began to bite at their skin. Schwab finally stood up and he slowly helped Rachel to her feet. He pointed at one of the chairs.

'Sit down and I'll get us something nice,' he said to her. And he went over to his oak cabinet and brought back an aged cut glass decanter which was nearly half full of ruby red port. He poured two good glasses and they both sat back in their chairs and eyed each other in the semi darkness of the office, comfortable and sipping their drinks. They continued to drink and talk, and they eventually finished off the port and then went on to drink the remaining wine that they'd left unfinished in the bottle. Once again the alcohol made them flush with anticipation, and once again the attraction that they had for each other was quickly rekindled. Rachel finally put her empty glass firmly back down on the table. Then she climbed onto Schwab and straddled him as he sat there naked, and they made love on the chair as she fell into his arms.

Breathless and happy, and still a little astounded at what had happened between them both, Schwab and Rachel sat there for some time and talked and kissed intimately. There was now an unbreakable connection between them both, their relationship had become a union. Eventually Schwab helped Rachel to put her clothes back on and then he too dressed. They switched off the lights and left the office and the factory, and then with no great plan they quite unintentionally walked back to Schwab's house. They chatted away happily, and when they arrived at Schwab's home, Schwab naturally invited her in. But suddenly Rachel's expression changed and she declined, and then she rather abruptly told him that she had to go home, and when Schwab obviously offered to go with her, Rachel flatly refused and she gave him a short excuse and then swiftly walked away.

Schwab was left rather dumbfounded. He stood there and watched her as she disappeared around the corner. And he was at a loss as to what had just happened. An hour previously they had been locked in each other's embrace, and now it all suddenly felt rather surreal.

And then the obvious hit him, and it hit him over the head like a hammer blow.

Yes, the absolute obvious.

Rachel Hartman was married. She was a married woman, and Rachel Hartman had a husband, and that husband was probably waiting for her back at their home. And tonight she would go to bed with that same husband and then god only knew what else. And Schwab's mind went into overload at the thought of Rachel being with someone else, even the thought of sharing her with anyone else made his head spin. And then the reality of what had just happened finally struck him.

Rachel Hartman was married, she had a husband. And it was he, Schwab, who was the trespasser. He was the intruder. He was the thief in the night.

The thought of it made him feel physically sick.

Rachel turned the corner and walked home as quickly as possible, she was flustered.

Yuri was away, away on one of his 'trips'. And she hoped with her life that he was still away. Rachel never knew where he would be, and in her mind she immediately thought up an excuse for being late, just in case he'd returned. And the thought of him made here shudder.

As she quickly walked home, she wondered to herself ...'What on earth she was going to do?'

She without doubt loved Schwab, of that there was no question at all. But there was always going to be Yuri, and if Yuri Hartman found out what was going on he would kill Ernst Schwab. Of that Rachel also had no doubt at all.

And as she walked along, alone and on her own, she suddenly shivered.

Schwab turned around and walked up to the front door of his house. And he looked around and he realised what a dark and lonely place it was. It was big house and it echoed, it echoed the memories of his past. After his mother had died Schwab had been left alone and had remained on his own for years. Now he felt as though those echoes were laughing at him and they were the reminders of just how alone he was.

He walked into the hallway and sat down there in the dark. He felt a despair that he didn't fully understand. He had just had the most wonderful encounter of his life, yet he felt so sad. He knew of course what it was. Rachel was a married woman.

And as he sat there in the dark, Schwab wondered how he was going to keep her.

Because he'd made up his mind. He simply could not let this woman go.

The next morning Schwab lay in bed thinking about Rachel and only Rachel.

Truth be known, he'd been thinking about her the most of the night, but as he lay there alone in his bed he remembered her beautiful body and their frantic love making in the office that previous night. Those erotic thoughts made him smoulder somewhat and in the end he decided that he would have to be more of a man, and that he would have to take hold of this woman and take charge of things. He would have to take a stance. A considerable stance.

He got out of bed, washed and dressed and immediately left his house and marched off to the bakery for breakfast. It was an obvious excuse. He wanted to see Rachel Hartman again as soon and as quickly as possible. On the way there his nerves began to get the better of him. What if last night had been a mistake, what if last night was just the result of too much wine? What if Rachel was now very embarrassed, and he suddenly wondered if she would actually be there at the bakery. What would he do if she never returned, and what would he do if he could never see her or make love to her again?

He approached the baker's shop and walked straight in through the door. The shop was completely empty and his heart missed a desperate beat. So he stood there for what seemed several minutes, eternal minutes, and still nothing. He was just about to call out, expecting to be met by the baker himself, when the bakery door suddenly swung open and Rachel entered, carrying a tray of fresh bread. She stopped dead in her tracks when she saw him, and for a moment she just stared at him. Then she dropped the tray of bread on the floor and dashed around the counter and threw her arms around him.

They embraced and Schwab felt the unbelievable joy of reassurance. Nothing had changed between them. Nothing at all.

In their excitement they both giggled and chatted and he kissed her profusely, in fact he couldn't stop kissing her and she eventually had to stop him. They laughed at what now seemed the ridiculous act of her now handing him his 'usual' breakfast. She promised to see him at lunch and Ernst Schwab strolled out of the baker's shop, a blissfully and happier man.

Lunchtime arrived and so did Rachel. They both laughed again and ate comfortably with each other and they kissed. Schwab's secretary, the wily Mrs Kausky, left them alone. His secretary had continued to observe her boss and young Rachel Hartman for some time, and she'd suspected that something was going on. Mrs Kausky was no fool, but today she realized there was something different. Her boss and young Rachel were suddenly so much closer, noticeably closer. Mrs Kausky had been Ernst Schwab's secretary for many years and had an idea about what had happened. She was definitely nobody's fool. For a long, long time she'd known that Schwab was a very lonely man, but now it seemed to her that at last, he had fallen unexpectedly into a pool of happiness. And that thought alone made Mrs Kausky smile.

Schwab and Rachel made plans, and that evening Rachel again arrived at his office after work with a meal for them both. A potato pie infused with beef and venison with a rich gravy and some minted peas, along with a blackberry and apple tart.

But that night they both made their way to Schwab's house and ate in the comfort of his spacious kitchen. Then they went upstairs to his even more spacious bedroom and rolled about ecstatically in his very spacious bed.

For once they were both happy and at peace, the peace that only love brings. They both got to know each other's physicality and their lovemaking had become something more. Neither of them having had a proper loving physical relationship had left them both somehow naive and untutored, but it was a void that was quickly bridged.

Almost immediately, their evening meal together became their new routine. They were more than comfortable together and it seemed the natural thing to do.

Schwab and Rachel had quickly gotten into their new daily habit, rightly or wrongly. But it was a habit and it was a mistake.

'Routine is a weakness'. And it was a weakness, but for Schwab and Rachel, their happiness was bliss and without giving it much thought, several weeks quickly slipped through their fingers.

However, life was never going to be simple and a darker cloud was about to blow in from an even darker corner, and it would completely and irrevocably turn their happiness into something far more desperate.

Yuri Hartman was never home. He was on a killing spree.

Under the orders of Manny Gotz, he had Moscow locked down.

The Ghost was everywhere and nowhere.

A greedy bank manager needed to be taught a lesson. Apparently he had been borrowing money from one of Manny Gotz's bank accounts and had stupidly thought he'd got away with it. Yuri Hartman simply walked into the manager's office via a back door, another weakness.

He clubbed the bank manager unconscious and then rolled him on top of the very prestigious desk which stood resplendent in the middle of the banker's very prestigious office.

Yuri then took hold of the manager's wrists and chopped off all of his fingers and thumbs with his trusty little sharpened axe. He then dropped the offending fingers and thumbs into the bank manager's oriental fish tank which stood on an adjacent table. The tropical fish were the bank manager's pride and joy and as his prized fish nibbled at the bloodied fingers, the bank manager awoke screaming in agony. The banker would never again lift a pen or turn a page, and never again would he borrow' anymore money from Manny Gotz's bank account.

In fact, the bank manager would have a problem in even being able to wipe his own backside.

A successful brothel owner, an overconfident slag of a woman who thought she was untouchable also had a surprise visit from the Ghost. She had rather mistakenly, tried to not balance her books correctly. And the amount money that was being returned to Manny Gotz did not balance with the amount of legs opened.

Yuri Hartman quietly visited the brothel, where he sat in a corner and drank some of their 'best' vodka, which was actually very good, and it stirred him. He then decided to have one of the girls, so he took a sixteen year old Albanian girl who wasn't much more than a child. What Hartman did to her was indescribable, and then he slit her throat. One could almost say it was a mercy.

He then walked into the brothel owner's private quarters, full of blood and lust. He seized hold of the brothel owner and sliced off her nose with his hunting knife and then cut off both of her ears. To stop her screaming he smashed her over the head with the butt of his knife and knocked her unconscious in order to shut her up.

Sitting there with his knife in his hand, he waited. The brothel owner's daughter would eventually arrive because she always did. And he knew that she would because he had been in the brothel before. And so he sat there and he waited and he watched.

Again, it was repetition.

The daughter was twenty two years old, dark haired and very beautiful. And as she walked through the door Yuri grabbed her and smashed her head twice onto a table. The poor girl was barely conscious as he lifted her skirt and raped her from behind.

As he copulated he had only one thing on his mind. It was Rachel. She was the only thing that aroused him, only Rachel. And his thoughts were only of her. When he'd finished with the girl he simply pulled her head back and slit her throat, and then in disgust he threw her body to one side.

She too, was nothing more than a piece of meat.

The word was out in Moscow. Manny Gotz was the King.

The King was certainly not dead and yes, long live the King.

And suddenly, nobody even thought of 'not' paying Manny Gotz.

You didn't argue with Manny Gotz and you didn't mess with Manny Gotz. You paid the man.

'For god's sake...pay the man.'

Manny Gotz was becoming a legend.

His plan had worked. Because he had the Ghost.

Yuri Hartman was invisible.

He spent most of his time in Moscow and he was Manny Gotz's invisible weapon.

He would sit in the corner of any bar or brothel, forever sipping his beloved vodka, just watching. Watching and waiting. He now knew the veins and the arteries of the Gotz Empire. He knew it all, absolutely everything, and he used that knowledge like a tool.

And now Yuri had money, so much money, the likes of which he had never known before.

Everyone who he'd slaughtered or maimed, he'd also robbed. And Manny Gotz never asked any questions.

There was one thing though, something that was totally unknown, even to Manny Gotz.

Yuri Hartman had acquired one of the smartest of apartments, right in centre of Moscow.

The apartment was contained within the magnificent 'Stutz Building' which was one of the most opulent residences in Moscow. The Stutz was so noticeably central and so obviously apparent that it rendered Yuri totally undetectable.

Yuri had moved himself in there in the most discreet fashion, nobody at all knew him and no one would ever think to look for somebody like Yuri Hartman in a place as prestigious as the Stutz Building. Anyone who lived in that fashionable block, and who were mostly the rich and the famous, probably thought that Yuri was just one of the caretakers.

Yuri had given all of this great thought. If he was invisible to Manny Gotz, Yuri truly was a free spirit and he knew it.

However, with the passing of time, Yuri Hartman was becoming a darker and more dangerous person. To Yuri, everyone was now dispensable. Anyone at all who irritated him was deemed to be 'killable'. Screaming women with cheeky children or anyone who was rude or insulting would quickly discover how easily their face could be slashed. There was always the one hapless person who jostled him or blocked his way. Anyone at all could be dispensed by his razor sharp blade. Yuri killed in a way that was so open and so obvious that incredibly, others failed to notice. To stick his hunting knife into a person's chest as he embraced them 'as a friend' was so laughingly simple. As they fell to the floor dying, he simply walked away.

Yuri had also discovered the joys of the gun, and once he owned one, his life became a lot simpler and a lot easier.

One evening he approached an unfortunate and misguided accountant who was walking his dog along the canal on their regular evening routine. The accountant had been unwisely fraudulent with some of Mr Gotz's money, which was never a good idea. As the accountant walked past him and nodded, Yuri simply shot him in the face. The accountant fell to the ground, dead. His face had exploded into a red mush.

Had it not quickly bolted, Yuri would have shot his dog too.

A week later Yuri Hartman caught the early morning train to Smolensk. It was a cold grey morning and Yuri sat waiting for the train to leave the station. He had his usual bottle of vodka with him which he sipped regularly and as he stared out of the window on that dull grey morning he thought of Rachel.

It was time to go home.

The train finally set off and Yuri began to think about his future. He without doubt hated living in Smolensk. He had acquired a taste for Moscow, a city that was alive and exiting. Living in Smolensk was nothing more than vodka and boredom, and it was Moscow that kept him 'busy'.

Yuri wanted to live permanently in Moscow and had decided to ask Manny Gotz if he could move back there. Manny would find him somewhere to live, Manny Gotz owned houses throughout Moscow so surely he would find somewhere out of the way and private for his Ghost...surely?

Yuri took another sip of vodka. Manny Gotz owed him big time, so Manny Gotz had better find him somewhere, and soon.

Yuri sat back and thought about his own secret apartment. It was fabulous. He had carefully refurbished the place, redecorated it and had it furnished. Yuri had made sure that everything was done in the middle of the day when most of the other tenants were out. Any tradesmen or furniture deliveries had to arrive after ten o' clock in the morning and the tradesmen would have to leave before three o' clock in the afternoon. There were to be no disruptions or interruptions, and therefore no questions asked.

Yuri had to make sure that Manny Gotz never found out about his hidden apartment. Yuri was fully aware that he was Manny Gotz's key assassin, but he also realised that if he ever put one foot wrong, or was deemed to have put one foot wrong, then Manny Gotz would turn on him like a wolf. And if things ever went wrong, Manny would send his henchmen and others to bring him in, or even worse. They would look for him in the streets and the sewers and they would look outside central

Moscow, they might even go back and scour Smolensk. But they would never think to look for him in the magnificence of the Stutz Building. They would never think to stop and look up and see him watching them from up above.

There was the money too. Yuri had quickly amassed a fair amount of money, enough to keep him going for a couple of years in reasonable luxury. After that, well, who knew?

Manny Gotz wouldn't be around forever. And Yuri would always have to consider his future.

The train rumbled on through the countryside whilst Yuri sipped his vodka and sat there silently watching the thousands of acres of the vast Russian plains pass slowly by.

As he stared out of the window he began to think about Rachel. He missed her in a strange sort of way, and sitting there quietly, he remembered how they had met.

Several years earlier he had arrived in her home village. He had been a quiet young man back then, plainly dressed, though he had already grown the beard and the long hair that he would always wear. Yuri had inadvertently spotted Rachel walking down the main street one Sunday morning and he was immediately attracted to her. Somehow she reminded him of his own appalling mother. His mother and Rachel both had the same deep hazel brown eyes.

Yes, his mother, and what a cow she had been.

Yuri had pursued Rachel and courted her. However Rachel's aging father was against it. He didn't like or trust Yuri Hartman, not one bit. He'd disapproved of Yuri from the start and when Yuri proposed to her, Rachel turned him down out of respect for her father.

After her mother had died, Rachel had been left alone with her father and he had never bothered to remarry. There had always been just her and her father and she adored him.

Yuri went to see Rachel's father to talk to him 'man to man', but the old man told Yuri in no uncertain terms that he would never allow Rachel to marry him. He continued to tell Yuri that his daughter could do so much better than the likes of 'Yuri Hartman' and that he must leave Rachel alone. With that said, he shut the door in Yuri's face.

Yuri had seethed with cold anger. He had been insulted and he wasn't taking it lightly. As he walked away, he started to plan his revenge.

Late that same night, Yuri returned to Rachel's home. He climbed silently into the house through the back kitchen window and made his way upstairs. Once at the top of the stairs he stopped to listen for a man's snoring. It was quite easy to recognise, and that particular sound was coming from the bedroom on his immediate left. Yuri quietly entered the room and spotted the old man asleep in bed. The moon was reasonably bright that evening and the bedroom was fairly well illuminated, things couldn't have worked out better. Yuri stood there for a moment and then he took a scrap of old rag out of his pocket. It was the rag that he used as a handkerchief. He then walked straight across the bedroom floor and climbed onto the bed and straddled the old man. Rachel's father woke with a jolt and he tried to struggle but he was held down by Yuri's weight. Yuri grabbed hold of the old man's face and then he jammed the whole filthy rag into his victim's mouth. The old man's eyes widened as he gagged and choked, but there was nothing he could do.

Yuri then leant forward and whispered the question.

'Do you know who I am?'

The old man just stared up at him, helpless.

'Do you know who I am?' he asked again.

Rachel's father nodded frantically.

Yuri continued quietly, 'So, now you 'will' listen to me old man, because I'm going to tell you something. When I came here today to see you, you insulted me and you shut your door in my face. You insulted and disrespected me. So now I'm going to kill you old man, but before I do, you really need to know something. After I've killed you, I'm going to go into your daughter's bedroom, and I'm going to rape her and rape her terribly...and then I'm going to slit her throat.'

Yuri stared down at Rachel's father and he quietly spoke to him.

'This is all because of you old man," he whispered, 'all because of you ...'

Rachel's father was in panic as he realised what Yuri had planned. He struggled with every inch of strength left in his aging body. But it was to no avail. Yuri was too strong for him and too heavy.

Yuri reached down and simply pinched the old man's nostrils together. Then he waited.

The old man tried to breathe but with his airways blocked, both his nose and his mouth, he realised that he couldn't. He began to thrash about trying to gasp for air, but there was none. His eyes turned red and bulged as he tried to shake off his assailant but there was nothing he could do, nothing at all. His heaving chest began to fail as he took a last fearful look at Yuri Hartman. And as he died that awful death, he could only wonder at what terror was going to be inflicted on his darling, darling daughter.

Within another couple of minutes, Rachel's father was dead.

Yuri pulled the rag out of the old man's mouth and closed the dead and staring eyes. Then he made him look peaceful. It was as though the old man had just died in his sleep.

After that Yuri stood up and silently left the house. He wasn't going to hurt or harm Rachel, he never was of course. Yuri had different plans for her.

Walking to work the next morning and after a bout of sneezing, Yuri reached into his pocket for his handkerchief. As he looked down at the filthy rag, he smiled to himself.

Yes, his plan would work. He immediately threw the dirty rag away and into a muddy puddle. He would have to use his sleeve for the rest of the day.

With the shock of the sudden death of her beloved father, Rachel found solace in Yuri's arms. In the beginning he was supportive and caring, he was also very cunning and within a short time had taken total control of her life.

Six weeks later they were married.

Rachel would never know how her father died and no one would ever suspect the truth.

On the train heading for Smolensk, Yuri took another drink of his vodka. And he smiled when he thought of what he'd got away with.

Meanwhile, over in Smolensk, his wife Rachel was in a state of shock and total despair. She had just made an appalling discovery.

She was pregnant.

And what for her should have been a moment of immense pleasure, had in fact, left her completely terrified and numb with fear.

She and Schwab had been sleeping together regularly for nearly two months and the catastrophe had struck when nature finally decided to take its true course. Rachel was utterly bewildered as to what she should do, and unfortunately her response to the problem was to do and say nothing at all.

That evening, Rachel had been around to Schwab's office as usual and together they'd walked back to his house. After they had eaten they made love. Schwab noticed that she was somewhat quieter than usual and put it down to her being tired. However in bed her love making had been somehow desperate and she felt tense. Later on she slipped away as he slept. Rachel had never stayed the night, ever, and Schwab had always known not to ask why.

Always in the back of her mind, Rachel realised that Yuri could arrive home at anytime, anytime at all.

So she went back at her dreary flat at around ten o' clock that evening and as she walked in through the doorway, a fist viscously smashed into her face. She was knocked to the floor dazed, then suddenly she was grabbed by her hair and dragged to her feet and thumped in the face again. Rachel tumbled backwards and this time she hit her head hard against the wall. She was once more pulled to her feet by her hair and had to strain to focus on the face that was staring at her.

It was her husband. It was Yuri Hartman. He was back.

Unfortunately for Rachel, not only had he returned, he was also drunk and he was angry, he was very angry.

'Where the hell have you been you bitch?' he bellowed at her.

Rachel couldn't answer, she was terrified. He hit her in the face once again.

'Where've you been you bitch?' he asked her once more and Rachel knew she would have to give him an answer or she would receive a more brutal beating.

'I've been working at the bakers,' she replied.

Again he slapped her across the face.

'Not till this time you haven't, you fucking liar.'

Rachel had to think, she had to think quickly and she had to come up with a feasible excuse right away. Yuri was in the foulest of tempers and she knew exactly what he was capable of. She had suffered cracked ribs and multiple bruising before because of his severe beatings.

Then suddenly from nowhere, an answer came to her.

'I've had to hide Yuri, there's been some men calling here, they've been looking for you.'

It was a shot in the dark but she would have tried anything.

He stopped for a moment.

'What men?'

'Two of them Yuri, big men, a couple of thugs, they knocked me about. They were looking for you.'

'Who were they?'

'I don't know,' she replied, 'they looked like Ukrainians.'

Now that was a stroke of luck for Rachel, because completely unknown to her, the Zwerner family had originated from the Ukrainian border. And though Rachel hadn't known any of that, Yuri certainly did. He relaxed his grip for a moment which gave her some relief.

She continued with her excuse. 'I've been staying late at the bakery, I was frightened. One of those men kept touching me and I was frightened that he would come back. I think he would have raped me Yuri.'

Those final words thankfully turned his anger in another direction, and he let her go.

'Bastards' he said out loud, and his twisted jealous nature started to make him burn inwardly.

'Make me some food,' he said to her, and then he went over to his bag and pulled out a bottle of vodka.

Rachel shuddered.

He ate in the kitchen in silence and then went to sit in front of the fire. As he poured another glass of vodka he sat there looking into the flames.

He had to think. He had to get out. Those bastards had found him.

Rachel disappeared off to bed as soon as possible. She lay there hoping against hope that Yuri would drink himself into a stupor and collapse. After her precious times with Schwab, the thought of Yuri coming anywhere near her had become a personal nightmare. As she lay there, she wondered if she was brave enough to take the kitchen knife and stab him to death, but no. Eventually she fell into an uneasy sleep. That was until an hour later when the crazed Yuri Hartman dragged her out of the bed and rutted and brutalized her in such a terrible fashion, that it would have been considered harsh treatment on even a farmyard animal.

The next morning Rachel lay almost paralysed in bed. She could hardly move because she was in so much pain. Yuri had woken earlier and had gone out. When she finally managed to get herself to her feet she went over to the mirror to examine her bruised face and her bruised and beaten body and the scratches and the bite marks. The thought of what she had been put through almost made her vomit. She somehow managed to wash herself and rinse away the blood. Then she put on some clean clothes and went over to change the badly stained bed sheets. Those stained sheets retold the story and Rachel had to steady herself as she remembered what he had done to her.

The door suddenly swung open and Yuri walked in. Rachel stepped back in absolute panic. However for Yuri it was as though nothing untoward had happened at all. He stared at her for a brief second and then issued his news.

'I'm going back to Moscow today. I'll return in a couple of days and then we'll be leaving Smolensk. We're going to go and live in Moscow. Pack up everything, and as soon as I get back we'll take everything we have and leave.'

With that, he picked up his bag and walked back out of the flat, slamming the door behind him. Rachel just stood there looking at the closed door and then, suddenly, she thought about Ernst Schwab.

She went over to the kitchen table, and sat down and openly wept as she thought about the only man she had ever loved and the baby that they had made together.

Three hours passed, three hours of torment and turmoil. Ultimately, Rachel had to make a decision, and it would have to be the right decision. She would have to make a choice that would be the best for everyone. Once she'd considered all the possible options, Rachel sadly decided on what was her only choice. She knew what she must to do.

And so she went over to their old wooden cupboard and opened the left hand drawer and took out a sheet of writing paper, an envelope and a pencil. Then she went back to the table and wrote a letter to Ernst Schwab.

In her letter she had to tell him that she was 'with child' and she expressed her unending love for him and only him, and that she had never loved any other man in her life.

In distress and in anguish Rachel continued to write and she told Schwab that her husband had suddenly returned home. She then tried to explain to Schwab what type of a man Yuri Hartman was. Rachel told him all about her brutal husband and their life together, what he did and what he was capable of. Her husband was a paid killer and there was no doubt at all that he would kill both of them if he ever found out about her affair with Schwab. She also told him that Yuri would be quite capable of murdering their baby too, if he ever found out that he was not the real father.

That was the reality of their situation.

She was frightened for their lives, for all of their lives.

She told Schwab that she couldn't continue to see him, simply because it would be far too dangerous. She knew that Yuri would kill Schwab and in her heart and in her mind she couldn't allow any harm come to him, ever.

Rachel asked Schwab to be in agreement with her wishes. She asked him not try and contact her. No good would ever come of it.

She did promise to write to him and tell him when the baby was born.

That was his right. He was the father, of course he was.

At the end of her letter she expressed her undying love for him and she told him that the last two months had been the happiest of her life.

She wouldn't have changed anything, anything at all, because she loved him.

Rachel put the letter into the envelope and wrote his name on the front of it.

She got herself dressed and then, slowly and painfully, she left the apartment and walked as best she could all the way to the bakery. She'd missed her morning shift, she couldn't have worked.

The baker was shocked when he saw the bruising on Rachel's face, but this was Russia and he knew better than to ask. He was however, even more upset when Rachel told him that she was going to have to stop working at the bakery. She told him that her elderly mother was very ill and that her mother lived in a village on the outskirts of Moscow and because of that she would have to go and live there with her for the foreseeable future.

She also gave the baker her letter to Schwab and asked him to pass it onto Mr Schwab when he called for his regular breakfast the following morning.

The baker agreed but seemed somewhat puzzled, until Rachel explained to him that Mr Schwab had been very kind to her and was going to sell her some furniture at a 'reduced' price. Now however, because she had to leave, she was going to have to turn down his kind offer but she wanted to thank him anyway.

That lie seemed to satisfy the baker, and before Rachel left he gave her a few roubles, a hug and a promise that her job would be here waiting for her, if and when she ever came back.

Rachel turned and walked out of the baker's shop.

Another chapter of her life, ended.

The following morning, Schwab walked into the baker's shop for his breakfast. More than that, he walked in to see what was wrong with Rachel. The previous morning when he arrived it was the baker's wife that had served him. When Schwab had enquired as to where Rachel was, the baker's wife simply threw her arms in the air and started to rant about how the girl hadn't bothered to turn in and how she'd had to get out of bed and had to come down to work in the shop, and how hard her life was and on and on.

Schwab left the shop slightly mystified.

At lunchtime, the baker's wife had hurriedly called at Schwab's office with his hastily prepared lunch. She was still complaining and eventually dashed off back to the shop.

Schwab sat there for a while with his untouched lunch and wondered what the problem was. In his mind he was worried.

So the next morning Schwab once again walked into the baker's shop for his breakfast. This time he was met by the baker himself, who was more than slightly flustered. It turned out that he and his wife had been arguing again, and she now refused point blank to work for her beast of a husband anymore.

The baker had apparently asked his own sister to help him out for a few days, but she'd not turned up either, so the baker was overworked and more than a little stressed.

As he rambled on about 'how on earth he was going to get through the day', Schwab asked the baker, 'where was Rachel, his usual assistant?'

The baker wiped some surplus flour off his face.

'Oh,' he replied, 'she had to leave. Her elderly mother is apparently ill. She lives in some village somewhere on the other side of Moscow.'

'Oh,' said Schwab, somewhat taken aback.

'Well,' continued the baker, as he placed Schwab's breakfast order on the counter, 'Well that's what she says, whether it's true or not is another matter.'

'And why's that?' asked Schwab, trying to sound little more than casual.

'She had a bruise on her face and a black eye, a real shiner. Somebody's given her a real good thumping. I didn't ask of course, well it's none of my business is it? Anyway, it was probably her husband. She'll have been up to something no doubt. Women, they're never happy. It's like my wife...'

At that point Schwab interrupted the troubled baker. He was upset when he heard about Rachel's injuries. Shockingly upset.

'So she's definitely left then?' Schwab asked nervously.

The baker, seeing Schwab's sudden change of manner, immediately and incorrectly interpreted the situation.

'Ah, is it the furniture Mr Schwab?'

'What" asked Schwab?

'The furniture, the furniture that she ordered, yes she's sorry about that. In fact she's left you a letter to apologize. I have it here somewhere.'

Schwab looked at the baker in some kind of disbelief.

'What on earth was the man talking about...and what furniture'?

Then the baker opened a drawer under his counter and produced an envelope with Schwab's name written on it.

Schwab took hold of the envelope and stared at it.

Nothing was said for a moment, then Schwab quickly scooped up his breakfast from the top of the counter and excused himself.

The baker, slightly mystified, scratched his head as he watched Schwab hurriedly leave the shop and came to the slightly sceptical conclusion that it was going to be 'one of those days'.

Schwab almost ran to the factory. He dashed up to his office and slammed the door behind him. After throwing his breakfast onto a nearby chair he then went to sit as his desk and desperately ripped open the envelope.

He sat there in silence as he read Rachel's letter, and he began to struggle. His hands started to shake as he read the letter once again. As he finished his lips began to quiver as he stared down at the most tragic letter that he had ever received in his life.

Sitting there, and in true despair, Ernst Schwab started to weep.

It was the hopelessness of it all, the utter hopelessness.

He was losing the greatest love of his life and with her the most precious thing...their child.

It was later that day, and Yuri Hartman had arrived back home as promised. He and Rachel, along with their four very full and battered old cases got onto a train and left the City of Smolensk for once and for all. They were heading back to Moscow to their new home.

The previous day Yuri had been to see Manny Gotz and they'd spoken at length.

Manny had been quite disconcerted when his Ghost told him about the two men who had arrived in Smolensk to find him. Manny couldn't understand how anyone would even know about the place, and he was left to consider the possibility that he may have an enemy within his own camp. Later, he would compile a list of the people in his organisation who knew about the hidden apartment in Smolensk, and then he would act accordingly.

His Ghost would have more work to do.

It also brought up the problem that if those two men were related to the Zwerner family in any way, they too might be on their way to Moscow. Moreover, they might already be in Moscow. After all, they somehow had all the information about Smolensk.

Yes, there were problems, there were problems indeed.

Manny decided that he would indeed, need to have his Ghost nearer to home. If the Zwerners wanted reprisals it would be better to have Yuri Hartman close to hand. The man saw things that others did not.

The Gotz family owned an empty house in the Druzhba district, a quiet suburb on the outskirts of Moscow.

Manny had given Yuri the address and the key. Yuri was to move himself in there and await further instruction. And so he'd gone back to Smolensk for his personal belongings, which also included his wife.

The trip back to Moscow was a quiet affair. Yuri just sat there, gazing out of the window as he drank his bottle of vodka. Rachel, bruised and still very sore, contemplated her future with this man, and how she was going to have to deceive him into thinking that her baby was his. Since she hadn't seen him for almost three months, there was not a chance of him believing her if she suddenly announced to him that she was pregnant. She would have to be cleverer than that. So she decided that his brutal attack on her the night before would have to be the 'moment in time' when she had apparently conceived. From there she would have to fool him. Rachel decided that she would wait a couple of weeks before telling Yuri the good news. Then she would worry about everything else at a later date. By then her vodka addled husband would hopefully have forgotten the day, the date and the time, hopefully.

As she sat there, Rachel's thoughts turned to Schwab. With a heavy heart she wondered how he'd taken the news when he had finally read her letter. She had to control her emotions as she thought about him, and that she would never see him ever again. In her heart of hearts she knew that she was doing the right thing. She had to protect him, and she had to protect their child.

Rachel leant back in her seat, closed her eyes and tried to blank out her thoughts as she listened to the steady rumble of the train as it roared on, ever northwards.

Several hours later they'd arrived in the City of Moscow and had located their new home.

It was a timber built affair that had seen better days, but it was a fairly anonymous house in a road of similarly worn properties. Ten minutes after arriving there and having given the place a look over, Yuri informed Rachel that he was going out. She was left to light the fire and get some warmth into the place. After that she would unpack and try to make the house as liveable and as comfortable as possible.

Yuri never returned that evening, Rachel knew he wouldn't and she thanked her god for it.

Two weeks later she informed Yuri that she was expecting a baby. In true form he demanded an explanation. When she told him that she had conceived on the night he'd arrived back from Moscow, he just grunted at the vague memory. Then for clarity, Rachel informed him that it had been the night he had arrived home and she had told him about the two men who had been looking for him, and then a couple of days they had finally left Smolensk.

Yuri struggled to think, but then he remembered her telling him about the two and he also remembered looking at her bruised face as they waited for the train at Smolensk train station. In the end though, he accepted the obvious conclusion.

Then once again Yuri left the house and he didn't return for another two weeks, their life would continue in that way and nothing would change.

Back in Smolensk, Schwab had decided to act. He had to do something, he couldn't lose Rachel, especially not now. Schwab had sat at night in his lonely house and given the whole situation a lot of thought. In the end he decided that he must find Rachel, whatever the cost. He'd considered his life, and everything that he had and who he was. And it didn't matter anymore.

He would find her and then they would run, and run anywhere. He had enough money, he could fund their disappearance and they could go anywhere in the world. He had thoughts about America, in particular Canada. He had read all about Canada and it had always seemed to be a similar country to Russia, full of wide open spaces with huge forests. He decided that he could start a business again in Canada, with Rachel and their new family.

It was a dream and that was how it would remain. Just a dream.

Schwab would spend days and nights walking around the Glinka district of Smolensk, trying to find Rachel. But she wasn't there. She never had been of course. Nobody in the neighbourhood knew her or remembered her and in the end Schwab realised the truth of it. Rachel had never lived there at all.

She would never discuss her home or home life with him and her living in the Glinka district was obviously a deception. Schwab could only wonder about Yuri Hartman, and the dark and dangerous figure that he must surely be.

Schwab eventually gave up and returned home lost,lonely and heartbroken.

In the end and in utter despair, he turned his attentions back to his work, and then he totally buried himself in his business.

Ten months later he received a letter.

'My dearest darling Ernst,

I have given birth to our daughter. She is so beautiful. I only wish that you could see her.

I truly love you with all my heart.'

Rachel.

That was all she could write. To say anymore would have been a torment for both of them.

And it would have been a final cruelty to the man that she loved.

CHAPTER 5

Twenty years later and on that Friday evening, an older and possibly wiser Ernst Schwab stood in his office gazing out of the window as he watched his young secretary, Anna, leave for the weekend. He stood there remembering his sorrowful past, and he sipped his brandy as he watched her walk away.

He'd just had his regular weekly meeting with his manager Koenig.

Good old Koenig, Schwab didn't know how he would manage without Koenig running the factory floor. They'd just had a good long chat, along with their usual glass or two of excellent French brandy. They'd discussed the week's production and then talked about the talents of young Pavel Bratz, the young apprentice who was an 'artist' with wood. Pavel Bratz was now working in the 'Marquetry and Parquetry' section of the factory and was demonstrating skills that had left the time served carpenters working there in complete awe. Pavel's natural talent had now come into play as he'd immersed himself in the artistry of inlaid wood. His fascination with the different techniques and intricate designs using exotic timbers had absolutely captivated him, and sometimes he would spend up to twenty hours a day in the workshop, frequently working late into the night.

For Pavel, it was a timeless and effortless joy.

So on that Friday evening, Schwab stood there with another glass of his favourite brandy in his hand. He'd already watched Koenig leave the factory and shortly afterwards his secretary Anna had bid him goodnight and he'd bid her a 'goodnight' too and told her to enjoy her weekend.

As Schwab gazed down he watched Anna walk towards the factory entrance. It was something that he always did. Schwab was a creature of habit.

As she approached the large wrought iron factory gates a young man suddenly came out of nowhere and grabbed hold of Anna as she walked past. Schwab gasped in fear for her, he was about to drop his glass and attempt to get himself down into the yard and try to stop whatever was going on. But as he looked on, he saw that the man was actually spinning her around in a very friendly manner, and that Anna had turned around and was laughing as she threw her arms around his neck.

Schwab was amazed. What was going on?

He stood there in his office and observed them as they embraced.

Schwab was rather taken aback. He'd never realized, never even considered that Anna was seeing someone. After all, she spent most of her time in his factory.

Schwab just stared at them both and he suddenly had a rush of emotion. He'd always been protective of Anna. And through the failing light he watched them both talking and laughing.

The young man had been waiting for her inside Schwab's factory and that rather annoyed Schwab, he considered it a form of trespass.

Suddenly the man turned sideways as he linked Anna's arm and kissed her, and that was when Ernst Schwab was somewhat astonished. Schwab saw the profile of the man's face.

It was the face of someone that he recognized immediately. It was Pavel Bratz.

Pavel Bratz, the boy, the apprentice. Schwab had to stop and think. Pavel Bratz wasn't a boy anymore, no, not any longer. Pavel Bratz was now a young man and seeing him with Anna, seeing him kissing Anna made Schwab feel quite uneasy, and for good reason.

That evening as Anna had left his office, Schwab had smiled at her as usual. She knew so little about her boss, so little indeed. But strangely, Schwab knew all and everything about Anna. He knew about her life and her past life. And he knew her dead parents, he knew all about them and he knew all their past little secrets too. He knew things about Anna's life that she herself didn't know and never would know.

But Schwab knew. Schwab knew everything.

And he knew the biggest secret of all, the one hidden secret that nobody else in the world would ever know, nor even consider.

Schwab looked down at Pavel Bratz and Anna and he saw their happiness and sighed, knowing that someday, one way or another, this would finally happen. As he watched Anna, so happy and smiling, he thought about her and how they'd first met. She was so beautiful, so very beautiful. The first time he'd met her she was only fifteen and he'd been stunned by her beauty even then and during the last few years as she worked for him, he'd learned to love her.

In fact, he'd decided to look after her for as long as necessary, and if possible, forever.

Yes, the one truth that the world did not know and the one truth that Anna certainly didn't know, was something that Schwab had kept as a lifelong secret.

Because Anna's name, her full name, was Anna Hartman....Anna Kristen Hartman.

Rachel Hartman had been her mother and he, Ernst Schwab was her father.

And Anna Kristen Hartman was in reality, Ernst Schwab's very own darling daughter.

She was his lost and only child.

Several years earlier Anna had turned up at the Schwab Factory together with a lawyer from Moscow, a Mr Jozeph Kleiner.

Mr Kleiner, a strict and dour man, had formally introduced himself to Schwab with a firm handshake. That done, Mr Kleiner then went on to explain that he worked for 'Messrs Meltzer and Forsch' who were a firm of lawyers in Moscow. Mr Kleiner was there under instruction from one of his clients, a client who had tragically died leaving behind a daughter, the young girl who was with him, her name was Anna.

Schwab looked down at the girl who stood there nervously with her head bowed.

Schwab was mystified. What on earth was this, and what did the solicitor actually want?

Mr Kleiner then explained that he had been instructed to bring the girl to Smolensk along with a letter of introduction. That was all he knew.

Mr Kleiner then coughed as he produced a white envelope from his inside pocket.

On the envelope were written the words...

'Personal'
To Mr Ernst Schwab
The Schwab Furniture Company
Smolensk

Mr Kleiner passed the envelope to Schwab who quickly ripped it open and started to read the letter inside. A moment later Ernst Schwab gasped, and he had to steady himself.

The solicitor, Mr Kleiner, watched as Schwab seemed momentarily unbalanced, then he observed how quickly he regained his composure. Kleiner considered the moment and he quite accurately surmised that whatever was written in the letter had been a total shock to Mr Schwab.

Schwab continued to read, but it was more than a shock. It was a tragedy. The letter said it all...

'My Darling Ernst'

'I have written this letter to you as my last will and testament.
If you are reading this, something has happened both to me and my husband
Yuri Hartman.
If so, my lawyers have explicit written instructions to contact you personally.
I hope that this letter will fully explain everything.
The young lady that hopefully accompanies the solicitor is our daughter.
She is 'our' daughter Ernst, you are her father and I am her mother.
Her name is Anna...Anna Kristen Hartman.
As I write, Anna is just ten years old.
She is a beautiful and intelligent little girl who has a good heart.
She knows nothing about you, nothing at all. But you are her father.

Whatever tragedy has taken place, please take care of her.
She is our flesh and blood.

Life has been cruel Ernst, but I have never stopped loving you. You have always been and always will remain the love of my life'.

'I love you'.
Rachel.

Ernst Schwab there stood for a moment, aghast.

The letter meant that Rachel had died. His one and only love was dead.

For the last sixteen years, not for one day had Schwab ever considered that he wouldn't see Rachel again. In his heart and in his dreams he'd always thought that she would come back to him. He'd always considered that Rachel's husband would finally die somehow, or that in the end she would find some way of leaving him and come back to live with Schwab here in Smolensk.

Time would be of no distance for Schwab, he would always love her because he always had. And even though the years had achingly passed by, he'd never lost hope. One day they would be together, and this time as a family.

Schwab clutched the letter, the letter that told him that Rachel was dead and that all of his hopes were dashed. He would never see her again, ever.

In shock he looked to Mr Kleiner, who just stared back at him, waiting for some sort of answer.

The three of them stood there in silence...the three of them. It was at that point, Schwab realised that the young girl standing in front of him was his child, his one and only child. Again he thought of Rachel, and now here in front of him was their precious daughter.

This shy young girl, with her head still bowed.

Schwab looked down at her and wondered 'what does she look like... and who does she look like'?

All he could see was the top of her head. She had dark auburn hair and Schwab remembered Rachel's beautiful white blonde hair.

Schwab spoke out softly 'Anna'...

The girl slowly looked up, and Ernst Schwab suddenly struggled for his breath, and he bit into his lip to stop himself from crying out.

There was a moment of silence as Anna Hartman looked up at him, and

Schwab had to try to control his emotions as he took one deep breath and then another.

Standing there in front of him was Rachel Hartman's double. The young lady facing him, his lost daughter Anna, was the absolute image of her mother. She had the same beautiful face and those same remarkably stunning hazel eyes. It was the face that Schwab remembered so well, the face that he'd dreamt about. Here was the reflection of someone that he'd wanted to see again after sixteen years of waiting, and sixteen years of yearning. It was almost as though it was 'his Rachel' standing there in front of him, almost.

Anna, beautiful Anna, had without doubt inherited her mother's face and her tawny eyes, but she'd also been left with a legacy from the 'Schwab family', and that was her beautiful dark auburn hair. And at that moment Schwab considered it a blessing, because if her hair had been the same striking blonde as her mother's, Schwab would have found it difficult not to throw his arms around her and weep.

There was a perceptible silence as the three of them stood alone in Schwab's office. Kleiner just stared at Schwab and took in the obvious shock and unease. Kleiner would have to think this one through.

The silence was broken by Schwab himself. In the short moments of panic he kept asking himself... 'What on earth he was going to do'?

Schwab suddenly leant over and pressed the buzzer on his desk. Within a couple of seconds the office door swung open as his secretary entered the room.

'Ah, Mrs Kausky,' Schwab smiled as he greeted her.

Mrs Kausky returned an enquiring smile.

'Err, Mrs Kausky, could you take young Anna here into your office and make her something warm to drink, some coffee or some of your lovely hot chocolate, if you have some of course.'

'Certainly Mr Schwab.' she replied.

'Oh, and could you possibly make me and Mr Kleiner some coffee too please?'

'Yes, certainly Mr Schwab,' again Mrs Kausky replied and then she turned to Anna.

'Just follow me dear,' she said and she smiled at Anna. Then suddenly, Mrs Kausky stopped dead in her tracks as she looked at Anna's pretty face.

Mrs Kausky stopped and then quickly looked back at Schwab. There was an evident look of shock on her face.

Schwab looked back at her, and as he stared directly at her his eyes widened, and straight away Mrs Kausky instinctively saw the signal.

'Err, yes if you could please Mrs Kausky,' continued Schwab, 'Mr Kleiner and I just have to sort some things out.'

Mrs Kausky responded with her professional smile.

'Yes Mr Schwab, I'll sort that out right away,' she replied efficiently and then turned to Anna,

'Right dear, come along with me, you can help me boil the kettle,' and with a pleasant smile she led Anna away from the office.

Once the office door closed behind them, Schwab turned to Kleiner.

'Please, sit down Mr Kleiner.'

Both men went to sit at Schwab's small table and wait for their coffee. Schwab himself almost slumped into his chair. The shock of the news that Rachel had died had hit him hard, terribly hard. And as they sat there, Schwab's mind was moving in several different directions. He was in a daze. Rachel, what had happened to Rachel? She'd died but how? What had happened to her? And now he would never, ever see her again. His hopes were completely and utterly dashed. And Anna had suddenly appeared from absolutely nowhere, and now she was here in his office, and in his life. What was he going to do, what on earth was he going to do with Anna?

Kleiner coughed for attention 'Are you alright Mr Schwab?'

Schwab immediately looked up.

'What happened Mr Kleiner? What happened to...to Mrs Hartman?'

Schwab had to struggle to control his voice.

'She died in a fire Mr Schwab, a house fire. Both Mrs Hartman and her husband perished when their house burned down. A tragedy I'm afraid.'

'Burned down...where?' asked Schwab.

'Oh, in Moscow, they lived in the Druzhba district in Moscow. It was a timber build house and of course when they catch fire they go up like a torch. But were you not aware of where they lived Mr Schwab?' asked Kleiner.

Schwab hesitated "Err no, we'd lost touch" and he remembered the time that he'd spent searching for Rachel in Smolensk, all of his wasted time.

'Hmm,' Kleiner continued, 'Yes well, the house burned down and the Hartman's charred bodies were found in the ashes. Probably started in the kitchen, it seems to be the cause of most fires these days.'

Schwab tried to stifle a look of despair as he thought about Rachel being burned to death. The thought of it threw him into a state of desolation.

Kleiner just sat there, and he watched as Schwab struggled with his emotions, and he wondered.

'Well Mr Schwab, when our office realised what had happened we had to act on Mrs Hartman's instructions,'

'Instructions?' asked Schwab.

Kleiner looked across the table at Schwab.

'You don't know anything about this do you Mr Schwab, you don't know anything at all?'

Schwab stared back at him 'No Mr Kleiner, I don't know a damn thing.'

'What was your relationship with Mrs Hartman?' Kleiner suddenly enquired.

This sharpness alerted Schwab somewhat, and he was immediately guarded.

'We were friends, years ago. I...I didn't even know that she had a daughter.'

Somehow Kleiner found that hard to believe. Jozeph Kleiner knew a lie when he heard it.

'Well Mr Schwab, it's a bit of a strange tale really. As I said, I work for 'Meltzer and Forsch' the law firm in Moscow. Anyway, your 'friend' Mrs Hartman walked into our offices, I think it would be about six years ago. She came into my office and sat herself down and presented me with a letter. It was the same letter that I've just given to you Mr Schwab. Mrs Hartman then instructed me that if anything happened to her and her husband, I was to find her daughter and bring her here to you in Smolensk, along with that letter, the letter of introduction. She told me that you would then be taking care of Miss Hartman's affairs.

Schwab just sat there, slightly taken aback.

Mr Kleiner continued 'I asked Mrs Hartman if she was in some sort of danger, or was she suffering from ill health, but no. Then she told me that her only living relative was her elderly mother who did suffer from ill health. She also gave me her mother's address.'

'Where did her mother live?' Schwab asked.

'About a hundred kilometres north of Moscow.'

Schwab shook his head. He'd never had a clue where to look for Rachel, and it would have been impossible for him to have ever found her or her mother. Not in the vastness of Russia.

Kleiner leant back in his chair.

'That's when things got a little stranger Mr Schwab. You see, I then asked Mrs Hartman how we would know if and when something did happen to her and her husband. There was obviously no family, so I asked her if she had a contact or a friend who would contact us. She hadn't. But she'd thought it all out. Mrs Hartman had a simple plan. On the first day of every month she would send us a letter and inside that letter there was a signed communication and a ten rouble note. She instructed me that if ever the letter didn't arrive, then I should act immediately. Over the years we continued to receive her monthly letter and her payment and we added it to her account. The expenses for our services are more than paid for Mr Schwab.'

'So how did you find the girl' asked Schwab?

'She was at her grandmother's house. The old lady had died years ago but Anna and her mother used to live there most of the time. I spoke to some of their neighbours. It seems that the Hartman's were a strange couple and I have a feeling that Mrs Hartman took her daughter up there so that they could get away from the husband. Apparently Mrs Hartman was under instruction from her husband that she had to return to Moscow every other weekend to do his washing and clean up the house. Anna would usually remain at her grandmother's. Her mother preferred it, and apparently her father never asked. Unfortunately, three weeks ago Mrs Hartman was back in Moscow with her husband when their house burned down. It was a blessing really that young Anna wasn't there. Anyway, it was my secretary who notified me that Mrs Hartman's monthly letter and the money hadn't arrived. I gave it another two days and then went around to the Hartman's house in the 'Druzhba'. You can understand my shock when I saw that the house was burned to the ground, so I questioned some of the neighbour's. However, no one seemed to know what had happened. In fact nobody seemed to know much about the Hartmans at all, other than the husband seemed to disappear from time to time. I then went to the authorities and was informed that the house had burned down before anything could be done to save it or the occupants, and the next day they'd found two charred bodies in what was left of the property.'

Schwab just stared at the floor as Kleiner continued.

'By the way Mr Schwab, our firm has fully taken care of the funerals. Meltzer and Forsch have paid all of the expenses,' said Kleiner with some degree of satisfaction.

'Oh, right Mr Kleiner, that was very good of you,' said Schwab quietly.

'Ah well, we felt that since Mrs Hartman was a long established client, we considered it the only right and proper thing to do.'

It was also the easiest way for Messrs Meltzer and Forsch to proceed and tie up a few untidy ends. To quickly and finally close the Hartman account, Yuri and Rachel Hartman had been given the cheapest possible funeral and were now buried in Moscow's Vvedenskoe Communal graveyard. Their graves were marked with two simple wooden crosses, wooden crosses that wouldn't survive more than a couple of Russia's harsh and bitter winters.

'The authorities knew nothing at all about the daughter,' continued Kleiner, 'and so I took it upon myself to travel north to the grandmother's old house, and I found young Anna there awaiting her mother's return. I had to break the news to her which devastated the poor girl. I then took her back to Moscow for a couple of days, to sign her mother's account and accept the small balance of the monies that remained. Then we both got on the train and came here to Smolensk to find you. And there you have it Mr Schwab. That's all I know.'

Schwab just sat there, slightly at a loss, when suddenly the office door opened. Both men looked up to see Anna carrying in a tray on which was a pot of coffee and a small jug of milk, along with two china cups and saucers. She walked over to the table and put down the tray and proceeded to pour out the hot, fresh brew. As she handed him his cup, Anna turned to Schwab and smiled.

'I've been helping Mrs Kausky with the coffee. She's asked had me carry in the tray because my hands are steadier than hers,' and she continued to smile.

Schwab just sat there, almost rigid in his chair. Looking at him was his Rachel, his beautiful, beautiful Rachel. That same face, those same hazel brown eyes and now she was back here at the same table, the table where she had fed him and served him coffee all those years ago, and the table where they'd first made love. He loved that face and his heart and soul wanted to scream out. Ernst Schwab felt like he wanted to reach out and hug this image of the woman that he'd loved and adored and lost.

Anna just stared back at him for a moment, and then with a feeling of slight embarrassment she turned to give Mr Kleiner his coffee.

Kleiner had seen the expression on Schwab's face too, and he found it all quite intriguing.

Schwab suddenly realised that he was acting irrationally and that he was drawing attention to himself. He immediately spoke out.

'Anna...I'm so sorry, but you are the image of your mother, you have quite startled me. You have darker hair of course, but you share the same eyes and face. It's quite remarkable. You do resemble each other so very much.'

Anna turned back to him, she suddenly smiled and the awkwardness was gone.

'Did you know my mother well, Mr Schwab?' She asked.

'Oh yes, quite well.' replied Schwab, 'we were quite good friends when she lived here in Smolensk all those years ago. Your mother used to work in the little bakers shop around the corner. I still get my breakfasts and my lunches from there. I'm a creature of habit you see.'

Anna chuckled.

And Schwab almost sighed out loud at the memory of it all.

'Your mother used to prepare my breakfast every morning Anna, and then later on she would bring me my lunch, here at my office. Every day I would order the same thing and your mothers used to laugh at me and try to get me to change.'

'And did she?'

Schwab looked back at the face he loved, and he smiled at her.

'Yes Anna she did, eventually she did.'

Anna smiled back at him 'My mother was like that, when I was little she could always make me eat my food, no matter what it was.'

'Yes,' said Schwab, 'she was very persuasive, and she was a lovely woman. Your mother always had time for a chat. She used to brighten up my day.'

'My mother told me that she once worked at a baker's shop. She loved to bake cakes, she was a very good cook.'

Schwab remembered the meals that he and Rachel had shared. He knew more than anyone what an excellent cook Anna's mother had been.

'Your mother was a really lovely person Anna.'

Anna turned to leave the office.

'Thank you Mr Schwab, thank you,' she replied, and then she left them sitting there as she closed the office door behind her.

Both men sat there in silence for a moment, and then Kleiner finally spoke.

'How well did you actually know Anna's mother?' he enquired, and there was a hint of suggestion in his voice.

'Well enough' replied Schwab. He'd picked up on what Kleiner was inferring and he was having none of it.

'And that's all?' continued Kleiner

Schwab gave the lawyer a serious look, 'that's all there is to know Mr Kleiner,' he said.

And Kleiner was sensible enough to realise that their conversation had all but come to an end.

They finished their coffee and then both men shook hands.

'I'll take care of things from here,' said Schwab, although at that moment he hadn't a clue what he was going to do with young Anna Hartman.

Kleiner nodded. 'I'll go and speak to her and wish her well Mr Schwab.'

Ten minutes later Mr Jozeph Kleiner walked out of the Schwab furniture factory. If he hurried he would be able to catch the early train back to Moscow. As he walked briskly back to the city centre he contemplated on what had just happened in Ernst Schwab's office. Kleiner gave some thought to Schwab's relationship with Rachel Hartman. He didn't know what had gone on. But he had a good idea

.

Back at his office, Schwab was still sitting at his table, pondering.

He heard a slight tap and Mrs Kausky popped her head around the office door.

Schwab turned as he heard her.

'Could I have a word Mr Schwab,' she almost whispered.

'Come in Mrs Kausky,' Schwab replied.

Mrs Kausky entered Schwab's office, and then she looked back into her own office to check if there was anyone there.

She turned to Schwab.

'Ah good, I've just sent Anna on a little errand Mr Schwab.'

Schwab nodded.

Mrs Kausky scuttled over to the table were Schwab was sitting. She always did walk in a peculiar sort of way. She stood in front of Schwab her head tilted to the left, as always and she took a deep breath.

'Can I have a word Mr Schwab? It's personal.' Mrs Kausky was quite a private person and this act alone was somewhat out of character for her.

Schwab looked up at his loyal secretary.

'Of course you can Mrs Kausky, of course you can.'

'May I sit down Mr Schwab?' she asked.

Schwab was almost amused. This was all quite unusual, especially from Mrs Kausky.

'Yes of course, please do sit down Mrs Kausky,' Schwab replied. He was a little mystified by all this.

Mrs Kausky sat herself down at the table, directly in front of Schwab. The thought suddenly struck Schwab that in all the years that he'd known her, he and Mrs Kausky had never sat anywhere together.

Mrs Kausky coughed to clear her throat and it was obvious to Schwab that she had something important on her mind.

'Mr Schwab, may I speak openly?'She asked him.

Schwab straightened himself up. He was now more than curious.

'Yes Mrs Kausky, please do.'

Mrs Kausky looked at her boss.

'I'd like to, as they say, put 'my cards on the table' Mr Schwab.'

Schwab just nodded.

'I've worked here at Schwab's Furnishings for over forty years Mr Schwab. I've worked for you for twenty years and before that I worked for your father for twenty years.'

Mrs Kausky then took a deep breath before she could continue.

'And I have to tell you Mr Schwab, that your father was an utter bastard,'

Schwab was so shocked by Mrs Kausky's turn of phrase that he almost burst out laughing. He'd actually never heard her swear in his life.

But Mrs Kausky was serious, very serious.

'Your father was one of the most awful men I have ever known. He was a bully, and he was dishonest and he would use people to whatever end he could. In fact, I think that he was the cruellest person that I've ever known.'

Schwab just sat there, almost spellbound at this outburst.

'Yes I worked for your father for twenty years before you came along Mr Schwab. And in those days, if you worked for your father, he owned you. He treated everybody who worked for him like a slave. The wages were poor and the conditions here were awful. There was no heating in the factory at all back then and when people became ill he would simply sack them. He didn't care about anyone.'

Mrs Kausky took another deep breath.

'Forty years ago I was a young woman Mr Schwab. Back then I was quite good looking. Men found me attractive. Your father couldn't keep his grubby hands off me and thought of me as his personal plaything. Every time he got me alone in the office he would try to force himself on me. It was a nightmare. Things finally began to get worse and I realised that on the nights that he'd opened the vodka bottle, there was every chance of me getting raped. I used to have to have my wits about me and when he'd been drinking I used to disappear. Usually the next morning he'd forgotten. But one evening he had something planned. As I came into his office, it was this same office Mr Schwab, and as I came in with some papers for him to sign, he simply stood up and walked over to the door and locked it. I was trapped and I knew it. The vodka bottle was on his desk, he'd been drinking. He came over to me, picked up the vodka and offered me a drink.

I don't drink Mr Schwab, I never have, but your father tried to force me. He put his hands on me and I pushed him away. It was then that he got angry. He told me to leave at once and that he was sacking me. I begged him not to. I lived on my own you see, I've always lived on my own and I've always had to look after myself. I needed this job and he knew it. I was at my wit's end. So I got clever, or so I thought. I knew that I needed to start smiling and I walked back over to him and I laughed. He put his arms around me and pulled me to him. I could smell the vodka on his breath and I realized that he'd had a lot to drink. Once he'd got hold of me he started to touch me, but I just kept laughing and tried to hold him back. I knew he would try to rape me so I started to talk to him. I told him he was a married man and he didn't like that, but to stop him getting angry I told him that I would be willing to provide him with 'services...'

Mrs Kausky stopped for a moment as she let the words dwell.

'Do you understand what I'm telling you about your father, Mr Schwab?'

Schwab nodded at her. He was horrified.

'And that was what I had to do. I performed the act on him and that finally seemed to satisfy him. I left your father that night with his pants around his ankles. His eyes were glazed over with the vodka. I went home that night and wept. The next day when I came into work nothing was said, he just grinned at me. That was the start of it. It continued, and it continued for years. Whenever he got the mood on him or whenever he'd been drinking I was called into the office and he would lock the door. Then I'd have to get down on my knees and service the bastard.

I should have killed your father Mr Schwab. I should have killed the bastard.'

Schwab just sat there, horrified and disgusted. That his father had abused this loyal and trusted woman utterly sickened him. He was just about to say something to her but she shook her head.

'No, I've started Mr Schwab, so please let me finish what I want to say. It all carried on for years. I had no choice. I needed to keep my job. Then twenty years ago you took over the company Mr Schwab. You ran the company and then your father disappeared and never came back. For me it was a blessing. You're a good man Mr Schwab and you always have been. You've been good to me and to everybody else who works for you. You're nothing like your father and you've taken this business and made it successful and you've done it honestly. I've watched you since you were a boy. I've seen you grow up from a nervous young man into the kind and well respected person that you are. And I've seen everything that's happened to you.'

Schwab looked across the table at his secretary, and he had an uncomfortable feeling in the pit of his stomach.

But Mrs Kausky just smiled.

'What I'm about to tell you will probably get me sacked Mr Schwab, but I have something important to say to you, and anyway, it's probably time for me to retire. I'm getting too old.'

Mrs Kausky chuckled and then she continued.

'So Mr Schwab, you started working here all those years ago, not much more than a boy. You were always very shy and you were very quiet. It was plain to see that your father had knocked all the confidence out of you. He was nothing more than a bully. Then you took over the firm and continued to run it after he'd disappeared. You were married to that terrible woman from Moscow. She was an absolute bitch, and truth be known, you'd just swapped one bully for another. And then she disappeared too, well she disappeared back to Moscow and never returned, thank god. And then you lived on your own for a few years, all alone and lonely.'

Schwab shifted in his chair. He felt a bit uncomfortable, but he had to acknowledge that Mrs Kausky obviously did know all about him. She'd always been there of course.

'Yes, you were lonely and alone and then suddenly, 'she' turned up.'

Schwab looked up quickly 'Who?'

Mrs Kausky smiled. 'You know who. It was Rachel...Rachel from the bakers. Young Rachel Hartman walked into your life Mr Schwab and you both fell in love. I saw it happen before my very eyes. I watched the pair of you together, you were both so very happy. I was so pleased for you Mr Schwab, at last you'd found the woman you deserved. I can still remember her, she was really beautiful. Back then I realised that you'd finally met somebody, somebody that you really loved. And I always expected that at some point you would marry her. Then one day, she was gone. I don't know what had happened Mr Schwab but you were inconsolable. For months you walked around in a trance. We kept the business running, both me and Mr Koenig. It took you the best part of twelve months before we could get you anywhere near back to normal. But you were never the same. You buried yourself in your work and the running of this factory. I saw it all Mr Schwab, I saw it all but there was nothing I could do. Neither could Mr Koenig. It was your own private life and it was nothing to do with us. 'Time' as they say 'is a great healer' Mr Schwab, and we've all had to get on with our lives. Yes, we've all got on with our lives...until today Mr Schwab.'

Schwab just sat there and stared at his secretary.

'Today Mr Schwab, Miss Anna Hartman has walked into this office and you looked as though a ghost had just walked back into your life. Young Anna Hartman is the absolute image of her mother, I can see that. Dark haired she may be, but she's Rachel Hartman's daughter, no doubt about it. I was shocked too, and I couldn't believe it either. But I've been watching you Mr Schwab and I saw the look on your face. This has shaken you to the core. This is not just the daughter of an old girl friend turning up, and I think I'm right when I say that there's more to it. I don't want to upset you Mr Schwab but for once I want to speak my mind. Knowing you all these years, I think that I probably know you as well as anybody, and something's just not right here. So I'm going to say something and I'll have to suffer the consequences.'

Mrs Kausky took a deep breath 'Mr Schwab, I think that Anna Hartman is your daughter. Your true daughter. I think she's the child that you and Rachel had after your brief affair. She's now sixteen years old and Rachel Hartman disappeared from Smolensk around sixteen years ago. I've been talking to Anna for the last hour and she's a really lovely girl. She's told me about both of her parents dying tragically. Yes, her last name is Hartman and she had a father, her family name is Hartman and always was. I don't know what happened and I don't know what's going to happen in the future Mr Schwab. But I think that young lady is your daughter and I think that you know it too.'

Schwab sat there in silence, and then he took a deep sigh and slowly ran his hands over his head.

'You're right Mrs Kausky, of course you are. And today, well today has been unbearable for me. Rachel's dead Mrs Kausky, she's dead and I don't know what to do. I know I'm stupid and I'm naive, but I've always hoped that one day she would come back to me. For years I've waited and waited, and I've never given up hope. You see Mrs Kausky, Rachel was the only woman that I've ever loved.'

That statement overwhelmed Schwab and suddenly a tear began to run down his cheek.

Mrs Kausky took hold of his hand, her touch was almost motherly. She'd always worried about his well being.

'It's alright Mr Schwab, I understand. The news of Rachel's death must have been a shock. I think you always knew that she'd had your child, didn't you? I take it that her pregnancy was the reason she disappeared?'

Schwab nodded as he tried to take control of his emotions.

'So what will happen now?' she asked him.

Schwab shook his head. 'I really don't know Mrs Kausky, I really don't know. That solicitor from Moscow has just dumped her here. What am I supposed to do? She doesn't know who I am, she hasn't a clue. What on earth am I supposed to do with her?'

Mrs Kausky smiled at her boss. She'd already given this a lot of thought.

'I have an idea,' she said.

Mrs Kausky got up from the table, simply because she suddenly needed to stretch her legs. She was approaching an age when her joints easily stiffened and she walked across the office and back, not just to ease the pain in her legs but also to gather her thoughts and consider how she was going to convey them.

She returned to the table where Schwab sat silently watching her.

'Right...' she said to him, 'This is the way I see things.'

Schwab just sat there, immovable and still waiting.

'Today Mr Schwab you've finally met your one daughter, your only child. I've spoken to her and she is a really lovely girl, just as her mother was. You may never have met her before Mr Schwab but that young lady is your flesh and blood. You and her mother loved each other dearly and she is the culmination of that love. Apart from this factory, she is the only thing you've got left. Please, please don't lose this child Mr Schwab. She's just walked into your life and Anna is your only link with Rachel, and every time you look at her you will see Rachel and that will warm your heart Mr Schwab, it will warm your heart. Having Anna here with you will be the next best thing to having her mother back. You've waited a long time Mr Schwab. Please, please don't lose this chance.'

Schwab sat there for a moment as he thought about Mrs Kausky's advice. Then he reached into his inside pocket and took out the letter that Mr Kleiner had given to him, it was Rachel's letter.

He passed it over to his loyal secretary for her to read.

Mrs Kausky opened the now slightly crumpled envelope and took out the letter. She read it and re-read it. Then she looked back at her boss.

'This is the letter from someone who knew something terrible was eventually going to happen. Rachel Hartman must have been in some sort of trouble, in this letter she has almost predicted her death. That's why she's asked you to look after Anna, she must have known about this for some time. Rachel was obviously making sure that Anna was looked after and protected because she herself wasn't going to be there.'

Schwab took a deep breath, 'It was her husband, Mr Kausky. It was her husband that was the problem.'

Now it was Mrs Kausky's turn to listen.

'Rachel was married to a man called Yuri Hartman, Mrs Kausky. He was a very, very bad man. When Rachel became pregnant she wrote me a final letter before she disappeared. In that letter she told me that her husband was a murderer, a 'paid' murderer. He was apparently working for someone in Moscow, and there are a lot of bad folk in Moscow. Hartman would be away for months at a time, then when he came home he would brutalize poor Rachel. She was absolutely terrified of him, so much so that when she found out she was pregnant she feared for her life, she feared for all of our lives. Apparently Hartman had a terrible temper and was uncontrollably violent. Rachel told me that if he ever found out about us, he would kill us all, and he would kill the baby too. She had no doubt in her mind about it and so she fled. But she obviously left Smolensk with her husband, because for years they lived together somewhere in Moscow.'

Mrs Kausky interrupted, 'Anna told me that she spent a lot of time at her grandmother's.'

'Yes,' said Schwab 'Rachel's mother lived somewhere north of Moscow.'

'Well Mr Schwab, Yuri Hartman's gone now and you have other things to think about.'

Schwab nodded in agreement, but he was still at a loss.

Mrs Kausky smiled at him.

'I've been thinking,' she said, 'and I've had an idea which might just work Mr Schwab.'

She knew that had to get his full attention.

'I've spent an hour this afternoon talking to Anna. She's a bright young thing, very bright in fact. Another fact is Mr Schwab that I'm getting old, and I'm getting too old to do this job. I've stayed on here at the factory because you're here and Mr Koenig's here too. For me it's almost been like working with my family. But these days I'm getting a little tired and I've been thinking that maybe I could do with a bit of help. So I wondered... what if I trained young Anna to do my job. It would take a couple of years to get her proficient of course, but by then I would probably be ready to retire. It would really help me Mr Schwab, it really would. And also, until we can find her somewhere to live, she can stay with me. I could do with some company. It would be quite nice actually. From there you would need to find somewhere for her to live permanently, an apartment would be nice. You could buy her somewhere and then charge her a minimal rent. Truth be known she wouldn't even have to know that you owned it, you could just tell her that you were paying her rent to a landlord directly out of her wages. I'm sure she would never suspect.'

Schwab just sat there, opened mouthed.

'Mrs Kausky, I think that you should have been a diplomat.' he said, 'I think you've had this whole thing planned from start to finish.'

Mrs Kausky stood there for an instant, she was a little taken aback.

'Well,' she replied haughtily, 'these things need to be sorted out. You men are hopeless. I've had to push both you and Mr Koenig for years. I don't know how you'd manage without me, really I don't.'

Schwab looked at his secretary and yes, she was probably quite right. Mrs Kausky had been the backbone of his company for years and she was also correct as to the subject of 'how' he was going to manage without her. Yes, Mrs Kausky was indeed right. He was going to have to find someone very special to be able to step into her 'trusted' shoes.

'What you've said makes complete sense Mrs Kausky, ' he replied, 'and we will at some point need somebody capable enough to take over your duties. It does obviously make better sense to start to train someone now rather than later. Yes, it's an excellent idea.'

Mrs Kausky smiled to herself. She was a wise old bird. But Schwab already knew that.

'Right Mrs Kausky,' he continued, 'if you'll bring Anna through, I'll sit and have a word with her.'

Mrs Kausky was just about to turn and leave when Schwab said something to her.

'I didn't think that I would smile again today Mrs Kausky, not today. But you've helped me get through it. Thank you Mrs Kausky, thank you so very much.'

At that moment Mrs Kausky trembled slightly, and she nearly showed her true emotion. But then she waved her hand at him as though she was too busy for all this nonsense, then she went through to the outer office to retrieve her new young protégé.

A moment later she reappeared with Anna. Schwab had gone over to sit at his desk, it seemed more appropriate, and Anna came in and sat on an office chair in front of him as Mrs Kausky once again disappeared.

He sat there and looked at her, and when Anna smiled back at him his heart fluttered as he looked at a face that he loved so much. So for his own gravity, Schwab immediately took the decision that it would have to be business as usual. It was the only way that he was ever going to be able to handle events.

'Now then Anna,' he said to her, 'I've been looking at things and I am trying to sort out the situation.'

Anna just sat there, but Schwab could see the look of worry etched on her young face. She was frightened. It was understandable.

'Your dear mother sent a letter of introduction to me via her solicitors in Moscow. It has been given to me by Mr Kleiner. You probably know that already?'

'Yes Mr Schwab,' Anna replied.

'In the letter your mother has asked me to look after your wellbeing. And I am prepared to do that Anna, for your mother's sake. I have discussed the subject with Mrs Kausky and we have come up with a plan which I hope will be suitable to you.'

Anna just nodded.

'I am prepared to find you employment here at the factory. You will become a junior secretary under Mrs Kausky's charge. She will teach you all you need to know. There is also the question of your accommodation. Mrs Kausky has kindly offered to take you under her wing for the time being. We will of course have to find you accommodation. I have an associate who rents out properties. We will find you somewhere suitable to live and the rent will be paid directly out of your wages.'

Schwab stopped for a moment.

'How do you feel about all of this Anna?' he asked her.

Anna looked up at him, and promptly burst into tears.

'Oh lord,' Schwab immediately uttered as he went to comfort the poor girl.

'I'm so sorry Mr Schwab,' she sobbed, 'I've been so worried. I didn't know what was going to happen to me. My mother has always looked after me...'

And with that Anna completely broke down.

Schwab, now totally out of his depth did the only thing possible.

'Mrs Kausky..!'

A second after he'd called out, Mrs Kausky almost charged into his office. It was patently obvious that she had been listening from behind the door and knew everything that was going on. She rushed over to Anna and put her arm around Anna's shoulder to comfort her.

'Don't worry dear,' she said, 'Everything is going to be alright.'

'I'm sorry Mrs Kausky,' Anna replied tearfully.

'Don't worry child,' replied the secretary.

Schwab then spoke, somewhat nervously.

'Why don't you take Anna into to your office and make her a warm drink.'

'Yes, come with me,' said Mrs Kausky taking control again, 'I'll make you some hot chocolate. Now don't you worry Anna because everything is going to be fine. You're going to work here with us and you're going to be alright. We're just one big happy family.'

And with that Mrs Kausky turned back to Schwab and gave him a sly wink.

Ernst Schwab stood alone in his office. For him it had been a day of tribulation and upset. His lost dream of ever having Rachel by his side again was gone, a broken hope, a hope that now felt like a pitiless stupidity. He was forlorn and somewhat bewildered.

But through all of this turmoil he now had a daughter with him, his only child and the one person who would always remind him of the joy he had with her mother.

As he stood there he contemplated his future. This was the only way forward. It was the best he could ever expect if he wanted to find some semblance of peace in his life.

But unbeknown to Schwab, the sought-after peace that he hoped for was about to be unequivocally shattered. There was trouble brewing. A problem was about to emerge and it was a problem that would eventually pursue him all the way to Smolensk to search him out.

It was as though the 'sins of the fathers' would never go away and never let go.

CHAPTER 6

One month before he burned to death, Yuri Hartman had been comfortably living his 'double' life in Moscow. In between the intermittent and violent contracts that he'd carried out for Manny Gotz, Yuri had time on his hands and he would spend as much of that time as possible at his luxury apartment in the Stutz building. Strangely, Yuri had taken to reading. In fact, he had actually become quite an obsessive reader.

For most of his violent life, Yuri Hartman had striven to get through every single day just to get hold of some form of income. Every day had been a battle, and one way or another he'd had to obtain enough money to get him through to the following day and then he had to start all over again. That was how his life had been. His only solace and his only respite in the past had been vodka. That colourless Russian liquor had always given Yuri Hartman some form of solace. With a bottle of vodka Yuri could forget his problems. He could forget everything.

But suddenly, Yuri had taken to walking the streets of Moscow, calling in at various bookshops where he would peruse the shelves for cheap second hand books. He started with simple novels, and he would even read children's books as his appetite for reading became voracious. He read the classics and famous autobiographies and he had even scrutinized some of the various mechanical and technical manuals. At one time he took to reading the bible, but found that he only favoured the more violent parts of the book. And the more books he read, the more he learned. It was the intricate plots in the writings that always fascinated him, especially the murders. In his particular field Yuri was always looking for fresh ideas and he considered that all of this instruction made him a better assassin.

Yuri liked to sit in the luxurious silence of his apartment at the Stutz with one of his good books. He had a large comfortable chair which he'd placed at the side of a window that received the maximum amount of sunshine. And he would sit there with a glass and a bottle of vodka on a small table at the side of him as he read.

Small coincidence though it was, the table and the comfortable chair that he preferred had both been made by 'Schwabs of Smolensk'.

Yuri would alternate between his secret apartment and his family home in Druzhba. His wife Rachel would arrive back there every couple of weeks to clean the house and do his laundry, and Yuri would have to make the place look as though he'd been living there at some point, even though he was hardly ever there.

'Coincidences'...can often be the cause or the catalyst of some of life's stranger events. In some cases they are uncanny, even bizarre. Coincidences, for one reason or another, may seem unfounded at the time. Sometimes it's as simple as a person being in either the right or the wrong place, and there is every possibility that it could be down to just good or bad luck, or even the timing. But sometimes, when a certain coincidence does happen, it can be forever life changing. And so it happened.

Manny Gotz was on his way to an important meeting. The meeting was a power play.

And the reason for this was that during that previous year Manny Gotz had encountered a serious problem, and it was a problem that wasn't going to easily go away.

The source of the problem was the highly venerated 'Guberman' family of St Petersburg.

St Petersburg itself lay some way to the west of Moscow and it was without doubt one of Russia's most beautiful and highly regarded cities.

The Guberman's were a family much alike the Gotz family, the similarity being that they were extremely rich, and that they too lived their lucrative and grossly illegal lives through coercion and crime. However, over the last year or so as the two family business empires had grown larger and crept even further, they had come to a point of overlap. In essence, both families were starting to tread on each other's toes. And the two families realised that each was beginning to step into the other's deemed territory.

One or two incidents had occurred, nasty little incidents that had made each aware of the other and a point had been reached where negotiations were judged to be the better way. Better than an all out war and the deaths of many, because that was what would have happened if a 'blood feud' had begun.

So it had been agreed that the heads of both families would meet to discuss what they considered were their own territorial rights.

Manny Gotz would of course act for the Gotz family. In the case of the Gubermans, it would be Arkady Guberman, who was the father and head of his own family.

It had been decided that both families would meet in Moscow and that decision also suited both parties, but for entirely different reasons. Manny Gotz was a true Muscovite, born and bred there. He'd travelled of course, in fact he had travelled extensively when he was younger. But his heart was in Moscow, it was the city of his birth and it was the city where he thrived. He knew every road and street and he appreciated it's security. So to make the Gubermans come to him in Moscow was more than just an accomplishment, it gave Manny a certain 'edge'. The Gubermans it seemed were already dancing to his tune and Manny Gotz certainly didn't want to travel to St Petersburg. If only for his own safety.

The Gubermans were there to visit him, so Manny would welcome them as a gracious host, and then he would lean on them and push them into a corner and they would have no other option but to bow to his will.

Arkady 'Ozof' Guberman was a large rotund man, probably in his mid fifties and as strong as the proverbial ox. He was known throughout St Petersburg as 'the Jew', though strangely he wasn't Jewish at all. Far from it in fact, though few knew it, Arkady Guberman was actually an Orthodox Christian. Arkady himself knew all the stories and knew all the anti Semitic insults and names by which he was referred to. But he quite enjoyed it that everyone called him 'the Jew'. For him, it added to the legend. People needed a symbol to respect, or fear, or simply despise. It was better that way, and as 'the Jew', Arkady Guberman ran St. Petersburg with an iron fist, much in the same way that the Gotz family ruled Moscow.

The Gubermans, very successfully had their 'fingers in the pie' in all and every illegal activity that took place in their fair city. There were no exceptions.

Arkady Guberman had one son, Anatoly, who considered himself, probably quite rightly as heir to the Guberman throne. Anatoly was a keen but slightly pampered young man who was continually pulling at his father's reins. It was the arrogance of youth. Young Anatoly thought he knew better, and he also thought he could do better and do it all a whole lot faster.

Young Anatoly Guberman desperately wanted to build his own little empire, and then he wanted more.

When over dinner, Arkady Guberman announced to his son that they would be going to Moscow to meet the Gotz family, Anatoly had been less than impressed with his father's decision. In fact, Anatoly was almost shouting at his father as they dined that evening

'Why do we have to go there to meet them? Why can't they come here to us for God's sake? It's an insult, and nothing more.'

Arkady Guberman continued to eat his meal, his son's eagerness was something he'd had to get used to and something he'd patiently learned to ignore.

'We don't want them here in St Petersburg,' Arkady simply replied.

'And why not,' asked Anatoly? 'Why do we have to go begging to them over territories that we already rightfully own?'

Arkady shook his head.

'We won't be doing any begging.' he said to his son, 'We just need to talk. It will be better and it will be simpler.'

'Huh' replied Anatoly sullenly as he sat there with his arms folded, his food only half eaten.

Arkady continued to eat his meal until the awkward silence finally got to him.

He picked up his folded napkin, wiped his mouth and then threw it down in front of his unfinished plate.

'Anatoly,' he started, 'You don't know these people. I unfortunately do.'

Anatoly sat there in silence, but he listened.

'The Gotz family are powerful and clever and devious. They're headed by Manny Gotz, who is the most ruthless bastard you could ever wish to meet. So listen to me son, we don't want the likes of Manny Gotz here in St Petersburg. Our city is the 'jewel in the crown' in Russia.

We run it and we run it easily. I've seen to it that we don't have a lot of problems. We have a business here that bears fruit, but to Manny Gotz we could be the apple that he would want to pick.'

'We could wipe the bastards off the face of the earth if they came here to us,' Anatoly seethed, and he oozed with youthful confidence. 'We could get them here if we gave them some sort of promise. Offer them a working partnership here in St Petersburg along with us. Tell them we've got too much on our plate. Those greedy Gotz bastards would fall for that. Once we got them here we could make sure that none of them ever saw Moscow again.'

Then Anatoly ran his forefinger across his own throat. It was an act that was supposed to impress his father.

Arkady Guberman looked across at his son and shook his head. He wasn't impressed, not one bit. Arkady picked up his fork and started to tap it repeatedly on the table top, he was thinking of what to say to his son.

Young Anatoly considered this as a sign that his father was of the same opinion as himself, and that they were finally seeing eye-to-eye on matters. Anatoly was just about to give out further instructions when his father spoke.

'Anatoly, my son...you are a fucking idiot.'

Anatoly, the 'fucking idiot', just stared back at his father. However, he knew when to keep his mouth firmly shut.

Arkady Guberman then continued.

'Let me tell you about the Gotz family, Anatoly. They are headed by Manny Gotz and are the most successful family in Moscow and possibly the most successful in Russia, if of course you take out the Tsar and the rest of those bloody Royals...those shithead Romanovs.

And Manny Gotz is without doubt a fucking snake, but believe me, he would not set one foot inside our territory without being totally protected. We would be fools to bring him here to St Petersburg, absolute fools.

Anatoly raised his arms in a gesture, 'What can he do for god's sake? Even if he brings twenty men with him we can take them out, we can take them all out. We have the resources.'

Arkady Guberman looked across the dining table at his son.

'He doesn't need twenty men Anatoly, he just needs the one.'

Anatoly Guberman stared back at his father.

'I don't understand you' he said.

But his father did. His father did understand.

'Manny Gotz has one man. He's known as 'the Ghost' and he's Manny Gotz's ghost. He's a living pariah who's owned by Manny Gotz and works only for Manny Gotz. He's an invisible assassin, and he is fucking invisible, believe me. The Ghost has slaughtered anyone and everyone who has opposed the Gotz regime in any way, and that's how Manny Gotz controls Moscow, he rules it by fear. Nobody knows who the Ghost is or where he comes from, but the man's a monster, he's a bloody maniac. There are stories about him that you don't want to know. He's capable of unbelievable acts of violence and he seems to have an instinct for trapping his victims when they're least aware, and by then it's too late. The man has an insane lust for mutilating and killing people, his methods are appalling. I don't want him anywhere near us and I don't want him anywhere near our family. Anatoly, I don't want the Ghost to ever come to St Petersburg.'

'He's only one man.' Anatoly scoffed, 'And we're supposed to be frightened of just one man?'

Arkady Guberman stared back at his son.

'Yes Anatoly, we are scared of this one man. This one man would kill us all. It doesn't matter if we kill Manny Gotz and all the Gotz family and all of the Gotz's henchmen. The Ghost would be waiting, he'd always be waiting. He would find us and he would stalk us. It could be days, or months, or even years but he would never give up. He's like a dog that's only ever had one master. He would torture and kill our women and he would mutilate our children. He would pick us off one by one. Murdering us would not be enough for the Ghost, he would want to exact on us the maximum amount of pain. We would spend the rest of our lives living in fear. We couldn't function and the end result would still remain the same, and that would be the inevitable destruction of this family".

Anatoly looked at his father 'You say this man would even kill our children?'

'Listen to me,' said Guberman. 'In the early days, Manny Gotz was having problems with some Ukrainians. They were bad bastards but they were fucking tough people, believe me.

Manny sent in his Ghost. The Ghost found out where the family lived, they were all brothers with their wives and families. The Ghost watched them and waited and planned. When he was finally ready, he caught hold of the wife of the eldest brother and chopped her head off, and then he took her head and left it outside their front door. The next day he burned down the house with everyone inside it. Most of them burned to death... the brothers, the women, and their children. Only a few of the family survived and they fled for their lives.'

Anatoly said nothing.

Arkady Guberman nodded to his son.

'Now you understand why we're going to Moscow to talk to Manny Gotz. We will deal of course, and we will try to get ourselves the best deal possible. I think that if we are prepared to share the middle territories with them, we can work something out. Manny Gotz is nobody's fool. He won't want a feud with us, it would be a waste of time, people and money.'

Anatoly still said nothing.

With that, Arkady Guberman slowly got up from the table.

'I'm going to bed,' he said, 'that's where I can best think things out.'

Anatoly watched his father leave the room, but he still remained at the table. He was deep in thought himself.

An hour later he took a sheet of paper and wrote a letter to a 'secret friend' in Moscow.

A friend that no one was aware of.

Two weeks later the Gubermans arrived in Moscow on the late morning train. It was a bleak and daunting day as the low cloud hung over the city like a damp grey shroud.

And it was on that particular day, that one of those strange little 'coincidences' unexpectedly came into play.

Manny Gotz, for no other reason than it being central, had decided to book the Gubermans into the 'prestigious' Stutz Building. Manny knew the owner of the building very well. In fact, the Gotz family actually owned a ten percent share in the Stutz Building. Manny Gotz had wisely lent the owner the money to build the property, and the owner had very wisely accepted that offer.

The Guberman party consisted of Arkady Guberman himself, his son Anatoly and two of Arkady's so called 'friends', who were actually his bodyguards. This was deemed an acceptable force. Manny Gotz completely understood that the Gubermans couldn't travel without some sort of security. That of course would be ridiculous, the Gubermans would have their own enemies back in St Petersburg, enemies who would gladly love to take down 'The Jew'.

So Manny Gotz booked the Gubermans into a large private apartment in the Stutz Building. There would of course be enough bedrooms for everyone and the building itself would afford them the privacy that a Deluxe Hotel certainly couldn't.

The meeting was going to take place later that afternoon and that would give Arkady Guberman an hour or two to ready himself.

Manny Gotz was on his way around to the Stutz after just having lunch with his faithful accountant. They had eaten in a diner just a hundred yards around the corner. It was a good little restaurant and they'd dined on salmon baked in fresh dill, the meal being washed down with a good bottle of Chablis. After some expensive brandy followed by coffee, they parted company, leaving Manny in a good mood and feeling quite competent in dealing with the task ahead. He was also fairly confident that he could manoeuvre the Gubermans into his way of thinking. In the end, what choice did they have? Manny of course would go through the usual blustering that was acceptable in any deal. But in the end he would have his way.

He was accompanied by his own two bodyguards, one of whom was Hendrik, Manny's trusted Ukrainian henchman who had loyally served him for years. There was also a newer younger man. Only twenty nine years old, but with a lifetime of experience, his name was Dmitri Karazin.

Karazin had risen rapidly through the ranks of the Gotz Empire, even though he'd only worked for Manny Gotz for approximately a year. It was Karazin's ability to retrieve money that had drawn him to Manny's attention. Suddenly, it seemed that it was always Karazin's name that was mentioned when someone rashly considered that they didn't need to pay their dues. Those people should have known better, the Gotz family would always demand their percentage.

So suddenly, it was Dmitri Karazin who was collecting the money and doing it very efficiently. For Manny Gotz it didn't take long to realise that he possibly had another 'Ghost' in the making. Karazin was ruthlessly and coldly efficient. He was a man of few words and even fewer vices. In fact, Manny had never even seen him take a drink. Nonetheless, he was certainly capable and his use of the gun and the knife were almost second to none...almost.

Good as Karazin was, in Manny Gotz's mind he would never equal the raw ruthlessness and brilliance of the Ghost. Not yet anyway.

And as things were, Manny didn't need to call on his ghostly assassin too often. The Ghost's reputation was generally enough to keep the more serious problems at bay. His retribution was usually a terminal experience, or if not it left any usurper damaged and crushed. The day to day problems were being dealt with by Karazin. It was simpler, mainly because Karazin was always at hand. Manny Gotz had wisely decided that he would only get in touch with his Ghost as and when things became more problematic.

But respect had to be earned, and one evening Manny Gotz finally and fully realised the value and worth of Dmitri Karazin.

It was after a business meeting. Manny Gotz was being escorted home by his two bodyguards, the ever faithful Hendrik together with Dmitri Karazin. They were two streets from Manny Gotz's mansion and Manny was talking to Hendrik as Karazin walked along behind them, he was following both men at a respectful distance. He realised that his boss and Hendrik were more like old friends and so he didn't want to be seen to be intrusive. Manny and Hendrik strolled along in deep conversation, Manny was in a good mood, apparently the meeting had been profitable.

As they turned the corner and continued home, Manny suddenly heard the words 'Down!' and he abruptly lurched sideways as he was violently pushed to the ground. As Manny Gotz keeled over and painfully hit the pavement he saw Karazin dash past him and to his utter amazement he suddenly realised that it was Karazin who had pushed him over. Angry and somewhat startled, Manny watched as his young bodyguard ran towards a man who had been walking towards them. The man was some twenty yards ahead, yet Karazin was running towards him at an incredible speed. Then at the very last moment Karazin leapt high into the air, his long coat opening up like a pair of wings as dropped straight onto the man.

It was like watching a bird of prey plunging onto its quarry. The man instantly fell to the ground with Karazin on top of him.

Manny Gotz looked on as he saw the man's legs shake in final rigor and he realised that Karazin had obviously killed him. Suddenly and almost immediately, Hendrik pulled his boss from the floor and then both men ran over ran to where Karazin was now kneeling.

'What the hell is going on?' Manny Gotz shouted.

Karazin stood up, but he was still looking down at the dead man lying there at his feet. Karazin's knife was embedded in the man's throat and the dark red blood was still pumping slowly out of his dead body. Karazin then turned to look at Manny and Hendrik.

'There was something, I don't know...just something.' he said slowly.

The two men stared back down at the man's body. He looked innocuous enough, just someone that you would pass in the street without giving a second glance. The dead man lay there strangely, with one arm reaching into an inside pocket. Hendrik went down on one knee and quickly unbuttoned the man's coat. As he undid the last button the coat fell open and there in the man's hand was a revolver.

'Bastard!' spat out Manny Gotz.

Hendrik checked the man's coat and he found a brown envelope stuffed into another pocket. He looked at it and then passed it up to Manny. Written on the front of the envelope was the word 'Gotz' with a cross underneath it. The cross indicated some sort of finality. Manny Gotz ripped open the envelope, inside there were two thousand roubles.

Manny Gotz erupted. He looked down at the body.

'Who sent you...you bastard?' he seethed, and in a fit of anger he turned and kicked the dead man in the face. There was the crunch of bone as the man's cheek and the side of his face collapsed.

Manny gathered his breath and looked back over a Karazin, who was standing there in silence.

'How did you know?' asked Manny.

'It was his body language,' replied Karazin, 'It was the way he walked, with one hand hidden in his jacket. This man wasn't going for an evening stroll. He had a purpose.'

Manny turned to Hendrik.

'Sort out the body' he said.

Hendrik nodded.

'I'll get you home first boss, then I'll bring back some men. Karazin, you drag the body over there into those bushes, I'll be back in ten minutes.'

Karazin nodded.

The two men set off as Karazin dragged the dead man over and into some bushes across the road.

As Manny Gotz and Hendrik made their way home, Karazin lit up a cigarette. As he exhaled the smoke into the cold dark night, he leant back against a tree and smiled to himself.

It had all been so, so easy.

Karazin had always known that he would have to make himself invaluable to Manny Gotz.

It was all part of the plan.

For the previous two weeks, Karazin had carried with him the brown envelope full of roubles with Gotz's name written on it, along with the spare revolver. He'd watched and waited, waited for just the right moment, and on that very evening everything had just dropped perfectly into place.

As Manny Gotz and Hendrik had walked along that evening, both in deep conversation, they hadn't noticed the man walking towards them in the distance. They hadn't seen him. But Karazin had, and Karazin realised that this was the very moment that he'd been waiting and planned for. The man was a nobody. Well to Karazin he was nobody. The actuality was that to a wife somewhere he was a husband, and to their child he was a father, but all that meant nothing to Karazin. It meant nothing at all. The man was on his way home after working late. The man needed the money. His family needed the money.

Karazin had knocked Manny Gotz to the floor and that act had seized Hendrik's attention. Then he'd silently sprinted towards his unsuspecting victim. Only at the last moment did the man look up to see Karazin heading for him at full pace. In those last few seconds the man just stood there paralysed, as Karazin leapt high into the air and knocked him to the floor. The man never saw the knife. He just felt the unbearable searing pain as Karazin's knife ripped into his throat and slashed through a main artery.

The man died almost instantly. simply because Karazin was a trained and efficient killer.

Everything had happened so quickly. By the time Hendrik had reached down to help Manny, Karazin had already unbuttoned the victim's coat and inserted the envelope into an inside pocket. He'd then quickly re-buttoned the man's coat, leaving the top buttons undone and then he'd placed the revolver into the man's hand and jammed his arm back into the gap in his coat.

Karazin had then stood back and let Hendrik inspect the body. It was all so obvious. There were never going to be any doubts.

Hendrik returned fifteen minutes later, he had two more men with him, they both carried shovels. They dragged the body though the bushes and back about one hundred yards to where the dense bushes finally turned into forest. Then the two men hurriedly began to dig.

Hendrik gave them their instructions

'Make sure it's deep enough,' he ordered.

He walked over to Karazin and took him to one side, they needed to talk.

'I never saw it,' said Hendrik, 'I just never saw it.'

It was an admission to a younger, faster man.

Karazin shrugged.

'I just got lucky,' he replied.

But Hendrik just shook his head and that too was an admission.

Karazin took hold of Hendrik's arm.

'Listen, I got lucky. If he'd have gotten closer to Mr Gotz, you'd have taken him down. The important thing is that Mr Gotz is okay.'

Hendrik nodded in reply.

Karazin continued, 'We need to work as a team, you and I. You have the experience, I'm still learning. Our priority is the Boss...okay?'

Hendrik reached out and shook Karazin's hand. There was nothing else to say.

They went back to where the men were still digging. As they stood there in silence, Karazin reflected on what had just happened. Hendrik now respected him too, and that was a tool he could use. Hendrik would now treat him as an equal and with that, Karazin could gather more information. Now he could ask Hendrik the questions and expect an answer.

Yes, everything was going to plan.

They buried the man deep, so deep that no one would ever find him. Not his wife, or his child or anyone else for that matter.

When they got back to the Gotz residence, Manny took Karazin directly into his study. He needed to talk to his young bodyguard privately.

Manny sat himself down at his expansive desk and made himself comfortable, and then looked across at his young henchman.

'Do you want a drink Karazin?' Manny asked.

'No thank you Mr Gotz,' he replied.

Manny shrugged.

'You did well tonight,' said Manny.

Now it was Karazin's turn to shrug.

'I was just doing my job, Boss,' he replied.

Manny opened the top drawer of his desk and took out the brown envelope bearing his own name and the cross. It was the so called assassin's blood money.

'Here,' he said as he slid the envelope over to Karazin, 'Here, you've earned it.'

Karazin nodded as he picked up the money.

Manny continued 'I think I'm going to increase your wages Karazin, you've worked well tonight.'

'Thank you Mr Gotz,' said Karazin and he nodded again.

'Okay,' said Manny Gotz as he reached into his desk for his brandy. It was a subtle hint. It was time for Karazin to leave.

As Karazin closed the doors behind him, Manny Gotz sat there and remembered a similar conversation fifteen years ago with the man who became his Ghost, and he considered that maybe history was repeating itself. Yuri Hartman was now an older man and frighteningly ruthless though he was, the Ghost was also getting older and one day, one day, his time would be over.

Manny smiled as he sipped his expensive brandy. He'd always known that one day he would have to replace his Ghost. Now he could.

As he walked away from Manny Gotz's office, Karazin reflected on the evening's events.

He'd almost laughed when Gotz had given him back his own money. As he thought about it, the whole evening's exercise had cost him nothing at all, even the revolver had been stolen.

The fact that he'd just murdered a totally innocent man never even registered in his mind.

Back at the Stutz building, and it was almost time for the meeting between Arkady Guberman and Manny Gotz to take place.

Coincidences...coincidences, yes sometimes it's just the wrong time and the wrong place.

Manny Gotz had just finished his lunch with his accountant and was making his way to the Stutz building with his two bodyguards, Hendrik and Karazin. He was in a confident mood, he'd had a very good lunch with just enough wine and brandy to make him feel energetic and so the three of them strode on purposely. Manny was ready for the confrontation, he intended to break Arkady Guberman because he was going to demand the lion's share. After all, what could Guberman possibly do?

They were just turning the corner to the square where the majestic Stutz building stood when Manny Gotz stopped dead in his tracks. Hendrik and Karazin nearly walked right into him.

Gotz stood there for a brief second and then quickly stepped back. His two bodyguards had to move sharply to get out of his way.

Manny Gotz just stood there in disbelief. He stood there and watched a man walk directly out of the entrance to the Stutz building. It was a man that he'd known for over fifteen years, the man was carrying a small brown paper parcel and he was walking away from the Stutz and away from where Manny Gotz was standing.

Manny couldn't believe it. The man shouldn't have been there, not in a thousand years should he have been there. But he was.

In utter confusion Manny turned to Hendrik. He grabbed hold of his bodyguard's arm and thrust him forward so that Hendrik could see the man too. Hendrik gasped and he looked back at his boss. Hendrik too, knew that this was all wrong. What was that man doing here?

He spoke the words out loud, too loud, and that was a mistake.

'It's the Ghost,' he said.

Karazin shot around and saw the man, saw him for who he was, and the hair stood up on the back of his neck. He stared intently at the man and he observed him closely, because he had to remember that face. Yes, he had to remember that face.

Finally, finally, he'd found the Ghost.

The three men stood there in a daze as they watched Yuri Hartman walk away. Nothing was said for a moment until Manny Gotz finally snapped back to life.

'Step back down there,' he said to his two bodyguards, and they all moved into a narrow backstreet. Manny turned to Hendrik.

'What the hell's going on? What's he doing here at the Stutz for god's sake?'

Hendrik looked at his boss and shook his head emphatically.

Manny Gotz clenched his fists.

'Why is he here? He must have met up with Guberman. That must be it. What do you think was in the parcel?'

Hendrik stared at his boss.

'Money?' he asked.

'Yes,' said Manny Gotz, 'Fucking money. The bastard's sold us out. He's sold us out to that fucking Jew.'

'What do we do boss?'

Manny stood there for a moment and gave the matter some thought.

'We go to the fucking meeting and see what happens. That's what we do.'

Then he turned to Karazin, 'You, be ready. If I give you the word, take the fuckers out.'

Karazin nodded and checked for his gun

Manny then took a few minutes to calm himself down, and then the three of them proceeded to make their way to their prearranged meeting with the Gubermans. But now Manny Gotz was in a different frame of mind. He would be guarded and he would now take an entirely different approach when he dealt with the Jew.

Yuri Hartman walked off down the road with the brown paper parcel tucked under his arm. But unfortunately for Yuri, he was completely unaware of what had just happened. He didn't know the Gubermans, not at all, and he certainly didn't know that they were staying at the Stutz. He'd heard of the Guberman family of course, they ran St Petersburg, but he certainly didn't know that they were at a meeting today with Manny Gotz, not there at the Stutz.

It was just one of those 'coincidences'.

Yuri was normally more than observant, but today his old friend 'routine' had turned the tables on him and had let him down badly. 'Routine and repetition' had turned to complacency and living at the Stutz had unfortunately given Yuri Hartman a false sense of security. The Stutz was his comfort zone, it was his hiding place and it was the place where he felt totally secure. Nobody at all knew that he lived there or even knew who he was.

Not until today.

Yuri also had other things on his mind.

That weekend his wife Rachel would be returning to Moscow, back to their family home in the Druzhba. Rachel lived up north at her mother's old house with their daughter but she would return every two weeks to clean the house and wash Yuri's laundry. Yuri actually hated the damn place, but Manny Gotz had put him there and it was there that he was expected to be if and whenever needed. Nobody knew about the Stutz.

No, not until today.

It had been the brown paper parcel tucked firmly under his arm that had held Yuri's attention that afternoon. Wrapped inside the parcel was a book, a book that had been delivered to his apartment that very same morning. It was a book that he'd been searching for and for quite a long time and now he finally had a copy.

The book was 'The Art of War' and was written by the Chinese military tactician Sun Tzu.

Yuri, now with the cherished book in his possession, was quite happy to make the trip to his house in the Druzhba. He could quite contentedly read his book and when Rachel did finally arrive she would cook and clean for him and, more importantly, keep out of his way.

Over the last several years Hartman's brutal and carnal tendencies towards his wife had waned with age. He no longer felt the desire, in fact he treated her more like an unpaid cleaner than his wife. There was never any conversation between them because there never had been. He would always ask about their daughter, naturally, but certainly very little else.

Rachel too never had much to say to her husband but that was simply because she hated him.

When he got to their house in the Druzhba later that day, he discovered that Rachel was already there and that she'd arrived there earlier that very same morning. Thankfully she'd lit the fires in the kitchen and the main living room and the house was already fairly warm. She simply nodded to him as he walked in through the front door and then she went into the kitchen to make him a pot of fresh coffee.

Yuri went into the living room and untied the parcel that contained his precious book and then he glanced through it. He sat down near the fire and started to read.

The coffee eventually arrived and was served in silence.

Later that day, as Rachel brought him a small plate of smoked ham and some bread, she commented that there was very little laundry for her to do.

Yuri just grunted and told her that he'd been working away. She knew not to ask.

He continued to read his book, he found it engrossing. The 'Art of War', written almost two thousand years ago was the platform on which the wisest and cleverest men in history had used when going to war. Confucius and even Napoleon had used the same book for guidance. The simple rules and tactics that the writer Sun Tzu had written about all those years ago were still relevant in today's modern world. As Yuri eagerly read Sun Tzu's text he began to consider just how much war and business were alike.

It was how you dealt with the enemy, or in today's world 'the competition' that still mattered.

As he sat back and read, Yuri realized that he too was a soldier. No, more than a soldier, in his own eyes he was a warrior.

The opening lines of the book said everything to Yuri Hartman.

It read 'If I fight...I win.'

Yuri spent the whole day reading, he was totally captivated by the book. Sun Tzu was a genius.

The book 'The Art of War' was thought by many to have been written around 450 B.C. It's author Sun Tzu, was a master tactician whose transcripts on military matters and strategies were seen as brilliant and timeless.

The 'Art of War' was a dedicated, practical handbook on how to successfully wage war and it contained thirteen chapters, with titles such as 'Attack by Stratagem', 'Classification of Terrain', 'Variation of Tactics' and 'The Use of Spies'.

Yuri was enthralled.

The 'Art of War' would be his handbook, the writings were an education and Yuri felt that the book could have been written for him alone.

Back in central Moscow Manny Gotz, Hendrik and Karazin had entered the Stutz building and were making their way up the several flights of stairs to reach the apartment where their meeting with the Gubermans had been planned to take place.

They finally arrived, and Hendrik knocked on the door for his boss then stood to one side.

The large, dark wooden door was opened by Arkady Guberman himself. It was a sign of respect and a show of future friendship. It was, however, a useless act because Manny Gotz had made his mind up. Arkady Guberman was now the enemy and a deadlier enemy than Manny had thought possible.

Arkady Guberman was now controlling the Ghost.

So what was this meeting all about and what was the use of these discussions if the Gubermans now had the Ghost in their employ. What was happening? A myriad of thoughts and threats were running through Manny Gotz's mind and they all culminated to the same conclusion. The Guberman's had the Ghost. The Ghost was a killing machine. The Ghost also knew all and everything about the Gotz organization and the Gotz family, and Manny Gotz knew exactly what the Ghost was capable of.

'Come in, come in my friends,' said an exuberant Arkady Guberman as he welcomed the Gotz party into his 'humble abode', even though the apartment that they were booked into was actually one of the most luxurious in the Stutz building.

Manny Gotz had seen to that.

Manny and his men walked into the apartment where they were met by three others. Arkady Guberman dismissed his two bodyguards as he introduced his son Anatoly, to Mr Gotz.

Hendrik and Karazin stepped back and took a seat on a large couch at the far end of the apartment. They were not intended to be party to these discussions.

Karazin once again felt for his gun, he had to be ready if needed.

As Anatoly shook Manny Gotz's hand, he stared back at him strangely. Manny didn't know whether this was fear, or something else.

But Arkady Guberman didn't seem to notice this, and he proceeded jovially and had fresh coffee and cake served. It was almost a party.

Unfortunately, Manny Gotz didn't think so.

Finally the pleasantries, along with the coffee and cake came to an end and it was time to get down to business. Arkady Guberman had come prepared. They cleared the table of cups and plates and Arkady then produced a large map which he opened up and spread across the large table top. The map was quite detailed and clearly showed St Petersburg in relation to Moscow and it covered the 'disputed territories' that were in between.

'We are all sensible men here,' Arkady Guberman shrugged casually, 'Russia is big enough for everyone.' and he laughed.

Manny Gotz didn't laugh. Strangely, neither did Anatoly Guberman.

Arkady then took a black crayon from his inside pocket and he leant over his map.

'As I see it,' continued Arkady, 'we are in the West and you the East. We are on the left side of Russia and you are on the right. So I am thinking that our little 'problem' can be solved quite simply.'

And with that, Arkady Guberman took his crayon and drew a long black line exactly between St Petersburg and Moscow. It was a practised move, Arkady knew precisely what he was proposing. The line accurately split the territory between the two cities equally.

'There,' he said as he put down the crayon and he looked across the table at Manny Gotz. Guberman considered the offer a fair one. There would be some obvious problems but Arkady was open to discussion and he was ready to haggle and offer to give 'something back'. In his eyes, the only possible problem could be Smolensk. That particular city lay to the west of Moscow and south of St Petersburg but it was a long, long way south and if truth be known, it was too far for the Gubermans to control. St Petersburg bordered on Estonia and Latvia where there were far easier and richer pickings.

Manny studied the map, it was interesting, or it would have been interesting, but not now.

Manny considered the moment and made an immediate decision. In a split second he determined that all of this was a lie. It was all a bluff, yes of course it was. The Gubermans were simply buying time. Otherwise, why was the Ghost involved?

Suddenly Manny Gotz became angry.

These people were trying to bring down his 'house'.

Manny reached across the table and picked up the crayon. Then he leant over the map and drew a thick black circle around St Petersburg.

There was a moment of silence as both the Gubermans looked on. They didn't understand.

But Manny Gotz was about to educate them.

'That's St Petersburg,' he told them, 'Get back there and stay there.'

Arkady Guberman just stood there open mouthed, but it was Anatoly who broke the silence.

'You must be mad,' he shouted, 'Most of this territory is ours anyway and we're not going to give it up just like that...you fucking fool,'

Arkady Guberman exploded, but his anger was aimed at his son.

'Shut up boy,' he bellowed and he snatched hold of Anatoly and with his massive strength he picked up his son and slammed him down onto a nearby chair. It was the final humiliation.

Arkady quickly turned back to Manny Gotz. Hendrik and Karazin had already stood up and were making their way forward. Karazin quite strangely, was beginning to twitch.

Hearing the commotion brought Arkady Guberman's two bodyguards out of the apartment kitchen and suddenly there was a tension that was about to erupt into bloodshed.

Arkady held out his arms.

'Steady everyone, steady. Everyone calm down please.'

For a few seconds there was some sort of standoff, then the moment passed and eventually everybody took a second breath.

Arkady Guberman turned back to Manny Gotz.

'Why are you doing this?' he asked Manny.

Manny stared back at him.

'You think you can get the better of me?' Manny replied sharply.

'I thought we were here to do a deal,' spluttered Arkady Guberman, 'we came in good faith. Why would we come all this way if not to deal, why?'

'He's damn crazy,' Anatoly interrupted from his seat and Arkady again immediately silenced his son.

'You'd better muzzle your pup,' Manny threatened, 'or I'll quieten him myself.'

'What is your problem Gotz?' Arkady asked, 'We came here to talk, to sort things out and now you don't want to know. Why?'

Manny Gotz turned away as he moved to leave, and Hendrik went to open the door. There were to be no further discussions. The meeting was over.

As he was about to leave Manny Gotz turned back to Arkady Guberman. 'Stop this game, and I'll leave you alone. Carry on...and I'll crush you.'

Guberman once again raised his arms, this time in resignation.

'What game?' he asked, 'I don't understand. What game are you talking about?'

Manny Gotz looked intently at Arkady Guberman. It was a look of complete hatred and distrust.

'Fuck you Guberman,' he replied. Then he turned and walked out of the apartment.

Gotz, Hendrik and Karazin left the Stutz building immediately. They were going back to the Gotz mansion. On the way out Hendrik asked Manny if he was okay.

'We should have sorted it out there and then,' Manny replied, 'we should have brought another couple of men with us and shot the bastards while we had them.'

There was a moment of silence, and then Karazin spoke.

'Yes, you should have,' he said.

Both men looked at him.

Karazin continued.

'I had them lined up, one, two, three and four. It would have taken four, five seconds at the most. Then your problems would be over Mr Gotz. It was an easy task, an easy task for me. You should have given the order.'

Hendrik held his breath. He couldn't believe that Karazin had dared to speak to Mr Gotz in such a way. He was almost chastising his boss.

But Manny Gotz didn't take the insult. He took it as the truth. He knew what he should have done, absolutely knew, and again he'd stupidly underestimated Karazin.

Once again he'd undervalued this man. But never again.
'When we get back to the house, I will speak to you Karazin.'

Back at the Stutz the Gubermans were in disarray. Father and son were at each other's throats as they argued over just about everything. Arkady Guberman still erred on the side of caution but Anatoly was incensed over what he saw as an insult to his family's name and standing. He was also disgusted with his father's ineffectual handling of the whole situation. He thought his father actions were weak and feeble. It almost bordered on cowardice.

In the end Anatoly stormed out of the room and went off to his own apartment, which was three doors further down the same corridor. He had, quite wisely in his eyes, booked his own private room, knowing that he and his father would continually argue over everything.

An hour in his father's company had become an hour too long.

Manny Gotz and his two men arrived back home at the Gotz mansion.

Manny immediately took Karazin into his study, and as both men sat down at his huge desk, Manny poured a large shot of brandy into his favourite crystal glass.

On the way home Manny had been noticeably quiet. He'd been deep in thought.

Manny Gotz drank half the contents of his glass and then he set it down on the top of the desk in front of him. He looked across at Karazin and after a moments silence he spoke.

'How good are you Karazin?' he asked.

Karazin stared back at his boss. He didn't even blink an eye.

'I'm the best,' he replied, 'the best you'll ever know.'

There was another short silence.

'No you're not,' said Manny Gotz.

Karazin sat there, impassive.

'This is about the Ghost isn't it Mr Gotz?'

Manny nodded.

Karazin continued. 'Your Ghost has just become your enemy Mr Gotz. He's sold you out and now he's about to become your nightmare. And that's because Mr Gotz, your Ghost knows every single thing about you. He knows everything.'

'Yes.' replied Manny, 'He knows absolutely everything.'

'What do you want me to do Mr Gotz?' asked Karazin, but he already knew the answer.

'I want to know what you are capable of Karazin.' Gotz replied.

Karazin just sat there, impassive as ever.

Manny continued. 'I want to know if you are capable of getting rid of him permanently.'

Karazin smiled, 'Of course I am. I've told you Mr Gotz. I'm the best.'

Manny Gotz slammed his hand onto the desktop.

'No you are bloody not,' Manny said out loud, 'You don't know the Ghost. You don't know anything about him. The man is a phenomenal killer. He has a natural ability. He sees things that others never do and by then it's always too late.'

Karazin took a breath, 'Yes Mr Gotz. I know how dangerous he is, or was. But he's now an older man and probably less cautious. He's had you as a sponsor for the last fifteen years, so life has been a lot easier for him too. You don't use him as often as you used to do Mr Gotz, and why? Because you've got me, and I'm good and I'm efficient and I'm younger. I'm better Mr Gotz. I'm the better man.'

Manny gave thought to what Karazin had just said and there was a certain amount of truth and logic in his words. Yuri Hartman 'was' now an older man and Manny knew just how much the Ghost liked to drink his vodka. Hartman had been a hard drinker fifteen years ago and in Russia it was a daily habit that was difficult to drop.

But Manny was still unsure.

'You need to understand me Karazin. If you don't manage to do the job, he'll want revenge. He'll come for me and mine.'

Karazin smiled 'Why on earth should he Mr Gotz? He can't relate me to you in any way. He doesn't know me, he's never met me. He doesn't even know I exist.'

How little did Karazin know and how little did he understand.

Manny Gotz ran his hand over his forehead. It was the moment to make a decision.

And suddenly, 'Do it Karazin,' he said, 'Do it and do it right, and I'll give you more money than you've ever dreamed of.'

'Where do I have to go to find him?' Karazin asked.

Manny smiled. 'He's right under your nose,' he said, 'I have him here in Moscow. He's always been at my beck and call, always.'

Manny then opened one of the drawers in his desk and carefully took out a blank white envelope. He slid it across the desk to Karazin.

'His real name is Yuri Hartman and he lives in the Druzhba District. In that envelope is the address. He lives in a house that belongs to me.'

Karazin opened the envelope and took out a sheet of white paper. He read the address, memorized it and then put the sheet of paper back in to the envelope and placed it in his inside pocket. He sat there motionless, trying to hide his feelings of total elation.

Finally, yes finally...he'd found the Ghost.

'Okay,' said Manny Gotz, 'I don't know what your plans are but take my advice Karazin, plan well. This is the most dangerous man you will ever come across. Take nothing for granted, nothing at all.'

Karazin stood up to go, the meeting was over.

'Just one more thing,' said Manny as Karazin was leaving.

'What's that Mr Gotz?'

'Don't carry anything at all that can connect you to me'.

Karazin nodded efficiently and then walked out of Manny's office.

That left Manny Gotz on his own, and he sat there and wondered about the wisdom of the decision that he'd just taken. Had he played it right and was Karazin capable of taking down an assassin who'd become a legend. Karazin was good, undeniably very good. He'd always reminded Manny of the young Yuri Hartman. However, deep in Manny's mind he still had to wonder if Karazin would be good enough.

Only time alone would tell.

Karazin left Manny Gotz's mansion and should have then made his way to the Druzba district. He should have gone there, if only to find Yuri Hartman's house. He should have gone there to observe, watch and wait and he should have gone there to formulate a plan. But he didn't.

After leaving Manny Gotz, Karazin made his way back into central Moscow. He had other plans on his mind, his own plans.

Curiously, he returned to the Stutz building. He walked cautiously around the back of the block and found the rear delivery entrance. It was used by the cleaners and various tradesmen who were forever working there and were simply not allowed to just wander in and out through the main front doors of the building, not one as prestigious as the Stutz.

No, definitely not.

He carefully tried the door to the rear entrance, and rather surprisingly, it opened. Had it been locked Karazin could have easily broken in, he had the skills.

He walked inside and quietly closed the door behind him. Then he turned and looked around and spotted the rear stairway. The stairs were there to be used by anyone who was working in the building and they were also the designated fire exits.

Karazin began to silently climb the stairs, he had to get to the floor where the Gubermans were staying and he didn't know the exact amount of security Arkady Guberman had in place. Though Guberman had his two bodyguards in the apartment with him, there could be more.

Karazin also realised that Guberman's guards already knew him and they knew he was one of Manny Gotz's men. The moment they saw him sneaking up those stairs they would probably shoot to kill and then it would all be over. They would obviously connect him with Manny Gotz, and then all hell would break loose.

Onwards and upwards, Karazin crept steadily on, floor by floor, but there was no one at all in sight. He finally reached the floor where the Gubermans were staying, and then Karazin pulled out his gun.

He was now in the most dangerous of situations. Anyone who came to visit Arkady Guberman or who left the apartment would immediately notice him. Karazin continued, silently hoping that his luck would continue. At the end of the corridor was Arkady Guberman's apartment. Karazin held the gun firmly in his hand as he moved forwards, but three doors down from the apartment, Karazin stopped. He straightened up and pointed the gun straight in front of him, and then he knocked on the door. There were a few seconds of silence and then the door opened. Standing there in the doorway was Anatoly Guberman.

Karazin stood there in front of him pointing the gun right at Anatoly's chest. There was a moment of complete silence, nothing was said, absolutely nothing at all.

Anatoly Guberman just stood there, motionless, looking directly at Karazin.

For Anatoly Guberman it was a moment in time. It was a moment that he would always remember.

He stared back at Karazin, and then he grinned and immediately took hold of Karazin's arm.

'Come in old friend, 'he said, 'Quickly...come inside.'

Back at his house in Druzhba, Yuri Hartman put down his book as he stood up and stretched.

The light was finally beginning to fade and he was finding it increasingly difficult to read. In the kitchen he could smell the coffee that Rachel had freshly brewed as she prepared his evening meal. Yuri picked up his book and walked through to the kitchen where it was warmer and well lit.

Rachel turned to look at him as he entered her domain, she went over to the stove and poured him a mug of hot coffee and then silently put it down in front of him as he sat down at the kitchen table.

'Bring me the vodka,' he said to her abruptly.

Rachel turned to a cupboard and took out a bottle of the colourless spirit. She then put that down on the table as well, together with a glass.

It was Yuri's habit to start drinking late in the afternoon and Rachel was quite glad of that.

The tide had turned in their relationship, Yuri would slowly drink himself into a stupor in the evening, and on every evening, and then he would fall asleep in the chair. He never came to bed anymore. A fact that Rachel was more than grateful for.

Whenever she came back to Moscow, Rachel would always make sure that she brought a couple of bottles of vodka with her. Her nightly routine was to feed him as he continued to drink his vodka, then she would disappear upstairs to their bedroom and read for a couple of hours, sure in the knowledge that her husband would remain downstairs.

Yet another routine.

Karazin worked for Anatoly Guberman, and he always had.

Fifteen months prior to what was presently happening there in Moscow, Anatoly had realised that there was going to be a problem with the Gotz family. These people had intruded into the Guberman territories with a view to taking over, and they were utterly ruthless. For young Anatoly Guberman, who wanted to ultimately take over and expand his father's business, this intrusion was completely unacceptable. He knew that eventually things would come to a head and the battle lines would be drawn. That time had now arrived.

Anatoly Guberman had met Karazin purely by accident.

Anatoly and a friend had been on a night out. The friend had a cautious father who had decided that his son should have a part time minder on nights such as this. The father didn't want two heavyweight bodyguards following his son around and his son certainly didn't. So he employed young Karazin, who was apparently 'very handy' but would remain low key. On that particular night, Anatoly and his friend had been out drinking and as they left the bar there were three men waiting for them. Actually they were waiting for Anatoly. They knew who he was, or rather, who his father was and they wanted some form of revenge.

Anatoly and his friend were then threatened.

'So you're the Jew's boy, eh?' one of the men said and then he spat into Anatoly's face.

'We're going to send you back to your father, all cut and bleeding, just to remind him to keep his fat hands in his fat pockets,' said another. Then the three men closed in.

All of a sudden Karazin strode out from a side alley. It was as though he'd appeared from nowhere. He straightaway smashed a bottle into the face of the first man and then turned to the second and struck him twice over the head with the slim steel bar that back in those early days, he always carried with him,. The third man turned and fled leaving his two compatriots unconscious, damaged and bloodied all over the pavement.

It was all over in a matter of seconds, but the speed, the delivery and the method of Karazin's attack astounded Anatoly. It also opened Anatoly Guberman's eyes to the world that he was living in. So Anatoly took Karazin into his employ, but nobody was to know about it, least of all his father. And although Anatoly never realised it at the time, he too had employed his own 'ghost'. However unlike Manny Gotz, Anatoly and Karazin worked as a team. And Anatoly was quite happy to discuss his own personal plans with Karazin, and Karazin quickly became embroiled with Anatoly's strategy for the future of the Guberman business empire, and he realised that he could be part of it. Anatoly Guberman was sharp and eager and keen to get on, and Karazin respected that. The two young men got on well together and eventually became good friends. Anatoly recognized this and he greatly appreciated Karazin's loyalty. For Karazin it was something that money could not buy. Not even Manny Gotz's promise of great wealth.

Back at the Stutz, Anatoly Guberman quickly closed the door behind him after he'd promptly ushered Karazin into his private room. Karazin pushed his gun back into his belt and both men began to laugh as Karazin shook his head.

'That was a close thing back there with your father and Gotz,' said Karazin as he jerked his head in the direction of Arkady Guberman's apartment, just three doors down on the same corridor.

'Yes,' laughed Anatoly, 'I thought I'd nearly overplayed it.'

'Overplayed it...yes my friend, you nearly did. At one point I thought your father's men were going to pull out their guns. I had to think quickly, I didn't know who to shoot first, your father's men or Gotz and that fucking Hendrik.

Anatoly laughed again, 'Maybe you should have shot all of them there and then, including my stupid bloody father. It would probably have saved us a lot of time in the long run.'

Karazin shrugged, he'd never actually considered killing Arkady Guberman. If he'd actually known the strength of Anatoly's feelings he would have undoubtedly done so. Killing everybody there and then would have solved a lot of problems, except for one.

The Ghost of course, they'd needed to find out about the Ghost.

Karazin grinned at Anatoly, 'Your actions however, did produce one result Anatoly.'

Anatoly was curious, 'And?' he asked.

'I know where the Ghost is,' said Karazin, 'I know where he lives and I know who he is, I even have the address.' And with that he pulled out the white envelope from his inside pocket and threw it onto the table in front of Anatoly Guberman.

Anatoly was astounded.

'Karazin...I don't believe it, how did this happen?' and he grinned with delight as he looked down at the envelope.

It was the final piece of the jigsaw.

Karazin continued, 'Well my friend, would you believe that I have just been instructed by Manny Gotz to kill him. It seems that Gotz wants his Ghost dead and buried.'

Anatoly looked up. This was a piece of information that he didn't understand. It just didn't add up.

'Why would Gotz want his top assassin killed?' he asked Karazin.

'You're not going to believe it,' Karazin continued, 'this afternoon when we were on our way here to the meeting, we turned the corner and Manny Gotz stopped dead in his tracks. The Ghost was actually walking straight out of this building. Gotz nearly had a fit. He put two and two together and reckoned that the Ghost was in league with your father. He was even carrying what looked like a parcel of money with him.'

Karazin hesitated for a moment, 'you don't think that your father is involved with the Ghost do you?'

Anatoly shook his head, 'No...No, I'm sure of it.'

Then he stopped for a moment, 'I wouldn't think so. I've always thought that my father was terrified of the man. That's why we we're here for the meeting. My father didn't want Gotz or the Ghost in St Petersburg.'

Anatoly had to think for a moment. The last thing he needed, or wanted, was his father to be having dealings with the Ghost. That man could become an adversary, an adversary that Anatoly would have a problem in dealing with, even with Karazin backing him up.

Karazin suddenly interrupted him. He just stared at Anatoly.

'The bastards found us.'

'What...' replied Anatoly?

Karazin looked at him, 'He's found us...the Ghost...he's fucking found us. That's what this is all about. Manny Gotz said the Ghost has a natural insight into things and that he's always one step in front. He sees things that others never do and by then it's too late. He's found us Anatoly. All this time he's been watching out for Gotz, and Gotz doesn't even know it. That's why he was coming out of the Stutz. He's been here and he'll know who you are and where you are and exactly which rooms you're staying in. Then he'll wait for his orders from Manny Gotz, and if Gotz gives the order, he'll have it all planned to take us out as quickly and efficiently as possible. He'll know you're only in Moscow for a few days.'

And with that Karazin shook his head.

'How do you know he'll do all this?' Anatoly asked.

'Because that's exactly what I'd do,' said Karazin slowly.

'I'd make sure I knew precisely where you all were, then I'd shoot you all and then I'd burn you. I'd set fire to the place, then there would be no evidence. It would look like an accident. By the time the fire was put out there would be just a pile of charred bodies.'

Anatoly was speechless. Yes, now he understood. The Ghost was onto them.

Karazin continued, 'I've learned a lot about his methods since I've worked for Manny Gotz. Gotz's men hold the Ghost in some sort of esteem, they like to talk about his exploits. He seems to come from nowhere and then kills and destroys. He likes to burn, he's done it before. Burning sends out a message, it breeds fear.'

Anatoly Guberman took a deep breath.

'And now Gotz wants you to kill this man?'

Karazin nodded.

'Can you do it? Anatoly asked.

Dmitri Karazin smiled back at his employer and friend.

'Of course I can,' he replied.

'Are you sure?' again Anatoly asked.

'I now know where he lives,' said Karazin, nodding at the envelope on the table, 'He thinks that nobody else knows that, except for Gotz of course. He'll never think it possible that somebody's going to turn up at his own home to kill him, never. He still thinks that he's invisible. But now I know that he's just a man called Yuri Hartman and he lives in a house in the Druzhba. I even know the road where he lives and today I saw that man and now I know his face. He's just a man Anatoly, he's just a man like the rest of us and he can be killed, just like anybody else. The legend that he's built for himself won't save him tonight.'

'You're going to do it tonight?' Anatoly asked.

'Yes, we're going take them all out at once. I'm going to kill the Ghost and rid ourselves of that threat, and you are going to take out Gotz and his men as we planned. We're going to strike them when they least expect it,' replied Karazin, 'I take it you've brought your men?'

'Yes. I've brought twelve good men with me, they're staying in rooms at three different hotels but I can get them together within the hour.'

'And transport?'

'Yes we've got horses and three carriages.'

'Good,' said Karazin, 'and the map?'

Anatoly went over to a cupboard and took a map from the drawer. He unfolded it and lay it across the table. It was an enlarged map of Moscow and it showed in detail, the roads and the streets and the numerous important utilities within the city.

Karazin leant over the map. He knew exactly where the Druzhba district was and he immediately found the road where Yuri Hartman was living.

'It's only a short road' he said, 'it won't be a problem.'

Then he pointed to another spot on the map. The Kirzhach district.

'And that's the Gotz Mansion, exactly there,'

Anatoly looked down and he smiled.

It had been earlier the previous year when Anatoly Guberman had first started to make his plans. The issues that they were beginning to encounter with the Gotz family were going to be an escalating problem, Anatoly had realised that. He and Karazin had discussed their predicament and decided that Karazin should go to Moscow to gather information on Gotz and his empire. Karazin later returned to St Petersburg where he and Anatoly had formulated a plan. Karazin would infiltrate Manny Gotz's organization and try to place himself in a position of confidence. Everything had gone better than planned. After Hendrik, Karazin had almost become Manny Gotz's right hand man and he'd become privy as to how the business was being run. Karazin would send a weekly letter containing all of this information back to Anatoly in St Petersburg. Then periodically he would return there by train for a day or two, to discuss their ever changing plans.

When Arkady Guberman informed his son that they were about to visit the Gotz family in Moscow, he was unaware that Anatoly had already made his own plans. Suddenly they would 'all' be going into 'the lion's den'.

Anatoly wanted his own empire. He hadn't got time to wait for his father to die, though he'd seriously considered helping the 'old man' on his way. And unfortunately, Arkady Guberman wasn't showing any signs of ever handing power over to his son.

Anatoly didn't want a 'turf war' with the Gotz family. It would take too much time and men and it held too many complications. Better to have Karazin good and up close to Manny Gotz and keep his eye on things. That was the better and cleverer way.

Anatoly knew that his day would come, and now that day seemed to have finally arrived.

Anatoly had picked twelve good men and had sent them on to Moscow where he'd sorted out their accommodation, and more importantly, the transport. The plan was to hit the Gotz mansion and kill Manny Gotz and any of his family, along with all of Gotz's henchmen.

Over the years Manny Gotz had become too complacent. The security at his home consisted of Hendrik and just four or five other bodyguards, one of which was Karazin himself. Karazin knew the layout of the house and he also knew where everyone slept.

Yes, Manny Gotz had become complacent. Never in a million years did he ever think that there would be an attack on his own home. After all, Manny Gotz ruled Moscow, didn't he?

He ruled Moscow and the Gotz Mansion was his palace.

In his apartment at the Stutz building, Anatoly discussed the evening's events with Karazin.

It was planned that they would all journey to the Gotz mansion in three carriages. There would be fourteen of them in all and Karazin would direct them there. Karazin would then take one of the carriages and make his way to Yuri Hartman's house over in the Druzhba, leaving Anatoly Guberman and his twelve men to take out the Gotz clan. It was all going to be taken care of quickly. Karazin had known everything about the house and how it was run. Manny Gotz had no exterior guards, everyone would be inside the mansion. The weakness was at the back, an unguarded and empty kitchen that led into the main building. From the kitchen there would be open access to the rest of the house.

Two hours later, Anatoly Guberman, Karazin and their twelve men from St Petersburg set off to Manny Gotz's mansion. It was past ten o' clock by then and it was dark. The three carriages made their way there and kept a good distance being between them so as not to draw any obvious attention.

Half an hour later they drove by the Gotz Mansion along with two or three other passing carriages. Nobody would have given them a second glance. They carried on for another two hundred yards and then they all stopped. From there they would wait for another hour. It would give them time to observe and prepare.

Anatoly and Karazin got out of the first carriage and the driver and another man also stepped down onto the pavement, leaving the carriage empty. As they rejoined the other men, Anatoly shook hands with Karazin and they both wished each other well. It was agreed that they would meet up later back at the Stutz, where they would celebrate their success and then lay out their plans for Moscow.

In each of the carriages they'd placed two small barrels of turpentine. Karazin had decided to use the Ghost's tried and tested method. Burning held a sense of finality and that in itself felt good.

Karazin climbed back onto his own carriage, took the reins, then set off in the direction of the Druzhba. He'd estimated that it would take almost an hour. He drove steadily as he considered his plans. There were variables of course, there would always be variables, but in his heart Karazin knew that he had the upper hand. The Ghost didn't know he was coming.

And suddenly Karazin had a thought, there wasn't a Ghost anymore, it was far more straightforward than that. Now all he had to do was find and kill a man called Yuri Hartman. It was that simple.

It took the best part of an hour but Karazin finally found the house were Yuri Hartman was living. At the same time Anatoly and his men were going into action.

Anatoly had moved one of the carriages closer to the Gotz mansion and he and five other men sat there patiently, watching as most of the household lights were slowly turned down.

When the time felt right, Anatoly and two of his men got out of the carriage and then the driver moved off up the road to meet with the others. From there they drove around the block and stopped as they approached the rear of the Gotz residence. After tying up the horses the men walked quietly to the rear gate. It wasn't even locked. They silently opened the large wrought iron gate and made their way through the garden to the rear kitchen door.

They stood there silently and waited. Waiting for the signal.

Anatoly and his two men walked across the road and up the steps to the Gotz mansion. The two men placed themselves on either side of the door so as not to be seen, and Anatoly lifted the large brass door knocker and struck it firmly. A couple of minutes later there was a movement behind the door. It was Hendrik, he was looking through the spy hole that had been specially fitted into the door, not everyone was welcome. Hendrik was trying to see who was calling at that late hour. The knocking had woken him up. He'd been dozing in a chair in the room next to Manny's study. Manny Gotz was as usual working late into the night, accompanied by a glass or two of his favourite brandy. Hendrik the ever faithful bodyguard would never leave his master until he'd seen him go off to bed.

As he looked through the spy hole, he saw that it was Anatoly Guberman standing there. Hendrik sighed.

'What on earth did this prick want...and at this hour?'

He was inclined to leave the 'Guberman boy' outside, but with youth came stupidity and Hendrik was concerned that if Anatoly kept on knocking he would probably wake up half the house. As he started to unbolt the door, Hendrik wondered if young Anatoly Guberman had come to personally apologise to Mr Gotz, or maybe he was drunk or maybe he'd been sent with a message from his father. Hendrik considered these options and figured that it would probably be the latter.

The large front door was then opened to a smiling Anatoly Guberman. This annoyed Hendrik.

The boy had been outspoken at their previous meeting and now here he was, grinning like an idiot.

'What the hell do you want?' asked Hendrik, 'Do you know what time it is?'

'It's time for you to die,' replied Anatoly, and with that he pulled out his revolver and shot Hendrik twice in the chest. Hendrik fell backwards onto the carpeted floor where he spent the next several minutes listening to the ensuing chaos before he finally died.

Those shots were the signal for the men waiting at the back of the mansion. They kicked in the kitchen door and immediately charged into the property. Guided by Karazin's instructions they dashed upstairs and immediately shot and killed Manny Gotz's remaining bodyguards. There were a couple of Manny's cousins and a nephew living in the house with him and they were killed too. Manny's actual family circle was quite small and it had just become a whole lot smaller. Though he had one or two other cousins and nephews who worked for him, they all lived in other parts of Moscow. Manny had never knowingly had any children and his one and only wife had died eleven years ago.

It had taken Anatoly's men less than five minutes to murder everyone.

Downstairs after he'd shot Hendrik, Anatoly and his two men walked quickly across the large hallway and straight to Manny Gotz's study. Anatoly then kicked the study door open. Manny was sitting at his desk, wide eyed, and for a moment in shock.

'You...' was all that he could say to Anatoly.

Anatoly walked around the desk, grabbed Manny Gotz by the ear then dragged him off his chair.

Manny Gotz howled in agony. He wasn't used to pain. It was Manny who usually doled out the punishment and he wasn't used to receiving it. Anatoly pulled him from behind his desk and into the centre of the room. Manny, who was now on his hands and knees, groaned with the displeasure and humiliation of it all. Anatoly then spun around and kicked him hard in the face. Manny Gotz moaned and keeled over. The three men then waited for a couple of minutes as Manny recovered.

Anatoly kicked him again, this time in the ribs, because he needed to get Manny Gotz's attention.

Manny gasped as Anatoly leant over him.

'Yes Mr Gotz, it's me...'the 'puppy'.

Manny Gotz just stared up at him.

'What's my name, Mr Gotz?' Anatoly suddenly asked him.

Manny looked up at him, 'You bastard' he said and he spat out the reply.

Anatoly leant across and put the barrel of his gun against Manny's kneecap, and then he pulled the trigger. There was a deafening shot and then the screaming as Manny Gotz writhed in agony. They gave him another couple of minutes to calm down and then Anatoly leant over him again.

'You have another kneecap that I can play with Mr Gotz,' said Anatoly, smiling at his victim.

'So I ask you again...what's my name?' And Anatoly waved the gun in Manny's face.

Manny Gotz lay there in distress. He'd never known suffering like this and definitely didn't want to go through it again. He looked up at Anatoly and he knew what he had to do.

'You're Anatoly...Anatoly Guberman,' he gasped.

Anatoly shook his head.

'No, no,' he replied, 'No, to you...I am 'Mr' Anatoly Guberman,' and he continued to smile down at Manny.

Manny took a deep breath. It was a sign of submission.

'Yes...you, you're name is...Mr Anatoly Guberman,' he spluttered.

Anatoly acknowledged that, and he nodded, then he took his gun and he shot Manny Gotz in the face.

Anatoly's men had already carried the barrels of turpentine into the Gotz mansion and had poured it liberally throughout the building. As they all left through the kitchen entrance, Anatoly's last job was to throw the lit match which would spark off the fire. As the kitchen burst into flames, Anatoly closed the door. They returned to the horses, got into the carriages and then drove around the block. As they passed the front of the Gotz mansion they looked on as the ground floor started to blaze. The fire would be unstoppable.

At around the same time that Manny Gotz's mansion was burning to the ground, Karazin had found exactly were Yuri Hartman lived.

He'd driven past the house a couple of times and observed.

The Ghost's house stood in its own garden and was set some way back. It was a distant sort of property, one that you could drive past and easily miss.

Karazin had stopped the horse and carriage and he tied it up about fifty yards down from the house. As he sat there he checked the time repeatedly. The evening was drawing to a close.

For an hour or so he had continued to sit there watching the house. There was only one light on and that was at the rear, it would probably be in the kitchen. Karazin sat there waiting. People were creatures of habit and again it was their routine. He knew that at some point the residents would go to bed, and that was when he would strike. When the light went out in the kitchen, a light would then be turned on in the bedroom and when that light went out he would be almost ready. He would wait another fifteen minutes or so to let the occupants fall asleep and then he would make his move.

Karazin had no intention of breaking into the house to try to kill Yuri Hartman in his bed.

No, that would be far too risky, almost foolhardy. He knew what the man was capable of.

So Karazin had chosen to burn the house down with Hartman in it. Fire caused panic and he would simply shoot dead anyone at all who survived the flames and tried to flee from the burning building.

It was that simple.

Inside the house, Yuri Hartman had spent all day reading his book while his wife had cooked and cleaned. As Yuri sat there in the warm kitchen he could smell the evening meal she was cooking.

Pork and potatoes, she always cooked pork and potatoes and luckily for her, Yuri enjoyed it. Not that he would ever praise his wife, no never, and Rachel Hartman would never expect him to. Yuri poured himself another glass of vodka, and observing this, Rachel once again refilled his mug with hot coffee.

An hour later he had eaten his meal and returned to his book and his vodka. Yuri was enthralled by what he read, he found the book fascinating and the writings were an education. Rachel had cleared away the pots and pans and had gone upstairs. It was her habit to sit in her bedroom and read a book for a while. Later she would go quietly down the stairs to the kitchen where her husband would be asleep in his chair. She would douse the kitchen lamps and then go back upstairs and extinguish her own bedroom light, only then would she would go to bed to sleep. The oil that ran the lamps was far too expensive to leave burning away all night long.

It was another routine, however this time it could also be a coincidence.

Karazin sat there and then he suddenly looked up as a light came on in the Hartman's bedroom. He waited for what seemed forever, and then he saw the kitchen light finally extinguished. The Hartman's were going to bed. Or so he thought.

A moment later the bedroom light went out too, and that was the sign that Karazin had been waiting for. He sat there for what seemed an everlasting fifteen minutes and then he made his move.

He picked up one of the barrels of turpentine from the back of the carriage and quietly carried it up the driveway to the house, and then he went back for the second barrel.

As he was walking to and fro, Karazin wondered how Anatoly and his men had handled things. There was no doubt in his mind that the attack would have been a success. Even so, Karazin had been giving the matter some thought and he was actually in a winning position. If Anatoly's attack on Gotz's mansion had been successful, Anatoly Guberman would take over and run Moscow, and Karazin would be his right hand man. If Anatoly had failed, he would have undoubtedly been killed, and Karazin would still remain Manny Gotz's golden boy. Especially after he'd rid Manny of the Ghost.

Karazin smiled to himself as he unplugged the barrels and then proceeded to pour the turpentine liberally all over the front porch of the house. He watched as the liquid ran under the front door. This was better than he expected. The turpentine was running straight into the house, and when lit the building would go up like a bonfire. He was originally going to pour the turpentine all around the house but he now realized that this method would be easier and certainly more efficient. He took the second barrel and once again emptied the turpentine over the front porch which was now almost flooded and was steadily draining under the door and into the house.

Karazin stood back as he struck a match, and then he threw it in the direction of the front door. There was a 'whoosh' as the turpentine burst into flame. He immediately stepped away from the tremendous rush of heat, and as the flames leapt up the front door he stepped back again. Then one of the lower windows suddenly turned yellow and gold as the interior of the house quickly turned into an inferno.

Karazin walked back a short distance and stood behind a tree as the house started to be consumed by the flames. As he stood there in the shadows he pulled out his gun. Anyone who staggered from the house would be quickly taken care of. He looked upwards and saw a red glow in the bedroom window. Within seconds it had turned yellow and the curtains had set alight.

Up in her bedroom Rachel died quickly. She woke up coughing as the room became engulfed with thick smoke. She struggled to get out of bed as the hot air began to choke her and in a blind panic she discovered that she couldn't find the door. The thick, black smoke enveloped her and was drawn into her lungs and Rachel Hartman's life ended very swiftly as she collapsed onto the bedroom floor. She was dead before the flames had even reached her.

Downstairs in the kitchen Yuri Hartman woke up with a jolt. Something was wrong. The natural instinct that had always worked for him had shaken him to his senses. His heart was beating and he was immediately alert. Then he smelt the smoke and he knew straightaway that the house was on fire. Yuri was no stranger to burning buildings. He instantly dropped to the floor where the smoke would be less dense and in a split second his brain began to work. His house was on fire. Why would it be on fire? There was plainly no reason.

The kitchen lamp had been doused. It always was when Rachel stayed. He knew that she always came back downstairs to douse the lamp. She was a creature of habit. He knew too that she always went back to bed, so the lamp in her bedroom was never left burning either.

The hair stood up on the back of his neck. Someone had found him.

Who could it be...and why?

Then the reality of the situation along with Yuri's sense of self preservation came into play. Someone had set fire to his house, it was the only answer, and that same someone would probably be watching, watching to make sure that he didn't get out alive.

And if they were watching, they were waiting.

Without another thought, Yuri crawled towards the kitchen door. He carefully opened it and then rolled outside. He expected to be attacked but there was no one there and that surprised him. He crawled silently across the garden and away from his burning house and he didn't stop until he got to the bushes that were part of the perimeter fence. He managed to crawl under the bushes and he slid into the garden next door. Only then did he turn around to see what had happened.

The front of the house was completely ablaze and Yuri immediately realised that Rachel was dead. He considered her death for a moment. She'd been a decent enough partner, decent in that she kept the house clean and her mouth shut. And of course she looked after their daughter. Apart from that, Yuri had no further emotion, other than the thought that someone had just destroyed one of his personal possessions.

He cast his eyes across the garden. Somebody had to be there, and whoever it was would have to make sure that he was dead, absolutely sure.

And then he saw it. Just a glimmer of a reflection, it was just for a split second, but it had been there. He'd seen a flash of yellow light. At the front of the house and away to the left he'd seen something. Then suddenly, there it was again. Only this time Yuri knew exactly what it was. The yellow light was from the fire and the reflection had come off the shiny barrel of a gun.

Yuri strained his eyes to look to the trees over in the corner of the garden and then another flash of yellow light guided him to the man who was standing behind one of those trees.

That man was an assassin and was obviously waiting to see if his work was done. Yuri realised that the man was waiting to see if anyone ran from the house and then of course, the man would shoot them. What he couldn't understand was why the assassin hadn't placed himself in a better position so as to cover the back door as well. It was an oversight, or it was over confidence. He also couldn't understand why the assassin had a shiny silver handgun.

Yuri Hartman only used guns made from dull dark steel. If need be he would rub mud or oil over a weapon or even wrap a rag around it. Anything at all that would keep it concealed.

These were strange thoughts, but it made Yuri concentrate his mind. Then suddenly, he had a plan.

Yuri silently crept along the back of the garden fence and eventually came up behind the assassin. He dropped back to his knees and without a sound slid under the bushes and back into his own garden. Slowly and noiselessly he stood up, and then he drew his hunting knife from his belt. The assassin stood there watching the house successfully burn. Not knowing for one moment that there was a Ghost standing behind him.

Karazin watched as the flames crackled. The front bedroom was ablaze. Nobody could have survived. No one had run from the house with their clothes on fire and nobody had leapt out of the window. His job was done.

He reached into his pocket for a cigar that Manny Gotz had given him. Karazin had already partially smoked it, smoked it a couple of times really. But now he could finish it off. Now he could relax. He took out a match, lit the cigar and then took a good draw on it. It smelled and tasted wonderful and Karazin smiled to himself as he thought about Manny Gotz. By now Manny Gotz would undoubtedly be dead. Karazin blew out the smoke and smiled again.

Then suddenly there was a flash of white light and a blinding pain in his head as Dmitri Karazin dropped unconsciously to the ground.

Yuri had stood there for thirty seconds, a lifetime.

He'd stood there, ten steps behind his assassin, waiting to make his move. But it had to be planned and it had to be right. Any movement or any noise at all could alert the assassin, the assassin who held a gun. The burning house cast long shadows that could be broken by any movement, even the dark grass that they were standing on could contain dried leaves or twigs that would snap underfoot. Even a reflection in the barrel that shiny gun would be a giveaway and a warning.

Yuri had just stood there with the knife in his hand and he'd watched as the assassin took a cigar out of his pocket. He'd watched him put the cigar in his mouth and then reach for a match. Now was the moment.

As the match struck, Yuri casually took five steps closer and then stopped. He'd watched as the assassin took a draw on the cigar and he knew that the man's attention would be on that first wonderful taste. With that, Yuri took the final five steps. And just as the assassin was about to exhale, Yuri raised his arm and viciously clubbed the back of the man's head with the steel butt of his knife.

The assassin dropped to the ground. He would never know what had hit him, until later.

Yuri took hold of the man's collar and dragged him from the trees and into the open garden. The garden was now lit by flames and Yuri could see everything. It was almost as bright as an autumn day.

He knelt down and took hold of the still unconscious man and rolled him over onto his back.

Yuri stopped and stared, because he couldn't believe what he saw.

The man lying on the ground in front of him was Dmitri Karazin.

Yuri Hartman recognised him straightaway because he already knew who Karazin was, and that he was in the employ of Manny Gotz.

Information was power and Yuri Hartman had always known that. Yuri used information as a tool and it provided him with the knowledge that could give him the upper hand. He took nothing for granted, nothing at all and neither did he trust anyone.

Life had taught him that lesson.

His information was sourced in two ways. It was either gleaned or it was observed and Yuri Hartman was a great observer. Manny Gotz might not have seen his Ghost for months at a time, however Yuri had made it his habit to see Manny at least once a week, though it was always from a distance and Manny never knew. For Yuri there had always been an element of mistrust with Manny Gotz. Over the years he had grown to know the man and had often wondered, if and when, this day would come. And now it had.

Keeping an eye on Manny Gotz had always been an act of self preservation. Yuri liked to know what Manny was up to and who he was mixing with, and so Yuri would keep an eye on Manny, always from a distance and always invisible.

It had been twelve months earlier when Yuri had first noticed Dmitri Karazin. Whenever Manny and Hendrik were out and about, Karazin seemed to always be there too. He hung on to Manny Gotz's tail like a faithful puppy. Yuri had made some enquiries but could find nothing about Karazin's past life. He did learn however, that Manny Gotz was using Karazin's skills quite regularly and that fact alone had always given Yuri something to think about.

And now this...this was an act of betrayal by Manny Gotz and Yuri couldn't understand why. The only possible reason could be that Yuri knew too much, and maybe that was true.

Yuri rolled Karazin back over so that he was face down and then he took out his hunting knife. It was time for him to start his work.

He took his blade and stabbed the unconscious Karazin deep into his left buttock and then he pressed down hard until he felt bone. From there he cut all the way down Karazin's leg until he reached the back of the knee joint. The knife, razor sharp as ever, made light work of severing the flesh. Yuri then punctured Karazin's right buttock and carried out the same procedure. He sliced through the muscle and the flesh, and the tendons and the ligaments. Dmitri Karazin would never be able to move his legs ever again. Neither would he ever walk again. But that wasn't going to matter.

Yuri stripped Karazin of his coat and then reached over and picked up his knife again.

He inserted the blade under Karazin's left armpit and pushed it in hard so that the knife went in under his victim's shoulder blade. Then with the skill of a trained butcher he cut all the way around the shoulder blade so that when he'd finished Karazin's arm was almost severed. He then carried out the same procedure on Karazin's right arm.

The whole process had taken less than couple of minutes. However the art to the whole thing was that Yuri never cut into any major vein or artery. That would have caused Karazin to bleed to death too quickly and Yuri Hartman didn't want that. No, definitely not.

Yuri then took a handkerchief from his pocket and stuffed into Karazin's mouth. Karazin was still mercifully unconscious, and in theory, would now die slowly.

But that wasn't going to happen either. No, definitely not.

Yuri then got to his feet and looked down at his handiwork. Karazin was totally immobile, he wouldn't be able to use his arms or legs and now he wouldn't even be able to scream.

Yuri stood there for a moment and then opened his pants, took out his cock and then pissed all over Dmitri Karazin's face.

Karazin woke and immediately tried to scream as he felt the agonizing and excruciating pain.

He shook his head wildly because that was all he could do. For a moment he couldn't understand why his arms and legs weren't working. His eyes widened as he looked up and immediately saw Yuri Hartman staring down at him, and what was left of Dmitri Karazin sagged at the realisation of what was happening. The Ghost...he was at the mercy of the Ghost.

Yuri grabbed hold of Karazin's collar and began to drag his paralysed body across the garden. The house was now well ablaze and the front of the building suddenly collapsed as the fire started to spread to the rear. Yuri continued to drag Karazin across the garden and into the smoke filled kitchen. He kicked the table over and then propped Karazin up against it so that his unfortunate victim was facing the open kitchen door. Yuri then picked up a chair which he took outside and then he sat down and looked back in at the helpless Dmitri Karazin.

Within minutes the kitchen caught fire. Karazin tried to cough but couldn't. He tried to move, but couldn't do that either. All he could do was lie there in a pool of his own blood as the kitchen began to burn. The only thing he could see was Yuri Hartman, sitting outside with his arms folded, watching. Before long the table caught fire and with it so did Dmitri Karazin. The first thing to catch fire was Karazin's hair and clothes. All he could do was shake his head over and over again as the flesh around his hairline turned red and then to a deeper brown. All he wanted to do was scream and scream again but he couldn't do that either. His shirt caught fire then his pants and he wanted desperately to shake the flames off, but he couldn't do anything because he couldn't move. All he could do was watch himself burn. The flames from Karazin's blazing shirt began to lick his face. His chest was on fire and now the flames were running up his neck and up to his already blackened head. Only his eyes showed the fear and the agony of what was happening to him. They were the eyes of a man who wanted the pain to stop and wanted the terrible, terrible pain to go way. He was a man who frantically wished that he could pass out because he wanted to die quickly, but the excruciating pain wouldn't let him.

Karazin's head shook wildly as his face suddenly caught fire and his head started to burn. The last thing he would ever see was the image of Yuri Hartman staring at him, and watching him with great interest.

Karazin's eyelids caught fire and his eyes began boil and then melt. Moments later he was dead.

Yuri stood up, he took hold of the chair and threw it into the burning kitchen. Then he slipped back into his neighbour's garden and quietly walked away as a number of people clustered around the front of the house, helpless to do anything to stop the blaze.

He walked off down the road, unseen. And now it was time for Yuri to make a decision. He had a variety of choices, and he began to think about the teachings of Sun Tzu, and then suddenly he stopped...'The book ...the damn book'.

Yuri suddenly realised that his treasured book 'The Art of War' had perished in the flames of the burning house. It was yet another possession destroyed.

And for the first time that evening, Yuri Hartman was angry and upset.

Yuri made a decision. He would go to Manny Gotz and he would kill him. He would have to ask Manny the question 'Why?' But then he would still kill him.

Yuri would enter the house through the kitchen, it was the obvious choice, he knew that.

He also knew he would have to do it tonight because if Karazin didn't report back to Manny Gotz that evening, Manny would know that Karazin had failed. He would know that Yuri was still alive and that would be an extremely dangerous threat. Manny Gotz would increase his security and surround himself with bodyguards. The job would be made harder. But Yuri would still kill him. It would just be a matter of time.

It took Yuri almost two hours to reach the Gotz mansion but when he arrived there he was dumbfounded. The building was virtually burned to the ground. The far wing of the house was still aflame and the rudimentary fire brigade of the time were still trying hopelessly to put out the remaining fire. There were men waiting to search through the still hot ashes, waiting until they could recover the bodies. More people were arriving, some of them were Gotz's own men and Yuri knew a few of them from previous days.. He spoke to some of them, they were quite subdued.

"It's all over" said one.

'What do you mean?' Yuri asked him.

'It's the St Petersburg mob, its Guberman the Jew. He's taken over, they've killed Gotz, his body must be in there somewhere,' and the man nodded in the direction of the burned mansion, 'I reckon Hendrik and the others must be in there somewhere too.'

'What are you going to do?' asked another.

The first man replied. 'I'm going to lie low for a few weeks because there could be more blood spilled. I'm going to lie low and after that I'll go to Guberman and ask him for a job. The way I look at it, we either work for one or the other. I don't care, I just need the money.'

The other men nodded in agreement.

'The King was dead...long live the King'.

Yuri walked away. He made his way back to the Stutz.

As he went up the stairs to his apartment and walked along the corridor he sawAnatoly Guberman coming out of his own apartment together with one of his men. It was time for Anatoly to speak to his father. Another of Anatoly's men had already gone to wake Arkady Guberman.

Yuri walked past Anatoly Guberman, neither of them knowing the other. But they momentarily glanced at one another as they carried on walking.

Anatoly turned to his man.

'Who was that?' he asked.

The man shrugged and replied 'probably the caretaker,'

Anatoly never gave it another thought.

It was now Anatoly Guberman's 'time'. He sat his father down and told him exactly what he'd done and exactly what had happened. Anatoly told his father about his plans for Moscow and his plans to amalgamate their crime syndicate in St Petersburg with Moscow. That would make the

Gubermans the most powerful crime family in Russia. They would have immense power.

At first Arkady Guberman was shocked, reticent even, but as his son explained his plans, Arkady became more enthusiastic. He could suddenly see the sense in it all. There was also the added bonus of Manny Gotz now being out of the way. What an arrogant and rude bastard he had turned out to be, he deserved to die.

There was still a problem though...a big problem.

'There is one difficulty that we will still somehow have to solve,' Arkady said to his son, 'and that is Gotz's man, his Ghost. He will come looking for us, I'm in no doubt of it and that man is trouble Anatoly. You don't know what he's capable of"

Anatoly Guberman smiled at his father. It was the other moment that he'd been waiting for.

'The Ghost has been taken care of father. He's dead. I've seen to that too.'

Arkady Guberman was astonished. He'd underestimated his son, greatly underestimated him. It was a moment of great triumph and Arkady knew that he would have to step back and let his son build his own empire. It was Anatoly's time to take charge. Arkady knew the feeling, because he too had been that same determined young man, many years ago.

The next day however, Anatoly Guberman wasn't feeling quite as confident, when he realised that Karazin hadn't returned home. He didn't know what had happened but he was increasingly beginning to fear the worst. Another problem was that although Karazin had the Ghost's address written down in his envelope, nobody else had read it. Anatoly remembered that Karazin had mentioned some district or other, but on that night Anatoly had been more interested in the whereabouts of the Gotz mansion and their evening's planned attack.

Anatoly Guberman was worried. He'd suddenly lost his right hand man and that alone was going to make things a whole lot more difficult. But now he had to think about the man who was the Ghost. That man was now on the loose and it was Anatoly who had just murdered his boss. Anatoly sent a message back to St Petersburg.

He would need another twenty hard men, at least.

He also decided not to inform his father.

Arkady Guberman left for St Petersburg and Anatoly quickly moved out of the Stutz. It was too high profile and if the Ghost wanted to find him there he would be easy meat. Anatoly moved to a more secure property, a large private house in the Troitsk District. The house stood openly within its own grounds, was highly visible from all sides and would be much easier to police.

Yuri himself stayed locked away in the Stutz. He was safe there and comfortable. It was time for him to look to his own future and he'd actually given it much thought. The Guberman family from St Petersburg had killed Manny Gotz and they were about to take over Manny's business interests in Moscow. He'd wondered why Manny Gotz had sent Karazin to kill him, and he decided to dismiss it all. His simple reasoning was that 'My enemy's enemy is my friend' and Yuri realised the truth of it. Manny Gotz had for some reason become the enemy.

Yuri also considered the reality of his life, he was getting older. It was maybe time to look elsewhere.

Yuri had enough money saved, enough to keep him at the Stutz for the next couple of years but after that, who knew? However there was one certainty. He never wanted to be a poor man again.

He spent the next several weeks contemplating his future but there was one nagging dilemma that kept returning to him. It could have been guilt or possibly shame, Yuri couldn't decide or even explain it. But he had one small problem, a problem that he couldn't dismiss.

And that was his daughter, his one and only child, Anna Kristen Hartman.

Yuri had never been a loving father, far from it. He actually held a great dislike of all children. However the girl was his flesh and blood and something deep inside his dark soul told him that he would have to go to her, if only to explain the death of her mother. He also reasoned that he would probably have to give her some money. He certainly didn't want her living with him there at the Stutz.

The following week he took the train north to the village and to the house where his wife and daughter lived and had lived. When he arrived at the pitifully small, run down cottage he found it empty. After making some enquiries with the neighbours it appearedd that a lawyer from

Moscow had turned up out of the blue and had spoken to Anna and had then taken her back to Moscow with him.

Yuri couldn't understand it. 'What lawyer?'

That evening Yuri searched the house, and in a bottom drawer in his wife's bedroom he stumbled across the paperwork that he was looking for. There were letters and receipts, all dating back years and all from a Mr Jozeph Kleiner of Messrs. Meltzer and Forsch, who were a firm of lawyers back in Moscow. There were receipts for monies that had been paid for what seemed like years and years.

Yuri couldn't understand it, but he smelt a rat. There was something going on and he was determined to find out what it was.

The next morning he returned to Moscow.

It didn't take Yuri long to find the building that held the offices of the old and established firm of Messrs. Meltzer and Forsch. He entered the building through some imposing double doors and then took the stairs to the first floor where the offices of Meltzer and Forsch were situated. Yuri entered the offices through a patterned glazed door to where a receptionist was sitting behind a desk, busily writing.

She glanced up at him and smiled. She seemed a pleasant young thing.

'Can I help you, sir?' she asked.

Yuri liked that, and those few words probably served to save her life.

'Yes,' replied Yuri, 'I would like to see your Mr. Kleiner, please.' He added the 'please' as a nicety.

'Can I ask you what it's about, sir?' she enquired.

Yuri was quite pleased with her attitude, she was being agreeable.

'Yes, it's family business,' he again replied.

This was all very sociable.

'Can I ask you what you're name is?" the girl asked politely.

Yuri had to think quickly.

'It's Mr Stein,' he said casually, and he smiled back at her.

The secretary stood up and went across the office to a door which had the name 'J. Kleiner' etched on it in gold letters. Yuri considered that perhaps he should have noticed that. Never mind.

The secretary knocked on the door, waited for a reply and then went in.

A moment later she returned but with a disappointed look on her face.

"I'm very sorry Mr Stein" she said "But Mr Kleiner is very busy and asks if you could make an appointment please".

Once again those good manners, but Yuri had no time for this and neither was he in the mood.

He had to think quickly.

Oh right,' he replied and then he frowned, 'The only problem is that I leave for Germany tomorrow. I have businesses in Hamburg and then I go onto Holland. I could be away for two or three months and I need to sort something out before I leave. It's in the form of a Trust.'

The mention of places 'foreign', together with the words 'businesses' and 'trust' impressed the young lady so much so that she felt she had to return to Mr Kleiner's office and repeat what she had just been told.

A few moments later she returned. She looked a little embarrassed.

'If you would like to wait Mr Stein, Mr Kleiner will see you. It's just that he's a little busy at the moment.'

She knew and Yuri knew that this was a lie and Yuri had to contain the rage that wanted to run and kick open that office door and beat Mr Jozeph Kleiner to a pulp.

However, Yuri needed the information, so he sat there and he waited, and inwardly he seethed. Nearly twenty minutes passed, twenty very long minutes and every so often the secretary would look up and smile apologetically.

She had witnessed it all before. It was Jozeph Kleiner's way of showing clients just 'who' was in control.

Eventually Kleiner's door opened and Mr Jozeph Kleiner himself finally made an appearance.

He looked across his secretary's office to where Yuri was sitting and gave a small and efficient nod of acknowledgment.

'Come this way please Mr Stein,' he said with casual authority.

The young secretary glanced at Yuri for just a second too long, then quickly returned to her papers.

Yuri stood up and went over to Kleiner's office. Kleiner had already turned and gone back inside and was sitting majestically behind his desk as Yuri walked through the door.

Yuri closed the door behind him.

'Sit down please Mr Stein,' said Kleiner and he nodded to the very obvious plain chair that was placed in front of his desk.

Yuri sat down.

Kleiner continued, 'Right Mr Stein, what is it that you actually want me to do?'

Yuri took out several of the letters together with the receipts addressed to his wife and placed them on the desk in front of Mr Jozeph Kleiner.

'I want you to explain these,' he said.

Kleiner picked up the letters and receipts and as he began to read them he frowned. He immediately put the letters back down on his desk and looked across at Yuri.

'What is this about Mr Stein?' he asked.

Yuri repeated his question. 'I want you to explain these,' he said again and he nodded towards the letters.

'I'm afraid those letters are private, Mr Stein,' said Kleiner, 'I can't discuss them with you.'

Then Kleiner paused for a moment, 'and I have to ask you Mr Stein, just how did you come by these letters? As far as I know, no one else is privy to these documents.'

'Ah,' said Yuri, 'Well you see Mr Kleiner, I am privy because I am Rachel Hartman's husband.'

Kleiner just sat there and stared back.

'But...you're dead.'

'It would appear not,' replied Yuri.

Kleiner shook his head as though trying to get his facts right. He was losing the control.

Then he suddenly thought of a response that would quickly put an end to this charade.

'So I take it that your name isn't Stein?'

'Obviously not,' replied Yuri.

'So you've lied to me Mr Stein, or Hartman, or whatever your name is,' said Kleiner, suddenly with a slight edge in his voice.

'Obviously Mr Kleiner. Yes indeed, I have lied to you,' replied Yuri. He was almost enjoying the moment.

'Get out,' Kleiner demanded, 'Get out of my office now. You've come here under false pretences and I'll have nothing further to do with you. Now go...get out.'

Yuri shrugged. He knew that it would probably come to this. So he stood up as though to leave. Kleiner just sat there with a look of disgust and anger written all over his smug face. He felt that he had won the argument.

Yuri looked down at him, almost sympathetically, but Kleiner just glowered back like the self righteous bastard he was.

Yuri turned to go, but to Kleiner's utter astonishment, he turned the wrong way. And instead of leaving the office, Yuri Hartman walked quickly around the desk and smashed his fist into Jozeph Kleiner's face. Kleiner toppled backwards off his chair and even before he hit the floor Yuri was on top of him. Once more Yuri produced a handkerchief, and he grabbed hold of Kleiner's nose and stuffed the rag deep into the solicitor's mouth.

Kleiner was completely stupefied, he was a stranger to both violence and pain.

In fact, Jozeph Kleiner had never been hit since he was a schoolboy, when he'd once been thumped by the school bully.

Shocked, gagged and with the weight of Yuri Hartman on top of him, Jozeph Kleiner suddenly entered a newer, different world. However, things were about to get worse.

Yuri then slid his knife from his belt and waved it in front of Kleiner's suddenly terrified face.

As Yuri looked down at the shocked lawyer he put his finger to his lips and whispered the word 'Sshh...'

It was an instruction. It let Kleiner know that he must lie still.

Yuri then laid the point of his knife onto Jozeph Kleiner's open eyeball. The solicitor let out a high pitched moan and but for the gag it would have been a scream.

Yuri Hartman knew his victim and saw the weakness.

It was a well known fact to Yuri. You had to find a man's personal weakness. In the past he'd dealt with and threatened much harder men, who weren't worried about being stabbed because they had been stabbed before. He'd known men who'd been stabbed in the stomach and the back and even in the hand and they'd shown no fear. There had been one man, who as Yuri Hartman's blade was cutting into his throat, had spat into Yuri's face as a final act of defiance. Yuri would always respect him.

But not this cowardly piece of shit that now lay in front of him, whimpering like a dog.

Yes, a knife pointed anywhere on Kleiner's body would cause fear. But the threat of a sharp knife being plunged directly into the eye usually terrified even the bravest of men.

Yuri spoke to him slowly and quietly.

'Mr Kleiner, you are about to tell me everything I need to know. Am I right?'

And he lifted the knife a fraction, just enough to allow the lawyer to nod.

'In a moment Mr Kleiner, I will remove the gag from your mouth. If you make one single noise, I will take out your eye. And if anyone comes through that door, I will immediately slit your throat. Okay?'

Kleiner nodded weakly.

'Another thing Mr Kleiner, if you tell me one lie or tell me something that I think is a lie, or you hold back any information at all, I will stab you in your left eye, and then in your right eye too. I'll cut out both of your eyes. You understand ...yes?'

Kleiner nodded again, this time a little more willingly.

Yuri removed the gag.

'Now then, tell me all about my wife.' he said.

Kleiner told Yuri everything.

He told Yuri about that first curious meeting with Rachel Hartman all those years ago and the strange system of payments that Rachel had set up back then. He told Yuri about his instructions as regards 'if or when' both of Anna Hartman's parents died and he told Yuri about collecting Anna and their subsequent trip to Smolensk.

Yuri was confused.

'Why Smolensk?' he asked Kleiner.

Yuri and Rachel had left there years ago and had never returned, ever.

Kleiner told Yuri about the meeting at the Schwab furniture factory with Mr Schwab himself and then about the letter of introduction. Mr Schwab was going to take care of Anna Hartman. It was an obligation.

Yuri was puzzled by these revelations. Why on earth did somebody from Smolensk be obligated to look after his daughter?

'And how would this Mr Schwab know my daughter?' asked Yuri.

'He didn't. He apparently knew your wife.'

Kleiner flinched. It was there, he'd said it. And he'd said too much.

Yuri stared down at the man.

'What do you mean by that?' he asked.

'Err, nothing, nothing. I just thought...it was nothing, nothing at all.'

But it was too late.

Yuri forcibly slammed his hand over the lawyer's mouth so as to stifle any sound. Then he placed the point of his blade right onto Kleiner's open eyeball. Kleiner tried to scream.

'You're lying to me Mr Kleiner and what did I tell you would happen if you lied?'

Kleiner nodded frantically. He now wanted more than ever to tell Yuri the truth, absolutely.

Yuri removed his hand but not the blade.

'Now you bastard,' he hissed, 'Now tell me what you know.'

It took Kleiner a moment to get his breath back and to try and contain his composure.

Not an easy thing when there is a knife pressing into your eyeball.

Kleiner would have blinked if he could, but he couldn't. He also knew that he would have to tell Yuri Hartman what he considered the truth. If not, he would be blinded for life or even worse. He was going to have to give some considered information to probably the most violent man he had ever met, and suddenly Kleiner realized the meaning and the consequences of Rachel Hartman's will. She'd had to live her life with this violence and that was what this was all about.

'I think there was possibly a relationship,' Kleiner stammered.

Yuri frowned. For a moment he had to think if his wife had any relations in Smolensk and of course she didn't.

'I don't understand you,' he replied.

Kleiner gasped for breath. He would have to say it.

'These things happen...you know what I'm trying to say.'

'Know what?' Yuri raised his voice. He didn't have the time for this.

Kleiner took another breath.

'I think that somehow it is quite possible that Anna Hartman is Ernst Schwab's daughter.'

There was silence.

Yuri had to figure this out in his head. Surely Anna was 'his' daughter, but now this man was telling him not. Then the penny suddenly dropped in Yuri Hartman's head.

His wife, she'd had an affair behind his back and she'd had a child and she'd lied, she'd lied for all those years.

Yuri Hartman suddenly felt hot and he felt uncomfortable. All those jealousies that he'd felt all those years ago suddenly returned and his temper rose as he thought about the deceit.

It had been a lifetime of deceit.

He felt the rage deep inside him and then he felt Kleiner squirm.

He had no time or use for this bastard anymore, especially now.

Yuri took the knife away from Kleiner's eye and the lawyer gave a sigh a relief. It would be the last breath he ever took. Yuri slammed his hand over Kleiner's mouth again as he reached down and pushed the knife deep into Kleiner's chest and straight into his heart. The lawyer died almost instantly. There was a look of complete shock on his staring face.

Yuri stood up and then went over to sit down on the lawyer's empty chair. He had to calm himself down, he knew he had to calm down. So he sat there for several minutes, he had to formulate a plan. In fact, he had to formulate a few plans.

He eventually stood up and went over to Kleiner's body and went through the dead lawyer's pockets. What he was looking for wasn't there.

He went back to the desk and rifled through the drawers and in the top left hand drawer he finally found it, a key. Yuri carefully and quietly tried the key in Kleiner's office door and it turned. It was a result. Yuri knew that Jozeph Kleiner would be a creature of habit. He went back to the desk and picked up some of the letters that were in the lawyer's 'out tray'. He then walked out of the office and as he turned to close the door he quickly slipped the key into the lock. His back was to the secretary and she didn't see him lock the door. He then turned around and went across to the secretary's desk, he was smiling.

'Thank you for everything,' he said to her.

'Was everything okay?' she asked, again very politely.

'Oh yes,' replied Yuri, 'although it's all a bit complex. I'm afraid I've left you're Mr Kleiner with quite a lot of work to do.'

The secretary smiled again. She was a lovely girl.

'Oh yes,' said Yuri suddenly, as though he'd forgotten something. 'Mr Kleiner asked me to give you these letters. He wants you to post them off... apparently 'right away'. He says they're important and he needs to clear his desk.'

The secretary took the letters and looked up at the clock.

'I'll take them to the post office now,' she said efficiently, 'It's time for my lunch anyway,' and with that she stood up to get her coat.

Yuri smiled back at her and nodded curtly as he turned and left the office and then the building.

When she returned from her lunch Mr Kleiner's secretary would at some point in the afternoon need to speak to her boss. But when she knocked on his door and got no reply and then discovered that the door was locked, she would undoubtedly presume that her boss was having a late lunch or had simply decided to go home.

As Yuri walked away from Messrs. Meltzer and Forsch he considered the outcome of his actions.

It could take one day, or it could take four days.

If Mr Kleiner had a family and didn't return home from work that evening then the family would contact Meltzer and Forsch the very next day. If however Kleiner lived alone, his first day's absence would be taken as illness and the second day too. By the third day there would be some sort of concern as the office tried to contact him, and by the fourth day it would be time to break down the door. That action may of course be accelerated, because of the smell emanating from a corpse that had lain in a nice warm office for four long days.

Yuri returned to the Stutz where he spent a day of angry contemplation. That 'bitch' of a wife had played him for a fool. All those years and she'd been laughing at him behind his back.

Someone would have to pay.

The next morning Yuri arrived early at Moscow's Rijskiy Train Station. He immediately got on the first available train, the train that would take him back to Smolensk.

As the train rattled south Yuri sat there brooding. He tried to speculate as to what had gone on and what had occurred to put him in the position he now found himself. He sat there silently for a while, then he pulled out his faithful bottle of vodka from the inside pocket of his thick coat, and as he sat there he wondered.

Everyone was dead. The Gotz family were dead and Rachel was now dead. Everyone was dead but his daughter. But she wasn't his daughter, or was she?

He would have to sort something out, he would have to find out about her, somehow.

Yuri had given the subject some thought. He only had Kleiner's words on the matter and Kleiner could have been wrong of course, but then there was also the matter of the will that his wife had written and paid for...for years. Something definitely wasn't right and there were things that Yuri Hartman needed to know.

There was also another slight problem, and that was his loss of earnings now that Manny Gotz was dead. Yuri had money stashed away for one or maybe two years, but after that his funds would start to dwindle and Yuri realised that he was no longer a young man. With that thought in mind he also recognised the fact that he didn't want to become an old man who had to struggle with poverty. Not him, not Yuri Hartman.

He needed a lot of money and quickly. He needed a rather large nest egg to fall back on because he'd become used to living in the comfort and the luxury of the Stutz, together with his collection of books. That standard of living was the one thing in his life that he didn't want to lose.

He sat there deep in thought for quite a while, and then from nowhere at all, a thought occurred to him. It was another possibility, another plan.

For hours the train trundled on and eventually, after he'd consumed about half the bottle of vodka, Yuri decided to get up and go to the toilet, which was at the end of the next carriage. He suddenly felt the need to relieve himself and so he stood up and walked back between the rows of seats. He observed everybody and nobody as he walked through the carriage. There didn't appear to be anyone who was a threat, they were all just common everyday people going about their everyday business. He entered the second carriage, at the end was the toilet which was small and basic but functional. He went through to see if it was empty and just as he was about to reach for the door handle, a large hand grabbed the side of his face and pushed him out of the way. A huge bear of a man had shoved

Yuri sideways, almost knocking him over. The man looked down at Yuri, he had dark brown hair sticking out from a thick woollen cap and a thick black beard to match.

'You can piss out of the carriage door,' he said to Yuri, and then he nodded towards the toilet, 'I need a crap.'

With that said he again pushed Yuri sideways, and almost as a matter of course he manoeuvred himself into the small toilet compartment and then slammed the toilet door shut.

It had only been a matter of a few seconds, but it made Yuri suddenly realise how vulnerable he had been and also his slowness to react. He was getting careless and he blamed the vodka. The man could have been yet another assassin. He could have been some half wit, half paid fool with a knife, and the man could have murdered him.

Yuri stood there for a moment. He would have to do better.

He would have to do so much better.

So Yuri took a deep breath. He counted to ten and then he reached forward and opened the carriage door and he stood there as the wind and the noise from the train suddenly invaded the toilet compartment. A couple of minutes later he heard the toilet door handle turn. And as the door opened Yuri stepped back and his right hand felt for the hunting knife that was always strapped to his belt, the knife that was his truest friend.

The big man emerged from the toilet and as he exited he heard the rush of wind and saw that the carriage door was swinging open. He grinned to himself when he saw Yuri still standing there.

'If you need more than a piss it's all yours, now,' he said and he laughed at Yuri.

At that moment Yuri Hartman leapt forward and punched the knife into the man's chest three times. The man staggered backwards and big as he was, Yuri had inflicted three mortally wounding blows. On the rebound from the third blow Yuri drew his knife from the man's huge chest and with one fluid motion he swung the knife in an upwards arc and stabbed the man under his chin, the blade went straight up through his mouth and into the base of his brain. The man was instantly paralysed.

As he withdrew the knife, Yuri twisted the blade in order to cause the most possible damage, and as he extracted the knife the blade caught the man's jugular artery and his blood spewed out like a tap. Because of his bulk the man just stood there, astounded at what was happening to him. And his final recognition that his life was over was when Yuri grabbed hold of his head and whispered in the man's ear.

'You should have let me piss,' he said, and then he pushed the man's huge bulk straight out through the flailing carriage door.

The man just disappeared and would most likely remain that way until some unsuspecting farmer discovered his rotting body, probably during the following spring. And that was only if the local wildlife had left anything other than a few bones for anyone to find.

As he walked back to his seat, Yuri did the numbers. Three stabs, three seconds, the slash to the throat, maybe another two or three seconds and then the brief but final 'little chat', that would be another couple of seconds, maybe even three. Then he'd pushed the fat bastard out through the carriage door, another two seconds at most. So roughly ten seconds in all, and he'd removed a man from history.

Yuri smiled to himself. Not bad for an aging assassin, not bad at all.

The train finally arrived in Smolensk later that afternoon and Yuri found a small hotel within a short walking distance. He booked himself in there for a week but doubted if he would be staying there that long. From there he made enquiries and soon found the whereabouts of the Schwab Furniture Factory. It wasn't hard since the company was very well known throughout Smolensk.

Yuri arrived at the factory late in the afternoon. What bit of sun there was had all but disappeared and it was beginning to go dark.

When he finally arrived he recognised the factory immediately. His wife had worked in the baker's shop which was still there on the corner. It was another piece of the jigsaw.

So Yuri watched and he waited, because that was what he did.

He saw the day come to a close at the factory and watched as some of the men left and went home and he saw the others go to their quarters. Those were the men who lived, ate and slept at the factory. The factory was their home. That was the way of things in old Russia.

At around six o'clock two women walked out of the factory gates. Even though it was dark by then, from where he stood across the road Yuri could see that one of the women was older and the other quite young. He thought they were probably mother and daughter until they walked past. It was only then that he saw the young girl's profile and his heart began to beat a little faster. It was the face, the face he would know anywhere. She was the double of her mother. It was Anna.

He turned and started to follow them, all the way home to Mrs Kausky's house. Anna had been living with Mr Schwab's elderly secretary until some accommodation could be found for her. It wasn't a problem.

Yuri noted where they were living and then he walked back to Schwab's Furnishings.

He slipped into the factory unseen and silently made his way around the yard so that he could understand the layout of the place. He finally went into the main factory building and moved cautiously between the industrial lathes and the saws and the high stacks of timber. Suddenly, he stopped. There was someone there. Yuri stepped back and slowly walked around some more piles of timber, then he moved forward again. When he reached the corner he carefully peered around it. There at the end of the factory a man was still working at his desk. It was Koenig the factory manager, working late as usual.

Yuri would wait, he could do that. It was the practised art of an assassin.

He looked to his right and he saw the stairs leading up to Ernst Schwab's office. The light was still on in there too and Yuri was correct in his assumption that the owner, Mr Schwab, was also working late. Yes, he could wait.

As he stood there between the different stacks of wood he took in the smells of the factory and realised that he must have been standing next to a pile of cedar wood. He inhaled its wonderful aroma, the smell was almost intoxicating and reminded him somehow of Manny Gotz. The makers of the best gentlemen's Eau de Cologne used cedar wood essence as one of its main ingredients. Manny Gotz used to use some kind of expensive Eau de Cologne and the smell would always linger in his office. It was something that Yuri would never consider using, because an odour was just like a movement or a sound. It could give you away and it could compromise your position. Stealth was never an option, it was a necessity.

Yuri waited patiently and at times such as these would think about his past. It was a good way of passing the time. As he leant quietly against the stack of timber, he began to think about the people that he'd killed.

The first person he ever murdered was his school friend Fredrik...Poor little Fredrik.

He and Yuri had been chums up to the age of ten, which was when Fredrik had suddenly decided that he wasn't going to share his lunch with Yuri anymore. Every day, Fredrik's mother would pack him some salami and some biscuits for his lunch at school. She tied the food up in a scarf, it was all very nice. Yuri's mother of course, made him nothing. In fact, he was lucky to get fed at all. So he'd befriended Fredrik and at lunchtimes Yuri would beg him for a little piece of salami or half a biscuit. One particular morning on their way to school both boys had walked across the fields as usual and they'd stopped on the bridge that overlooked the local river. It was their habit to throw small stones into the river below and gaze down into its flowing waters.

Yuri was hungry, very hungry indeed. When he'd arrived home from school the previous day his mother was in bed drunk, and there was no food at all in the house. She was still in bed the following morning and Yuri still hadn't eaten a thing.

As both boys played on the bridge, Yuri's thoughts turned to the lunch that Fredrik had wrapped up in his school satchel. So without further ado, he tried to explain to Fredrik why he was so hungry and he asked his best friend for some of his food. Fredrik refused, he wanted to eat at lunchtime. Fredrik of course had already eaten a decent breakfast. Unfortunately, the boys ended up in an argument which turned into a bit of a tussle. And in a fit of temper, Yuri grabbed Fredrik's satchel and threw it over the bridge. Luckily it landed on the riverbank below. But Fredrik was so angry, that he gave Yuri a wallop in the face which knocked the boy to the floor and made him cry.

Fredrik then leant over the bridge and spotted his satchel down on the riverbank. So he went around the side of the bridge and made his way carefully down to the river. Yuri followed, and he was sobbing as he tried to apologize, but Fredrik was having none of it. Fredrik started to shout at him and told Yuri that they were no longer friends. Yuri was devastated. Now he would have no friends and no food and he couldn't stand it. As Fredrik knelt down to pick up his satchel, Yuri looked around for a stone that he could manage to pick up in his small hand. He found one, picked it up and smashed it over Fredrik's little blonde head. Fredrik fell over screaming, so Yuri hit him over the head again twice, this time to shut him up.

Poor Fredrik, he died right there and then. Yuri sat himself down on the riverbank and opened the satchel. He ate the food ravenously because he was starving. As he ate he looked down at Fredrik. His blonde hair was now red with blood but apart from that he looked quite peaceful.

Yuri Hartman was only ten years old at the time but he realised that he would be in trouble over his actions. Even at the tender age of ten Yuri was already starting to think things out. He needed a plan, he would always need a plan and this was where it all started. Yuri finished the salami and the biscuits and then threw the satchel into the flowing river. He stood there for a while and watched as it rapidly floated away. He then went over to Fredrik's body and rolled Fredrik into the water too. Yuri stood there for a few minutes as his friend slowly disappeared around the river's bend. Then he ran, and ran like he'd never done before in his whole life. He ran all the way to the school at full pelt. Yuri ran straight into the classroom where his teacher was getting ready to start the day's lessons. He ran in there screaming and breathless, very upset and panting. He told the teacher that he and Fredrik had been playing on the bridge and that Fredrik had climbed up onto the side of the bridge and had fallen over the edge. At that point Yuri was crying hysterically.

The teacher raised the alarm and the local men went out to search the river and found Fredrik's body late that afternoon. He was found floating between some tall river reeds.

It was nothing more than a tragedy.

Yes, even from that early age Yuri Hartman had found it quite natural to live his life in a world full of violence. He was almost born to it.

Standing there in the quiet shadows of the Schwab factory, Yuri tried to remember the others that he'd killed but found that he couldn't even remember half of them. For him it was just a job, it was how he earned a living. After all he was only carrying out somebody else's orders. If he didn't do it, well, somebody else certainly would. During his professional career, Yuri had rarely killed for retribution. However, all that was about to change.

As Yuri stood there he thought about the two people whose throats he could have willingly ripped out. One was Manny Gotz. After years of loyal service that bastard had turned on him and would have happily seen Yuri dead and buried. The second was his wife, Rachel. And Yuri started to grimace as he thought of the years of lies and deceit.

The utter treachery from the pair of them began to make Yuri Hartman's blood boil.

Another hour passed by but Yuri didn't care. It just gave him more time think about what he was going to say to his new friend, Mr Schwab.

Koenig finally stood up, his working day now at an end. He folded some papers and collected some others and made his way to Mr Schwab's office. Yuri stood back as Koenig walked right past him and went up the stairs to see Mr Schwab. Several minutes later Koenig came back down the stairs scratching his head, he was checking some figures that he didn't seem to understand. In the end he dropped the papers back onto his desk and grabbed his hat and coat and walked briskly out of the factory.

Yuri watched him go and then waited for several minutes. Now was the right time.

He walked out from behind the stacks of timber and went directly up the stairs and into the office. Without knocking or waiting, Yuri opened the door and walked straight in.

He didn't bother to close the door behind him, and that was perhaps a mistake.

Sitting there behind his desk was Ernst Schwab.

With his wife's adultery in mind, whatever picture of virility Yuri Hartman had conjured up in his brain, the man sitting in front of him certainly wasn't it. Tall, thin and bald, Ernst Schwab just sat there looking at Yuri curiously.

In a slightly indignant voice Ernst Schwab asked, 'Can I help you?'

'Ah Mr Schwab,' Yuri replied, 'Yes, I think you can.' and with that Yuri pulled up a chair and sat himself down.

Schwab was rather confused. Nor was he too happy with this stranger's attitude.

'What do you actually want Mr...What is your name please?' asked Schwab.

'Ah, quick and to the point Mr Schwab, I like that,' Yuri responded, and then he leant back in the chair.

'You see Mr Schwab, I'm at rather a disadvantage. Would you believe it that up until a day ago I'd never even heard of you? However Mr Schwab, it seems that you've known all about me for years and years".

Schwab was now even more confused.

'Who exactly are you?' he demanded.

Yuri slid the hunting knife from his belt and placed the razor sharp blade on top of the desk.

Schwab's eyes widened as he looked down at the weapon. This was something that he didn't understand and a hundred questions went through his head, but not one answer.

He looked back at Yuri.

'What do you want?' he asked.

'Oh, I want plenty Mr Schwab, I want plenty. But first of all I think that I should introduce myself.'

Schwab just stared at him.

'My name...is Yuri Hartman. And I believe that at one time Mr Schwab, you used to fuck my wife.'

Ernst Schwab went rigid in his chair.

His mouth suddenly felt dry and he almost started to twitch. But there were no words, there was nothing at all for him to say. Schwab then felt physically sick as he realised that he was probably going to die. The knife in front of him, when wielded by Yuri Hartman was going to stab, cut and slash him to death. Schwab had always known about Yuri Harman and he also knew the sadistic nature of the man and what he was capable of.

'Are you...are you going to kill me?' Schwab asked, almost naively.

'Well, we'll have to see about that,' replied Yuri, 'because now it's not just about you is it?

Now there's also the question of our 'little' Anna.'

Schwab's heart nearly stopped.

All he could say was 'No, no...Please no.'

'Ah, but...yes, yes.' replied Yuri.

He then continued. 'So, Mr Schwab...you took my wife and you fucked her, whilst all along knowing that she was a married woman. You did, didn't you Schwab?'

Ernst Schwab felt like weeping but he was too scared.

He just nodded at Yuri.

Yes he'd known she was married, of course he had, but it didn't seem to matter at the time.

But now, suddenly, it did.

Yuri continued once more, 'So you fucked my wife and then you got her pregnant. Am I right?'

Schwab again nodded, and there it was, at that moment Yuri Hartman had all the evidence he needed.

Yuri stood up as he felt the blood rise in his veins and the rage...oh yes the rage.

In his mind he was about to leap over the desk and hack the bastard to death. He was going to stick his knife down into Schwab's mouth and rip out his tongue and then another thousand things besides. His brain was pulsating, Yuri was about to go into a frenzy.

Schwab sat there and saw the change in Hartman and he nearly fell backwards off his chair in fear. The man was turning into a raging animal right in front of him and Schwab knew that he was going to die.

Then Yuri heard his own voice, a voice from inside his head.

'No Yuri...Stop it ...Don't do this, stop right now and calm yourself down Yuri. Think about it...think about your plans.'

It was a warning. It was a message to Yuri's brain. This was not the plan, this was definitely not the plan.

Yuri stopped. He tried to catch his breath. And then he did catch his breath and he steadied himself.

'Get clever Yuri,' he said to himself, 'get clever".

And he once again looked down at the terrified figure of Ernst Schwab.

'We need to talk Schwab,' he said, smiling.

Ernst Schwab just sat there trembling with fear.

Yuri Hartman stared down at him.

'So Mr Schwab, you had an affair with my wife, even though you knew that she was married to me. Then you got her pregnant and for all these years you and my wife continued to let me think that Anna was my daughter, and now I find out that she isn't.'

Yuri continued to stare at Schwab. 'Am I right?'

Schwab just sat there and nodded. It was a capitulation of the truth.

'So tell me, who is the dishonest person here, Mr Schwab?' Yuri asked.

The memories of Rachel flashed through Ernst Schwab's mind, but there was only one answer to Yuri's question.

I am Mr Hartman. I am the dishonest person,' he said sadly.

'That's right Mr Schwab, you are the dishonest person. Now we've got that out of the way and now that we both agree that I've been wronged, it's time for you to pay Mr Schwab. And you are going to pay dearly.'

Schwab looked at the knife again. 'Are you going to kill me?' he asked.

Yuri smiled, 'Oh no Mr Schwab, it's nothing like that. However, the way I see it is that I've had to look after young Anna for sixteen years, and that's sixteen years of my life and sixteen years of my time, plus the emotional stress that I am now suffering. All this has cost me Mr Schwab, it has cost me a lot. And now I shall want paying for all my effort and hard work.'

Schwab blinked. Hartman was actually offering him his life back and for what...Money?'

Was this all about money? Yes it was, of course it was.

Schwab knew immediately that he would have to pay, and he would pay. Just to get Yuri Hartman out of his life.

Schwab gulped. 'How much do you want Mr Hartman?'

Yuri stared back at Ernst Schwab.

'I want a million roubles Mr Schwab. I want a million roubles and I want it quickly.'

Schwab stopped for a moment and he swallowed.

'I don't have that kind of money. I...I don't have it,' he stuttered.

'Well you're going to have to find it Schwab. You're going to have to go and ask your friendly bank manager for it or you're going to have to steal it. I don't care what you do, but there's one thing for sure Schwab. That's the amount you're going to have to pay me.'

'But it would bankrupt me,' Schwab tried to explain.

Yuri shook his head, 'You arrogant bastard Schwab. Do you think I'm bothered? You've lived well for all these years, along with your dirty little secret, and you think I'm bothered? And now you've got my 'bastard' daughter under your roof and you're quibbling about some fucking amount of money.'

Yuri was getting angry again. He'd had enough of Ernst Schwab.

'Listen to me Schwab, because this is what is going to happen. Tonight, before I came to see you, I followed Anna and an older woman all the way home. So now I know exactly where they live.'

Schwab's eyes widened when he heard that information.

Yuri continued. 'So I'm going to leave here now and I'm going to go back to their house. I'll stay there for two days. While I'm there I'm going to tie them to their beds. You will have two days to bring the money to me. After that I will slash the old woman to pieces. Then I'll move on to Anna. She's now your little Ann, and she'll be tied to the bed and that will be very inviting. She's such a pretty little thing. She's actually the double of her mother, and I used to have a lot of fun with her mother's body, but so did you no doubt. You see Schwab, little Anna's not my daughter anymore, she's your daughter, and she's now your flesh and blood, not mine. She's nothing to do with me anymore, and I'm now quite happy to rape her in the most terrible way while she's still tied to the bed. In fact Schwab, I'm quite looking forward to it. I used to rape her mother you see, and that was just wonderful, and now it looks like I'm going to be able to do the same again, if you see what I mean. They're both so very much alike. The only thing is that this time when I've finished raping her, I'll slit her throat wide open. And that will be fun too.'

Ernst Schwab shuddered in horror as he listened to Yuri Hartman's threat.

'And then Mr Schwab, I'll be coming for you, and once I've killed you I'm going to burn your precious factory to the ground.'

Yuri smiled. He'd managed to say it all. Well, everything that needed to be said.

Schwab sat there, stunned and in shock. The very thought of anything violent happening to his beautiful daughter upset him so much that it almost made him vomit. He wanted to weep. And there was Mrs Kausky too, and the factory and himself. Everything was going to be destroyed, everything and all because of this animal, this Yuri Hartman. Rachel had told Schwab what her husband was capable of but Schwab really had no idea.

No, not this.

'I ... I'll get you the money,' Schwab stuttered, 'Somehow I'll get you the money. Just please, please don't hurt Anna".

Schwab had to bite his lip, he'd nearly said 'My Anna' but he knew that could throw Hartman into another rage and he surely to god didn't want that.

'Two days Schwab...just two days,' said Yuri. The threat was there and now firmly in place.

Yuri Hartman then turned and walked out through the open door. He went down the stairs and proceeded to walk through the factory building. He had things to do. He would go at once to the house were Anna and the old woman lived. He would kill the old woman immediately of course. Then he was definitely going to tie Anna to the bed and rape her straightaway, and that would only be the first time. All that talk about raping her as he was threatening Schwab had somehow stirred him and now he was eager and ready. He remembered the acts he'd performed on Rachel and he wondered if this was going to be as pleasurable. He would have two days to find out.

It had been a long time since he'd felt like this, a very long time.

Yuri had decided that once Schwab turned up with the money he would drag him in through the open door and cut his throat, or maybe something a bit slower. He would have to make his mind up on that one. That 'bastard' Schwab had a lot to answer for, he'd had his filthy hands all over Rachel and for that he would definitely have to pay. Suddenly Yuri had an idea. Yes, the first thing he would do would be to cut off Schwab's dirty, filthy hands and then he would torture him badly. And after he'd finally killed Schwab, he would go upstairs to Anna and then he would kill her too. If he hadn't done it already.

As he walked through the factory, Yuri once again he thought about Anna, and it was those thoughts that made him momentarily lose his concentration and with it his natural awareness. He felt the movement in the air, it was immediate and Yuri started to turn as he heard the 'swish' coming towards him. Every instinct in his body told him to duck and drop to the floor. But it was too late.

For an instant, Yuri saw a split second of absolutely blinding white light. For him it was even brighter than the sun. That flash of light was then followed by a moment of agonizing pain as his skull was crushed and he collapsed to the floor.

After a lifetime of murdering the innocent and the guilty, Yuri Hartman's time had finally come.

The 'Ghost'...Yuri Hartman, was finally dead.

A man stepped out of the darkness. He had been standing behind one of the stacks of timber and he'd been waiting. In his hand he held an oblong length of wood, it was about a metre long and would eventually be turned on one of the factory lathes to become a table leg. The man had smashed it down onto Yuri Hartman's head, edge first. He didn't want to simply knock Yuri Hartman out. No, he wanted to kill him. Using all his strength he had hit Hartman knowing that the sharp edge of that piece of wood would chop through the bone and crush Yuri's skull.

The man leant down and took hold of Yuri Hartman's collar and then dragged the lifeless body back into the darkness. He knew exactly where he could hide a body in this factory.

Well he would. After all, he ran the place.

It was Koenig.

Coincidences, sometimes they can change a life.

That evening when he'd finished his work, Koenig had taken some figures up to Mr Schwab for him to check and sign. They were estimates. Unfortunately the figures were wrong, because the price of the imported timber they were using had risen by three percent. Mr Schwab apologized, he thought he'd already told his manager about the price rise but it turned out that he hadn't and now all the figures were wrong. A wasted afternoon's work for Koenig, who was justifiably annoyed but as usual said nothing. Mr Schwab had apologised profusely and told Koenig to go home and not to worry. Koenig took him at his word and decided to go home. After all, he was tired. So he'd left the factory and was making his way home. However Koenig being Koenig, the figures began to play on his mind. He knew that he had other jobs to attend to the following day, other equally important jobs and having to do those figures again would set him behind. Koenig also knew that when things played on his mind he couldn't sleep. He knew he would be kept awake most of the night and the next day he would be exhausted. It had happened before.

So after walking for five or so minutes, he turned around and made his way back to the factory. He was trying to make the decision on whether to pick up the papers and take them home with him, or should he stay at the factory and do the work there. He finally decided to do the paperwork at the factory. The factory was warm, and his house would be cold. If he went home he would have to cook something but at the factory he could get Kibble, his foreman, to make him a meal. Living on his own wasn't much fun and he often wondered about asking Mr Schwab if he could sort out some separate living accommodation there at the factory. He obviously couldn't live in the worker's quarters, after all, he was the manager.

With all those thoughts running through his head, Koenig walked back into the main factory building and it was at that precise moment he saw something move.

A man had stepped out from behind a stack of timber and he was walking toward the stairs that led to Mr Schwab's office. Koenig stood there and watched as the man walked straight into the office without even knocking. Something was wrong. Koenig moved quickly, he went to the foot of stairs and then crept up them silently. The stairs didn't creak, Koenig had personally overseen their construction several years before, and anything at all that was made in the Schwab factory certainly did not 'creak'.

In his haste, the man had left the office door wide open and Koenig heard it all.

When the man had picked up the knife in anger, Koenig had readied himself to charge in there and suffer the consequences. However the man had eventually calmed down and Koenig listened to the threats and the blackmail and when he heard who Anna actually was, everything started to slot together.

The one thing that Koenig did know was that this bastard wouldn't be happy with just the money. This man wanted revenge. This man wanted bloodshed and destruction and the bankrupting of the company. But when the man spoke of his plans to burn the factory down, Koenig made a decision. Schwab's Furnishings was his life and Koenig was prepared defend it with his life. Nobody but nobody was going to touch his beloved factory.

So Koenig had stepped away and had gone back down the stairs where he found himself the right piece of timber. He knew where it was. He knew where everything was.

He had gone back and had waited in the darkness. As the man started to come down the stairs, Koenig had already raised his 'club'. The man walked straight past him and it took exactly one second for Koenig to heave the club with all his might and smash it down onto the man's skull. It all happened so fast that the man didn't utter a sound. The only noise was the dull crunch of broken bone as the hard timber made contact. Yuri Hartman's body had just slumped to the floor.

In a past life, a much younger Koenig had served for ten years in the Russian army. It was a brutally tough existence. He had been well trained and had seen death on many fronts. He'd had to kill or be killed. And Koenig knew exactly what it took to kill a man.

Several minutes passed and Koenig stayed there in the darkness. It wasn't long before a very worried Mr Schwab almost dashed out of his office and quickly made his way home. Koenig felt sorry for him, Mr Schwab had always been a good man and didn't deserve this.

Not one bit.

Koenig waited for another ten minutes and then he dragged the body around to the furnace room.

The working heart of the Schwab factory was the furnace. All the machinery in the factory and all the heating ran from the steam and the hot water that the furnace produced. It was an enormous steel affair that ran on a never ending supply of waste timber and was backed up with industrial coal and coke. Every evening the furnace was charged with slow burning coke that would continue to burn all night long. The furnace was never allowed to go out and it was in continual use for every single day of the year.

Koenig opened the huge steel door to the furnace's fire box and stood back as the heat and flames burst out. He pulled Yuri Hartman's body onto the small cart that was used to tip the wood, coal or coke into the flames. Koenig simply tipped the body into the red hot furnace, and then he closed the door and let it burn. He left it the best part of an hour and he stood there as the sickly smell of burning flesh spread throughout the building. An hour later he opened the furnace door again and raked out the skull and the larger bones which were now burned and charcoal black. He once again took his wooden 'club' and smashed the skull and the other bones into smaller and unrecognizable pieces. Then he tossed them back into the fire. They would soon become undistinguishable from the pig bones and the other animal waste that Kibble threw into the furnace every day.

Koenig turned around and made his way home. He would have to do his paperwork tomorrow.

The next morning Ernst Schwab went back to his factory. It was early, very early.

He'd not slept, he hadn't wanted to. All through the night and into the early morning he'd scribbled numbers down on sheets of paper. He could do it, together with some help from the bank and he could do it. It would mean him selling his house, but that didn't matter. He had to pay Hartman, he had to get rid of him. The house was a small price to pay, even more when he thought about Anna, Anna and Rachel, and poor Mrs Kausky.

He'd gone into work early to sort out some papers and look at the securities that he would need to take to the bank with him. He would go to the bank later that morning and talk to the manager about 'expanding the business'. He couldn't just ask for a million roubles, the manager would be suspicious, he wouldn't hear of it, and then everything would be a total disaster.

Schwab had completely lost track of the time, when suddenly there was a familiar knock on his office door, he looked up in shock and bewilderment

And Mrs Kausky popped her head around the door.

'Good morning Mr Schwab, Anna's just putting the coffee on for you.'

Schwab just stared at her. It was as though he'd seen a ghost.

Mrs Kausky looked back at her boss.

'Is everything alright Mr Schwab?' she asked.

Schwab couldn't understand what was happening.

'You...Mrs Kausky, you're here.'

'Yes Mr Schwab.'

'And Anna is with you?'

"Yes of course Mr Schwab, she's making the coffee.'

Schwab was desperate now, 'Mrs Kausky. Did a man come to your house last night?'

Mrs Kausky was puzzled.

'No Mr Schwab.'

'You're sure Mrs Kausky? Now listen to me, this is very serious. Did you go out last night? Were you both out at anytime last night?'

The tone of Schwab's voice was now giving her some concern.

'No Mr Schwab, we stayed in all night. What's all this about?'

At that point Ernst Schwab thought that his mind was going to explode. He ran his hands over the top of his head and his eyes widened as he stared down at his desk. He had to think clearly.

'Mr Schwab, what on earth is wrong?'

Schwab quickly looked up.

'Go to Anna and tell her to leave the coffee. And then Mrs Kausky, I want you to come back in here immediately.'

Mrs Kausky saw the panic on his face and almost dashed out of the office. A few seconds later she returned.

Schwab sat her down and told her everything, every single detail.

Mrs Kausky sat there with her hands to her face. She was horrified.

'What are we going to do Mr Schwab, what are we going to do?' There was an understandable panic in her voice.

Schwab twitched and fumbled. What to do? What was he going to do? He stared around the room. Then suddenly he had the answer.

He went over to the office safe, opened it and took out a dark blue cotton bag. It was full of money. He turned to Mrs Kausky and gave her the bag.

'You must both go to Moscow straightaway. When you get there, book yourself into the Timor Hotel. I've stayed there before. You must both stay at that hotel until I come for you.'

'What should I tell Anna?' asked Mrs Kausky.

'Tell her anything. Tell her that I've decided to treat you both to some new clothes and a short break. Tell her that I'm coming over to Moscow next week for a conference. Tell her anything at all. But you mustn't go back home, he could be there waiting for you.'

Mrs Kausky visibly shuddered.

Schwab looked at the office clock.

'I'll get Koenig to take you to the train station.'

'What about you Mr Schwab? What about you?'

'Never mind about me,' he told her, 'I'll sort something out. I'll find a way to pay him the money. I just need to get you both safe and out of harm's way.'

And that was it. Koenig took them both to the train station. Strangely, he never asked Mrs Kausky any questions or even the reason why. In fact, Mrs Kausky found him rather quiet.

It took four weeks before Schwab dared to go to the Timor Hotel in Moscow and then he brought them both back to Smolensk.

To Schwab's utter amazement Yuri Hartman never returned. He just never came back.

Schwab would never understand it.

And he would never know the reason why.

CHAPTER 7

Back to the present time.

It was Saturday morning and Sarah Lawton was feeling quite excited.

Two weeks had passed since Sarah's husband, John Lawton, had discovered the mysterious opal ring hidden away in the roof cavity of a house which was due for demolition.

She and John had taken the ring to be valued at the local jewellers, Lancaster's Jewellers in the town centre.

They had both been quite amazed by the reaction of the owner Mr Paul Lancaster when he'd been shown the ring. The ring had intrigued him. It was such a wonderful piece of jewellery.

Paul Lancaster had in turn taken the ring and shown it to his retired father. Old Harry Lancaster's lifetime hobby was antique jewellery. He was most knowledgeable on the subject and had immediately recognized the work of the master craftsman who had made this quite remarkable opal ring.

So on that sunny Saturday morning John and Sarah made their way down to the town centre to Lancaster's Jewellers. They had decided to walk there. Even though Sarah was blind, she really did enjoy walking with her husband. John would link her arm and describe all and everything around them as they walked. For Sarah it was a treat. She was stuck in the house all day long, usually on her own, and to go for a walk outside and feel the sun on her skin was a delight.

They entered the jeweller's shop at around eleven o' clock and straightaway walked over to the reception desk. The young girl there

275

remembered them and immediately picked up the telephone and rang upstairs to Paul Lancaster's office. A couple of minutes later the upstairs office door opened and Paul Lancaster and his father, Harry, came out of the office and down the stairs to greet John and Sarah.

Coffee was ordered and the four of them made their way into a small viewing room where they could have a bit of privacy.

The coffee arrived and they all sat down at a small desk which was covered in dark blue felt. The dark felt was used as a contrast, and it helped to display the jewellery, especially the diamond rings. Small but powerful spotlights shone down from the ceiling so as to enhance the colour and cut of the diamonds and bring out their natural beauty.

Paul Lancaster produced the small black box that contained the opal ring. He opened the box and the light from the spotlights hit the opal and the diamonds and the ring lit up, shimmering under the bright lights.

For a moment, John Lawton held his breath, and then he smiled. He had almost forgotten the beauty of it. The ring was almost hypnotic.

'My God,' he said, 'It's absolutely stunning,' and he held Sarah's hand. Sarah smiled.

'It certainly is Mr Lawton,' replied Harry Lancaster, 'It's a beauty. It's actually one of the finest opals that I have ever seen.'

John nodded.

'My father has had a look at the ring,' said Paul Lancaster, 'and he thinks he remembers it.'

Harry Lancaster smiled at John and Sarah.

'Yes I do. It must be over fifty years ago, but I can still remember this ring. You never do forget a really beautiful piece of jewellery. I remember seeing it in a catalogue all those years ago and I was so impressed with it, even back then. When the jewellery trade in London had something out of the ordinary, something like this, it was often catalogued and offered to a few of the more prominent regional jewellers. There was always the possibility that one of the regionals may have had a wealthy client on their books. Someone who could afford something a little bit special.

Anyway, that was back then and back in those days the ring would have had an intrinsic value. It's a beautiful opal and diamond ring, and believe me, it would have been quite expensive. However, though opals are extremely beautiful stones, and let me tell you, this is one the best that

I have ever seen, they will never command the same price as an equivalent size, top class flawless diamond. It is strange, but that's the way it has always been. As I've said, all those years ago the ring would have been valued purely for its physical worth. However things have changed. There is now a market for certain types of antique jewellery, especially from the famous makers such as Cartier and Bulgari and Boucheron. Their antique jewellery can now command enormous prices and the market is actually quite buoyant.'

Paul Lancaster then spoke to them 'My father has looked into the history of this ring and we think we are onto something rather special here.'

'This is really exciting,' said Sarah, 'It's a bit of a mystery isn't it?'

'It certainly is,' Harry Lancaster continued, 'I do have an idea who made the ring, but to be absolutely positive we are going to have to send it to London to a specialist. We need to know what we are dealing with and we will need their expertise.'

John was amazed. 'So who actually did make the ring?' he asked.

The Lancaster's looked at one another and Paul nodded for his father to continue.

'The ring was originally made in London, somewhere around 1950, by the jewellers Albemarle and Skeet of Bond Street. They were a small but influential company at the time who produced some of the very best quality jewellery. Although Albemarle and Skeet may have disappeared some years ago, some of their work has caused quite a bit of interest recently. Albemarle and Skeet at one time employed the skills of a Russian émigré, he was reportedly a jeweller who had fled from Russia at the time of the 1917 Revolution. His name was Vasily Orlof Bratz.'

John Lawton shrugged his shoulders. 'To be honest with you Mr Lancaster, I know nothing at all about jewellery. If this man was famous, well I've never heard of him.' and John laughed.

Harry Lancaster smiled.

'Though you may never have heard his name, you will have undoubtedly heard of where he trained and worked. You see Mr Lawton, Vasily Orlof Bratz was once one of the most skilled craftsmen at Faberge, the famous Russian jewellers who made jewellery for the leading royal families all across Europe. It was Faberge who made the famous Royal Eggs for the Romanov's, the Russian Royal family. Those fabulous jewelled eggs were presented to the Royal family every Easter. At one time Vasily Orlof Bratz was part of the team who made the eggs. He was without doubt a craftsman of the highest repute.'

Paul Lancaster then spoke. 'What we have here is possibly a great find Mr Lawton. Russia is now a wealthier country and there are some very rich Russian businessmen who are dedicated to buying back all things Russian. Russian art and jewellery and other iconic works have been purchased at great expense and have been taken back to Russia and to the Russian people. Every one of those famous Faberge jewelled eggs that have come onto the market in the last thirty years have immediately been bought and returned to Russia for huge and undisclosed sums. With this opal ring we could possibly have a link to one of Faberge's top craftsmen. However, we will need professional guidance. What we want to do Mr Lawton, is to send it to London were a specialist will appraise the ring and hopefully confirm that it was made by Vasily Orlof Bratz. From there, well who knows? We would of course ask for guidance as to its worth as a historic piece of jewellery that was originally made by one of Faberge's best.'

John and Sarah just sat there in stunned silence.

Harry Lancaster tapped the top of the desk with his forefinger.

'We could be talking about a sizeable amount of money here Mr Lawton.' he said.

John Lawton nodded as he gripped his wife's hand firmly.

'In that case Mr Lancaster,' he said, 'we'd better send it off to your man in London.'

The Lawton's left Lancaster's Jewellers and made their way to the central bus station. They had decided to visit their daughter's grave on the way home. Their baby daughter Louise had died almost ten years previously, very shortly after being born, and on most weekends Sarah and John would visit her small, simple grave.

As they walked arm in arm to the bus station, they discussed their visit to Lancaster's.

'What do you think John?' Sarah asked.

'I don't know love. I really don't know,' he replied, 'but I think we need to find out.'

'Yes,' said Sarah, 'All this about Faberge and the Russian jeweller. What was his name again?'

'Orlof Bratz or something,' said John and he frowned for a moment. But Sarah remembered.

'Yes that was it 'Vasily Orlof Bratz', I wonder who he was John?'

'I don't know, but if the Lancaster's are right we're shortly going to find out.'

They both walked on in silence.

Then John spoke, 'There is one thing that puzzles me though Sarah.'

'What's that?'

'Do you remember the message that came with the box? The handwritten note that was inside the envelope with the ring, it was written by someone called T. McCall.'

'Yes I do.' said Sarah quietly.

'That's what slightly worries me about all of this. The man who wrote that note was desperately unhappy. He was giving the ring away to anyone at all. In the letter he wrote

'You've found this ring and now it's yours, you can have it.' He certainly didn't want the ring and I've got the feeling that he didn't care anymore. And the last line in his letter...'and now I've lost everything'. It worries me somehow. Something happened to that man and it wasn't good.'

John Lawton turned to his wife, 'That ring has a history Sarah. There's something definitely strange about it.'

Little did John Lawton realise the truth of his words.

Later that afternoon, the Lawton's finally made their way home after visiting their daughter's tiny grave. They left some flowers there. A small bunch of bright white carnations, their purity was almost a symbol.

They left the graveyard arm in arm, always arm in arm. As ever, there was a short silence before either of them spoke. It had always been a moment of reflection on what could have been and what should have been.

'We could have passed the ring on to Louise,' said Sarah suddenly, it was almost as though she was thinking out loud.

'That would have been nice,' John replied, 'You mean like a family heirloom?'

'Yes.' said Sarah.

'We could have called it 'The Lawton Opal'...and John laughed at his own suggestion.

'Yes,' replied Sarah, 'It could have been handed down through the family...'

And then Sarah stopped talking, because she realised the stupidity of her words and she immediately felt foolish. There would be no handing down of anything. Not to daughters or granddaughters or great granddaughters. There would be no one.

Both she and John realised emptiness of her words and John clutched his wife's arm as they both walked on in silence.

CHAPTER 8

Anna Hartman had only been working at Schwab's furniture factory for around twelve months, when the seemingly young and slightly nervous Pavel Bratz arrived there to start his apprenticeship. On that first day he was accompanied by his rather strange and ill-tempered father, who turned out to be Mr Ivan Bratz. Once Mr Bratz had left his son and the factory, Anna had taken Pavel down to the factory floor to meet Mr Koenig. They had both walked there in silence. Anna was seventeen and Pavel was sixteen and at that time they seemed worlds apart.

Once she'd introduced Pavel to Mr Koenig, Anna had quickly retreated to the safety of her office, she was still unsure about being around men who did nothing more than stare at her. However, time had passed and she was now quite comfortable with her job at the Schwab factory. The aging Mrs Kausky who had been the previous secretary had trained her well. In fact, Mrs Kausky would still call in at the factory most Thursday afternoons and if Anna had any problems at all, Mrs Kausky would solve them there and then and Anna was always grateful. She knew the old lady came in every Thursday for just that purpose, though nothing was ever said.

When Anna had first arrived in Smolensk and been introduced to Mr Schwab at the factory, she had been very frightened and alone. Her parents had died in a house fire in Moscow, and Anna had been left at her grandmother's house and had only found out about her mother's death when a lawyer arrived from Moscow to inform her of the bad news. The lawyer had finally taken her to Smolensk to meet Mr Schwab, who it turned out had been a family friend of her mother's. Mr Schwab had kindly looked after her and had given her a job. At first, she'd lived with Mrs Kausky, who had treated Anna like a long lost granddaughter. The elderly secretary had spoiled Anna, just as her mother did, and those first three months living at Mrs Kausky's house had helped Anna to get through a tragically hard time in her life.

Mr Schwab had finally found Anna a small flat which wasn't too far from the factory. It was only a short walk really. Mr Schwab apparently knew the owner of the flat and they had come to some sort of friendly agreement as to a minimal rent. Mr Schwab had sorted it all out for her and he just took the rent out of her wages. She was amazed how little it cost. When Anna eventually made friends with other girls, she had been quite surprised at how much everyone else seemed to be paying.

Time passed and under Mrs Kausky's tutelage Anna had become quite adept at her job. She was comfortable too, Mr Schwab was a good boss, and so was the factory manager, Mr Koenig. Anna was quite happy, she almost felt as though she was part of the family business.

How strange?

Every Friday afternoon Mr Koenig would arrive at Mr Schwab's office for their weekly meeting and Anna would as always make them both a pot of freshly brewed hot coffee. If they ever needed a refill she would make them another. On these occasions as she flitted in and out of Mr Schwab's office she would 'pick up' on certain snippets of information. The one subject that gradually began to intrigue her were their constant references to Pavel Bratz.

The young boy that she had once taken down to meet Mr Koenig suddenly seemed to have both men consumed with admiration. Apparently he was some sort of genius with wood, whatever that meant, and every week as she served Mr Koenig and Mr Schwab their coffee, they always seemed to be talking about young Pavel Bratz.

Anna found that the subject actually annoyed her and fascinated her at the same time. She found it all quite frustrating and didn't understand why. When she'd led him down into the factory Pavel Bratz had never spoken a word to her. In fact, Anna had found him most uninteresting and had dumped him there and immediately left. But now the constant mention of his name was making her somewhat inquisitive. She hadn't seen anything of Pavel Bratz for quite some time, he seemed to have kept himself hidden away in one or the other of many workshops within the factory. However her memory of him was of that sullen young boy. After all, he was probably only sixteen years old back then.

However, the time spent at Schwab's factory during the last couple of years had certainly made a difference to Pavel Bratz. Having now turned eighteen, he'd unquestionably grown somewhat and could no longer be described as just 'a boy'.

Pavel worked like a man, and therefore ate like a man. Constant physical work along with regular meals had always produced generations of hardy Russian men and Pavel Bratz was no exception. He was now physically strong and capable of doing hard and laborious work for hours at a time. Physically strong he may have been but because of his unrelenting attitude to work, Pavel rarely left the factory. In fact, he actually led quite a sheltered existence.

One day at lunchtime, Pavel Bratz was making his way back to the men's quarters for his midday meal. He was hungry, and was ready to eat whatever Mr Kibbel had cooked up. Kibbel was Mr Koenig's right hand man and general dogsbody, and he prepared the meals for the men from whatever he could get his hands on. For once, Pavel was early. It was his usual habit to either miss his lunch or at least be very late. Kibbel would always chastise him for his bad timekeeping, but when Pavel was working on one of his projects he would completely lose track of time. Kibbel was fond of the lad and he too recognised Pavel's dedication to his work, as did everybody else. Kibbel would usually fill a plate of food for him and leave it in the oven. It would always be hot and ready for Pavel when he did eventually turn up.

However that morning, Pavel had finally finished the inlaying on a new tabletop. It was a masterpiece, a creative design using teak and maple together with cherry wood. Pavel had finished early because he'd worked late into the night on the previous evening and that morning he'd started early and glued the final intricate strips of wood into place. They would now need twenty four hours to set and dry at a very stable temperature, so as to avoid shrinkage.

Pavel walked into the men's quarters and into pandemonium. Kibbel was shouting, and shouting loudly. However, he was shouting at himself.

Kibbel turned around when he heard Pavel walk through the door and he raised his hands in the air in panic and frustration.

'And now this bloody man arrives early,' he shouted, 'Bloody hell.'

Kibbel was without doubt, slightly agitated.

Pavel had to stop himself from smiling. He was used to Mr Kibbel's ranting, possibly because Kibbel ranted all the time.

So Pavel walked over to the kitchen area with a sympathetic look on his face.

'What's wrong Mr Kibbel?' he asked, almost innocently.

Pavel still called him 'Mr Kibbel'. It was a sign of respect and Kibbel still appreciated it.

But Kibbel was unrelenting.

'What's wrong...What's wrong?' he shouted again, 'everything's wrong.'

Pavel just stood there, waiting for the inevitable reply to his question.

Finally he got an answer.

'The bloody ovens gone out,' shouted Kibble, 'why in god's name, I don't know. The wood must have been damp or something, but now I'm behind with everything and the men will be parading in here in the next half hour, all hungry and shouting for food and now nothing's ready. If the men are late going back to work and Koenig finds out, he'll shoot me.'

Pavel was just about to speak when Kibbel suddenly threw his arms up in despair again.

'Oh Christ no...The bread...The bloody bread.' he yelled.

'What about the bread?' Pavel asked.

'I've forgotten to go to the bakers for the bread. The order's there waiting to be picked up and I've not collected it because I've been trying to relight this damn oven. Oh hell! The men will go mad if there's no bread, oh my God.'

At that point Pavel stepped in.

'I'll go for the bread Mr Kibbel.'

Kibbel blinked. He saw the logic in it. That would solve one of his problems immediately.

'Good lad, Pavel,' he replied and he almost smiled, 'Go around to the bakers right now, the order will be ready for you. Just pick it up and get back here as soon as possible.'

Pavel about turned and immediately set off to the bakers shop. It was just down the road, just a short walk from the Schwab factory.

At that very same time, Anna Hartman was also making her way to the bakery.

She went there every day for Mr Schwab's lunch. As always, she smiled to herself when she thought about her boss. Mr Schwab had the same lunch every day, it never changed.

Nothing ever changed.

Anna would go to the bakers every day where she would get Mr Schwab his usual 'potato pie and a small custard cake'. In the past she'd asked him if he would like to try something different, but of course he wouldn't. He would tell Anna again and again that he was just a creature of habit and they would both laugh about it.

What Anna didn't realise or understand, was that the highlight of Mr Schwab's every working day was when Anna popped into his office with his usual lunch. For him it was a returning memory, it was almost as though Rachel had returned. Young Anna was without doubt the double of her mother and Ernst Schwab had realised long ago that this was the nearest he would ever again be to the only woman he'd ever loved.

Anna stood in the baker's shop behind the small queue of lunchtime customers who had steadily gathered there. She was in no particular hurry. Mr Schwab was no stickler for timekeeping, not with her anyway, and it was nice to get out of the office from time to time and walk in those brief intervals of early afternoon sun.

As Anna stood there daydreaming, a young man burst through the shop doorway. He was breathless because he'd to had run all the way there and was quite startled when he saw that there were several people already in the shop, all waiting to be served. He took a few deep breaths to try and stop himself from panting and it was at that moment he finally glanced to his left and noticed the young lady standing at the side of him.

Pavel Bratz stopped panting.

Anna Hartman recognised Pavel the moment that he dashed in through the shop door. As soon as she saw his face she had known that it was him, she remembered him as the boy he had been. But now she had to look again, because he wasn't a boy anymore. As she stood there next to him, Anna could feel the heat from his body. Standing so close to Pavel, together in that small shop made her aware of his personal odour, it was earthy and honest and it caught her unawares. Anna was quite taken aback. It was the first time she had ever felt this way.

It was a physical attraction, and without any other thought in her mind she openly looked at his body and had to suddenly catch her breath.

She turned to him, only to find that he too was looking directly at her and she immediately started to blush.

Pavel was looking back at Anna, but he didn't notice her blushes. He just saw the prettiest thing he had ever seen in his life and he just stood there slightly bewildered, trying desperately to say something. But he couldn't.

They both just continued to stare at one another, and even some of the other customers turned around to see what was, or wasn't, going on. Two of the older women in the queue smiled at one another, they still had the memories of what once was, and when a boy meets a girl.

It was Anna who finally spoke, if only to cover her embarrassment.

'You're...you're Pavel Bratz.' she managed to say.

Pavel's eyes widened.

'Aren't you Mr Schwab's secretary?' he replied awkwardly.

'Yes I am. Do you remember me?'

Pavel nodded. 'You took me down to see Mr Koenig on my first day at the factory.'

'Yes, you were only a boy back then,' and Anna stopped abruptly, feeling that this could be seen as an admission. She had of course been staring at him.

Pavel smiled at her.

'Yes I was a bit young back then. I'm nineteen now, well nearly.'

'Oh I'm nineteen too,' Anna replied eagerly and then bit her lip. Another stupid admission and she felt like kicking herself.

But Pavel kept on smiling because he just couldn't stop looking at her.

'I'm here for Mr Schwab's lunch,' Anna continued, 'I come here every day, every day and always the same order. Mr Schwab always has the same thing for his lunch, he never changes.'

Pavel laughed, 'He's a good man Mr Schwab, and Mr Koenig too.'

Anna nodded in agreement.

'I'm here on an emergency,' said Pavel, suddenly looking around at the dwindling queue, 'Mr Kibble's had a bit of a disaster. The oven went out and he's behind with his cooking. He's sent me here to collect the bread because he'd forgotten all about it.'

'Oh,' said Anna, 'Oh in that case you'd better get served before me or there'll be trouble,' and with that she stepped aside and manoeuvred him in front of her.

'Are you sure?' he asked.

'Oh yes, it's alright. Mr Schwab's never in a hurry.'

'Oh, thank you...err,' and Pavel stared at her awkwardly. He suddenly realised that he didn't even know her name and then he too started to blush.

Anna saw this, she saw it all and it suddenly made her tummy flutter.

'Anna' she said to him softly, 'My name is Anna Hartman.' And then she stared up at him.

Pavel looked back at her. He couldn't stop looking at her, he couldn't help himself, but had to finally turn away. Mr Kibbel needed the bread. He moved forward to the counter.

'I've come for the bread for the Schwab factory,' he said to the girl behind the counter.

'Oh right,' she said, 'It's here for you,' and the girl turned around and picked up a tied hessian sack which obviously contained the loaves of bread for the men.

She dumped it onto the counter.

'Right,' she said to him, 'and next!'

That was it, Pavel was instantly dismissed. He picked up the sack as the assistant spoke to Anna and then went off to prepare her order.

Pavel turned to Anna. What could he say?

They both looked at one another.

Then with a pang of regret he said, 'Okay, I'll have to get back. I'll see you sometime.'

Anna smiled, 'Yes, okay.' It was all she could say and as he walked out of the shop she sighed and wondered.

Anna then had to wait for the assistant wrap up Mr Schwab's potato pie and then his custard cake. It seemed to take ages because the assistant kept on returning to the bake house. Anna finally left the baker's shop and had given up any hope at all of catching up with Pavel Bratz and his sack of bread. She walked out of the shop door into the sunshine, ready to make her way back to the factory, when she suddenly stopped dead in her tracks. Leaning against the wall was Pavel, the sack of bread on the floor beside him.

He looked at her and grinned sheepishly.

'I'll walk with you back to the factory.' he said.

Anna smiled back at him.

'I thought you had to dash back with the bread?'

'They can all wait, I'll blame the baker,' he said.

Pavel laughed and Anna began to giggle as they both strolled back to the factory at a most leisurely pace.

Kibble complained, but Pavel didn't care. For the first time in his life he'd just discovered something far more beautiful than wood.

It was the start of their romance, and another romance that had started in that same baker's shop.

History was almost repeating itself.

Pavel started to go to the baker's shop every day, always for 'something or other', and where he would coincidently always happen to meet up with Anna Hartman who would be collecting Mr Schwab's lunch.

Anna saw to it too, that she went to the baker's shop, always at a specific time, so that she could see Pavel Bratz every day. It wasn't long before they were both meeting outside the factory gates and both walking to the baker's shop together.

Then Anna began to work later every night. She would still be there when Mr Schwab was leaving to go home and when he began to express some concern, she told him that she was 'just finishing off' and would only be working for another ten minutes or so. This soon became the normal practice and Mr Schwab no longer questioned her.

However, Anna wasn't working for an extra ten minutes. She was actually staying there in her office for another two hours.

Neither was she working. She and Pavel had started to meet there after work and they would sit together in her warm office, talking and laughing and drinking mugs of hot chocolate.

Before long they were talking and laughing and kissing and having mugs of hot chocolate.

Then one evening after work they both returned to Anna's flat. She needed some shelves putting up and while he was there Anna promised to cook Pavel a meal.

The shelves were never put up and nor was much of the food eaten either. Anna did however lead Pavel to her bedroom where they made love for the very first time.

Before long Pavel and Anna were spending every night together back at her comfortable flat. They soon became inseparable, as young love does.

Pavel's problem was that he had to be seen to be back at the factory every morning and Kibbel's last job every night was to lock and chain up the factory gates. Timber, after all was a valuable commodity. So was the furniture.

Pavel's answer to the predicament was to construct his own special ladder, and with it he could climb back over the factory's high brick wall and silently creep back to his own bed in the men's quarters under the darkness of night. He'd made the ladder in his spare time, and had constructed it from a very lightweight pine. The ladder was extremely narrow, not much wider than a man's hand and each rung could accommodate just one foot. But that was all that Pavel Bratz needed. Once he'd finished the ladder he mixed some thin varnish with a few handfuls of dark grey ash from the furnace. He then stained the light pine ladder with the greyish brown mixture and after a few coats of this his new ladder eventually attained a 'dirty' and worn look.

It was perfect, because it was now invisible.

Then one lunch time, Pavel quietly threw his ladder over the factory wall and then walked out of the factory gates to find where the ladder had landed. He carried the ladder to an obscure area along the outer wall where there were some scrub bushes. Pavel dropped the ladder behind these bushes and it almost disappeared. His camouflage had worked. If anyone came across it, the dirt stained narrow ladder now just looked like a piece of old wood.

From then on and after midnight, Pavel would leave Anna's soft warm bed and her soft warm body and make his way back to the factory. He would lean his ladder against the wall and carefully climb up it. Once he was sitting on top of the wall he would kick the ladder over and back into the bushes, then he would lower himself to the ground and quietly sneak back into the men's quarters, unnoticed.

Koenig knew what was going on of course, Koenig knew everything. But he'd had seen them fall in love and he quietly admired it. He was fond of these two young people. He had also never forgotten the life and the love he'd once shared with his darling wife Ingrid, the wife he had lost.

Kibbel also had a good idea of what was happening, but chose to keep his mouth shut. Pavel, unlike the other men had always shown Kibbel respect, and he still called him 'Mr Kibbel'.

And Kibbel always liked that.

But now however, Mr Schwab was aware of what was happening and it was happening right under his nose. On that particular Friday night he'd watched Anna leave work, and then as she was walking out through the factory gates she'd laughingly fallen into Pavel Bratz's loving arms. Ernst Schwab had seen it all.

Schwab had watched them as they embraced and immediately realised that this was far more than just a casual friendship. He also appreciated that Anna had her own flat and with it her own bedroom. As the couple walked away arm in arm, Schwab began to understand how far there relationship had blossomed.

What was he to do? He was after all, Anna's father, but she didn't know that and never would. No one would ever know his secret, no one at all.

Schwab was of course unaware that Koenig knew all and everything. But that was Koenig's little secret too. And that same little secret was dead and buried, or more accurately had been killed off, and was dead and then burned and buried a couple of years ago.

Ernst Schwab sipped his brandy. He considered himself a fool. He had no say at all as to whom Anna should or should not see. As far as Anna was concerned, he was her employer and nothing more. Certainly not her father.

And what on earth did he expect? Anna was a beautiful girl and of course young men would be chasing after her affections.

Hadn't he done exactly the same thing when he'd first met her mother?

Maybe he should be happy that she'd met someone like Pavel Bratz.

Pavel's father may have been a contemptible bastard, but the son was a likeable enough and honest lad.

Schwab frowned when he thought about old Ivan Bratz. That man could be a problem.

And with that in mind, Ernst Schwab poured himself another glass of his fine French brandy and decided on his actions.

He would do nothing.

He would do nothing at all and let nature take its course. What more could he do?

What would be...would be.

Unfortunately, 'what would be' was at that moment written on a sealed letter that was heading for Schwab Furnishings in Smolensk. The letter was addressed to Pavel Bratz and had been written and sent to him by his indomitable father, Ivan Bratz.

Two days later that same letter finally landed on Anna's desk.

Anna looked at the handwriting and the name written on the envelope and was curious. Never before had a letter ever arrived for Pavel Bratz at the Schwab factory. By his own admission, Pavel had admitted to her that his family never kept in touch. In fact, Pavel hadn't seen or heard anything at all from his family since the day he had arrived at Schwabs and that had been three years ago.

At lunchtime, Anna met up with Pavel as usual outside the factory gates and they walked together towards the baker's shop. Anna opened her bag and handed Pavel his letter. Pavel was curious, he wasn't used to receiving letters. Truth be known, he had never received a letter in his life. So as they walked along, Pavel ripped open the envelope and then took out the letter and started to read. A moment later he stopped dead in his tracks.

'Oh no,' he said quietly and immediately looked at Anna.

Anna stared back at him, and at that instant she had a slight feeling of anxiety.

'What is it Pavel?' she asked.

Pavel just stood there looking at her, the letter still held in front of him.

'It's from my father. He wants me to go back home. He says that I've spent enough time here and he needs me back at the factory.'

Anna just stood there in shock. And a multitude of thoughts began to run through her mind.

Pavel too, suddenly realised the enormity of it all.

Neither of them had ever considered that things would ever change, and now their blissfully happy life was about to be turned into turmoil. Pavel had happily worked away in the factory for the last three years, totally engrossed in his craft. Then he had met Anna and his life had become just about perfect. Even climbing over the factory wall every night had become a laughable routine. Now this. He'd become complacent, but he was in love.

Pavel Bratz had two loves in his life. Anna of course was the first, and crafting exotic timber at the Schwab factory was his second. And though he'd never realised it, Schwab's had become his home and it was the home that he loved.

They both just stood there then Anna burst into tears.

'You're going to leave me,' she sobbed, 'I'm going to be on my own again.'

Pavel suddenly felt a rush of protective emotion and it made him feel angry, but he was helpless. The letter was from his father and his father was Ivan Bratz.

'What are we going to do Pavel?' Anna asked him.

Pavel just shook his head.

'I don't know, but I'll think of something.'

They called at the bakers for Mr Schwab's lunch. But Pavel found he had lost his appetite.

On the way back to the factory Anna talked to him and asked him question after question. She was looking for answers but Pavel didn't have any. His head was still spinning.

When they arrived at the factory gate he kissed her on the cheek and told her not to worry, which in itself was a ridiculous statement. They eventually agreed to meet in Anna's office after work to try and work something out. With that Pavel turned away and doggedly walked off back to his work. Anna stood there watching him go. He was her only love.

She was heartbroken.

Pavel went back to his workshop. He had been cutting and shaping some beautiful scrolled table legs that he would finally inlay with teak and mahogany to form an exquisite design. As he once again began to work with his beloved timber, his mind began to work. And as he carved out the intricate shapes into the wood with a tiny razor sharp chisel, he gradually became calmer and more positive. There had to be an answer, there had to be.

Exactly one hour later, and almost to the minute, the answer to all Pavel's problems suddenly leapt into his brain. He actually stopped working for a moment, and he put down his tools and stood up and smiled to himself. Then he burst out laughing. It was all so simple. It was all so very, very simple.

Shortly afterwards Pavel began to search through his stock of exotic timbers. He knew exactly what he was looking for and he knew where it would be because he'd tucked it away for that one 'special' job, that special job that would occasionally merit only the finest of timbers and this was a piece of timber with that one unique colour. Finally, he found it.

It was just a piece of wood, just half a foot in length, only a small piece really but it was so very special.

Pavel examined the small length of the hardest and possibly the darkest section of ebony wood that he had ever come across. It had arrived with a parcel of other exotic woods from the Far East and the untrained eye would have probably used it to fire the furnace.

But Pavel didn't have an untrained eye. Pavel had the gift.

He took that one special piece of ebony and carefully sanded it on one side. It had been as resilient and as hard as a lump of stone. Pavel realised that this wasn't just a length of freshly cut timber, this was something that had been cut years previously, or had been broken off a tree at some time and had lain in the sun and slowly hardened. It had probably been picked up off the ground by someone to add to a bundle of other woods. Pavel had sanded through the remnants of the bark and into the inner wood and had seen its promise. Then he oiled the sanded timber and wiped it down and was astonished by what he saw. Within the wood's patina were a multitude of colours running through the grain of the ebony, they ranged from black to the deepest brown, and also contained within it was a flash of red...blood red.

It was amazing. The pattern was exquisite, absolutely exquisite.

Originally, Pavel had taken the piece of ebony and stored it away somewhere safe. He'd always known that one day he would use it for something special.

So on that afternoon Pavel forgot about the scrolled table legs and he turned his mind to other things. He took his smallest and sharpest saw and began to work on the piece of ebony. After an hour's labour and careful concentration, he then went off to find a lathe.

That same evening he and Anna met up in her office. Mr Schwab had gone home and everybody else had finished their day's work, although Koenig would probably still be in the factory somewhere.

Pavel walked into the office to find Anna sitting there behind her desk. She was red eyed, tearful and still upset. Mr Schwab had been quite concerned for her, but Anna had lied and told him that she had a stomach ache, a woman's 'problem'. Schwab knew not to ask and was slightly embarrassed, but he'd told Anna that if she wasn't well she should have the next couple of days off. She thanked him and immediately felt guilty. She had never lied to Mr Schwab.

As Pavel walked through the door, Anna stood up and almost dashed around her desk. She desperately hugged Pavel and then clung to him. As he held her he could feel her body shaking.

'What are we going to do Pavel, what on earth are we going to do?' she was almost crying.

To her complete surprise, Pavel kissed the side of her neck and then picked her up and spun her around.

She looked at him and was mystified because he was actually smiling. Anna didn't understand.

'I have the answer Anna,' he said and then he kissed her on the cheek.

She was dumbfounded. She had been so upset, they both had, but now here he was, all smiles and happy. Pavel turned and picked up a chair and sat her down. Anna just looked at him, he was still smiling. Suddenly he got down on one knee and took hold of her hand.

Then he spoke to her.

'Marry me Anna...marry me. Be my wife.'

She looked at him for a moment as her mind tried to take in what he had just said to her, and for a split second she didn't understand. Then she did.

Anna started to cry as she leant down and held his face close to hers. She looked into those honest eyes and then kissed him once.

'Yes, I'll be your wife Pavel Bratz,' she said, 'it's the only thing I've ever wanted.'

They stood up and embraced, and then Pavel stood back and fumbled in his inside pocket.

'I have something to show you,' he said and with that he produced a crumpled handkerchief which he began to carefully unwrap.

'It's not finished yet,' he said, 'but I want you to see it. It's something special.'

He slowly opened the handkerchief to reveal a ring, a ring made out of the most wonderful piece of ebony wood that Pavel had ever seen or ever worked with.

'I know that it's different and it's not a jewel or anything, but it's made from the most beautiful piece of ebony and it's so special. I've got to do more work on it, I want to engrave our names on the inside and it needs to be oiled and waxed over and over again to really bring out the colours. I just wanted you to see it.'

He looked at her, 'What do you think?'

Anna picked up the ring and gazed at it as she held it up to the light. The colours amazed her. She turned the ring into the light to see the pattern of natural colour. The ebony black was mixed with a deep tobacco brown, but the immediate and most startling colour which ran through the grain of that dark and most mysterious of woods was the presence of a deep red hew. The blood red stain ran through the wood like an opened vein.

Anna stared at the ring, mesmerized, and then looked up at Pavel.

'It's beautiful,' she said, 'Oh Pavel, it's so beautiful.'

'Yes,' he said to her, 'It's made from a special piece of ebony that I found. I've never seen anything like it. It needs more work on it, but when it's finished it will be as hard as steel. It will never split or break...never.'

Earlier that afternoon, Pavel had taken the length of ebony and had meticulously cut it into three sections. He had planed and sanded the wood and checked the variation in the pattern. Eventually he had picked out the middle section as his choice, it was where the colouring in the grain of the wood was at its best. Pavel then went to the lathe department and set his piece of ebony onto a small lathe. From there he began to turn it, skilfully reducing the timber with a sharp chisel as the ebony spun evenly on the lathe. Once he had reduced it to an optimum size, he took the now smooth piece of ebony and set it in a clamp on an industrial drill. He used the smallest drill bit to start drilling out the centre section and once he had drilled it through he used larger drills to slowly and skilfully enlarge the inner section so as to fit a finger's width. Eventually Pavel was left with a short tube of beautifully coloured ebony. He then took his tiny razor sharp tenon saw and cut the tube of ebony into three further sections. Now he had three rings of black ebony with the blood red stain running through them. Pavel sat there and examined them closely, and then he chose the perfect one.

It had the perfect grain and it would make the perfect ring.

He then picked up the other two rings and smashed them into small pieces with a hammer.

There would be no second bests. Pavel took the ring back to his workshop and started to rub linseed oil into the wood with a soft cloth. The ebony began to shine, almost in gratitude. Pavel sat there for over two hours, applying coat after coat of oil. It would be a long process that would take weeks, if not months to complete, as the oil seeped deep into the ebony.

But Pavel knew that. Pavel knew exactly what he was doing. Pavel had the gift.

That evening Pavel and Anna discussed their future plans as they sat in front of the open fire back at her flat. They both realised that once married, they were going have to leave Smolensk and go and live back in Pavel's home town of Zhumyov, a prospect that was rather more daunting for Pavel than his future wife-to-be. Pavel had grown up in Zhumyov and his memories of the place hardly instilled any sort of enthusiasm. The thought of being back home and living under the iron will of his dominating father was also slightly more than disconcerting. Pavel had been freed from his family and from Zhumyov for more than three years, three very important years. He had gone from a 'boy to a man' in Smolensk and at the Schwab Factory he was well known and respected. Back in Zhumyov his status would be diminished and he would simply be known as the 'youngest brother' in the Bratz Family. Working once again for his father would be a different life, a lot different than working for Mr Ernst Schwab.

Pavel had tried to portray family life in his hometown of Zhumyov as something far more agreeable. But Anna knew Pavel's ways and she knew that he was trying to make things look credible for her, and that gave her some concern.

In the end they decided that Pavel would write to his father and tell him of their intentions.

It was also decided by the young lovers, that if Pavel's father disagreed with their marriage in anyway, then they would immediately get married in Smolensk and suffer the consequences when they finally arrived back in Zhumyov.

The Bratz family could jump up and down and scream and shout, but by then it would be all too late.

Anna's next task was to inform Mr Schwab about her relationship with Pavel Bratz and of their decision to marry and move away.

Anna had always felt a little guilty about seeing Pavel in secrecy. She hadn't intended to go behind Mr Schwab's back but it had all just turned out that way. Mr Schwab had always been very good to her. He'd been her Guardian and had taken her in after her parent's tragic deaths, and he'd found her employment and her own place to live.

So Anna took the decision to 'come clean'. Mr Schwab deserved to know the truth and Anna wanted him to be the first to know. After all, he had been like an uncle to her.

Strangely, she almost felt that he was 'family'.

The following day Anna went to the bakers shop as normal for Mr Schwab's usual lunch.

When she returned she entered his office and placed the pie and the cake on his desk. And as usual he smiled at her and they exchanged their usual banter. Anna then took a deep breath and asked him the question.

'Can I have a word with you Mr Schwab?'

Ernst Schwab stopped smiling for the briefest of moments. He was curious. This was slightly different from their regular lunchtime conversations, and as he looked up at his young secretary he saw her very serious face. Suddenly, Ernst Schwab lost his appetite.

'Whatever is it Anna?' he asked.

Anna just stood there with her hands behind her back, almost subservient.

'I have something to tell you Mr Schwab, something that I should have told you before and I'm really, really sorry.'

Ernst Schwab then lost his appetite completely.

'What on earth is it Anna. What's wrong?' he asked again.

Anna's lip started to tremble slightly but she continued.

'I've...I've been seeing Pavel Bratz, Mr Schwab. We're courting. We've been courting for some time now Mr Schwab and I'm really, really sorry, I know I should have told you, I know I should.'

Her words tumbled out in all of a rush.

Ernst Schwab stared back at his secretary. Part of him wanted to laugh out loud but he knew he mustn't. He'd known for a long time about Pavel Bratz and Anna's romance and had kept it to himself. He'd had to stand back and take a position of neutrality, and he would continue to do that.

'Oh, I see.' was all he said.

Anna just looked back at him. She hadn't known really what to expect. There was a moment's silence.

'I love him Mr Schwab, I really do.'

Schwab had already observed it all from afar, but he wasn't going to admit it to her.

'Well Anna,' he replied, 'Pavel Bratz is a really good boy and I like him too, we all do.'

Anna looked back at him, she hadn't known what he would say, and in fact she was a little surprised at how calmly he'd received her news.

'Thank you Mr Schwab, thank you very much.'

Ernst Schwab inwardly took a sigh of relief. The crisis was solved and now everything was out in the open and things would get back to normal. Wonderful.

But Anna still stood there in front of him, still looking sheepish, and Schwab suddenly realized that there must be something else.

'What is it Anna?' he asked her again. And he suddenly wondered about the possibility of her being pregnant. That would actually make him a grandfather, and he suddenly saw a future where there would be his daughter and a grandchild and then he could look after everybody forever. But no, it was not to be.

'It's Pavel's father,' she said, 'Pavel's father has written to him and told him that he has to go back home. He needs him there to work.'

Ernst Schwab clenched his teeth. That cheeky bastard Ivan Bratz had almost begged Schwab to give young Pavel Bratz an apprenticeship, and now he wants his son back, now that Pavel was an accomplished carpenter.

There had been no letter written to Ernst Schwab, asking for Pavel Bratz to be released from his contract. No, no letter at all. This discourteous and ill mannered attitude was typical of Ivan Bratz. Schwab considered the man, and as ever he realised that he was dealing with a 'peasant'.

Schwab took a deep breath.

But Anna continued.

'I love Pavel, Mr Schwab, and he loves me and we won't be parted.'

Schwab stared back at her.

'What do you mean?' he asked.

'Pavel wants us to get married Mr Schwab. He wants me to marry him so that I can go with him back to Zhumyov. He's written to his father telling him of our plans and if his father doesn't agree we're going to get married anyway. We want to be husband and wife.'

Schwab sat there, dumbfounded.

Anna stood in front of him, breathing heavily. She'd done it, she'd finally got everything out in the open.

But Schwab was still speechless. He could let go of a skilled craftsman, even the likes Pavel Bratz. And he could let go of a very proficient secretary, there were always other secretaries. But he could not lose his daughter, not again.

'What am I going to do?' he suddenly said out loud.

Anna, who totally misinterpreted the outburst, simply replied.

'We'll have to find you a new secretary, Mr Schwab.'

The very next day she and Pavel sent a letter back to Zhumyov, informing the Bratz family of their intentions.

It took two weeks for Ivan Bratz and the Russian postal service to finally send a letter back to Schwab's Furnishings. It was addressed once more to

Pavel Bratz and Anna recognized it immediately. She fidgeted all the way through till lunchtime, and then she almost ran to the factory gates to meet Pavel. She handed him the letter in silence. Pavel looked at her as he ripped open the envelope and then he started to read.

A couple of minutes later he stopped reading and sighed, then he handed Anna the letter.

As she too started to read, Anna quickly realised that she was marrying into a family whose relationships were definitely not built on love. The letter immediately informed Pavel that he was not in a financial position to consider marriage at this time. However, when he did come back home to Zhumyov, Pavel would be expected to work in the family factory. And if he did want to bring his bride-to-be with him, Anna could work in the office along with Ivan Bratz and she could handle the company paperwork and the accounting. Pavel and Anna would have to live with the family. Pavel's eldest brother had married and moved out and so there was now some extra space for the pair of them in the family home. Ivan Bratz then went on to inform his son that he could have a word with the local priest and get the young couple 'married off' quickly.

Anna was not impressed. In fact, she was fearful. Her happy life it seemed, was about to take another turn for the worse. But what could she do? If she wasn't prepared to go and live with the Bratz family in Zhumyov she could lose Pavel forever.

The next morning Ernst Schwab walked into his office. He took one look at Anna and knew instinctively that something was wrong. He could read her like an open book.

Ten or so minutes later she came into his office with his usual first coffee of the day. He studied her for a moment, Anna was trying her best to make the normal and established early conversation, just as she did every morning. But today her heart wasn't in it and Ernst Schwab could see it wasn't. In the end he asked her to sit down and asked her what was wrong. Anna immediately burst into tears as she told her boss about the letter from Pavel's father.

Ernst Schwab sighed. Ivan Bratz was a callous bastard. Not only that, he was a 'cheap' callous bastard. Bratz was going to have Anna married off as quickly and as cheaply as possible and then she and Pavel would become another of his assets. Then he would be in control, he would have them both locked away and greedily stored under his own roof.

Anna left Mr Schwab's office, leaving him sitting there seething and inwardly cursing.

What was he to do?

In Ernst Schwab's mind, Ivan Bratz was stealing his only child from him, and he was powerless to do anything about it. Again, what could he do?

Anna loved young Pavel Bratz and if they were married she would have to follow him as his wife. That was the nature of things and Schwab's hands were tied. Even if he openly and quite wrongly told Anna that he was actually her father, things would still not change. Anna would still have to go with her husband and live in Zhumyov.

It was a long morning for Ernst Schwab.

The thought of not seeing Anna again every day and the memories of her mother troubled him greatly.

Schwab got up from his desk and went over to the large safe that sat in the corner of his office. He took out a key from his inside pocket and opened the safe, then he reached inside and took out a worn white envelope. On the front of the envelope were written the words...

'Personal'
To Mr Ernst Schwab
The Schwab Furniture Company
Smolensk

The white envelope was worn with time and use, because it had been opened so many times. Inside the envelope was a letter that was similarly worn with time. It was the letter that Rachel had written to Schwab as her last will and testament, his darling Rachel.

Schwab took the envelope over to his desk and sat down. He opened it and took out the letter, the letter that he had read a thousand times. He read the words again, and although he knew its content off by heart, he still had to read it.

Rachel's last will and testament prophesied the possibility of her death, and it was also used as an introduction to their daughter Anna, who as a young girl had accompanied the letter all the way to Ernst Schwab and to his factory in Smolensk.

He read the letter, and when he finally got to the most significant sentence, the message that Rachel had written long ago. Those few words helped Ernst Schwab to make a decision.

'Whatever tragedy has taken place, please take care of her.
She is our flesh and blood'

That afternoon when Anna appeared at Mr Schwab's office with his lunch, Schwab was feeling somewhat calmer. He knew what he had to do. Anna entered his office still looking quite pale and upset. She was obviously still quite ill at ease.

'Ah Anna,' he said to her, almost casually.

Anna looked up and gave him a weary smile.

'Anna,' he continued, 'later this evening when Pavel has finished his work, I would like you both to come and see me.'

Anna was slightly confused.

'Is there anything wrong Mr Schwab?' she asked.

'No Anna, nothing at all. I just wanted a quick chat with you both, that's all.'

Ernst Schwab picked up his pen and returned to his paperwork. Anna stared at him for a moment and then turned and went back to her office.

As he continued to write, Ernst Schwab smiled.

At around six o' clock that evening there was knock on Schwab's office door. Schwab knew of course who it would be.

'Come,' he said out loud.

The door opened and Anna walked quietly into his office, followed by Pavel Bratz.

'Ah, hello you two,' said Schwab.

'Hello Mr Schwab,' Pavel replied.

Anna smiled half-heartedly, she was still slightly perplexed and wondered what this was all about.

'Right,' Schwab continued, 'Take hold of a couple of chairs and come and sit yourselves down.'

Pavel and Anna took two chairs over to Schwab's desk and then sat themselves down in front of their boss. They were unsure what he was going to say to them.

Schwab looked at them both, he knew they were worried.

'Now then,' he said to them, 'I want to talk to you both.'

Pavel and Anna just sat there, not knowing what to expect.

Schwab continued, 'Anna, you came here four years ago when you were nothing more than a child. Your mother, as you know, asked me to take care of you and from there on I appointed myself as your sole guardian.'

Anna nodded in agreement.

'We have had a happy four years I think, and in fact Anna, I've always look upon you as the daughter I never had.'

As she smiled at him, Schwab's chest heaved with emotion. There...he had finally said it, and that statement was the nearest he was ever going to get to telling his daughter the truth.

He continued, 'Now I can see that you two are very much in love, and therefore you want to get married. And that's good, very good, and you both have my blessing. So, where do we go from here? Pavel, your father wants you to return home and obviously you will want to take Anna with you and eventually you will be married.'

Now it was Pavel's turn to agree on the events, and he hardly looked positive. Pavel had always known his own father's traits.

Ernst Swab smiled. 'Well Pavel, since Anna is like a daughter to me and that I am also her guardian, I shall continue with the promise that I gave to her mother...'to look after her'.

I hold a responsibility and therefore I have decided that if you two are to be married, the responsibility will be mine. You will be married here in Smolensk and I will pay for the wedding. You Pavel, will write to your parents and inform them what is happening. We will sort out all the arrangements and your parents and family will have to come here to Smolensk.'

Anna stared at him for a moment and then burst into tears. She stood up and walked around the desk and hugged him. For Schwab it was a moment of immense pride.

He had done the 'right' thing by her.

'Thank you Mr Schwab, thank you so very, very much,' she said to him, between the tears.

Pavel stood up and shook Schwab's hand.

He just smiled his boyish smile and said 'Thanks boss.'

For Schwab, that was enough.

Ernst Schwab was a happier man but he hadn't finished. He had Anna and Pavel sit down again and then he continued.

'Starting married life under another man's roof is hardly ideal. It can cause friction, especially when that man's roof is your father's, Pavel.'

Pavel Bratz raised an eyebrow. He knew exactly what Mr Schwab meant. The thought of having to live once again with his family and under the rule of his dominating father was daunting. Pavel had escaped from Ivan Bratz and the Bratz's family regime and he'd become used to being his own man.

'I have therefore decided,' continued Schwab, 'to buy a property in Zhumyov. I shall buy a decent house which you can both live in and you can pay me a reasonable rent, once you can afford it. We'll sort something out and it will be an investment for me. What do you think?'

Anna and Pavel were stunned. This was something they'd never expected, neither was the wedding, and Pavel stood up and once again shook Schwab's hand.

'Thank you Mr Schwab. Thank you very, very much. This will change our lives.'

Anna of course, continued to cry.

Schwab gave a wry smile.

'Pavel, your father doesn't like spending money. And me spending some of mine should actually make him happy. However, I feel that it might aggravate him too. But who cares?'

Ernst Schwab then burst out laughing.

So the plans were made and letters were exchanged.

Ivan Bratz of course, immediately agreed to Schwab paying for the wedding, he was actually quite amazed. But he was rather more than amazed when he found out that Ernst Schwab was buying a property in Zhumyov. That proposition certainly did set off a number of puzzled questions in Ivan Bratz's suspicious mind. However none would ever be answered. Circumstance would see to that.

The wedding took place four months later. The happy couple were married in the Smolensk's beautiful St Michael's Church, which was one of the city's oldest and grandest churches.

The celebrations took place later in the city's resplendent Grand Lafer Hotel. Schwab, true to his word, gave Anna a wedding day that had no expense spared. It was a beautiful sunny day, and it was warm and all went well.

Ivan Bratz and his family were given accommodation in the Grand Lafer, once he'd arrived with his wife Martha, his daughter Lera and his second son Nikolai. The elder brother, Yakov, was to remain in Zhumyov. Ivan Bratz had no intention of closing his factory for a wedding or any other family celebration, and that included births, marriages or even deaths. Eldest son, Yakov, was by that time married and his wife would shortly be expecting their first child and that had been Ivan Bratz's excuse for his son's absence.

Schwab knew better, and so did Pavel.

Strangely, or maybe not, Ivan Bratz was by this time actually quite a wealthy man.

His business had without doubt grown and his 'Baltic' extending ladders had been a great success. They were in great demand and were sold in many of the surrounding states. Together with his ladders there had also been a market for his basic but functional furniture. Bratz had quite skilfully set up a large chain of distributors who sold his products and he used the railways as an efficient way of delivering his goods.

A wealthy man indeed. However, great wealth often goes hand in hand with greed and it was Ivan Bratz's ultimate plan to become a great deal wealthier.

He craved wealth, and with it the power. That was the adrenaline of the rich.

Ivan Bratz wanted to expand his business and Ivan Bratz had a plan.

It was the evening of the wedding celebrations. The guests had eaten and drank and were merry, and music was being played and there was dancing.

Schwab sat at the top table, which had been reserved for the family.

As he sat there on his own he enjoyed a cigar and a full glass of brandy. His thoughts as ever returned to Rachel. She would have been happy that day. She and Schwab should have been there together to see their daughter married. And who knew, there could have been other children too. Schwab sighed. It wasn't to be and he knew that, it was just an ever recurring dream for him, but it was a dream that had lingered for over twenty years.

There was the sudden scraping of a shifted chair, and Schwab turned to his left and was rather surprised to see that Ivan Bratz was sitting down next to him. Bratz had a large glass of vodka in his hand and he too was enjoying a cigar. For once Ivan Bratz smiled, it was the first time Ernst Schwab had ever seen him smile and that fact alone worried Schwab somewhat.

'A good wedding,' Bratz commented.

'I think so,' replied Schwab, 'We've done her proud.'

'Yes, damn good,' said Bratz as he looked down at all the guests and considered how much money he'd saved because of Schwab's generosity.

There was a short silence between them. But Bratz had to ask.

'Why did you insist on paying for everything Schwab?'

Ernst Schwab felt the knot in his stomach, it was as ever the warning sign, the warning sign that made him wary and it made him cautious.

Schwab knew immediately that he should take control of the situation.

'It was my duty of course. I am Anna's guardian after all, and it was a promise to her mother.'

'You knew her mother well then?' Bratz enquired.

'Oh yes,' Schwab replied, 'She was an old family friend,' he lied casually. And then he suddenly thought about it...'Who the hell was going to know any different anyway?'

'Hmm, it seems a lot of expense for a 'friend,' Bratz continued his questioning.

'Ah well,' said Schwab, now on the defence, 'I have a lot of money Bratz. I'm a wealthy man and I may as well spend some of it on the things I enjoy. I enjoy a good party and I enjoy a good wedding. There's not enough of them these days, especially at my age.'

And Schwab chuckled, more to himself really.

But Ivan Bratz still had more questions

'The promise of a house in Zhumyov was also very generous of you Schwab, possibly an extravagance?'

Schwab leant back on his chair. He drew on his cigar and inwardly sighed. Bratz wasn't going to let things lie.

'It's an investment really Bratz,' he countered, 'For quite a while now I've been buying cheaper properties outside the Smolensk area and I've been renting them out. It's quite profitable really. You should look into it, it's very lucrative.'

Schwab suddenly felt quite pleased with himself. Lying was quite rewarding when t was Ivan Bratz who was the unfortunate victim.

Bratz said nothing. Renting property was something he had never thought of. He suddenly realized that he'd been too busy making ladders.

Schwab continued. 'Buying a property in Zhumyov makes sense. First of all it will give Anna and Pavel their much needed security, and secondly, I'll make a decent return on my money. I always do. In fact, I may buy several other properties when I visit Zhumyov with Anna and Pavel. You see, I want to find them something quite nice.'

Ivan Bratz bristled at Schwab's statement. First of all was the suggestion of Pavel's 'much needed security'. Who on earth did Schwab think he was? Ivan Bratz could sort out his own son and his own family's security. Then there were Schwab's plans to come to Zhumyov and start buying up all the property. Ivan Bratz wasn't having any of that. When he got back home Bratz would straightaway be looking into the property market himself.

Ernst Schwab smiled to himself. He knew exactly what he was doing. He'd stopped Ivan Bratz asking any more possibly awkward questions. Schwab could read Ivan Bratz like a book, he'd had to deal with men like Bratz all of his life. Ernst Schwab's own cruel and dominating father had been a man just like Ivan Bratz, and Schwab remembered everything.

The two men sat there quietly watching the ongoing wedding celebrations. They both smoked their cigars in silent contemplation, but it was all part of Ivan Bratz's plan. He'd waited all day to speak to Ernst Schwab, when they were finally on their own. He'd waited until the time was right, and now he felt that this was the moment.

'Schwab?' he said slowly.

Ernst Schwab turned in his seat, 'Yes Bratz?'

'I want to buy your company Schwab. I want you to sell me your business.'

And finally, that was Ivan Bratz's plan.

Schwab just sat there. He was dumfounded. He had never, ever, expected this. He'd never even considered it.

Before Schwab could even utter a word, Bratz continued with his well prepared speech.

'I need to expand my business Schwab, and I need to be in Smolensk. You see, I need to be nearer the railways.'

Schwab was momentarily confused.

'We're a furniture business Bratz. You make ladders.'

'Yes,' replied Bratz, 'but we also make a range of budget furniture, and I want to expand that side of the business too. And I want to produce a range of top quality furniture.'

Ernst Schwab almost laughed. It had taken the Schwab Furniture Company almost a century to build its reputation for excellence. And now this 'peasant' all the way from the backwoods of Zhumyov wanted to walk in and take over a business that he knew absolutely nothing about.

Schwab shook his head and Ivan Bratz saw it.

It was now time for Bratz to sell his idea.

'I put it to you like this Ernst. None of us are getting any younger. Nobody can go on forever.

If you were to sell me your company, I would leave that side of the business to you, to be run as it always has been. Your men would all retain their jobs and nothing at all would change. My son Pavel could stay here and work with you and learn about the business side of things. And eventually, as he got older and more proficient, he could take over the reins. I would have my second son Nikolai come and work here and we could set up part of the factory to increase the production of our Baltic Ladders and with it we could also increase the production of our own budget furniture.'

Ivan Bratz continued to preach about the whys and the wherefores of them working together and he continued to talk about the great opportunities that could be achieved.

But Schwab had stopped listening. He had stopped listening straight after Bratz had spoken about Pavel remaining at the factory and eventually 'taking over the reins'. A thought suddenly materialised in Ernst Schwab's mind. If Pavel Bratz remained at the factory, then Anna would remain at the factory. He would still be able to see his daughter every day. Nothing would change, and nothing would ever have to change.

Suddenly, there was another future.

Ernst Schwab swallowed and took a deep breath. He needed to think and he needed time.

He turned to Ivan Bratz, who was still extolling the virtues and wonderful possibilities of 'what if..?'

'Bratz,' Schwab interrupted.

Ivan Bratz stopped talking.

'Bratz, we are at a wedding and now is not the time to talk business. We're here to celebrate. If you want to talk business come to my office tomorrow.'

Ivan Bratz just sat there, his mouth slightly open. He didn't know how to take this. Was this an insult to shut him up, or a possible opening? Maybe, but maybe not.

Bratz forcibly smiled at his host.

'Yes, of course Ernst,' he replied, 'of course.'

And he sat back in his chair and raised his glass of vodka.

'To the happy couple' he said out loud, and he smiled.

The wedding celebrations went on till late, and it was the following afternoon before Ivan Bratz felt that he was in any condition to go and talk to Ernst Schwab.

Bratz finally arrived at the offices of Schwab Furnishings at around three o' clock.

Schwab had used the surplus time to think, plan and resolve most of his thoughts.

He showed Ivan Bratz into his office and offered him a seat. Schwab then poured them both some freshly brewed coffee and then filled two glasses with his finest French brandy.

Ernst Schwab didn't stock vodka.

After the wedding celebrations had finished the previous evening and the guests had finally all left the Grand Lafer Hotel, Schwab had made his way home and had sat up into the early hours, deliberating the past and a 'possible' future. He'd eventually made his way to bed but awoke early in the morning, still contemplating and still deliberating. His mind was full of possibilities, but also full of doubts. What was he going to do?

Both men sipped their coffee. There would be time for the brandy later.
Eventually, and after a few of the obvious niceties, it was Ivan Bratz who broached the subject.
'Well Ernst, what do you think about my proposal?'
Schwab smiled to himself. Bratz was keen and eager to get on with things, and that was good. It meant that Ernst Schwab could sit back and let Bratz 'sell' him the deal.
'To be truthful, I never expected any of this Bratz,' said Schwab, 'I didn't know you were thinking of expanding your business. Things must be going well if you want to come here to Smolensk.'
'They are,' replied Ivan Bratz, 'we are at full production but we are also stuck in Zhumyov. My company needs to grow and I need to be nearer the railways. I'm permanently waiting for my timber to arrive and then we have a distribution problem. It takes far too long to get our products to the main railways. Everything that comes in or out of our factory has to be transported long distances by horse and cart. It all takes time, too much time.'
Ernst Schwab nodded. He completely understood Bratz's problem. Having a factory in Smolensk would make sense. The city of Smolensk did have excellent railway connections and there were direct routes to Moscow, and from there the rest of Russia.
Yes, Schwab could understand Bratz's plans to expand.
'So I have to ask you Ernst,' Ivan Bratz continued, 'have you given any thought to my offer, would you consider selling me your company?'
Schwab looked at Bratz. Here was an impatient man, a man who wanted an answer. It was Bratz's way of course. But Schwab could also see a hint of desperation. Ivan Bratz must have been thinking about this for a long time, maybe even when he had first brought Pavel to the factory as an apprentice, all those years ago. Nothing about Ivan Bratz would surprise Ernst Schwab, nothing at all. But it was the manner in which Bratz had approached him that gave Schwab the upper hand.

Should he sell or not sell? And ultimately, at what price? Did Bratz have the funds?

However, it had been Bratz's comment on 'not getting any younger' and that nobody could go on forever that had struck a note in Ernst Schwab's mind. For quite a while he'd wondered what the future would have in store for him, especially now that he had Anna to consider. He would of course make financial arrangements for her, in fact he already had. Now however, she was married to Pavel, and if Ivan Bratz got a whiff of the money, then Ivan Bratz would steal that money. Ernst Schwab had no doubts about that at all.

But it was Bratz's original plan, that he would want his son Pavel to stay in Smolensk and continue to work at the factory that was central to Schwab's thoughts. Schwab would see Anna every day, and eventually there would be children, no doubt about it. They would be his grandchildren and he could die a happy man.

'What would be your plans for my factory?' Schwab asked.

Ivan Bratz smiled. This was progress and that question alone meant that old man Schwab had considered his offer. Bratz's only problem was how much money that 'old bastard Schwab' would actually want. Bratz would have to come to some sort of agreement with him. He knew from past events that Schwab was a competent adversary when it came to haggling.

So Bratz would have to sell him 'his plan'.

'Nothing would change Ernst, nothing at all,' Bratz quickly replied, 'You would continue to run things as you always have. You would still be in total control. The workforce is yours and would remain that way. Schwab's would continue to make the finest quality furniture, as one would expect. But your factory is huge, you have the space and I would want to set up ladder production somewhere here, along with our 'basic' furniture.'

It was true. Schwab's had only ever used around two thirds of its huge factory and grounds and Ernst Schwab acknowledged that, though he did wonder just how Ivan Bratz had attained that knowledge. Maybe it was from Pavel, but for some reason Schwab doubted it.

Their conversation carried on for another hour until it finally became an exchange of ideas. Then the final question, the issue that both men had skirted around. How much?

'What's your company worth?' Ivan Bratz finally asked.

Schwab smiled at his adversary.

'What it's worth, or what I want for it?' he replied.

'Come on my friend,' Bratz continued, 'we both know that we have to agree a fair price.'

Schwab stopped smiling. 'Well the way I see it Ivan, is that you do really want to buy my business. However, I'm in such a position that it doesn't matter to me either way. I'm a wealthy man. I don't have to or need to sell my business at all.'

Ivan Bratz bristled at that. Had he read Schwab wrong?

'But,' Bratz started.

'But nothing,' Schwab interrupted.

Schwab was enjoying this. It was his plan. He needed to retain the upper hand when dealing with the likes of Ivan Bratz, because Bratz was a bastard. Schwab realised that he would always have to take control when dealing with this man. Ivan Bratz could ruin everything.

Schwab tapped the top of his desk with his pen. It was an act of contemplation, and both men sat there in silence. Bratz moved in his chair in frustration.

'Four million roubles,' Schwab suddenly announced, and Ivan Bratz gasped.

'How much?' Bratz was astounded.

'Four million,' replied Schwab casually.

'Never,' Bratz blurted out, and then he wished he hadn't. Emotion could be seen as a weakness and that was something that he didn't want to show.

Ivan Bratz had done his figures. He was a fairly wealthy man. Ever since his ladder business had taken off, Bratz had been prudent. Once a month he would travel to Moscow with a large amount of money, which he would deposit in the Moscow Principal Bank. He now had over a million roubles deposited there and he'd built up a good working relationship with his bank manager.

Ivan Bratz had prepared for this day and after discussions with the bank, it was agreed that they would loan him a million roubles to go with the million he already had deposited there.

So Bratz had a fighting fund of around two million roubles. He also had an amount of money hidden away in a large safe in the cellar of his

house back in Zhumyov which nobody knew about. Not even his family.
However Ivan Bratz wanted that money to remain were it was.

Bratz had wanted to offer Schwab a million roubles. He knew that actual
amount was very low, but then he was prepared to haggle and would have
eventually raised his bid to one and a half million. If need be he would
have finally capitulated and offered the whole two million roubles. It
would still be worth it, eventually.

For Ivan Bratz, this was far more than just a business deal. For Ivan
Bratz this was about power. It was something he had dreamed about
for years. No longer was he just the simple worker from downtrodden
Zhumyov. Bratz had worked hard to get where he was and what he'd
accomplished. He had been successful but he knew he would always be
labelled as a peasant, a humble peasant from bloody rotten Zhumyov.
But Ivan Bratz wanted more. Ivan Bratz wanted respect, and to become
the owner of the highly esteemed Schwab Furnishing Company would
give him that respect, immediately. He wanted to live in Smolensk and
he wanted a better life for himself. Ivan Bratz craved the admiration and
respect that only wealth and power could bring.

But now this. Four million roubles. And that four million roubles would
blow Ivan Bratz's hopes and dreams clear out of the water.

'Damn you Ernst Schwab...Damn you'.

Ivan Bratz looked up at Ernst Schwab, his adversary.
'I can't pay you that amount,' he said to Schwab, 'I haven't got the funds.'
'Oh,' Schwab replied, 'Oh I see.'

There were another few agonizing moments of silence. Agonizing
for Bratz.

'How much were you thinking of offering me?' Schwab asked. He was
enjoying all of this.

Bratz sighed, he was a beaten man and he suddenly felt out of his depth.

'I was going to offer you one and a half million roubles,' he lied, 'but you
could have pushed me to two million.'

There was once again a strained silence.

'Hmm,' said Schwab.

Bratz looked down at the floor.

Finally, Ernst Schwab spoke.

'I may have a deal for you Bratz,' he said, 'I may have a deal for you, but there will be conditions and limitations. The deal I propose will have to be followed to the letter. However, in the long run you and your family will benefit greatly".

Bratz looked up again. He was possibly being thrown a lifeline. He took a deep breath.

'What is it Schwab?' he asked.

'For two million roubles I will sell you half of my company, but with that there are certain conditions.'

Bratz nodded.

Ernst Schwab continued. 'My company will be run by me and only me. I will train and educate your son Pavel so that at some point he could take over my furniture business without any problems. I will teach him everything. Your other son will come here and we will set up the production of your Baltic ladders and your range of furniture. Your son Nikolai and Pavel will jointly run these ventures. You Bratz, will have nothing to do with any of this. You will remain in Zhumyov and look after your business there.'

Bratz was about to protest. He had never heard anything more ridiculous in his life. Ivan Bratz 'was' the Baltic Ladder Company, and he certainly wasn't going to hand over two million roubles for a company that he would have little or no part in running.

Schwab held up his hand to stop Bratz from saying something that he could possibly regret.

'Listen to me Bratz,' said Schwab, 'You were right when you said that we weren't getting any younger, and I've been giving this some considerable thought. What you also need to realize is that I look upon Pavel as almost a son. He's the son I unfortunately never had. I'm childless of course. I took Pavel under my wing as a boy and I've watched him grow into a man, and he's a good man. I respect him, and as you know he has a talent with wood and the love of the craft. Pavel would continue to produce the quality furniture that has always borne the Schwab name. Of that I am confident. We can accommodate your business here Bratz, and you're right of course, we do have the room to expand. However, you and I cannot work together. You are used to being your own man and so am I. A business cannot have two bosses with conflicting interests, and believe me Bratz, you and I would end up in conflict and that would be to the detriment of both our companies. It simply would not work. You and I will not be working together under the 'same roof'...ever.'

Ivan Bratz shrugged, but Schwab saw the look of quick anger in his eyes. It was time for Ernst Schwab to dangle the 'carrot'.

'However, I have a plan,' Schwab continued, 'and it's a plan that could work to our mutual benefit.'

Bratz looked dismissive. He'd heard enough and what he had heard sounded more or less an insult.

But Ernst Schwab suddenly spoke in a different tone. It was almost threatening.

'Listen to me Bratz and listen well,' he said, 'because I'm about to give you something, an offer that you can't refuse.'

Ivan Bratz just sat there, he was open to anything.

Then Schwab made his play.

'I will sell you half of my company for two million roubles and we will run the company as I've stated. We will continue to run it that way until my death, whenever that's God's will. And then Bratz, upon my death, I will leave all and everything that I own to your son Pavel.

I will leave him my business, my house, my properties and my money. Everything will go to him. As you know I have no one else to leave it to, so it might as well be Pavel. He has a gift, he is a master carpenter, and I feel that he will continue to run this company in the same manner that I always have.'

Ivan Bratz couldn't believe what he had just heard. He almost shook his head to make sure that he wasn't dreaming. Did Ernst Schwab realise what he had just proposed? He was going to give everything, absolutely everything to Pavel. And everything was the business, the property and all of the money. Bratz nearly burst out laughing with incredulity. Silly, stupid, old Schwab was going to give it all away, and he would be giving it all to the Bratz family.

Bratz would eventually get back the two million roubles that he was going to have to pay Ernst Schwab for the business. He was going to get Schwab's for nothing. He would get all of his money back, plus the Schwab

Furnishing Company, plus Schwab's house and all his properties, along with all of Schwab's money.

Ivan Bratz nearly leapt out of his chair as he went to shake Ernst Schwab's hand.

'It's a deal Ernst,' Bratz almost shouted. He tried his best not to sound over excited, but his obvious greed was so apparent.

'Good,' said Ernst Schwab, 'I'm glad we've come to a positive compromise. It will nice to know that my company will be left in safe hands. No one can live forever Bratz, and I can't take my money to the grave with me. As they say...'You come into this world with nothing, and when you leave, you leave everything'. So this is my legacy, my legacy to Pavel.'

'Yes, yes, of course,' Bratz quickly agreed. His mind of course, was on other things.

'Give me the rest of the week, and I will get the two million roubles to you straightaway.'

Bratz was eager to seal the deal. He certainly couldn't risk Ernst Schwab having a change of heart.

Schwab reached into his desk and presented Bratz with a sheet of paper.

'There is the name of my bank and my account details. Send the money there and I will have my solicitor sort out all the details.'

Bratz took the piece of paper from him and jammed it into his inside pocket. There wasn't much more to say and after a few more formalities and some small talk about the 'happy couple', Bratz once again shook Ernst Schwab's hand and then excused himself.

There were things that he had to attend to.

Once Bratz had left his office, Ernst Schwab returned to the drinks cabinet and refilled his brandy glass, it was possibly the largest brandy Schwab had ever poured himself. He went back to his desk, raised his glass and made a toast to himself. Then he laughed out loud.

'Bratz, you're a greedy bastard...a greedy, greedy bastard.'

It had worked, his plan had worked.

For a long time Schwab had worried about Anna's future. Her future when he wouldn't be there to look after her. True, he could have left her a large amount of money in his will, but once word got out that she was a rich and very attractive young woman, there would very quickly be a line of unsuitable suitors knocking on her door. Anna was naive and Schwab could envisage some sharp young 'blade' whisking her off her feet and eventually leaving her penniless. He had seen it all before. Then she had suddenly fallen in love with Pavel Bratz and it was an honest love. Pavel loved Anna for who she was, there was certainly no motive. Anna was simply Schwab's secretary, there was no wealth and no one knew about the past.

But it was also a simple fact of life that he couldn't just leave everything to Anna. That would leave many unresolved questions. Schwab preferred it that Anna thought of him as an 'uncle'. It was too late for Schwab to be her father.

Leaving Anna a working factory was to leave her with innumerable problems, she would be swamped by problems. No, that was not the answer. However, leaving her husband the factory and all that went with it was something else. It stopped a lot of questions and for Schwab it resolved a lot of problems. Anna would be taken care of and of that he was sure. She would be taken care of and hopefully live a happy life. She and Pavel would remain in Smolensk. They could live there permanently and would never have to live in the shadow of that dreadful Bratz family in a backwater called Zhumyov.

Schwab took a good, straight drink of his brandy and laughed out loud again.

He was a happier man

The next day he would visit his solicitor and together they would hammer out a contract that would tie up Ivan Bratz's greedy hands for years to come.

Everything had gone to plan.

Pavel and Anna began their happy married life together and a year and a half later Anna gave birth to their first son, Victor Andrei. Three more years passed by before their second son was born. They named him Vasily Orlof...'Vasily Orlof Bratz'.

And he too would have a gift.

CHAPTER 9

Ten more years passed by, and for Pavel and Anna Bratz they were very happy years.

Ernst Schwab's plans had worked and had worked well. The partnership between the two companies had also worked. Both businesses had merged together almost effortlessly. Nikolai Bratz turned out to be an affable sort of lad and he and Pavel had no problems in working together. In fact, the whole workforce integrated well and Pavel and Nikolai both had the common sense to let Mr Koenig rule the roost. Experience is a priceless commodity and Koenig's common sense approach once again turned out to be invaluable. It also suited Koenig, who would have never stepped down to some new, young usurper. Koenig had always commanded respect and he rightfully deserved it.

One of the smarter and cleverer of Ernst Schwab's plans had been the insistence that Ivan Bratz was to have nothing at all to do with the Schwab Factory. Schwab and his solicitor had put together an iron clad contract confirming that. Ivan Bratz had been in so much of a hurry to give Ernst Schwab the two million roubles to buy into Schwab's highly profitable company that he hadn't bothered to take any professional advice. Too late he discovered the error of his ways, and his two million roubles had been long deposited in Ernst Schwab's bank account before Bratz finally went to find a solicitor who explained the 'small print' in the contract to him, and that his deal with Schwab had left Bratz quite powerless.

Ivan Bratz was infuriated when he found out that he'd been duped, or considered he had. After all, the money was still flowing into his bank account at an ever increasing rate.

But for Bratz that wasn't enough. He had visions of power and authority. That was what he'd always hungered for. Bratz had an image of himself at the helm of Schwab Industries, and of being 'one of the elite' in Smolensk, just as Ernst Schwab was. Now those visions had been dashed and Ivan Bratz was incensed. In his mind he felt that he'd been robbed and almost straightaway he'd had a huge argument with Ernst Schwab. Schwab retaliated by having Bratz escorted from the factory. That was the ultimate humiliation for Bratz, who in temper then went directly to the Smolensk train station and caught a train to Moscow were he got drunk for the best part of a week. He finally returned to Zhumyov and spent another month there licking his wounds. Zhumyov though, had lost its attraction for Bratz. There were no challenges anymore in Zhumyov, together with the fact that Ivan Bratz was by then a very wealthy man. Within the month he was back in Moscow. Whilst he was there he bought himself a decent apartment in a reasonable district and would stay there for weeks at a time, drinking good vodka and using bad whores. In the end the vodka and the whores finally got the better of him. After several years of irreverent living his health began to decline, even though his bad habits didn't. One night, and after a particularly heavy bout of drinking, he took a large busty Romanian woman called Olga back to his apartment. She threw him onto the bed and then threw herself on top of him. Her antics and her sexual appetite finally got the better of Bratz and he suffered a massive heart attack.

One could almost say that Ivan Bratz died a happy man, maybe not.

Olga, the Romanian 'beauty' was completely devastated by the loss of her new lover.

Bratz could have been her ticket to a better life for her. However, it wasn't to be.

Once she realised that her man had died, the poor woman was positively distraught. So she quickly and efficiently went through Bratz's apartment and found the ten thousand roubles that he had hidden in a small leather bag in a bottom drawer. It was the cash that Bratz used as spending money.

Suddenly poor Olga wasn't so poor anymore, and she pilfered all of the money along with Bratz's gold pocket watch, and a bottle of vodka.

On leaving the apartment, Olga turned to Bratz. He was on the bed, dead and staring at the ceiling.

'Twat'...she muttered in Romanian, and then she and the money quickly left the building.

Life without Ivan Bratz somehow made life a little easier for everyone, especially for the Bratz family. In truth, they all quietly gave a sigh of relief, especially his wife Martha, who had spent a lifetime living under her husband's rule and putting up with his awkwardness and complete indifference.

The three Bratz brothers found that they worked well together and the Bratz and the Schwab partnership also worked very well. Production at both factories continued to rise and sales and profits gradually increased. The overheads at the Zhumyov factory were extremely low and the Smolensk factory was ideally placed for the distribution of all of their products.

The old adage 'If it's not broke, don't fix it' comes to mind.

Pavel, Anna and their two boys were extremely happy. They owned a good house and Pavel was doing the job that he loved. He and Anna had taken on board the running of the company through the tutelage of Ernst Schwab. 'Uncle Ernst', as he had become, soon realised that it would be Anna who had the business brain. The two brothers, Pavel and Nikolai, looked after production and quality control, together with Mr Koenig who was by then ten years older and happier to take a slower pace of life. Koenig considered that his work was done and he was quite happy to hand the reins of Schwab's furniture production over to the two brothers. He still went into work every day but he started a little later, and finished a great deal earlier.

Ladder production had been astounding. Baltic Ladders were now distributed throughout the whole of Russia and the market for them had begun to open in parts of Europe. The secret of their success was their robustness. The Bratz brothers had decided that no corners would be cut when it came to the quality of their Baltic Ladders. The brand name itself had become synonymous as a superior product. Baltic ladders didn't break, and Baltic ladders didn't rot.

Other companies had tried to reproduce their own versions and copy the ladders, but they couldn't compete on price, quality and availability.

Hence, the family thrived.

Pavel's two sons, Victor Andrei and Vasily Orlof, were by then thirteen and ten years old respectively.

The two brothers were as different as 'chalk and cheese'. Victor, the elder, was the more robust sort of boy. Dark haired and tall, he was the more physical and would spend most of his spare time at the factory with his father and his Uncle Nikolai. He was given free range there and being the boss's son meant he was never really going to be chastised by anyone. Except of course, by Mr Koenig.

Young Victor Bratz very quickly realised he would have to give Mr Koenig a wide berth.

Vasily Orlof, the younger brother of the two, was a quieter boy all together. Very fair haired and slim, he had his mother's looks and a head of blonde hair that had been inherited from his grandmother Rachel. Anna recognized this, and for very different reasons, so did Ernst Schwab. He was very fond of both boys. After all, he was in truth their grandfather.

However, the bustle of the timber factory was not for young Vasily Orlof, he was happiest staying at home with his mother. He had always been considered the baby of the family and there was never been any pressure on him to do anything at all really. Because his mother, Anna was permanently involved with the business, they decided they should employ a family cook and a maid. So the young Vasily Orlof Bratz was left at home for hours at a time, and left to his own devices.

Anna Bratz had possibly one great weakness, and that was her utter fascination for jewellery. For years Anna had bought and had been bought an assortment of the most diverse and beautiful pieces of jewellery. Some were expensive, some were not, but Anna had a good eye and she knew what she liked. As the years passed, she had accumulated quite a large, mixed collection of 'costume' and other more expensive jewellery. The expensive pieces were locked away in the family safe, but Anna's cheaper costume jewellery filled many of the drawers in her and Pavel's bedroom.

Anna's hobby had always amused Pavel, and he would chastise his wife every time he had to have another little set of drawers constructed to hold her ever expanding collection of jewellery.. But his wife was beautiful and he loved her, and whenever they attended one of the many functions in Smolensk, Pavel would smile when he saw the other women staring at Anna's jewellery and quietly nudging one another.

Pavel Bratz and his wife had come a long way, Pavel had almost unknowingly achieved the respect that his Father had craved, but never found.

Young Vasily Orlof too shared his mother's love for jewellery. He adored it. As a young boy he would often go into his parent's bedroom and search through his mother's jewellery for some special bead or stone or anything else that took his eye. On sunnier days he would lie on top of their large bed and hold the different jewels up to the light. He was fascinated by the shape of the facets which were cut into the coloured glass and crystal and he would spend hours gazing through the glass of the jewels at a world which suddenly became a different colour. He would lay his mother's beads, brooches and jewelled rings on top of her white linen bedspread and watch as the sun shone through the jewelled glass and threw a spectrum of colours across the clean white sheets.

His fascination eventually turned into a passion. And as he got older his mother trusted him with her more expensive jewellery and he would spend hours sketching and then colouring his drawings of her prized gems. The quality of his artwork became so accomplished that his mother began to have the pictures put into expensive frames and had them hung on the more prominent walls throughout the house. She was proud of her son, very proud.

Strangely however, the one piece of jewellery that Vasily Orlof never once showed any interest in was his mother's unique wedding ring. Made by Pavel Bratz from the hardest piece of ebony, the ring would shine black and red and the darkest brown on his mother's third finger. With the passing years the ring had acquired an ageless and enduring beauty. But for Vasily Orlof, it was just a piece of wood. And unfortunately, Vasily Orlof Bratz would never have any love for wood or for timber, or for anything at all to do with his family's business.

Anna Bratz's favourite day, was without doubt Saturdays. Anna never went into the factory on Saturdays and she had always considered it her 'special' day. On Saturdays, Anna would go into Smolensk city centre to visit the jewellers' shops, most of which were situated in the well known Krasninsky district. Once there she would flit from shop to shop, ever searching for that one special piece of jewellery. From there she would go to the different markets and peruse the many jewellery stalls there, always looking for that one piece of jewellery that would catch her eye.

Saturday became Vasily Orlof's favourite day too. He began to accompany his mother every weekend and together they would wander around the city centre looking for things to do or something special to buy.

If they couldn't find any jewellery that took their particular interest, Anna would turn her attention to the various clothes stores and haberdasheries. She would always have to buy something, if not for herself, then certainly for Vasily. They would then enjoy a late lunch at their favourite restaurant.

'Dmitri's' was run by an old Greek émigré family. The restaurant was situated in the centre of Smolensk and had been there for decades. It was an old family business that had been continually passed down from father to son and with it the skills of preparing excellent food.

Anna and Vasily would always have the grilled fish. It didn't matter to them which or what grilled fish it actually was, and that was part of the fun. The fish was seasonal, sometimes it was down to availability and sometimes it was 'whatever' had arrived at market. But no matter what fish it was, Dmitri's would cook it to perfection. After their main course, Anna would have a delicious slice of cake with a cup of special Greek coffee. But for Vasily it was always the ice cream. Dmitri's made their own sumptuous ice cream, which again would be flavoured by the season's different fruits. Anna would always smile as Vasily took his first mouthful and then giggle at the pleasure of it.

As he got older, Vasily became more discerning over his mother's choice of jewellery. He too knew what he liked and his preference for quality precious stones soon became evident. He began to influence his mother to such a point, that Anna had stopped telling Pavel just how much her little 'hobby' was beginning to cost. Vasily was fussy and becoming fussier. He and his mother were no longer visiting the jewellery stalls at the different markets. Vasily described the pretty displays of glass costume jewellery there as 'rubbish' and told his mother that she 'must' wear the real thing. Anything else was worthless.

It wasn't simply arrogance, the boy was far from arrogant. It was just his fascination and a true passion for excellence.

By the time he was fifteen, most of the jewellers in the Krasninsky district recognised young Vasily Orlof Bratz. Strange as it may seem, the boy was respected. The 'trade' had realised that young Mr Bratz had a good eye and it was an eye for quality. It was seen as a talent.

Others may have said it was a 'gift'.

Whenever they went into the city, Anna and Vasily would always call in at 'Blesks the Jewellers', one of the most prestigious jewellers in Smolensk. The shop was owned by Rubin Blesk himself, and it was without doubt their favourite jewellers.

Rubin Blesk would only stock the finest and the best. Vasily Orlof knew that and respected that fact. Over the years, Vasily's mother had bought many pieces of jewellery from Rubin Blesk and she was a highly valued customer. The doors of Blesks the Jewellers were ever open to Mrs Anna Bratz. After all, her husband was the owner of Schwab Furnishings of Smolensk.

It was on one of their trips into Smolensk that Anna and Vasily had gone to Blesk's to view some new jewellery there. Anna, Vasily and Rubin Blesk were in conversation when Rubin turned to Vasily.

'You really do have a great interest in fine jewellery, don't you Vasily Orlof?' he said, and he smiled at Vasily.

'Yes I do Mr Blesk,' Vasily replied, 'I find it fascinating. I love the preciseness of the cut and the ability to bring out the colouring in the different stones. It's a work of art.'

Rubin Blesk laughed, 'You remind me of when I was a boy. I too had a fascination for precious stones. As I remember it was diamonds and emeralds that were my favourites. My father used to let me play with the most valuable of gems. It makes me shudder now when I think about how I used to handle them.'

'Vasily was the same as a small boy,' said Anna, 'He used to play with all my old costume jewellery. He used to do sketches of it all, in fact he still does. Every time I purchase something new, Vasily will draw it. We have his drawings hung all around the house, they're beautiful.'

Rubin Blesk turned to Vasily, who was by then looking more than slightly embarrassed.

'I would really like to see them,' said Rubin Blesk.

'They're nothing really Mr Blesk,' replied Vasily, who was feeling slightly perturbed.

But his mother intervened. 'Yes they are Vasily, they are really beautiful Mr Blesk. Everyone who visits the house always comments on them.'

Rubin Blesk was intrigued. For years he'd watched young Vasily Orlof and had seen his fascination for really good jewellery, and he knew that here was a possible talent.

'I would actually really like to see them,' Ruben Blesk asked again.

'Why don't you come around for tea next Saturday afternoon Mr Blesk,' said Anna suddenly, 'you could look at Vasily's drawings then.'

Vasily shot his mother an embarrassed glance, this was something he wasn't expecting.

But Ruben Blesk was quite taken aback. When he had asked to see Vasily Orlof's drawings, he expected Mrs Bratz to bring one or two of them to his shop when she next called. Never did he expect to be invited to their house. Ruben Blesk was gratified.

'Mrs Bratz, that would be an honour,' he replied.

The following Saturday at three o' clock Ruben Blesk arrived, as agreed, at the Bratz home.

He was met at the front door by Anna and was shown into their large living room where Blesk, Anna and Vasily Orlof spent the next hour dining on neatly prepared sandwiches and beautifully baked cakes, along with a couple of pots of 'English Tea'. Their conversations flowed easily, and eventually the topic of conversation naturally turned to jewellery. Ruben Blesk has already noticed the four or five drawings of prominent pieces of jewellery that were hung in the room. They were as exquisite as the jewellery they portrayed. Blesk was more than impressed and finally drew the conversation as to the quality of Vasily's stunning drawings. Anna, who was very proud of her son's work, and immediately offered to show Blesk around the house so that he could see the rest of Vasily's work.

Vasily Orlof was quite overwhelmed. Nobody he knew had ever really taken any notice of his drawings before, apart from his mother. His father certainly never had, neither had his brother. All they ever spoke about was wood and timber and that awful factory. But now, here was Ruben Blesk, a man who Vasily Orlof admired and respected and this man was showing a great appreciation for Vasily's work. Eventually they made their way back to the living room and Anna had the pot of tea replenished. They were all sitting there comfortably when Rubin Blesk decided to ask Vasily a question.

'What do you intend to do with your life Vasily?' Blesk asked.

Vasily shrugged, 'I don't really know,' he replied, 'I've never actually given it much thought.'

It was an honest enough answer.

'Will you go into the timber trade and make furniture alongside your father?' Blesk asked.

'Hardly,' replied Vasily, and he shook his head, 'I have no intention of ever working in 'that' factory.'

Anna smiled at her son, 'Vasily has no interest in making furniture Mr Blesk, no interest at all,'

Vasily Orlof shrugged, 'I hate the damn place,' he added.

Anna Bratz raised her eyebrows somewhat.

'Have you considered becoming an artist?' Rubin Blesk asked him, 'You certainly have a talent, and your drawings definitely show great promise.'

'Thank you Mr Blesk,' Vasily replied, 'Unfortunately, I only seem to have a talent for drawing jewellery. I've tried landscapes and even portraits, but somehow I can't find the same passion. Do you understand what I mean Mr Blesk?'

Rubin Blesk did understand, completely.

'Yes I do Vasily,' he said, 'I really do.'

There was a moment of silence, and then Rubin Blesk spoke again.

'Have you ever considered becoming a jeweller?' he suddenly asked.

Vasily Orlof sat there speechless.

It was as though someone had just opened a hidden door. 'A jeweller'... To become a jeweller was something Vasily Orlof Bratz had never even considered, never in his life.

He turned to his mother, but she was sitting there looking just as amazed as her son.

'A jeweller Mr Blesk, but how?' Vasily asked.

Rubin Blesk smiled.

'I'm offering you a job Vasily Orlof. Come and work for me and learn the craft. I will teach you everything. I have skilled workers, craftsmen who work with silver and gold and some of the most beautiful of precious stones. It's a world of diamonds and sapphires, and emeralds and rubies. It's a world you would love, I can see that, and I believe you have a definite talent Vasily Orlof. It is very hard work, very hard indeed, and very intense and time consuming. However, if you have the talent, I will find it.'

Vasily turned to his mother, his eyes were wide with excitement.

'Can I mother, can I go and work for Mr Blesk?'

Anna suddenly had to control her emotions. Of course she would love to have Vasily work for Rubin Blesk, because Anna certainly did understand her son's love of jewellery. However, 'her' son was also Pavel's son, and she would have to discuss Vasily's future with her husband. Anna informed Mr Blesk about speaking to her husband, but she promised to talk to Pavel as soon as he returned home that evening.

Half an hour later, Rubin Blesk left the house after shaking hands with both Anna and a very excited Vasily Orlof.

As Blesk walked away he wondered what the outcome would be.

Rubin Blesk was of course, a Jew.

That evening, Anna and Pavel sat in their dining room enjoying their evening meal. Anna had the cook prepare a strongly flavoured goulash, dressed with cabbage and beetroot. It was one of Pavel's favourites. As they both sat at their large candlelit table, Anna listened to her husband talk about factory production as he dunked lumps of dark grained bread into his food and drank his customary glass of beer.

Vasily Orlof was in his bedroom, Anna had instructed him to keep out of the way for a while. Their other son, Victor Andrei would probably still be at the factory.

In fact he wasn't. He was as usual out with some of his friends, drinking in some of the local hostelries and chasing any woman who would let him.

Anna sat there patiently listening to her husband, who was telling her all about some beautiful imported oak that had arrived at the factory that day. She waited for him to finish and then chose her moment.

'I want to talk to you about Vasily,' she said to him.

Pavel stopped eating for a moment, and he wondered why that particular subject had suddenly come up in their conversation. Pavel had been talking about the timber business and the beauty of good oak. Now his wife suddenly wanted to talk about their youngest son.

A wiser man would have smelled a rat.

'What about him?' Pavel asked.

'What are we going to do with him?' Anna replied.

Pavel started to eat his meal again, and that gave him a moment to think.

Pavel had a problem with his youngest son. They hardly ever spoke to one another. Vasily was so unlike Victor Andrei, his elder brother. Victor Andrei was a very open and likeable lad, who had always readily worked in the factory and had a great interest in carpentry. Pavel could talk to Victor Andrei all day long. But it was never the same with Vasily Orlof., and Pavel had always found it difficult to communicate with his youngest son.

Anna was aware of the problem. She knew that Victor Andrei would always work with his father, and in all probability would end up running Schwab Furnishings. But that was all in the future. Anna' worry was for her youngest son. She and Vasily were close, very close, and she'd always known that Vasily would have to tread a different path.

Schwab Furnishings was not for Vasily Orlof Bratz.

Anna looked at her husband.

'You know that he has no interest at all in carpentry or making furniture, don't you Pavel?'

Pavel Bratz just grunted. It was his typical response and Anna smiled, it was what she expected.

But she continued, 'Something's come up Pavel, Vasily's been offered a job. It would be the beginning of a new career and I think that it's something that would suit him.'

Pavel looked up at his wife. This was actually interesting news, because Pavel knew, deep in his heart, that Vasily Orlof had no love at all for carpentry and never would.

'Oh really, 'he said to her, 'and what is this job?'

Anna took a deep breath.

'Ruben Blesk, the jeweller has offered to take Vasily Orlof under his wing and teach him the jewellery trade. He thinks that Vasily has a talent and he will train him to become a master craftsman. It's something that Vasily really wants to do and...'

At that point Pavel Bratz cut his wife off in mid sentence.

'Is this some sort of joke?' he asked.

Anna looked at her husband, 'No Pavel,' she replied.

Pavel stared at her, and then he shook his head, 'I'm not having my son work for a Jew and I'm not having him work in the jewellery trade either.'

Anna was somewhat taken aback. She realised there may have been a difficulty in telling her husband that their son wanted to be a jeweller, but she never considered that the bigger problem would be that Mr Blesk was Jewish.

'And what's wrong with Mr Blesk?' she asked.

Pavel just shook his head.

Anna tried to continue, 'Mr Blesk wants Vasily to train and work in his shop with his other skilled jewellers. It's the chance of a lifetime.'

'He won't be working for Blesk, ever.' Pavel was suddenly becoming agitated.

'And why is that?' asked Anna.

'Because no son of mine is working for a bloody Jew,' he snapped back. Pavel was becoming annoyed. 'Do you expect me to let our son work down in the Krasninsky district? They're all Jews down there. All those jewellers' shops are owned by the Jews.'

Anna looked at her husband in amazement.

'Of course the jewellers are owned by Jews you idiot. How do you think 'jewellery' got its name?'

Pavel blinked for a moment, he'd never even considered the connection.

In an act of defiance, Pavel folded his arms, and that obstinacy began to anger his wife.

Anna stared back at him.

'Our son has a real talent Pavel, and just like you he has a gift.'

Pavel just smirked at her, which made Anna even angrier.

'A gift...what gift?' he replied abruptly, 'I have a talent with wood and with timber, I know that and I always have. But jewellery? No, that's not a talent, it's nothing more than a whim. He can't make jewellery. What would everybody think?'

Anna was infuriated.

'Why can't he make jewellery? And who is 'everybody' for god's sake?'

Pavel was suddenly becoming very annoyed.

'Everybody Anna,' he said loudly, 'Everyone we know. What would people think if they found out that the son of Pavel Bratz was working for a Jew and playing about with jewellery? No, no son of mine is going to make jewellery for a living. It wouldn't be right.'

Anna stared back at him.

'And what's wrong with making jewellery?' she asked.

Pavel scowled, 'I want him to do a proper job, I want him to do a man's job and do man's work. Not playing around with damn baubles and making stupid women's rings.'

There was a moment of silence, and then Anna quietly stood up. She leant forward and they were now facing each other. The only thing between them was a lit candle, it burned brightly and Anna could feel its heat. She slowly lifted her left hand and held it at the side of the burning candle. Her hand was in front of Pavel's face, and in the bright light the polished ebony wedding ring on her third finger gleamed like a black diamond, with its scarlet grain still vivid and blood red.

'You once made me a piece of jewellery Pavel Bratz. You once made this 'stupid woman' a very beautiful ring,' Anna said quietly.

Pavel stared at the ring as the light from the flame illuminated its dark irridescence. Yes, the ring was still absolutely stunning. It had been crafted from the most beautiful piece of ebony that Pavel had ever seen.

'What is wrong with you Pavel?' she asked him, 'Have you changed so much?'

Pavel couldn't reply. He just kept staring at the ring he had once made for her, the most beautiful ring, for his beautiful wife. Yes he had once made jewellery, and he suddenly realised his own stupidity.

Anna took his silence as obstinacy and she was angry.

And angry people say hurtful things and angry people use words as weapons.

"You were once 'a nobody' Pavel Bratz. Do you remember that?' she said to him, 'You were a nobody. And it was Uncle Ernst who gave you your chance, just like he gave me a chance, and that chance changed our lives. Without Uncle Ernst you would never have had anything, no house and no business. He believed in you and he saw your talent, he saw 'your gift'. And now you have a son who has a talent, a talent in a different direction but nevertheless a talent. But you are so pig headed that you can't see it, or moreover, you won't see it. Rubin Blesk has faith in Vasily and he wants to give him the same opportunity that you had. But no, not the son of 'Mr Pavel Bratz'. Why not Pavel, why not? Remember your own father Pavel, remember how he treated you? He dominated you...and you're going end up just like him.'

Pavel sat there and bit his lip. He didn't like that comparison, not one bit.

'You've said enough Anna.' he growled.

But Anna hadn't said enough.

'Don't you dare talk to me like that? I'm not like your mother. I won't be treated like some peasant woman.'

Pavel immediately stood up. The mention of his mother had provoked him.

'Don't you ever call my mother a peasant.' Now he was shouting.

There were suddenly tears in Anna's eyes, but they were tears of anger and frustration.

'You once told me Pavel, you told me that everyone in Zhumyov was a peasant and that you never wanted to go back there. You're forgetting where you come from Pavel Bratz and the truth hurts. But you know as well as me...You were all peasants, all of you.'

And with that Anna turned and stormed out of the room.

Pavel stood there and watched his wife slam the door behind her. He clenched his fist but he didn't know what to do with it. Pavel Bratz had never been a violent man. He couldn't stand falling out with his wife, and in truth, they hardly ever had a cross word between them.

After all, Anna was not only his wife, she was his closest friend.

Pavel sat down at the table again, but he found that he'd lost his appetite. He sat there tapping the table with his fork, contemplating what had just happened. He had to think things through, however, in his mind kept seeing the ebony wedding ring he had made for his wife all those years ago. He remembered making the ring, and he remembered carving it out of that one special piece of ebony, and he also remembered the joy that it had given him.

Suddenly Pavel Bratz realised the depth of his own stupidity. His son, Vasily Orlof, was fascinated by fine jewellery in the same way that Pavel had always admired the finest timber. The beauty of the different coloured woods that Pavel loved to work with was akin to Vasily's admiration for precious stones. It was suddenly all so very obvious. Pavel sat at the dining table mulling things over in his mind. If Vasily Orlof wanted to become a craftsman jeweller, then he should work and train with the best, just like Pavel did at Schwab's.

Rubin Blesk was one of the best, one of the best in Smolensk anyway and Pavel knew that.

He sat there staring at the still burning candle. Anna had been right all along, of course she had. And Vasily Orlof would never make a carpenter, ever.

Pavel snubbed out the candle and made his way upstairs to bed, only to find that his bed was empty. Anna had decided to sleep on her own in their spare bedroom.

After lying there on his own for over an hour Pavel finally got up and went to find his wife in the spare room. He climbed into bed with her and put his arm around her waist. Anna lay there in silence but Pavel knew that she was still awake. He leant over and spoke to her.

'You were right Anna, and I was wrong. Vasily can go to Blesk's and learn the jewellery trade. I'm sorry for upsetting you, I'm an idiot.'

Anna turned to him and smiled

'Yes you are. You're an idiot,' she whispered, and then she kissed him.

A week later Vasily Orlof Bratz started work at Blesks the Jewellers down in the Krasninsky District of Smolensk. On his first day there, Rubin Blesk took Vasily Orlof into his workshop. This was a separate older red brick building, which was set at the back of the shop. There he was introduced to Blesk's three craftsmen jewellers. Two of the men were in their late sixties. One was Uncle Sholem, who was actually Rubin Blesk's uncle. The other, 'Mr Nathan', was a small wiry man who everyone seemed to call 'Nat'. The third and younger man was Maurice Broch. Maurice was in his early forties, he was an intense looking man who had an overgrown head of curly black hair, and wore, almost matching in colour, a pair of thick, black horn-rimmed spectacles.

Vasily Orlof was immediately welcomed into the group and would in time learn to respect and even love these three men. They all had the same passion, the art of cutting precious stones and the creation of stunningly beautiful jewellery.

For the first three months the only thing Vasily Orlof was required to do was observe, and he loved it. In between the observing he had to clean and wash and sweep of course. And he also had to make endless cups of tea and coffee, depending on the drinker's preference, and he made sure that everybody ate. None of which was a problem for Vasily Orlof. He was totally addicted to his work. He was in a world that he loved, and it wasn't long before he was spending six or seven days a week at Blesk's workshop, working late into the night. It was almost an addiction, and he wasn't alone. Though the two older men would leave at a reasonable hour, Maurice Broch had a younger man's passion and he and Vasily Orlof would stay late into the night and continue with the day's work whilst discussing the colour and the clarity of cut stones.

For the first three months Vasily Orlof would watch those three men work miracles with silver and gold and with diamonds and pearls. It was a stupendous artistry.

Every new piece of jewellery was a joint project, the men all worked together as a team. From the initial design, right through to the end product, each step of the process was discussed. Above the workshop a set of creaking stairs led up to the first floor to an area known as 'the office'. The team would meet there and sit around a large circular wooden table to plan, prepare and develop the upcoming pieces of jewellery. Rubin Blesk headed the team. He was the master artist and would arrive there with spectacular drawings of his fabulous designs.

Every three or four months Rubin Blesk would gather his craftsmen together to examine his latest consignment of precious stones. It was a time of great excitement for the team and a experience that Vasily Orlof would never forget. The jewellers would all go and sit around the large circular table up in the office. Then the table would be covered with a dark linen cloth and Rubin would arrive, carrying with him his dark brown leather bag. He would open it and then empty small cotton bags full of brilliant diamonds and other coloured gems onto the linen covered table. The team would then sift through the 'treasure' and admire or discard the different gems.

Vasily Orlof had never imagined anything like it in his life.

Rubin Blesk was not only a jeweller, he was also an astute businessman and an important part of his business was the trading and wholesaling of diamonds and other precious stones. Blesk would travel to Antwerp in Belgium three or four times a year. He would take the train and travel west, all the way to Antwerp to the city's famous diamond markets. Antwerp had steadily become the largest diamond marketplace in Europe. Its influence had grown after huge amounts of diamonds were discovered in South Africa in 1866. Before then most of the world's diamonds had originated from India. But in 1888 the diamond company known as 'De Beers' Consolidated Mines had been established after De Beers and its backers bought up most of the competition.

De Beers suddenly held a monopoly, and most of the diamonds that were hacked out of their famous Kimberly Mines were eventually sent on to Antwerp.

Rubin Blesk would travel to Antwerp to buy diamonds and other precious stones and then he would bring them back to Smolensk where he and his craftsmen would pick out the very best. Blesk would then sell the surplus stones to the jewellery trade in the Krasninsky District. However, the demand for diamonds in Moscow and St Petersburg had also begun to increase and Blesk realized that there were lucrative business opportunities there too. He began to buy larger amounts of precious stones and he accepted the fact that in the near future he may have to visit Antwerp every couple of months, possibly even more. The problem lay in getting his diamonds back home to Smolensk. He could only physically carry a certain amount of diamonds without drawing attention to himself.

And with that in mind, Rubin Blesk had taken matters into hand.

The trip to Antwerp was long and arduous trawl. From Smolensk, Blesk had to travel by train to Warsaw in Poland, and then onwards through Germany to Berlin and then onto Cologne. From there he would continue west until finally arriving at Antwerp's famous Rijfstraat Train Station.

Blesk would never seek any accommodation. He would immediately make his way directly to the diamond trader's halls on the Pelikaanstraad. These were the original traders, the historic 'Diamantclub' diamond traders of Antwerp. After dealing there, Blesk would move on, just ten doors up to number 62 Pelikaanstraad, to the newly opened 'Vrije Diamanthhandel'. This was where a set of breakaway, mainly Jewish traders who had founded their own trading hall, simply because they could not meet the strict admission requirements set up by the politically correct members of the original Diamantclub.

In essence, the old brigade didn't want any of those 'Jews' muscling in on their territory, even though in private they were quite happy to trade and take money off anyone at all who practised the Jewish faith. The hypocrisy was recognised by all, but was never spoken about.

Once again Rubin Blesk made plans to travel to Antwerp.

On hearing the news, Vasily Orlof became quite excited. He relished the thought of once more sitting around the table with the other men as Rubin Blesk emptied the cotton bags of diamonds onto that dark tabletop.

Vasily Orlof made a point of finding Mr Blesk before he left Smolensk. He wanted to wish him a safe journey.

Blesk thanked him and smiled as Vasily Orlof walked away. He had made the right decision in choosing Vasily Orlof as an apprentice. He'd always known that the boy had a talent, as did the rest of his team. They'd already spoken to Rubin and told him as much.

Blesk set off for Antwerp on the Monday morning. He took an early train that initially headed for Warsaw, from there the trip to Antwerp would take two to three days there and then back again. On these trips he always took his old brown leather bag with him. Blesk would never carry something as conspicuous as a briefcase or a secure attaché case. No, that would draw too much attention. Inside his old leather bag were a few toiletries, plus a few other basic necessities. However, tucked away in the bottom of the bag there was a small fortune in diamonds and gems and precious stones. But nobody ever knew. Nobody ever gave that worn old leather bag a second glance. And why would they?

The train eventually set off and after Blesk had been travelling for a couple of hours he decided to go to the W.C to relieve himself. As he walked along between the rows of other passengers he glanced left and right to observe who was travelling with him. It was an old habit, Rubin Blesk had to be on his guard at all times. He was only half way down the carriage when he glanced at the two men on his left. They were about five or six rows back and on the opposite side from where Blesk had been sitting. The two men were dressed almost identically and could have almost been brothers, both men had dark hair and matching Russian beards. However, one of the men was quite tall and the other was rather small.

It was almost comical.

As he passed them he instinctively looked down at them again. Suddenly something caught his attention. Both men were staring directly forwards. Not left and not right, and neither were they talking. Both men just stared straight ahead, unsmiling and silent and somehow tense. Blesk entered the W.C and was slightly perplexed. However when he walked back down the carriage to his seat, both men had disappeared. Before he sat down Blesk glanced back again, but the men were nowhere to be seen.

He took off his hat, held it to his chest and scratched the top of his head.

It was a strange thing to do, but there you go.

Blesk finally arrived at Antwerp mid morning on the Wednesday. As he was walking out of Rijfstraad Train Station he stopped at a kiosk to buy a newspaper and a cigar. As he stood there waiting for his change he looked through the glass kiosk and saw two men walking past and out of the station. They were both dressed similarly to the two men on the train. One was about six and a half feet in height, the smaller man, around five and a quarter. They looked like the same men, but Blesk wasn't sure and he took off his hat and once again scratched his head. Maybe it was intuition.

Once he was in Antwerp's centre, Blesk visited both of the famous diamond markets. First he went to the Diamantclub where he bought six expensive bags of beautiful white diamonds, which even in their raw state possessed the most amazing clarity. Then he went on to the Vrije Diamanthandel where the dealing was a little easier...for a Jew. There he bought from the various dealers and finally ended up with ten bags of mixed gems, some of which contained some of the most fabulous jewels.

The art was to buy the 'very good' along with the not 'as' good. That way he could always get a deal. He could clear the 'not as good' gems through the wholesale side of his business, it was never a problem.

It was the middle of the afternoon when Blesk left the Vrije Diamanthandel. He'd paid his bills, which was also never a problem

Blesk had bank accounts at Antwerp's well respected Antwerpse Diamantbank which was also very handily situated at 54 Pelikaanstraad, exactly between both of the diamond markets. Blesk was well known to most of the dealers, they knew that he was good for the money. Rubin Blesk's cheques certainly did not bounce.

As he walked out of the Vrije Diamanthandel Building into the bright sunlight he glanced to his left and then his right. Suddenly he stopped and looked left again, but they were gone. When he had first looked left he was sure that the two men from the train had been standing there looking at him. It was the tall man and the short man. But when he'd looked again they'd both disappeared, vanished. He wondered if he was imagining things and he took off his hat and scratched his head again as he wondered what to do. Suddenly a passing tram stopped right in front of him and Blesk leapt onto it. He didn't know where it was going but one way or another he needed to get away. Wherever it stopped didn't matter, Blesk could always make his way back to the Rijfstraat Train Station where he would get on the train and then make the long trek home.

An hour later he was on a train heading out of Antwerp and out of Belgium. Over the next two days he would travel back through Cologne and then onto Berlin. From Berlin he continued to travel east back to Poland and he eventually arrived in Warsaw where he would pick up his final train, the train that would take him directly to Smolensk. Blesk stood there in Warsaw's Central Train Station and sighed to himself. His last train would of course be a Russian train and that meant very little heating and generally very inadequate plumbing. Russian trains were infamous for their unreliability.

With just under half an hour to go before his train arrived, Blesk decided to pay a final visit to the toilet. It was around nine o' clock in the evening and the station was beginning to close down. Several people seemed to be waiting for the same train as Blesk but not many more. As Blesk walked around to the back of the platform and approached the toilet block, two men stepped out of the adjoining cloakroom. It was the same two men that had been on the train, the same two men that he had seen in Antwerp. It was the tall one and the short one and suddenly it all made sense. They'd followed him of course, and they had watched his every move. The smaller man suddenly pulled out a revolver and his partner then produced a gleaming blade from within his jacket.

The small man smiled.

'Go into the toilet Mr Blesk,' he said amiably.

Blesk stood there, and then he took off his hat and scratched his head as he stared at them. They knew him and they knew who he was, of course they did. They must have been from Smolensk, a couple of chancers who had sat and planned it all out. And there was only two of them, because organised crime would have sent several men and they would have just shot him openly in broad daylight somewhere and seized the diamonds. But not these two, these two must have figured out just why he went to Antwerp three or four times a year. But how? It would more than likely be 'loose' tongues. It could have been anyone, anyone working in the ticket office at the train station in Smolensk, or even a lowly cleaner working at one of the jewellers in the Krasninsky District, someone or anyone who had overheard a snippet of information relating to Rubin Blesk. All of those thoughts were going through Blesk's mind, when the small man spoke to him again.

'Get into that toilet you fucking Jew, or my friend here will slit your rich Jewish fucking throat.'

The tall man never said a word, he just stared at Blesk.

Blesk put his hat back on his head and walked into the toilet. He had no doubts at all that these two men intended to kill him. He walked into the toilet and towards the farthest wall. He stood there with his back to them, his brown leather bag still in his right hand. He knew their intentions would be to stab him. Stabbing was a silent act, but a gun made a loud noise and could summon attention and there was always a chance that someone would see them. No, it would be the tall man with the knife who would do the deed.

The two men followed Blesk into the toilet and watched him walk over to the wall and stand there with his back towards them. The smaller man frowned, he didn't expect that, and in truth he didn't understand it.

'Turn around,' he said.

Blesk turned around.

'Throw your bag over here,' the small man demanded.

Blesk looked at the small man, and then he dropped his bag to the floor at his own feet.

The small man was getting angry now.

'Kick it over here or you're a fucking dead man,' he hissed.

Blesk was certain then that they intended to stab him, otherwise the small man would have already pulled the trigger.

Blesk stepped forward, put his foot against the bag and then slid bag about a foot along the tiled floor. The small man gave a sigh of annoyance and both of them stepped forward to retrieve the bag full of diamonds. It was going to be the answer to all their dreams.

At that moment the toilet door swung open and in walked a man holding a pistol. The pistol was a Luger, one of latest handguns specifically designed for the German Army.

For a split second, Blesk's tormentors just stood there, astounded.

The man immediately shot the smaller man in the face. That was the gunman taken care of. The tall man spun around and was about to lunge at him, but the man with the Luger shot him in the chest at point blank range.

The bullet that came out of the tall man's back took a lump of flesh the size of a clenched fist with it. The man with the Luger then leant over and shot the tall man in the back of the head, just to make sure.

Blesk stood there and looked at the man holding the Luger. For a split second both men just stared at one another in complete silence.

'Thank you Mr Vodle,' said Rubin Blesk.

He then retrieved his bag from the floor, thankfully there was no blood on it. Blesk was quite fond of his old brown bag. He stepped over the two corpses and then went back outside to wait for his train.

The man with the Luger, Mr Vodle, dragged the tall man into one of the closets and sat him on the lavatory. He then dragged the smaller man in there too and propped him behind the door so that the man's weight jammed the door shut. It would be the following morning before one of the cleaners discovered the 'problem'.

Mr Vodle then went back onto the platform and waited for the train to

Smolensk. It was the same train that Mr Blesk was waiting for. The two men stood fifty feet apart, as they always did. Once the train arrived both men sat in the same carriage. Mr Vodle sat several seats behind Ruben Blesk because he always did...always.

Herman Vodle had once been a sergeant in the German Army. He was Prussian by birth and from being a small boy all he had ever wanted to be was a soldier, just like his father.

He joined the German Army when he was fifteen years old and by his own tenacity rose to the rank of corporal and then went on to become a sergeant, a very well respected sergeant.

His father had also been a sergeant, and in the same regiment. And his father was extremely proud of his son's achievement.

But, unfortunately, it would all go wrong.

It all began when Sergeant Herman Vodle went to check on his men late one evening. When he went into their barracks he discovered that one of his men was missing. The missing soldier turned out to be a young lad who was only fifteen, the same age that Sergeant Vodle had been when he joined the Army. Vodle demanded to know where the boy was and was informed that the notorious Lieutenant Officer Gunter Hauptmann had been into the barracks and had commandeered the boy, just half an hour earlier. Herman Vodle went sick to the pit of his stomach. There were rumours, nasty rumours, about Lieutenant Gunter Hauptmann's 'antics' with some of the younger men in the regiment, violent and sexual antics.

Sergeant Vodle immediately marched around to Lieutenant Hauptmann's private quarters where he heard a young man's screaming. Vodle kicked in the door and found Gunter Hauptmann trying to sodomize the boy. Hauptmann had the young soldier naked and face down on his bed. The soldier's back and buttocks were ripped and bleeding. Hauptmann was standing there, sweating profusely. He too was naked, except for a damp open shirt. He just stood there in bewilderment as Vodle burst into his room. Vodle walked across the room and smashed his fist into Gunter Hauptmann's face, and Hauptmann collapsed to the floor. Vodle then picked up a heavy wooden chair and repeatedly smashed it over the officer until the chair fell to pieces. In temper Sergeant Vodle then kicked Officer Hauptmann several times in the lower abdomen and the testicles. In doing so he ruptured Hauptmann's stomach and lower intestine and he crushed both of Gunter Hauptmann's testicles, irreversibly.

When Vodle had calmed down, he sent the boy back to his barracks and then sat on the edge of Hauptmann's bed and contemplated his future. It was over. There would be no future. In the darkness he listened to Gunter Hauptmann's unconscious breathing, so at least he'd not killed the bastard. There was only one thing to do. Sergeant Herman Vodle stood up and marched around to his Major's quarters and knocked on the door. The Major was quite surprised to see Sergeant Vodle standing there at that time of night, but Vodle felt that he knew the Major well enough and that he could speak openly to him. Once he'd explained what had happened, the Major had Sergeant Vodle arrested immediately. A week passed and rumours abounded. Finally, a hearing was arranged and Vodle was brought before a General. The Major also attended the hearing, which was strangely, quite a small affair considering the nature of Sergeant Vodle's offence.

Sergeant Vodle was quickly informed that he was to be drummed out of the army, never to return. It was as much as Vodle expected and he was surprised that he didn't also receive a prison sentence of sorts. Under the General's orders he was immediately stripped of his rank. The General then stood up, and without saluting walked out of the room. That left the Major and Vodle alone.

'Since you are no longer in the Army I feel I can speak freely,' said the Major as he lit himself a cigarette, 'My hands were tied on this one Vodle I'm afraid.'

Herman Vodel just nodded in reply.

The Major continued, 'Hauptmann was a dirty vile bastard and we are glad to see the back of him. You may never be a soldier again Vodle, but if it's any consolation to you, neither will Hauptmann. In fact, and if the rumours are correct, he will never be a man again either.'

The Major then threw his cigarette to the floor, stood to attention and actually saluted the civilian, Herman Vodle.

Vodle was then escorted to his barracks where he was able to collect his personal effects. It was there that he managed to stuff his beloved Luger into a folded jacket without anyone noticing.

The barracks were completely deserted as Herman Vodle walked out of the main gates for the last time. There was not a man in sight. The men had been ordered that no one should be there to bid him farewell

But worse was to come. Vodle then returned home and had to face his father's wrath. Vodle's father would not listen to any explanation. He considered his son a disgrace, a disgrace to the family and a disgrace to the regiment. Vodle senior then told his son to leave the house.

Life after that became a lot harder for Herman Vodle. Like most ex soldiers he went from job to job, he was mostly employed in throwing bad drunks out of rough bars. Then one way or another he ended up in St Petersburg in Russia, working for the Guberman Family who were the heads of organised crime there. From St Petersburg he was sent to Moscow to work for the same people. Moscow was a different call altogether. Moscow was violent. In Moscow he had to shoot people.

Then out of the blue he'd been sent to Smolensk to find a man who owed the Guberman Family quite a large amount of money. Vodel recovered the money. He'd found the man and shot him. Suddenly Vodle was in favour, and because he quite liked Smolensk, he asked if he could stay there. It was agreed that he could, but under the proviso that if he was needed, Vodle would return to Moscow immediately. Vodle agreed, and he had to return to Moscow on several occasions to earn his wages, but he hated the place and was always glad to return to Smolensk where it was always rather more peaceful.

Herman Vodle took a view on life. There were two types of people, good people and bad people. The good people were the ones who paid him. The rest could all go to hell.

Eventually he'd been introduced to Rubin Blesk by someone who knew that Blesk was looking for some low key personal security, as and when it was needed. When he'd first met Blesk, Vodle had been somewhat sceptical. He had no intention of becoming a shopkeeper's guard dog. But the more he'd spoken to Rubin Blesk, the more impressed he had been. Rubin Blesk was a very clever man. And from the very beginning, Mr Blesk had put Vodle on a weekly retainer, it didn't matter whether Vodle had worked or not. That pleased Vodel, and it also bought his loyalty.

It was Ruben Blesk who had thought up their 'strategy'. When Vodle was working with Mr Blesk, in particular on their trips to Antwerp, it was agreed they would never make contact either physically or verbally. Both men would wait at the train station, but separately. When Mr Blesk sat in his carriage, Vodle would sit in the same carriage but a few rows behind and from there he would watch everyone. Nobody had a clue they were working together. Whenever Mr Blesk walked from one platform to another to catch the next train, Vodle would be twenty feet behind, seemingly looking the other way so that no one would ever notice. Once they reached Antwerp he would stand across the road from the diamond markets and pretend to read a newspaper. To the people walking up and down the busy Pelikaanstraad he just looked like someone who was waiting for a tram.

It had been Mr Blesk who had conjured up the 'warning' sign. If for any reason at all Rubin Blesk was unsure of something, or if he ever needed Vodle's attention or help, then Blesk would simply take off his hat and scratch his head. It was so simple, but it was also virtually unnoticeable to anyone else.

When Blesk had first spotted the two men on the train after leaving Smolensk, Blesk had taken off his hat and scratched his head. The two men had then left the carriage, but Vodle had already seen them go and he later found them sitting further down the train, deep in conversation. He'd kept a check on them and had followed them off the train as Mr Blesk once again scratched his head as they walked past him at the kiosk at the train station in Antwerp. Vodle had stood outside the diamond markets on the Pelikaanstraad and had watched those same two men stand across the road, waiting for Mr Blesk to leave. He'd seen Mr Blesk scratch his head once again as he'd fleetingly recognised those same two men. When Mr Blesk had leapt onto the tram, Vodle had immediately jumped on behind him and promptly turned his back to Mr Blesk. Rubin Blesk had never even known he was there. Once their train had left Antwerp's Rijfstraat Train Station, Vodle had walked up and down the carriages until he spotted the two men again. He found it curious that wherever they sat, the tall man always sat next to the window. It was an indication to Vodle that it must the smaller man who was in charge. He kept an eye on them on every train they travelled on, as they all headed back to Smolensk. However Vodle knew it would be at Warsaw where they would finally attack and rob Mr Blesk, it had to be Warsaw.

Warsaw train station was their last stop before catching the train to Smolensk. It would be there when the two men would attempt to steal Mr Blesk's diamonds, then they could get on the train and return to Smolensk. It had to be Warsaw. Their plan was good. Warsaw was a quieter station, especially at that time of night. Yes, their plan was good. Even as they had their gun pointed at Mr Blesk and watched him scratch his head in shock, they still hadn't a clue as to what was really happening. And even as Vodel shot them both, the two men still didn't really understand.

But Vodle understood and Mr Blesk understood. It was really all so simple.

If Rubin Blesk had walked around with a personal bodyguard by his side, the first action by any assailant would be to take out the bodyguard. Kill the bodyguard and the principal target would then be left helpless. In the game of chess, it was the first rule.

Once they'd arrived back in Smolensk, Vodle followed Mr Blesk home and then returned to his own residence, a small flat in a quieter part of the city. Herman Vodle was a happy man. It had been a good trip, eventful, but not really a problem. He had been dealing with amateurs really. And Vodel knew that sometime during the following week, Mr Blesk would present him with a nice bonus for his excellent work.

He liked Mr Blesk. Mr Blesk was a very clever man.

Vasily Orlof Bratz would eventually spend six wonderful years at Rubin Blesk's, and in those years he would become not only an accomplished craftsman, he would also show all the signs of becoming a genius.

But sadly, during those six years there was also going to be a family tragedy. It was a death that was more of a fond farewell for Vasily Orlof and his brother, but for their mother, Anna, it caused absolute heartbreak.

'Uncle' Ernst Schwab, their mentor and protector, had finally passed away.

Schwab was by that time an old man and well into his eighties. His health had deteriorated somewhat but he still tried his best to keep active. Life however can be cruel, and in the end Schwab became immobile and had to depend on a wheel chair.

Anna would call in to see him every day, usually at lunchtime, and she would still bring him his same potato pie and his custard cake. Nothing ever changed. Schwab employed a cook and a cleaner but his cook was made redundant when it came to Ernst's lunch. Evenings and weekends however, were a different matter.

If for whatever reason, Anna couldn't get to Uncle Ernst's house at lunchtime, she always made sure that his pie and cake were delivered there by one of her staff. On those occasions Anna would call in to see him on her way home. Nothing at all must change, and Anna made sure of that. Ernst Schwab had been good to Anna and he'd always been good to her family.

Ernst Schwab had saved her life.

On Friday afternoons after lunch and weather permitting, Anna would take Uncle Ernst around to the factory in his wheelchair. She would wheel him around so that he could still observe production and have a chat with the men. Then he would meet up with Koenig who was still pottering away at his desk, though Koenig too was an older man by then. Two of the workmen would lift Mr Schwab and his wheelchair up and into the office where he, Pavel and Koenig would then spend an hour together, talking business. Anna would make them all a pot of coffee and Pavel would pour them the same French brandy.

Nothing must change. Anna always made sure of that.

It was only a matter of time however, before Russia's oldest tormentor took its toll.

Schwab caught a chill, and that chill turned into a cold. From there the cold went on to become influenza and that illness then took it's a natural progression. Schwab caught pneumonia.

Ernst Schwab was dying and Anna moved into his house to nurse him through the nights.

After five long days and nights, Schwab's life began to slowly slip away. He mostly slept, but every so often he would have moments of consciousness and clarity.

Late in the evening, of what would become Ernst Schwab's final day, Anna was leant over him, wiping his fevered brow and face with a cool damp cloth. It was the only comfort she could give him. Though unconscious,

Schwab had been rambling in his sleep for more than an hour. Anna knew what was coming, but she still tried to do her best for him.

He had always done his best for her.

Anna stroked the side of his face and recounted on how they'd first met. She had only been a girl. She thought about how her mother had written to Schwab, asking him to look after her. And he'd been a true friend to her mother. With no questions at all asked, he had taken her in and taken care of her.

As she stroked his face, Schwab slowly opened his eyes and looked up at her. For a moment he was confused as he stared up at Anna, and then he smiled.

'Rachel...' he whispered, 'Rachel.'

Anna looked down at him, she was startled by this, but she knew he was confused. Not wishing to upset him, she continued.

'Yes Ernst,' she said to him, 'It's alright, I'm here.'

He stared at her again, 'Rachel...Rachel.'

Once again Anna spoke to him, 'It's alright, I'm here Ernst.'

And a tear suddenly rolled out of Schwab's left eye and ran down his cheek.

Schwab tried to form more words, in his mind he was trying to speak. And then in an act of sheer desperation he suddenly managed to grab hold of Anna's arm.

Though his vision was clouded, he could see 'his' Rachel, he could see her again, finally.

'I love you ...I always loved you,' he whispered, and Anna leant closer as she heard what he was saying.

Suddenly, in a moment of final clarity, he said it...he said it all. They were his last words.

'I looked after her Rachel, like I promised...our baby.'

And with that Ernst Schwab slipped back into unconsciousness.

Anna looked down at him in wonder. She was mystified. What did he mean by 'our baby'? Ernst Schwab had never had any children, she didn't understand it. And what did he mean by 'he'd looked after her'? He'd looked after who?

She still struggled to comprehend the meaning of what he'd just said, and she stared at him for a moment.

And then suddenly, she understood. And she realized what he'd actually meant, and what he was saying to her. And everything suddenly burst into Anna's brain.

It was as though someone had just pulled back the curtains and she'd seen the light.

'Our baby...our baby' It was her. The baby was her...it was Anna. The baby that he'd always looked after had to be her. And for all those years he'd loved her and looked after her because it was her. He wasn't her guardian or even her uncle. Ernst Schwab was her father, he was her true, true father.

She held onto his arm in shock

'Why didn't you tell me?' she almost shouted, 'Why didn't you ever tell me...why?'

But there was no reply and there was no answer and there never would be.

Anna looked down at him, and she began to cry.

If only he'd told her...if only he'd told her, there could have been so much more.

Within the next hour he passed away. Ernst Schwab never regained consciousness and in the end he slipped into a peaceful death.

Anna sat there with him until daylight was breaking. She sat there thinking about everything.

Ernst's final words kept going through her mind, 'I love you, I love you'.

Ernst thought that he was speaking to her mother, Rachel. She and her mother were the image of each other and Ernst had been very confused. But when he'd said 'I love you', those precious words were meant only for Rachel.

And Anna realised that as she also realised that she was their baby. There could be no doubt. She sat there and she wondered about them both. They'd been lovers, obviously. So what went wrong? And after a while she started to think about the times and the dates and she started to work out the figures. She knew what year her mother got married and she knew her own age of course. From there it was easy to deduct that her mother had been having an affair with Ernst Schwab whilst she was still married to her father, or the man that she had always thought of as her father. Yuri Hartman. What a strange, cold hearted man he had been and always had been. She knew her mother didn't love him and he in return never showed any affection to either of them. Anna began to wonder if he had known, or even suspected that he wasn't Anna's true father. But the thought of that made her shudder. Yuri Hartman was a brutal man, and if he'd suspected anything at all he would have probably killed her mother. So why hadn't she run away with Ernst Schwab, he was after all rich and successful. But as Anna thought things through she realised that if that had happened, Yuri Hartman would have found them and probably murdered them both.

She shuddered once again at the mere thought of him.

Later that morning Anna wearily returned home to inform the family that 'Uncle Ernst' had passed away. Pavel was heartbroken, but Anna was devastated. It would take her another three days before she could talk to Pavel about her discovery.

They were sitting having their evening meal, but instead of facing each other across the table, Pavel had moved his chair so that he could sit by his wife's side. He had been really worried about Anna, she had been so upset. He knew Anna's past and he'd always known that Mr Schwab had taken her under his wing when Anna had lost everything. Her grief was understandable. They finished their meal and Pavel replenished their wine and as the moment mellowed, Anna took hold of his hand and suddenly began to weep.

Pavel took her hand and stroked her fingers.

'It's alright Anna,' he said to her, 'It's good to cry, really it is.'

She looked at him. 'You don't understand Pavel. It's not what you think.'

Pavel looked at her. 'What is it Anna?' he asked her.

'I've something to tell you Pavel,' she replied.

And with that she told him everything that she knew. When Anna finished telling Pavel her secret, he just sat there and quietly shook his head. He was amazed, but as he thought about it he realised the obvious. For years it had all been staring them in the face.

'This does actually answer a lot of questions really Anna, we just never saw it.'

'What do you mean?' she asked.

Pavel continued and he smiled at her.

'Uncle Ernst always did have a soft spot for you. You were always his favourite. Whenever you walked into the room you always made him smile.'

Anna didn't know what to say.

'Well, we all saw it Anna, but we just took it as normal. Then when you first moved here to Smolensk, he installed you in an apartment that turned out to have the cheapest rent in the whole of Russia.'

Anna smiled, and yes, it had taken her a few years to figure that one out.

'Think about it Anna. He actually paid for your wedding, and that must have made him so proud.'

Anna stared at her husband 'You're right Pavel, he did. 'My father' did pay for my wedding day.' and she started to sob and the tears began to run down her cheek. Pavel took out a handkerchief and dabbed his wife's eyes. She leant on his shoulder, remembering her wedding and that happiest of days.

Pavel hugged his wife.

'You know something Anna, your father was a very clever man, very clever. In fact, he was a genius.'

Anna turned to Pavel and gave him a quizzical look.

'Anna, when we first decided to get married, we were going to have to go and live in Zhumyov, do you remember?'

Anna nodded.

'Your father must have been devastated. He was even going to buy us a house there to live in.'

'Yes,' said Anna, 'He didn't want us to have to live with your awful family.'

Pavel laughed, 'I don't blame him, I didn't want to live with them either.'

They both laughed, and it lightened the moment.

'But your father came up with a master plan Anna, it was brilliant. He tied my greedy father up with a business deal that kept me here in Smolensk. And if I was here, you would be here too. So he never lost you.'

Anna thought about it, and she agreed.

Pavel laughed. 'He stitched my father up with that deal and he also told him that he was going to leave everything to me. And my father fell for it. Ernst Schwab knew that there were a good few years in him, and that there was every chance of him outliving my greedy father. And he did.'

"Yes he did 'thank god'. Your father would have made our lives a living hell.'

Pavel smiled. 'Don't worry, I'd have had Mr Koenig throw him into the furnace.'

They both laughed at that. But Pavel and Anna would never know just what Mr Koenig was actually capable of.

Pavel continued, 'But the beauty of your father's plan was that he told us that he was going to leave everything to me, and we've always known that.'

'Yes,' said Anna, but she didn't really understand what Pavel was trying to tell her.

'In leaving everything to me Anna, he was actually leaving it all to you. Think about it. If he had died and left you a factory and a house and money and properties all over the place, well somebody would have figured it out, figured it out that you were his illegitimate child, and after all those years? Think about it, nobody leaves everything to their secretary, not 'everything'. Tongues would be wagging and people would be thinking all sorts of things. Your father was a proud man Anna, and you know he wouldn't have wanted that. He wanted you to be respected. So he tied it all up in a business deal, and really, he left everything to us both. And don't forget he had grandchildren too. He had years of happiness with us all as a family.'

Anna put her arms around Pavel and hugged him.

"Thank you Pavel, and yes, you're right,' and she sighed to herself, 'I suppose I realise that now. He always did look after me, always. I only wished I'd known more.'

Pavel Bratz kissed his wife.

'He had a good life Anna. Your father had a wonderful life.'

Ernst Schwab's funeral took place the following week and many of the good people of Smolensk turned out to show their respects. Ernst Schwab had been a popular man and had been one of the city's main benefactors. It was a sunny day and the church was full. Hymns were sung and prayers were said. But for most of the people there, Ernst Schwab would be remembered for one thing alone. And that was for being the good person he was.

The factory closed for the rest of the week as a sign of respect. On the Friday morning Pavel and Anna went into work to start sorting out Ernst

Schwab's private papers. Schwab's safe still stood in the corner of the office. It had remained there untouched and unopened for several years. Pavel had his own personal safe installed in the office and Ernst Schwab had given him his old safe keys for Pavel to look after. Pavel had put those keys in his own office drawer and forgotten about them, intentionally.

So it was with some trepidation that they came to open Ernst Schwab's private safe.

It had felt strange that morning, walking through a factory that was suddenly silent. Neither of them had ever known it. They walked in through the gates, laughing at the memories. They remembered their secret meetings and Pavel having to climb back into the factory late at night so that no one would know about their secret romance.

As they walked into the office, Anna turned to Pavel.

'I can still remember your father bringing you here for the first time.'

Pavel nodded. 'It seems a lifetime ago doesn't it?'

They entered the office and Anna shuddered, even though it wasn't particularly cold.

Pavel laughed, 'Yes I know, it's eerie in here when its quiet isn't it?'

He stood there and looked around the room and smiled.

'You know something Anna...'If only walls could talk'.

They would never know the truth of it.

Pavel emptied his office drawer, and he finally found the key to Ernst Schwab's safe.

He passed it to Anna.

'Don't you want to open it?' she asked him.

'No. He's your father Anna. There are to be no more secrets, not between us two anyway.'

Anna went over to the safe and inserted the key into the lock and turned it. The safes inner bolts slid free and she turned the large brass handle with a resounding clang and pulled the door open. It creaked and then slowly swung open to reveal piles of large envelopes and stacks of papers, all tied up with string or ribbon. Anna turned to look at her husband. He just shrugged.

'Well, we've got to start somewhere,' he said.

Anna began to empty the safe and Pavel stacked the various papers into different piles for the different types of documents. There was a pile for bonds, another for stocks and shares, and another for the deeds to various properties. There was a stack of accounts, and another for what they listed as 'various'. Pavel whistled when he saw some of the papers.

'My God,' he said, 'your father owns a fortune.'

Anna laughed, 'He always was prudent with money.'

Once they began to empty some of the papers it became evident that the safe contained three large metal shelves.

'Hey look at this,' she said to Pavel as she lifted the last papers off the top shelf. Under the sheaf of papers was a small metal drawer set into the safe itself.

'I wonder what's in there?' she said.

'It's probably full of diamond rings,' quipped Pavel.

'If it is, we'll give them to Vasily,' Anna replied with a sly smile.

Pavel raised his eyes and shook his head.

'Yes, and if there's a gun in there, we'll give it to Victor.'

Anna pulled her face at him.

'Is it locked?' he asked.

Anna reached into the safe and pulled the metal drawer's slim brass handle, the drawer slid open effortlessly.

She looked inside.

'No valuables in here, just an old white envelope.'

Anna reached in and picked up the worn old envelope. It had turned yellow and was creased with age and wear. On one side the envelope had split, but there was some writing on it.

She looked at the faded words written on the front.

'Personal'
To Mr Ernst Schwab
The Schwab Furniture Company
Smolensk

Inside the envelope were two very creased letters. She picked out the smaller one first. It wasn't much more than a note. Anna read it out loud.

'My dearest darling Ernst

I have given birth to our daughter. She is so beautiful. I only wish that you could see her.

I love you with all my heart'

Rachel.

Anna just stood there and stared at Pavel. She couldn't believe what she had just read. Pavel too was amazed and for a moment he didn't know what to say. They both just stood there in silence.

It was Pavel who spoke first.

He looked at Anna. "What about the other letter?"

Anna looked inside the envelope. The letter inside was worn...worn as though it had been read a thousand times.

She looked back at Pavel.

'I don't know if I can read it,' she said.

Pavel took a deep breath.

'Only you can read it Anna. Ernst Schwab was your father and Rachel was your mother.

They were your parents Anna, whatever happened, they were your parents. If you don't read the letter it will leave you wondering for the rest of your life. No more secrets Anna.'

Anna reached into the worn envelope and took out the creased old letter. She coughed and then read the letter out to him.

'My Darling Ernst

I have written this letter to you as my last will and testament.
If you are reading this, something has happened both to me and my husband
Yuri Hartman.
If so, my lawyers have explicit written instructions to contact you personally.
I hope that this letter will fully explain everything.

*The young lady that hopefully accompanies the lawyer is
our daughter.
She is 'our' daughter Ernst, you are her father and I am her mother.
Her name is Anna...Anna Kristen Hartman.
As I write, Anna is just ten years old.
She is a beautiful and intelligent little girl who has a good heart.
She knows nothing about you, nothing at all. But you are her father.*

*Whatever tragedy has taken place, please take care of her.
She is our flesh and blood.*

*Life has been cruel Ernst, but I have never stopped loving you.
You have always been and always will remain the love of my life'.*

'I love you'.

Rachel.

Anna's voice cracked as she read out the last few lines and then she started to cry. Pavel went to his wife and took hold of her.

'They loved each other Pavel, they really loved each other.'

'Yes they did Anna, they truly loved one another. Your father must have kept on reading that letter all of his life.'

Anna looked up at him, 'I'm not just something that was the result of some cheap affair, they really did love one another didn't they?'

'That letter says it all Anna. Yes, they loved one another. In his dying breath, all your father could think about was your mother and you'.

And Anna remembered that moment, and it comforted her.

'I don't know what went wrong Anna, and we never will. But now it's over. Your mother and father loved each other just like we love each other. So let's be happy. We're blessed.'

And with that, Pavel Bratz put his arms around his beautiful wife and he kissed her.

CHAPTER 10

It was the year 1913.

Vasily Orlof Bratz crunched through the fresh white fallen snow as he made his way to work on another cold and early morning. It was Monday, but that didn't make much difference to Vasily Orlof. He could have been going into work on any day. In fact, he did go into work on most days simply because Vasily Orlof Bratz loved his profession. After six years, he'd not only become a craftsman jeweller, he'd managed to become a craftsman jeweller of outstanding ability.

Working at Blesks the Jewellers, Vasily Orlof would spend his every day turning raw precious stones into the most incredible pieces of jewellery. He could take a lump of fine translucent carbon and turn it into a spectacular diamond after spending months of cutting and grinding a multitude of polished facets into its surface. Those facets would reflect the light deep into the diamond's centre and that same light would reappear like small flashing stars. He worked continuously with the purest gold and silver and other precious metals.

In fact, Vasily Orlof had access to the quantities of gold that would make most men rich.

And that was the passion of jewellery. Not only was it beautiful, it was physical wealth.

As he walked in to the workshop Vasily Orlof heard a noise and he realised that he was not alone. Maurice Broch, another of Blesk's craftsman jewellers was already at his work bench.

Vasily Orlof and Maurice were at that moment working on a joint project. Rubin Blesk had returned from Antwerp with a large 'raw' ruby that had immense potential. Vasily Orlof had studied the ruby for the best part of a week before he could proceed with the first initial cut. It would take weeks to cut the ruby into the required shape and after that there would be more months of work, grinding the intricate pattern of facets into the ruby and then, finally, the polishing.

He and Maurice Broch had decided to create a brooch using the ruby as the centrepiece. Maurice Broch was making the mount for it. He was constructing it from platinum and white gold, a twisted 'basket' of precious metals. There was no immediate rush. It had taken Vasily Orlof months to prepare the ruby, together with the adjoining stones that would be used in the brooch's design.

The ruby would be cut and ground into a 'pear' shape that when set into the brooch would be laid on its side. It would have five sizeable 'brilliant cut' round diamonds set around it's perimeter, but at the narrow 'stalk' end of the stone Vasily Orlof would place an exquisite square cut emerald. The contrast in colour and shape was ingenious, the ruby would radiate, as would the emerald and the twisted platinum and white gold setting that the jewels were to be mounted on would complete the whole effect. The ruby was a superb stone. Deep set and shimmering red, it simply glowed.

Vasily and Maurice Broch bid each other 'good morning', as was their habit. Vasily Orlof looked at the stunning setting that Maurice was producing. It was a woven basket of white gold and platinum, arranged in such a way that the colours from the ruby and the emerald reflected back on themselves. It was an ingenious exercise in the use of precious metals and after a short discussion, both men turned to their work.

Within the hour, the other two craftsmen jewellers arrived together, along with the new apprentice, the 'new boy'.

Rubin Blesk's uncle, Uncle Sholem and Mr Nathan would always arrive at work together since they both caught the same tram every morning. The new boy, the 'apprentice' ran into to the workshop five minutes behind them. He was late, again.

Peter, or 'young Peter' as he would be forever known was always late. And it was becoming a bad habit.

Uncle Sholem began to tut and he chastised the boy.

'Again Peter...Again. And now it's every morning you're late. You might as well turn up at dinner time. Maybe you should just turn up at dinner time and then just work for an hour. Why bother? You don't care, of course you don't. In my day I would have been thrashed... thrashed and sent home in disgrace. But you young people today, you're all the same, you just don't care anymore.'

Peter, as usual, stood there looking down at his feet. He had no answers and no explanation.

'Go and put the kettle on Peter' continued Uncle Sholem, 'Do something useful for once, before we all die of thirst.'

Vasily Orlof smiled to himself. This same exchange took place every morning and it seemed that young Peter was never going to learn. Not yet anyway.

The morning came and went and it was early afternoon when Rubin Blesk walked into the workshop. He nodded to his uncle and both men had a short conversation.

Young Peter the apprentice immediately made himself scarce.

Rubin Blesk then went over to his other craftsman, Mr Nathan and again had a short conversation. Those two old men had been the foundation of Rubin Blesk's business and age and wisdom had always earned respect.

Blesk then went over to Maurice Broch and Vasily Orlof. He'd been following their progress on the ruby brooch with great interest. It would be a masterpiece, a masterpiece that would earn Blesk a small fortune when he took it to St Petersburg or Moscow were he would sell it to one of the leading jewellers there. Smolensk itself was quite a well to do city, but in St Petersburg and Moscow there was 'real' wealth.

After examining the delicate cutting of the ruby, Blesk congratulated both men on their work.

Then he turned to Vasily.

'Come to my office later this afternoon. I need to speak to you.'

Vasily Orlof took a quick glance at Maurice Broch, but Broch just shrugged.

Rubin Blesk just smiled and he turned and left the workshop.

'What's that about?' Vasily said to Maurice.

'Search me,' Broch replied, 'He's probably going to sack you. The standard of your work is bloody awful these days,' and he laughed to himself as he returned to his platinum and gold.

Over the last several years, Rubin Blesk had greatly expanded his business. The jeweller's shop in Smolensk was now only a part of his exclusive business empire. Blesk had been very successful in becoming a major wholesaler in diamonds and precious stones and he now travelled regularly to Antwerp, sometimes up to two or three times a month. From there he would return to Smolensk with his new cache of precious diamonds and gems and would sort out the stones that needed, and put aside the parcels of stones that he did not.

He would then travel to St Petersburg where he had steadily built up a relationship with a number of the city's most important jewellers. The leading jewellers there were 'Bolin's', 'Konstantin's' and 'Nicholls and Plincke'. And eventually, even the great House of Faberge had opened their doors to Rubin Blesk.

Faberge's links to the Romanov Royal family were legendary and it meant that Faberge's required a continuous and unvarying supply of quality stones. Ever year, the House of Faberge was commissioned to produce the Royal Easter Egg, which was an elaborate jewel encrusted affair that the Tsar would present to his delighted wife on every Easter Sunday.

It was essential that the House of Faberge maintained a constant supply of very high quality diamonds along with other opulent gems. These precious stones were needed to produce the priceless Royal Egg every year, along with a continuous array of jewellery for the Royal family and their entourage, and the rest of St Petersburg's wealthier residents.

Blesk soon realised that he was more than capable of supplying the 'House of Faberge' with the top quality diamonds and gems that they so desperately needed. And even better for Ruben Blesk, the price was secondary. When it came to Faberge, quality was 'King'.

With the increased regularity of his trips to Antwerp, Blesk had been advised by his bodyguard Herman Vodle to improve his personal security. Blesk had immediately given Vodle the go ahead. Herman Vodle, it seemed, knew an old comrade that he had previously served with in his regiment in the German army. He and Erich Groener were long and trusted friends.

However, the other reason for Vodle's choice had been Erich Groener's physical appearance. The man had the same build and stature as Rubin Blesk. Even in character they looked very similar.

Vodle had decided that their future trips to Antwerp would be supervised differently. Vodle would still follow Rubin Blesk at a distance, but Groener would walk ten or fifteen paces in front of Blesk, along a predetermined route to the diamond merchants in Antwerp's Pelikaanstraad. On these trips, Rubin Blesk would always carry his old brown leather bag. Under Herman Vodle's instruction, Blesk had also purchased himself a beautiful grey woollen coat and a black Homburg style hat. The coat had been made to combat the cold Russian winters and it sported a large black bearskin collar. It was a very stylish piece of clothing

Just as in the past, the three men never communicated at all during their trip to Antwerp. Once there, Rubin Blesk would go about his business, buying large amounts of diamonds and precious stones. They would then return to Antwerp's busy Rijfstraat Train station and await their train. Once they'd entered the station, Erich Groener would head straight for the toilets. Blesk would wait for a couple of minutes and if Groener didn't come out straight away it meant that everything was clear and the toilets were empty. Blesk would then follow him in there and they would both exchange coats, Groener would also put on Rubin Blesk's black Homburg hat. Both men carried the same style brown leather bag, and a moment later Erich Groener would walk out of the toilets looking the exact double of Rubin Blesk. The hat, the coat and the brown bag being Blesk's signature apparel. The only difference being that the brown bag Groener carried was full of Rubin Blesk's favourite boiled sweets.

A minute later Rubin Blesk would leave the same toilets wearing Erich Groener's plain brown coat and a woollen worker's cap. The brown leather bag containing a small fortune in jewels would be casually thrown over his shoulder.

Only once had they ever had a problem, and that had been at the train station at Antwerp.

A tall ruddy faced man had been spotted loitering on the Pelikaanstraad near the Vrije Diamanthandel diamond merchants.

The man was doing absolutely nothing, and that was how he'd drawn attention to himself.

In Russia, no one had the time to do nothing.

Rubin Blesk walked out of the Vrije Diamanthandel with his brown bag full of gems and the man had immediately followed him. The same man followed Blesk all the way to the train station, but stayed his distance. Once Rubin Blesk entered the Rijfstraat Station he and Groener made their way to the toilets to carry out their regular 'switch'.

Vodle hovered. He had already surmised that the man was working alone. However, he couldn't afford take any chances. When Blesk and Groener had entered the toilet, Vodle placed himself a short distance away from the toilet entrance. Had there been a show of force by a number of individuals, he would have been ready to spring into action.

But nothing happened. Groener left the toilets and went to stand by himself on the platform. To all appearances he was waiting for the train. Vodle just stood there and waited until Rubin Blesk had walked safely away, unnoticed.

It was then that the lone robber struck.

Unfortunately, the man that he was about to rob was not Rubin Blesk. Vodle had started to follow the man as he pulled out a knife and approached Erich Groener. The man walked right up to Groener and demanded that he handed over the bag of jewels immediately. He then began to poke Groener in the stomach with the knife. It was a pathetic attempt really.

Vodle strolled over and coshed the 'would be' robber over the head with the butt of his Luger. He then caught the man in his arms as he fell backwards and then 'helped' the man to a nearby bench. One or two inquisitive people stopped to watch, but Vodle just shook his head.

'Another stupid drunkard' he said out loud, and that was enough to quell everyone's interest. Most people were too busy and had other more important things on their mind.

The train arrived and Vodle watched Rubin Blesk and Groener get on it.

As a parting reminder, Vodle slid his own blade from his belt and then he leant over the unconscious man and pushed his knife into the left side of the man's rib cage. The wound was away from the man's heart and vital arteries, but the blade punctured the man's left lung. Vodle then twisted the knife so as to make a sizeable internal gash. The robber would survive the injury, but would never again be able to do anything physically strenuous.

That would always be a problem, when you had a hole in your lung.

So later that afternoon back at the workshop, Vasily Orlof Bratz washed his hands and made his way to Rubin Blesk's office. He knocked on the office door and was bid to 'enter'.

'Ah Vasily,' said Rubin Blesk as Vasily Orlof entered his office, 'Come in Vasily, come in and sit yourself down.'

Vasily Orlof sat down. And though he wasn't particularly worried, he did wonder what Rubin Blesk wanted. He also wondered what Rubin needed to say to him that he couldn't say it in front of the others. After all, they all worked as a team, a very close knit team.

Rubin opened a drawer in his desk and produced a couple of his favourite boiled sweets. He slid one across the desk.

'Have one,' he said.

'Thank you Rubin,' Vasily replied and put the sweet into the breast pocket of his shirt.

'I've not long had my lunch, so I'll have it later.'

Rubin nodded and continued to smile as he popped his own sweet into his mouth.

'They're very good Vasily. I get them from Antwerp.'

Vasily Orlof nodded back, and he wondered just where this conversation was going. He was in the middle of grinding and polishing the new ruby and this break from his work slightly annoyed him. All he wanted to do was get back to his work.

Rubin sat back in his chair.

'I want to talk to you Vasily,' he said.

Vasily Orlof looked back at him.

'An opportunity has arisen Vasily. An opportunity that is the chance in a lifetime.'

Vasily Orlof said nothing.

So Rubin Blesk continued.

'These days Vasily, I do a lot of business in St Petersburg. I'm dealing with some of the finest jewellery houses there. They are phenomenal, and lately I've started to work with the House of Faberge. I've managed to make some contacts there, some very good contacts. And an opportunity has arisen Vasily, an opening has become available. Due to their contracts with the Royal Family, Faberge's are heavily committed to producing a constant stream of jewellery, in particular the Royal Easter Egg, which they have to produce every year. The House of Faberge are desperately in need of craftsmen of a 'certain quality'. They only use the finest master craftsmen because the standard of work that is required has to be absolutely flawless. I have spoken to the people at Faberge on your behalf and they would like to meet you.'

Rubin Blesk grinned enthusiastically. For him, it was as though the deal was already done.

But Vasily Orlof was left speechless.

'What do you mean?' he said in his usual naive manner.

Rubin Blesk eagerly continued.

'Vasily, you can go to St Petersburg. You can go to the House of Faberge. You can become a 'master craftsman' at the House of Faberge. It will be the pinnacle of your career.'

'But what about my work here?' Vasily Orlof asked.

Rubin Blesk saw the worried look on Vasily Orlof's face, and he suddenly realized that his plans may be about to falter.

'Your work here is not a problem Vasily,' he replied, 'If you want to, you can finish off your ruby brooch first and then I'll sort out all the arrangements.'

Vasily Orlof was dumbfounded. 'Finish off the brooch'...of course he wanted to finish off the brooch. It had been the only thing on his mind, the only thing he ever thought about. His passion and his intensity for his work necessitated that whatever project he was working on, that work completely took over his life. And what about Blesks? What about all the future projects that he and Maurice Broch had planned. Between them they had produced a sketch book of dazzling designs. They were designs for the future, and for the future of Blesks.

'Do you want me to leave Rubin' Vasily asked quietly, 'Is that it. Do you want me to go?'

Rubin Blesk suddenly stopped smiling. Something was wrong. This wonderful chance that he was offering Vasily Orlof was obviously not welcome. There was no enthusiasm and no elation for the remarkable opportunity that was being handed to him. Then all at once, Rubin Blesk suddenly understood. It was fear. Fear of the unknown and the fear of something new.

Rubin immediately understood, and cursed himself for his own stupidity. Vasily Orlof had always led an insular life and a life of limited experience. Rubin wondered if Vasily Orlof had ever even ventured out of Smolensk and came to the conclusion, probably not.

'Vasily,' he spoke softly, 'No, I don't want you to leave, not one bit. I know we are like family here and I know that you are very comfortable, we all are. But Vasily, you are destined for greater things in a greater world. You could quite easily stay here in Smolensk. But Smolensk is just Smolensk and always will be. There's a whole world out there Vasily and you have a rare talent that the world needs to see. You can go so much further Vasily, and you can do so much more. At Faberge's you would be working with the finest jewellers in Russia...'The best of the best'. Outstanding master craftsmen who would show you things that we here at Blesks could only dream of Vasily. You would be working with some of the greatest craftsmen in the world.'

Rubin Blesk's words resounded in Vasily Orlof's head. Blesk had hit a note, and suddenly Vasily had to think. He would love to work with the finest jewellers, and he began to wonder. Could he do it, could he work for Faberge? Slowly, Vasily began to understand what Rubin meant, he wanted Vasily to improve himself, and here before him he was being offered something, another plan, and maybe another life.

'Do you think I'm good enough Rubin?' he asked nervously.

Rubin Blesk smiled to himself. He'd possibly just sold Vasily Orlof a future, thank God.

'Yes Vasily.' Rubin slowly replied, 'Yes Vasily, you are good enough. You have a blessed talent Vasily, a gift, and you need to take that talent and do so much more with it. We will always be here for you here in Smolensk. If for any reason you are unhappy in any way, you can always come back here to us, you know that. We are like a family. We will always be here for you, always.'

Vasily Orlof nodded in gratitude.

'Thank you Rubin,' he replied.

'So Vasily, how long will it take you to finish the ruby brooch?'

Vasily Orlof considered the question, 'If I work nonstop, probably a month, maybe six weeks.'

Rubin Blesk smiled back at his protégé.

'I was hoping you could do it in two or three weeks.'

Verily Orlof gulped. He still had an enormous amount of work to do on the ruby, along with setting the diamonds and that one special emerald. However, those stones were already cut.

'I still have quite a lot of work to do on the ruby,' said Vasily, 'It has to be perfect.'

'Yes. Of course,' said Blesk.

Vasily Orlof then continued, 'Maurice has already done most of the work on the mount. He will finish that sooner than me. I will try my best Rubin, I'll work a bit later and I'll come in at the weekends.'

Rubin Blesk laughed, 'But you already do come in most weekends Vasily.'

Vasily Orlof shrugged his shoulders, 'Maybe I should sleep here too" he replied, and he grinned back at his boss.

'In about a month's time I shall be going back to St Petersburg,' said Blesk, 'I want you to be ready and I want you to come with me".

Vasily Orlof considered the moment and he considered what was being offered to him. To work with the 'best of the best'. Yes, that's what Rubin had called them, 'the best of the best'.

He knew he had to take up the offer, he just had to. His quest to make beautiful jewellery had to continue. Never in his wildest dreams had he ever thought that he would work for the House of Faberge.

Vasily looked at Rubin Blesk.

'I'll inform my parents that I shall be going to work in St Petersburg. And I will finish the ruby brooch for you Rubin. It will be a wonderful piece. I 'will' go to work for the House of Faberge, but I can never thank you enough Rubin for my training here. The years here at Blesks have without doubt been my happiest, I owe everything to you. Had it not been for you, I would have never become a jeweller.'

Both men stood up and shook hands. It was quite an emotional moment.

Rubin Blesk spoke.

'It's been my pleasure Vasily Orlof, and I want you to go to St Petersburg and make us all proud.'

'I shall certainly try my best,' replied Vasily Orlof, 'but now I have a ruby to cut and polish.'

He smiled at Rubin Blesk and then he turned and left the office.

As the door closed, Rubin Blesk took a short sigh of relief. For a moment there, he thought that Vasily Orlof was about to turn down his offer and refuse to go. That could have had serious implications. Rubin sat down again and reached into his drawer for another boiled sweet.

Over the last several years, Rubin Blesk's business interests had changed considerably. His jewellers shop in Smolensk had become only a small part of his growing empire. Though his craftsmen were producing some incredible pieces of jewellery, those pieces of jewellery were no longer being sold in Smolensk. Smolensk was indeed a large city, but it had by no means the same fiscal wealth as St Petersburg or Moscow. There was a lot of wealth in Russia, but the 'real' money lay in those two great cities.

Rubin Blesk's business interests lay in two areas.

Firstly, he had become a diamond merchant of some repute, and that reputation was growing. Blesk had always had a 'good eye', he was very astute and he knew and understood the market for diamonds and other precious and semi precious stones.

Secondly, he himself had been producing some wonderful jewellery from his own workshop in Smolensk, jewellery that had been sold in St Petersburg and in Moscow, and at double the price of what he could have ever achieved in Smolensk.

But it was his first business, the supplying and wholesaling of the diamonds and other stones that now took his preference. It was certainly the easier, and in the long run, the most profitable.

Individual pieces of jewellery took a long time to produce, and cutting and polishing the raw stones took forever, no matter how profitable. Whereas Rubin Blesk's wholesale operation simply involved those frequent trips to Antwerp, however long and arduous they might be. It was a quicker and simpler way of making a profit, and making huge profits.

Blesk was committed to St Petersburg, and he had gradually become committed to the House of Faberge. There was a lot of money to be made from Faberge's, and because of that, Vasily Orlof Bratz had unknowingly become embroiled in Rubin Blesk's master plan?

Blesk had started to supply the House of Faberge with precious and semi precious stones. Faberge's of course had several suppliers who all dealt with one man. His name was Gustav Stoltz and he was the head buyer for House of Faberge. Over the past twelve months Rubin Blesk and Gustav Stoltz had steadily built up a relationship that was proving to be highly profitable for both men. It was quite simple really. Blesk would supply the House of Faberge with diamonds and other precious stones at highly inflated prices. Gustav Stoltz would agree the price and then he and Blesk would share the profit margin. The Faberge family trusted Stoltz implicitly, he had worked there for years. And because the Faberge family themselves were so involved with production, along with keeping the Tsar and the rest of the Romanov's happy, it meant that Stoltz's decisions were never questioned. At that time, the House of Faberge was almost 'eating' precious stones, the demand for them had become so high. Together with this there was a shortage of skilled craftsmen, only the most skilled master craftsmen jewellers could ever work for the House Faberge. Only the best of the best.

Rubin Blesk had met Faberge's owner, Mr Carl Faberge, on several occasions and Blesk was very keen to advance that relationship. Blesk's objective was to become Faberge's principal gem supplier. Blesk and Gustav Stoltz had discussed this at length and it was quite obvious to both of them that the more jewels and gems that Rubin Blesk supplied, the more money they would both make. Blesk and Stoltz had also discussed Carl Faberge's biggest problem, the lack of highly skilled labour, those master craftsmen who could work to Faberge's exacting standards.

Rubin Blesk realised that he had the answer to Carl Faberge's problem. Rubin Blesk had Vasily Orlof Bratz.

Vasily Orlof Bratz could walk into Faberge's and immediately start to produce the astounding creations that the House of Faberge was so famous for. Blesk had lied to Vasily Orlof when he'd told him that 'you can go so much further and you can do so much more'. Faberge's could teach Vasily Orlof Bratz nothing. In fact, the reverse would be nearer the truth and Rubin Blesk knew it.

Vasily Orlof Bratz had a rare talent. Vasily Orlof had a gift.

So a plan had been devised. Gustav Stoltz, the trusted head buyer for the House of Faberge would speak to Carl Faberge and extol the virtues of Rubin Blesk. Stoltz would inform Mr Faberge of the excellent service that Rubin Blesk was providing and how Blesk was procuring some of the 'most wonderful' gems. That was just what Carl Faberge needed to hear. Quality was all important. Carl Faberge had been trained as a jeweller in Paris when he was a younger man and he thoroughly understood the beauty and the wonder of precious stones, but unfortunately, not the price of those same stones.

Gustav Stoltz then went on to tell Mr Faberge about the wonderful young craftsman that Rubin Blesk had 'discovered'. The young man was in Blesk's employ and worked only for him. Stoltz then told Carl Faberge about Vasily Orlof's remarkable talent and all about the amazing jewellery that he was creating. The young man was a prodigy, an absolute genius.

The story had intrigued Carl Faberge. He was fascinated.

Stoltz continued his tale. He said that he had asked Rubin Blesk if he would allow his young 'protégé' to come and work for the House of Faberge. Rubin Blesk had of course refused. Blesk was after all a businessman and knew when he was on to a good thing. Stoltz told Carl Faberge that the House of Faberge desperately needed a talent such as Vasily Orlof Bratz. Their order books were full and there was always the looming problem of having to produce the Royal Easter Egg every spring. Carl Faberge readily agreed with his head buyer. They did indeed need more skilled craftsmen and this young man sounded ideal. He would be an asset to the firm. But what could they do?

Gustav Stoltz took Mr Faberge to one side.

'We need to persuade Rubin Blesk sir, in one way or another,' he'd told Carl Faberge. 'We need to present him with an offer that would be far more appealing.'

'What might that be?' Carl Faberge asked.

Gustav Stoltz considered the question for a moment, then he looked up at the ceiling as though deep in thought. It was a very good act.

'Well...I just wondered,' Stoltz continued, 'Blesk has been continually supplying us with some of the very best diamonds and other top quality stones, and he has been supplying us steadily for over a year now. I wonder if it would be more 'practical' to make him our main supplier. It would only be a title of course, as head buyer I would obviously continue to monitor him, as I do with all our suppliers. However, if he was to be given the title of 'Official Supplier' to the House of Faberge, that title would afford him a huge reputation. He would be recognised throughout Europe".

Carl Faberge looked at Stoltz

'Do you think that would persuade him?' he asked.

'Yes sir, I do. That official title would gain him huge respect. If the House of Faberge used Rubin Blesk, so would others. That recognition could earn him a fortune.'

Carl Faberge nodded.

'Could you organise this Gustav?' he asked.

'Yes of course sir. I'll speak to Mr Blesk. I'm sure he'll see the sense in it. After all this is St Petersburg, not Smolensk. Smolensk is just a city full of peasants.'

Carl Faberge smiled, and he acknowledged Gustav Stoltz's wisdom.

Stoltz was a good man. Very dependable.

Gustav Stoltz would go and find Rubin Blesk and speak to him. Then they could celebrate, of course they could. Their plan had worked perfectly.

Rubin Blesk would be the main supplier to the House of Faberge and from there he and Stoltz would share the fabulous profits from their illicit dealing.

Five weeks later, Rubin Blesk and Vasily Orlof Bratz made their way to St Petersburg.

For Vasily Orlof, it had been a tearful farewell from his mother and he promised to write to her regularly and keep in touch. His father had respectfully shaken Vasily's hand and he wished his son well, but as a father and son they had never been close. Their conversations together had always remained 'difficult'.

It seemed that timber and jewellery would never mix.

Vasily's brother, Victor, never even made an appearance.

And as the train finally pulled away from Smolensk's bustling train station, it would only be Anna Kristen Bratz who stood there crying.

On arriving at St Petersburg, the capital city of the whole of Russia, Vasily Orlof Bratz had been completely amazed and astounded.

From the moment he stepped off the train at the then named 'Nicholaevsky' train station he felt as though he had just entered another world.

And who could have blamed him?

The city was so full of energy and vitality, and the city was immense. St Petersburg was the where the Russian Royal family presided, it was also the centre of finance and within its city walls were some of the most opulent buildings and parks that Vasily Orlof Bratz had ever seen, most of which he could have never imagined. However, more than that, there was the wealth. In St Petersburg there was a sweet perfume in the air, and it was the smell of money.

And in the whole of St Petersburg, there was one undisputedly recognised institution, one place that symbolised the city's great wealth, and with it its opulence and its privilege.

And that place was the 'House of Faberge'.

On arriving at Faberge's, Vasily Orlof Bratz felt as though he had entered the beating heart of his world. Rubin Blesk had wasted no time, from the Nicholaevsky train station they had gone directly to Faberge's exclusive premises on the 'Bolshaya Morskaya'. Blesk had introduced Vasily Orlof to Gustav Stoltz and from there Gustav Stoltz took over. Vasily Orlof was then given a tour of the building. It was a huge place. He was shown the extensive showrooms that were the retail side of Faberge's. There were cabinets filled with some of the most beautiful jewellery Vasily Orlof had ever seen. It was the sheer amount that impressed him the most, cabinet after cabinet, filled with luxurious necklaces and brooches and some of the most magnificent objet d'arte jewellery. As Vasily Orlof stared at all the jewellery that was on display, the one thought passed through his mind. There was nothing there that he himself could not create. He also realised, that given the right materials he could create so much more, and better and finer. That one thought gave him the belief in himself and the much needed confidence, the confidence that he had all the skills that the House of Faberge would have need of.

After the tour of the showrooms Gustav Stoltz took Vasily Orlof to the

Faberge workshops. Once there he was introduced to the skilled jewellers who he would be working with. He was enthusiastically welcomed into the company by craftsmen who had the same kindred spirit. Craftsmen who lived for their work.

Later that afternoon he was taken to meet Carl Faberge himself. Vasily Orlof sat in Mr Faberge's lavish office and he spoke to his new employer for over an hour. During that time Carl Faberge talked to Vasily about his own love of jewellery. Faberge was also a master craftsman, who as a young man had also been trained by the 'best of the best' in Paris. Carl Faberge went on to discuss his company's planned projects. He explained to Vasily Orlof the importance of the Royal connection and the value of the famous Faberge Easter Eggs.

When Vasily Orlof finally left Carl Faberge's office that afternoon he was a much wiser and better informed young man.

Carl Faberge stood and watched Vasily Orlof leave his office. He stared at the door as it closed behind his new employee. And he realised that the young man he had just spoken to for over an hour had something rather special about him. He had a passion, a gift.

The House of Faberge provided affordable housing for those of its employees who needed accommodation. Faberge's held the lease on a small block of local apartments on the edge of the Bolshaya Morskaya district. These apartments were only a short walk away from the Faberge main building, and the company rented the apartments to their employees at very favourable rates, ridiculously favourable actually. Mr Faberge had always realised that having underpaid and poorly housed employees would never advance his business. Not one bit.

Gustav Stoltz took Vasily Orlof there himself and showed Vasily his new lodgings. Normally he would have given the task to someone else. But, for some reason, Stoltz had decided to keep an eye on Rubin Blesk's young protégé.

Blesk may have been Gustav Stoltz's accomplice, but he was an accomplice who needed watching.

Once he'd handed Vasily Orlof Bratz over to the readily appreciative hands of the House of Faberge, Rubin Blesk disappeared.

He made his way to the other major purveyor of jewellery to the Russian Royal household.

That company was the 'House of Bolin'.

History would consign the firm of C.E Bolin to the history books. But in its day the company, which was wholly owned by Carl Edward Bolin, was the only potential contender that could challenge Carl Faberge for his crown.

Blesk arrived at the House of Bolin, he had an appointment to see their buyer, a Mr Leonid Barsov. The two men met in Barsov's office and exchanged greetings, then they got down to the business in hand.

'You have it with you?' asked the somewhat curious Barsov.

'Yes I have,' replied Blesk, and he reached into his inside pocket and produced a small leather pouch.

'And is it as good as you described it?' asked Barsov.

'Look for yourself,' replied Rubin Blesk, and he slid the pouch across the top of Leonid Barsov's eye-catching and beautifully crafted desk. The desk was hand made from mahogany and had been inlaid with larch wood. It was one of the most stunningly remarkable pieces of furniture that Blesk had ever seen.

As Barsov leant forward to pick up the pouch, Blesk sat back and appraised the desk's extraordinary craftsmanship. It was something that Rubin Blesk himself would have loved to own, Blesk had an eye for quality and he readily appreciated that the desk must have cost a small fortune.

Leonid Barsov slowly unfolded the soft leather pouch and slid its contents onto the top of his desk. Then he visibly gasped.

There in front of him lay one of the most striking pieces of jewellery that he had ever seen.

A large ruby which had been cut with fantastic precision was surrounded by five brilliant cut round diamonds, and at one end there was a stunning square cut emerald of the most amazing clarity. The stones were mounted on a twisted setting made from platinum and white gold. It was incredible, but the beauty in it all lay in the shape of the ruby, it was pear shaped and was laid on its side. The sparkling emerald had been placed where the 'stalk' would have been.

It was the ruby brooch that Vasily Orlof Bratz had devotedly created for his master, Rubin Blesk.

Leonid Barsov carefully picked up the brooch and held it up to the light. As he stared at it, he appreciated its beauty and fully admired the skill of the man who made it.

'It's absolutely perfect,' said Barsov. He could say nothing else.

Rubin Blesk smiled.

'Yes, it is,' he replied, 'it's fabulous.'

Leonid Barsov continued to stare at the ruby for another full minute before finally returning the brooch to its leather pouch.

'It's all you said and more, Blesk.'

'To describe it as less would have been almost ridiculous,' replied Blesk, 'but my dear Leonid, surely you know me better by now. I will always give an honest appraisal. To understate or overstate would be a complete waste of everyone's time.'

Barsov nodded in agreement. Yes, dealing with Rubin Blesk had always been straightforward. Nobody got the upper hand and because of that, everyone made a profit.

Leonid Barsov continued.

'From your written description of the brooch, we have searched our books and we think we may have found a buyer, a very wealthy industrialist in Moscow who must really love his wife.'

'Or maybe his mistress,' quipped Blesk.

Both men laughed.

'You may be right Blesk,' said Barsov, 'Stranger things have happened. Anyway, we have a possible buyer. However, he lives in Moscow, and fortunately for us, we do have our other branch there. So my friend, you're going to have to make the long journey all the way to Moscow with this beauty,' and Leonid Barsov once more stared at the leather pouch as he considered what it contained.

Blesk nodded in appreciation. Bolin's had done their work and come up trumps, he couldn't complain.

'Moscow it is then my friend,' replied Blesk.

Leonid Barsov began to frown at Rubin. 'You know, you must take care Blesk. There are always thieves about, everyone from the pickpockets to the organised gangs. You're vulnerable, you really should have some security. It's not safe out there, and you are of course carrying something that's worth a fortune.'

'Don't worry Leonid, everything will be okay, believe me,' replied Rubin Blesk.

But Rubin Blesk didn't have to worry, not one bit. Because as always, out there somewhere were Vodle and Groener. Rubin Blesk didn't know where they were, but Vodle and Groener did. And if Blesk didn't know their whereabouts, neither did anyone else.

Both men stood up and shook hands. A deal was in the making and money would be made.

As Blesk was about to leave the office, he turned to Barsov.

'Your desk" he said "I can't help but admire it. It's a beautiful piece of furniture.'

'Ah yes, it certainly is,' Barsov agreed, 'It came from Schwab's of Smolensk.'

Rubin Blesk smiled.

'Most things do,' he said, 'most things do.'

Vasily Orlof flourished at Faberge.

From the first day he started, Vasily realised that he had access to the most wonderful trove of diamonds and gems he could have ever imagined. For Vasily Orlof, it was as though he had just been given the world.

His passion would become almost an obsession, almost an infatuation.

Days would become weeks and the weeks quickly became the months that turned into years. Without realising it, three of those years easily floated by.

During that period, Vasily Orlof produced some of Faberge's most wonderful creations, and he had also been commissioned to work on some of the more delicate intricacies of the famous Royal Easter Eggs.

Throughout Faberge's, Vasily Orlof had become recognised and respected. Even within the inner sanctum of the House of Faberge, he was accepted as one of the best.

It was during that third year, in the late autumn, that Vasily Orlof first met the Royal Family.

It had been arranged that the Tsar Nicholas, his wife the Tsarina Alexandra and their four daughters would pay the House of Faberge an official visit.

Unofficially, the Tsarina Alexandra and her daughters had already paid numerous visits to their favourite jewellers on numerous occasions, but that was unofficially. The Romanov women loved Faberge's and it was apparently a true fact that they even had rows of diamonds sewn into their corsets.

As was usual, all the Faberge employees would respectfully line up to greet Tsar Nicholas and his family. Carl Faberge himself would then personally give the Romanov's a guided tour of his company.

As was also usual on these visits, anything appertaining to the Royal Egg would be discretely put away so as not to spoil the Easter surprise.

The Tsar's four daughters, Olga, Tatiana, Maria and Anastasia all attended the visit that day. The Romanov's did have a fifth child, a young son Prince Alexei. However, the unspoken tragedy was that the boy, who one day would be the heir to the whole of Russia, had an incurable illness. Prince Alexei had inherited haemophilia, a curse from his mother's side of the family and from which he suffered agonizing bouts of protracted bleeding.

The young prince did not attend that day, but that was hardly surprising. Apart from his illness, no twelve year old boy would have any great interest in jewellery?

Unless of course, he was Vasily Orlof Bratz.

So the Royal tour of the House of Faberge began. All the staff lined up to greet Tsar Nicholas and the rest of the Royal family, all except one, and that was Vasily Orlof Bratz.

Vasily Orlof had heard some of the other members of staff muttering something about a Royal visit, the details of which had gone completely out of his head. Vasily Orlof had better things to do, he was busy. His thoughts at that particular moment were entirely concentrated on the sapphire ring that he was working on.

A stunning sapphire, recently imported from India, had arrived at Faberge's. And as soon as he'd seen the jewel, Vasily Orlof had asked for permission to work on this fabulous stone. Permission was granted of course, Faberge's were no fools. When Vasily Orlof saw promise in a new project, the House of Faberge were quite happy to stand back and let him get on with it.

Vasily Orlof had taken the sapphire and to make the most out of the stone he had cut it into an oblong shape. From there he encased the sapphire inside a larger piece of the blue lapis lazuli gemstone. The effect was spectacular. The mix of the two contrasting blue stones was nothing more than a brilliance of design. The stones were set onto a pure silver mount which had been engraved with tiny Greek scrolls.

Yes, Vasily Orlof was busy.

The Royal family continued its tour. The four Romanov girls had of course been around the House of Faberge a hundred times, but they kept their council, if only to keep their father happy. As they inspected the Faberge workshops it was the second eldest girl, Tatiana, who lagged behind the others. She was bored. The making and the production of jewellery didn't interest her one bit. It was only the finished article that fascinated her. So, as she ambled along some distance behind the others, her mind was elsewhere. And it was at that moment she heard a noise. To her left was a half open door to a smaller workshop, and inside was a young man who was working studiously. Princess Tatiana stood there for a moment, watching as the young man leant over something that dazzled in the light. Curiosity finally got the better of her and she quietly entered the room and walked over to the bench where Vasily Orlof was working.

'What are you doing?' she asked him.

Vasily Orlof nearly dropped his tools on the floor. He turned suddenly to see a raven haired young lady standing there and looking directly at him.

'What are you doing here?' he said to her, quite abruptly.

Princess Tatiana said nothing. She was quite unused to being spoken to in such a tone.

'You can't come in here,' Vasily Orlof continued, he was quite unaware as to who the young lady actually was.

And at that moment, her 'Royal Highness' Princess Tatiana, daughter of the Tsar of the whole of Russia, decided not to tell him.

'I'm a bit lost,' she said in a deliberately subdued voice, 'My parents are around here somewhere talking to Mr Faberge.'

'Oh really,' said Vasily Orlof. He came to the conclusion that the girl's parents must be customers.

He wasn't wrong.

Suddenly she looked over Vasily Orlof's shoulder and saw the glittering sapphire ring.

For a moment she held her breath in awe.

'My goodness,' she said, 'that is absolutely stunning.'

And before Vasily Orlof could do anything, she reached over to the ring.

'Don't touch it,' he said in panic.

'Why ever not?' she asked.

'Because it's not finished.'

'It looks finished to me,' she said.

'Well it's not,' Vasily Orlof replied.

'Why, what's wrong with it?' she continued to ask.

'There's nothing at all wrong with it, I just need to finish it. It has to be perfect.'

Vasily Orlof sighed. This outspoken young lady somehow irritated him.

'Oh I see,' said Princess Tatiana. But she didn't really.

She just stood there and gazed at the sapphire ring.

'It is really beautiful,' she said.

Vasily Orlof turned to look at his work.

'Yes it is.' he said.

And then for some strange reason he asked her a question.

'Do you know anything about jewellery?'

Tatiana knew when to keep her mouth shut. But she was quite enjoying this little game.

She pointed to the ring 'I know that's a sapphire,' she told him, 'and isn't that lapis lazuli?'

Vasily Orlof nodded.

Yes it is, you're right,' he said to her.

'And the band, is it made from platinum?' she asked him.

'No, I've made it from silver. There's a subtle difference in the colour of silver from that of platinum. I think that silver works better with the blue stones.'

Tatiana stared at the ring.

'You must be right,' she said, 'because it's absolutely beautiful.'

As they both gazed at the sapphire ring, Vasily Orlof suddenly became aware of her presence. She was quite close to him, closer than any woman had been since his mother had kissed him goodbye at Smolensk train station. He could smell Tatiana's fresh perfume and it strangely affected him. At that moment he quickly glanced at her, he looked her dark brown hair and he noticed that she had the most beautiful shaped eyebrows.

'What's your favourite gem?' she suddenly asked him, 'Is it diamonds?'

That brought him back with a jolt. This girl was full of infuriating questions.

He looked at her and smiled, 'To be honest with you, I love them all. I find them all beautiful.'

And it was that answer that caught her. Tatiana looked at the young man who she had tried to annoy and suddenly she saw something else. She saw a gentle passion.

She stared back at him. Nothing was said, but suddenly her emotions started to make her blush.

To cover her embarrassment, she suddenly blurted out 'I really love opals!'

'What?' he said, he too was in some sort of trance.

'Opals...I really love opals.'

'Ah, yes, opals,' Vasily Orlof replied, and he was suddenly back in the real world again.

'Opals are truly beautiful,' he continued, 'they're formed differently from diamonds and other stones, but nevertheless they do have a priceless beauty all of their own.'

'I love all their different colours,' said Tatiana.

'Yes, no two opals can ever be the exactly same, there is always a variation in the colour. That's the nature of opals.'

Tatiana thought about that for a moment.

'Would you make me an opal ring?' she asked.

It wasn't a command, it was a request.

Vasily Orlof smiled at her again.

'Yes I can,' he said, 'but you had better go and ask your parents first. Apparently my work is quite expensive.'

She looked at him and suddenly she decided to stop all the tomfoolery.

'If you do make me a special opal ring, can I come here every so often and see its progress?'

For once, Vasily Orlof burst out laughing.

I can see that you are determined to make my life a misery.'

Tatiana giggled. She liked this young man when he laughed.

'I think we will become friends,' she said to him. 'What is your name?'

'My name is Vasily Orlof Bratz,' he told her, 'and you will only see me again if your father can afford my work.'

And then Vasily Orlof's good manners got the better of him.

'I'm sorry. Of course we can be friends,' he said, smiling at her, 'Tell me, who are you?'

'I am Tatiana...Tatiana Romanov,' she replied.

Vasily Orlof smiled at his new friend, but something in the back of his confused mind told him that something wasn't right.

Tatiana smiled, she was enjoying herself.

'Tatiana Romanov' she said again, and shrugged her shoulders as if to question him.

But Vasily Orlof just sat there looking at her, mystified and clueless.

She tried to give him a hint. 'You'll have probably heard of my father, he's quite famous. We own quite a lot of land.'

'Why, who is he?' Vasily Orlof asked.

She stared at him. 'My father is the Tsar Nicholas, Head of the Romanov Dynasty and the Ruler of the whole of Russia...' And then she saw the look on Vasily Orlof's face and she burst out laughing.

Vasily Orlof just sat there, speechless.

At that moment the door burst open, and Carl Faberge charged into the workshop. There was a look of total panic on his face, but when he saw the princess standing there he stopped dead in his tracks. Though he was the sweating somewhat, Carl Faberge gave Tatiana a deferential bow.

'I'm sorry to interrupt you Lady Tatiana, but we've all been looking for you.'

'Oh,' replied Tatiana, she was completely unaware.

'Err, yes,' Carl Faberge continued, 'Your parents thought you were lost, they are quite concerned. There's been a bit of a panic I'm afraid.'

'Oh I see,' said Tatiana again. She still had no idea that the whole of Faberge's had been frantically searching for her.

'Mr Faberge,' she asked in the most obliging of ways, 'I want Vasily Orlof to make me a ring. Could you please bring some of your finest opals to the palace?'

Carl Faberge and Vasily Orlof both exchanged stunned glances.

Carl Faberge was somewhat taken aback. 'What the hell had been going on here?'

'Of course your majesty,' he replied straightaway. What else could he possibly say?

'Right' said Princess Tatiana. She was again taking complete control of the situation.

'Come Mr Faberge,' she said, 'let's go and find my parents.'

As she left, she turned to Vasily Orlof and gave him the cheekiest of winks.

'I'll hopefully see you soon, my friend' she said.

Throughout all this, Vasily Orlof hadn't spoken a word. As the door closed behind her, he began to wonder if his brain had just conjured up something completely ridiculous.

Words failed him.

It took a week.

One week later Carl Faberge visited the royal residence, the Alexandra Palace, and he took with him a purse full of the most beautiful opals that the House of Faberge had in stock.

Princess Tatiana looked at them all and admired their individual beauty. Glistening and shining, their colours were exquisite. They really were the very best. The following week she returned once again to Faberge's, this time unannounced.

Once again the House of Faberge was put into a flutter. That was until the word got around that the visit was 'unofficial', and was then deemed gratefully acceptable. Faberge's had become quite used to the Romanov women arriving 'unofficially'. It was actually quite profitable.

The princess was immediately escorted to Vasily Orlof's workshop where she charged through the doors and nearly caused Vasily Orlof to slip, just as he was about to cut a minor facet into a diamond that was worth a small fortune.

'Oh God,' he said out loud, before he realised just who he'd said 'Oh God' to.

'Oh I'm so sorry your royal highness. I didn't know it was you,' he continued rather nervously.

All of this went completely over Princess Tatiana's head.

Vasily Orlof jumped up, then bowed, and then graciously offered her a chair.

Princess Tatiana stood there with her hands on her hips and she looked at him.

'Right Vasily Orlof,' she said, 'You can stop all that 'Royal' rubbish right now. When we're on our own I'm just Tatiana. I'm here to see you as a friend and I'm going to call you Vasily.'

This headstrong young lady had Vasily Orlof in a whirl. Before he could say a word she reached into her bag and produced a small leather purse.

'I've got them,' she said eagerly, 'I've got them here.'

'Got what?' he asked.

'The opals of course, silly.'

Suddenly Vasily Orlof realised that her request for him to make her an opal ring was not just a royal whim.

She waved the purse at him.

'Do you want to have a look?' she said. She was almost provocative.

Vasily Orlof's natural enthusiasm immediately got the better of him and he smiled back at her.

'Yes, yes. Come and sit here at my bench and let me see what you've brought.'

Vasily Orlof took the purse from her and she sat down beside him. He reached over for a green velvet lined tray and poured the contents of the purse onto it. A dozen perfect little opals bounced across the velvet and sparkled in the bright jeweller's light. They were all turquoise blue, with flecks of sapphire and red and gold and they were all perfectly matched.

'Mr Faberge says they're the best.'

Vasily Orlof immediately agreed with her and he examined them through a small eyeglass, his jeweller's loupe. As he turned them around with a small pair of tweezers, Tatiana watched him closely.

'Mr Faberge said that they are colour matched and that you would understand.'

Vasily Orlof once again agreed with her. Carl Faberge had understood exactly what would be required. Mismatched opals would have been a disaster. It was the continuity of pattern that was most important.

When Carl Faberge had presented Tatiana with the opals she had sworn him to secrecy. She wanted the opals to be a surprise. Carl Faberge would of course obey her royal wishes.

Vasily Orlof gazed at the twelve glittering opals.

'They're beautiful Tatiana,' and he suddenly stopped when he realised that he'd just used her first name.

She just smiled at him, because that was what she wanted.

'Yes they are,' she replied, 'I knew you'd like them.'

It was a though she was giving him a present, and in a way she was.

As Vasily Orlof studied those beautiful opals, Tatiana Romanov was studying Vasily Orlof. For some strange reason this young man intrigued her. In her perfect world where every single person was agreeable and false, here was a young man who had more important things on his mind. Important to him at least, and she admired that trait. Vasily Orlof was quirky and he was naive, but most of all he was honest.

'Vasily,' she said softly.

He turned to her and smiled, and that warmed her heart.

'Will you be able to make a ring from those opals?'

He smiled at her again.

'Tatiana, I'm going to make you a flower, a beautiful flower.'

Ever since he was a young boy, Vasily Orlof had been totally intrigued by the effect of sunlight on precious stones. And as a child he used to play with his mother's expensive jewellery in her bedroom, and he would hold the jewels up in the natural sunlight and watch as coloured patterns formed across the white cotton sheets of her bed. Sometimes he would take the largest of his mother's brilliant cut diamond rings and watch the white light from the sun transform into the colours of the rainbow as the light refracted across the bed sheets.

In the springtime, young Vasily Orlof would sit at his bedroom window and study the icicles as they began to melt in the weak Russian sun. He was fascinated by the sun's rays as they passed through the slowly melting icicles and projected thin shafts of light onto the wall behind. It was something he had never forgotten, and the memory of it had always lingered somewhere in the back of his mind. And as a jeweller, he had always wondered if it was possible to direct nature's light through a pure diamond and then direct that light to a specific place.

While he'd been at Faberge's, Vasily Orlof had access to an almost unlimited amount of diamonds, and he'd used his spare time to continue his quest, to find a way to control the direction of light through a diamond. And he'd had some success.

By cutting minute triangular ridges along the base of a quality diamond, he'd discovered that those ridges acted like small prisms. As light entered the diamond, it hit the prisms and then reflected inside the stone. The facets of the diamond then mirrored the light inwards, as opposed to outwards. The result being that a tiny beam of intense light radiated out of the diamond. Vasily Orlof's only problem was that he was unable to predict the direction of the light as it left the stone. The small intense beam of light that emerged from the diamond was unpredictable. It would appear like a tiny torchlight, but from any side and out of any facet.

Slowly but surely though, he'd been making progress.

And now suddenly he'd been given the chance to put some of his findings into practice. Tatiana had presented him with twelve perfect opals and an open script to do anything he wanted with them. Her only request being that it should be a ring.

Vasily Orlof was determined to make her something beautiful, something as rare and beautiful as she was.

Little did he know it at that time, but it was to become a labour of love.

During the next weeks and then months, Princess Tatiana would become a frequent visitor to the House of Faberge. So much so, that when she arrived it was hardly an event any more. Everyone there knew that Vasily Orlof had been personally commissioned by the princess to make her a special piece of jewellery. And as a result of that, and because everyone at Faberge's knew the exacting standards of the Romanov family, Vasily Orlof was actually given quite a lot of sympathy. It was considered by many that the constant intrusions must be driving Vasily Orlof mad. It would have certainly been hampering his work.

Even Carl Faberge himself was reluctant to ask.

Tuesday morning arrived, and with it so did Princess Tatiana Romanov.

She strolled through the building with her usual vigour. A Faberge assistant was as ever on hand to open and close every door behind her.

When they arrived at Vasily Orlof's workshop the assistant hurriedly dashed forward, knocked on the door, opened it and immediately announced the impending presence of 'her ladyship, Princess Tatiana'.

Vasily Orlof immediately stood up and bowed in a show of deference as he openly welcomed 'his Royal Highness'. The assistant bowed too, and then left as quickly as possible.

As the door closed, Tatiana and Vasily Orlof were left alone. And being alone, they continued to act in exactly the same manner as they had for the previous couple of months.

Vasily Orlof walked over to her, smiling.

'Good morning darling,' he said to her. And then they embraced and kissed passionately.

It wasn't yet a full blown affair, but it was getting there, and quickly. Their love for each other hadn't yet been consummated, but lovers they were and it would only be a matter of time.

It all began after their very first meeting, each of them had been immediately attracted to the other and before long Tatiana was visiting him two or three times a week, sometimes more. They would sit next to each other at Vasily Orlof's workbench and he would explain the intricacies of the beautiful piece of jewellery that he was making for her. He would go through it step by step and Tatiana would gaze at him dreamily. He too had been finding it hard to concentrate. For some strange reason he couldn't stop himself from looking at her pretty face and those beautiful eyebrows. They were dark and exquisitely shaped and seemed to have a texture all of their own. Sitting so close to one another, every so often their legs would touch. And that physical contact was like a mild electric shock to both of them. Then one day it happened once more, and this time neither of them moved their legs away, and that was the physical connection that required a response. Vasily Orlof continued to talk as Tatiana just sat there staring at him. Then the heat of the moment got to him too and he suddenly stopped talking. They both just sat there looking at one another.

Finally, Tatiana sighed.

'Vasily...kiss me...please.'

Vasily Orlof reached for her and kissed her passionately.

After a few moments they stopped and looked at one another and then started to giggle. They'd finally done it, they had finally crossed the impasse and with that they continued to embrace.

So on that Tuesday morning in one of Faberge's workshops, Vasily Orlof was kissing Tatiana fervently whilst fumbling with the intricacies of her blouse. She started to laugh and in the end she helped him along. The extent of their fondling usually ended up with them both being semi unclothed, however it would have been risqué and foolhardy for them to end up fully naked. At any moment someone could knock on the door and require Princess Tatiana's attention. Vasily Orlof had a chair jammed under the door handle so as to stop any immediate intrusion, but they had to be very careful not to arouse any suspicion. If anyone ever found out about them and word got out, then the Royal family would become involved and there would be a scandal. Princess Tatiana would be banned from ever visiting Faberge's again. In fact the whole relationship between the House of Faberge and the Romanovs would become strained, possibly irrevocably.

There was also the possibility that the princess would have had to leave St Petersburg, perhaps indefinitely. So with all that in mind they both had to be extremely careful. Yet they yearned for one another. Neither of them had ever had any experience at all of the opposite sex and this 'first love' held them like a drug.

Eventually their fondling came to an end and they both sat on their chairs, breathless and hot. They giggled at their own audacity and Vasily Orlof started once again to kiss Tatiana's neck as she tried to dress. After several slaps on the wrist he eventually gave up and got up from his chair and fastened his pants. After another ten minutes of playful conversation they finally returned to the supposed reason for her visit. Vasily Orlof opened a drawer in his workbench and took out a small wooden tray. On it was his 'creation'. He held the ring up to the light and watched as it shone with a life of its own.

'What do you think?' he said to her.

Tatiana clapped her hands with delight.

'Oh Vasily, it's wonderful, it is a flower and it glows like you said it would. I can't believe it.'

But she could, because Vasily Orlof had told her all about his project, step by step.

'I've spent all weekend putting it together,' he told her, 'It only needs the finishing touches.'

In fact, after Tatiana's visit on the previous Friday, Vasily Orlof had hardly been home.

He'd worked nearly twenty hours a day over the weekend and on the Monday because he needed to finish the ring. He needed to see if it worked.

Truth be known, the ring should and could have been finished over a month ago, but because of the couple's philandering it had all taken a little longer. He and Tatiana had discussed this. They both knew that once the ring was finished they would no longer be able to see each other at their little hideaway within the House of Faberge. However they were determined that they would find a way, they loved each other, and love always finds a way.

Along with Tatiana's twelve opals, Vasily Orlof had searched through Faberge's stock and had picked out twenty four small diamonds of extremely high quality. It had taken him several weeks to cut the tiny prism shaped ridges into the bottom of each stone. It had been painstaking and laborious work that had required immense concentration. One minor mistake and the diamond would be rendered useless. There would be no room for error.

For the band of the ring he'd used pure platinum, nothing less would do. And on that band he'd hand carved an intricate pattern of floral stems. If the jewels were going to be a flower, the band was going to be the stem. It was so simple, but yet it worked.

Out of the opals and diamonds, Vasily Orlof had created a shape similar to a small flower. Within that circular shape he had alternatively placed opals with diamonds.

He'd studied each individual diamond and found where the light emitted from it, and then he'd set each stone so that its light shone directly into the corresponding opal. The effect was unbelievable as the opals lit up and seemed to shine with a life of their own.

Tatiana kissed him as she left on that Tuesday afternoon. She promised to return on either the Thursday or the Friday. As she walked out of Faberge's her only thoughts and concerns were what was going to happen next. Now that Vasily had finished her beautiful opal ring his work was done. She would somehow have to find a way to continue seeing him, she had to find a way. In her mind she had decided that their love would have to continue, it had to.

Waiting outside Faberge's along with her carriage was Princess Tatiana's personal bodyguard, Spiridon Dronzi. At over six and a half feet tall, Dronzi was built like a bull. Though he was tall and muscular, strangely for a man his size he possessed the thinnest of faces, it was almost weasel like. His strangest feature however were his eyes. They were a very pale grey and the whites of his eyes seemed to have a yellow tinge to them. The whole effect was that he seemed to possess the eyes of a corpse.

Spiridon Dronzi acknowledged the princess with a nod as she walked out of the building.

'Hello Spiridon,' she said to him quite merrily, 'I'm ready now.'

He opened the door to the carriage and they quickly got in. Then the carriage moved off as it made its way back to the Royal residence.

Though everyone else was rather nervous around Spiridon Dronzi, it seemed that the Princess was not. She was the only person to ever call him by his first name. Spiridon Dronzi had been her bodyguard for the last ten years, since she was a child really. In fact she found it difficult to remember a time when he had not been her bodyguard. And although she knew that everyone was a bit frightened of him, she herself considered Dronzi akin to a big old dog whose bark was probably worse than his bite.

How little did she know?

And lives were going to change, as history too was about to change its course.

Princess Tatiana returned to Faberge's on the Thursday, she couldn't wait another day. But when she arrived at Vasily Orlof's workshop she found him not full of embraces, but full of a cold. He actually looked rather ill and Tatiana was quite concerned. He showed her the finished ring and she immediately christened it her 'flower' ring. That joy however was short lived when Vasily Orlof went into a fit of coughing and sneezing. He told her that it would probably be better if she left, he certainly didn't want her to catch his illness. In those days in Russia, a bad cold could be terminal. She hesitantly agreed, since there was very little she could do at that point. Vasily told her that he would pass the ring onto Carl Faberge, who would then handle things with the Royal Family by way of the usual protocol.

He sadly bid her good bye and she told him to keep warm and that she would call back to see him there at Faberge's on the following Monday.

By the early afternoon, Vasily Orlof wasn't feeling well at all. He was by then running a high temperature, so much so that he left Faberge's and made his way home.

On the Monday, Princess Tatiana arrived back at Faberge's, but as they made their way to Vasily Orlof's workshop a nervous assistant hinted that Vasily Orlof may not' be there. Vasily had apparently been off work all over the weekend and the assistant hadn't seen him at all on that particular morning. Tatiana immediately dismissed the assistant and made her own way to Vasily's workshop. She walked in through the open door only to find the workshop empty. That wasn't like Vasily Orlof at all. Tatiana was just about to turn and leave, when she stopped. She walked over to his workbench and opened the drawer. Lying there on the tray was her 'flower' ring. As it gleamed in the light, Tatiana was suddenly struck by the obvious. If Vasily hadn't passed the ring on to Mr Faberge, he must have left on the Thursday after she'd visited him.

She picked up the ring and on an impulse, she slid it onto her finger. Then she went to see Mr Faberge.

Carl Faberge welcomed her into his office with open arms.

'So nice of you to call in and see me your majesty,' he said graciously.

'Yes it is,' she replied rather sharply, and then, 'Tell me Mr Faberge, where is Vasily Orlof Bratz?'

Carl Faberge gave a fleeting look of concern.

'Vasily Orlof, oh he's rather ill your majesty. I've actually had one of my assistants call around to see him this morning and he's really not well. But be assured your majesty, as soon as he's up and fit he'll be back at his work and we'll get your opal ring finished for you as soon as possible.'

Tatiana stuck out her hand, right in front of Carl Faberge's face.

'Here is the ring,' she said.

Carl Faberge looked at the ring on her finger and he was astonished. He'd never seen anything like it. He continued to stare at it and he was absolutely amazed at what Vasily Orlof had managed to accomplish. It was incredible.

Princess Tatiana needed to get his immediate attention.

'I'm not bothered about the damn ring.' she said loudly, 'I want to know if Vasily Orlof is alright?'

Carl Faberge was rather taken aback.

'Well as I said your highness, he is quite ill.'

Tatiana had no time for all of this silliness.

'I happen to know where Vasily Orlof lives Mr Faberge. Just tell me the number of his apartment please.'

Carl Faberge looked quite horrified. The thought of royalty making a personal visit to his staff was absolutely unheard of.

'Err, this is quite an unusual request your Majesty,' he started to say.

'This is not a request Mr Faberge,' she replied firmly, 'It's a command.'

Carl Faberge blinked.

'It's apartment twenty two your Majesty.'

Princess Tatiana turned and quickly left his office.

Once the door had closed behind her, Carl Faberge felt that he had to sit himself down.

'What the hell was going on?'

Tatiana walked out of Faberge's and was immediately escorted to her carriage by Spiridon Dronzi. She then gave instructions to be taken to the block of apartments in the Bolshaya Morskaya district where Vasily Orlof lived. Dronzi was slightly puzzled by his majesty's latest request, but he gave the driver his orders and he got into the carriage with his mistress.

Nothing was said between them, but that was the usual way of things. After all, Dronzi was just her bodyguard.

However, things were not always as they seemed, certainly not for Spiridon Dronzi anyway. Dronzi had been given the position of Princess Tatiana's personal bodyguard when she was just ten years old. At that time she was a precocious young girl with all the antics of a young lady who desperately wanted to be a teenager. As a child Tatiana never saw the malevolence that Spiridon Dronzi personally exuded. Most of the royal staff were quite frightened by him.

Dronzi had originally been in the Russian army where he was well known for being a very hard man. He was also a man of very few words. When requested, his commanding officer had readily signed Spiridon Dronzi over for royal duties, basically just to get rid of the man. Dronzi was a loner and always had been, and his silence intimidated the rest of the men.

In the army Spiridon Dronzi had no friends, none at all. And that had been the same for most of his life really. As a child and for most of his school years he'd been mercilessly bullied by the other boys. Dronzi hadn't always been as physical as he later became. At school his weasel like features had given rise to permanent scorn from his classmates. Boys would be boys, and it was considered an acceptable sport to 'bully the weasel'.

Along with all that began the habitual beatings from one specific group of young bloods. There were six of them and they were in some sort of gang and were constantly causing trouble. They also made life hell for Spiridon Dronzi. The 'weasel' was targeted for regular beatings and it finally reached a point where Dronzi couldn't turn a corner without checking who was there first. That kind of furtive behaviour hardly helped his cause either.

At fifteen Dronzi discovered boxing and he joined a local gymnasium. For Spiridon Dronzi, boxing became a religion and along with this the gymnasium became his church and his place of worship.

He started to spend most of his free time there and he learned the art of boxing whilst building up his physique. The bullying still continued and Dronzi still lived his life in fear, but that was because it had become a habit. The fear had passed the physical stage and it was now a mental progression, but Dronzi just couldn't see through it.

Suddenly Dronzi grew and had a very good physique, but his tormentors didn't take any notice because they saw him every day at school and they'd just got used to him being big stupid Dronzi. Dronzi the weasel.

At sixteen they all left school, but on the streets of Dronzi's home town the bullying continued. However, at sixteen something happened to Spiridon Dronzi. He grew up.

It all started at the gymnasium. One of the better boxers had needed a sparring partner and Dronzi was called into the ring. The boxer was a popular young man, very well respected and regarded as a possible professional. Unfortunately, he held a personal dislike for young Spiridon Dronzi. Dronzi had never mixed with any of the other boxers, he just trained on his own, but he never stopped training. So Dronzi was called into the ring and the other boxer's supporters all stood around, watching and sniggering.

As they both squared up to one another, the boxer goaded Dronzi.

'I'm going to beat you to a pulp, you weasel,' he said. It seemed that even he knew Dronzi's nickname.

The fight started and for the first two rounds Dronzi was knocked steadily around the ring.

The watching supporters all laughed, they considered Dronzi a clown and told him as much from the ringside. Round three started and Dronzi walked straight into a punch that flattened him. As he lay on the floor of the ring the onlookers started to chant 'Weasel, Weasel'. It was at that moment in an act of sheer contempt and stupidity that the other boxer decided to kick Dronzi in the leg and he told him to get up. The referee was standing outside the ring and he somewhat meekly chastised the boxer for his actions. But that was all. In reality he should have disqualified the boxer, but the referee was never going to do that. After all, it was only Dronzi, 'the weasel'.

Whilst lying there, Spiridon Dronzi realised the unfairness of it. Boxing was an art, it had a code, and a code that should be respected and followed. That was what he had learned, and now suddenly, that code had been broken. As he lay there with all those supporters cruelly chanting his nickname, Spiridon Dronzi felt a strange emotion running through his body. He had never felt it before and it made him feel very hot. The emotion was anger.

Dronzi stood up, flexed his muscles and twisted his neck sideways to steady himself and regain his balance.

The other boxer squared up to him and grinned.

'So you want some more, eh weasel?' he said, and then he stepped back, ready to deliver his final blow.

That would be the last thing he remembered.

Dronzi leapt across the ring and smashed the man in the face. Then with a tirade of punches he forced the boxer into the corner where he continued to rain blows to the man's face and head. The boxer dropped to his knees but Dronzi didn't stop, he couldn't stop.

All the anger at being bullied over the years erupted from his fists. The boxer collapsed to the floor but Dronzi wasn't about to stop, he jumped on top of the boxer and continued to beat the man's face to a pulp. Crimson red blood poured onto the canvas and covered Dronzi's gloves, but still he wouldn't stop. The referee jumped into the ring and physically tried to stop Dronzi, but Dronzi knocked him out of the way and continued to savagely smash his fists into the other boxer's face over and over again. The onlookers frantically climbed into the ring and it eventually took several of them to drag Dronzi off his unconscious opponent.

It was over.

Dronzi was thrown out of the gymnasium, banned and told never to return. The other boxer eventually lost an eye, a career over before it even started.

However, Spiridon Dronzi hadn't finished. That wasn't the end, it was just the beginning.

He then planned his revenge on the gang of school yard bullies. For Dronzi it was a spiritual and mental cleansing.

One by one he found them and beat them mercilessly. A lifetime of being bullied had exacted its toll. After giving three of them a very brutal thrashing, the leader of the little gang and his two remaining followers decided to get clever. They could see what was coming. So the leader met up with Spiridon in the centre of town and offered to fight him in the local park that very evening. It had been snowing and it was cold but that didn't matter. The park would be deserted. The plan being that the leader would turn up early with his two accomplices who would be hiding in the trees. When Spiridon eventually turned up, the other two lads would come out from behind the trees and together the three of them would give Spiridon Dronzi a beating that he would never forget. And that would be the end of it.

So they went to the park an hour earlier than the arranged time and placed themselves strategically, ready for the fight.

They also brought with them three wooden clubs, they intended to do the job properly. They'd seen what Dronzi had done to their three friends and they wanted blood.

The leader went over to a large rock and sat on it, but before that he hid his wooden club in the snow just in front of his feet. Then he was ready.

The three bullies may have turned up with their wooden clubs, but Spiridon Dronzi turned up with a steel bar. He had also turned up an hour before the bullies and he'd already witnessed their devious intentions.

Once everybody had settled down, Dronzi silently crept up behind one of the lads who thought he was cleverly hidden in some snow covered bushes. Dronzi smashed him over the head with the steel bar. The 'would be' assailant was unconscious for over twenty four hours. He was the lucky one.

Dronzi then crept over to the other side of the park and attacked the second accomplice. This time he hit his victim three times in the side of the face with so much force that the steel bar ripped off the lad's ear. He was left comatose and bleeding in the snow.

Dronzi then silently made his way back around the park and until he finally stepped out onto the field directly opposite the leader.

When the lad saw Spiridon Dronzi walking towards him he remained sitting on his rock.

Full of arrogance, he considered himself 'the king of his castle' and by remaining there on the rock he exuded an air of confidence.

Spiridon continued to walk towards his old tormentor, the person who was wholly responsible for his lifetime of misery. Dronzi appeared to have arrived empty handed, and that made his opponent very happy. Unfortunately for him, little did he realise that Dronzi had slid his viscous steel bar up into the sleeve of his thick jacket.

He finally stood up as Dronzi approached.

'So Weasel, you finally want to make a go of it,' he said, brimming with confidence.

Dronzi just nodded.

His opponent then ducked down and pulled his wooden club from beneath the snow.

'You don't know what you've let yourself in for weasel,' he then sniggered.

And with that he stood back, waiting for his two other avengers to storm out of from behind the trees.

But nothing happened.

Spiridon just stood there silently.

'They're not coming,' he said.

His opponent stared at him for a moment, then he looked left and right, but no one appeared. He called out their names, but still no one appeared.

'They're sleeping,' said Dronzi, and then he slipped the steel bar from out of his sleeve.

When the young lad saw the steel bar, his eyes widened and he looked at the wooden club in his own hand and it suddenly appeared useless. And it certainly was.

In an act of 'good faith' he threw the club to the ground. Then he started with some kind of pathetic laughter.

'Okay Dronzi, you win...Fair enough, the fun's over.'

'No...No it's not,' Dronzi slowly replied.

'Come on Spiridon, we're just having a laugh, it's only a bit of fun.'

'No it's not,' Dronzi said again, and it struck him that this was the first time he had ever been called Spiridon by any of these bastards.

The opponent began to panic and the fear showed in his eyes.

'Now you begin to understand,' said Dronzi, 'now you understand what fear is, when you're all alone.'

'What are you going to do?' stammered the opponent, and his voice was raised in fear.

'I'm going to give you pain,' said Dronzi, 'pain like you've never known before.'

The opponent stepped back in terror but Dronzi grabbed him by the ear. The lad screamed but there would be no escape.

Dronzi dropped the steel bar into the snow as he smashed his fist into his opponent's face, the boxer's trained punch completely breaking the lad's nose. The opponent howled in agony, but Dronzi still kept hold of his ear. He dragged the lad over the rock and then smashed his head onto it several times until the lad's face became a pulverized mess. Dronzi then went to retrieve his steel bar. He took his opponents right hand and laid it on top of the rock and then smashed it with the steel bar over and over again until every single bone was broken and the hand would remain forever useless.

Dronzi wanted him to remember and remember why.

For that escapade Dronzi was chased out of town. If some of the locals had their way, he would have been shot.

After a couple of fairly desperate years, Dronzi finally enlisted into the Russian Army and from there his professional training began. Four years later he had become an efficient killer, and was destined for higher things.

But other events had also taken place. There was an air of dissatisfaction within the brigades of the Russian Army and an underground elite had formed. The underground were looking for others to join their inner ranks, other dissatisfied soldiers. Loners like Spiridon Dronzi were exactly the type of people they were looking for. They wanted empty vessels that they could fill with a passionate hatred for the present system of government.

They were the Bolsheviks.

Princess Tatiana and Dronzi finally arrived at Vasily Orlof's block of apartments and Dronzi helped the princess out of the carriage. She turned to him and told him to stay and wait for her there with the carriage.

That wasn't usual.

'There are many dangerous individuals about these days mistress, it would be better if I come with you,' he told her.

'No Spiridon. Stay here with the carriage please,' she replied with authority, and before he could say another word she quickly turned and walked away in the direction of the building.

She entered through a double set of doors and went up two flights of stone stairs and eventually found apartment twenty two. She took a deep breath as she knocked on the dark wooden door. There was no answer, so she knocked again and still there was no reply. What was she to do? Then a thought suddenly struck her. She was the Princess Tatiana of Russia and the House of Romanov. She could go wherever she liked. And with that thought in her mind she turned the door handle and walked into Vasily Orlof's apartment. What she saw horrified her. The small apartment was in darkness and in his bed in the corner lay Vasily.

He looked dreadful. Even from the doorway she could hear him wheezing, he sounded as though he was broken. His eyes were thin slits and were watering. His skin was pallid and white, except for his nose which was red and blistered and sore. But worst of all he was sweating profusely, but when Tatiana felt his forehead it was freezing cold. That wasn't good. It was the beginning of pneumonia, Mother Russia's biggest killer.

There was hardly any food in the apartment but Tatiana managed to make him a mug of black sweet tea and then managed to get some of the hot dark liquid into him. He had the onset of a fever so there was no time to waste. She left the apartment and quickly returned to the royal residence. Once there, she summoned the royal surgeon immediately. She instructed him that he must go immediately to Vasily Orlof's address and attend to him. She explained to the doctor that Mr Bratz was her personal jeweller and that he worked for the House of Faberge. Tatiana then went on to tell the doctor about the wonderful jewellery that Vasily Orlof had produced and that it was imperative he resume his good health because of his involvement in making the Royal jewellery. The smokescreen worked. Tatiana also asked the doctor to act discreetly. It would be frowned upon if one of the Faberge's staff were seen to be favoured by royalty.

The doctor took the hint.

Tatiana then ordered the kitchen to prepare a container of chicken soup which was to be put into a picnic hamper and delivered to Vasily Orlof's address straight away. The doctor would be there to receive it.

The next day Tatiana returned to the apartment. The doctor had already informed her that he had administrated the appropriate drugs and that now it would be up to nature to takes its course. Unfortunately he hadn't managed to get Mr Bratz to eat any of the soup.

Tatiana went to visit Vasily and once again she left a perturbed Spiridon Dronzi with the carriage as she went up to Vasily's apartment. He wasn't much better, but she warmed the soup and managed to get him to eat some. For the first time in her whole life she actually lit a fire and managed to get some heat into the room.

Sitting alone in the carriage, Dronzi began to brood. He didn't understand all this mystery and he didn't like it, not one bit. His official position was to guard Princess Tatiana, but in his own mind he was more than her protector, he saw himself as her 'knight in shining armour'.

Dronzi had watched his precocious little princess grow up into a stunningly beautiful young woman. With her raven dark hair and the Romanov beauty that she shared with her sisters, she was in Dronzi's eyes every inch a princess. More than that, Dronzi had a fascination with her, a fascination that was becoming unhealthy.

Dronzi hadn't had much experience with women, his one attempt at love had been a complete disaster. As a young man on his travels he'd met and fallen for the charms of a young prostitute. He'd pledged his undying love for her, but the following week when he walked into her bedroom and found her 'working', he realised the error of his ways. In a spat of fury he beat the unfortunate customer to a pulp and then he took hold of the love of his life and had throttled her to death. Once again he had to disappear.

But now Princess Tatiana Romanov had unknowingly become the target for his affections, and unfortunately, affection could easily turn into obsession for a man like Spiridon Dronzi.

He was devoted to her and in his own simplistic way he adored her. He knew of course that he could never, ever have a relationship with Princess Tatiana. But in truth, Spiridon Dronzi was lying to himself.

Deep in the recesses of his dark and misunderstood mind, he dreamt of the day when his princess would suddenly realise that she loved him too. One day it would happen. So he would wait, he was ready to wait because he too knew that true love would always find a way.

Nearly two hours passed by before the princess reappeared and returned to the carriage. During the trip back to the residence Tatiana never spoke a word, though she looked quite pensive. So much so that Dronzi felt that he couldn't ask.

Those visits suddenly became part of their new routine, whenever possible Princess Tatiana would slip away to Vasily Orlof''s apartment. It could be in the middle of the afternoon or even in the early evening, and everything had to be worked around her family and her other royal commitments.

After two weeks of this coming and going, Dronzi made a discovery. They'd arrived at the apartments early one evening, just as the light was beginning to fade. The princess as usual entered the apartment building on her own. A minute or so later Dronzi happened to look up and he noticed that a light had just been turned on in an apartment on the second floor.

A few days later they arrived again and at a similar time. The princess once again entered the building, but this time Dronzi was already looking up at the apartment on the second floor. A minute later the same light suddenly appeared in the same apartment..

Dronzi quickly worked out where that apartment was within the building, and he walked away from the carriage and into the apartment block. He quietly ascended the two flights of stone stairs and walked down the dark corridor. At the end of the corridor a light shone under a door.

Dronzi moved forward and put his ear to the door. He could hear voices, it was mostly mumbling but the one voice he could make out was that of Princess Tatiana.

He looked up at the door. It was apartment twenty two.

Dronzi made his way back to the carriage and he stayed there. Now he knew where she was. It was a matter of security of course. He had to know where his princess was at all times.

Of course he did.

Another two weeks passed and the visits stopped, or rather, the official visits with Dronzi accompanying her stopped. Vasily Orlof was well again and had returned to work. Obviously Princess Tatiana couldn't keep visiting Faberge's because the commission to make her the 'Flower' ring had been completed and documented.

So Tatiana then took things into hand. Three or four times a week she would have her official driver take her around to the apartments on the Bolshaya Morskaya in a very unofficial carriage. The driver was a wily old retainer, who in a lifetime of dealing with the Romanovs had fulfilled many unexplained duties. The added bonus of a few roubles would always buy secrecy along with his silence.

No one was to know. Not even her royal bodyguard, Spiridon Dronzi.

It was during this time that Vasily and Tatiana finally became lovers in the true sense of the word. It was always going to happen, but it was always about the time and the place. Now they both had the time and they also had the place.

But other things were happening around them, things were taking place of which they were both completely unaware.

Russia was on the edge of a Revolution that would change the nature of the country for evermore. Unfortunately the last people to realise this were the Romanov Royal family.

The working class populace of Russia were becoming obsessed with the politician Lenin. For many, his preaching's had almost become a religion and he and his party were rapidly gaining an ever growing mass of fervent followers.

The Bolsheviks were coming and they had sourced information which would eventually lead them to power. They even knew what was happening inside the royal residence.

And how? Through Spiridon Dronzi of course.

Drozni may have had feelings towards the princess, but he detested the rest of the Romanovs and their friends, who he saw as a band of leeches. He'd seen what went on and had watched for years the privilege and the squandering and the waste, whilst outside the palace gates there were people who were starving and struggling to keep warm.

It was the age old problem. Those above who were supposedly in charge had lost touch with the ordinary people. Not only were they blissfully unaware of what was actually staring them in the face, they also had the arrogance not to even bother looking.

There was unrest on the streets as the mood of the people began to turn. Anger and resentment had been taken up with a new confidence and there was a general feeling of discontent. Things were beginning to boil.

Tsar Nicholas was seen by many to be at fault and in the end he lost the respect of not only the common folk but also his armed forces.

His disastrous leadership of troops during World War One had left the Russian army broken, battered and bleeding. It was something that his once loyal soldiers would never forgive and never forget

He had also failed to change the ancient feudal system in Russia, which let the landowners bleed the peasants dry. These were the peasants who tilled the land and grew the food, and yet they still starved.

The Russian people wanted reform, together with political rights and a fairer system of government. Workers, peasants and soldiers, they were all becoming weary and impatient and restless. It was an open door for dissidence

Finally it happened. The Revolution began and there was rioting on the streets and there were mass demonstrations which led to the shootings between the Bolshevik troops and the troops still loyal to the Tsar. Total pandemonium broke out and eventually the Tsar's royal residence, the Alexander Palace, was seized and along with it the Romanov family.

For quite a long time, Spiridon Dronzi had been in cohorts with a man called Yakov Sverdlov. Yakov Sverdlov was one of Lenin's disciples and would become one of his principal advisors after the revolution. Sverdlov had shown Spiridon Dronzi 'the light'. He'd coached him and taught him the ethics of Lenin's preaching's and with it the promise of a brand new world.

Dronzi, and others like him, would attend secret meetings with similar thinking 'brothers in arms', where they were all lectured, lied to and promised a slice of power once they'd taken over and Lenin was in control.

Spiridon Dronzi had passed on all and any of the information that Yakov Sverdlov required, and Sverdlov had then dutifully passed on that information to Lenin, the master.

Spiridon Dronzi knew all along what was going to happen. The revolution would take place and with his help the palace could be easily entered and the Romanovs would all be arrested.

However, 'all' was going to be a problem for Spiridon Dronzi. It meant that Princess Tatiana would be arrested too, and that wasn't part of the plan, not Dronzi's plan anyway.

In his deluded mind, Spiridon Dronzi was going to save the day. He was the 'knight in shining armour' who was going save Princess Tatiana from her fate.

Once the Romanovs had all been arrested, Dronzi was going to use his position to secure her release. Failing that, he would simply kidnap her. He would save her life and carry her off to safety and she would then realise how much she loved him and how much he loved her and they would disappear and live happily ever after.

It was a fairytale of course, but a very dangerous one.

As the Bolshevik troops overran the palace, Dronzi took it upon himself to go and find the princess. He knocked on the door to her private rooms but there was no answer, the door was locked, but he continued to knock. Finally he kicked the door in. The princess wasn't there but two of her maids were still there, hiding in a dressing room within the princess's bedroom. Dronzi demanded to know the whereabouts of the Princess, but the maids, who were absolutely horrified at everything that was happening around them, told Dronzi that they didn't know. It was only when Dronzi, in a fit of temper, picked one of them up by the throat that they both decided to tell him exactly what they knew. Terrified, they realised that Spiridon Dronzi was not a man to provoke.

It seemed that the princess frequently disappeared, at least three or four nights a week. And this was happening every week. Dronzi was completely amazed, how had he not known. How could this be happening, and furthermore, where was she going?

Then his brain sparked. It was of course to the Bolshaya Morskaya. Apartment twenty two.

Spiridon turned and stormed out of the bedroom, leaving the maids to the whims of the occupying Bolshevik soldiers and the likely prospect of eventually being raped.

Dronzi found a driver and a carriage, and amid the panic and disarray on the streets he made his way to the apartments on the Bolshaya Morskaya. Everywhere was confusion and disorder as hysteria began to take rule, but he finally managed to get there. He jumped out of the carriage and ran into the building and up the two flights of stairs. When he got to apartment twenty two he started to bang on the door, he heard voices and so continued to beat on the door in desperation.

His princess needed saving, yes she did.

The door swung open and a young man stood there in front of him, dressed only in his underclothes. Suddenly, Dronzi was confused.

The young man too was confused, and he asked Dronzi 'what on earth' he wanted.

Dronzi could only reply 'The princess...I've come for Princess Tatiana.'

At that moment he heard a voice call out, 'Is that you Dronzi?'

He looked over the young man's shoulder, only to see his princess getting out of the young man's bed, and she too was only wearing little more than her underclothes.

Dronzi pushed the young man out of the way.

Grabbing her dress, Princess Tatiana began to shout.

'What the hell are you doing here Dronzi?' It was again not a question, it was a command.

Spiridon Dronzi just stared at her, but through simple habit he replied.

'You must come with me your majesty, there's rioting on the streets, you're not safe,'

And then his brain suddenly began to work, he had to think quickly and he had get her away. 'Your family have ordered me to come and find you,' he told her.

Tatiana and Vasily Orlof exchanged worried glances. If the family had found out what was going on there could be trouble.

'Close the door and stand outside Dronzi, I need to get dressed,' she said to him. It was yet another command.

Dronzi closed the door and stood outside and waited, but in his mind he was going crazy.

Moments later the door opened again and Princess Tatiana appeared. She turned to Vasily Orlof and smiled at him, and he smiled back at her and that was all. But seeing that one single act, that one act so obvious, was the catalyst that finally started to make Spiridon Dronzi's blood begin to boil.

He and the princess made their way back to the waiting carriage in complete silence. He helped her in, but just before he got in himself he turned to his princess.

'Mistress, I think I should just go back and warn your friend as to what is happening on the streets. The mob are burning and looting everywhere. He needs to stay inside and keep his door locked.'

Without waiting for a reply, Dronzi quickly turned and made his way back to the apartment. Two flights of stairs and up to apartment twenty two. Dronzi knocked on the door, and again the door was opened by the same young man, who once again looked at Dronzi with some surprise.

Dronzi smashed him in the face with a punch that could have knocked the door off its hinges.

He then walked in and picked up the half unconscious Vasily Orlof and dragged him across the floor. Dronzi took hold of Vasily by the hair and started to slap his face to bring him out of shock. Once Vasily's eyes opened, Dronzi grabbed his ear and began to twist it. Vasily Orlof cried out in agony. He stared up at the giant of a man who only moments ago was supposedly protecting Princess Tatiana. That was what she had told him before she'd left. He was her bodyguard. Now that same man was back here and attacking him.

'Who are you?' Dronzi demanded.

'I'm Vasily Orlof Bratz' was all he could manage to say.

Spiridon Dronzi squeezed Vasily's ear.

'I'm Vasily Orlof Bratz. I'm from Smolensk,' Vasily tried to answer.

Then Dronzi slapped him so hard that for a moment Vasily Orlof saw only white light.

Then he felt the pain.

'Who the fuck are you?' Dronzi asked him again, 'How do you know the princess?'

'I'm...I'm her jeweller. I work for her, at Faberge's,' Vasily Orlof stuttered.

Dronzi stared at him, and suddenly everything fitted into place. All those hours that he'd had to spend waiting and hanging around outside that damn jeweller's, his princess had been inside there fucking one of the staff. This member of staff.

Jealousy is a human trait whose failing has no bounds, and in Spiridon Dronzi that jealousy was the key to unlocking a terrible and violent anger.

Spiridon Dronzi stared down into the face of the man who had defiled his dream. Dronzi let out a scream of hatred as he spun Vasily Orlof around and smashed his face into the cast iron fireplace. Vasily Orlof moaned as he once again slipped into unconsciousness. And that was probably a blessing, because Spiridon Dronzi then went completely berserk.

He repeatedly stamped all over Vasily Orlof's unconscious body, over and over again, until his rage of jealousy was finally sated.

Dronzi stormed out of the room leaving Vasily Orlof with a broken face and smashed nose. All of Vasily's ribs were broken and damaged and he'd suffered a fractured hip.

Vasily Orlof would never fully recover from that one night's brutal attack.

Dronzi returned to the carriage where Tatiana was still waiting. He got in and ordered the driver to take them back to the palace. Princess Tatiana was livid.

'You had no right to just barge in there,' she exclaimed angrily.

Dronzi turned to her and slapped her in the face so hard that it knocked her head into the side of the carriage door. She was so shocked, that for a moment it left her speechless. She had never felt pain like that, not in that way.

'What...what are you doing?" she finally uttered.

Spiridon Dronzi grabbed her by her raven coloured hair and dragged her off her seat. He was just inches away from her face.

'You dirty fucking whore.' he said to her. And in an act of total disgust he then spat into her face.

'You filthy fucking bitch.' he said, and then he thumped her in the face with a blow so hard that it knocked her onto the floor and into the corner of the carriage. She lay there numbed and terrified and she didn't move until they reached the palace. Once there, Dronzi physically dragged her out of the carriage and threw her onto the ground. Then he turned to some of the smirking Bolshevik guards, now victorious, who were standing around waiting.

'Take this little cow and throw her in with the rest of her fucking family.' Spiridon Dronzi's love affair with his princess was finally over.

The Romanov family were placed under house arrest in the Royal Palace for a few months and eventually they were sent into exile. They were taken to Tobolsk, a small town right on the edge of the Siberian border. It was a place far enough away for them to disappear, no longer to be seen or heard from. Once they were gone they would no longer be in the public's view or the public's thoughts.

Out of sight and eventually out of mind.

During the next few months, Spiridon Dronzi was given a certain amount of power as a reward for his valuable assistance. Russia was inflamed and in crisis, and all over the country warring factions of the old and the new were fighting one another. The Cossacks had become involved and they were fighting against the Bolsheviks in a new war between the 'red' and the 'white' armies. Mayhem was spreading across Russia, and in the madness, some of the major cities were being sacked and burned. It was as though Russia itself was aflame.

Spiridon Dronzi was sent to fight for the cause. He was given position and power, and now it was he who commanded the troops.

After a period of success he was called back to St Petersburg. Once he had returned there he was called upon by his old mentor, Yakov Sverdlof.

Sitting in Sverdlof's new office, Sverdlof spoke to Dronzi about an ongoing problem. Over two mugs of hot coffee both men discussed an issue that wouldn't go away.

It was the Romanovs.

The question of the Romanovs was a difficult one. What to do with them?

Their ignoble royal cousins from all across Europe no longer wished to be associated with the Russian royals because of the political backlash. Even the British Royal Family, to their ever dying shame, had refused their closest of relative's a sanctuary. It was shameful.

It was as though the Romanovs had become the family pariah.

And now Sverdlof deemed that the time was right.

'Anything can happen in Russia at this point in time my friend,' he said to Spiridon Dronzi, 'anything...anything at all.'

Dronzi nodded in agreement.

Sverdlof continued, 'And it's up to men like us to make things happen in these difficult times. Men like us have to forge a future if we want to see Mother Russia survive.'

Dronzi again nodded, it was this sort of dialogue which stirred his blood. He would have done anything for Sverdlof, anything at all. And now he was about to be tested.

Yakov Sverdlof looked Spiridon Dronzi straight in the eye.

'So now is the time my friend, time for us to get rid of one particular problem for once and for all, a problem that won't go away. The Romanov family must be removed Dronzi, they must be executed. The White Army are fighting for the return of the Romanovs, but if the Romanovs were no longer there they would have no one to fight for. They would surely lose heart. This is a war we need to win my friend, we need to stop the divide.'

When this was explained to him by Yakov Sverdlov, Dronzi could of course see the logic. The strategy would work. It was so simple, take out the leader and the followers would eventually crumble.

Sverdlov gave Spiridon Dronzi his orders.

'You must go to Tobolsk. I have a man there, his name is Goloschekin. He's there with some of his men and he's holding the Romanov family there under house arrest. Go to Tobolsk with my orders and put an end to the Romanov dynasty.'

Sverdlof put his hand on Spiridon Dronzi's shoulder.

"Finish the job my friend, let's finish it.'

Spiridon Dronzi left Yakov Sverdlof's office with the mission firmly on his mind.

The only problem with the mission was that Dronzi would have to see Princess Tatiana again. He had put her to the back of his mind and with all the current fighting and disruption he'd almost managed to forget her. He'd been a very busy man.

But she was still his one weakness, and in his heart he knew it.

On his trip to Tobolsk, Dronzi once again began to falter. He thought about Princess Tatiana, he could save her, he knew he could. But should he...after all she had cheated and lied to him and she' acted like a whore. But maybe, maybe, it was all the fault of that sweet talking bastard Vasily Orlof Bratz. Maybe that little swine had managed to persuade her into doing those awful things, and maybe it was because she was naive to the ways of men. Dronzi knew she was inexperienced, he'd accompanied the princess for most of her life and he knew for certain that she had never been with any other man. Maybe it had all been a mistake. Maybe he could forgive her.

All of those questions ran through his mind as he made the long trek to Tobolsk, were he had to arrange the assassination and murder of the family that had ruled Russia for over three hundred years.

Vasily Orlof should have died. He nearly did die, but it wasn't to happen. He was however terribly damaged, and it would take weeks and then months before his body would recover. Vasily Orlof never went back to work at Faberge's. After the revolution, the House of Faberge was taken apart and quickly closed down by the Bolsheviks, once they'd pilfered most of its treasures.

Vasily Orlof lay in his bed for months trying to recover. Had it not been for the services of an elderly caretaker, who for a price, brought him soup and black bread every day, Vasily Orlof would have probably starved to death. For some strange reason, Tatiana never returned. Vasily was worried and he'd always wondered why, until the caretaker informed him about the ongoing revolution. The caretaker also told him that the royal family had disappeared, and Vasily Orlof had the notion that someone must have whisked them away to safety.

Thank God for that.

But what about the man who had attacked him, that madman Spiridon Dronzi?

Tatiana had told him that Dronzi was her bodyguard. So why had he come back and beat Vasily so badly. Why?

Vasily Orlof still didn't understand.

The Romanov family were being held captive in Tobolsk in a secluded former Dacha, known by the locals as the 'Apatiev' House,

Spiridon Dronzi travelled all the way to Tobolsk and when he finally arrived there he was met by Sverdlof's man, Filip Goloschekin. Up till that point, Goloschekin had been in complete control of everything, but one look at Spiridon Drozni and Goloschekin took a step back. Dronzi would now be in charge.

Dronzi wasn't going to waste anyone's time, especially his own. He immediately assembled the men together. They were a gang of deluded, 'so called' Bolsheviks, half of whom had never even read Lenin and the other half who probably couldn't even read at all. But now, since having acquired their new 'Bolshevik' title, they thought that they were entitled to strut around the town, bullying people and settling old scores.

Goloschekin introduced the men to Spiridon Dronzi and then he disappeared. He wanted no part in what was about to happen.

Dronzi picked out two men, two complete bastards who were weak, but willing to do anything.

Those men were YakovYurovsky and a probable psychopath whose name was Peter Ermakov.

It was arranged that Yurovsky would organize the killing of the Tsar, the Tsarina and their son Alexei. Those three poor innocents were subsequently dragged out of their house and tied to three separate trees to await their execution.

Meanwhile, Peter Ermakov had the Romanov girls herded into a cellar. However, there were only three of them. Olga, Maria and Anastasia.

Princess Tatiana was awaiting a different fate.

Tatiana sat on her bed alone. She was in her bedroom wondering what was happening, when suddenly the door opened and in walked the instigator of all her nightmares. It was Spiridon Dronzi. She immediately shrank backwards in fear as he looked directly at her with those lifeless, almost colourless pale grey eyes. There was something about him that was almost feral.

Dronzi just stared at her. He despised her for what she'd done to him, yet strangely in his twisted mind, he did still love her.

For Spiridon Dronzi, it was going to be the moment of truth.

Princess Tatiana moved backwards on the bed as Dronzi approached her. She was terrified of him. He looked down at her, he didn't want her to be frightened of him, he wanted her to love him.

'I can save you Princess,' he said suddenly. He still couldn't call her by her first name, it was a strange, almost pitiable habit.

Tatiana just stared at him.

'I can save you,' he said again.

'What do you mean?' she said.

'We can run away, we can start a new life together.'

Princess Tatiana was totally mystified as to what he meant. She shook her head.

'I don't understand you Dronzi,' she stuttered. 'What do you mean...a new life?'

Suddenly, Spiridon Dronzi couldn't stop himself. He had to tell her.

'You and I, we could run away. I could find us somewhere and we would be happy. You know that I love you.'

He had finally said it. After years of frustration and hope, he'd finally told her about his feelings towards her.

Princess Tatiana sat on the edge of her bed, astounded.

There was a moment of silence between them.

Dronzi saw the look on her face, and then he asked the one question that he needed to know the answer to.

Almost childlike, he asked her, 'Could you ever love me princess?'

But before he had even taken another breath, she answered.

'No, of course not.'

And she said it with such disdain, that he suddenly felt a flicker of an insult.

'Why?' he asked her. It was such a stupid question.

She looked at him in amazement and he felt the sting of it.

'Love you. Why would I love 'you'? Don't be ridiculous,' she replied.

And suddenly she'd said it. Those last three little words 'don't be ridiculous' would ultimately seal her downfall.

In that instant, Spiridon Dronzi felt angry, and he felt humiliated and embarrassed.

Dronzi then retaliated. 'It's him isn't it? It's that bastard, that little jeweller friend of yours?'

Tatiana held her breath as she stared at him, and he knew that he had suddenly hit the target, the target that Princess Tatiana had always tried to protect. He saw the look in her eyes.

So Dronzi continued, 'Little Vasily Orlof Bratz, your little lover.'

The words stung her. He knew her secret, of course he did.

She said nothing, but Dronzi continued, he he had to. And then he grinned at her.

'But your lover will be your lover no more your majesty. Because when I finished with him he was broken and smashed. I doubt if he's even still alive. But if he is, I can promise you one thing. He's now a cripple.'

And as he uttered those words Dronzi's eyes brightened at the memory of it, and he smiled.

Princess Tatiana just sat there in shock at what Dronzi had just told her.

Vasily. Her beautiful, tender Vasily.

What had this man done to him? She suddenly started to cry.

However, those tears only angered Dronzi.

'What are you crying for you stupid bitch?' he seethed, 'He was only a boy, just a stupid little boy.'

Heartbroken and angered, Tatiana turned on him.

'You fucking oaf. He was a better man than anyone. Better than you will ever know.'

Dronzi felt the heat rising within him, the uncontrollable heat.

'What...just because he fucked you?' he shouted.

But Tatiana shouted back at him, she would treat Dronzi like the imbecile he was. But she didn't see the danger.

'Yes,' she screamed, 'yes, because he fucked me. He fucked me better than anyone.'

She wasn't going to let him win. She wasn't going to let a traitor like Spiridon Dronzi intimidate her. She wasn't going to let him triumph over her, never.

But Dronzi was quick to reply.

'No princess, you don't know it yet, but I'm the one that's better than anyone.'

And with that, Dronzi grabbed hold of her and pulled her to him. With both hands he took hold of her dress and ripped it open. Tatiana tried to scramble backwards bur Dronzi was far too strong. He grabbed her again and tore the dress off her back, and then he ripped off her white cotton blouse. He stood there for a moment staring at her nakedness and her pale breasts. Then he pushed her backwards and pulled off her dress completely. Down and past her legs and then he threw it onto the floor. The princess was in shock as she lay there on the bed, spread-eagled and wearing only her knickers and stockings.

Dronzi leered at her as she lay there, so soft and naked and delicious, and his body began to stir.

Princess Tatiana looked up at him. She knew what was about to happen. And she also realised with a terrible finality what her fate would be.

And at that moment, three hundred years of ancestry and three hundred years of Romanov blood and pride and dignity came into play.

She was a Romanov, and she would fight and die like a Romanov.

Dronzi started to undo his belt, he was breathing heavily and all he could do was look down at her perfectly nubile body.

Suddenly she spoke to him.

'What are you going to do Spiridon, stick it in me?'

She spoke with an air of confidence, it was almost mockery.

For a moment it shocked him. It was something he didn't expect.

'Well let's get it over with,' she said. 'You certainly won't be the first, but you know that already don't you. You do know that I've been fucked before and I know exactly what it feels like. I only hope you can do it better.'

Dronzi stared at her. He continued to unbutton his pants but he couldn't think of a reply.

'Come on Dronzi,' Tatiana continued, it was almost a command. 'Get it out and let's have a look at it. I hope it's big enough?'

Dronzi stopped, he knew her game, but still he stopped. This was not what he expected.

She looked up at him and smiled.

'And when did you actually 'fall in love' with me Dronzi?' she asked him mockingly, and then she laughed and shook her head dismissively.

For Spiridon Dronzi it was the final insult.

He grabbed her by the neck and pulled her towards him. All of his hopes were dashed. He was inches away from her face and in one last desperate attempt, he tried to kiss her. She turned her head away and tried to resist him, but he was too strong. So at the last moment she turned to him and delivered her final insult.

'Before you kiss me Dronzi,' she said softly, 'remember that I've had his cock in my mouth.'

Spiridon Dronzi stopped and looked at her. This was history repeating itself. It was the prostitute all over again, it was the whore and it was the deceit. What he had wanted was purity, untouched purity, untouched by any other man. And once again he'd deceived, just like the prostitute had deceived him when he was a young man.

Dronzi began to shake her by the neck and his hands clenched and tightened around her throat. He screamed at her in anger and he shook her and he squeezed and squeezed.

And after a moment he stopped. He stopped and he looked down, because she was dead.

He'd crushed her throat and with it her windpipe. He'd strangled her to death.

Dronzi stepped back, and he fastened his pants. Then he just stood and stared down at her.

It was over. Finished.

Outside, things were going no better. Assassinating the Romanovs, three innocent people, a father, a mother and their young son was not going to be a simple task.

At the last moment Yakov Yurovsky lost his nerve and his accomplice Peter Ermakov had to be called up from the cellars. Ermakov would do the shooting and he would probably enjoy it.

Peter Ermakov had joined the Bolsheviks for all the wrong reasons, but because the Bolsheviks were now in control and Ermakov had already been a party member, he was given a limited amount of power together with a gun. The gun was a Mauser type pistol and Ermakov had taken it upon himself to swagger around the town checking up on people and generally ordering them about. He regularly patrolled the streets with his pistol visibly stuck in his belt, it was an unsubtle reminder to anyone who thought that they possibly had an opinion.

And just like any man who had ever owned a gun, Ermakov wanted to shoot it. He generally wandered around the forest taking pot shots at anything bigger than a sparrow, and most of the time he missed. However, just lately he'd found bigger quarry. His latest target had been the local dogs. Any dog in the locality that dared to bark at Peter Ermakov was shot. Ermakov felt justified in his actions, after all those dogs could be dangerous. The dog's owners on the other hand, felt that Ermakov was altogether the bigger danger. Most of them had lived in the town of Tobolsk all of their lives and knew him for the vicious lunatic that he was.

So, suddenly Peter Ermakov had a modicum of power and now he was being asked to take charge of an official death sentence. Yes, he was now a very important man.

As he stood there with his Mauser pistol in his hand, Ermakov had to decide which of the Romanov's to shoot first. He finally decided that it should be in order of importance, so he walked straight up to Tsar Nicholas and shot him in the temple. It was a clean shot and the Tsar died instantly. Ermakov was also aided by that fact that Nicholas had enough royal dignity to stand there and not move a muscle. The Tsarina however was going to be a different prospect altogether. She started to scream and shake her head which unfortunately made her a harder target. Eventually, and for ease, Ermakov shot her twice in the chest, then he blasted her in the face just to make sure.

The other four soldiers who were there to assist, grimaced as they watched. They all thought they were there to be part of a firing squad, the final act that would give the Romanov family a dignified death, if there ever was ever such a thing. But Ermakov's handling of the whole affair was turning it into a blood bath. However, when it came to the shooting of young Prince Alexei, Ermakov's choice of order could certainly be questioned. Tied to a tree and having just witnessed both of his parents being murdered in the most barbaric fashion, Prince Alexei started to howl in fear and he screamed out in terror at the pain that was about to be inflicted on him.

It was more than the squad of men could witness. Two of them walked away and the other two turned their backs. Ermakov hadn't time for all this nonsense. He simply walked up to the young prince, grabbed him by the hair and shot him in the head.

Prince Alexei Romanov, son and heir to the Russian throne, died instantly.

Ermakov then made his way back down the cellar stairs. He had left three of the other guards watching over the royal sisters.

History would have us believe that those sisters were shot and quickly disposed of.

However, reality is usually a lot different from what the history books would have us believe. And it would be doubtful if the truth of what happened would ever be revealed, let alone acknowledged.

The three sisters cowered before their captors as the men looked at them greedily. Those three royal beauties were the prettiest girls they had ever seen. So fine and so untouchable, they were the forbidden fruit. They were also considered the spoils of war. So the men decided that they could do anything they wanted with them, and they would.

Before their deaths, the three royal sisters were systematically raped and terribly abused in ways abhorrent to anyone remotely civilized. In the end, as the four semi naked men looked down at their poor bloodied victims,

Peter Ermakov retrieved his pistol and then stepped over the sisters and shot each one of them in the head.

The obscenities of what happened that day would be watered down by future historians to justify the acceptable. But to all those who were involved, and to all those who could have done something and should have done something to stop what happened and saved that poor family... all should have hung their heads and lived with the undying shame.

Spiridon Dronzi closed the bedroom door. Before he left he'd wrapped Princess Tatiana's body in a bed sheet. Why, he didn't know. Possibly a feeling of guilt or error, who would ever know? He walked out of the Dacha where he was met by Yurovsky and Ermakov. Yurovsky had his men cut the three dead bodies from the trees they'd been tied to, and those bodies were then laid side by side on the grass.

Ermakov looked at Dronzi.

'The other three are in the cellar sir.'

'All dead..?' Dronzi asked.

'Yes sir, of course sir.'

Dronzi looked at them both.

'There's another body upstairs,' he said to them.

Peter Ermakov was tempted to grin, but then he thought better of it.

Dronzi again took control.

'Load all the bodies onto the back of a cart and cover them up.' Then he looked at Yurovsky, 'I take it you've made arrangements?'

'Yes sir,' stuttered Yurovsky, 'We've already dug a pit in the forest sir.'

'Good. Load up the bodies and get some shovels, and then we'll go and have a look at your pit,' said Dronzi.

'You're coming with us sir?' Yurovsky asked nervously.

'Of course,' Dronzi replied, and he gave Yurovsky a look that let the man know not to ask anymore stupid questions.

A horse and cart were found and the seven bodies were loaded onto the back of the cart and covered with an old canvas sheet. Dronzi, along with six of the other men then made their way into the forest. Yurovsky led the horse by its reigns and Dronzi sat on the cart, he'd no intention of walking. The other men, including Peter Ermakov, walked along dutifully behind the cart. Ermakov was beginning to feel quite disgruntled. He felt that it was he who had done most of the work, but it seemed that Dronzi was only prepared to deal with Yurovsky. Just one hour after murdering most of the members of the Russian Royal family, Peter Ermakov was beginning to sulk. They turned the cart off the forest path and continued for another half an hour until they came to a small clearing were there was evidence that someone had been digging. The cart stopped and Dronzi stepped down and went over to examine the workings. It was a pit, about twelve feet in diameter and several feet deep.

Dronzi looked down and shook his head. He turned to Yurovsky.

'Get three of your men down there with shovels, I want it digging three or four feet deeper.'

Yurovsky did as he was told.

Dronzi turned to the other men.

'I want you to collect some stones and small boulders, and I want you to dig up some small bushes. And be careful with them, they'll be needed for replanting.'

After an hour Yurovsky went over to Dronzi, who was leaning on a tree smoking a cigarette and looking slightly pensive.

'I think everything's done sir,' he said.

Spiridon Dronzi exhaled some smoke and nodded.

Yurovsky stood silent for a moment, and then he asked Dronzi a question.

'If I may ask sir, what are the rocks for? Aren't we supposed to be hiding the grave, sir?'

Dronzi looked at Yurovsky.

'They're not for the top of the grave, they're for on top of the bodies,' and then he took another draw on his cigarette, 'I've seen it before. If the wolves get the smell of carrion you'd be surprised how far they will dig. The wolves may get through the soil, but they can't get through the layer of rocks.'

He took one last draw on his cigarette and threw it into the bushes.

'Bears however, are a different problem altogether,' he remarked, and he walked off to inspect the work.

One by one, the bodies were thrown into their final resting place. Strangely the last body was that of Princess Tatiana, she was still wrapped in the bed sheet.

Dronzi stared down at her body, almost in wonder at what he had done. Yurovsky came over to him. 'Should we start to throw the rocks in now sir?'

'In a minute,' Dronzi replied, and he continued to stare down at the body wrapped in the cotton sheet. Dronzi then looked up at the men. They were all standing around the edge of the grave expectantly.

Spiridon Dronzi gave the moment some thought, and then he reached into the inside of his coat and pulled out a revolver. He pointed the gun at Peter Ermakov and shot him twice in the chest.

Ermakov still had the look of complete surprise on his face as he fell into the grave together with the other bodies. The rest of the men just stood there, paralysed with fear. Was this part of the plan? Was Dronzi going to murder them all so that there would be no witnesses?

It actually did make sense.

But Dronzi slowly put the revolver back into his coat pocket.

'I didn't like the man, he said to Yurovsky, 'now throw the rocks in and cover the bodies, and then fill in the grave with the rest of the soil. After that I want you to carefully replant those bushes on top of the grave so that nothing can be seen, nothing at all.'

The men looked at one another, they took a deep sigh of relief and then started to fill in the grave as Dronzi walked back to the tree and lit another cigarette.

He thought about Ermakov, and he knew he had done the right thing. He'd known men like Peter Ermakov all his life. Little men, little nobodies who were full of their own self importance and who liked to brag. And it would only be a matter of time before Ermakov would open his big mouth and want to tell somebody all about his exploits. And as ever, somebody, somewhere, would be listening.

The next day Dronzi prepared to return to St Petersburg. The Dacha had been scrupulously cleaned and cleared of any evidence. It was shut down and made to look as though no one had lived there for quite some time. Several windows were then smashed to allow the weather and the local wildlife to take its toll.

Spiridon Dronzi returned to St Petersburg. He now had only one mission in life and that was to serve the party. He was a driven man, and God help anyone who got in his way.

Vasily Orlof was still recovering.

His bones had begun to knit together and heal, however his face and nose would never be the same again. Dronzi's handiwork had robbed him of his looks, and it wasn't helped by the fact that Vasily Orlof had lost almost half of his bodyweight.

Vasily had stopped going out of his apartment altogether. Since that fateful night he had stayed inside and permanently lived off the weak soup and bread which his caretaker provided. It was all he could afford. Every so often he would peer out of his window, but when he saw the angry crowds and the ensuing chaos he just turned down the lights and returned to his bed. In his bed he could sleep, and he could dream about Tatiana, his only love. In his dreams she was always there. He could almost reach out and touch her.

Late one morning he was woken by the sound of heavy banging on his door. He began to get out of bed but then sank back again. It was Spiridon Dronzi, it had to be. He'd come back, he must have decided to return and murder Vasily Orlof. It had to be him. With that in mind, Vasily just sat there quivering with fear. There was a muffled shouting outside the door followed by the continual banging, it wouldn't stop. Vasily Orlof sat there full of horror and panic at what was about to happen to him. He felt like picking up a pillow and covering his head, the banging just wouldn't stop. Then door started to rattle, Dronzi was trying to kick down the door, and suddenly Vasily Orlof wanted to scream, he wanted to scream out loud because he couldn't go through that physical pain again, he couldn't.

The door burst open and slammed back against the wall, and Vasily wanted to roll up into a ball and die. He closed his eyes tightly. 'Let it be over, just let it be over'.

'Vasily...Vasily, it's me. Vasily.'

He heard the voice, it was a long forgotten memory, but he heard the voice.

Someone put an arm round his shoulder and turned him over.

'Vasily, it's me.'

Vasily Orlof laid there and slowly opened his eyes. He strained to see who it was.

Looking down at him was a familiar face, the face of an old friend. It was Rubin Blesk.

'My god Vasily,' said Blesk. 'What have they done to you?'

Blesk lifted him up and sat him on the side of the bed. There were also another two men in the room, and one of them quickly approached him. It was Maurice Broch, Vasily's longstanding friend and workmate from Smolensk.

Maurice Broch came forward and took hold of Vasily Orlof's hand.

'Vasily,' he said, 'what on earth has happened to you?

'I was attacked,'" Vasily Orlof replied, 'and beaten up by a man called Dronzi.'

Rubin Blesk suddenly stared at Vasily Orlof.

'Spiridon Dronzi? You know Spiridon Dronzi...how?'

'It was through Faberge's...through the royal family. I did work for them.'

'You know that bastard Dronzi?' Blesk again asked.

Vasily Orlof nodded.

'Oh my god Vasily,' said Blesk and then he looked around the room, 'We've got to go, we've got to get you out of here now.'

'Why?' Vasily asked.

"Because Dronzi's coming for us, he's looking for us and has probably linked us to you. He knows we're all from Smolensk, he could be on his way here right now.'

The third man, who'd quietly stood there listening to them, walked over to Rubin Blesk and took him on one side.

'We've got to go Mr Blesk. We've got to leave right now.'

That third man was Herman Vodle. He was carrying Rubin Blesk's old brown leather bag and at that moment he was very concerned.

They got Vasily Orlof out of bed and hurriedly dressed him. Then they left the apartment and went down the two flights of stairs and dashed outside to their waiting carriage. Without any delay, they made their way to the still named 'Nicholaevsky' Train station.

Earlier that day, Spiridon Dronzi had been called into Yakov Sverdlov's office.

Sverdlov was seething.

'Sit down Dronzi, sit down,' he said.

'You are upset comrade Sverdlov, what's wrong?' Dronzi asked.

Yakov Sverdlov slammed his hand on the top of his desk.

'It's that bastard Carl Faberge. We've just found out that he's disappeared.'

At the mention of the name 'Faberge', Spiridon Dronzi bristled.

Sverdlov continued. 'Though we've already confiscated most of the jewellery from the House of Faberge, we've been keeping our eye on Mr Carl Faberge. He's undoubtedly got a stash of something hidden away somewhere, his type always do. We've been having him followed, but he's given our man the slip.'

Where do you think he'll go?' Dronzi asked.

'I think he'll run,' said Sverdlov, 'probably west, he'll probably try to get himself and whatever he's stolen from the state and make his way to Paris.'

Dronzi mulled over the information.

'Another piece of information is that Rubin Blesk's arrived in St Petersburg,' said Sverdlov.

Dronzi pondered for a moment. Somewhere he'd heard mention of that name.

'Who's Rubin Blesk?' Dronzi asked.

'He's a very rich Jewish diamond merchant. He hails from Smolensk, apparently he carries a fortune in diamonds around with him in an old leather bag. He and Faberge have had many dealings. I think he's possibly here to help get Carl Faberge out of the country.'

The word 'Smolensk' rang in Spiridon Dronzi's ears and it stuck there, Jewellery...and the city of Smolensk. And suddenly Dronzy understood everything. The one thing that brought all of this together, the central figure to it all had to be that little bastard, Vasily Orlof Bratz. Vasily Orlof Bratz had told that he was 'a jeweller from Smolensk'. There had to be a connection. Dronzi had always considered that when he had the time he would go around to Bratz's apartment to see if he was still alive. If he was, Dronzi would kill him. And suddenly, the thought struck Dronzi. If you wanted to hide in this city, hide before you ran, where would it be? Why of course, Vasily Orlof's apartment on the Bolshaya Morskaya, that would be the perfect place.

That was where Carl Faberge would be, Spiridon Dronzi would have bet money on it.

But he would have lost.

Carl Faberge had already left St Petersburg. He was on one of the last safe trains heading for Riga in Latvia. From there he would travel south and eventually end up in Switzerland. He had escaped.

Carl Faberge would live in Switzerland for the rest of his natural life, which unfortunately for him, turned out to be only two more years before dying through illness.

Spiridon Dronzi immediately left Yakov Sverdlof's office, promising that he would apprehend Carl Faberge come what may. His confidence was of course, misguided.

He took a squad of ten men and they made their way to the apartments at the Bolshaya Morskaya. To Dronzi's dismay however, the birds had already flown.

Dronzi stood there in Vasily Orlof's empty apartment, wondering what to do next, when suddenly one of his lieutenants ran through the door.

'We've just had word sir, the office has been trying to get hold of you.'

'What is it?' asked Dronzi.

'Apparently there's been a shooting at Faberge's sir. One of our own men has been killed whilst trying to apprehend three others.'

'And who were these men?' Dronzi demanded.

'We think one of them was called Rubin Blesk sir. We think he's a Jew.'

Dronzi stood there in amazement. The pieces of the jigsaw were starting to come together.

Of course, Blesk must have come to see Carl Faberge and one of Dronzi's men had been suspicious. Somehow they must have all fled, and one of them could possibly be Vasily Orlof Bratz. But where would they go? They obviously weren't here in Bratz's apartment. Suddenly, Spiridon Dronzi understood, he understood it all. They would run and Spiridon Dronzi knew where too. He needed to get his men to the 'Nicholaevsky' train station.

Dronzi hated that name.

Rubin Blesk had indeed gone to the House of Faberge. He went there with Maurice Broch and Vodle after having to leave Smolensk, another city in total chaos and self ruination.

Blesk wanted to speak to Carl Faberge, not realising the situation there in St Petersburg.

Faberge wasn't there, but four armed guards were. When Blesk enquired about Carl Faberge one of the guards had become suspicious and they were questioned.

'I'll need to contact my superior, Comrade Dronzi. He'll need to speak to you,' the guard said.

'Is that Spiridon Dronzi?' Blesk had asked casually.

'You know him?' the guard asked.

'I've heard of him,' Blesk had replied, again very casually.

Rubin Blesk knew all about Spiridon Dronzi. The man was a psychopath and Blesk had already heard the stories. He knew exactly what Comrade Spiridon Dronzi was capable of.

Rumours were already beginning to surface about the extermination of the royal family. Someone in Tobolsk, or maybe even from Yakov Sverdlov's own office had talked, and the rumours were rife.

'You will all be placed in an office,' said the guard, 'and you will have to wait for Comrade Dronzi to get here".

The guard clicked his fingers and one of the other guards came forward.

'Lock these men up in one of the offices,' he said as he smiled at Rubin Blesk.

Blesk, Maurice Broch and Vodle were led down a long corridor and were shown into an unused office. The guard held the door open and ushered the three of them in. Vodle was at the rear. As he walked in, Vodle suddenly grabbed the guard by the neck and threw the man to the floor. In an instant Vodle whipped out his Luger, he pressed it close against the guard's chest and fired. The guard died almost instantly. And though the noise from the shot had been somewhat contained, somebody must have heard it, because as the three of them came back out of the office they heard someone shouting. They then ran down the corridor to the end of the building and escaped out of a back door.

Blesk made up his mind to go and get Vasily Orlof, and then they would all have to get out of St Petersburg and out of Russia.

When Blesk and the others finally got to Nicholaevsky train station, Spiridon Dronzi was already there.

The station itself was heaving with desperate people, all trying to leave St Petersburg. Most were trying to leave forever, or at least until the upheaval had died down.

Earlier, when Dronzi and his troops had dashed into the station, there were many there whose stomachs turned sick with worry. Each thought that Dronzi and his men had come to arrest them personally. The people fleeing from St Petersburg had money and valuables with them that they didn't particularly want to hand over to the new 'shared' system of communism.

In their eyes, 'all were definitely not equal'.

Two trains were waiting in the station that afternoon. By far the busiest, was the train going west to Riga. People were frantically queuing to get on it, and if possible, get a seat for themselves and their families. It was turning into complete mayhem. There should have been two trains going to Riga that day but already the inefficiency and incompetence of the communist system was becoming all too evident. Worse was to come.

On the other side of the track was a smaller train. This train was going north to the Karelia region and would have usually been filled with lumberjacks, all going up there to the forests to cut timber. For the moment however the revolution had put paid to all that. In fact the train was less than half full and though it should have left an hour earlier, nobody seemed to be in any sort of a hurry. The fireman had been slowly building up the train's steam pressure and was steadily shovelling more and more coal into train's firebox, but the driver was still leaning against one of the carriages, talking to an inspector.

As they walked down the steps to the station, Blesk suddenly stopped as he saw the troops going from carriage to carriage. The four of them froze and that was when Vasily Orlof spotted Spiridon Dronzi. He went rigid with fear, just seeing the man put him back into some sort of shock and he immediately grabbed hold of Rubin Blesk's arm.

'That's...that's him Rubin,' it was almost a whisper, 'That's Spiridon Dronzi.'

Rubin shot around to see where Vasily Orlof was looking. He saw Dronzi immediately, a big brutal man, dressed in army issue uniform and barking orders at his men. Even the troops were frightened of Spiridon Dronzi.

Dronzi's men were causing complete chaos, climbing through the carriages and knocking people in all directions in their desperate search for Blesk and his accomplices.

Rubin Blesk, along with Vasily Orlof, Broch and Vodle hid behind a pile of sacks which were full of grain. The four of them stayed there, low and out of sight.

Vasily Orlof looked at Rubin.

'We're never going to get on that train,' he stammered, 'it's impossible. Dronzi's going to catch us, he'll see us straightaway.' Vasily's voice was beginning to tremble.

'We're not getting on that train,' replied Rubin Blesk.

Vasily Orlof just stared at him.

'We're getting on the other train Vasily. We're not going west, we're heading north.'

Vasily stared at Rubin Blesk, so did Maurice Broch.

'Everyone's heading west,' said Blesk, 'and that's the problem. We're going to go north and we're going to go the long way around.'

'To where..?' Vasily Orlof asked.

Rubin Blesk looked at him.

'To England Vasily, God willing. We're going to England.'

Once Spiridon Dronzi realised that Blesk and his friends weren't at the station, he had his men strategically conceal themselves. They stood behind the station pillars and the mass of mounting cargo and they tried to generally keep out of sight. Spiridon Dronzi stood back and waited, his eyes were everywhere. They had to come here, he was sure of it.

He would wait. Blesk and that 'bastard' Vasily Bratz would eventually turn up and hopefully they would have Carl Faberge with them. That would really be the icing on the cake.

Dronzi too would also stay low and wait. After all, Blesk and his little gang didn't even know that he was here at the station looking for them. Did they?

Twenty very long minutes later, the driver of the train heading north to Karelia stopped talking and decided to get onto his engine. He pulled some levers and the train began to belch out thick black smoke. It moved forward slowly for about ten feet and then it stopped again.

Rubin Blesk wiped his hand over his face.

Spiridon Dronzi looked over at the leaving train. It was half empty and he had already had his men check it twice. Dronzi should have known better.

The train jerked and once again began to heave forward but nobody was really interested.

The train heading west to Riga was packed to capacity, when it was suddenly discovered that there was no driver. There were normally two drivers, but neither of them had been given any specific instructions and so both of them had subsequently gone home.

It was communism working at its disorganised best.

From behind the sacks of grain, Rubin Blesk watched as Spiridon Dronzi glanced back once more at the slowly departing train. Their escape was doomed to failure, it all seemed useless. Then suddenly, Dronzi looked away.

Blesk made an immediate decision. This was it, now was the moment. Blesk quickly turned to his friends.

'Come on,' he said, 'we've got to run for it...now!'

The four of them set off at a pace, the train was still moving slowly and they desperately needed to run to get on it, it was life or death and they all knew their situation. Blesk got there first, even though he was carrying his leather bag, he was tall and lean and easily outstripped the others. He got to the penultimate carriage, grabbed the door handle and pulled it open. He threw his leather bag into the empty compartment and turned to see Maurice Broch right behind him. Blesk seized hold of Bloch and bundled him into the carriage.

Then he looked back.

Herman Vodle and Vasily Orlof had been right behind them, but when Blesk looked around they were still half way along the platform. It was Vasily Orlof, he couldn't run. He was still far from recovery and all the physical exertion had taken its toll on him. He was exhausted.

Vodle had been running right behind Maurice Broch when he'd suddenly realised that Vasily Orlof had fallen back. He had turned and grabbed hold of Vasily but they were still struggling to catch up with the others. Rubin Blesk spun around and immediately ran back to help them.

But at that precise moment, disaster struck.

The driver of the train had looked across at the driverless Riga train which was still stuck in the station and he laughed to himself, his own smaller and somewhat insignificant train was now happily on its way to its destination. There had always been a touch of bravado between the train staff and the drivers. It was all down to who could be the most efficient and who could get the upper hand, and in a moment of euphoria the driver pulled the train's whistle as a show of his superiority. The sound of it echoed loudly throughout the station.

All heads turned, including that of Spiridon Dronzi, and what he saw he couldn't believe.

A tall Jewish man was running down the opposite platform towards two other men who were struggling to catch the train. Once the man had caught up with the other two, they all set off together to try and get on the slowly moving train. They were almost dragging one of the men as they moved towards an open carriage door. It was an act of desperation.

For a split second Dronzi just watched in amazement, and then suddenly he saw the face of the man that they were dragging along the platform. It was Vasily Orlof Bratz.

Dronzi suddenly realised what was happening and he screamed at his men as he pointed across to the opposite platform.

'It's them. Catch them, catch them now.'

The troops set off running and there was an immediate sound of gunshot, Dronzi had started shooting. He'd taken out his revolver and had started firing it at the three fleeing men. The other soldiers quickly followed suit.

Blesk jumped into the carriage and literally dragged Vasily Orlof in off the platform. Bullets spattered everywhere as the soldiers ran towards them. The train continued on its way but it just wasn't going fast enough. The soldiers were going to catch them.

Blesk threw his hand out to Vodle to pull him in, but to his utter amazement, Vodle appeared to be slowing down.

Herman Vodle stared up at Rubin Blesk.

'Be on your way Mr Blesk,' he shouted to Rubin, 'It's always been my job to protect you.'

And with that, Herman Vodle stopped running.

Blesk was horrified. He watched as Herman Vodle turned and jumped behind a pillar and then took out his beloved Luger. He took aim and started to fire. Five of the soldiers nearest to Vodle were killed before he finally ran out of bullets.

For Herman Vodle it was the moment of truth. He knew what his life had been. After he'd been drummed out of the army he'd spent the most of his life running, until he met Rubin Blesk.

Vodle had been a respected soldier in the German Army. He was Prussian and he was proud and he knew that he was better than this Russian scum.

He walked out from behind the pillar and pointed his empty gun at the oncoming soldiers in a final effort to slow them down. He was almost immediately cut down by a hail of bullets.

Herman Vodle had made his final decision. He wasn't going to be captured and interrogated, and he wasn't going to be tortured and then butchered by those bastards.

For Herman Vodle, it was a soldier's end.

Rubin Blesk stood looking out of the carriage door. He just stood there and watched in complete awe at Herman Vodle's brave sacrifice.

The train was pulling out of the station and was starting to gather momentum. They were on their way. But things were not to be.

At that moment Spiridon Dronzi burst out of nowhere. He'd stopped to reload his gun and then he'd set off running again. He leapt over Herman Vodle's bullet ridden body and then hurtled down the platform after the slowly moving train.

Dronzi was a big man and he was as fit as any athlete and at that moment he was actually catching up with them.

Rubin Blesk was aghast, he physically willed the train to go faster.

They were coming to the end of the platform, another thirty feet and the platform came to a sudden halt which ended in a ten foot drop. Blesk slammed the carriage door shut but Spiridon Dronzi was still running after them at a phenomenal pace. Then suddenly, Dronzi too realised that the platform was coming to an end and in a final act of anger and desperation he pointed his revolver at the carriage and fired off every bullet.

Blesk realised at once what was about to happen and shouted 'Down...

Get down,' as he threw himself on top of Vasily Orlof. The bullets hit the carriage squarely and blood splattered over the opposite window. But the train kept going. It rumbled out of the station but not before Spiridon Dronzi finally ran out of space and leapt off the end of the platform and rolled onto the gravel below. Winded and with his face scratched and grazed, he threw his revolver after the departing train in a fit of anger.

The train rattled on and it took a minute before anyone moved.

Blesk got his breathing under control and rolled sideways and looked at Vasily Orlof.

'Are you alright?' he asked.

Vasily Orlof nodded.

'Are you alright Maurice?' Blesk again asked, but there was no answer from Maurice Broch. Blesk looked across the compartment and it was then that he saw the top of the blood splattered window. His heart sank and he got onto his knees and turned to see what had happened. There, propped under the bloodied window was Maurice Broch. He was dead. Part of his face had been blown away by Spiridon Dronzi's final shots.

Vasily Orlof got to his knees and he stared at Maurice's body. For a while both he and Rubin just sat there looking at their dead comrade.

Broch was a quiet, beautiful man. He had been a wonderful friend to everyone.

The reality of it all was appalling to Rubin Blesk and Vasily Orlof. They had both just lost two of the finest men they had ever known. But worse was yet to come. Worse for both of them.

Eventually it was Rubin Blesk who had to make the decision.

'We have to do something Vasily. It's a terrible thing, but it has to be done.'

Vasily Orlof just stared back at him.

'We have to get rid of Maurice's body Vasily. We have to clean up this mess before the blood starts to congeal and set.'

Vasily Orlof didn't know what he was supposed to do or even say.

Blesk started to undo Maurice Broch's jacket.

'Come on Vasily, quickly, help me,' he urged.

He and Vasily pulled off Broch's jacket and then used it to wipe down the carriage windows and scoop up the bits of flesh and the gore. Finally they wiped up the remaining blood from the floor. Blesk then went over to the carriage door, opened it and threw the bloodied coat out into a passing field. He then turned, but he didn't close the door.

He looked at Vasily, 'It's got to be done.'

Vasily Orlof stared back at him.

'You don't mean..?'

'Take hold of one of his arms Vasily,' Blesk said firmly. But Vasily Orlof didn't move.

'We can't Rubin,' Vasily replied quietly, 'he's our friend.'

Rubin Blesk blinked.

'Listen Vasily, we have to get rid of Maurice's body. We don't know what's ahead of us. I don't know this line but there may be more stations in front of us with more soldiers. If a station guard looks into our carriage and sees a dead body we're in trouble, and all this will have been for nothing. Maurice and Vodle would have done exactly the same. If we get caught Vasily, their deaths will have all been in vain. Think about that Vasily.'

Vasily Orlof said nothing, but he reluctantly took hold of one of Maurice Broch's arms and they both dragged the lifeless body of their friend to the carriage door. In the end they took hold of his legs and simply tipped him out of the moving carriage. Maurice's body bounced as it rolled down the embankment and into a field.

Their only hope was that at some point a farmer would possibly find the body and bury it.

It was a poor and unfitting end to one of Russia's finer craftsmen jewellers. A true talent.

But for Vasily Orlof, the real nightmare was about to unfold.

The train rumbled on, and they sat there in silence for almost half an hour until finally it was Rubin Blesk who spoke. It was time to talk, and it was time to tell Vasily Orlof the truth of what he knew.

'Vasily, I need to talk to you about something,' he said slowly.

Wearily, Vasily Orlof looked across at his old mentor.

'What is it?' he asked.

'Smolensk,' replied Blesk, 'It's about Smolensk.'

Vasily's eyes widened.

'What is it Rubin?'

'They've burned Schwab's to the ground Vasily. I think your parents may have perished.' Vasily Orlof just stared at Rubin Blesk, he couldn't take in what he was being told.

Rubin Blesk took a deep breath, 'The Bolsheviks arrived in Smolensk Vasily, and a mob of lunatics joined them and they went on the rampage. The mob got larger and more enraged and they suddenly got it into their heads that anyone who had a business was a filthy capitalist. Then they marched down to the Jewish area and around to the Krasninsky district and they looted and then burned down all the jeweller's shops there. They smashed and burned most of the Jewish businesses. By then the mob was running amok. They went on to torch half of the businesses in Smolensk. Schwab's went up like a bonfire, it was full of timber obviously, but from there some of the deluded bastards went around to your parent's house and set fire to that too. The last news I heard before I left was that nobody had seen anything of your mother or your father.'

Vasily Orlof stared into space, all he could think about was his mother, his poor dear mother.

Rubin Blesk shook his head and sighed.

'I don't know how all this is going to end Vasily, the whole country's aflame. And now the royal family's gone there is no one left. That bastard Lenin has a lot to answer for, there's been thousands killed and murdered".

Vasily Orlof just sat there, suddenly not really listening to Rubin Blesk. He was thinking about his mother, his mother who had loved him with all her heart, his mother who had doted on him and spoiled him. She was the woman who had the tenacity and strength to understand that her son had 'a gift', and she was the woman who made sure that he followed his dream.

But then, something suddenly clouded his thoughts. It was something Rubin had said, he'd just said something, something about the royal family. Vasily suddenly looked up.

'What did you just say about the royal family Rubin?'

Rubin looked across at his young friend.

'The royal family...the Romanov's, they're gone. Didn't you know Vasily?'

Vasily Orlof knew nothing. He'd been locked away in his apartment for months.

'What do you mean 'gone'..?' Vasily asked urgently.

Rubin Blesk looked at Vasily Orlof strangely. He didn't understand the significance.

'The Romanovs Vasily, they're all dead.'

Vasily Orlof just sat there in horror, Rubin's words echoing in his head.

Rubin continued, still not understanding just what he was telling Vasily Orlof.

'Lenin's lot had the Romanovs exiled to some place in Siberia and then they sent that pig Spiridon Dronzi up there to murder them. They're all dead Vasily, the Tsar and Tsarina, the four daughters, even young Prince Alexei. All slaughtered by Dronzi. That man should rot in hell Vasily".

But Vasily wasn't listening. He was suddenly crying.

Tatiana, his beautiful Tatiana gone, murdered. It just couldn't be.

He couldn't take it in and he didn't fully understand. At that moment his mind was trying to shut it all out. But he could still see her face. And his mind was drowning, and the beautiful memories of her kept leaping into his brain. The only thing that had kept Vasily Orlof alive for the last few months was the single thought that he would see her again. Always, that he would see her again. She was his life. His love. Then suddenly he was being told that she was dead, and never again would he see her or hold her in his arms. And for Vasily, it was as though he'd only seen her yesterday, and that all this was all a lie, or a mistake. But it wasn't.

And there in the middle of all the upset and distress was the one constant memory that wouldn't fade away. That of them being in his bed together and him running his fingers over her beautifully raven coloured eyebrows, and how they fascinated him with their beautiful sculptured shape, they could have been drawn by an artist. In his mind he looked into her dark eyes, and he heard her laughing so clearly that he could hear her voice again. Always her voice, lyrical, beautiful, and then he realised that he would never hear her voice again, ever. The voice of his lover and his friend, his best friend. Never again would he have the intimacy, the closeness. He'd never been with any other woman before, Tatiana had totally consumed him, they had consumed one another and now he would never know that intimacy ever again. He was so close to her, closer to her than he had ever been to anyone in his life. Not the mother's love that he knew so well, it was the love between a man and a woman, unique and so very personal. She was the love of his life.

It would never be the same.

Tatiana wasn't going to be there anymore and he couldn't come to terms with it. He would never come to terms with it. He'd lost her. His love was lost and was never coming back and his mind was bending and breaking and in the absolute turmoil of it all. He wept until he could weep no more. Then in dark despair, his mind finally closed down.

Rubin Blesk had sat there and watched Vasily Orlof mentally break and fall apart right in front of his very eyes. Blesk was completely overwhelmed. To see another human being, a friend, go to pieces and shatter and snap right there in front of him was something he could never think possible. He couldn't comprehend what Vasily Orlof was going through and he felt powerless to do anything. Vasily Orlof had become inconsolable, then hysterical, and then finally he'd blacked out and collapsed.

Rubin laid Vasily across the bench seat of the carriage and put his thick coat over his young friend. He was at a loss to understand what had happened. The upset over Vasily's parents in Smolensk was quite feasible, he could have accepted and understood that. But it was the mention of the death of the Romanov's that had deeply affected Vasily.

He was distraught, so distraught that he was almost out of his mind.

Rubin Blesk sat back and pondered their situation. There was something seriously wrong with Vasily Orlof and it was something that could affect the both of them. They had a long way to go and there were weeks of constant travel in front of them. He would have to plan well.

Rubin started to wonder what had happened between Vasily and the Romanov family.

Something definitely had, and it was obviously something very deep and personal. Maybe he shouldn't ask. In the end, he never did.

Rubin Blesk thought once again about Smolensk, it had been terrifying. There had always been the few anti-Semitic elements in Smolensk, Blesk knew that. Always the few arrogant zealots who preached anti-Jewish activities. It was almost a religion itself, fed by ignorance, jealousy and greed.

When the Bolsheviks had arrived to stir things up, even Rubin Blesk had been shocked by the anti-Jewish feelings that lurked beneath the surface of the city, the city that he had lived in all of his life. The mob had burned his business to the ground along with others. He'd had to leave, but before the mob had incinerated his shop, Blesk had opened his safe and filled his leather bag with treasure, some of the best diamonds and precious stones that he had in stock. He only took the best, and he still had to leave behind large quantities of gold and platinum and other valuable metals simply because of their physical weight. The metals were far too heavy to carry. Pound for pound, diamonds would always be the best bet.

His biggest worry was for his Uncle Sholem and old Nathan, his other two craftsman jewellers. He'd implored them to go with him, but both had refused, their reasoning being that they were too old. Blesk had left Smolensk in the final hours, taking with him Maurice Broch and of course his most faithful of bodyguards, Herman Vodle.

Blesk thought about what had happened to his two comrades and wondered if he'd made the right decision. Maybe his actions had been wrong, maybe those two men would still be alive if he had stayed in St Petersburg. He wondered too about his Uncle Sholem and Nathan. Had they survived? Rubin Blesk would never know.

His hatred for the Bolsheviks and the mob was overpowering.

He would never return to Smolensk and he would never return to Russia.

When Vasily Orlof finally awoke, Blesk was still sitting there, staring at him. Blesk had never slept for a moment.

But the Vasily Orlof of several hours ago was now gone, suddenly here was a different man. He just lay there, vacant and in some form of shock. The last few months had obviously taken their toll, but after hearing about the Romanov family, a dark curtain had closed around him. It was a mental breakdown in the making. Blesk tried to talk to Vasily but there were no answers, only the occasional glimpses of reality which then ended in tears.

Their train journey together continued relentlessly.

It would actually turn out to be several train journeys. They wouldn't be heading up to the forests of Karelia, Rubin Blesk and Vasily Orlof would veer away and go west on a train to Finland, and all the way to Helsinki. From there they would travel on another train, down to Finland's southwest archipelago where they would cross the Baltic waters to Sweden on an aging wooden fishing boat. From the value of the diamonds that Rubin Blesk paid for the crossing, the owner would buy himself a newer, better boat.

They finally arrived in Stockholm but continued onwards and northwest, all the way into Norway. It would have been much easier to go south and head for Denmark and then down and into western Europe. But Europe was still in turmoil and Rubin Blesk was wise enough to realise that a Jew wandering around with a bag full of diamonds had every chance of being robbed and then their plans would be over.

So Norway it was. They arrived in Oslo only to take another train and head south all the way down to the Skagerrak gulf and then onto another boat which would sail them across the North Sea to land on the east coast of England at the small port of Whitley Bay.

Rubin Blesk and Vasily Orlof simply stepped off the boat and onto the small harbour there. They then caught a bus to the nearest train station and from there they travelled to London.

London, where men were free and minds were open and fair.

And London, where Rubin Blesk had friends.

Rubin soon found those friends and he and Vasily took lodgings in Golders Green. It was a small flat but it was cosy enough and the rent was more than fair. The flat was owned by a Jewish gentleman who would have let them have it for free, but Blesk had insisted.

During the next few months Rubin Blesk found his feet, whilst at the same time he nursed Vasily back into some sort of health. Vasily Orlof however would never be the same man again and Rubin Blesk quickly realised that. Eventually there was a return to short conversations, followed by long periods of silence. Blesk didn't mind, at least Vasily was still alive. Vasily Orlof was Rubin Blesk's only link to a past life, a life that he too had lost.

Six months later, Rubin Blesk took Vasily Orlof to one of the most prominent jeweller's shops on Bond Street in central London. He was introduced there to the owner, a Mr Louis Skeet.

Louis Skeet was the sole proprietor of the firm 'Albemarle and Skeet'. Mr Skeet having bought out Mr Albemarle several years previously. Louis Skeet was Dutch, but not of a Dutch family. His parents were originally both Russian and had moved to Holland over half a century before. The firm Albemarle and Skeet were jewellers of the highest repute and were well known by London's richer and well heeled elite. Only the best and the finest were available from Albemarle and Skeet.

Louis Skeet was also Jewish, and he also spoke Russian. He and Rubin Blesk had originally met and became friends when Skeet had been visiting Antwerp. He was there to buy diamonds, and they had both been introduced to one another. Rubin had acquired a parcel of exquisite diamonds for Louis Skeet and Skeet in turn had been appreciative. Favours through friendship.

Back in London, Rubin Blesk had explained Vasily Orlof's problems to Louis Skeet and had assured him that Vasily was one of the finest jewellers that he had ever known. Vasily Orlof had after all worked for Faberges, and he'd even worked on the famed Romanov Easter Eggs. However, Vasily would need coaching back into work, slowly but surely and with no pressure put on him at all. If that were to happen and Vasily could recover and make a successful return to his beloved craft, then Louis Skeet would have one of the finest jewellers in Europe working for him.

Skeet agreed. He agreed because Rubin Blesk was his friend.

The following week, Vasily Orlof entered the workshops of Albemarle and Skeet. For Vasily it would be the third and the last jewellers that he would ever work for. There were three other skilled craftsmen also working there. One man was Dutch and the other two were both English. Louis Skeet had informed them that Vasily Orlof had been though hard times and was not yet fully recovered. The men understood and decided that they would leave Vasily Orlof to get on with it. None of them spoke Russian anyway, so communication was always going to be a problem.

Returning to his craft was a blessing for Vasily Orlof, it was his anchor. It was the second most important thing in his life.

If his craft had been a gift, it now turned into an obsession. Vasily Orlof dedicated his life to his work. He would toil late into the night, every night, on almost every day of the week. In the end, Louis Skeet had to order Vasily Orlof to stay at home on Sundays. Skeet's long suffering wife kept complaining about him going off to work every Sunday to 'open up the shop'. Why couldn't he take up golf like other successful men?

But before long, Louis Skeet and his other three craftsmen jewellers began to realise and understand something quite significant. That they were working with a genius.

Rubin Blesk would eventually return to Antwerp, the pull of the diamond markets was too strong and in the end he moved there permanently and for the next twenty years he ran a very profitable business.

However, history has a habit of repeating itself. Twenty years after those terrible men had led the mobs and had taken over in Russia, a new breed of the same type of men had surfaced and with it another breed of mob. The Nazi party had broken out of Germany and were intent on ruling the world. And it was a world in which there would be no room at all for the Jewish people.

Rubin Blesk was arrested in 1943 and was shipped off to the infamous Auschwitz-Birkenau concentration camp. Along with thousands of other good and honest and talented folk, he was murdered there by people whom only history could judge

The Second World War came and went and Albemarle and Skeet managed to survive, if only for the prudency and good management of Louis Skeet himself. Two of his English jewellers had been called up for war, only one had returned. But life went on and after a few years followed by a lot of rationing, things began to return to normal. Especially for the affluent, who seemed to return to normal a lot faster than the rest of the population.

Jewellery and fancy goods were once again being bought and sold, and suddenly, for some, the world seemed a brighter place.

It was an evening in late 1949 when Louis Skeet almost ran into the workshop, for a man in his late seventies, it was a good attempt. It was late, but Skeet knew that Vasily Orlof would still be there. Louis Skeet was so excited that he had to talk to someone, and that someone had to be Vasily Orlof Bratz. Only with Vasily Orlof could he share his treasure. Only Vasily Orlof would truly understand.

'Vasily my friend, thank god you're still here,' Louis Skeet gasped.

Vasily was always there, where else would he be.

Vasily Orlof was himself by then in his sixties. He was a loner who lived a lonely life. In truth, the only person he ever really spoke to was Louis Skeet. Vasily had never really bothered to take up the English language and Louis was the only person that he knew who spoke fluent Russian.

But Vasily had never lost the skill of his craft, in fact, he'd never worked better. With the modern tools now to hand, Vasily Orlof could produce the most exquisite jewellery. His attention to detail was extraordinary, always a never ending compulsion. He did however suffer from bouts of complete depression. All of which were triggered by deep memories and always because of Tatiana. At the height of those periods Vasily couldn't work. He would just lie in his bed, still there in his little flat in Golders Green. He would have to lie there in the dark until his mind finally began to function again properly.

Once that had happened and he felt that he was somewhat recovered, Vasily would return to Albemarle and Skeet's to work as normal.

Louis Skeet understood. He could wait.

Vasily Orlof would in due course always return.

That evening, Vasily Orlof looked up as Louis Skeet burst in through the door. Skeet was jabbering away in English and Vasily Orlof could hardly understand half of what he was saying. He shook his head and Skeet immediately switched to Russian and started to tell Vasily Orlof what had happened, in a language that both of them understood.

It seemed that one of Louis Skeet's suppliers, 'De Wint Diamonds' over in Hatton Garden had something that they wanted Louis to see. Burti De Wint, one of the dealers there and a nephew of the De Wint family, knew that Louis Skeet was always looking for something 'special'.

Burti also knew the quality of jewellery that Albemarle and Skeet produced and he had something special in his possession, something that needed to be worked on by only the best.

Louis Skeet had been so excited at what he'd been shown, that he immediately did the deal with Burti De Wint and then returned to his workshop to speak to Vasily Orlof.

'Vasily my friend, I have something to show you. I think it's good. I think it has promise.'

Skeet's enthusiasm was always contagious and whenever he found something very special he acted in the same way. It was something that always made Vasily Orlof smile and enjoy. It was the unknown and it always reminded him of the happy times when Rubin Blesk would return to Smolensk from Antwerp with another hoard of precious stones and they would spread them out across the old table and examine them with glee.

Louis Skeet put his hand into his left hand jacket pocket and slowly pulled out a cloth wallet. It was made from soft velvet and was a rich purple colour. He placed the wallet in front of Vasily Orlof with a triumphant look on his face.

'Open the wallet Vasily, see what I've found.'

Vasily Orlof flipped open the wallet and reached inside. When he removed his hand, there in his palm was the largest raw opal that he had ever seen in his life. He was amazed. The stone had been partially polished to show off its potential, but it was far from cut or finished. When Vasily held it up to the light, he actually gasped. The internal colouring was astounding. There was a whole world of colour inside the opal, a world of light blues and dark blues and gold, and in its centre was a red fire that shone like a small sun.

Louis Skeet watched Vasily Orlof intently, he had never seen him so moved. This too was a first and it only served to increase Skeet's eagerness.

'What do you think Vasily, what do you think?' Skeet asked him excitedly.

Vasily Orlof never moved, he just stared at the stone.

'I think it is the most beautiful opal that I have ever seen,' he slowly replied.

Skeet laughed and almost did a jig, almost.

'It will need cutting,' said Vasily Orlof.

Skeet nodded.

'It will need cutting correctly,' Vasily Orlof continued, 'and then we'll polish it and cut it again to get to the inner colour. There can be no room for error.'

Skeet continued to nod.

Vasily Orlof looked at him.

'Put the opal in your safe Louis,' he said, 'It will take me the rest of the week to finish what I'm doing at the moment. On Monday I'll make a start. I need time to think.'

As Vasily Orlof left the workshop that evening, Louis Skeet bid him goodnight, but Vasily Orlof just mumbled something and made his way home. He was in deep thought.

Skeet watched Vasily Orlof walk away and smiled to himself. He had never seen Vasily show any emotion over anything. Maybe this was a new start.

Little did he know.

Vasily Orlof returned to his flat that evening but he didn't sleep, he couldn't sleep. Over and over in his mind he kept seeing the opal and he kept remembering the colours. It was the start of his obsession, simply because it was an opal. Opals were always Tatiana's favourite stone, he'd always remembered that. And he remembered the flower ring that he had first made for her with those twelve beautiful opals which Mr Faberge had found. He remembered how happy she had been and how much in love they both were. He'd never forgotten that. And he wondered where that ring was now.

Vasily Orlof spent the rest of the week with nothing but the opal on his mind. He'd not slept properly and that was because of the design he had in his mind. He lay there in his bed every night thinking about it, constructing it and seeing it come to life.

For years, in his private little world, Vasily Orlof had continued to work on his quest to find a way of passing light through a diamond in a given direction. Finally he'd succeeded. He'd learned with success how and where to cut the tiny prisms, so that they would emit a beam of light out of a diamond like a small torch. He'd never used the technique, but why would he? He had first used this skill on Tatiana's flower ring and its inspiration had become something very personal to him. Nobody else must know that joy, it was something he had produced for her and her alone. His beautiful, beautiful Tatiana.

Vasily Orlof was becoming fixated with the opal. In his heart and his mind he was totally captivated by it, but it was a mind that would always be fragile. As the days and nights passed by, he became engrossed with the idea that by using this opal, he would create the finest piece of jewellery he had ever made.

In his mind, he was making the opal ring for Tatiana.

When Vasily Orlof walked into work early on Monday morning, Louis Skeet was already there waiting for him.

Skeet went into his safe and took the opal to Vasily Orlof at his workbench. Vasily once more held it up in front of his jeweller's light and sat there looking at it intently, staring into the raw stone. It was stupendous.

'Is there anything you need Vasily?' Louis Skeet asked apprehensively.

Vasily Orlof put the opal carefully back down on his bench and he turned to Skeet.

'Louis,' he replied, 'I will need some of the finest 'brilliant' cut diamonds that you can find.'

Louis Skeet went back to his office and Vasily Orlof sat there for a while. He stared at the large raw opal on his bench and he gazed at it in wonder as he contemplated the task ahead. His plans for the ring were incredible.

But in his mind there was also another line of thought, and another plan. It was almost a hidden agenda. Yes, he would make the ring. But the ring would be for Tatiana, because opals were always her favourite stone.

And once again, it would be a labour of love.

Vasily sat at his workbench and he looked down at the unrefined piece of opaque stone.

It was magnificent, a natural splendour that had been cut out of the rock, deep from under the ground.

And as he stared down at the stone, his thoughts drifted for a moment.

'Where have you come from...?' he wondered.

CHAPTER 11

Coober Pedy District, South Australia 1948-49

Kalyo knelt in silent anticipation. Hidden under two small eucalyptus trees and concealed by the waist high spear grass, he lay there in the heat and waited. He knew that if he stayed there long enough and silent enough, the wildlife that surrounded him would once more go about its business and peace, quiet and normality would return to the bush.

For over three hours Kalyo had lain in the hot shade, but it didn't bother him. His aboriginal body had been hardened over the generations of thousands of years to be able to endure the blistering heat of his birth land.

Kaylo was from the 'Nunga', a tribe of aboriginal people who had lived in that same territory for what seemed all of time. He was forty years old, coal black and wirily muscled. He was a hunter and it was his job to find the food to take back to his settlement for his family and his people, so that they could eat.

Kaylo had laid there, half listening, half dreaming, in a state of inner trance. It was his natural ability as a hunter to wait for his prey. Just like the Eskimo who patiently sits for hours on the frozen ice, waiting for a seal to surface through the blow hole to breathe, so was the skill of the aborigine. The art was to let your quarry come to you.

In his dreamworld, Kaylo spoke to his ancestors. Deep in his mind he could see his father and his grandfather and the elders of his ancient tribe. They were the Nunga, 'the great tribe', the tribe that had walked the lands forever. In his dreams Kaylo saw his people, gone but never lost, never lost.

And as he lay there he thought about his wife Naata and his two children, both boys who would one day be men. He thought about his ageing mother and he wondered how long it would be before she joined the great tribe in the sky.

The 'Nunga', the great tribe who had walked this land from the beginning

The thoughts in his mind were suddenly broken. He felt it at first, he felt the vibrations coming through the ground and though his body...thump, thump, thump. They had finally arrived. They were here, just like he had always known they would be. Then he heard them, their grunting and the clicking sound. They'd found their food, they had found the long grass that they needed to survive on.

It was the kangaroo. They had finally arrived and were there to feed.

Kaylo listened, but he didn't move. It was best to let the kangaroo settle, settle and begin to eat the nutritious long grass that was so sparse in that desperate land.

They were the 'Kangaroo' and they were the brothers of the Nunga, because they had lived side by side forever.

Kaylo reached for his spear, the short spear known as the 'dooull'. It had been his grandfather's spear, given to him when Kaylo had become a man. The colouring on the ornate shaft ran in bands of charcoaled black and red ochre and on it was carved the white snake pattern in the traditional aboriginal design. The spear was his to hunt with by right, and one day he would pass it on to his first grandson, in the same old way.

Kaylo slowly rolled over and lifted his head. The kangaroo were there in front of him, six of them. One was a Joey, a younger male about one year old who was smaller than the rest and slower.

He would be the one.

Kaylo was downwind from the group and they couldn't smell him and they couldn't see him. He was invisible.

He knelt there and watched them as they ate. He would wait until they'd had their fill and then they would lie down and rest and maybe sleep. That would be the moment, the moment he would strike. That was when he would have the advantage.

Kaylo knew the habits of his brother kangaroos so well.

The sweltering heat combined with their full stomachs made the kangaroo weary and sluggish, and eventually they began to droop and finally they sank to the ground. As they lay there in the heat, two of them slowly rolled over in the dust, disturbing the flies.

Kaylo stood up.

He started to breathe deeply, to slowly fill his lungs and fill his blood with the oxygen that his body would need for the chase ahead. It was the way of the hunter, his father and his grandfather had taught him well.

When the moment was right, Kaylo leant forward in a stance, ready for the sprint. He took one final breath and broke out from beneath the eucalyptus trees. H'd run a dozen steps at speed before the kangaroo felt those same vibrations. With loud warning grunts they immediately leapt up and started to bound away. It all happened in a matter of seconds but Kaylo kept running after his chosen target. The 'Joey' had been the last one to move, it was young and inexperienced and Kaylo chased after it as it veered off and away from the others. Without the elders to follow, it went left and then right, not knowing which way to turn, but Kaylo ran straight and true, he knew that the youngster would bound away in a zigzag pattern, they always did.

He was gaining on his quarry as it approached the longer grass and that was better for Kaylo because the long grass would hamper the young kangaroo and slow it down. The time was right and Kaylo raised his spear, his 'dooull', he was almost ready to strike. It would take four more steps and then he would launch the spear with all his strength. He was almost there.

In that instant, the ground suddenly disappeared before Kaylo's eyes and he was falling. He fell through space and into darkness and at that moment he didn't understand. Then there was an immediate flash of light and pain as everything suddenly stopped and then went very dark.

Several hours passed and eventually Kaylo regained consciousness. His head throbbed and hurt and his shoulders and right leg were sore. He rolled over onto his back and tried to focus. At first he didn't realise what he was looking at, all he could see was a rough circular pattern of white dots amid the blackness. His eyes finally focused and he realised that he was looking up at the night sky and that those little white dots were actually the stars.

As Kaylo lay there he remembered the series of events. He was chasing the kangaroo, the smaller one, the 'Joey', and suddenly he was falling into the blackness. He knew straightaway what had happened, he had fallen into a hidden sinkhole.

Sinkholes could appear anywhere and hidden in the tall grass, they were almost invisible until you were right on top of them. His eyes adjusted to the darkness and as he looked up he could see the outline of the top of the hole. It was fairly circular but looked quite a distance away and that meant that the sinkhole was fairly deep. He moved his arms slowly and suddenly felt something on his right side. He stopped for a moment, and then reached out again. He touched something, and at first he thought it was a length of wood, but then he realised that it was something else. It was a bone.

Kaylo wasn't the first creature to fall down this sinkhole.

He rolled onto his knees and spread his arms across the ground. And then he finally he found it. It was his grandfather's spear, his dooull. He sat there for a while and cradled the spear in his arms. He had to think, he had to think of a way to get himself out of the hole or he would die, because no one would ever find him down there until it was too late.

His head was still aching, but he had to think. He began to feel his way around, there were plenty of bones and he was careful not to trip over them. He squatted down again. There had to be a way, there had to be. Then Kaylo stood up and reached out his arms, and he felt the walls of the sinkhole. Though it was rock, it contained a mixture of sand as well and Kaylo took his spear and pressed into the rocky wall. The spear penetrated the rock wall. He pushed it harder until it felt quite solid, then he slung his leg over the spear and sat on it. The spear held his weight.

Kaylo suddenly had an idea. He got back down on his hands and knees scrabbled around on the floor, feeling for the longest bones. He found several. They must have been the leg or thigh bones of some unfortunate and larger animals. He piled the bones in what he perceived was the centre of the sink hole and just as he turned to continue his search he smashed his head on a protruding rock. For a moment he saw even more stars as he fell to the floor again. He was dazed and he felt the warm trickle of blood running down his forehead. He sat there for a few minutes, trying to clear his head and then he slowly stood up and carefully felt around for the overhanging rock. Finally he found it. He felt the shape of the rock and pulled at it. It moved ever so slightly. He pulled at it again and again it moved. Kaylo continued for the next ten minutes until the rock finally came away from the wall.

He held it in his hand, it was the size of an emu egg and he felt its weight. For the first time that evening he smiled. He looked up at the distant stars. His ancestors had not forgotten him.

Kaylo sat in the dark with the pile of long bones and he took his sharp spear and he honed the end of each bone into a point. It took him over an hour, but finally they were done. He stood up and picked up one of the sharpened bones and using his rock he hammered it into the side of the wall. It went in, and when Kaylo stood on it and it held his weight. He took another bone and as he stood on the first bone he again knocked it in with his stone, and again it worked and took him higher. From there he took the other bones and did the same, eventually building a crude ladder that would get him to the surface. He was almost there when he found there were none of the longer bones left. He had a final idea. He took his grandfather's spear and with his rock hammered it into the wall. It was difficult because nearer to the surface the ground had become a lot rockier and harder. It took several attempts before his spear finally felt solid enough to take his weight and when he climbed onto it the slim spear gave slightly. The stars were shining and there was a half moon, just enough light for him to be able to see. The edge of the sink hole was about a foot above his reach, it was too far. It was then that Kaylo made a decision. He tossed the rock up and out of the hole, the lighter he was the better. He then took a half crouch and a deep breath and leapt straight upwards.

He felt the spear move under his feet but as he made the leap up to the surface he managed to grab hold of some of the long grass that grew along the edge of the sinkhole. He hung on to it, hoping for his life that it wouldn't come away from the looser, sandy ground. Luckily it held and slowly but surely Kaylo pulled himself up and out of the hole. He was back on solid ground.

He lay there in the soft warm grass, utterly exhausted, and he stared up at the stars.

'My ancestors,' he whispered, 'thank you for not forgetting me.'
And with that, Kaylo closed his eyes and slept.

Several hours later, Kaylo awoke. He had turned over in his sleep and something sharp had caught him in the chest. When he opened his eyes he saw it was a sharp rock. When he took hold of it he realised that it was the rock he had used as a hammer. He could still remember the feel of it through all those hours in the darkness. Then he remembered the sinkhole. He dropped the rock and slowly stood up. Though his head was still aching he felt somewhat better, considering the ordeal he had just been through. He looked around for the opening to the hole, but he was wary of once again falling into the dark pit. It was then that Kaylo remembered his spear. It was still stuck in the wall of the sinkhole. He went over to the edge and looked down. He could see the patterned handle below him, it was sticking out of the rock wall at an angle but it was too far down for him to reach. Kaylo looked around, and apart from the two eucalyptus bushes there was nothing else there at all, nothing that he could use to help him retrieve his grandfather's old spear, his beloved dooull.

Kaylo thought about it for a while, and then he realised what he needed. It was the white man's rope. He would have to get some rope and come back with two or three of the men from his village. It was the only way.

He surveyed the surrounding landscape and realised how barren and featureless it was. It was just grassland littered with rocks and similar outcrops of the same small eucalyptus bushes. It would have been easy to lose his bearings and if that happened he would lose his spear forever. He would have to mark the place.

So Kaylo looked around and decided to build a pile of rocks between the two eucalyptus bushes as a marker, so that he could tell the place apart from others. It was that simple.

It was as he looked around for some rocks that he once again picked up the rock he had used in the sinkhole as a hammer. It lay there at his feet, so it was obviously his first choice. He had not taken much notice of the rock because there had been other things on his mind, but when Kaylo picked it up, the rock suddenly flashed in the sunlight. It made him stop for a moment, and as he slowly turned the rock in his hand it again flashed in the bright morning sun. He was quite amazed.

He looked down at the rock and examined it closely. On one side there was a thick vein of blue crystal which ran straight through the rock and came out at the other side, though somewhat narrower. He again turned the stone to the sun and once again the blue crystal flashed. Kaylo walked out from the eucalyptus bushes and he picked up another couple of rocks which he found lying on the ground. One was quite large and flat, the other was smaller and wedge shaped. He squatted down and placed his 'blue' rock on the larger flat rock and then started to chip away at it with the other smaller one, using this as a chisel.

After an hour he'd managed to chip off most of the surplus and was left with a rough blue crystal that was the size of a man's thumb. Kaylo held the stone up into the sun and he looked closely at it. Even in its rough state he could see all the different tones of blue, but as he looked deep into its centre, he saw the red glow within.

Kaylo laughed out loud and threw the stone into the air and caught it again with glee. He had found the stone that the white man called 'Opal'. Yes the white man, who had dug tunnels under Kaylo's land and scurried about like rats, burying deep down into the ground just to find this stone. And now Kaylo had been blessed again, and he lifted the opal to the skies and once more thanked his ancestors.

Kaylo knew just how much the white man valued this precious stone. He had heard the stories about men earning fortunes from opals that were a lot smaller than this. He tucked the opal into the small purse that was tied around his middle and then he gathered together the rocks that would mark the two eucalyptus trees where he could once again find his grandfather's priceless spear.

The 'dooull' was worth far more to Kaylo than any silly coloured stones.

Kaylo looked up at the sun and figured out its direction. Then he took a bearing and set off for the township they called 'Coober Pedy'. In the aboriginal language it meant 'white man's hole'. The description wasn't too far wrong.

Kaylo walked all day and part of the night, and then he found a rocky outcrop where he made a fire and slept. The next morning he set off again.

It was early in the afternoon when he finally arrived. The small township of Coober Pedy was bustling, it was as usual full of white men who seemed to be either drinking, fighting or talking about opals.

Kaylo walked straight over to a horse trough and drank his fill, and then he wandered around the town two or three times to see if any of his tribe were there too. But on that particular day there were none. He went back to the main street and sat on the side steps of Kooabarra Pub. Experience had taught him not to sit on the front steps, the white men didn't like that and some of them would kick you out of the way. The white men were strange people with some strange habits, and in Coober Pedy, though it seemed peculiar, each and every aboriginal man was only known by one name, and that was 'Blacky'.

Kaylo sat on the side steps of the Kooabarra Pub and he looked across the main street, there directly opposite the pub was O'Gorman's Opal Shop.

Joe O'Gorman was the main opal buyer in Coober Pedy and Kaylo's simple logic told him that it would be the best place to go. So he sat there and he waited. He watched people enter and leave the shop for most of the afternoon, but Kaylo stayed where he was, and he waited until O'Gorman's was finally empty. He then stood up and casually ambled across the dusty main street. He went up three very worn steps and walked into the shop.

Sitting wearily behind a counter sat Joe O'Gorman himself. He was a big gruff silver haired man who was used to getting his own way. And why not, Joe O'Gorman had the money and it was he who set the prices for opals in Coober Pedy. There were other opal shops in Coober Pedy of course, but they all followed Joe O'Gorman's lead.

Greed is a great institution.

Sitting at an old wooden table at the side of O'Gorman's counter and playing cards were two rogues. They were Boswell and McCreedy and they were the two men who Joe O'Gorman loosely termed as his 'security'.

Kaylo quietly closed the door behind him.

O'Gorman looked up over his silver rimmed glasses and the other two men gave a quick glance before returning to their cards.

O'Gorman stared at Kaylo and gave a long sigh.

'And what do you want Blacky?' he said, 'The bloody grog shop's across the road.'

The other two men chuckled and shook their heads.

It was a well known fact that the aborigine's weakness was alcohol. They weren't used to it and they couldn't handle the drunkenness. Unfortunate as it was, 'the drink' and its consequences had been the downfall of many of the native Australians.

Joe O'Gorman continued with his business as Kaylo walked up to the counter and stood there in silence. He looked at all the fascinating things that surrounded Mr O'Gorman. There was a set of fine brass scales that were used to weigh the miner's hard earned opals, and there were ledgers and lists and yellowing old newspapers. He stared intently at the variety of pencils and pens in glass pots, and the different bottles of red, blue and black coloured inks. Everything in there belonged to a world that Kaylo had never seen before and he didn't understand.

However, the one thing that Kaylo did understand was that he had something special in his possession, and something that Mr O'Gorman would without doubt want to buy. Kaylo knew that he would have to keep his wits about him, because all the white men he had ever known had been thieves and cheats and liars.

Kaylo also realized that his opal was something very special. He had listened to the white men talking about their successes. Most opals were the size of a man's thumbnail. Kaylo's opal was the size of a man's thumb.

Joe O'Gorman finally put his pen down and looked at the small black man standing in front of him. Kaylo's silence was beginning to irritate him.

'What do you want Blacky? I'm bloody busy,' said O'Gorman gruffly. It wasn't a question, it was more a statement.

But Kaylo stood his ground.

'I gotta opal mista, biggest bloody opal you've ever seen.'

'Oh really,' O'Gorman replied. He had seen it all before. Bloody stupid blacks with tiny chips of opal that were absolutely worthless. All they wanted was some money to buy some more grog. Once they got their hands on some cash, they went straight across the road to the Kooabarra to buy themselves another bottle.

'What have you got?' said O'Gorman wearily.

Kaylo looked at Joe O'Gorman, and then he reached inside his purse and felt for the opal. He took hold of it and then stretched out his arm over the counter and opened his hand. There in Kaylo's palm lay the biggest opal that Joe O'Gorman had ever seen in his life.

'Strewth almighty,' said O'Gorman. At that particular moment it was all he could manage say.

He stared down at the opal, mesmerized. He'd been in the opal trade for most of his life and had never seen anything like it. Not only was the stone huge, it displayed an intense colour, even though the opal was still in its raw state. O'Gorman had heard all the stories about bigger opals, everybody had. All the ridiculous tales that up in the north there were opals the size of hen's eggs. O'Gorman had never really believed it. Nothing that size had ever turned up at Coober Pedy, not yet anyway.

O'Gorman reached for the opal but Kaylo stepped back.

O'Gorman looked up at him, he was a little mystified.

'Give it to me,' he said to Kaylo.

Kaylo shook his head.

Joe O'Gorman was a bit put out by that.

'Give it to me,' he said again, 'Let me look at it.'

Kaylo once again shook his head.

'You already seen it Mista. It's a big one, biggest you've ever seen.'

O'Gorman stared back at Kaylo. Joe O'Gorman wasn't used to a black fella talking back to him. And he didn't like it, not one bit.

'Just pass me the bloody opal Blacky,' he said, 'I need to look at it.' His voice was becoming slightly louder, and there was an edge of a threat.

But Kaylo took another step backwards. He knew the white man, and he knew what he was capable of. If O'Gorman got hold of his opal he would keep it, and wouldn't give it back to Kaylo.

At this point Boswell and McCreedy had stopped playing cards and were watching events closely. Kaylo saw the two men turn to look at him. Now there were three white men and only Kaylo, and he realized he was outnumbered and that these men could easily take his opal from him. So he turned around and walked straight out of the shop.

As the door closed behind him he heard O'Gorman shout 'Blacky, get back here now...'

But Kaylo walked across the main street and once again went to sit on the side steps of the Kooabarra Pub. He would have to think this one out.

Back in O'Gorman's opal shop, things were getting a little tense. As the door closed behind Kaylo, Joe O'Gorman slammed his fist on the top of the counter so hard, that all the pens and pencils bounced out of their pots.

'The bastard...damn the little black bastard,' he bellowed.

Boswell and McCreedy sat back. They didn't fully understand what had gone on other than it was something to do with an opal. They had been busy playing cards, but their boss's outburst had more than caught their attention. It was Joe O'Gorman who paid their wages, and like two obedient dogs they immediately stood up.

Boswell was a big man, though he was actually more fat than muscle. His partner McCreedy was just the opposite. He was smaller and leaner and intimidating. If McCreedy was the brains behind their little partnership then Boswell was definitely the brawn.

McCreedy moved swiftly to the door, just in time to see Kaylo walk back across the street and sit down on the side steps of the pub.

He turned to Joe O'Gorman.

'What was all that about Boss?' he asked.

O'Gorman just stood there, he was still staring at the closed door but McCreedy's question suddenly caught his attention.

'Did you see it? Did you see that bloody opal?' Said O'Gorman.

'No Boss,' said McCreedy.

'What opal Boss?' asked Boswell. Boswell had the habit of asking the unnecessary.

'That black fella,' O'Gorman continued, 'that bastard's got an opal, it must be two inches long. Biggest bloody opal I've ever seen.'

'Well he's over the road at the Kooabarra,' said McCreedy, 'he's just sitting there on the steps.'

Joe O'Gorman went over to the door to look for himself. He could see Kaylo across the street, he was just sitting there on the side steps of the pub, prodding the sandy ground with a stick.

O'Gorman stood there staring out of the window, he was deep in thought.

'I've got to get hold of that opal.'

And though he'd said it out loud, in his mind he was talking to himself.

'How will we do that Boss?' asked Boswell. He was ignored by all.

Joe O'Gorman continued to stare out of the window and then turned to McCreedy.

'Get that opal off the little bastard,' he said and then looked at McCreedy. 'And do it quietly, I don't want any fuss.'

McCreedy nodded. He opened the door and walked out of the shop. Boswell followed him closely behind.

Both men walked across the street and up the front steps and into the Kooabarra Pub.

In the coolness of the pub they ordered two glasses of beer, and as they drank McCreedy told Boswell his plan. Boswell just nodded and smiled. They then ordered three glasses of beer and went back outside.

McCreedy and Boswell strolled across the pub's veranda and over to the side steps where Kaylo was sitting, still playing with his stick.

'G'day mate.' said McCreedy.

Kaylo turned in surprise. He was only used to abuse from the white man. He was actually a bit confused for a moment and then realsed who the two white men were. He recognized them immediately. The two men looking down at him were the men from O'Gorman's opal shop. They'd been sitting at the table when Kaylo had gone in there and had been playing cards.

McCreedy took the lead.

'Here you go mate,' he said, 'Mr O'Gorman asked us to come and find you and buy you a beer.'

And with that he thrust the glass of cold beer into Kaylo's hand.

'Cheers mate,' said McCreedy, and he raised his glass. So did Boswell.

Kaylo looked at the white man's beer. He knew how good beer tasted, he'd drunk it before and he knew that it made you feel good. He looked down at his glass, the beer was lovely and golden and so very, very cool.

'C'mon mate,' said McCreedy.

Kaylo took a mouthful. It tasted delicious.

McCreedy smiled.

'Nice one matey.'

Kaylo took another drink.

McCreedy continued, 'Y'know Blacky, Mr O'Gorman's a good man and he's really sorry. He just wanted to look at your opal. He wants to give you top dollar for it.'

Kaylo shrugged his shoulders and took another mouthful of beer.

'Why don't we finish our drink and then go back to the shop?' asked McCreedy.

Kaylo just turned and looked up at him.

'Maybe tomorrow,' he said and then shrugged. He was nobody's fool and he wasn't about to be bamboozled into walking back into O'Gorman's shop with these two men.

Kaylo took another drink of beer.

McCreedy looked across at Boswell. He lifted his glass and nodded, and Boswell went back into the pub and purchased three more beers.

When Boswell returned he handed a beer to McCreedy and another to Kaylo. Kaylo smiled.

'Y'know Blacky' said McCreedy again, 'If we went back to the shop Mr O'Gorman could tell you what the opal's worth.'

Kaylo again shrugged his shoulders, the beer tasted so good.

'Maybe I go and ask da' other folk what it's worth first,' Kaylo replied, and he took another drink.

'Okay Blacky. Drink your beer matey, no problem,' said McCreedy, and he looked at Boswell and again nodded.

Boswell went back into the pub and returned with three more glasses of beer. Kaylo belched as he was handed yet another glass.

McCreedy changed the conversation and started to ask Kaylo about his village and the hunting and his family, anything at all but opals. McCreedy kept talking, and Boswell kept returning from the bar with more beer.

'I need a piss,' announced McCreedy, and with a knowing nod, 'how about you Boswell?'

'Yes I need one too' replied Boswell, and with that in agreement both men went back inside the pub.

Once inside McCreedy instructed Boswell to go to the bar and buy some grog.

Kaylo watched as both McCreedy and Boswell went back into the Kooabarra Pub. He sat there and watched them go and then he picked up his stick. Kaylo knew what was happening, he realised that these men were getting him drunk and he was already starting to feel the effects of the alcohol. Their little trick was beginning to work on him and Kaylo knew that once he was drunk these two men would rob him. He put down his glass of beer and took his stick and began to prod the ground between his feet. Once he found a soft spot in the sand he took his stick and dug a shallow hole. He looked around again, McCreedy and Boswell were still in the pub. Kaylo reached into his purse and took out the opal, he gazed at it for a moment and then leant forward and dropped the precious stone into the hole, and then he kicked some sand over it and pressed it down gently with his foot.

Kaylo picked up his glass of beer and smiled to himself. The two white men would bring him more beer and the opal would be right there under their noses and they would never know it. He took another drink and he laughed out loud. He was beginning to feel drunk but it didn't matter anymore.

When McCreedy and Boswell returned, Boswell was carrying another three glasses of beer and McCreedy was holding a bottle of Bundaberg Rum.

'Here ya go Blacky,' said Boswell as he handed Kaylo a beer. Kaylo emptied his glass and gladly accepted yet another.

'We're going to go now Blacky,' said McCreedy, 'We'll probably see you tomorrow.'

Kaylo looked up at them, he didn't fully understand but by then he was feeling slightly drunk.

'No more beer?' he asked.

'No matey, no more beer,' said McCreedy, 'but Mr O'Gorman's told us to give you this,' and he handed Kaylo the bottle of Bundaberg Rum.

Kaylo's eyes brightened as he took hold of the bottle and he started to laugh. He had their booze, but they still didn't have his opal. Kaylo thought it was hilarious and he just sat there on the steps laughing.

McCreedy and Boswell finished off their beers and then walked back across the street. As they reached the steps to O'Gorman's opal shop, McCreedy turned to his partner.

'Stupid black bastard,' he said, 'One way or another Mr O'Gorman is gonna end up with that bloody opal, believe me.'

Unfortunately, forthcoming events might prove McCreedy right.

They sat in Joe O'Gorman's shop and watched Kaylo for nearly three hours. O'Gorman himself had gone home hours before, and in his absence McCreedy and Boswell had dragged the table over to the window where they kept an eye on Kaylo as they both played cards.

As they played, Kaylo drank. He sat on the steps and continued to sip the rum all afternoon and he carried on until the sun began to set.

Kaylo was in his drunken dreamworld. He sat on the steps of the pub, singing and humming to himself. He spoke to his ancestors and he talked to his invisible people about the hunting and the trekking. He was in a stupor, he was drunken and lost. Finally as the sun went down, he managed to stand up.

On seeing this, McCreedy and Boswell did the same.

Kaylo stood up and steadied himself, and then he walked down the side of the pub building. He'd only managed a dozen steps when he dropped his empty bottle and collapsed to the ground. Lying on his back he looked up at the stars, they were all fuzzy and he couldn't make them out. So in the end he rolled up into a ball in the cooling sand and finally he passed out.

McCreedy and Boswell stood there looking down at Kaylo as he lay there, rolled up and in deep sleep.

'He'll do,' said McCreedy.

Then he leant over and ripped the purse from where it was tied around Kaylo's waist. They walked back into the light of the street where McCreedy opened the purse, only to find it empty.

'The sneaky black bastard's hidden it,' he hissed.

Boswell looked back down the side street at Kaylo.

'I'll beat it out of him, I'll make that bastard tell me where it is,' he said.

McCreedy considered his partner's suggestion. He also considered the reality, that Kaylo was by then so drunk that an immediate beating may not work.

'It's too early yet,' he said to Boswell, 'we need it to get darker and let the pub get busier and noisier. That way no one will hear us. We'll go and shut up the shop and then go for a few beers. He'll be right, he's not going anywhere.'

Boswell nodded in agreement.

Three hours and several drinks later, they both walked back out of the pub. Not drunk, but very refreshed. They walked down the side of the Kooabarra where Kaylo still lay asleep.

As they picked him up, both men were laughing.

'Come on you little black bastard,' said McCreedy, 'It's time to go for a walk.'

Boswell picked up Kaylo's empty rum bottle, he undid his pants and urinated in it, filling the bottle to the top.

'He might not like his next drink,' said Boswell. Both of them found this comment highly amusing.

They dragged Kaylo down past the back of the pub, to a dry riverbed that only flooded after the winter rains. It was bone dry and full of sand and rocks. They laid him on the dry and dusty bank and began to slap him. Kaylo groaned, but they still couldn't get him to wake up. In the end Boswell poured the bottle of urine into Kaylo's mouth and over his face. Kaylo finally woke up coughing and spluttering and immediately started to vomit into the sand. He lay back on the bank and tried to comprehend what was happening to him.

McCreedy slapped him about the face so hard that Kaylo reeled backwards.

'Where have you hidden it you black bastard?' he shouted, and he grabbed hold of Kaylo's hair and shook his head about until Kaylo howled.

'Where's that bloody opal you bastard?'

Kaylo just stared up at him.

McCreedy kicked him in the shin and when Kaylo keeled over he smashed his fist into the side of Kaylo's face. Kaylo groaned and then fell over completely. McCreedy grabbed his hair once again and dragged him upright.

'Tell me where you've hidden that bloody opal?'

But Kaylo just continued to stare back at him.

He took hold of Kaylo's ear and started to twist it. Kaylo howled at the pain as his ear started to rip and bleed, but still he wouldn't answer.

McCreedy stood back and shook his head at Boswell. But Boswell smiled.

'Let me have a go,' he said with glee.

Boswell strode over to Kaylo and kicked him in the testicles. Kaylo collapsed in distress and as he rolled over on the ground Boswell began to kick him in the anus. He continued to kick him several times as Kaylo screamed in agony. By then Kaylo was face down in the sand and Boswell leant over him and knelt on his head. Kaylo began to choke in the sand, he couldn't breathe and his arms and legs started to flail. Boswell held him there just long enough and then he dragged Kaylo up by his hair and back onto the side of the bank.

'Now then you bastard, where is it?' Boswell hissed. He was close up to Kaylo, and Kaylo could smell his stinking breath.

At that moment something strange and implausible took hold of Kaylo's mind. His breathing slowed and he suddenly felt at peace. He looked past Boswell and he looked up to the sky. As he looked up he saw the stars shining bright in the dark sky, and he knew their shapes and he knew their intricate patterns. He saw his ancestors walking across the land, so proud and so free. It was all so beautiful, so very beautiful.

Then he looked back at Boswell, another stinking white man that had fed his people with lies and booze and insults.

Kaylo felt Boswell's hand around his throat.

'Tell me where that opal is you black bastard,' Boswell snarled.

Kaylo looked up at him, and he smiled and shook his head.

'No' said Kaylo. And then he spat in Boswells face.

Boswell erupted.

He head butted Kaylo and then in a fit of temper he grabbed up the empty rum bottle and started to hit Kaylo over the head with it until the bottle smashed. McCreedy tried to stop him but it was all too late. Boswell continued to hit Kaylo with the broken bottle until his face and neck were a mass of bloody gashes.

Kaylo never moved, he died in an instant.

Both men just stood there breathless and panting.

'Oh Christ,' said McCreedy finally, 'You've killed the bastard.'

'Yeah,' Boswell answered, and then he looked at McCreedy. 'What are we going to do?'

McCreedy thought about it for a moment.

"We'll make it look like an accident" he replied, 'Come on.'

They found some larger rocks and piled them up at the bottom of the bank. They then laid Kaylo on the rocks with his head at a suitable angle. They picked up the pieces of broken glass and scattered them around together with the broken bottle. To all intents and purposes it looked as though Kaylo had fallen down the bank whilst drunk, and somehow managed to smash his face on the rocks, or on the bottle, or both.

And it worked.

Two days later some children discovered Kaylo's body, which by then was a mass of congealed blood, insects, maggots and infestation.

The obvious was quickly concluded by one and all. In addition to that, someone had seen Kaylo sitting on the steps of the Kooabarra with a bottle of Bundaberg rum.

Well, what would you expect. It was just another bloody aborigine full of booze.

And with that, things returned to normal and two more weeks passed by.

John Williams walked into the bar of the Kooabarra Pub and ordered yet another beer. Unfortunately for him, and the way that his luck was going, he might not be ordering many more.

John Williams was a twenty eight year old Englishman who had set sail for Australia two years previously. With every promise of finding wealth and prosperity in the opal fields of Southern Australia, John had decided to leave his young wife back in England, together with their two children. They lived in a small industrial town in the north of England, and whilst John set sail for warmer climes to try and make his fortune, he left his poor wife at home all alone and struggling with their children. She was short of money and she was miserable.

John Williams was a fool.

He had finally arrived at Coober Pedy in the land of opportunity, but he was soon to have his hopes fairly well dashed. Though he'd begun his quest full of enthusiasm and determination, he was soon to realise that he had actually arrived at 'hell on earth'. And he wasn't the first.

Like many others before him, John Williams failed and failed badly. The much spoken about opals weren't just lying around to be simply picked up, neither were they just a couple of feet under the ground. To his astonishment John found there were miners in Coober Pedy who were digging tunnels fifty and a hundred feet deep, and having to remove thousands of tons of rocks and red earth. Poor John couldn't comprehend it all, he couldn't even make a start.

He went to work for a miner, digging in the deep tunnels underground.

However the Australians were a tough breed, a lot tougher than John, and in the end he was sacked simply because he couldn't physically keep up with the rest of the men.

From there he did many different jobs, anything at all to keep him going, and of course to keep him going to the pub.

John had worked as a clerk at one or two of the local opal dealers, but he soon realised that this was the nearest he was ever going to get to those precious stones.

In between drinking there, he also helped out at the Kooabarra pub. For a pittance he would sweep up or collect and wash the glasses, and sometimes when they were short handed, the owner would let him serve behind the bar. For that John could have free beer and keep his own tips.

Luck was smiling on John Williams that afternoon, because as he ordered his second beer the owner asked him to work the bar. Yet again somebody or other had decided not to show up, and so John worked all afternoon until six o' clock and then he took a break. He poured himself a 'free' beer and went outside onto the pub's veranda to take in the last of the sun. At around that time it became cooler and pleasanter, and for John this was the only thing about Coober Pedy that he actually enjoyed.

John wanted to go home. He wanted to go back to England, back to cool and green England where the people were nicer and where he could at least earn a decent living. He missed his wife and he missed his children and he missed the comforts of his home, the home where his poor wife cooked and cleaned for him and attended to his every beck and call. He knew that he should have written to her more and let her know how he was, but he'd been so busy, what with all the drinking and trying to find work.

John Williams had one major problem. He was absolutely broke. So even though he wanted to return to England, he couldn't afford it. He'd considered going to Perth or Melbourne or even Sydney and boarding a ship and working his passage. However he didn't even have the money to make the trip across Australia to a suitable port.

So in the fading sun, John stood there on the veranda of the Kooabarra pub drinking his beer. He put his hand into his left pocket and felt for the coins there. They were his tips. The bar had been quite busy because a couple of miners had been in celebrating their luck. As John rummaged in his pocket he realised that the afternoon may have been quite profitable. He strolled over to the side steps of the veranda and sat down. He then put his beer on one of the steps and started to count his money. As he counted, he put the coins into stacks of one dollar and placed them at the side of his glass. John smiled to himself, he'd done really quite well.

At that moment there was a commotion. Two men came out of the pub onto the veranda and they were arguing. They'd apparently been playing cards and one of them had accused the other of cheating. Both men had been drinking and one of them started to punch the other in the face. Chaos ensued, until some of the other men who had also been playing cards broke up the fight.

As John turned to see what was happening, he caught his glass with his elbow and he knocked the drink and most of his coins off the step and into the sand. He cursed and immediately got down on his hands and knees to try and recover his hard earned cash.

The beer had mixed with the coins and everything was buried in the sand. So John knelt down and carefully began to dig up his lost earnings out of the wet sand. As he found his coins he placed them on the bottom step, he would have to wipe and clean them afterwards and then recount his money. The problem was that the more he dug, the more the coins seemed to sink and disappear, and in the end he was grabbing handfuls of sand in an effort to try and retrieve the rest of his cash. He reached down into the sand again and then he felt something. He pulled out a handful of sand and tipped it onto the step. There were just three coins there and something else. It was a small rock, just a piece of stone. John was just about to flick it away when the light from the setting sun suddenly caught it, and there was an immediate flash of blue.

John just knelt there in the sand staring at it. What on earth was it? He picked up the stone and held it up in the warm sunlight, and then his heart suddenly missed a beat.

It was an opal, the likes of which he had never seen before.

He took a sharp intake of breath and quickly looked around. The few people who were there on the veranda were taking no notice of him, and why would they? So he put the opal into his left pocket and then scraped up the remaining coins from the step and for whatever reason, he put them into his other pocket.

John stood up and walked away from the pub. He returned to the small room that he rented above some aging washrooms, once there he switched on the light and locked the door. He sat on the edge of his worn, grubby bed and he took the opal out of his pocket. In the glare of the bare electric light bulb, John marvelled at his find and held it up to the light in wonder. How on earth had an opal ended up under the steps of the Kooabarra pub? John could only come to one conclusion, at some time it must have belonged to a miner who had dropped or lost it. The miner was probably drunk. It must have been a while ago because John had never heard any stories about anyone losing such a valuable stone. Maybe the miner didn't want anyone to know?

John lay back on his bed and again he held up the stone to the light. This was his ticket, this would be his ticket to go home. He would sell the opal, and with the money he would get himself out of this god forsaken country and back home to England. He would put this misadventure behind him and start again.

But he would have to be careful, and he would have to make a plan.

As he lay there on his bed, John smiled to himself as he came to one definite conclusion.

'Yes...there was a God'.

The next morning John Williams had got himself up and out of bed bright and early. For once he hadn't got the thick head that resulted from a hangover. He'd actually lain in bed for hours, trying to formulate his plans as he stared at the precious opal. At nine o' clock he was dressed and had left his room and made his way down Coober Pedy's main street in the direction of O'Gorman's Opal Shop. John had chosen O'Gorman's over the other opal buyers in town simply because O'Gorman's was the main dealer. O'Gorman's set the prices of course, but more importantly, Joe O'Gorman had the money.

John walked into the shop and looked around. The shop was empty, there were no customers in there and that suited John. Sitting behind the counter as usual was Joe O'Gorman. It was a well known fact in Coober Pedy that the only person in O'Gorman's shop who handled the money or the opals, was Joe O'Gorman himself. And playing cards in the corner were Joe O'Gorman's two henchmen, McCreedy and Boswell. John knew well to give those two thugs a very wide berth.

Joe O'Gorman looked up and once again sighed.

It was that 'bloody glass collector' from the pub, the one that was always mithering Joe for a job.

'No,' said O'Gorman off handily, 'there's no jobs,' and he shook his head as he continued to write something into one of his ledgers. McCreedy and Boswell didn't even bother to look up.

'I don't want a job today Mr O'Gorman,' said John. He spoke in a tone that he felt was slightly more in command than his usual subservient mumblings.

It cut no ice with Joe O'Gorman, he never even bothered to look up either.

'What the bloody hell do you want then?' O'Gorman asked.

John coughed, 'I have an opal that I want to sell.'

Joe O'Gorman glanced up over his silver rimmed glasses. Well this was different. He knew that John Williams had been a failure as a miner, everyone did. Coober Pedy was a small town full of gossip and everybody knew each other's business.

'You...have an opal?' O'Gorman asked.

'Yes I do,' John replied, and he took the opal out of his pocket and held it out for Joe O'Gorman to see.

Joe O'Gorman nearly burst a blood vessel.

At that moment the shop door burst open and in walked three of Coober Pedy's better known characters. All three were miners and they'd made their way into the town that morning with the sole intentions of selling their hard earned finds to O'Gorman and then moving across the street to the Kooabarra pub and getting as drunk as possible.

'Top of the morning O'Gorman, you thieving old bastard,' shouted one of them as the other two burst out laughing.

When one of them saw John standing there, he quipped, 'Who're you robbing now Joe, you thieving old git?"

Once again the others continued to laugh.

Joe O'Gorman was thrown into a quandary. In front of him was the missing opal. His two stupid, stupid employees had managed to murder the only lead to its whereabouts, and now this idiot comes waltzing into his shop and flashes the opal right under his nose.

The three miners walked up to the counter and immediately spotted the opal in John's hand.

'Strewth Almighty,' said the first miner, 'That's the biggest fucker I've ever seen in my life.'

The other two looked on in awe.

'Jesus wept,' said one of them as they crowded around John.

Joe O'Gorman realized that things were getting out of hand. Even McCreedy and Boswell had left their cards and had come across to have a look. They instantly shot a look at O'Gorman, they knew that it had to be the opal. Joe O'Gorman rubbed his forehead and realized that he had to take control of the situation. So he opened his cash drawer and pulled out a ten dollar note.

'Right you lot,' he said to the miners, 'Here's ten bucks. Fuck off to the pub and get yourself a drink. I've got some business to sort out with this young fella, so I'll stand you all a beer.'

The miners looked at one another, it seemed a fair enough deal.

'Go on,' said O'Gorman, 'Bugger off and come back in an hour.'

One of the miners snatched up the ten dollar note and they went to leave.

Before they left the shop the first miner turned to John.

'Whatever that old bastard offers you, ask for double. He's a thieving old twat.'

The miner winked at John and then they all left and headed across the street to the pub.

As they left, one of them called back. 'Come over to the pub after, and we'll all celebrate.'

That left John Williams alone, to deal with Joe O'Gorman and the opal.

O'Gorman gave McCreedy and Boswell a dismissive nod and they both returned to their cards like the two obedient dogs they were.

'Right then,' said O'Gorman.

He'd missed the opportunity, missed it by minutes. If he'd have known that John had the opal he would have simply taken it off him. He'd have asked John to pass him the opal so that he could assess its value, and then he would have pocketed it. Then he would have had McCreedy and Boswell throw John out onto the street. There would be no witnesses, so there was nothing that John could have said or done. But now, every bugger in the pub knew about it. And in another hour, half of Coober Pedy would know about the opal.

Deep inside Joe O'Gorman raged. That bloody 'blacky'. If he was still alive O'Gorman would have killed him. Joe O'Gorman didn't see the irony in that.

John Williams stood there with the opal in his hand, like some stupid innocent. Joe O'Gorman looked at him and then he took a deep breath and tried to calm himself down.

'Can I look at it?' he asked civilly.

John passed him the opal and O'Gorman actually quivered when he felt the weight of it.

When he held it up to the light and he saw its unique colouring, he started to blink. He stared at the stone and tried to maintain his calm.

'Where did you get it?' O'Gorman asked John casually.

'I acquired it.' John replied, he was ready for that one. Everyone in Coober Pedy knew that he wasn't a miner and he realized that he would have to keep his wits about him.

'Hmmm,' replied O'Gorman nonchalantly. It was all part of his bluff.

And so, the game began.

'Even though it's of a size,' said O'Gorman, as he peered at the opal through his jeweller's loupe, 'It'll need cutting down to show off its true colour.'

'Yes I know,' said John. He didn't, but it sounded good and that comment made O'Gorman glance at him. Now it would be Joe O'Gorman who would have his wits about him.

O'Gorman casually put the opal down on his counter, it was a reluctant move. He didn't want to lose the opal again.

The game continued.

O'Gorman sniffed and shrugged at the same time.

'Three hundred dollars,' he said outright, 'It's worth three hundred dollars, give or take.'

'Yeah, right,' said John, and he reached across for his opal. He'd worked for a couple of opal dealers in the past as a clerk, before being sacked, and so he did have a rough idea as to what the dealers paid.

Seeing John reaching for the opal, the opal that Joe O'Gorman considered was his by right, caused him to relent somewhat.

'Okay, okay,' he grumbled, 'I did say 'give or take'. How much are you looking for?'

John swallowed and he tried to look calm. It was a good act. He'd been practising it all through the night and most of the morning.

And so he looked Joe O'Gorman straight in the eye, it was a practised move.

'A thousand dollars' he said.

Even McCreedy and Boswell stopped playing cards when they heard that.

O'Gorman just stared back at him. He was used to negotiations going up or down in multiples of ten or twenty. Not seven hundred.

'Bugger off,' said O'Gorman in shock. And he immediately regretted it as John leant over and picked up his opal

'There are other buyers,' said John, another practised move.

'Hold on a minute,' said O'Gorman, 'Let's see what we can do.'

And the game continued.

O'Gorman realized he'd have to up his bid.

'Hold on a minute son,' he said, 'I'm a fair man, and I don't care what anybody says. Go on then, I'll give you five hundred dollars. You can't ask for fairer than that?'

John Williams stood there for a moment and he listened to O'Gorman's patronizing bullshit. And for the first time in a long while, he became angry.

'Mr O'Gorman,' he said, 'Please don't call me 'son'. It's a fucking insult. I am not your son. And just let me tell you something else. I've come to you plenty of times in the past, and I've almost begged you for a job, and you Mr O'Gorman have treated me like a piece of shit. And now, I have something that 'you' really want. So stop fucking me about . Buy the opal or don't buy the opal, I don't give a shit either way.'

And that was it, game advantage.

Joe O'Gorman went red in the face, and he looked back at John,

'Eight hundred and you're a rich man. It's the best deal you'll ever get, anywhere.'

'No' replied John, 'I won't be a rich man and it won't be the best deal I can get.'

At that point, Joe O'Gorman's mind was already working in two different directions. He would eventually have to sort this out, legally or illegally, because old habits died hard.

'Nine hundred..?' O'Gorman asked, but he already knew the answer.

John Williams simply shook his head.

'You're a piece of shit,' said O'Gorman as he finally capitulated. He turned around and walked over to the office safe.

'Carry on like that Joe, and we'll really fallout,' said John in good humour. But for a brief moment O'Gorman's inner anger boiled over. He'd made a decision, and it would be back to the old ways, and the old habits.

Game over. Maybe.

O'Gorman stacked ten bundles, each of one hundred dollars onto the counter in front of John.

Both men nodded in agreement, and John handed over the opal as O'Gorman threw the money into a brown canvas bag.

It was either stupidity or providence, but as John turned to go he said something rather inane.

'Call in at the pub later on,' he said laughing, 'and I'll buy you all a drink.'

O'Gorman simply turned his back to John.

'Enjoy it while you can,' he quietly muttered.

John glanced at McCreedy and Boswell and he saw their stare.

And at that moment, John Williams knew that his troubles were far from over.

It took all of his willpower, but John kept the silly grin on his face.

'Okay then, I'll see you all later,' he said, and he walked out of O'Gorman's opal shop and straight across the street to the Kooabarra Pub.

McCreedy quickly moved over to the window and watched John Williams walk merrily through the doors of the pub.

'He's in the Kooabarra,' he said.

'Let the bastard have a drink,' said O'Gorman, 'let the little bastard drink himself stupid, and then take him somewhere and get my fucking money back. And then give him the hiding of his fucking life.'

McCreedy and Boswell nodded.

'And Boswell,' O'Gorman added.

Boswell looked at his boss.

'This time, don't kill the fucker.'

John Williams walked into the Kooabarra pub. Thankfully the three miners were in a corner talking to another group of men. They were actually talking about the large opal that they'd just seen in O'Gorman's shop and in doing so they completely failed to notice John walk in through the front door. But John never stopped, he walked straight through the pub and out through the back. He then made his way down to the stockyards. It was the stopping off point for everything that came into Coober Pedy. Live sheep and cattle, grain and the flour, cheese and butter and beer, it all had to be brought in by road. John soon found a driver, the owner of a truck who was willing to take him out of Coober Pedy quickly.

And for the amount of money that John was willing to pay, immediately. Game, set and match.

John sat back in the truck and silently waved Coober Pedy goodbye. He finally had enough money to get him back home.

The truck driver drove him due south to Port Augusta, where John could catch a boat to Melbourne. From there he got on a decent ship and sailed back to England in relative luxury. Later, as he relaxed on the bow of the ship in the warm mid ocean, with a glass of cold beer in his hand, John Williams considered himself a lucky man.

God however, had other plans.

John had been away from home for more than two years. He'd left his wife and his two young children on their own, and he'd left his wife to fend for herself with the promise that he would finally return a richer man. His letters had been few and far between and then they'd finally stopped altogether. His wife didn't know if he was dead or alive, or even if he was ever coming back.

She was a pretty young thing and she worked in the local butchers, serving the customers.

Mr Entwistle, the butcher, had a roving eye and he'd always had a bit of a thing for young Mrs Williams. However, she'd always been happily married and Mr Entwistle had always known his place. But after a year or so he'd noticed the change in her. She was lonely and she missed male company. Stuck at home on her own with two young children night after night was wearing her down, and she was working every god given hour just to pay the rent. And though she chatted away to the customers in her usual friendly manner, she missed the closeness of another human being. In the evenings, when the shop was closed, she'd started stay behind and talk to Mr Entwistle, she enjoyed the conversation. He in turn enjoyed her company, and he also enjoyed looking at the shape of her ample young body. He began to treat her. At the end of the night he would wrap up a pound of sausages for her to take home, or a piece of ham or beef. Just little bits of meat, little gifts, and all for free. And then one Friday night when they'd had to work late, Entwistle brought out the bottle of scotch whiskey that he always kept in his fridge, just for Friday nights. They both shared a glass and the alcohol began to work. She'd worked with Mr Entwistle for a long time and she was used to being close to him. The whiskey made her warm, and it made her restless. She ached for a man's touch, she'd missed it so, so much. Entwistle too was both obsessed with her and with her body. Leaning over her at the counter everyday and briefly touching her buttocks had always made him more than aroused. She of course knew what he was doing and at times it made her tremble.

So on that evening he poured them both a second drink and she began to giggle and pout. He enjoyed that, he really enjoyed that and he began to get playful. She liked that a lot, and she suddenly stopped and stared directly at him.

'What?' he asked her as he smiled.

She too just stood there smiling, and then she undid the buttons on the front of her white overall and let it fall to the ground. Underneath she was completely naked. She stood there breathing heavily, and so was Entwistle. Then she put her hands under her firm breasts and offered them to him. She just smiled at him and said, 'What are you waiting for?'

He reached over and took hold of her, and he lowered his head sucked her breasts until she was delirious. He ran his hand down her thigh and in between her legs and her pleasure turned into ecstasy as she started to squirm at his touch. She in turn undid the front of his pants and then reached in and took hold of him, by then there was no going back. Her hands on him made his hips go into involuntary thrusts. She knew what was happening and she undid his pants and slid them off him. She then pulled him to the floor and fed him into her and moaned at the sheer pleasure of it all.

She left the shop that night fulfilled and calmer, so much so that she forgot her sausages.

She also began to forget her husband.

The months continued and so did the sex. It was a strange thing, but they never kissed, never at all. In between serving the customers, they would perform all sorts of sexual acts alone in the back of the shop. Though it was never love, it was just sex and lust.

But greed and stupidity finally got the better of young Mrs Williams. It all started whenever Entwistle had to go out with deliveries and leave her alone in the shop. She started to dip into his till.

Entwistle of course, soon discovered the discrepancy in his takings and he sacked her.

He considered her thieving as an act of betrayal.

He was willing to share 'his meat' with her, but definitely not his money.

By the time John Williams finally got back to his home town in the north of England his wife was long gone and with her his two children.

She was living in Scotland, and was by then playing at being somebody else's wife.

McCreedy and Boswell scoured the whole of Coober Pedy looking for John Williams. But he was gone, he'd disappeared. He'd jumped ship in more than one way or another.

Joe O'Gorman was infuriated. He'd let someone else slip through his fingers, however this time he did have the opal.

A week later and after a lot of time and effort, Joe O'Gorman finally got off the train at the Central Railway Station in the bustling city of Sidney, in New South Wales.

Dressed in a badly fitting suit and carrying a cheap canvas suitcase, he made his way directly to the offices of Oscar Roth. Sidney was becoming an internationally recognized city and Oscar Roth were Sydney's best known and most successful importers and exporters of diamonds and opals. O'Gorman had dealt with them on a regular basis. Once he'd concluded his business there he would make use of Sydney's excellent banking services, and from there he would make use of Sydney's excellent brothels, and their services.

Joe O'Gorman sold the opal to Oscar Roth for a considerable profit. And as he walked out of their offices he suddenly decided to stay in Sydney for a month, or maybe longer. He was certainly in no rush to return to barren delights of Coober Pedy. Not one bit.

The opal was finally sent to England, to London, and to the famous Hatton Gardens.

It was bought by the diamond importers 'De Wint Diamonds' and it was their nephew, Burti De Wint who had contacted Louis Skeet at Albemarle and Skeet. He had sold the opal to Louis Skeet and Louis Skeet had in turn presented it to his finest craftsmen. Possibly one of the finest craftsmen in the world.

And that was how the opal fell into the hands of Vasily Orlof Bratz.

CHAPTER 12

It would take Vasily Orlof Bratz ten months.

Ten months of incredibly hard work and immense concentration to create an opal and diamond ring of astonishing quality. It was a feat of extraordinary craftsmanship.

It was a ring worthy of a princess.

Ten months may have seemed a long time, but in reality it was only forty weeks and during that time Vasily Orlof had consistently worked for six or seven days a week. He spent his time constantly hunched over at his workbench till all hours, creating the most wonderful piece of jewellery of his life.

Vasily's first task was to cut the opal down to a certain size and shape. He decided to cut it into an oval, which would make the most of the opal's length. But the skill and the expertise in the whole process was in the accuracy and the precision of cutting the opal absolutely right and to be able to bring out its truly exceptional colour. It was a fine art.

If too much of the opal's surface was retained, then there was always the possibility that some of its stunning colouring could be missed or obscured. Cut off too much and the opal would be ruined. It was down to the obvious skill of the craftsman.

And then there were the diamonds.

Louis Skeet had found Vasily Orlof twenty stunningly beautiful 'brilliant' cut diamonds, all matching and all with perfect clarity. Louis had once again visited De Wint Diamonds at Hatton Gardens and had again dealt with the nephew, Burti De Wint. A deal was struck, but at a price. The one thing that held Louis Skeet to the deal was that he had that spectacular opal. He also had Vasily Orlof Bratz.

Skeet knew that he would have to get the best for Vasily Orlof, anything less would have been an insult and folly. Quality would have to be paramount. Albemarle and Skeet had built their reputation by selling only the finest, their good name had always been synonymous with excellence.

Louis Skeet had handed his valuable diamonds over to Vasily Orlof. If he had realised what Vasily was going to do with them he would have possibly had a heart attack.

Vasily Orlof would spend months working on the opal, slowly but surely cutting it down and constantly inspecting its internal colours. He could eventually recognize every fragment of colour within the precious stone.

For Vasily Orlof, it was like examining the picture of a loved one.

In the end he cut, ground and polished the opal to perfection.

Every colour shone through, the blues and the golds and the turquoise, all the way to the heart of the stone and its red fire.

Vasily Orlof then started to work on the diamonds.

He took Louis Skeet's valuable and costly diamonds and chopped them into a totally different shape. When he'd finally ground and polished them, he had twenty spear shaped diamonds. They were like small pointing fingers. It then took months for Vasily Orlof to cut the minute inverted prisms into the underside of each stone. Vasily collected and saved all the tiny pieces of chipped diamonds that were produced during of cutting process, and he stored them in an old marmalade jar.

Once the prisms had been meticulously cut into those unique spear shaped diamonds, Vasily took a piece of blue velvet cloth from his drawer and laid it out on the bench in front of him. He took the diamonds and laid them in a small circle, each with the pointed ends facing inwards. He placed the opal in the middle of them and then pushed each individual diamond close up to it so that they almost touched. From there, he took his jewellers lamp and placed it over the diamonds, and then he turned on the light.

As the bright light shone down, the diamonds lit up and each one threw a tiny beam of light into the centre of the opal. The opal itself radiated and its colours and lit up like a rainbow.

Vasily Orlof stared down at the wonder of it.

"Hello my love" he said to his opal. And he smiled.

However, time and the task involved in the making of the ring had taken a definite toll on Vasily Orlof. He was becoming weary.

The nonstop physical and mental concentration of having to make sure that the opal was absolutely perfect, and cutting the diamonds, all to their exact shape, was exhausting.

However, it was the mental toll that would have a far more reaching effect on him.

Vasily Orlof had started to talk to the opal as he worked on it. He was having a conversation with his beautiful opal and his mind was becoming mixed up as he was slowly failing to comprehend reality.

Once he'd arrived at work every morning he would immediately take the opal out of the small cardboard box where he kept it inside his workbench. Then he would start to talk to it. The other jewellers who worked there all saw what was occurring, but they thought that Vasily Orlof was simply talking to himself, the fact that Vasily only spoke in Russian didn't help either, none of the others did and so they didn't even know what he was saying.

But in his mind, Vasily was talking to Tatiana.

In his muddled state, Tatiana's soul was alive within the opal, it had to be, because opals were Tatiana's favourite stone. And this was the most beautiful opal he had ever seen and Tatiana was the most beautiful person he had ever known.

It was the only logic he could understand, and so even though Vasily Orlof's skills were at their pinnacle, his mind was slowly beginning to deteriorate. But he continued to work flawlessly.

After all the arduous work on the opal and the matching diamonds, Vasily then started to make the band and the setting for ring.

With the opal placed in front of him, he began to talk to the precious stone about his design.

He chose to use platinum, only the best would do for his darling opal, only the best for the best. To him it was as though he was designing a wonderful outfit for his Tatiana, some fantastic gown for her to wear.

He worked and shaped the platinum band and it was then that Vasily Orlof's artistry and ingenuity came into play. He took all the diamond chips that he had stored away in his marmalade jar and painstakingly set each and every tiny diamond fragment into the ring's platinum band. It took over a month. The tiny mixed diamond chips gave an astonishing 'frosted' appearance to the whole creation. The jewel encrusted ring band was a work of art in itself.

Vasily Orlof then painstakingly set each of the spear shaped diamonds onto the band. Every single one of them had to be set at the correct and critical angle. Finally he picked up his opal and kissed it before very carefully setting it into the centre of the ring.

The skills that Vasily Orlof had spent a lifetime in learning, all of his skills and all of his flair and his creative talent, came together in that one single moment. His jeweller's lamp shone down on the ring and radiated through the diamonds to send tiny beams of light directly into the centre of the opal. The opal instantly lit up as though it had a life of its own.

For Vasily Orlof it was as though the morning sun had just begun to shine.

A small tear rolled down Vasily's cheek as he stared down at his creation.

'You look so very beautiful my dear.' he said.

He was in love with the impossible.

Maybe he always had been.

The next day, Vasily Orlof presented his opal ring to Louis Skeet.

He took the ring into Louis Skeet's office. It was wrapped in a piece of the blue velvet cloth and Vasily placed it on Louis' desk. Louis Skeet slowly unfolded the cloth and for an instant he stopped breathing. He stared down at the opal ring that Vasily Orlof had created and he couldn't believe his eyes, it was incredible. Louis Skeet was absolutely stunned.

Never in his life, and in a life that lived for jewellery, had he seen anything like it.

He looked up open mouthed at Vasily Orlof and was speechless.

'It's the best,' Vasily said to him, 'It's the best I could ever do.'

It was a statement of fact. And for Vasily it was a personal acceptance of the truth.

Louis Skeet just nodded, and once again he looked down at the opal ring that lay on the desk in front of him. He shook his head

'Vasily...it's a masterpiece.'

He could say nothing less.

The next day Vasily Orlof didn't turn in to work.

Louis Skeet didn't mind, how could he?

Louis spent the day rearranging his shop window. Louis had a new star, a new star that he wanted to show to the world. Louis Skeet would once again exhibit the excellence that only Albemarle and Skeet of Bond Street could create.

He used the opal ring as the centrepiece for his whole display. He placed the ring on a simple black velvet cushion in centre of the window and then he directed the strong display lights down onto the ring. The effect was stunning as the whole ring lit up. It was spectacular.

And it wasn't long before people began to stop outside the shop and stare.

Louis Skeet just smiled and watched them as they gazed in wonder at the ring, and then eventually they passed by.

He knew that none of them could possibly afford it.

The following day Vasily Orlof returned to work.

He was late, late for Vasily Orlof, who was normally at work at around seven o' clock in the morning. It was nine thirty but Vasily Orlof was completely unaware of the time.

He was slightly disconcerted and very unsettled. He'd had a bad night.

Vasily Orlof was somehow lost. He'd finished the ring, his ring, and now he was at a loss as to what he was doing. He'd lain awake all night with the strange feeling that he had lost the opal, simply because he'd given the opal away to Louis Skeet. For Vasily in his confused state, it was as though he had once again lost Tatiana. It was as though he had somehow deserted her.

But when he approached the shop and looked in the window, there she was, waiting for him. She was beautifully displayed, she was of course the most beautiful thing in the whole display, without doubt. And she seemed to be smiling at him, and he smiled back at her.

'Good morning my love,' he said, 'you look so beautiful today.'

It made him feel good to see her again. And he smiled and went into work.

That same evening when he left, he went around to the front of the shop and spoke to her.

After ten of minutes of intimate conversation, he turned and made his way home, he felt happier and somewhat contented.

But it was the beginning of a downward spiral.

From then on, Vasily Orlof would arrive at work every day and stand outside the shop talking to his opal ring, and in the evening he would do the same before leaving to go home.

People walking by would glance at the old man who was gazing into the jewellers shop window and muttering something in Russian. Most ignored him, or shook their heads and quickly walked past, none of them realising that the old man standing there had actually made some of the finest and most beautiful pieces of jewellery that were in that shop window.

Vasily Orlof had begun to stand in front of Albemarle and Skeet's shop window for more than an hour at a time before Louis Skeet finally realised what was going on. One of his shop assistants had observed Vasily Orlof outside the shop. She was slightly concerned and had informed Mr Skeet. Louis had gone outside and brought Vasily back into the workshop and had sat him down with a cup of tea. Louis too was concerned. He knew from the past that Vasily Orlof had problems and wasn't well. Since he'd finished the ring, Vasily had done hardly any work at all. But that didn't matter to Louis Skeet. Louis held a loyalty for Vasily Orlof. Vasily Orlof had repaid his wages a thousand times. Vasily Orlof Bratz had made Louis Skeet a richer man.

But there was more than that. There was an older, Russian loyalty, and there was a memory of a lost friendship, with a man named Rubin Blesk.

From that day and every day, Louis would go outside every morning and bring Vasily Orlof into the workshop. And in the evening he made sure that his dedicated old craftsman would be safely on his way home.

It was more than a kindness, it was a respect for the finest craftsman Louis Skeet would ever know.

On a sunny afternoon, five weeks later, newly married Peter Cunningham and his much adored young wife Rebecca were strolling down Bond Street, arm in arm and very much in love. Peter Cunningham was a very lucky man. Not only had he married the woman he loved, he was also the only son of an extremely wealthy man and was the heir to a considerable fortune.

His father, Angus Cunningham, had made his first fortune after the First World War. Angus Cunningham's own father had been a horse dealer and during the war he'd been awarded a very profitable contract to supply the army with horses.

Unfortunately, or perhaps fortunately, Angus's father had died during the war years and young Angus Cunningham had to take over the business.

At the end of the war there was very little call for horses, the motor car being the way forward. So Angus Cunningham took his father's quite significant profits and ploughed the money into land and property. By the end of the Great War most of the land and property had become fairly worthless since no one had any money and nobody could afford it. Angus Cunningham did have money, and plenty of it. So he went on a spending spree. He also had the good sense to come up with the idea of buying cheap land on the outskirts of London. His line of thought being that when things got better, so would the price of any of the land he had bought. Things did get better, considerably better and in turn Angus Cunningham had made himself a considerable fortune.

As the Second World War approached, history repeated itself. Well it certainly did for the Cunningham family. As the war ended, Angus Cunningham, along with his son Peter, had purchased properties all along the south coast and had also bought large areas in northern England. In particular Lancashire and Cheshire.

The Cunningham family also invested in cheap parcels of land throughout the bombed out remains of London, many of which were just piles of bricks and rubble. Those investments were shrewd and fortunes were made several times over.

The old Jewish maxim, 'Buy land son, they've stopped making it' should have been the Cunningham family motto.

The fifties had just arrived and with it a new decade of promise.

Peter Cunningham had first met his wife-to-be at University and from there they had never looked back. Peter had left university and gone straight into the family business. It had always been the plan.

Peter Cunningham was a wealthy young man, he had a large bank account, a very good business and suddenly he had a beautiful and loving wife.

Paris had been their honeymoon destination where they had spent a blissful week before returning to London to the Cunningham family home in Mayfair. Their stay in London however would only be short lived. Peter and Rebecca, with the help of some family funding, had bought a mansion in Cheshire.

It was a planned strategy. Rebecca's family lived in the same county, and from there Peter Cunningham could run their northern estates. Their new acquisition was Worsley Manor, a palatial mansion surrounded by a hundred acres of farm and woodland. Compared to the steadily rising prices in London, its half a million pound purchase price was looked upon as a 'snip'.

That afternoon, as Peter and Rebecca Cunningham strolled arm in arm down Bond Street, there couldn't have been a more contented couple. Their world was a happy place.

Earlier, they had been aimlessly walking around London looking at various shops, though with nothing particular in mind. Peter had treated them both to lunch at the Ritz, where they had some exceptional food and a very good bottle of champagne to celebrate not only the end of their honeymoon, but also their forthcoming move to Cheshire. Rebecca was very excited at the thought of moving back to her home county, where she could keep in close touch with her immediate family.

So they sauntered down Bond Street looking at the different shops and finally they came to Albemarle and Skeet's jewellers. As Peter Cunningham looked through the window at the latest Rolex watches, his wife Rebecca was looking at diamond rings.

A woman's preference, and a man's curse.

Suddenly, Rebecca held her breath. There in front of her, placed on the central display in the shop window was the most unbelievable ring she had ever seen in her life. It was of course, Vasily Orlof's opal. So taken was Rebecca Cunningham by it's incredible beauty that she could only utter the words.

'Oh my god!'

Peter Cunningham turned to his wife. 'What is it darling?' he asked. Maybe it would have been wiser if he hadn't.

'Oh Peter,' she said to him, 'Look at that ring. It's unbelievable.'

He leant over to see what she was looking at. And then he saw the ring too.

'My Lord,' he said, 'Now that is one phenomenal piece of jewellery.' And he made the age old mistake of agreeing with his wife over something that was not only beautiful but was also for sale.

They both just stood there, gazing into Albemarle and Skeet's shop window.

'Look at the colours Peter, just look at that opal. And look at all those diamonds and the diamonds on the band too.'

Rebecca was enthralled. More than that, she was completely captivated.

'I think it's the most beautiful thing I have ever seen Peter.'

They stood there in silence, and then Peter Cunningham slowly turned to look at his wife. He just stood there thinking, and he smiled to himself. 'God...she is so, so pretty'.

And he was right. His wife was beautiful and he did consider himself a very lucky man.

Peter Cunningham had married the love of his life. From the moment he had seen her standing there in the great hall of his university, he'd known that she was the one. He had gone straight over and spoken to her, and that was it. Within a week they were an item. Within another week they were lovers and Peter Cunningham knew that there would never be anyone else. She would be his partner and his wife and his very best friend for the rest of their lives.

Peter was still looking at his wife, and he was still smiling.

'Come on,' he said to her, 'let's go and try it on.'

Rebecca shot him a sudden glance. 'No...No Peter. I didn't mean...'

Peter laughed. 'I know you didn't.'

'No Peter,' she said, 'I've got my beautiful engagement ring and my wedding ring.'

Peter grabbed her in his arms. 'Be quiet woman,' he said playfully, 'your husband wants you to try on a ring, that's all.'

She stared at him. 'But I don't want you to buy me another ring.'

Peter laughed at her, 'I didn't say I was buying it, I just said that I wanted you to try it on.'

Rebecca Cunningham burst out laughing. She knew her husband better than that.

They both walked into Albemarle and Skeet and were immediately approached by a young lady assistant.

'We would like to look at the lovely opal ring that you have in your window,' said Peter Cunningham rather pleasantly.

The assistant's eyes widened slightly, she knew exactly which ring he meant.

'I'll just get Mr Skeet,' she replied, also quite pleasantly, 'He deals with the special items.'

And with that she quickly went to get her boss.

The young assistant had been instructed never to hand over valuable pieces of jewellery to strangers. On more than one occasion in London's Bond Street, some suave criminal had walked out of one of the jewellers shops with more than just a diamond or two tucked away in his or her pocket.

Louis Skeet swiftly appeared, and he was in full sales mode. He immediately recognised Peter Cunningham, Louis knew all about the Cunningham family, and their assets. It was always good practice in London to know 'who was who'.

Not that Louis Skeet would make a fuss, not one bit. It was professional etiquette to treat all customers as though they were all new arrivals.

'Good morning sir...madam,' said Louis Skeet, and he gave a nod that was almost a bow.

"I believe that you are interested in our opal ring?' he asked.

Peter Cunningham nodded. 'Yes we are.' he replied, 'My wife quite likes the look of it.'

Louis Skeet nodded and went over to the window display.

He returned with the opal ring, still on its black velvet cushion.

Louis turned to Rebecca, 'Would you like to try it on madam?' he asked and without waiting for a reply he picked up the ring and slid it gently onto the middle finger of Rebecca Cunningham's outstretched hand. The ring fitted her like a glove. Rebecca looked at the opal and took a deep breath as she felt the physical beauty of it. With the exception of being married to her husband, she had never wanted something so much in her life. Rebecca knew it was a weakness, after all, she was a woman.

She looked up at Peter and gave a little smile. Peter Cunningham readily accepted the inevitable.

'How much is the ring Mr Skeet?' he asked.

This was the moment of truth.

Albemarle and Skeet the Jewellers didn't do prices. There was not one price tag on any single item in the whole of the shop. Such was their exclusivity. Albemarle and Skeet only dealt with the privileged and the privileged didn't want the common public to know what and how much they were spending. If a customer came into Albemarle and Skeet to look at a piece of jewellery, then it was taken for granted that they would have more than enough money to pay for it.

Louis Skeet looked at Peter Cunningham.

'That piece would be fourteen thousand pounds sir,' he replied politely.

Rebecca stared across at her husband. She couldn't believe what she'd just heard. For a moment she felt a little dizzy as she again glanced down at the stupendous opal ring on her middle finger. She felt that she should take it off and immediately hand it back to Mr Skeet. Rebecca Cunningham came from a working family in her small home town in Cheshire, and in that town you could buy a decent terraced house for less than a thousand pounds. And even that seemed a huge amount of money to her.

Rebecca Cunningham stood there in silence, almost dumbfounded.

Her husband, Peter Cunningham, just smiled.

'Right Mr Skeet, I think we'll take it,' he said.

Rebecca Cunningham nearly fainted.

Louis Skeet nodded once more.

'Should we have the ring delivered sir...to Mayfair?'

That last 'touch' made Peter Cunningham smile. He turned to Rebecca.

'Unless you want to wear it now darling?' he asked her.

Rebecca Cunningham was horrified at the thought, and quickly handed the ring back to Louis Skeet.

'Probably a wise choice madam,' he said, 'you never know do you?'

Peter and Rebecca Cunningham then left the shop.

Not one penny had changed hands. No notes, no cheques, not even a shiny coin had been exchanged. But Rebecca Cunningham was suddenly the very excited and very proud owner of an exquisite opal and diamond ring that was worth an unbelievable amount of money.

That was the way of the privileged.

The ring would be invoiced and it would be paid for. And that was the way of things.

The next morning at ten o' clock. Vasily Orlof Bratz slowly made his way along Bond Street. He was beginning to lose track of time. For Vasily it could be either morning or evening, he never really looked at a clock anymore.

As he approached Albemarle and Skeet, he stopped as usual to talk to his 'darling' opal ring. But when he looked through the window he could see that she wasn't there. He was confused. Where could she be? And instead of walking around to the rear of the building and into the workshops, Vasily Orlof walked straight into the shop through the front door.

The assistant looked up, she vaguely recognised Vasily Orlof. The girl knew that he worked in the workshop with the other jewellers, but that was as much as she knew. She didn't know any of the other jewellers either.

Vasily Orlof shuffled over to her, he was quite confused.

'Where is she?' he asked.

The assistant didn't understand.

'Who?' she replied.

'My...my opal, where is she?'

The assistant still didn't understand.

Vasily Orlof was becoming quite distressed. He pointed to the window.

'What have you done with her, my opal?'

Suddenly the assistant realised what Vasily Orlof was talking about.

'Oh you mean the ring, the opal ring in the window. Is that what you mean?'

'Yes, yes,' Vasily quickly replied, 'my opal ring, where is she?'

'Oh it's gone,' she replied, 'Mr Skeet sold it yesterday. He sold it to some rich couple. I don't know who they were.'

Vasily Orlof didn't understand, 'It's gone...gone where?'

The young assistant was becoming slightly annoyed. She was busy and hadn't got time for all of this, and so she started to speak to Vasily Orlof in a louder tone.

'It's gone. It's been sold' she said to him again.

'She's gone?' Vasily asked again.

The assistant nodded her head. 'Yes, that's right, she's gone, she's gone away.'

It was a callous thing to say, but the assistant didn't know any better.

Vasily Orlof stood there for a moment, he didn't fully understand and so he turned and slowly shuffled out of the shop.

The assistant watched him go and she just shrugged. She didn't really care, the assistant had enough problems of her own. The night before she'd discovered her boyfriend kissing one of her best friends, and worst of all, it was on the night that she'd decided to tell him that she was pregnant.

Vasily Orlof was lost. He didn't know what to say or who to ask. He stood outside the shop for a while and he looked through the window at the empty display where his opal used to be.

He started to cry. She'd gone, she'd gone away again, and now once more, he was left all alone. After half an hour he turned away, heartbroken.

Vasily Orlof slowly made his way back home to his little flat in Golders Green.

He went home and he went to bed and he stayed there. His mind was in a state of distress.

He slept and he dreamt of Tatiana. But when he awoke she was gone and he was alone again.

He started to cry out. 'Don't leave me' but she wasn't there, she was never there.

In the end all he wanted to do was sleep, and dream, and see her again. And again he would wake up and she wasn't there, she wasn't ever going to be there and she was never coming back. And there were tears and he was in distress, deep distress.

He lay in bed for three days, never eating or drinking. He began to hallucinate and in his mind Tatiana was in bed with him and they were back in his flat in St Petersburg all those years ago, and he would be talking to her and laughing. And then her image would disappear and he would be left staring at an empty pillow.

And again, 'Don't go, don't go...don't leave me.'

But she did. She always did.

And Vasily Orlof's body and mind began to close down.

He lay there in bed for another day, and then finally he died from a heart attack.

Dehydration and the lack of fluids were in the end too much for him. Or maybe it was a broken heart.

One of the greatest craftsman jewellers that Russia would ever know, died quietly in his sleep.

Two days later Louis Skeet went around to Vasily Orlof's flat in Golders Green. Louis was quite concerned, he'd not seen Vasily Orlof for nearly a week. He knocked on the door, but of course there was no reply. So he quietly let himself in. He could see that Vasily was in bed and Louis went over to him, only to find that Vasily Orlof had died.

Louis Skeet organised Vasily Orlof's funeral. It was at London's Russian Orthodox Cathedral. The Cathedral of the Mother of God and All Saints was located in a quieter part of Knightsbridge. The funeral itself was a very small and private affair.

Vasily Orlof was later buried.

Louis Skeet had a small headstone prepared. It's inscription was simple, but it was the truth.

Vasily Orlof Bratz

Master Craftsman

CHAPTER 13

The year 1996.

Peter and Rebecca Cunningham lived a full and happy life. They had two sons, Edward and Alan, and they spent many happy years watching their two sons grow up in the rural Cheshire countryside.

Peter Cunningham became 'Sir Peter Cunningham' and was rather embarrassed about it, but he laughed it off and life was good.

Eventually however, and with the passing away of grandfather Angus, the Cunningham family had to move back to London to the family house in Mayfair. Business commitments were such that Peter Cunningham would have to return to the capitol where their central offices were located. The Cunningham's empire was huge and they now held vast swathes of land and property throughout England and also in South Africa.

Worsley Manor in Cheshire had been closed down and left empty for several years. The only people employed there were the grounds men whose job it was to keep the extensive gardens from quickly turning into a jungle. The house itself however began to deteriorate as the northern weather and the damp invited themselves into the building.

Peter and Rebecca Cunningham put their sons through university and after that the two brothers joined the family business.

Edward, the eldest, had moved to South Africa to manage their estates there. The family owned several large farms there and were profitably involved with agriculture. They had also ventured into the wine making business and owned a beautiful vineyard in the Stellenbosch Region where they produced very high quality wines.

Younger brother Alan had stayed in London, he married his wife Joyce and they had a son Timothy, who at that time was nine years old.

He and his wife then decided that they'd had enough of London. Or rather his wife Joyce had decided that they'd had enough of London. Joyce Cunningham had been born and bred in rural Norfolk and after ten years of hectic and very urban life in the City of London, she had just about had enough. Joyce Cunningham wanted their son Timothy to grow up in the same healthy environment that she'd had. She missed the land and the farming but most of all she missed her horses and the riding. Her past life in Norfolk had involved stables and horses and gymkhanas, something that she'd regrettably had to give up when she became 'Mrs Alan Cunningham' and moved to the city.

She and Alan had discussed their future and it was Alan who mentioned that they owned a mansion 'somewhere' in Cheshire. A place called Worsley Manor.

A week later they were in a Range Rover and heading up the M1.

Joyce Cunningham swooned from the moment she saw the rambling old place. One look at Worsley Manor and she absolutely loved it. They drove around its hundred acres and Joyce imagined herself riding again, and the horses, the stables and the wonderful life that they could all enjoy.

Alan had managed to find the keys to the old place and they almost had to break down the front doors to get inside.

The house was a bit of a mess. Slightly more than that, it was a disaster.

There was damp and mould everywhere. A series of leaks due to burst pipes had caused some of the ceilings to collapse. Moreover, a succession of winter storms had blown quite a few of the old roof tiles away and the weather and the wildlife had got in. One or two of the bedrooms were actually littered with dead pigeons.

To many, all of that may have been off putting, but not to Joyce Cunningham. No, she was made of sterner stuff. She had wonderful plans. Joyce Cunningham had plans in her head to restore Worsley Manor to its former glory and more.

They booked themselves into a 'decent' local hotel and then went to find a reputable local architect.

There future, however, held one small dark cloud.

Tony McCall was an out and out thief.

He was one of those insidious people who would burgle and rob and steal from anybody, and had no qualms about it at all.

Before he'd met his wife, he had been sent to prison twice, both times for burglary. The first time was for a month, the second time for three months. But as with most things and with the passing of time, he got a little bit cleverer.

Married to his wife Jenny and with an eight year old son, Barry, Tony McCall had two jobs. Firstly he was a plasterer, and secondly, he was a thief.

During the last few years Tony had quietly turned his burglary business into a nice little earner. Tony McCall had found himself a niche.

Tony worked for several building firms. Well, he did when the price was right. As was usual in the building trade, a tradesman would generally work for the firm who was paying the most, and from there everyone worked for everybody else. The building firms which Tony McCall usually worked for were generally medium sized companies who employed up to a dozen men. The work usually comprised of building extensions or loft conversions, or rebuilding people's houses. And that was where Tony McCall had found his little niche, his little window of opportunity.

Tony McCall had realised something quite interesting really. It seemed that at any given time the owners of the properties were always ready to talk to the joiners or the painters and decorators about the job in hand. They were always ready to talk to the electricians about the planned lighting and the position of their plug sockets. Plumbers too were high priority, the clients were always prepared to have a detailed discussion with the plumbers about their proposed new bathroom, or even their new kitchen sink.

However, when it came to the plasterer, no one wanted to know.

Plasterers it seemed, were invisible people. Plasterers were simply tradesmen who had a job to do, and there was no particular design or style required. When it came to plastering, the only thing the client ever required was smooth straight walls. Truth be known, in most cases the plasterer was just a prerequisite to the decorator.

Nobody ever spoke to the plasterer, it was just a job that had to be done. Tony McCall would just turn up, do his work and leave

But having that invisible status meant that he was never really noticed, not one bit.

Tony realised that he could wander around a house freely, and as long as he had a bucket in his hand, nobody ever gave him a second glance.

So he started to pinch things, just little things really, at first. It all started one sunny afternoon when he had finished his work for the day and was ready to go home. He was in the garage of the house that he was working on and he was cleaning up and he was thirsty. There was a large fridge in the corner of the garage which was full of cans beer and bottles of wine. Tony helped himself to a beer. It tasted good. The fridge was full of beer, so Tony put another couple of cans into his plastering bucket and stuck his overalls on top of them. Nobody ever noticed. And that was the start. The next day he had helped himself to another two or three cans, he also pinched a bottle of wine. He and Jenny drank it with their dinner that night. Jenny appreciated his little treat, not knowing that it had been pilfered.

Come the weekend, the family who lived in the house had replenished their beer and the wine, never realizing that some of it had been stolen, they never even noticed. By the end of the following week, Tony's work there was finished. But during that week he had pinched several cans of beer and a couple more bottles of wine, and on his last day there he stole a large bag of chicken breasts and a joint of beef from the family's freezer.

Jenny again, was more than appreciative. It wasn't like her husband to bring home good food and wine. She should have known better.

Jenny McCall was the typical long and ever suffering wife. She had married Tony because she'd found out that she was expecting a baby, their son Barry. The wedding had been a disaster, Tony was drunk, and Jenny's mother had cried for most of the day.

It was doubtful if Tony McCall remembered much of his wedding day, his wife certainly very quickly forgot most of her wedding night.

But Jenny had become Mrs Jenny McCall and would try her hardest to make the best of what life had given her.

Jenny McCall was a scrimper and saver, she had to be. And it had always been Jenny's dream for them to one day buy their own home and have the security that went with it. She had one problem though. Her husband Tony was bone idle.

Every time Tony McCall got some money, he stopped working. He would go to the pub and basically stay there until his money ran out. Then he would go and find himself another plastering job, or rob somebody. So Jenny McCall had to be more than a little careful with her money. She worked at the local supermarket in between looking after little Barry, and because of that she obviously couldn't do any overtime. Her only bonus was the bit of unspent money she found in her husband's back pocket when he came home drunk from the pub.

Very soon though, and on every job, Tony McCall began to steal more and more food and drink. He was actually quite amazed that no one ever noticed.

Then one day, Tony was called into to do a job on a house that had been recently flooded. It started when the elderly lady who owned the house had a problem with a central heating radiator in one of the bedrooms. A pipe had burst in the middle of the night and when the old lady got up the next morning and went downstairs, she found that her living room was full of water and the ceiling had collapsed. The firm that Tony was working for had been called in by the insurance company. The living room was to be fully renovated with a new carpets and a new ceiling and then fully redecorated. Tony's job was to replace and re-plaster the ceiling. When Tony had arrived to do the job, the nice old lady who owned the house had told Tony to help himself to tea or coffee. Tony took her at her word, and more.

Midweek, when he was going through her kitchen cupboards, he discovered something. He had already stolen a jar of coffee and a box of tea bags. Small fry really, but the old lady didn't own a fridge full of wine and beer and Tony wasn't too keen on sherry. Since she lived on her own, the old lady didn't have a freezer full of meat either. So Tony was looking through her cupboards to see what he could find. Nothing more extravagant than tinned peaches and garden peas really. It was then that he spotted an old tin tea caddy, pushed away at the back of the cupboard. He wasn't even going to bother looking at the worn old caddy, it probably contained some old loose tea leaves. But for some reason curiosity got the better of him, and he reached over for the caddy and took off the lid. Inside, to his amazement, was a folded wad of money. Tony took out the money and quickly counted it. There was over five hundred pounds. His first instinct was to put it in his back pocket. Then he thought about it. He would be leaving himself wide open. If someone noticed that the money was missing, the suspicion would straightaway fall on him. Who else could it be?

So Tony McCall got clever. That night before he left he stole the old lady's house key. As he drove home in his van, he stopped off at a locksmiths shop and had a couple of keys made.

It was that simple. The next day he brought back the original key.

Tony finished his work on the house that weekend and he left. Three weeks later, and the old lady's living room had been totally refurbished. The decorators had been in and put up new wallpaper and repainted the doors and skirting boards. Then a week later a new carpet had been fitted and the old lady had been delighted.

A week after that, in the very early hours of the morning, Tony McCall returned.

He quietly unlocked the door and walked straight in. He turned on his small torch and made his way straight into the kitchen and to the cupboard which held the tea caddy. He took the money out of the tea caddy and then walked silently out of the house, remembering of course to lock the door behind himself. On the way home he threw the house keys out of his van window.

It had been, so easy.

That was the start.

From there and on every job, Tony started to saunter around and 'stumble' onto things. He would find out what sort of rich pickings the customers owned and where they were kept. He was surprised how similar people were when it came to hiding their valuables, especially their money. The bottom of the wardrobe was a good old favourite, normally something hidden in a boot or a shoe. Or the sock drawer, for some reason people thought that no one would ever think of looking for something wrapped inside an old sock in the back of a drawer. Sometimes money was left in the pocket of a tatty old jacket, once again in the back of the wardrobe. That was an obvious one. Why on earth would you want to keep a worn old jacket? Wads of money, wrapped in plastic bags and left in the fridge freezer was another good one. No one would ever think of looking in there, would they? Strangely, a woman's preference seemed to be behind the bottom drawer of some cupboard or other. It was usually some jewellery that their husband's weren't aware of. Whereas men it seemed, favoured the loft or the garage. So many times there was money hidden in the bottom of a toolbox, surely the only place in the house where their wives wouldn't bother to look.

People always left keys lying around, which meant that Tony could pinch them, have copies made and then return the originals the next day. People would also write down the numbers of their burglar alarms in the strangest of places, but Tony could always find them. Sometimes they would even tell him the alarm number 'just in case' they were out. And they would of course tell him about the key under the plant pot or the doormat. And why not?

Another easy touch was 'the holidays'. People were always so keen to talk about their holidays and where they were going for two weeks, and when. Oh definitely, yes tell Tony McCall when your house would be empty for two weeks. That one would work every time.

And that was how it was done. Tony would learn the family's routine and then would finish the job and leave. But a couple of months later he would return. People didn't readily change their habits and Tony knew that. He always left it for two or three months so that there would never be any suspicion. If he'd returned a week or two later the police would check on everyone who'd had access to the house. They would put two and two together and look to the builders as the possible link. So Tony would always wait and bide his time.

If ever Tony McCall stole somebody's valuable jewellery, he had to find a way to sell it.

And he'd found someone.

He'd discovered Freddy Pope, a pawnbroker who ran a shop in one of Manchester's rougher districts. Pope's pawnbroker's shop had always been highly illegal, the police knew all about it of course, but when it came to Freddy Pope they could never seem to make anything stick.

Freddy's little trick was that when anything at all 'dodgy' arrived at his shop, he would move it on and move it on quickly. So whenever the police came to search his premises they never found a thing. Very frustrating for them, very profitable for Freddy.

Tony McCall would call in to see Freddy Pope whenever he had something interesting or valuable to get rid of. Freddy paid decent prices and wasn't over greedy. 'Little and often' was Freddy's view on things, and that motto kept his highly illegal little enterprise quietly and successfully profitable.

Jenny McCall, Tony's wife, had one slight problem.

She just couldn't understand where the money was coming from. Or maybe she could.

Over the last several months their lifestyle had changed somewhat. Her husband suddenly seemed to always have some money. They had meals out and had even talked about a holiday in Majorca. But more importantly than that, they were no longer renting a house.

Earlier that year they had finally managed to buy their first house. Jenny had scoured the property pages in the local papers for what seemed forever. But suddenly, she'd found something that appeared to be a bargain. A house on the nearby Meadows Estate had come up for sale and at a reduced price. The couple who owned it were emigrating to Australia and their visa application required that they had to move out there within the next six months. Failing that, their visa would be cancelled. Time was running out, the couple were desperate and so was Jenny really. This house could be her golden opportunity, she had always wanted a proper home for little Barry.

Jenny had sat down with Tony and they'd discussed things and then they went off to look at the house. Jenny loved it. It was the house she had always wanted.

It was fairly new, apparently it had only been built four or five years ago, but most of all there was a lovely garden at the back. It would be somewhere for Barry to play.

They agreed a price with the owners and shook hands on the deal. Then Tony and Jenny went off to their building society to sort out a mortgage. They had an account there so it shouldn't have really been a problem really.

They were immediately refused.

Since Tony had never had a record of his true income, there was no real proof of his earnings. Money came and went out of their building society account, naturally, and then there was Jenny's regular wage going in too, but the figures really didn't add up. Their joint earnings were considered 'a little vague'.

However it was the nineties and getting a mortgage was becoming easier. Plus the fact that the young man to whom they had spoken was desperate to earn his bonus, because he too had a house to buy. So he informed Tony and Jenny that if they could put down a 'decent' deposit, he would then sort them something out. When they asked how much the deposit would be, he told them that they would require six thousand pounds. Tony gasped and Jenny almost burst into tears.

They left the building society with Tony telling the young man that he would 'see what he could do'. When they got outside Jenny could have hit him. How ridiculous. Where on earth would they get six thousand pounds? At that moment, Jenny McCall would have had a problem finding even six hundred pounds.

They had an argument and then went home. Tony then went to the pub.

As he sat there with a pint of beer in the corner of his local 'tavern', Tony McCall had time to think. It was time for him to get organised.

Six months previously, the building firm that Tony had been working for at the time had been contracted to build an extension on a rather grand house. The house was owned, surprisingly, by a car dealer. The owner was a bit of a flash bastard in Tony's eyes, always arriving in some posh Mercedes or Jaguar, and sometimes in a Porsche that the dealer always struggled to get in or out of.

Tony had of course perused the house and he'd discovered a steel safe in the loft. Then he'd found a key in a drawer in the car dealer's office desk that he was sure belonged to the safe. The only problem was that he'd never had the opportunity to try the key to see if it fitted. When Tony had finally finished the plastering on the extension, his work complete and he was obviously no longer needed. But the thought of what could be in that safe stuck in Tony McCall's head. Two months later he'd returned during the day. He parked his van away from the house and waited. He watched as the car dealer's wife finally left for the hairdressers or wherever and then he waited another twenty minutes. Finally he got out of his van, but before he made his way to the house he took a bucket out of the back of the van and put a number of tools in it. He then wandered around to the back of the house, looking for a loose window or an unlocked door. Then suddenly he heard a voice.

'Excuse me. Can I help you?'

Tony spun around.

It was the lady from next door. She had come outside to put some rubbish in her bin and had spotted Tony over the fence.

Tony had to think and think quickly.

'Oh hello there.' he replied heartily, 'how are you doing?' he then asked her.

This greeting slightly confused the woman. Tony was speaking to her as though he knew her.

Tony walked casually towards her but stopped before getting too close.

'I've just called back,' he continued, 'our firm built the extension. We've left some tools here, I've just come to pick them up,' and with that he held up the bucket.

'Oh I see,' said the lady. It seemed reasonable enough.

'I've just been looking inside,' he said, 'It looks lovely now it's decorated. They've done a good job.'

'Yes it's very nice,' the neighbour replied, 'Well, they can certainly afford it,' she said, and she gave Tony a knowing look. It was her way of telling Tony that the car dealer was not only a flash bastard, he was a rich bastard too.

'It's alright for some,' Tony laughed as he strategically walked away.

'Bye love.' he called out.

'Bye bye,' she replied pleasantly.

An hour later she'd forgotten all about Tony McCall.

But that little comment 'they can afford it', had stuck in Tony's head.

And now he suddenly needed some money to buy a house. And fast.

So he made a decision to return to the car dealer's house once more. He actually went back there several times, and always at night. He would sit there for hours, watching and waiting and thinking.

Then Saturday night arrived and it was perfect. Tony watched the 'flash bastard' and his wife drive off in their huge, silver grey Mercedes Benz. They were going out for the night.

Tony sat there for almost an hour, just in case. Then he got out of his van and he grabbed the bucket which contained his tools. There was a crowbar, a hammer, a screwdriver and a torch. He went around to the back of the house and jemmied open the patio door. Once he was inside, he quickly went to the desk in the car dealer's office and found the all important key, it was still lying there in the drawer. He then went upstairs to the loft door. He flipped it open and drew down the wooden ladder. Once he'd climbed into the loft he quickly went over to the safe and inserted the key into the lock, and lo and behold, it opened.

Tony looked inside. It contained envelopes and paperwork and also some jewellery. There were three or four expensive rings, all in their boxes, one of which was a stunning sapphire and diamond. There was also a longer box which contained an emerald and diamond necklace, and that too was beautiful.

In the bottom of the safe there was a large blue canvas bag, Tony opened it and then shone his torch inside. For a moment he just stared at the contents. There were bundles of money, mostly twenty pound notes, and all tied with elastic bands. There must have been ten thousand pounds.

Tony had to stop himself from shaking. He immediately threw the jewellery into the canvas bag with the money and he got out of the house as quickly as possible without being seen by anybody. As he drove off he had to calm himself down and contain the urge to speed away. Getting stopped by the police or possibly crashing the car would have been an act of total stupidity.

But Tony managed to arrive home safe and sound. He went straight upstairs and hid the canvas bag in the bottom of his wardrobe. Where else?

The next day Tony didn't bother to go to work. His excuse to Jenny was that he had gone back to work the previous evening to finish off a job, and he'd had to work late, which in a strange sort of way was the truth.

Jenny left the house taking little Barry to school and then she went straight to work at the supermarket. As soon as he heard the door slam, Tony leapt out of bed. Even though he'd not slept well that night, he was wide awake. He immediately took the canvas bag out of the wardrobe and tipped the contents onto the bed. He couldn't help but laugh out loud.

Bingo! He'd cracked the bloody jackpot.

He put the jewellery to one side and counted the money. In that one singular moment, Tony McCall was actually having the best time of his entire life.

Twelve thousand pounds. Twelve thousand unbelievable pounds, and Tony McCall rolled back onto his bed and looked up at the ceiling and laughed uncontrollably.

After twenty minutes and a couple of cups of coffee, Tony began to think things out.

He had to get rid of the money. Well, he had to get rid of some of it. If Jenny found it she would definitely ask questions. He couldn't just leave all that money lying about in the house. They might get robbed.

An hour later he set off for town. He walked into the building society and deposited eight thousand pounds into their joint account and then spoke to the young man there and told him to proceed with the mortgage. He then went around to the estate agents who were selling the house on the Meadows Estate and told them to take it off the market. He and Jenny had a mortgage in place and they intended to buy the house. The estate agent then rang the owners who in turn were highly delighted.

Tony McCall walked back home a happier man. He felt that he had done the right thing. With the eight thousand in their building society account the mortgage was sorted, the extra two thousand would pay for the solicitor and all the other extras. It turned out that their mortgage repayments would actually be less than the rent they were presently paying, so another result for Tony McCall. He considered himself a bit of a financial genius. It was all a piece of cake really. Besides which, he still had four thousand pounds to play with. And he still had all that jewellery to sell.

When Jenny came home from work that night, Tony told her his big surprise. They were going to buy the house on the Meadows Estate, the house that she really wanted. However instead of throwing herself into his arms as he expected, Jenny just stood there, she was rather taken aback. When she asked him about the money, he told her about the eight thousand pounds that he'd deposited into their account.

Jenny was absolutely staggered, and she immediately asked Tony where the money had come from. He told her that he'd had a big win on the horses. Somebody in the know had put him onto a winner, a dead 'cert'.

Jenny didn't believe him, not one bit. But what could she do?

And she really did want that house.

In the end, she'd kept quiet. They moved into their new house, and all was well for the time being. But she didn't trust Tony, she didn't know what he'd been up to but she had a good idea. She had always known he was a thief and would steal anything, it was a weakness. Jenny would have to keep her eye on her husband, because things just didn't add up.

But life goes on and time went by.
However, Tony McCall was about to make two colossal mistakes.
First of all he got greedy. And secondly, he acquired a gun.

After he'd robbed the car dealer, Tony had gone to Freddy Pope's pawn shop over in Manchester to get rid of the stolen jewellery. Freddy Pope was a fat, balding man who always wore a grubby white shirt with an even grubbier off white vest underneath it. Freddy's eyes widened when he saw the stolen jewellery. There was a profit there for him, definitely. And now it was all down to a matter of negotiation. He and Tony started to barter. Tony of course was clueless and totally out of his depth, and Freddy Pope of course knew that. In the past Tony McCall had brought in the odd ring and the odd trinket, but never anything like this. Finally, clever Freddy offered Tony half the amount he would have normally offered, and stupid Tony McCall almost agreed to it.
'Come on Freddy,' he said, 'You can do a bit better than that.'
Tony would have said the same whatever Freddy had offered him, because he always had.
'I'll give you another fifty pounds,' Freddy said to him, just as a gesture really, 'It's the best I can do. I've got to shift this stuff you know, and quickly. I can't leave this sort of gear just lying around. What if the police turn up?'
The mention of the law cooled Tony's ardour somewhat. Really he was in no position to argue. And in any case, he did have all the other stolen money at home.
Once last try.
'Can't you give me a little bit more Freddy? Come on, anything.'
'Anything' was probably the worst word that Tony McCall could have ever said.
Freddy considered things for a moment and then stepped back and looked under his counter.

'Since you seem to be going on to bigger things Tony, you might need this.'

From under his counter Freddy produced a gun, it was a revolver. He put it on top of the counter and slid it over to Tony, who just stared at it.

'Sometimes you need protection,' said Freddy, 'Wave this in somebody's face and they'll stop chasing you.'

Tony was still looking at the gun, but what Freddy said made sense. He had always had a fear of getting caught. Tony wasn't a big man by any stretch of the imagination and if he was ever apprehended he was always going to have problems trying to escape.

Then a strange thought crossed his mind.

'Have you got any bullets for it?' he suddenly asked.

Freddy Pope frowned. He wasn't too sure about handing over any bullets. He'd only intended to give Tony the gun.

'Come on Freddy,' said Tony, 'If I've got a gun, I want to have a go at shooting it,' and then he added, 'There's a forest near me, I can set up a target.'

Freddy saw the logic. He once again reached under his counter and produced a box of shells.

'Be careful with these,' he said, '...very careful.'

'Don't worry Freddy, I will,' Tony replied, and the deal was done.

Freddy Pope handed over a couple of thick wads of money and Tony McCall was a happy man.

So was Freddy Pope, and of the two of them Freddy was probably the happier. The deal would make him a lot of money when he sent the jewellery down to London the next day.

As Tony left the shop Freddy Pope called after him.

'And don't shoot anybody,' he said light-heartedly.

Tony McCall should have listened.

So the McCall family had moved into their new home. All went well and Tony returned to work, eventually. Well he had to. When Jenny once again started to question him about where the money was coming from, he decided to return to plastering. Once he was back at work he had all the excuses he needed.

One day, seemingly out of the blue, Tony received a phone call from a firm of builders that he had previously worked for. They'd been contracted as part of a team to undertake a huge renovation job and they needed skilled labour. The contract would be for three or four months, maybe even longer. Bricklayers, joiners and decorators, and of course good plasterers, were all needed fairly urgently. Tony listened. The wages were good, very good in fact. The job would start in a couple of week's time and would he be available?

Yes he would.

The contract was for the complete renovation of a huge rundown mansion somewhere in Cheshire. A place called Worsley Manor.

Alan and Joyce Cunningham had big plans for their new home. Well, Joyce certainly had. Alan as usual, stood back and let his wife take control of the whole project. Joyce had harangued the architect and beat him into submission over every last detail of the renovation. She had been quite fastidious over every little thing and, in her eyes, quite rightly.

Worsley Manor was going to be their family home, so Joyce naturally wanted everything to be perfect. The plans were finally drawn up and she had eventually approved them, something that gave the architect a huge sigh of relief. Dealing with Mrs Joyce Cunningham was an experience that he didn't particularly want to repeat.

Worsley Manor was to be completely remodelled and renovated from top to bottom. Money was obviously no problem. Joyce Cunningham knew that her husband would let her spend whatever she wanted, and in truth, that was because Alan Cunningham wanted a first class job too. The Cunningham's never skimped on the things they valued.

Joyce had decided that they should live 'on site'. So they brought in a huge mobile home that cost a fortune. It had more amenities than any normal house, but Joyce still felt that it was rather cramped.

Their initial plan was to completely revamp the first floor of the manor. Joyce wanted to move in there as soon as possible so that she could be on hand to personally oversee the rest of the development. She was determined that no corner would be cut and that there should be no shoddy workmanship.

One of the rooms would be fitted out as a temporary kitchen and living room, so that all the facilities would be on hand. After that a couple of bedrooms were going to be made ready, along with a bathroom, and then an office for her husband. Once all of these were finished Joyce would have the three of them move in straightaway.

Young Timothy thought it was all wonderful. From the word go his mother had bought him a good pair of wellington boots and he would tramp around the place and talk to the workmen.

He had been very excited when his mother told him he could eventually have his very own pony. And once the house was finished Joyce had plans to build some extensive stabling for the horses. The architect didn't know about that yet.

Tony McCall started work at Worsley Manor on the Monday morning. He'd found the place quite easily, it was rural Cheshire and the traffic was never that bad. All he had to do was drive through a series of small towns and villages. But when he finally arrived there he was quite taken aback when he realised just how huge Worsley Manor actually was. Tony walked onto the site and met up with his foreman. The foreman in turn took him for a quick inspection around the manor so that Tony could get his bearings. Tony smiled to himself. Three to four month work, no way. It would take more like six to twelve months, easily.

And then he wondered if there would be anything for him to steal?

He smiled again. There would always be something.

Two months later and the Cunningham's living quarters on the first floor were finished, and the family decided to move in. It wasn't as big a problem as was first envisaged. Joyce Cunningham had decided that everything was to be brand new. From the large king-size bed to the large king-size kitchen table, everything was delivered directly by van from various upmarket shops and stores based anywhere between Cheshire and Manchester.

Everything from televisions to kitchen utensils, everything was bought in and brand new.

In truth, the only things that came from their house in London were their personal belongings. Clothes, shoes and books, all had to be boxed up and sent north.

Alan Cunningham had his business files, his business papers and his ledgers all transferred to his new office at Worsley Manor. And along with all that came some of the family valuables, which also included a quantity of Joyce Cunningham's jewellery.

Ten years before, when Alan and Joyce Cunningham were married, Rebecca Cunningham gave her daughter-in-law a very special wedding present. She gave Joyce her jewellery.

Rebecca Cunningham had decided that she was of an age when she didn't really need a lot of jewellery anymore and she wanted to pass it on to the family and to someone who would have the opportunity to actually wear it. There were four or five diamond rings, several stunning bracelets and brooches and a particularly beautiful pearl necklace of timeless quality. And there was also the spectacular opal ring that her husband Peter had bought her all those years ago when they were first married and living in London.

Rebecca Cunningham's beautiful jewellery had spent too many years locked away in the family safe and she had felt that it was time to let it go.

Newly married Joyce had been delighted. But when she saw the opal ring she had been overwhelmed. She too realised that the ring was more than just exceptional. It was unique.

Work was in full flow at Worsley Manor, three months in and the place was teaming with workmen. And that suited Tony McCall down to the ground. Once again he could become the inconspicuous plasterer, and once again he could become a thief.

The only problem being, that there was actually very little for Tony to steal. Worsley Manor had been empty for some time and the family had only just moved back in. After a couple of weeks a sizeable quantity of wine had been delivered and Tony started to pinch a bottle or two but nothing much more, good as it was. He felt slightly let down when he realised that there weren't going to be any deliveries of beer.

The Cunningham's didn't do beer.

There was also another problem. Tony McCall was beginning to realise the depletion of his funds. In other words, his money was running out.

Jenny had spent what he considered a small fortune on the house. Jenny McCall had wanted new things too. Along with that, Tony had become used to going out for meals and going out for more than just the odd pint of beer. There was the usual overspending at the local bookies and he had also put a deposit on a family holiday to Majorca. Jenny had decided they should go there for two weeks and not just the one. So he was faced with having to find the balance for the holiday and also the spending money.

Tony McCall had unfortunately gotten used to living slightly above his means.

He'd also got used to having what seemed like an unlimited amount of money, money that was now dwindling fast.

Money in a bag in the bottom of his wardrobe

Tony McCall was suddenly, once again having to work for his money. And that too was a problem. Tony McCall didn't like working. Tony was lazy.

Another month or so passed by. And by that time everyone on the site, including the Cunningham's themselves, had realised that the work was going to take a lot longer than was first estimated.

As was normal in the building trade, there were always a multitude of minor problems that continually hampered everyone's progress.

However the Cunningham's had resigned themselves to it. They had become quite used to it all by then. Living with twenty or thirty workmen began to seem quite normal. On most weekends the Cunningham's had started to go back down to London to give themselves a break. Nearby Manchester had excellent rail connections to London, and if they caught an express they could be back in the capital within two to three hours. In fact, Alan Cunningham had become a regular commuter, he'd quickly realised that the rail service was a lot quicker and much easier than driving all the way down south and then back again.

One afternoon Alan Cunningham was working in his makeshift office at the manor when the phone rang. He had been putting some papers into his 'newly arrived' safe and when he heard the phone he went back over to his desk to answer it.

The safe itself was brand new. It was quite large and stood nearly five feet in height. Alan had ordered it from a company in Birmingham and when it had been delivered several of the workmen had struggled to get it up the stairs and into Alan's first floor office.

The safe contained stacks of documents along with Alan Cunningham's private papers. On the top shelf were the family valuables, including his wife's jewellery. There was also several thousand pounds in cash.

As Alan Cunningham spoke on the telephone to a business associate down in London, he was flicking through some papers that appertained to the sale of some agricultural land in Kent.

If only he'd looked up.

Back on the landing and just out of sight stood Tony McCall. He had been wandering around the house and was passing the office door when he suddenly heard Alan Cunningham talking to someone. He'd naturally looked in as he walked past and it was then he'd seen the open safe.

Tony McCall stopped dead in his tracks and then he stepped back and stared. The open safe was in full view and Tony immediately saw the stacks of money.

Tony McCall felt a sudden thrill. The sight of all that money made his pulse quicken. Once again he remembered the feeling, when he'd opened the safe at the car dealer's house. It was that wonderful feeling, all that money just lying there, waiting for him.

Tony watched, and Alan Cunningham still hadn't noticed him. Then Tony saw something. The top left hand drawer in Alan Cunningham's desk was open. Maybe for no reason at all, or maybe there was a simpler explanation?

Tony McCall smiled to himself, and 'bingo'!

That would be the drawer were Alan Cunningham kept the safe key. Tony would have bet money on it, Alan Cunningham's money.

A week later Tony was once again passing the same office door, he'd started to make it a regular habit. He knew that at some time or other there would be no one there. That would be his chance to slip in there unseen. And now, here was his chance.

The office was obviously empty, the door was wide open and without even breaking stride Tony walked straight in. He immediately went over to the desk and quietly slid open the same drawer. There, right at the back of the drawer was a brand new shiny key, a key that would fit a brand new shiny safe. No doubt about it.

He quickly closed the drawer and walked straight out of the office. He immediately turned left and headed for the stairs and away.

If he'd looked right, he would have seen Joyce Cunningham staring at him.

Joyce was just walking out of the kitchen and she was annoyed. She was going to have to go to the local shop once again because this time she'd run out of milk. Joyce was making a mental list of all the other things she might need while she was there. She'd also decided to ask the local grocer if he could possibly start to deliver their groceries. She hadn't got time for all this coming and going.

As Joyce Cunningham walked out of the kitchen she suddenly looked up. There in front of her was Tony McCall. He was walking away from her and towards the stairs.

But where had he come from?

The office and the bathroom were both next to one another and both doors were open. Joyce just stood there and watched Tony McCall as he went down the stairs. She went into the office, nothing seemed amiss, but why would there be? There was nothing in there.

Then the thought suddenly struck her. That cheeky bloody plasterer had been using their bathroom. He must have been in there and used their toilet, it was obvious. Joyce went into the bathroom and instinctively flushed the loo and then sprayed bleach around the bowl.

She went back onto the landing and this time she closed the bathroom door behind her.

Joyce Cunningham suddenly decided that she would have to keep an eye on that man.

Yes she would.

Work on the manor was falling behind. They were now four months into the renovation and at the present rate of progress it looked as though it would easily take another four months, if not longer, to get anywhere near to finishing the restoration. But that was the nature of things and that was the building trade.

Unfortunately Joyce Cunningham wasn't in the building trade, never had been, and she was finding it all more and more frustrating. Every time she looked at the calendar on the wall in her husband's office she would sigh and take a considerable intake of breath.

She'd started to scowl a lot too, especially at any of the workmen who she considered weren't pulling their weight.

One of the major problems had been the damp. A decade or so of being empty and exposed to the elements had certainly taken its toll on the building. It had been decided that every single wall would have to be stripped back to the brickwork and then waterproofed and re-plastered.

It would all take time, a lot of time. And a possible part of the problem was that they were employing a plasterer who habitually took his time.

In truth, Tony McCall was actually quite a decent plasterer, but the trouble with Tony was that he wasn't over fond of his job. Then again, Tony McCall wasn't over fond of work at all, in any way, shape or form. Tony would always be the last man to arrive on the job and be the first to leave. And rather noticeably he also had the unfortunate habit of always arriving late and always disappearing early.

The term used was 'lack of commitment'.

The plastering seemed to be taking forever. Joyce Cunningham was aware of that and she was also aware that the plasterer never seemed to be doing his job. Every time she went to inspect Tony's work he seemed to have 'gone off' somewhere or other. He was always wandering about carrying an empty bucket.

Suddenly, Tony McCall wasn't invisible anymore.

Suddenly, Tony was getting noticed.

After another three weeks of not a lot being accomplished, Joyce Cunningham threw up her arms in despair. On the Friday lunch of that week, Joyce went to the foreman to have a word with him. She told him in no uncertain terms that she wanted the plasterer sacking. The foreman had raised an eyebrow, good plasterers were hard to find. However, even he'd noticed the lack of progress. He'd tried to push Tony but it was hard to get a full day's work out of a man who came to work late and then went home early.

So later that afternoon, before Tony sloped off home again, the foreman took him to one side and gave him the bad news.

Tony was indignant. He was sacked at a moment's notice, paid up and asked to leave.

When he'd asked 'why', the foreman just replied, 'Boss's orders, Mrs Cunningham pays the bills and she's not happy with your work.'

Tony took that as a personal insult and he stormed off to his van and drove away.

The foreman just shook his head. He wouldn't be using Tony McCall again.

But Tony McCall was angry.

As he drove home that afternoon he realised he had problems. Firstly, he was suddenly unemployed, and secondly, he'd run out of money. The canvas bag in the bottom of his wardrobe was finally empty. The last hundred pounds had been spent at the bookies on a horse that was as worthless as Tony himself.

But now Tony was seething. That stuck up Cunningham bitch had made the foreman give him the sack. What was he going to do? He would find another job of course but all that took time and of course he would have to work a week in hand so he would be once again waiting for his wages. Tony McCall needed money, and he needed it straight away. He had bills to pay, and there was the holiday and whatever spending money he was going to need. He'd also got used to leading a slightly different lifestyle. Going to the pub regularly and meals at nice restaurants every weekend had become the accepted habit.

And what was he going to tell Jenny? She thought that they were comfortable in their new home and their new life, and suddenly it was all coming to an end. Tony was going to struggle just to pay the mortgage.

He kept asking himself why he had stupidly promised Jenny and Barry that damn holiday.

After another two weeks things weren't going much better. Tony had managed to find work but it was only a short contract, a couple of terraced houses that needed plastering. Tony had managed to drag the work out, it took him ten days to finish a job which could have easily been done in a week. Then he was only given part of his wages because the builder was waiting to be paid too. It was all typical of the building trade

Tony McCall needed cash and quickly. And at the back of his mind he knew where he could find money, a lot of money.

Back at Worsley Manor there was the safe and it was full of money, and Tony knew exactly were the key to that safe was kept. It had always been in his thoughts, always. Tony knew that at some point he would return to the Manor, he knew he would. He couldn't resist it, and maybe he just couldn't help himself. He was a habitual thief and the burglary he had done at the car dealer's house had been like a drug to his addiction. It was that wonderful feeling of getting hold of a great deal of money and fast.

Normally Tony would have waited two or three months before he returned to rob someone, but Worsley Manor was different. At Worsley Manor there were twenty or thirty men all working there at any one time. Tony had left the site almost a month before and by now he would have been replaced and forgotten. There was no doubt about it.

Tony made up his mind. He knew what he had to do.

That weekend he drove over to Worsley Manor, it was a Saturday night. When he got there he turned off the main road and drove slowly down the drive to the house. He immediately switched off the van's lights so as not to draw anyone's attention. Tony knew that the Cunningham family often went back down to London for the weekend and that the partially renovated property was normally left empty. When he arrived at the house he noticed the first floor lights were on. He could only presume, quite rightly, that the family were there too.

Tony slowly turned his van around and returned home. It wasn't a problem, there would always be next week.

In the back of Tony's van was his bucket of tools, a crowbar, a hammer a screwdriver and his small torch. There was also his gun.

The next weekend he returned, again on the Saturday night and once again when he got there the first floor lights were on. The family were obviously in residence, so he turned his van around again and then drove home. Once again, not a problem, Tony could wait. He could always wait, wait and bide his time. That was what he did.

When he drove down the drive on the following weekend, all the lights were switched off, every single one of them. As Tony parked his van in a dark corner of the site his pulse began to quicken. It was the thought of that safe, and all that money.

On that particular weekend it was planned for the Cunningham family to visit London and spend a few days there. One of Joyce's oldest friends was having a birthday party, and Alan Cunningham had an important business meeting on the Monday morning which he needed to attend. After that, and with a bit of luck and good timing, the three of them could then enjoy a good lunch at their favourite restaurant before finally getting on the late afternoon train and returning to Cheshire.

But it was not to be. Joyce and Timothy had both started with a cold, a heavy cold. Joyce felt dreadful and young Timothy wasn't much better. After a lot of deliberation it was decided that Alan should go on his own. He would have to go to the birthday party, which would be full of people that he wasn't very fond of, and then on the Monday morning he would attend the business meeting and speak to people who were rather more interesting.

Alan had waved them both goodbye as he set off late in the afternoon, leaving Joyce feeling rather despondent. So after a miserable dinner and with both of them feeling grim, Joyce and Timothy had gone to bed early.

Tony McCall stepped quietly out of his van. He collected his bucket of tools and put on his leather gloves. Then he stuck the gun into his belt.

He remembered Freddy Pope's words, 'Wave this in somebody's face and they'll stop chasing you'.

He liked that, because there was always the possibility of someone catching him, always.

The thought of getting caught was his worst nightmare, getting caught and going back into prison.

He would lose everything, absolutely everything.

He walked straight into the building, and of course everything was open. It was after all a building site. Tony made his way easily through the house because he knew the place like the back of his hand. He then silently climbed the stairs up to the first floor. All was clear.

Tony took out his torch, he had to find the right door. It was next to the bathroom but he soon found it. He turned the door handle and quietly walked into the office. There wasn't even a lock. He closed the door behind him and then went over to the desk and opened the drawer. Right at the back of the drawer was the key, the shiny new safe key.

Tony once again smiled. These people almost deserved to get robbed.

Then he felt a moment of anxiety. What if he was wrong? What if this wasn't the key after all? He quickly picked it up, went over to the safe and inserted the key into the lock. The key went in smoothly and as he turned it the lock's mechanism suddenly clicked open.

Bingo again.

He pulled the heavy safe door open and shone his torch inside.

It was all there, just as he remembered it. It was all there in front of him, stacked on the top shelf, bundles of lovely money. It was all going to be so easy. Tony had to stop himself from laughing out loud.

He was back in clover. He was back in the money and with it all his problems would disappear. The mortgage, the holiday and the return to his comfortable lifestyle, everything would be solved.

Tony put the torch between his teeth so as to leave his hands free, and then he took his faithful old canvas bag out of his jacket pocket and started to fill it with the cash.

There was ten thousand pounds.

Tony justified his actions with the assumption that this was just spending money for the condescending bloody Cunningham family, and that toffee-nosed bitch of a woman.

There was no remorse, no guilt, none whatsoever. Why should there be?

Once he'd put all of the money in his bag he looked back into the safe. There were some boxes in there too, jewellery boxes. Tony had a flashing image of greedy Freddy Pope and even though he had the torch wedged between his teeth he still managed to smile. He reached for the nearest box and opened it, then he angled his head with the torch so that he could see what was inside.

He couldn't believe his eyes. The bright torchlight shone down onto a ring. The ring had large coloured opal in its centre which shone bright blue and gold and red. The stone was surrounded by diamonds that seemed to make it come alive in the darkness. For a brief moment Tony was mesmerized by the sheer beauty of it. He had to blink as he returned to his senses, and then he closed the box and threw it into his bag. He turned back to the safe to see what else was inside.

Then suddenly he heard it.

He heard something, a sound, a noise. It was the door handle.

Somebody had turned the handle and was about to open the office door. As Tony shot around to see who it was the torch flew from between his teeth. It bounced onto the hard wooden floor and immediately went out.

Tony McCall was left there, kneeling in the darkness. It was pitch black and he was trapped.

Joyce and Timothy Cunningham had gone to bed early because they were both feeling ill. Later that evening young Timothy woke up feeling quite poorly, his chest and throat were rather sore and his head felt muzzy, but he'd woken up because he needed to go to the toilet. It was dark by then and Timothy was feeling rather muddled. He got of bed and made his way to the bedroom door. Though it was dark he instinctively knew where the door was, and because his head was hurting didn't want to turn on the bright light. He stepped onto the landing and slowly made his way to the toilet. In the darkness he mistakenly walked past the bathroom and opened the door next to it, the door to the office.

Timothy stood there in the dark, unaware of just where he was. He didn't feel well at all.

Then he heard a man's voice call out, but he didn't understand what was happening.

At that moment his chest suddenly erupted and he let out a barking cough.

Tony McCall pulled his gun from his belt.

He was in complete darkness. He'd heard the door handle turn and then he heard the office door open, and then there was silence. Somebody was there and Tony realised that the house wasn't empty and at any moment someone would switch on the light and find him robbing the place. He envisaged the struggle, there would be a fight and there would be violence as someone tried to apprehend him. He wanted to get away and he wanted to keep the money.

Then he'd remembered the gun and Freddy Pope's advice.

Tony pointed the revolver in the direction of the door.

'I've got a gun...don't come any nearer,' he called out.

But there was no answer, just silence.

Tony felt his finger on the trigger. Maybe he should fire the gun into the air, a warning shot to let whoever it was know that he meant business. Tony listened, waiting for the inevitable.

Whoever was there, they were going to attack him, he was sure of it.

Suddenly there was a loud noise. And in that absolute instant, Tony thought it was the shout of an angry man coming to attack him. He pulled the trigger and the gun fired, and after a moment's echo there was silence again.

What was the noise?

It was just the sound of a small boy coughing.

The landing light suddenly came on and there was a scream.

Tony stared into the doorway which was suddenly lit up by the landing light. Lying there in a pool of blood was a young boy. The back of his head had been completely blown off.

Joyce Cunningham heard the shot and immediately leapt out of bed. She knew instinctively that something was wrong, but in the back of her mind she thought that something electrical had blown up. Her first thought was for her and Timothy's safety, there could be the possibility of fire. She dashed out of her bedroom and immediately switched on the landing light. As she looked down the landing she saw Timothy's body lying there on the floor...and she screamed.

She dashed towards her son, she could only see Timothy's legs and his body because he had fallen into the office. When she reached the door she was completely aghast at what she saw. Her young son was face down in a large pool of vivid, red blood. The back of his head was entirely blown away. As she looked down at him she went sick to the pit of her stomach. Timothy was dead. There could be no doubt about it.

She just moaned and staggered slightly as she stared down at her son. She was in shock. What had happened to him?

Then she heard a noise and looked up. Standing there in the half light was Tony McCall, it was the plasterer she had sacked and he was holding a gun. He had just shot and killed her darling boy.

'You...' she screamed...'You bastard.'

And in a frenzy of anger, hatred and despair she launched herself at her child's murderer.

Tony McCall had shot his gun into the darkness, not knowing who his would-be assailant was. It was only when the landing light came on that he saw the body of young Timothy lying there. He'd just killed the boy. Tony went into complete panic, he hadn't meant to pull the trigger, he didn't know that it was Timothy who had been standing there.

How was he to know?

All the excuses in the world, but it could never justify what he had just done.

Joyce Cunningham had run into the room. She'd looked down at her son and then across at Tony McCall and she'd screamed something at him. Then she ran to attack him.

Tony pulled the trigger twice. The two bullets hit Joyce Cunningham square in the chest and knocked her to the floor before she even had a chance to get near him.

She too died in an instant.

Tony McCall stood there for a moment, almost paralysed. Then he suddenly realized what he had just done. He'd killed two people. He had killed a woman and a child.

What on earth had he been thinking of?

He staggered for a moment and then steadied himself. He had to get away, had to get away.

He threw his gun into the canvas bag that held the money and the ring. To steal the rest of the jewellery would have been a waste of time, it would all be far too hot to handle. Tony stuffed the bag into the bucket with the rest of his tools. He was already beginning to panic. He quickly stepped over the two bodies. He couldn't bear to look at them. Then he ran down the landing and almost threw himself down the stairs. He quickly got out of the building and sprinted towards his van. He was running so that he wouldn't get caught, but then it suddenly struck him. There must be no one else there. If Mr Cunningham had been there, he would have become involved too. He stopped running, and in the stillness Tony took a deep breath as he got to his van. But he was still shaking and he tried to calm himself down as he stood there in the dark.

He had to calm down. Breathe and calm down. He got into the van and he put his bucket of tools on the floor in front of the passenger seat. Then he started the van, but as he set off he immediately stalled the engine.

He stopped for a moment.

'Calm down...Calm yourself down.' He was almost shouting at himself.

He set off once more and then stalled the van again.

He sat there and counted to twenty. His hands were shaking. They didn't even feel like his own hands any more. He counted twenty again and then set off once more.

He drove home carefully, never more than thirty five miles an hour. All the way home he kept reliving the night's events. The boy with the back of his head blown away. And the look on Joyce Cunningham face as he'd shot her. What had he done? God, what had he done?

Tony McCall had just become a murderer. He'd just murdered two innocent people, a mother and her young son. Two lives ended, irreversibly.

When Tony McCall finally arrived home it was late. He sat in his van for a while, trying to think things out. He would need a plan. He took the canvas bag out of the bucket and went into the house. His wife Jenny was in bed asleep by then, and so he crept into their bedroom and quietly tucked the bag down at the back of the wardrobe.

But Jenny stirred, he'd woken her up.

'Where've you been?' she asked him. She was tired and she yawned sleepily.

'Err, just sorting out some work with a bloke. We ended up having a drink.'

Nothing new there then, and Jenny rolled over and went back to sleep.

Tony went back downstairs. He was going to put the kettle on but then thought better of it. Instead, he reached for the whiskey bottle.

The next morning Jenny McCall woke up in bed on her own, again nothing new.

She went downstairs to make herself a cup of tea, only to find her husband collapsed on the living room floor. There was an empty bottle of whiskey on the floor at the side of him.

She shook her head in disgust and asked herself once again 'why' did she put up with Tony's antics. He was an idiot, an idiot who was lazy and unreliable.

He was also something else, he was a thief. Jenny never wanted to admit that to herself, it was something she had always turned a blind eye to.

But she knew.

Jenny made Barry his breakfast. When the young lad came downstairs, like most children he immediately switched on the television. He wanted to watch the children's programmes.

And that woke Tony up.

He lay there for a moment, his head was raging with alcohol and he was still half drunk. He closed his eyes and he tried to think. Then his memory began to work, and he suddenly remembered the events of the night before. He had murdered two people. He'd shot and killed them.

Then he remembered the bag of money that he'd stashed upstairs in the wardrobe. The money and the opal ring, and the gun.

Tony got up off the floor and propped himself on the settee. He could hear Jenny banging about in the kitchen and talking to Barry.

He called out to her, 'Make me a cup of coffee, love.'

There was a silence

'Jenny' he called out again.

'Alright, alright.' she replied. There was an edge to her voice but Tony decided to ignore it.

He picked up the television remote and switched the channel. Barry's cartoons weren't helping things at all. Then suddenly he went rigid. The news channel appeared and there on the screen in front of him was an aerial shot taken from a helicopter. It was flying over somewhere that Tony McCall knew very well. It was Worsley Manor.

The television newsreader was commenting on the savage murder and tragic death of Joyce Cunningham and her son Timothy, who were members of the wealthy Cunningham family. Both had been shot, apparently during a robbery. The police would only say that a large amount of money and some jewellery had been stolen from the house. However, they were following a possible lead.

Tony sat there in shock as another close up of the house appeared on the screen.

'Here's your coffee,' said Jenny.

Tony's head shot around in surprise. He was wide eyed. He had forgotten about the coffee, he had forgotten about a lot of things. At that moment his mind was well and truly back at Worsley Manor as he remembered what had happened.

He immediately turned the television off.

Jenny looked at him strangely.

'Here, here's your coffee,' she said again.

He just stared up at her.

'For Christ's sake Tony. Do you want it or not?'

Jenny was now getting more than slightly annoyed.

'Err, yes, thanks,' he finally replied. And as he took the hot coffee from her his hands shook and some of the brew spilled from the cup and onto the carpet.

'Oh bloody hell, sorry,' he said to her.

Jenny looked down at her husband. He was still half drunk, his breath reeked of whisky and his hands were shaking. Beads of sweat were forming on his forehead and Jenny stared at him in disgust.

'You're a waste of space Tony,' she said to him. And then she turned to go back into the kitchen. But something wasn't just right. She'd seen him drunk before, many times, and they had always gone through their same routine. Tony McCall was quite verbal and aggressive after he'd been drinking, and they usually ended up having a big row and not speaking for several days. But this morning was different. There was no verbal abuse and no nasty replies. Not even any anger, none at all. She turned around again to look at him. He was just sitting there. He'd turned the T.V off and he was still staring at her.

'Are you alright Tony?' she said him. But he just turned away. He couldn't make eye contact.

Jenny shrugged and went back into the kitchen to make sure that Barry was eating his breakfast. As she closed the door behind her, she heard the television come back on again.

She put a couple of slices of bread into the toaster as she thought about Tony. Something was definitely wrong. Maybe he was seeing another woman. Maybe that was it. Well he had been out late, and of course he was drunk.

Jenny gave that some thought. If he was seeing somebody else, did she care? Actually, no.

The problem would only arise if it went a step further and he decided to leave her. What would happen then, and who would pay the mortgage? She bit her lip. She needed the bastard, she knew she did.

The toaster clicked and two slices of toast popped up. Against her better judgement she buttered a slice of toast and put it onto a small plate and then took it into the living room.

Tony was still watching the news, once again the report on the murders at Worsley Manor. Once again the newsreader was repeating the police statement 'A large amount of money and some jewellery had been stolen from the house. However, they were following a possible lead'.

Tony just stared at the screen. 'A possible lead' ...what possible lead? He tried to think about what the newsreader had said and what the police had meant by it. He didn't understand and this damn hangover wasn't helping. He couldn't think straight.

As soon as Jenny opened the door, he turned the television off again and shot her a look.

'I've made you some toast,' she said to him, in a more compromising tone. He just stood up and shook his head.

'I don't want any bloody toast,' he said coldly, and he turned away and walked out of the room and went upstairs.

Jenny stood there and watched him go. She didn't understand what was going on.

But she did wonder.

Tony went into the bedroom and opened the wardrobe door. He got onto his knees and reached into the canvas bag. The money was all there, along with the box containing the ring and the gun. He took out two hundred pounds and stuffed the notes into his back pocket. Then he pushed the canvas bag into the back of the wardrobe once again.

He went back downstairs, put on his jacket and then walked out of the house.

As the front door opened Jenny called out to ask where he was going. But Tony just slammed the door behind him.

'Bastard' she shouted angrily, but there was no reply.

Tony was going to the pub. He needed to get away from the house and he needed to think. He'd always worked things out while he was sitting in the pub. It was without doubt the best place to be, on his own and with a pint of beer, always. He walked over to check his van, it was just a routine really. He had things on his mind, 'The police were following a possible lead'. What the hell did that mean?

He checked his van and he and put his bucket of tools into the back. He tipped everything out onto the floor of the van, his crowbar, the hammer, the screwdriver. No gun of course. That would have been stupid.

He slammed the van door shut and walked off to the pub. A few drinks would cure his hangover.

Young Barry McCall finished his breakfast and with the 'okay' from his mother, he went back into the living room and switched on the television. He put the cartoons on once again and settled back whilst his mother got on with her usual chores. Jenny washed the pots and cleaned up the kitchen and then prepared the roast for their dinner. She then went upstairs and made the bed and generally tidied up. She came back downstairs with the washing basket and then filled the washing machine. That done, she put the kettle on and proceeded to make herself a cup of tea. While she waited for the kettle to boil, she sat down at the kitchen table and wondered just what her husband was up to. There was definitely something wrong.

She considered all things and finally decided that it must definitely be another woman.

The kettle boiled and she made the cup of tea. Then she looked into the living room to see if Barry wanted something to drink, but he'd disappeared upstairs. So Jenny grabbed a couple of biscuits and along with her cup of tea went into the living room and sat down on the settee. She decided that she'd done enough. She needed a rest, and why not? After all, that bastard was in a pub somewhere, probably with his fancy piece.

She took a sip of her tea and picked up the television remote. The cartoons had finished and there was another kiddie's programme on with some idiot dressed up as a duck. She clicked over to another channel and the news came on. There was something about a murder somewhere, and a robbery, Jenny wasn't taking much notice really. She was wondering if she should go to the pub and find her husband, and then smack his new little slut in the face. Maybe not.

Suddenly she heard the words 'Worsley Manor'. The words caught her attention. 'Worsley Manor'. Where had she heard about Worsley Manor before?

Then she remembered. Worsley Manor. That was the place where Tony had been working about a month ago. She continued to watch the news as she wondered what had gone on there. And as she watched the television and listened to the reporter talking about the two murders and the robbery, Jenny's stomach began to tighten with a feeling of dread.

She sat there for a moment as the reporter repeated the horrific events, a mother and her son brutally murdered, two innocents slaughtered.

Jenny carefully put down her cup of tea and stood up. Then she went up the stairs and into their bedroom. She walked over to the wardrobe and took a deep breath, and then she opened the wardrobe door. She knelt down and reached into the bottom of the wardrobe, and found the canvas bag. She took it out and emptied the contents onto their bed.

There were stacks of money, thousands of pounds, and a jewellery box and a gun.

Jenny stared down in disbelief. Strangely, the first thing she did was pick up the gun and examine it. The barrel smelled like a spent firework, and she realised it must have been fired recently. She dropped it back onto the bed in dismay. She then picked up the jewellery box and opened it, and she blinked. There inside was the most beautiful ring that she had ever seen in her life. It was stunningly beautiful, and at any other time Jenny would have loved to try it on. But no, not now. Because she now realised that her husband had killed a woman and her young son for that ring, and for that money. He'd murdered them both. She closed the box and threw it back onto the bed. She looked at the money lying there on their bed, and she just stared at it. All that bloody money.

Jenny turned and sat on the edge of the bed. She put her head in her hands and began to cry. Her husband had murdered an innocent woman and her child. That little boy, he'd been the same age as their own son, Barry.

For a while, Jenny just stared down at the floor.

Maybe she should have seen this coming. Maybe she should have put a stop to it all before it went too far. Because Jenny McCall had always known about her husband. She'd always known that Tony was a thief, always.

When Jenny had first started going out with Tony McCall, one of her best friends had taken her to one side and told her about Tony having been in prison. Apparently he had been in there twice. Her friend had known somebody who knew somebody else and whatever.

Jenny however, rather naively believed that she could somehow change him, and anyway it had all been in the past and everyone deserved a second chance. Tony had been a bit of a charmer at the time, and Jenny had enjoyed the passion. It was only when she'd become pregnant and married him that she had discovered how lazy and useless he was.

They had been poor from the word go really, and Jenny always had to be careful with their hard earned cash. Then every so often, Tony would suddenly get his hands on an amount of unexplained money. He had always told her that he'd dropped onto a good job, or that one of his horses had come in, and it was always at the odds of a hundred to one, always. Tony could sure pick 'em.

In her heart, Jenny had known what he was up to, she just knew it. But they needed the money, and sometimes they needed the money badly.

Then the chance of getting the house had come along, and she'd wanted that house more than anything. Then suddenly once again, Tony had the money, lots of money.

She had asked him where the money had come from but he had given her all the usual excuses. And in the end she'd kept quiet because of the house.

But one day Jenny had been cleaning up in their bedroom, and as she was putting Tony's shoes into the wardrobe, there stuffed at the back was a canvas bag. She didn't give it much thought, but then it struck her that it might be full of old socks or dirty underpants, or god knows what. So she picked up the bag and looked inside, and then she stood there in shock. The bag was full of money. And at that moment her thoughts were confirmed. Her husband was a thief, always had been. She should have done something about it there and then, but she didn't. She'd turned a blind eye to it because she wanted a house and a home. That was all she'd ever wanted.

And now this.

Jenny sat there for the best part of an hour. She knew what she had to do. It was over.

Finally she went into their spare bedroom and brought back two suitcases. The two suitcases that she'd bought for their dream holiday to Majorca.

She filled the cases with her and Barry's clothes. She gathered up the money and then stuffed five hundred pounds of it into her handbag. She put the rest of the money back into the canvas bag and put the bag into one of the suitcases.

She was going to take the money, and run.

She went downstairs and took a sheet of paper and a pen from out of the cupboard drawer. And she wrote Tony a final note.

> *'Tony,*
> *I know what you've done. So I'm leaving you and I'm taking Barry with me. You are a rotten, lousy bastard and I hope the police catch you and lock you away for life. I've always known you were a thief and I've kept my mouth shut, but now this. What you've done is unforgivable. You've murdered that woman and her son. You're not fit to be Barry's father.*
> *Think about the little boy you've killed. He was the same age as our Barry.*

I have a friend in Scotland and I'm going to go and live there.

You will never see us again.'

She left the note propped up on the mantelpiece. He would see it when he got home.

If he was sober.

Jenny then phoned for a taxi. She wanted to be taken to the train station.

The line in her note about going to Scotland was of course a lie. She had no intention of going to Scotland, no intention at all. One way or another she was going to get herself and Barry down to the south coast, to Hastings. When she was a young girl and her parents had still been alive, they'd spent their family holidays there every year. They'd been some of the happiest times of her life. Now she was going back there.

Jenny had thought about what would happen to them once Tony got caught. And he would get caught, of course he would. She would lose the house, no doubt about it. She couldn't afford the mortgage, not on her own. She also knew where she would end up, living in some rough area in a rented flat. Barry deserved better than that.

And people would talk about her and stare, and what about Barry when he went to school?

Kids could be so cruel.

She had no family except for her son. Both her parents were now dead. She had friends of course, but not that many. She could start again.

With ten thousand pounds, she could start again.

Jenny took the money, but not the ring.

Money was anonymous, but jewellery. Jewellery always belonged to somebody.

Tony McCall sat in the corner of the pub. He was nursing his second pint of beer.

His hangover had subsided somewhat and he was sitting on his own because he wanted to be alone. He was trying to think. In his mind he was still trying to churn things over.

'The police are following a possible lead'.

What on earth did it mean?

The police had nothing on him, he was clean. It was years ago that he'd got himself into trouble and ended up in prison. The police couldn't have gone through the company's records at work that quickly and pulled out his name. Not the next day, not in less than twelve hours, that was impossible.

He had even considered the possibility that Freddy Pope could have grassed him up, but he couldn't see it. He'd not had any dealings with Freddy for a while, and anyway, Freddy Pope didn't even know that Tony was working at Worsley Manor. No, it couldn't be Freddy.

Maybe it was a ruse. Maybe the police just said those things to buy themselves some time.

The thought of that made Tony feel a bit better and he went to get himself another pint. He sat down again and thought things through. No, the police had nothing. Nothing at all.

No fingerprints, he always wore gloves. He'd been fastidious, he always was. He always worked the same way and always to the same plan. That was why he'd always been successful. Not this time though. He had really thought that the house was empty. Damn it! He took another drink from his glass.

As he sat there he remembered the shooting. He'd not meant to do it. It was sort of an accident. He'd not known that it was the boy who was standing there in the dark. And when his mother had run in screaming, the gun just went off in his hand.

There was something in that thought. Something that made him think again, but for the life of him he couldn't see the connection. In his mind he could see the two bodies in front of him. He shuddered for a moment, then he remembered grabbing the bag and putting it into his bucket of tools and getting out of there. Once again there was a connection, but he still didn't understand it.

And then suddenly, in dismay, he did understand.

He understood it all, all and everything and then he understood why the police did have a 'possible' lead.

The boy had been standing there in the dark. And Tony hadn't known that it was the boy.

But why was that?

Because the boy was in the dark. Tony couldn't see him, because as he'd spun around he'd dropped his torch and it had clattered onto the floor and then gone out. His torch, he'd picked up everything else and then he'd got away. But he had forgotten to pick up the bloody torch.

He'd left it there. When he emptied the bucket in the back of his van everything had been there but his torch. But he hadn't given it a thought.

Stupid. Stupid. Stupid.

Tony felt like smashing his hand onto the pub table.

The bloody torch.

Tony McCall went sick at the thought. The police would be on to him. The police could trace his finger prints. His prints were on record because he'd been in prison.

Tony started to panic, he had to get home and he had to get away. He had to get them all away. He stood up and almost ran out of the pub.

On his way home he was panting with the effort, every so often he would break into a short run. He kept wondering what to tell Jenny. Maybe he could tell her that he wanted to take them away for weekend to anywhere, anywhere at all. If he could only persuade her, he could get her and Barry into the van and he would drive them somewhere. After all, he had ten thousand pounds. That would buy him some time. He would have to think of something but he just needed more time.

Fifteen minutes later he arrived back home, sweating and out of breath.

He walked straight in. Jenny hadn't even bothered to lock the door.

As he came into the house he called out her name, but there was no answer. He went to the bottom of the stairs and called to her again, but still no answer. He called out to Barry, he wasn't there either. So he went upstairs and walked into their bedroom. There on the bed was his gun and the jewellery box. Tony just stood there, he couldn't believe it. Jenny had found his gun. He felt a moment of dread. He opened the wardrobe door and looked, but it wasn't there. The canvas bag and the money had disappeared, along with his wife and son.

In a panic he ran back downstairs shouting her name. He went to into the garden, hoping against hope that she would be out there burying the stolen money in some hole.

He really was a stupid man.

He went back into the house, and it was then that he saw the note propped up on the mantelpiece. He grabbed hold of the note and read it. He just stood there and stared.

It was all over. There was nothing he could do.

It was debatable whether he was more upset about losing his money, or his family

So pathetic a man, was Tony McCall.

He slumped onto the settee and once again read Jenny's letter. He'd lost the money and he had lost his wife and his son. He was also going to lose his house and everything he had ever worked for. If you could call it work.

Eventually, he was going to lose his freedom too, because the police would find him. And even if they didn't, Tony knew that his wife would eventually tell them. She wouldn't be able to live with the guilt. That he did know.

He sat there for a while and he stared at the carpet. Finally he went over to their drinks cupboard and opened it. Inside, there was a half bottle of whiskey and a bottle of brandy. He took out both bottles.

Tony McCall sat back on the settee and poured himself a glass of whisky.

He tried to think of a away to get out of his situation. But there was none.

'What was the use'? It was over. It would be a waste of time trying to run, the police would eventually catch him. No one would hide him. Nobody wanted to know a child killer.

He'd wondered about going to Freddy Pope with the ring, but Freddy wouldn't want it. Nobody would touch that ring now.

Tony continued to drink until the half bottle of whiskey was emptied. Then he opened the bottle of brandy. After an hour or so the alcohol had started to do its work. Tony was now feeling sorry for himself and he'd started to cry as he thought about Jenny and never being able to see his son ever again. It was truly pathetic.

At no point did he give any thought to the son he'd murdered, or about his two victims and their poor families. ·

As ever, the only thing that mattered to Tony...was Tony.

He staggered upstairs to the toilet and then went back into their bedroom. Still on the bed were the jewellery box and the gun. He picked up the box and opened it, and he looked at the ring. It was stunning. It would have looked so beautiful on Jenny's finger. He should have given the ring to her, he really should have.

And that was another drunken lie.

He never had any intention of giving her that opal ring, not a chance. Tony would have taken it to Freddy Pope's and got the best possible price for it.

Jenny McCall would have never even seen the ring.

But Tony was by now quite drunk and his logic was becoming slightly askew. He decided that if his wife couldn't have the ring then neither would anyone else.

He staggered back downstairs and got a sheet of paper and a pen, and another large glass of brandy, and then he went to sit down at the kitchen table.

After taking swig of the brandy, he started to write.

'You've found this ring and now it's yours. You can have it'.

T. McCall

'And now I've lost everything'

He added the last line in an act of self pity.

He folded the note and put it into the box with the ring. Then he snapped the box shut.

His drunken arrogance was unbelievable.

He actually did consider that it was he, Tony McCall, who had lost everything.

As a man and as a human being, he was a disgrace. The lowest of the low.

He found a large brown envelope in a drawer in one of the cupboards. It was just what he wanted. He took the envelope back over to the table and then leant over it and wrote.

'To the finder...To whom it may concern'

He put the jewellery box inside the envelope and sealed it. Then he went back to the cupboard and found some string, some rough green twine. He folded the envelope and tied it with the string. Then he gulped down another mouthful of brandy.

Tony stared down at the envelope, his drunken mind was beginning to wander.

'What was he going to do with it'?

Suddenly he smiled.

'I know what to do with you my little beauty,' he slurred to himself.

He went to the front door and stood outside for a moment, breathing in the cool fresh air. Then he went across the road to his van. He returned a couple of minutes later with a hammer and some nails. After another swig of brandy, he picked up the envelope, the hammer and the nails and he made his way back upstairs.

It took a bit of effort, but Tony eventually managed to open the loft door and pull down the aluminium loft ladders. After struggling, he finally climbed the ladders and got into the loft. He clicked on the light and looked around. Then he looked up.

'The very place,' he said out loud, and he stopped to catch his breath at the effort of it all.

He grabbed an old wooden stool which was stored up there and he stood on it. Then he took the parcel and nailed it to the inside of one of the uppermost beams. He then stepped back off the stool and looked up. The envelope couldn't be seen, it was completely hidden.

Smiling at his own success, Tony went back downstairs again after closing the loft door.

He went back into the kitchen for his brandy. He drank what was left in his glass and then went back into the living room to polish off the rest of the bottle.

In his drunken haze, Tony McCall would never remember going up into the loft to hide the ring. He sat on the settee and continued to drink until the alcohol completely addled his brain.

In the end he passed out. He keeled over and slept there until the morning.

That was when six policemen opened the door and charged in, dragging him off the settee and onto the floor. They had him handcuffed before Tony was barely conscious.

As they pushed him out through the front door, one of the policemen picked up the letter that had been left on the floor at the side of the settee. It had been written by Jenny McCall, and in it she accused her husband of murder and theft.

The policeman folded the letter and put it into his inside pocket.

They'd caught the right man.

Alan Cunningham never fully recovered from the death of his wife and his son.

He moved back to London where he remained. He tried to put everything behind him.

He didn't bother to report the stolen ring to the police, or even make an insurance claim for the money or the ring. In his mind they were the cause of his wife's and his son's deaths and he wanted nothing to do with any money or rings. His wife and his child were priceless.

Worsley Manor was quickly disposed of.

It was sold to a firm of property developers and was eventually turned into one of the plushest and most successful golf clubs in the North West.

Alan Cunningham could never live in the place. It would become a distant reminder of happier days, and of what could have been.

Five years later, Alan was killed on the M1 motorway as he was leaving London. His chauffeur driven car was involved in a motorway pile up when a petrol tanker jack-knifed and hit the central reservation.

Parents Peter and Rebecca Cunningham eventually passed away, and the Cunningham family lineage came to an abrupt end when the eldest son Edward was killed during a robbery at an off licence in Johannesburg.

He had stopped off there to buy some beer whilst making his way to a friend's family barbeque. He was unfortunately in the wrong place at the wrong time.

The Cunningham Empire would eventually disappear.

It was taken over by the banks and the various trusts, who would systematically cut it up and take it apart. The divided business would technically disappear, only to be run by firms of corporate accountants and huge investment companies.

It would become invisible, but still highly profitable. That was how the system worked.

CHAPTER 14

Back to the present time.

It was another bright July morning and John Lawton stretched in his bed and yawned. It was another day and it had all the possibilities of being a good one.

He slowly glanced over to the bedroom window and saw the yellow tinge from the sun as it seeped through his bedroom curtains, and that was always a good sign...

Every day was the same for John Lawton.

He got out of bed and showered, then went downstairs to make the usual couple of slices of toast accompanied by his favourite marmalade and a cup of tea.

When he had finished, he took the sandwiches out of the fridge which were for his lunch. Today he would be dining on cheese salad. John smiled to himself. His wife Sarah had prepared them for him the night before, as she did most nights.

'Nice one love' he thought to himself, as he did most mornings.

John then went around the house making sure that everything was in its expected location. Nothing had to be out of place, nothing at all. Mistakes could lead to accidents.

Sarah Lawton was blind and she and John had anticipated a few problems when Sarah began to lose her sight. However, the change in their lifestyle had only become apparent when Sarah finally lost her eyesight altogether.

So she and John had formed a routine, and their optimistic little plan had actually worked.

It was quite simple really. Everything had its place and everything had to be in the same place all of the time.

John had always joked with his wife that he could walk around the house with his eyes closed. And they would laugh about it. There was no embarrassment and no awkward moments, John and Sarah had faced their problems. They had openly discussed everything and they fully understood their predicament. Then they made the decision that they had to get on with their lives.

John Lawton truly loved his wife and they were happy, in their own way.

John was still working on the demolition of the Meadows Estate though they were now on the final phase. A month, maybe six weeks, and that would see the project come to an end. Because of John Lawton's commitment, he and his loyal team of workers were actually ahead of schedule and that would keep the bosses at Connell Construction happy and smiling. It would also stand John in very good stead, not that he needed it. The men at the top already knew the value of John Lawton.

John, as usual was the first to arrive at work. But within the hour, his team of men would also arrive and by then he would have a schedule of work prepared for them and the demolition of the Meadows Estate would continue.

After their first brew of the day, his men went off to work and John returned to the site office. He had some paperwork to finish. He sat down at his desk and he looked at the stack of letters and assorted forms and memos in his 'in tray' and he took a deep sigh. This was the hard part of the job. He'd always considered that the manual side of his job was relatively easy. Well it had been easy when John was younger, but now? John had realised, quite a while ago that his days of repeatedly climbing up and down ladders had come to an end. He would still help out of course, when needed, but he had stepped up into management and with that came the responsibility. Unfortunately, along with responsibility came the copious amounts of paperwork, absolutely never ending paperwork.

John sat back and again sighed. He looked out of the window and shook his head.

There was something wrong, John knew there was something wrong and he'd known it for a while.

In truth, he'd had enough.

The realisation of that simple, solitary truth had hung over him for weeks. He'd had enough of work and working, and he'd had enough of the never ending paperwork and the reports in which he had to justify his every action, and he'd had enough of the repetition of it all.

John knew that it was the modern way of doing things. But it wasn't his way of doing things.

Well, not for much longer.

As he sat there, he suddenly made the decision that would hopefully change his life. After the Meadows contract, he would retire. Game over.

John would have to talk it over with Sarah of course. But he had plans, exciting plans.

Certain events over the last few months had changed John's attitude, and for John and Sarah those events were possibly life changing.

Only a couple of months before, John had been contacted by Mr Paul Lancaster, the owner of Lancaster's Jewellers. John had previously discovered a stunningly beautiful opal ring and he and Sarah had taken it to Lancaster's for valuation.

The ring had caused a bit of a stir.

Paul Lancaster's father, Harry Lancaster, had then got involved. He was an expert on antique jewellery and he had recognised the ring and had realised immediately that it was something special. Paul and Harry Lancaster had in turn recommended that the ring be sent down to an expert in London for an unconditional verification as to its origin and its maker.

If Harry Lancaster was right, it was quite possible that the ring had been created by one of Russia's finest jewellers, a craftsman and a genius. Vasily Orlof Bratz.

So John had got the call and on the following Saturday he and Sarah had gone down to Lancaster's Jewellers to meet up with Paul Lancaster and his father. On arrival they were greeted by Paul Lancaster and were taken upstairs to the first floor to Paul Lancaster's private office. That they were being taken into a private office made John aware that something significant had happened.

Sitting there in a large leather chair and waiting for them was Paul's father, Harry Lancaster. Greetings were again exchanged and everyone was seated and coffee was served. Once the pleasantries had been exchanged, Paul Lancaster opened his desk drawer and took out the black and gold jewellery box that contained the infamous opal ring. He opened the box and the light shone on the ring and it once again sparkled in front of them in all its glory.

'There you have it,' said Paul Lancaster 'Your opal ring has finally returned home.'

He made his statement in an effort to involve Sarah too, and John appreciated his good intentions. John reached over and took the ring out of the box and slid it onto Sarah's middle finger. He too wanted her to be involved as much as possible and as Sarah ran her finger over the spectacular opal she smiled.

'It feels so beautiful,' she said.

And then everyone smiled.

'Yes it is beautiful,' Harry Lancaster agreed, 'and it's got a history.'

'Yes,' continued Paul Lancaster, 'we've had verification from our man in London and the ring is all my dad said it was and more.' Paul then nodded to Harry Lancaster.

In truth, he wanted his father to tell the tale.

'I've been doing a bit of research,' said Harry Lancaster as he made himself comfortable in his leather chair, 'but first of all let me tell you that our expert in London confirms that the ring was definitely, one hundred percent made by Vasily Orlof Bratz. There is absolutely no doubt about it.'

Paul Lancaster looked across at John and he just shrugged good naturedly and smiled. John in turn took hold of Sarah's hand. He wanted her to enjoy all of this too.

Harry Lancaster continued, 'Vasily Orlof Bratz was Russian. His early life is a bit of a mystery, but we're almost sure that he was born in Smolensk and that he was apprenticed and learned his craft there. He must have shown great promise at an early age, because he left there to go straight to St Petersburg and to work for Faberge's. We know he created some outstanding jewellery there and that he was also involved in the making of the priceless Faberge Eggs which were made for the Tsar and the Romanov royal family. Then the Russian revolution came along and Carl Faberge and most of his family fled from Russia, and so did Vasily Orlof Bratz. Somehow he ended up in London where he worked and lived in obscurity, although he still went on to produce some of his finest work, if not the finest".

Harry Lancaster was of course speaking about the opal ring.

Vasily Orlof Bratz died somewhere around 1952, probably not longer after creating your opal ring. There is no record of him working on anything else after that.'

'That seems so sad,' said Sarah and once again she ran her finger over the opal.

'Yes,' said Harry, 'He was buried in the Russian Orthodox Cathedral in London. I believe it's in Knightsbridge. No doubt there's a gravestone there somewhere.'

'We do however have more information on your opal ring,' said Paul Lancaster.

'Yes we do,' Harry Lancaster continued, 'According to our man in London, the ring was definitely made by Vasily Orlof Bratz in 1951 whilst he was working for the London jewellers 'Albemarle and Skeet'. Albemarle and Skeet ceased to trade years ago and we can find no record at all of whom they actually sold the ring to. We only know that it was catalogued, so in theory it could have been sold anywhere in the country, and probably was. And that's how it probably ended up in the north of England. Who knows, Mr Lawton?'

There was a moment of silence.

Paul and Harry Lancaster sat there, and they were looking directly at John. They wanted an answer to the mystery. After all, they'd done the groundwork and they'd found the history of the ring and its maker. But there was a huge gap in between and it intrigued them.

John Lawton smiled.

"I've come prepared" he said. And he reached into his inside pocket and took out a note. It was the note written by T. McCall. Tony McCall.

'I realised that it may come to this,' said John, 'and here is the only evidence I can give you to prove that I've not stolen it.' He passed the note over to Harry Lancaster.

But Paul Lancaster laughed, 'Oh we know you've not stolen it Mr Lawton, we do already know that.' he said.

John was slightly mystified, so was Sarah.

Paul continued. 'When something valuable like this comes up for valuation, it's immediately checked on the police records. The ring has never at any time in its entirety been stolen or gone missing. There has never been a criminal or police record appertaining to it at all, ever.'

Harry Lancaster read John's scribbled note, he was mystified by it and he handed it to his son to read.

'The simple truth is that I found the ring,' said John, 'I'm a builder and I found the ring in a building that was awaiting demolition. It was tied to a rafter and wrapped in an envelope. I have the envelope at home, written on the front of it are the words 'To the finder...To who it may concern', and inside the jewellery box was that letter.'

John nodded to the letter that Harry Lancaster was still holding.

Everyone sat there expectantly, waiting for Harry Lancaster to give his verdict.

'Reading this,' said Harry Lancaster, as he held the letter in his hand, 'reading this, I don't see a problem. Whoever this T. McCall was, legally he left the ring to the finder, which fortunately happened to be you Mr Lawton. Since the ring was not stolen or missing, it would appear that it certainly doesn't belong to anyone else. And so, as 'the finder', the ring is yours Mr Lawton. I doubt if legally anyone could say any different.'

Sarah suddenly burst out laughing, and it broke the mood.

'Well that's a blessing,' she said, 'we've always wondered about that, it's been a bit of a worry hasn't it John?'

'Yes,' John replied "It certainly has. We always wondered whether it was something illegal.'

'Not according to our records,' said Paul Lancaster, 'and as far as we're concerned the ring is legally yours. We will prepare the valuation on the ring, and on that valuation it will state that the ring belongs to you. Then everything will be official and above-board.'

'Thank you for that" John said to him, 'It's a weight off our minds, it really is.'

Harry Lancaster once more sat up in his chair and made himself comfortable. He hadn't finished, not by a long chalk.

'Right Mr Lawton,' he said, 'About the ring and the ring's value.'

It was the moment of truth.

'The report states that the ring is constructed from a platinum band set with diamond chips. The opal in the ring is of an outstanding and exceptional quality, our expert in London says that he has never seen better. The opal itself is surrounded by twenty 'brilliant' diamonds, all of exceptional clarity. The diamonds are a bit of an anomaly. Their shape is of a non standard design. Vasily Orlof Bratz cut them into their exact 'spear shape' for a reason. He'd discovered an incredible technique, the ability to throw light through a diamond and in an exact direction. How he accomplished it is a mystery.'

'We have no way of discovering how he did it,' added Paul Lancaster, '... and other than taking the ring apart there is no way of finding out. And really, that's not viable. It could completely destroy the ring's integrity. If it was damaged, or if the diamonds couldn't be realigned correctly it would be a disaster.'

Harry Lancaster agreed wholeheartedly with his son and then he continued.

'So there we have the ring. As I've said, it's made from a platinum band which is beautifully set with diamond chips. There are twenty of the highest quality diamonds which surround one of the finest opals anyone has ever seen.'

Harry Lancaster took a deep breath.

'Your opal ring Mr Lawton, has been valued at one hundred thousand pounds.'

Sarah gasped, and John once more grabbed hold of his wife's hand. John then shook his head in complete amazement.

But that wasn't the end of things.

'However,' continued Harry Lancaster, 'There is more. There is now a huge amount of interest in historic jewellery, especially from places such as Russia, which is now a country of great wealth. There are many prosperous and affluent people there who want to return Russia to its former glory. A movement has formed to preserve Russian art in general and also to seek the return of any of its lost and missing artefacts. This has been fuelled by the return of the Faberge Royal Eggs. Many of the Faberge eggs have been reacquired and are now back in Russia in private collections. In fact, anything at all related to Faberge has become phenomenally valuable. Our source in London informs us that because of the connection with Faberge, any jewellery made by Vasily Orlof Bratz is now greatly sought after. In fact, it's becoming highly collectable by 'certain' individuals.'

Harry Lancaster stopped for a moment to catch his breath. John and Sarah were totally enthralled, but Paul Lancaster sat back, he knew what was coming.

Harry Lancaster continued.

'Our man tells us that if the ring was put into a specialised auction in London, say at Bonham's or Christies, and if enough publicity was created and the private buyers became involved, he believes there would be every chance of the ring more than doubling its price.'

John Lawton stared at Harry Lancaster.

'You mean..?'

'Yes Mr Lawton,' said Harry, 'Two hundred thousand pounds, maybe even two hundred and fifty thousand.'

'But that's a quarter of a million pounds,' uttered Sarah, she was almost speaking to herself.

'Yes it is,' said Paul Lancaster, 'Anything at all associated with Faberge is highly sought after.'

Sarah felt the ring on her finger, and she carefully ran her finger over it, suddenly aware of its importance.

'Vasily Orlof Bratz was one of Faberge's master craftsmen,' Harry Lancaster continued, 'It seems that there is a similar ring in a private collection in St Petersburg. It too is attributed to Vasily Orlof Bratz. The ring is of a comparable design, a succession of opals illuminated by small diamonds using the same technique. Vasily Orlof Bratz truly was a genius. The ring in Moscow originally belonged to one of the Tsar's daughters, she was one of the murdered Romanovs. Apparently it's known as the Flower Ring.'

'My goodness, all this history,' said Sarah Lawton.

'Jewellery has always been timeless Mrs Lawton,' said Harry Lancaster, 'Absolutely timeless.'

"So there you have it" said Paul Lancaster. Suddenly it was back to business, and he needed to talk openly to John Lawton.

'I know that this is a lot to take in Mr Lawton, and we realise that. So we will prepare the valuation for you and then it's up to yourselves. Whether you decide to keep the ring or sell it is entirely your decision, but you will need the valuation for insurance purposes.'

John Lawton nodded in agreement.

'However,' Paul Lancaster continued, 'business is business Mr Lawton. And if you did ever decide to sell the ring, I would ask if you would consider using us as your agents. We could organise everything from here and liaise with the auction houses down in London. That's your choice of course.'

John Lawton sat back in his chair and once again took hold of Sarah's hand.

'Mr Lancaster,' he said, 'At this moment in time I don't know what we're going to do. My head's in a bit of a whirl. But I will tell you something. As far as I'm concerned, you've done all the groundwork and we appreciate it, we really do. Without you we would have been absolutely clueless. And so, if we ever do decide to sell the ring, we will without doubt contact you and place the sale in your hands.'

The Lancaster's and the Lawton's then shook hands and the deal was done.

Just as they were about to leave, Sarah turned to her husband. 'John,' she said.

'Yes love?' he replied.

She lifted up her hand and smiled at him.

'Put the ring back in the box John.'

That had been two months ago, two very long months.

When they got back home from Lancaster's jewellers that afternoon, John made them both a cup of tea and they sat down at the kitchen table to discuss things.

In the end they decided to do nothing, a typical human failing. They decided that they didn't need the money desperately and that the ring would be some sort of an investment. It would be a form of insurance in case anything went wrong. Anyway, if they changed their minds, they could always sell it.

Life however, had other plans for the Lawton's.

And so, on that evening as he drove home from work, John Lawton mulled things over in his mind. He had to talk to Sarah. He would tell her his plans to retire, and he just hoped that she would agree with him.

John had thought long and hard about the ring. What actual use was it?

Yes the ring was beautiful, but his poor wife couldn't see it and she never would. It was never going to be a family heirloom, they had no children. They had only ever had one child, their little baby Louise who had sadly died shortly after being born.

As John drove home he began to think about Louise, the young girl and the young woman she never became, and the good times they should have had, and the birthdays and the weddings and the grandchildren, and so very much more.

And suddenly John was angry. He was angry at the injustice of it all and how his life was being gnawed away. And the fact that he'd not been able to do a thing about it. He'd had to keep his head down and keep working day after day, and he'd had to leave Sarah on her own and alone and waiting for him to come home every night.

But not now damn it. Oh no, not now. Suddenly they had a chance.

John walked into the house and straight through to the kitchen where he knew Sarah would be, as usual. They sat down and ate their evening meal and John told her about his day, again as usual, and Sarah sat there smiling.

When they'd finished eating, John cleared the table and made Sarah and himself a fresh cup of coffee. John then sat back down at the table.

"I need to talk to you" he said.

Sarah just sat there, still smiling but also a little apprehensive. She knew by the tone of John's voice that this must be something important. Then came the question.

'What are we doing with our lives Sarah?' he asked her.

It was the question she couldn't reply to. She had no life. She could never say anything to John because she didn't want to upset him. But in truth, she had no life really, just the everyday repetition of sitting in the house and listening to the inane rubbish on the television and the radio. Hardly anyone ever came to see her anymore. The circle of so called friends she had once socialised with had all but disappeared. Her blindness had become their embarrassment. Every day she just sat there, waiting for John to come home.

In the end there was only one true response.

'What life?' she replied.

It was a question, and it was a statement.

John took hold of her hand.

'I know love, and I know you don't have much of a life. But I may have an answer, I've had an idea that I need to talk to you about".

Sarah said nothing. She just sat there.

So John continued, 'I've been thinking, and I've been thinking long and hard about our future.

Where are the next ten years taking us? Well I'll tell you something Sarah, they're taking us nowhere. The next ten years will see us ten years older and that's it. I'll have probably retired by then but we'll have been stuck in this routine for so long that I doubt if we'll be able to change. And I don't want that. I want us to do something Sarah, I want us to do something with our lives and I want to get off this daily merry-go-round and start to live again. I'm sick of work and I'm sick of working Sarah. I want to do something else, and I want us both to do something else. In the past, I've had to work. I've had to work to pay the bills. But now we've been given a chance and we now have an opportunity to change things.'

'You mean because of the ring, don't you?' said Sarah.

'Yes I do" he replied, 'I want to sell the ring and after that I want us to travel. We can both travel the world. I know you can't see the sights Sarah but you can smell and you can taste. I want to take you to restaurants all around the world, and I want us to dine everywhere and try the different cuisines in each and every country. I want us both to lie on sandy beaches and feel the sun on our skin. We can swim in the sea and we can eat and drink out in the open air. I want us to live again Sarah. And then, when we've done all of that, I want us to buy a second home. Somewhere sunny and warm were we can go for walks in the evening and spend some good times together. That's what I want Sarah. That's what I want us to do.'

The tears welled up in Sarah's eyes.

'I didn't know you were so unhappy at work.' she said.

'It's not just work. Work becomes an everyday routine. I'm unhappy for both of us Sarah. We lost Louise and you've lost your sight. It's just not fair and I don't want us to go on like this.'

John bit his lip as his own emotions began to rise.

Sarah held his hand tightly, she needed to tell him the truth.

'John, I'm so unhappy. I hate what's happened to me and I've always felt as though I've let you down. You have to do everything for me, and I just sit here at home, day after day on my own, just waiting for you to come home and talk to me. I'm so lonely John, I can't explain how lonely I am.'

And with that she burst into tears.

They both sat there for a moment as Sarah wiped her eyes. John Lawton looked at his wife, and he wondered how on earth it had all got to this. And suddenly he knew he was doing the right thing.

'Let's do it Sarah, let's sell the ring. Sell the ring and live again.'

In those last few minutes he'd opened up a world of possibilities for her and the chance of a new life together. With tears still in her eyes she smiled, and then she laughed.

'Yes, alright John,' she said to him, 'let's do it!'

Friday afternoon finally arrived, the last day of the week.

'Thank God for that' thought John Lawton, as he tried to finish off his week's work. His men had all gone home and John had been left on his own.

He was the last man there, as always.

He'd had to resend a report to head office because they'd somehow managed to lose it, and John had mistakenly not saved it onto his computer's file. It was sloppy practice on both sides really. Unusual for John though, and he recognised his mistake and that aggravated him. He was going to be late going home. Finally he'd finished his report, locked the gates to the estate and set off home. Then there was a traffic jam, and more aggravation. John looked at his watch. He was going to be late. He was going to be just half an hour late.

Sarah was sitting in her bedroom, casually listening to the radio. There had been an afternoon play on but she hadn't been paying much attention to it, the plot had been a bit over dramatic and she had sort of lost interest.

Sarah had other things on her mind.

She and John had talked about selling the ring at auction. Tomorrow was

Saturday and they planned to go and see Mr Paul Lancaster at Lancaster's Jewellers and ask him to proceed with the sale.

Sarah was excited. It was the beginning of their new start. John had told her that they could go to London when the ring went to auction and sit in the sale room and listen to the figures.

Then John would retire, or perhaps by then he may have already retired. He'd told her that he was finishing work once the demolition of the Meadows estate was over, and there wasn't much of the work left to do.

Sarah reached over for the jewellery box and once again took out the opal ring.

She knew that she would be losing her fabulous jewel but the reward would be worth it. In the end, she and John would have a new life.

She stroked the opal, and she could almost feel its worth. Then she took a tissue and began to carefully polish it. Strangely, it was something that she'd started to do. In her mind she wanted the opal ring to look its best.

On the radio the play came to an end, and the presenter announced the time and then started with the day's news. Sarah suddenly realised what time it was. John was late, he must have been held up.

Sarah immediately stood up, she had to go and start making John's tea. She still had the ring in her hand but her mind was suddenly on other things. Downstairs, the potatoes were already chopped up and in a pan of salted water. They were ready and waiting to be boiled. All she had to do was turn on the gas.

Sarah got to the top of the stairs and reached out for the banister, and then suddenly realised that she still had the opal ring in her hand. It was a simple decision. At that moment she tried to stop and swap the ring into her other hand, but she had already taken the first step. She tripped forwards and had nothing at to hold onto. As she fell into open space she clutched the ring tightly in her hand. Nothing must happen to the ring, nothing. The ring was their future. She had to protect it.

She somersaulted forwards and as her head hit the sixth step it snapped her neck. She was killed instantly. She tumbled down the rest of the stairs and her body landed against the front door.

But by then, Sarah Lawton was already dead.

When John finally arrived home he sat in his car for a moment and took a deep sigh.

'Not much longer' he thought to himself. The sun was still shining and he suddenly decided that he would open a bottle of their favourite white wine and he and Sarah could sit out in the garden and take in the last hours of the sun as they talked about their future plans.

That would be nice.

He put his key in the front door and tried to open it. But nothing happened. So he pushed, and then he pushed again, and still nothing happened. The door wouldn't open. Why?

So John put his two hands on the door and pushed it as hard as he could. The door moved five or six inches, but no more. John shouted through the gap to Sarah, but there was no reply. And suddenly he began to worry. This time he got his shoulder behind the door and pushed with all his might. The door very slowly began to open. Then John stopped.

He stopped when he saw Sarah's arm fall from behind the door, and in horror he realised that there'd a terrible accident. Sarah was injured. What had happened? He had to try and do something. He had to.

In that split second of blind panic, John would always remember looking down at Sarah's arm, only to see that she was still holding the opal ring tightly in her hand.

Sarah Lawton had died tragically.

The funeral took place three weeks later.

Many people attended, including all of her friends of course.

John had sat there in a daze. The thought crossed his mind of how strange it was that these people couldn't visit Sarah when she was alive, and yet they all came to see her when she was dead.

But he wouldn't say anything. It wasn't worth the fuss.

After the funeral he just went home. Again, he didn't want the fuss.

The previous three weeks had been quite harrowing for John. The unfortunate nature of Sarah's death meant that the police had to be involved and there had to be an inquest.

It was all quite simple really, the police had understood the nature of what had happened. It had been an unfortunate accident and there had been no suspicious circumstances. Even so, John had still been interviewed by them on two or three occasions.

All that procedure had taken time, and John had to sit at home for those three weeks, distressed and in a daze.

The funeral people had been very good. They'd taken care of all the arrangements for John.

It was understandable, that was their job.

Another six weeks went by, and people quickly stopped calling round to see John. Workmates, colleagues and friends, they all faded away after they had visited him once or twice.

In truth, John didn't want to see any of them. He wanted to be left alone. When he was on his own he could think of Sarah. He would sit with their favourite photographs and would run his finger around the outline of her face, remembering how beautiful she was and all the happy times that they'd had together, and he missed her.

John Lawton loved his wife. And then there would be tears.

John's dark days began to turn even darker.

John Lawton was lost. He knew he was.

On the Saturday morning John got into his car and went to the local supermarket. He bought three bottles of very good champagne. His and Sarah's favourite.

He also bought two packets of aspirin and two packets of paracetamol.

At the cashier's till he was told that they were only allowed to sell two packets of painkillers at a time. It was company policy. John apologised and handed two of the packets of pills back. After paying the cashier, he went back to his car and drove to another five shops.

At each shop John bought another two packets of the painkillers.

When he got home he immediately put the champagne into the fridge. Sarah had always insisted that champagne only tasted good when it was really cold.

He put the kettle on and made himself a cup of tea. He sat back and watched the lunchtime news on the television and sipped his brew. Once the news had finished, John went back into the kitchen and washed his cup. He dried it with a pot towel and put it back into the cupboard. The folded pot towel was then placed neatly at the side of the sink. Everything had to be tidy, just as Sarah liked it to be.

John had already realised what he needed to do.

He went upstairs to his and Sarah's bedroom. There on the dressing table was the black and gold jewellery box which contained the opal ring. He picked it up, took it back downstairs and placed it on the kitchen table. Then he went into the living room and opened the cupboard drawer. He took out the sheet of paper and an envelope and a pen.

Everything was organised.

He went back into the kitchen, took the pen and paper and began to write the obvious, but this time with a subtle difference. It was tragic, and at the same time it was almost inevitable.

He wrote

'You've found this ring, and now it's yours. You can keep it. I've lost my everything.'

John Lawton.

John then took the envelope and wrote on it *'To the finder...To whom it may concern'.*

He then folded the letter and put it into the jewellery box with the ring, and then he put the box into the envelope and sealed it.

John went back upstairs and up into the loft. He moved some of the boxes until he finally found one that he could stand on. He stepped up onto it and reached up to the rafters. There was a small gap between the beams and John stuffed the envelope in there.

Once that was done, he closed everything up and went back down the stairs, the stairs that had killed Sarah. Every time he went down those stairs he imagined her falling, and he remembered her body lying at the bottom of those stairs, damaged and broken.

He couldn't stand it.

John went into the kitchen, to the fridge, and he took out one of the bottles of champagne. It was by then lovely and cool. He took the cork out with the expected 'pop' and then poured himself a glass full.

He took the bottle and glass into the living room and sat down on the settee.

He then proceeded to drink the whole bottle. Along with the last two glasses he also swallowed the contents of two of the packets of painkillers.

That done, he went back into the kitchen to the fridge and opened another bottle of champagne, then he went to sit in the living room once more. The champagne tasted so good, and he smiled to himself as he remembered Sarah giggling whenever she drank it.

With every glass he poured, John continued to swallow more and more of the pills. By the time he'd finished the second bottle, most of the pills were gone. He stood up to go to the fridge again but this time he staggered. Now the alcohol was running freely through his veins. He opened the fridge door and took out the last bottle. He had to struggle to get the cork out this time, but finally he managed it. Rather unsteadily, he went back into the living room and slumped back onto the settee. There was just one packet of painkillers left. He emptied the pills into his hand and swallowed all of them as he drank the champagne from the open bottle.

Then he sat there and drunkenly considered that it was a job well done.

John sat there for the next hour, sipping the rest of the champagne and letting those little pills get on with their job.

The pattern on the wall was the first thing he noticed.

It was the pattern on the wallpaper right in front of him that was the first thing to change.

The pattern began to pulsate, first of all it was larger, and then it was smaller and then it began to swirl. John didn't care, he was past caring. He lifted the bottle and drank the last of the champagne, and then he let the bottle fall onto the carpet. He sat there smiling, he was actually at peace. It was the first time he'd known peace for weeks and weeks.

He sat there for another ten or fifteen minutes, just staring at the wall. Then for some reason, it began to snow. It seemed ridiculous, John knew of course that it couldn't possibly be snowing in his living room, but yet it was, and it all seemed so obvious and so acceptable. It was as though he was dreaming, but he wasn't dreaming.

As he looked through the snow, the living room wall disappeared in front of him, it suddenly wasn't there. John sat there in complete wonder, because now he was looking out into a forest, and the forest was thick with pine trees and the snow was falling quite heavily. Everything looked so natural and it was so quiet, the snow seemed to deaden all of the noise. John stared into the forest and through the pine trees and suddenly, in the distance, a figure came into view, and the figure was heading towards him. Someone wearing a hooded jacket was trying to make his way forwards but the wind had begun to blow and the figure was struggling through the snow. The wind was getting quite strong but the hooded figure fought relentlessly against it, onwards and onwards and always coming closer. The figure was only twenty or so feet away when the hood blew back. It was a man. As John peered through the snow he recognised the man but he couldn't understand it. The man was his father.

But it was his father as he was at fifty years old, and how John remembered him when he too was just a boy. It should have felt strange and it should have been a dream, but no, it wasn't. His father stood there strong and vibrant, he was dark haired and windblown. Not the eighty year old man who John had watched wither and die in a hospital bed.

His father stood there and waved and then came forward again. As he got close to John he called out.

'Come on John, come on. We're waiting for you.' and he stretched out his hand.

John stood up and went forward, he walked into the forest and into the snow but somehow he didn't feel the cold. He followed his father, who kept turning and smiling at him and ever bidding him onwards. They didn't seem to walk for long before the wind fell away and the snow stopped falling, and suddenly there was no snow at all as they both walked out into a clearing. It was so beautiful. A field of rich green pasture with a stream flowing through it at the other end. In the distance there was a crowd of people who were all waving to John.

His father again bid him forward.

'Come on John,' he said, 'We're nearly there.'

They both walked on through the pasture to meet everyone. And as he got closer, John realised that he knew everybody. His mother was there and she kissed him, his grandparents were there too, his uncles and aunties and his cousins. They all welcomed him and they were laughing and John was so happy to see them all again. He had missed them, they were his family and he had missed them all so much. Suddenly they all moved to one side and John looked over and for the very first time couldn't believe his eyes. It was Sarah, his Sarah.

She was walking towards him and she was smiling, and in her arms she had a little girl, a little girl who was barely two years old and had curly brown hair and her mother's face.

Sarah laughed and she smiled at him.

'Look John,' she said softly, 'I've found her...I've found Louise.'

John looked at them both, he was so happy, he reached over to touch Louise's cheek.

And at that moment, alone in his sitting room, John Lawton died.

In the last moment of his life, it could be said that John Lawton did die a happy man.

He was in his own personal heaven.

CHAPTER 15

Another year passed by.

Once the solicitors and the banks, the insurance companies and the estate agents had all had their way and taken their obligatory fee, John and Sarah Lawton's house was finally sold.

It was a young married couple, Nilesh and Kalpna Chandry, who finally bought the house. And at a fairly decent price.

For them it was their first step onto the property ladder. They'd been married for nearly two years, and just like the previous owners, they too were very much in love.

Two years spent in a rented property had always seemed like a waste of time and money to Nilesh and Kalpna, and it was their parents who had finally sat them down and told them that they needed to buy their own house. It would be an investment and it actually did make sense.

Nilesh worked for one of the major banks and Kalpna was a designer at a web design company. Both were keen to get on and this house was going to be their start.

Their idea was to extend and remodel the house. They had no long term plans to stay there. Hopefully the house was going to be their first move on to bigger and better things.

Nilesh took out a mortgage with his bank at favourable employee rates, and they were both delighted when they realised that their mortgage repayments were actually going to be a fair bit less than the rent they had already been paying. History repeats itself, and all seemed well.

So they moved in there and began to get on with things. Their plan was to remodel the house bit by bit. A new kitchen and new bathroom were a must. They decided that whenever there were any major renovations to be done on the house, they would simply move back in with their parents until the work was finished.

After three months a new kitchen was fitted. Next was the bathroom, but it would have to wait because they would need to save the money to pay for it. Kalpna was keen to get it done, and she must have spoken to her mother about it because Kalpna's parents suddenly offered to lend them the cash. Nilesh flatly refused. He was independent by nature and the thought of owing money to his wife's parents was something that he didn't really relish. It would make him accountable to both of them and Nilesh firmly intended to remain his 'own man'.

He was also very aware of the amount of power an Indian mother-in-law held in sway.

Oh dear me no.

Nilesh had told his wife they would have to manage it on their own. Kalpna however, wasn't entirely happy about it. Nilesh had finally appeased her by taking her to pick out some new furniture and carpets for the living room. They decided to paint and decorate it themselves. The kitchen had been a great success, and so peace would be maintained, at least for a short time.

Nilesh had plans to extend the house upstairs. Although the house already had three bedrooms, it also had a sizeable loft. One of Nilesh's cousins had recently extended their own property by building something called 'a dormer' in the loft. Basically the roof had been extended to make it square instead of sloped and then windows were fitted. Nilesh had called to see his cousin's house and was amazed at the amount of space it had given them. He had taken Kalpna around there too, and she had been more than impressed. So they looked to doing the same thing with their own property. Kalpna had come up with the idea that if they did convert the loft it would make a large enough bedroom to incorporate an ensuite bathroom. It was a brilliant plan. It would turn their three bed room house into a four bedroom house and with two bathrooms. With two brand new bathrooms and a spanking new kitchen the value of their house would definitely increase.

So that was the plan.

It took them another month to get the living room ship shape but when that was finished Kalpna was still keen to have her new bathroom. Nilesh however saw more sense in having all the major work done upstairs in the attic, and with it the extra bedroom and a bathroom.

In the end he went back to the bank to find out the maximum that he could borrow. He was quite surprised. Over their evening meal they discussed the possibilities, and Kalpna of course was keen to go ahead.

They would have to get a builder and possibly involve an architect too, they may even need to obtain planning permission. Nilesh rang his cousin for advice and also mentioned they were considering fitting an ensuite bathroom up there too.

'How big is your loft?' his cousin had asked.

Nilesh didn't have a clue. He'd only ever been up there twice. There was a light up there and when he'd switched it on the loft had looked gloomy and full of dust.

'You'll need to measure the space,' his cousin advised.

'Oh hell,' said Nilesh, 'it's bloody filthy up there.'

'Do yourself a favour then,' said his cousin, 'Get up there with the vacuum cleaner and clean it all up. If you don't you'll have dust all the way through your house. It happened to us and it was a nightmare.'

'Right,' Nilesh agreed, 'I'll have to get it done.'

'I don't think you'll get a bathroom up there,' his cousin warned him.

'You don't know my wife,' Nilesh replied.

After he put down the phone, Nilesh laughed. He quietly suspected that his cousin was a little bit jealous.

The following weekend Nilesh and Kalpna put on some of their oldest clothes and prepared to attack the loft. Nilesh had bought a long electrical extension cable and a far stronger light bulb than the one that was already up there. They both climbed into the loft, taking with them the vacuum cleaner and the extension cable. Once the light bulb was changed they had the chance to have a good look round. Yes, it was filthy. The house had been cleared and emptied before being put on the market and there was nothing at all left in the loft but the dust and the cobwebs. Kalpna shuddered, she hated spiders. Nilesh wasn't over fond of them either.

But they buckled down to the job and for an hour they continually lifted the vacuum cleaner out of the loft and downstairs so that they could empty the dust straight into the bin. Eventually they made headway and underneath all the dust the remaining flooring was actually quite good. Just as they were about to start clearing away all the cobwebs from the roof timbers the telephone rang downstairs. Kalpna looked at Nilesh and she grinned at him as she nodded sideways.

That was the signal for 'You get it'.

'It'll be your mother...again,' Nilesh exclaimed.

'All the more reason for you to answer it then' said Kalpna. 'Just tell her we're busy.'

Nilesh shook his head and his wife laughed at him.

As he climbed down the loft steps he nodded in the direction of the vacuum cleaner.

"Go on then...carry on,' he said to her, and then quickly ducked out of the way before she managed to hit him with something.

Kalpna switched on the vacuum cleaner and began to wave the long hose around the rafters. She wasn't really happy about it. It was because of the spiders and she realised that maybe she should have gone and answered the telephone after all.

Suddenly the vacuum cleaner started to make a high pitched whirring sound. It was the noise it always made when it became blocked. She lowered the hose, only to see a small paper package stuck on the end. It was some sort of envelope.

It was, of course, the opal ring.

In that moment, Nilesh and Kalpna Chandry's life would change, irreversibly.

They discovered the ring when they opened up the package, and they too were absolutely bowled over by its beauty.

In the end they had taken it to show both their parents and the ring's value had been enthusiastically discussed by one and all.

Events do have the habit of repeating themselves, sometimes.

Rather remarkably, Nilesh and Kalpna Chandry then took the ring to Lancaster's Jewellers for a preliminary appraisal. They just wanted a 'rough idea' of what the ring could possibly be worth.

The assistant took one look at the stunning opal ring and rang Mr Lancaster immediately.

A moment later, Paul Lancaster came down the stairs from his office to see what all the fuss was about. When he opened the box and saw the ring he gasped in amazement.

Paul Lancaster looked at Nilesh and Kalpna Chandry, who by then were both feeling rather intimidated by all the fuss. Nilesh began to wonder if they should pick up the ring and simply walk out of the shop. But Paul Lancaster was as suave and professional as ever and he took complete control of the situation. He introduced himself to Nilesh and Kalpna and they in turn reciprocated.

'I would really like to speak to you in private,' he said, 'I think I have some information about this ring that may startle you.'

Nilesh and Kalpna were intrigued, and Paul Lancaster seemed pleasant enough, so the three of them went upstairs to his office where Paul as usual ordered them all some coffee.

'Can you tell me what you know about the ring?' Paul had finally asked.

Nilesh produced John Lawton's letter from his pocket.

'We found the ring in our house Mr Lancaster, along with this letter.'

Paul Lancaster read the letter and was again stunned by what he read.

'I knew Mr Lawton and his wife, before they err...passed away.' Paul was reluctant to go into the details, but Nilesh and Kalpna did quickly glance at one another.

Paul Lancaster sat back in his chair

'Let me tell you what I know about the ring,' he said.

Half an hour later Nilesh and Kalpna Chandry both sat there, wide eyed. Not only were they suddenly aware of the name 'Vasily Orlof Bratz', but Paul Lancaster had just informed them that the unbelievable one hundred thousand pound ring that they had discovered could possibly be worth double that amount. Even a figure of two hundred and fifty thousand pounds had been mentioned.

Nilesh and Kalpna were astounded, they couldn't believe it.

'The ring was gifted to you Mr and Mrs Chandry, just like it was gifted to John Lawson. Simply put, the finder in this case is the keeper. I do know that the Lawson's had no dependents, so there is no one at all who could lay claim to it.'

'What actually happened to Mr Lawson and his wife?' asked Kalpna.

'I'm afraid they both died rather tragically Mrs Chandry,' Paul Lancaster replied. He didn't want to go into detail. The facts were too upsetting and besides, Paul Lancaster had been quite fond of John and Sarah Lawson. He felt it was better not to dwell.

Paul Lancaster then continued, 'So, you are the owners of a very rare and expensive piece of jewellery. I can only repeat to you what I told the Lawson's. If you wish to sell the ring for the best price, we would be only too happy to act as your agent. We would liaise with our man in London and approach one of the major auction houses down there. The ring would have to go into a specialized auction of course and buyers worldwide would have to be informed. There would be the need to create interest, but that's actually the job of the auction houses themselves".

Peter Lancaster looked across his desk at Nilesh and Kalpna.

'I suggest you take a week or two to mull things over before you make any possible decision. Take your time and think about it. You may decide to keep the ring, who knows? Whatever happens, we will always be here to assist and guide you. As I've already said, the decision should be yours and yours alone.'

Nilesh and Kalpna went home in a bit of a daze. They sat in their brand new kitchen and Kalpna boiled some water in their brand new kettle and they both had a cup of tea.

Nilesh looked across the table at his wife.

'What do you think?' he asked her.

'We should talk to our parents,' Kalpna quickly replied.

Nilesh raised his eyes to the ceiling.

'Why do we always have to talk to your parents? What's it got to do with them?'

'I didn't say my parents, I said 'our' parents,' she replied.

'My parents, your parents...what difference does it make?' said Nilesh, 'They always interfere.'

Kalpna sat there for a moment. She knew he was right. Their parents had an opinion on absolutely everything. It had taken Nilesh and Kalpna two weeks to get everyone to agree on what colour they should paint their own living room.

'Anyway,' said Nilesh, 'you know what they'll say.'

'Yes of course I do,' Kalpna replied, 'they'll tell us to sell it.'

Nilesh's eyes widened for a moment and Kalpna saw that look.

'But what do you want to do?' he asked her, 'If you want to keep the ring, we will. After all it is very beautiful, just like you.' And he laughed.

But Kalpna wasn't fooled, not one bit.

'Nilesh Chandry, you think you're clever, but I know you. You want to sell the ring too, I can see it in your eyes,' and she laughed at him.

He shrugged, 'It's a lot of money Kalpna. Just think what we could do with it.'

She looked at him, and then she was suddenly quite serious.

'Nilesh, that ring is very beautiful. It's the most beautiful thing I think I've ever seen, and any woman would love to own it. But everyone who has ever owned it seems to have had bad luck. Mr Lancaster told us about the first letter and now we have a similar letter and then we find out that something awful happened to those Lawson people. I don't like it Nilesh, and I don't think I would ever feel that the ring really belonged to me. That ring has a past.'

Nilesh tried not to smile.

'So you don't want it then?' he asked her.

'No, I don't want it,' said Kalpna, and then she grinned at him 'Let's sell the damn thing and take the money. And you're right. Just think what we could do with all that cash.'

Simply put, the decision had been made. They would sell the ring.

The next day they rang Paul Lancaster to tell him their decision. Paul Lancaster was delighted at the news. Business of course, was business.

The following Saturday Nilesh and Kalpna Chandry took the opal ring into Lancaster's Jewellers and personally handed it over to Paul Lancaster himself.

Paul explained the course of action. The ring would be sent to their man in London, a Mr Peter Giles. He would liaise with the auction houses and make the crucial decision of who to go with. The ring would obviously have to be put into a specialist auction and the whole procedure could take up to six months and possibly longer.

The Chandry's were quite happy with that. If truth be known, Nilesh and Kalpna were actually quite glad to see the back of it. They felt that the ring was a liability.

Better to let it go and enjoy the money.

It did take six months to get the ring to auction.

Down in London, Peter Giles had decided to go with the renowned auction house, Christies.

A date was set, and Paul Lancaster informed Nilesh and Kalpna Chandry and gave them all the details of the sale. Nilesh and Kalpna had decided do go to London and they were going to attend the auction. Paul Lancaster had wholeheartedly agreed with their decision. It was always better that the owners of the ring were there at the point of sale.

Who knew what could happen when large amounts of money were involved?

They were about to find out.

CHAPTER 16

For once, it was quite a sunny day in St Petersburg, Russia.

At the head offices of Verkel Industries, Vladimir Verkel sat and stared at the screen of his laptop computer. He was not a happy man. Oil and gas prices worldwide were plummeting and as a result, everything else seemed to be following suit. His own company shares were dropping too. Verkel Industries had been devalued by something less than one percent, and though that may not have seemed a lot, in real terms it amounted to millions.

Not that Vladimir Verkel should have worried. He had another dozen or so huge companies that were equally as successful as the one bearing his own name. What was hurting his pride was that Verkel Industries had been his first business. Verkel Industries had always been his personal 'baby'.

Vladimir Verkel sighed. That was there way of the world, up and down and unpredictable.

But Vladimir Verkel needn't really have worried. He had plenty of money. In fact he had mountains of money. In Russia and throughout the world he was infamous for his wealth. Vladimir Verkel was in fact one of Russia's richest men. He was known as an oligarch and in Russia that stood for someone who was a multi millionaire. Vladimir Verkel, however, had done slightly better than that. Vladimir Verkel was a billionaire.

The intercom on Vladimir Verkel's handcrafted antique desk began to buzz loudly. Verkel answered it. It was his secretary, it was always his secretary.

'Mr Pasternak's here to see you sir,' she said in her wonderfully sexual Czech accent.

'Okay Sonia,' he replied, 'Send Viktor in will you please.'

Vladimir loved the sound of his secretary's voice, and he also loved the shape of her body. His secretary was sensationally beautiful, and Vladimir Verkel realized that because of his riches, he could quite easily turn the beautiful Miss Sonia Neff into the next Mrs Vladimir Verkel. That he did know. Fortunately, he was at an age where he was quite content with his life. To take on the likes of Miss Sonia Neff at this point would be a personal lie. and he wouldn't allow himself the deceit. It was a lesson that a lot of rich men would never learn, the rich and the vain and the totally misguided.

There was a tap on the door and into the office walked Viktor Pasternak.

Pasternak was Vladimir Verkel's long serving and long suffering chief accountant. He had been with Vladimir from the very beginning, from those early days when Vladimir Verkel had been gobbling up companies like a hungry wolf.

Victor Pasternak himself was possibly everybody's idea of what an accountant should look like. He was in his late fifties and of average height and build, he had silver grey parted hair and wore steel rimmed spectacles. Victor Pasternak had always worn charcoal grey suits, always. Vladimir Verkel couldn't remember him ever wearing anything else. The only thing that ever changed was the colour of Viktor Pasternak's tie.

'Good morning Viktor,' said Vladimir Verkel as he looked up and greeted his accountant.

'Good morning Vladimir,' Pasternak replied efficiently.

Viktor Pasternak was the only person in the whole of Vladimir Verkel's vast business empire who was allowed to call his boss by his first name.

Even his bank manager called him 'Mr Verkel'. And quite rightly too.

'I'm concerned about our stock prices,' said Pasternak immediately.

Vladimir smiled. This was typical Viktor Pasternak. Never was there anything informal from Viktor, never any social chat or even 'How are you today Vladimir?' It was always business as usual with Victor Pasternak and had been from the word go. In all the years that Vladimir Verkel had known him, he had only met Viktor's wife twice, and Viktor Pasternak had two children whom Vladimir had never met at all. It was only because of the photograph on Pasternak's desk that he knew that his chief accountant had two teenage daughters.

Vladimir sat back on his chair.

'I don't think we've anything to worry about Viktor,' he said casually.

But that reply wouldn't be enough for his chief accountant and Vladimir Verkel knew as much.

Pasternak more or less ignored his boss's comment.

'We're down nearly one percent,' Pasternak exclaimed. He had the worried look of a man who had just lost his wallet.

'I know,' said Verkel.

'It'll cost us millions,' Pasternak continued.

'We've got millions,' Vladimir Verkel replied. He was trying to appease his accountant, but Pasternak just rubbed his forehead.

'I don't like it, I don't like it one bit,' Viktor Pasternak replied.

Suddenly, Vladimir Verkel's laptop computer made a noise. It was the sound of an e-mail arriving. Verkel looked down at the screen and raised his eyebrows. The e-mail was from Christies Auctioneers in London. Vladimir Verkel had a contact there. The e-mail read 'We have something that may be of great interest to you. Please e-mail us for details'.

Verkel immediately buzzed his secretary on the intercom and the lovely Sonia Neff replied almost immediately.

'Yes Mr Verkel?'

'Ah Sonia" he said, and couldn't help but smile at the sound of her voice, 'Will you e-mail Christies in London for me. Tell them that I may be interested and ask them to e-mail a brochure immediately. As soon as it arrives, print it off to a decent size and bring it in to me please.'

'Okay, I'll do it straightaway Mr Verkel,' the lovely Sonia replied.

Vladimir Verkel looked at his chief accountant who was staring back at him stone faced.

'Not again?' said Pasternak.

'What do you mean Viktor?' said Verkel in mock surprise.

Pasternak frowned. 'This obsession of yours, you've spent millions. It's quite ridiculous.'

'But I've got millions,' Vladimir Verkel replied, 'I'm a billionaire for god's sake Viktor.'

He knew this sort of talk infuriated his chief accountant but he really did enjoy watching Viktor Pasternak get agitated.

Pasternak stood up.

'Buying all these baubles and all this jewellery does not make this company any money. It's all costing a fortune. I do not condone it Vladimir.'

'I know Viktor, I know...just humour me old friend. It's my only weakness.'

Vladimir Verkel had used the same excuse a hundred times. And once again his faithful accountant sighed and shook his head dismissively, and then he turned to leave.

Verkel watched him go.

As Pasternak reached the door, Verkel called after him. This time more seriously.

'If the stock drops another half a percent Viktor, call me immediately.'

Viktor Pasternak almost smiled. It was back to business. Thank god.

As Pasternak closed the door behind him, Vladimir Verkel considered his accountant's advice. It was true, buying all those 'baubles' would not make the company any money. But as he ran his hand over the top of his large antique desk, he reflected. The desk was superbly crafted from mahogany and inlaid with larch wood, a stunningly beautiful piece of furniture.

The desk had been rescued from the old firm of Bolin's the jewellers in St Petersburg and Vladimir Verkel had it lovingly restored. It was over a hundred years old and was apparently, originally from Smolensk.

Vladimir loved it, and that was because he loved only the best.

He sat there in a moment of contemplation.

'No Viktor' he thought to himself. 'You're wrong my friend'.

Vladimir Verkel had two passions. One was making money, vast amounts of money.

His other was a passion Russian Art.

Verkel was a proud man who was even prouder of his country. He had lived through a difficult period, when Mother Russia had finally broken free from the strangulation of Communism. That freedom had allowed people like Vladimir Verkel to once again breathe in the sweet smell of capitalism and with it, success.

Verkel's plain and simple philosophy was that man was a hunter, a trader or a dealer. Man's natural instinct was to acquire, whether by strength or by guile, it didn't matter which. It was the survival of the fittest and the cleverest that made the greatest of leaders. He had always been of the opinion that Communism was nothing more than mass manipulation. Those self-righteous hypocrites who talked their way to the top had never achieved their position by merit. Lenin and Stalin were just shameless bullies who fooled and then controlled the masses. Once they took control they made themselves and those around them beyond reproof. It was the same the world over. From Lenin to Stalin to Brezhnev, all of them, along with the other higher ranks of the communist party. They never went hungry when the rest of Russia starved.

In the Far East, Chairman Mau did exactly the same. He was the fattest man in China.

In Vladimir Verkel's eyes, man should be a free spirit, not an ant.

Vladimir Verkel's love of Russian Art was world renowned.

He was originally thrust into public limelight when he completed a deal to buy several of the legendary Faberge Royal Easter Eggs from an American collector. They were bought for an undisclosed sum but the cost was estimated to be at around a hundred million dollars.

Viktor Pasternak nearly had a fit.

Verkel had them installed in his private museum in St Petersburg, along with his other precious artefacts. There were beautiful paintings, fine ceramics and dazzling jewellery, all created by the finest Russian artists and craftsmen. All were collected and stored and displayed there.

Vladimir Verkel had a true appreciation of his country's artistic culture. Those artefacts and that culture had been stolen and lost and misappropriated. Vladimir had always known that he had more money than he could ever spend, and long ago had decided that he wanted to be remembered as a philanthropist and not just a wealthy tycoon. He wanted to give something back to Mother Russia. His gift would be to try and return some of his country's unique artistic heritage back where it belonged.

Vladimir Verkel was born in the fifties and brought up in the sixties.

At that time the Russian people were living under President Khrushchev's cosh, and life in the USSR was more than bleak. Everyone queued for food in shops that had empty shelves. The men at the top had more important issues to deal with. Russia was quickly losing out on the 'space race' with America, and rather regrettably, it had also suffered the embarrassment of being caught out by the USA when trying to ship nuclear missiles into Cuba through the back door. That caused an international incident and the world had held its breath as President Kennedy's finger hovered over the nuclear red button. Khrushchev then suffered the humiliation of having to turn his ships around and bring them back home with their tails set firmly between their legs.

That incident would also ruin America's relationship with Cuba for another fifty years.

Thirty years later, relations between Russia and Cuba would also be tested, when the Russian leader Mikhail Gorbachev dispensed with communism altogether. Up until then Russia had subsidised the whole of the Cuban sugar industry, and most of that sugar was then exported back to Russia. Communist Cuba had vast areas of land dedicated solely to the growing of sugar cane, specifically for the Russian market. However with the collapse of Russia's economy in 1991, all that came to an end. Russia's demand for Cuban sugar ended and with it Cuba's entire economy collapsed too.

The end of the sugar industry devastated Cuba's finances and made the country even poorer than it already was.

Anyone who could fled to the USA via Miami, which was almost within spitting distance.

The rest of the population just sat there and waited for President Fidel Castro to die.

Communism, an impossible dream for some and a complete disaster for everyone else.

But for Vladimir Verkel, everything had started to fall into place.

Verkel was a devotee of all things Russian, except for its one national institution. Whilst the rest of his countrymen and women habitually drank vodka in copious amounts, Vladimir Verkel would never touch a drop. In fact he was an adamant teetotaller and throughout his life would never touch alcohol at all.

Verkel was born and brought up the small industrial town of Podolsk. Though the town was fairly well populated, it was a grimy and non eventful sort of place which lay a hundred kilometres south of Moscow. He and both of his parents lived in a cramped apartment there in one of the many nondescript state-built tower blocks.

The town's main employer was the local state run steelworks. Vladimir Verkel's father had worked there for most of his life. Apart from the steelworks there was nothing much else in the way of employment in Podolsk, and at the age of fifteen Vladimir started working there too. Vladimir's father worked in the foundry at the steelworks. As for his mother, she did very little else but drink.

Vladimir Verkel's parents both drank habitually. In the town of Podolsk on a Saturday night there wasn't much else to do. On most weekends, a bottle of vodka would be placed on the kitchen table and was then consumed, and then another, until his parents were both senseless and one of them would usually collapse.

In the end it was the vodka that killed his father. Verkel Senior staggered into work one Monday morning still half drunk. He and Mrs Verkel had been celebrating her birthday the previous evening which had involved drinking even more booze than usual. During the morning Mr Verkel had a dizzy turn, he inadvertently pulled the wrong handle and was immediately engulfed in a stream of red hot molten iron.

The company paid for the funeral.
After the funeral, the company issued the widow Verkel with some worthless company shares as a form of compensation. At some point, it was deemed that the shares could be handed back and they were considered to be a form of pension. At some point.

Following that incident young Vladimir Verkel became the family breadwinner. As a token gesture the company did promote him. They took him off the shop floor and into the offices. For Vladimir it was a start.

It was the beginning.

Russia in the sixties and seventies was without doubt a depressingly austere country to live in. Poverty, corruption and a general shortage of just about everything made most people's lives utterly miserable.

Like everyone else young Vladimir Verkel had to live with it. Unlike everyone else however, he wasn't ready to accept it.

Working in the offices had enlightened young Vladimir. Instead of working on the shop floor where all he ever did was carry, lift or move things. He now had time to reflect and he was suddenly working with figures and numbers, and it all fascinated him. He also had more time. At that point and almost by accident Vladimir Verkel decided to start up his own business.

One Friday evening as he was walking home from work, Vladimir was passing the state run liquor store. He would have been around eighteen years old at the time.

A man was unloading a truck and stacked on the back of the truck were cases of vodka. The vodka had come from the local government warehouse and there was a regular delivery to the store. As he walked towards the truck Vladimir took notice of the man's timing.

It was as simple as that.

The man, the driver of the truck, would pick up a case of vodka and carry it through to the back of the store, then he would come back out and repeat the process. As Vladimir walked past the truck, the man had just picked up another case and was carrying it into the store again. It was just an impulse really, but as the man disappeared through the door, Vladimir lifted one of the cases of vodka off the back of the truck and disappeared around the corner with it. In a country full of inefficiencies, the vodka was never even missed.

On the Saturday night, Vladimir sat in his bedroom and waited until around ten o' clock. He knew Russia's drinking habits and he knew by that time most of his countrymen would already be drinking. Those who could afford it. His case of stolen vodka contained twelve bottles. He put the bottles into two bags and went out of the apartment up a flight of stairs to the next floor.

He knocked on the first door and a man in a vest appeared. Vladimir offered him a bottle of vodka at three quarters the normal state fixed price. For some reason, the man looked over Vladimir's shoulder, it was a Russian habit. The man nodded and went to get him the money. Once the transaction had taken place, Vladimir moved on to the next apartment.

The same thing happened again, Vladimir handed over the vodka, and no questions asked.

After he had knocked on ten more doors he had sold the lot. He then went back downstairs and back to his own apartment and counted the money in his bedroom. It made him laugh out loud, it had been so easy.

The next Friday, he dared himself to do it again. He did, and successfully. On the Saturday night he once again knocked on those same doors and again the money was readily handed over, no questions asked.

Later in his bedroom, Vladimir Verkel understood one thing. That he suddenly had a business.

He also realised something else. He would somehow have to change his supply.

It was fairly obvious to Vladimir that at some point he would definitely get caught.

So the following week Vladimir approached the driver of the truck and offered him cash for a case of vodka. He offered him what was a decent price for stolen goods and then waved the money in front of the driver's face. They did the deal and this was the start. The following week the driver agreed to bring him two cases of Vodka and that was the beginning. More was to follow. Six weeks later Vladimir greased the right person's palm and got his own ground floor apartment, it was perfect for deliveries.

His regular driver would load up the truck and deliver the cases of vodka straight to what had become Vladimir Verkel's ground floor 'warehouse'.

Within six months he was supplying vodka to most of the apartments in his block and the block next door. He had one rule however, he would only sell them one bottle at a time.

The money was beginning to roll in.

Two things happened to Vladimir Verkel during that time and both would influence his life.

Firstly was that, on the odd occasion, some of his regular customers were a little short of money. It had been his very first customer, the 'man in the vest', who on finding himself short of cash offered Vladimir some of the steelwork company shares as part payment. By that time, things in Russia were so bad that employees everywhere were being paid part cash, part shares. Vladimir accepted the shares and that was that.

Word got out that Vladimir Verkel would sell his vodka and take payment in cash, plus a few shares. Since he couldn't spend them, Vladimir ended up with quite a lot of shares. He looked upon them as a form of future investment.

Ultimately, someone would want to buy them, surely.

The second influence in his life was 'old man' Leiber.

Mr Leiber lived up on the seventh floor. He was a seventy year old Jewish man who liked to take a drink of vodka at the weekend. He didn't buy vodka from Vladimir Verkel because it was cheap, he bought it because he could have it delivered to his door. Mr Leiber was of an age where he didn't want to keep struggling up and down the stairs anymore.

The first time Vladimir met Mr Leiber, the old man had invited him into his apartment. When he entered Vladimir had been astounded. The place was packed full of books and photographs and everything in the apartment appertained to Russian antiques and art and sculpture. Vladimir Verkel had been fascinated by it all. It turned out that Mr Leiber was originally a history teacher before he retired, and researching Russia's lost artefacts and lost artwork had been his lifelong hobby. Vladimir took an interest, and before long he and Mr Leiber became good friends. Vladimir would spend many an hour talking to the old man, who in turn was happy to teach him all about Russia's artworks and history. Vladimir would sit and learn all about Russian culture as Mr Leiber opened up his books and showed Vladimir the most wonderful photographs.

Vladimir had been completely spellbound by it all and it was a fascination that would never leave him.

It was Mr Leiber's tuition in those early years that instilled in him a true sense of the importance of art. Russia's lost artwork and its lost culture was important.

And as a result of that Vladimir Verkel became an avid collector.

But suddenly, Vladimir's Russia was becoming restless and everything was about to change.

Russia's youth was looking to the west and they liked what they saw. They saw it all. The fashion and the music and the style, it all seemed so exciting and so very different.

Vladimir Verkel too saw the opportunity and then began to deal in 'black market' goods. He got wind of a truck load of contraband 'western' brand jeans. The man who owned the jeans wanted to offload them and very quickly. Vladimir was in a position to buy them and buy them all, because Vladimir Verkel had the cash.

He bought the whole truckload, including the truck, and in doing that he'd spent a great deal of his hard earned money. But within two weeks he'd sold the lot and as a result had tripled his money. Vladimir Verkel was on a roll, and now he owned a truck too.

It was time to expand. He started to buy more black market contraband. Music cassettes and cassette recorders, western t-shirts, portable radios and stacks and stacks of jeans. Instead of trying to sell everything himself he started to employ 'agents' who could sell them for him.

He also started to 'lend' money at favourable rates, favourable of course for Vladimir Verkel.

His agents would lend small amounts and collect the repayments on weekly basis. Interestingly, if the borrowers at any time couldn't make their payments, Vladimir would allow them to hand over Steelwork company shares in lieu of payment for that particular week. Failing that, they would have to pay double plus a percentage on the following week.

Most lenders gladly handed over what they considered worthless bundles of papers which they usually had stuffed away in some bottom drawer somewhere.

By the end of the eighties the communist system was starting to falter and President Gorbachev's long term plan was beginning to work He issued his famous 'Glasnost' treaty, which was a proclamation for change. Suddenly the Russian people were given freedoms they had never known before. It was the beginning of free speech and a less controlled state press, and also the opportunity to start new and independent businesses.

In effect. all businesses were suddenly allowed to go into private ownership.

Vladimir Verkel understood what was happening and he saw a future, or at least one possible future. He took the chance and suddenly realised that those worthless company shares could now be worth something.

He immediately let the good people of Podolsk know that they could buy their vodka and anything else from Vladimir Verkel, and pay him with those worthless shares.

In 1991 the Russian economy collapsed and the country descended into free fall.

In Podolsk the board members of the Podolsk Steelworks held an extraordinary emergency meeting to discuss their future.

The members of the board however, were more than slightly shocked when Vladimir Verkel stormed into the meeting followed by ten of his 'agents' who were each carrying boxes full of company shares. They were even more shocked when they found out that Verkel was now the major shareholder. As his agents returned with more boxes of shares they suddenly realized that Vladimir Verkel was in complete control of their company.

Verkel immediately sacked the board, but he offered to buy their remaining shares at a reasonable price. The growing instability taking place in Russia managed to sway their pride.

In effect, they took the money and ran.

In a slight twist of fate, one of the 'agents' who had carried those boxes of shares into the board meeting that day would continue to work for Vladimir Verkel for many years to come. Vladimir had already noted that the young man was very good with figures, he could be useful. He could be an asset.

His name was Viktor Pasternak.

The following twenty years had been a white knuckle ride.

Vladimir Verkel along with Viktor Pasternak had bought and sold companies, and then bought them back again. It had been twenty helter-skelter years of dealing and financial arm wrestling and Vladimir Verkel had loved every minute of it. Together with Pasternak, he had bought up company after company, ever onwards and ever upwards. When the oil and gas markets opened up in Russia, he was cash rich and he stepped right in. Vast fortunes were made. It was virtually impossible 'not' to make money.

Vladimir Verkel became a multi millionaire, then a billionaire and then his companies became conglomerates and Verkel's personal wealth was reckoned to be astronomical.

With that wealth came the lifestyle. Properties all over the world, the helicopters, the private jet and a multitude of prestigious vehicles of all shapes and sizes.

But for Vladimir Verkel all those things were just trinkets. A rich man's trinkets of course, but trinkets nevertheless.

In truth, the only thing that Vladimir Verkel really ever vied for was Russia's lost art.

Old Mr Leiber's teachings had never left him and he had never forgotten.

And Vladimir had never forgotten the occasion, when one evening Mr Leiber had admitted that he had always wanted to live in Israel, but didn't have the money.

In later years, and to Vladimir Verkel's complete amazement, when Mr Leiber finally died he left everything in his apartment to Vladimir. The books, the photographs, everything.

In consequence, and almost in guilt, Vladimir Verkel had Mr Leiber's body flown to Israel where he was then buried in a cemetery overlooking Jerusalem.

That was when Vladimir Verkel's quest for lost Russian art and Russian artefacts had begun. He travelled the globe in a quest to buy back Russian history and Russian culture. He paid agents and contacts around the world and at all the major auction houses.

If it was Russian, the person to contact would be Vladimir Verkel.

His masterstroke had been in buying the collection of Faberge Easter Eggs before they went to auction. The art world had been stunned and the alleged amount paid for those fabulous jewelled eggs was unheard off.

Verkel acquired a sizeable building in St Petersburg and turned it into his private museum.

One section of the museum was dedicated to all things Faberge and it gave Vladimir Verkel a great sense of pride when anything appertaining to the House of Faberge was put on display there. For Verkel there was the immense satisfaction in Faberge's work being brought back to the city where it originated.

The one person however, who didn't get any satisfaction at all from Vladimir Verkel's single minded quest, was his chief accountant Viktor Pasternak. He could understand Vladimir's obsession had there been any profit in it, but to spend fortunes on all that gold and silver, and the paintings and the porcelain, and then to put everything into glass cases just to look at, seemed totally ridiculous to Pasternak. He'd had to fly around the world with Vladimir and watch as his boss signed cheques for precious artefacts for amounts of money that would have bought good small companies.

Viktor Pasternak missed the good old days when he and Vladimir were fighting to keep their heads above water and were doing deals that would make other men's eyes water. When those deals were successful he'd felt like screaming out with the excitement of it all. Those were the good old days. Nowadays Verkel Industries literally consumed companies. It had become all too easy.

So why did he stay? Viktor Pasternak had asked himself that question a hundred or more times on as many occasions. There were a number of reasons really. The money was phenomenal, as was the lifestyle. Jetting all over the world with Vladimir had always been quite exciting. And he really did enjoy Vladimir Verkel's friendship, even with all Verkel's faults.

Viktor Pasternak realised that he was too used to his way of life. He knew of course that he could retire whenever he wanted, but that would mean him spending more time at home with his wife. And unfortunately, she was a woman who he wasn't particularly fond of.

The intercom in Vladimir Verkel's office buzzed.

Verkel leant over and pressed the intercom's button.

'Yes Sonia?'

'I've got the brochure for you Mr Verkel,' said his secretary, she almost purred.

Vladimir Verkel smiled.

'Okay Sonia, let's have a look at what they've got.'

Sonia Neff clicked off the intercom. She already knew what they'd got.

Sonia had already received the electronic brochure from Christies and had printed off the photographs in the brochure directly onto high gloss photographic paper. As the prints slowly emerged from the printer Sonia picked them up and stared in awe.

There were six photographs of the most beautiful piece of jewellery she had ever seen. An opal and diamond ring that was so spectacular, the sight of it actually made her blink.

Sonia printed the description notes along with the ring details onto regular paper and then put everything into a binder before speaking to Mr Verkel on the intercom.

Everything had to be done professionally, and everything had to be done just right. Sonia Neff knew exactly what she had to do. She had to keep her boss happy, and hopefully her efficient manner might one day pay off. If Vladimir Verkel ever got his act together and finally put his hand on her leg.

As Sonia walked over to the intercom on her desk she wondered if it would ever happen. She looked the part and she dressed the part, Sonia Neff knew that. She also knew that if Mr Verkel ever laid a finger on her, she would of course, succumb.

After speaking over the intercom, Sonia went into Mr Verkel's office with the Christies brochure. She placed the brochure on the desk in front of him, like the good girl she was.

'Ah thank you Sonia,' he said, 'Now let's see what it is.'

'It's very beautiful,' said Sonia.

Verkel glanced up at her. She had already seen the brochure, obviously. And as Vladimir Verkel looked at her he couldn't help thinking 'and you are very beautiful too, Miss Sonia Neff'.

Then he opened the brochure, and suddenly his mind moved to other things. He stared at the photographs of the most incredible ring he had ever seen, and he couldn't believe it. He quickly thumbed through to the back pages to the ring's details and history and what he read made him grip the brochure in excitement. It was there, it was all there.

'The opal and diamond ring...accredited to Vasily Orlof Bratz...Faberge's Master Craftsman'.

It was what Vladimir Verkel had been looking and searching for. It was Vasily Orlof Bratz.

He looked up at his secretary.

'Sonia, find out the date of the auction. Sort out the flights and book me into The Savoy in London three days before the sale. Cancel everything else for that week. Everything.'

'Right away Mr Verkel' she said, as efficiently as ever, and she turned to leave.

As Vladimir watched those lovely legs walk away he suddenly called after her.

'And Sonia, contact Mr Pasternak will you please, let him know what's happening,' and then he smiled at her.

Sonia turned and leant her very supple body against the door.

'Whatever you say Mr Verkel.'

She smiled back and looked at him, for just one or two seconds too long.

Six weeks later Vladimir Verkel and Viktor Pasternak landed in the company private jet at London's Heathrow Airport. They were immediately taken by a Mercedes-Benz limousine to the Savoy Hotel, located on the Strand in London's bustling city centre.

On arrival they were installed in the penthouse suite. Vladimir didn't even wait for his suitcases to be brought up, he immediately picked up the phone and rang the Christies auction house and made an appointment to view the opal ring the following morning. He was going to be busy. Vladimir Verkel had plans.

Khalid Abdulla Singh looked down at his expensive gold watch. It was time to go.

Khalid Singh too was booked into one of London's more exclusive hotels. In his case it was The Ritz in Piccadilly. Khalid Singh had also flown into London, but on the previous day, and he was there with one intention on his mind.

His family, the Singh family, were one of the largest diamond merchants and specialist jewellers in Asia. They were based in the legendary 'diamond city' of Surat in India, along with many other jewellery companies there who were all plying the same trade. The city of Surat is in the Gujarat District in the north west of India and is famous for being the diamond centre of the 'new world', with an annual output larger than Antwerp or anywhere else in Europe or abroad.

In the diamond city of Surat, the Singh Diamond Company had become the largest and the most well known. There were three Singh brothers, who had inherited the business from their father when all he owned was a small but busy jewellers shop. They had taken that one small business, shaken it up and then pushed it to the top of the tree, and now their turnover was measured in millions of dollars.

The Singh Diamond Company traded and manufactured quality cut diamonds and precious stones which were sold all over the world. Back in Surat they employed over five hundred people, and added to that was their busy sales offices in central Mumbai.

And it was whilst he was in sunny Mumbai, that Khalid Singh had received a phone call from his contact in wet and windy London.

His contact had important information and at the end of their conversation Khalid Singh was given one definite piece of advice.

Get yourself over here as soon as possible.'

He had to go to London and he had to go to Christies.

Khalid Singh was on a personal mission. Two years before, he had missed an opportunity and it had been the opportunity of a lifetime. It had been the chance to make his company famous and it could have made the name 'Singh' an international brand and put them in the same league as Cartier or Bulgari, or hopefully, maybe even Faberge.

It would have also made the Singh family millions.

There were two reasons why he'd missed that golden opportunity.

The first was that Khalid Singh had not been aware of the potential.

The other was because of Vladimir Verkel.

Two years earlier, Khalid Singh had attended another auction at Christies. He had flown in from Mumbai with the intention of bidding for a spectacular ruby that had originally been mined in Burma. When Khalid Singh had inspected the gloriously deep red stone he'd been astonished by its clarity and quality, and had realised straightaway the possibility of creating something stupendous from it, once he got it back to his craftsmen in Surat. Khalid Singh knew his market and he immediately knew who would want to buy a fabulous piece of ruby and diamond jewellery. Because Khalid Singh dealt with the Arabs.

The ruby had caused a bit of a stir and at the auction that day there were several bidders who had enough money to give Khalid Singh a problem. Among them was Vladimir Verkel.

Heads turned when Mr Verkel walked into the auction room. Everyone present realised that the stakes had suddenly been raised. At that moment Khalid Singh realised that he had more than a problem. Not only could Vladimir Verkel buy the ruby, Vladimir Verkel probably had enough money to buy Khalid Singh's whole company.

The bidding started and a large coloured image of the ruby was projected onto the wall behind the auctioneer. The auctioneer himself was busy giving a brief description of the stone. The actual seller was unknown, but that was quite usual in high bidding auctions where people respected one another's anonymity. One by one the various buyers fell away and shook their heads as the price increased and the ruby floated away and out of their grasp.

In the end there were only two bidders left, it was down to Khalid Singh and Vladimir Verkel.

Khalid Singh glanced across at his opponent and then he stopped. Vladimir Verkel was looking directly at him and smiling. More than that, he was grinning. Singh put in another bid but Verkel just raised his arm, Singh put in another bid and Verkel raised his arm again. There was a hushed silence and an air of expectancy throughout the room. Khalid Singh was already fifty thousand pounds over his intended price but he was determined to try and wipe that stupid smile off the Russian's face.

'Bastard' he thought to himself. If Verkel wanted to play that game, then Khalid Singh would make him pay and pay dearly. He would keep on bidding and then at the last moment he would bow out and that would be that. At least he would have the satisfaction of knowing that the 'great' Vladimir Verkel had paid too much, far too much. If he could manage to speak to Verkel later, Khalid Singh intended to tell him with added glee, how he had been duped.

Khalid Singh nodded to the auctioneer and added another large amount to his bid. He then stood there and folded his arms. There was complete silence in the room.

'Mr Verkel? asked the auctioneer.

There was still complete silence in the room.

Khalid Singh once again glanced at Vladimir Verkel.

But Vladimir Verkel was taking no notice of the auctioneer at all. He had actually turned around and was having a discussion with his accountant.

'Mr Verkel, would you like to raise your bid?' asked the auctioneer again.

Vladimir Verkel glanced around and just shook his head, and then turned back to speak to his accountant.

'Sold to Mr Singh,' the auctioneer suddenly called out.

The room erupted.

Khalid Singh just stood there, he didn't understand what had just happened. Suddenly he was mobbed by some of the surrounding buyers who were all trying to shake his hand. But Khalid Singh was in a bit of a daze when he suddenly realised just how much he had paid.

Ten or so minutes later the fuss died down and Khalid Singh and several other of the more serious buyers had by then left the room. Curiously, Vladimir Verkel and Viktor Pasternak remained. Another two or three pieces of jewellery were auctioned off, including a beautiful diamond necklace made by Cartier, and it made decent money.

Then the next object then came up for sale. The auctioneer gave a report as the image of a stunning ring, which was crafted from diamonds and small opals, came into view on the screen behind him.

The auctioneer continued with his description.

'A beautiful diamond ring, intermixed with twelve small opals to produce a stunning effect. Thought to be Russian in origin, the ring arrived as part of a parcel of other Russian artefacts which will be sold at a later date. A rather vague history I'm afraid, but I have to tell you ladies and gentlemen that this ring is of a phenomenal design. When the light reflects through the diamonds, the opals seem to light up. The whole effect looks like a glistening flower, and I have to say, I have never seen anything like it in my life.

Now then, who will start the bidding?'

One or two bidders put up their hands, but quickly ran out of steam. The big money had already left the room.

Vladimir Verkel bought the ring for a snip.

After the auction Viktor Pasternak went off with Vladimir's chequebook to pay the Christies office for the ring.

As Vladimir stood in the foyer examining the beautiful ring, he smiled to himself. He'd done it, he had managed once more to achieve his ambition, and once more he'd acquired another important piece of Russian history. Because in his hand he held a lost ring, a ring that was once christened 'The Flower Ring'. A hundred or so years ago it was created by one of Faberge's master craftsmen, that man was Vasily Orlof Bratz, and the ring had once belonged to the Princess Tatiana Romanov, one of the daughters of Tsar Nicholas, Ruler of all Russia.

At that moment Khalid Singh strode into the Christies foyer, and instantly spotted Vladimir Verkel. He had been looking everywhere for Verkel and at that moment Khalid Singh was a very angry man.

He strode right up to Vladimir Verkel and challenged him.

'What the hell were you playing at?' he demanded.

Vladimir looked up at him.

'Ah, Mr Singh,'

'Why did you bid against me?' Khalid Singh continued angrily, 'You obviously didn't want the damn ruby.'

'No I didn't,' Vladimir Verkel replied, 'but I did need a diversion.'

'A diversion?' asked Khalid Singh, 'A diversion for what?'

'For this, Mr Singh,' and Vladimir Verkel took the ring between his finger and thumb and held it up to the light.

Khalid Singh stared at the ring, and he couldn't believe his eyes. He saw how those small diamonds reflected light back into the opals and he was amazed. He wondered how on earth it worked. Khalid Singh was totally captivated by the ring but more than that he was furious that he'd missed it.

'How the hell did you manage it Verkel?' he said, 'the details of the ring must have been hidden somewhere at the back of the catalogue.'

'I managed it because you were looking the other way Mr Singh. You all were.'

And then the penny dropped. All the fuss and attention had been drawn to the sale of the ruby. Vladimir Verkel had managed to create a diversion by raising the bidding and everyone else had missed the 'real' treasure.

Vladimir Verkel grinned, 'But you got your ruby Mr Singh. Surely that was what you wanted?'

'Yes Verkel. But I paid far too much for it and all because of you.' Khalid Singh was seething.

'Ah yes,' replied Vladimir Verkel, 'but if I remember rightly, you too were pushing up the price Mr Singh, and you were attempting to leave me high and dry and you also wanted me to pay too much. The only thing was Mr Singh, I stopped bidding first.'

Khalid Singh's eyes widened. He had been caught out. Verkel was right.

He glanced again at the ring. He should have bought it. He knew he should.

Khalid Singh sneered at Verkel.

'This isn't over yet, just you wait and see,' he said in a low threatening voice.

'Quite possibly,' Vladimir Verkel replied, rather mysteriously. And then he saw Viktor Pasternak approaching.

'Goodbye Mr Singh,' said Vladimir Verkel and he turned and walked away.

Khalid Singh just stood there. He was shaking with anger.

Back in India, Khalid Singh was the 'big' man, and everyone there danced to 'his' tune.

Vladimir Verkel had treated him like a fool, and Khalid Singh had fallen for it. He stood there and clenched his fists. It wasn't over yet. There would be other auctions and there would be other times, and next time he would be prepared.

Unfortunately for Khalid Singh, he'd been right. It wasn't over yet.

He took a deep breath and calmed himself down. He had to get his mind working again. For one, he would have to explain to his brothers why he had been so stupid, and why had he paid such an inordinate amount of money for the ruby. And though the ruby was indeed truly beautiful, he had paid far too much for it.

Khalid Singh turned and made his way to the Christies accounts office.

As he walked in and took out his chequebook, the cashier and the auctioneer were both talking to one another.

'Ah Mr Singh,' said the auctioneer as the cashier returned to his desk, 'A very good auction. Your ruby is a stunningly beautiful stone.'

'Yes,' replied Khalid Singh, though at that moment he wasn't feeling particularly excited about it.

'I'd better pay you,' he said, and he started to write out a cheque.

'Thank you Mr Singh,' said the auctioneer and he nodded to the cashier to print out a receipt.

As the printer whirred and clattered, Khalid Singh turned to the auctioneer.

'Could I ask you, who was the seller?'

'Yes,' said the auctioneer, 'the seller was Vladimir Verkel.'

Khalid Singh stopped, and stared.

'What?'

The auctioneer didn't understand.

'What did you say?' Khalid Singh asked again.

'Your ruby Mr Singh, it belonged to Mr Verkel.'

'What do you mean it belonged to Mr Verkel?' Khalid Singh suddenly demanded.

The auctioneer frowned, 'It's quite simple Mr Singh. Mr Vladimir Verkel asked us to sell his precious ruby at our auction, which we did. And you bought it.'

'But he was bidding for it too.' Khalid Singh was by then almost shouting.

'Ah well, that's Mr Verkel's prerogative. If you hadn't bought it Mr Singh, Mr Verkel would have sold it to himself and he would have still had to pay us our commission.'

Khalid Singh was speechless.

'Excuse me Mr Singh,' interrupted the cashier, 'but Mr Viktor Pasternak has just been in here. He's Mr Verkel's accountant. He's left you a note.'

And with that he passed a small white envelope to Khalid Singh.

Khalid ripped it open. Inside on a small piece of paper was a message:

'Thank you for your business'

Vladimir Verkel.

That had been two years ago and Khalid Singh had never forgotten.

He had never forgotten the ring either. He'd had go back home and explain the events to his brothers, but he'd also told them all about the 'flower' ring and the way the diamonds illuminated the other stones. Nobody knew how to do that, nobody. It had taken the best part of a year for Khalid Singh to find out about the origin of the ring, and finally its maker and creator. It was Vasily Orlof Bratz, one of Faberge's finest.

The Singh brothers had set up a laboratory in their company buildings in Surat in an effort to recreate the effect, but they'd had no success at all and finally they closed it down. But a decision had been taken. If ever something similar by Vasily Orlof Bratz ever came onto the market, then they must buy it. The plan then was to recreate the ring and from there promote their own 'house' as one of the finest and most unique jewellers in the world. Nobody could make jewellery like that, nobody, and the other Jewellery Houses would just look on and gasp in amazement.

And now Khalid Singh had been given a second chance.

On arriving in London he had immediately rung Christies Auction House and asked for an appointment. They knew Mr Singh of course, over the years Khalid Singh had been a regular buyer and seller at their jewellery auctions.

Mr Singh was interested in an opal and diamond ring that was coming up for sale. He believed that it was attributed to be by Vasily Orlof Bratz, who at one time worked for the House of Faberge in Russia. Lastly, could he come and view the ring prior to the auction.

The answer to all those questions had been a positive 'yes!'

The next day Khalid Singh arrived at Christies on King Street and was shown through to one of their private offices. One of the auctioneers and an assistant entered the office with the ring. When the jewellery box was opened and he saw what was inside, Khalid Singh, like many others before him, gasped in amazement. He had never seen anything like it before in his life. The opal was the largest he had ever seen and its internal colours were absolutely spellbinding. The turquoise and the blue and the gold, and right there in its heart, was an explosion of deep red fire. But it was the illumination of the opal that made it so remarkable. The surrounding diamonds seemed to radiate light into centre of the stone. It almost seemed to be alive.

When he got back to the Ritz Hotel, Khalid Singh made an international phone call. He rang his brothers back in India, in Surat. Khalid Singh talked to them and explained what had happened and exactly what he had seen. The ring was perfect for their plans, absolutely perfect. They unanimously decided that they must have it, whatever the cost, they must have it.

Khalid Singh and his brothers saw the ring as the future for their business. They wanted the name of 'Singh' to be recognised as one of the finest and the best.

Their future plans however, could be deemed by many to be flawed.

Khalid Singh and his brothers needed to know just how Vasily Orlof Bratz achieved his process of illumination. They needed to understand the physics of it all but to achieve that it would be necessary to take the ring apart. They planned to dismantle the ring and take a closer look at those diamonds and try to determine how it was done, if they could.

They had also discussed using the diamonds separately to illuminate different stones in different rings. They had even considered the possibility of chopping up the opal itself into thirds or quarters and making three or four rings out of it. That idea would be put on hold and was for future discussion. They would have to sit down and work out the figures.

At no point did they ever appreciate that they were destroying a work of art. And at no point did they consider that they could never reconstruct the ring, let alone understand its method.

Their plan was to discover Vasily Orlof Bratz's secret and then look at the possibility of patenting the process. Once that was done they could sit back and watch the money roll in. Which in truth, was what they'd already been doing for most of their lives?

Man's greed. It is beyond belief.

But first of all, they would have to acquire the ring.

In London's Arab Embassy, just across from Kensington Palace, Bashir al Hakim also had an interest in the ring.

He too had made a phone call. The previous week Bashir al Hakim had made a long distance call to his master in Saudi Arabia.

Bashir al Hakim was not a happy man. For quite some time he'd felt as though he had become his master's forgotten aid, and he felt that it was time to move on. But to achieve that, he would need to be looked upon with favour from his master.

Bashir al Hakim worked for Prince Hassan bin Siad, a member of the Siad Royal family, who were based in Southern Riyadh in Saudi Arabia.

Hassan bin Siad was an extremely rich man. It could have been greed, ego or just his own self importance, but it seemed to many that Hassan bin Siad was forever in the news endorsing his latest acquisition. Basically that meant anything that cost a fortune. Be it racehorses or property, football clubs or famed artwork. If anything of any value or worth came onto the market, Hassan bin Siad would attempt to buy it. Along with his vast wealth, he could just about buy anything. Unfortunately, Hassan bin Siad also considered himself a bit of a playboy, and it seemed obvious to everyone else that he had to constantly prove it.

Bashir al Hakim had made the call. He had told his master about the specialist jewellery auction at Christies and all about the opal ring. Hassan bin Siad had been dining at the time and had not been overly interested. He was also rather annoyed at being interrupted while he ate. That was until Bashir al Hakim presented him with a little more information. Information that made Hassan bin Siad put down his plate.

He was told that Vladimir Verkel would also be attending the auction.

Prince Hassan bin Siad suddenly gripped the phone and started to shout.

'That lying, cheating bastard...Vladimir Verkel'!

Over the years Vladimir Verkel, along with Verkel Industries, had stepped on Hassan bin Siad's very rich toes for far too many times. Verkel it seemed had the ability to snatch up everything that Hassan bin Siad had been interested in. Valuable acquisitions all over the world, and mostly from right under Hassan bin Siad's very greedy nose.

The whole sorry affair had started years before and culminated in the very public 'Emerald Oil Affair'.

Vladimir Verkel's company, Verkel Industries, actually owned the group that owned the Savoy Hotel, together with several other leading hotels in London. Hassan bin Siad and his entourage had been staying at one of the suites at The Savoy, when Hassan bin Siad had assaulted one of the members of staff there. The member of staff being an attractive young girl who Hassan bin Siad had taken a fancy to. He had ordered room service and when the young lady had arrived had tried to work his charms on her. When she declined his not very tempting offer, Hassan bin Siad had flown into a temper and he beat the girl quite badly. He and his entourage had then immediately left The Savoy and also the country. Charges were never pressed, unfortunately that was the way of things. However, Vladimir Verkel got to hear of the incident and he went round to the young lady's flat, where he found her with a broken nose and a badly bruised face. He compensated the young lady appropriately, together with a promise to her and the vow that one day he would get even with Mr Hassan bin Siad.

Following that incident Hassan bin Siad bought himself a huge private property in Knightsbridge where he could then assault anyone he wanted.

Vladimir Verkel's company owned an oil rig off the coast of Aberdeen in Scotland. The oil platform had been listed through a subsidiary company known as Northern Oil. The oil rig itself was named the Northern Star. And after several years of working one particular field, the oil in that area was beginning to run out. Then Northern Oil suddenly announced that it was pulling out of the Aberdeen field altogether and that the Northern Star oil rig was to be towed over to the Irish coast, five miles off Donegal, and then it was going to start drilling for oil. The government had immediately given Northern Oil a licence to drill for oil there, in an area that became known as the Emerald oil field. There had been great hopes. Once oil was discovered it would bring great prosperity to the area. Nine months later they struck oil.

However things were not that simple. During those previous nine months, Hassan bin Siad had been secretly buying every share in Northern Oil that he could get his hands on.

Hassan bin Siad had in his employ a very bright young accountant who had been personally advising him. Mahmoud Baktar was a smart young man who had approached Hassan bin Siad with some 'insider information'. Apparently Mahmoud Baktar had a cousin who worked for Northern Oil, and who had told Mahmoud, in confidence, that an oil strike at the Emerald field had been in the planning for a couple of years and that along with the huge amounts of oil there would also be huge amounts of profits. Hassan bin Siad had immediately put Mahmoud Baktar in charge of acquiring all and any shares that he could get his hands on. Mahmoud had been successful and within six months had managed to acquire more than sixty percent of the shares. By the time the Northern Star had struck oil in the Emerald field, Hassan bin Said owned nearly seventy percent of the shares. In effect, he almost owned the whole company. He then called an extraordinary board meeting which resulted in a shouting match between himself and Vladimir Verkel. Verkel was apparently astounded when he discovered that Hassan bin Siad had snatched one of his very well publicized successful companies right from under him. As a final act of arrogance Hassan bin Siad had offered to buy the remainder of Vladimir Verkel's shares. Verkel had stormed out of the meeting leaving his accountant Viktor Pasternak to agree the sale. Suddenly, Hassan bin Siad owned Northern Oil lock, stock and barrel and along with it the Emerald oil field.

They immediately began to pump oil. Two weeks later, it ran out.

Apparently the Emerald oil field turned out to be 'a drop in the ocean'. There was no real field. Apparently, there are tiny pockets of oil all over the world but most of them are never of any great consequence.

There was uproar. The tabloid newspapers had a field day with headlines such as

'Rich Arab runs out of Oil' and 'The luck of the Oilrish'. But it was the leader in the Times that really stung Hassan bin Siad. Plastered across the front page were the headlines

'Verkel outsmarts rich Arab Royal...once again'.

Hassan bin Siad was absolutely livid. But things were about to get worse.

He flew back to Riyadh to explain events to his family and also to confront his young accountant, Mahmoud Baktar.

Hassan bin Siad had every intention of throwing the stupid young man into prison where he could rot indefinitely.

However Hassan bin Siad was in for a shock. During the previous week, the youthful Mahmoud Baktar had departed from Riyadh airport and had then flown to London.

Apparently he had gone there to work for Vladimir Verkel at Verkel Industries.

Needless to say, Mahmoud didn't have any cousin working for Northern Oil either.

Hassan bin Siad had taken it all as a personal insult. He would not have the world laughing at him. And with that, he too, promised to exact his revenge.

After listening to Bashir al Hakim's ramblings, Hassan bin Siad made an immediate decision. He'd made it his priority to discover Verkel's weaknesses, and he's discovered that Russian artefacts were Vladimir Verkel's Achilles heel.

He then gave Bashir al Hakim his instructions.

'Arrange everything at your end and ring my office to sort out the flights. And inform Christies that we will attend the auction.'

Hassan bin Siad then put down the phone and he frowned.

'Vladimir Verkel...damn that bastard,' he said out loud.

Then he leant forwards and picked up his plate of food.

'This time I'll beat you Verkel. No matter what the cost.'

Bashir al Hakim rang Christies to make all the arrangements. By then he was beginning to sweat a little as he began to wonder...'Have I done the right thing?'

The auction took place four days later at one o' clock in the afternoon.

On that day the auction room at Christies was full to capacity as buyers had arrived from all over the world. This was a specialist auction and some of the world's finest jewellery was about to be bought and sold.

Khalid Singh was sitting in the central seating area where he felt he could observe most of the other buyers and get a feel for how the auction was proceeding. Very often, prices were driven on purely by the enthusiasm of the audience. He stared around the packed room, it was quite hard to see everyone. It was then that he caught a glimpse of Viktor Pasternak. Khalid Singh took a deep breath. That meant Vladimir Verkel would be about somewhere.

Vladimir Verkel, the enemy...'the bastard'.

Hassan bin Siad sat at the back of the auction room with his brother and a favourite cousin. Sitting with them was Bashir al Hakim. Bashir had specially reserved those seats. His masters required a degree of space and privacy, and could not be allowed to be confined like cattle and be jammed in with the rest of these infidels.

Through his dark sunglasses, Hassan bin Siad looked around the room and he sniffed.

All of these people looked the same to him.

The auctioneer started at one o' clock on the dot. For more than an hour some of the most beautiful jewellery in the world was sold at phenomenal prices. Images of the incredible jewellery were displayed on the large colour screen behind the auctioneer. It was all very entertaining.

But it wasn't entertaining for Khalid Singh, and certainly not for Hassan bin Siad either, as both men reread the catalogue and waited for Lot 17 to finally come up for sale.

Lot 17. Described as a stupendous opal ring, surrounded by inclusions of diamonds, and attributed to the master craftsman, Vasily Orlof Bratz, of the House of Faberge...etc, etc.

That was the description in the catalogue, and by the time Lot 17 came up for sale, both men were beginning to breathe heavily in anticipation.

Let the performance begin.

The auctioneer picked up his notes.

'Lot 17...ladies and gentlemen.'

Khalid Singh and Hassan bin Siad both looked up as the auctioneer continued.

'Lot 17 has been withdrawn from auction. We believe that it has been sold by prior arrangement.

And now please ladies and gentlemen...Lot 18.'

Khalid Singh just sat there, he couldn't believe what had just happened. He tried again to take in what the auctioneer had just said. Then he spun around in his seat. His first instinct was to try to locate Vladimir Verkel and Viktor Pasternak, but they weren't there. Khalid Singh turned again in his seat, still trying to find Verkel and Pasternak. There was suddenly a loud commotion, as the Arabs sitting at the back of the auction stood up and stormed out of the room.

The auctioneer stopped speaking for a moment and raised his eyebrows at the Arabic version of rudeness and bad manners.

The auctioneer made a sharp comment, 'You just can't put a price on 'class' ladies and gentlemen. You've either got it, or you haven't.'

At least that got a laugh.

Khalid Singh sat there for several minutes before he managed to excuse himself and leave.

Once he was out of the auction room he stood in the corridor and took out his mobile phone and rang one of his brothers in India.

He had to tell him what had happened but he had little to offer by way of an explanation.

'Do you know who bought it?' his brother asked.

'No,' replied Khalid Singh, 'I haven't a clue.'

'Who were the other buyers at the auction?' his brother again asked.

'It was packed,' said Khalid Singh, 'I couldn't see everyone. Vladimir Verkel was there somewhere...'

And then he stopped and the blood drained from his face.

Vladimir Verkel wasn't there. He never had been. His chief accountant, Viktor Pasternak had shown up to watch the fun and had then disappeared. But Verkel had never been there, and Khalid Singh new the reason why.

Because Vladimir Verkel had already done the deal.

Outside Christies auction house, a chauffeur held open the door of the silver grey Rolls Royce which Hassan bin Siad and his brother and cousin were about to get into.

Before he got into the car Hassan bin Siad turned to stare at his aid, Bashir al Hakim.

'Get out of my sight you imbecile,' he hissed.

Then he got into the back of the car.

That left Bashir al Hakim wondering about his future, as he stood there on the pavement and watched the silver grey Rolls Royce drive off into London's busy traffic.

Nilesh and Kalpna Chandry had travelled down to London on the previous day. They'd travelled there by express train and were accompanied by Paul Lancaster and his father Harry.

They were all booked into the Grosvenor Hotel in Westminster, where they were met by Mr Peter Giles. Peter Giles was Paul Lancaster's agent in London and he had prepared and organised the sale of the ring through Christies.

The five of them enjoyed an evening meal together at their hotel, where they discussed the following day's events. Eventually of course, the topic turned to money and the price that the ring might be expected to reach at auction the following day. Even though the true value of the ring was around the one hundred thousand pound mark, because of its maker and the links with Faberge it was expected to reach much more.

'Do you really think it will make over two hundred thousand pounds Mr Lancaster?' Kalpna Chandry asked Harry Lancaster.

Harry wiped his mouth with a napkin.

'Yes I do,' he replied, 'and I think the ring's historic provenance will bring out the buyers. The link with Faberge will be the key. And I also think that those same buyers may be starting to realise the talents of Vasily Orlof Bratz.'

'Anything linked to Faberge is becoming increasingly collectable Mrs Chandry,' added Peter Giles, 'Christies are really quite excited about it.'

'Do you think that a quarter of a million pounds is feasible?' Nilesh asked him.

Peter Giles took a deep breath.

'It's hard to say really, auctions can be unpredictable. Sometimes it's down to the buyers and it's also all about who turns up. If the ring bore the Faberge stamp and had come directly from the House of Faberge, then it would be a different thing altogether. But at the moment we're running on conjecture. There are links of course, but not absolutely direct links.'

'To be honest with you Mr Giles,' said Nilesh Chandry, 'we would really be happy with anything we get. After all, we did get the ring for free.'

Peter Giles stared at him for a moment. 'Just how much would you accept Mr Chandry?'

'Anything over two hundred thousand would be nice,' Nilesh replied with a grin.

Paul Lancaster glanced across the table at Peter Giles and looked at him for an instant.

It was a very strange question. 'Just how much would you accept?' Paul Lancaster thought about the question and also noticed the slight change in the tone of Peter Giles's voice.

It had been a serious question. But how serious, and why?

At the end of the evening everybody wished each other a good night and went to their separate rooms. Everyone was full of anticipation for the forthcoming day.

Peter Giles jumped into the back of a waiting black cab and gave the driver his home address. As the taxi set off into the slow moving traffic, Peter Giles pulled out a mobile phone from his inside pocket. He scrolled through his contacts until he came to the right name. Then he pressed a button and the phone began to ring. Several seconds later, someone picked up.

'Hello Peter.'

Peter Giles smiled.

'Hello...and yes, we need to talk.'

'Then you'd better come over right away.'

It was Vladimir Verkel.

Peter Giles switched off his phone and then called out to the taxi driver.

'Change of plan. Take me to The Savoy.'

The next morning at ten o clock Nilesh and Kalpna Chandry were sitting nervously in their room. They'd already had their breakfast. A young girl in uniform had arrived with a trolley stacked with bread, toast and boiled eggs. There was jam and honey and marmalade and a large pot of freshly brewed coffee. Nilesh and Kalpna had indulged themselves, they weren't really used to hotel luxury. Then they had showered and readied thmselves for the day ahead, it was all a bit daunting. Nilesh wore his best suit and tie and Kalpna had applied some extra makeup, just in case.

There was a knock at the door and Nilesh opened it. It was Paul Lancaster and his father Harry. Both men were dressed smartly and that made Nilesh feel a little better.

'Come in, come in,' said Nilesh, and he offered them some coffee. Both men declined.

'Actually I've ordered some more.' Kalpna said to her husband, 'that pot's gone cold.'

'It's okay,' said Paul Lancaster, 'there's plenty of time. We've just got to wait for Peter Giles to arrive. He said he would ring me when he was in the foyer downstairs.'

A minute or two later the same uniformed young lady arrived with their coffee. As Kalpna was sorting out the cups, Paul Lancaster's mobile phone rang.

It was Peter Giles.

'Good morning,' said Paul Lancaster.

'Yes hi,' came the reply, 'Where are you Paul?'

'We're in Nilesh and Kalpna's room, we were just waiting for you to call. Do you want us to meet you down in the foyer?'

'Ah, so you're all together then?' said Peter Giles, 'That's good. And no, I need to come up and speak to you all. What room is it Paul?'

Paul Lancaster told him the room number and the phone clicked off.

Paul looked at his phone and then at his father.

'That's strange. He's on his way up here. He wants to speak to us.'

'You think something has gone wrong?' asked Harry.

Paul Lancaster looked at them all and he shrugged his shoulders.

A couple of minutes later there was a tap on the door and Paul Lancaster instinctively went to open it.

Standing in the hallway was Peter Giles. With him were two men.

Paul Lancaster stood there for a moment, he wasn't expecting this.

Peter Giles was the first to speak. 'May we come in please?'

Paul Lancaster just stood there as the three men walked into the room.

'I would like to apologise for the intrusion,' said Peter Giles, 'but we need to talk to you before we go to the auction. Nilesh, Kalpna, Paul and Harry, I would like to introduce you to Mr Vladimir Verkel and Mr Viktor Pasternak".

It was all slightly surreal, but they all shook hands.

'Mr Verkel would like to speak to you,'said Peter Giles.

With that, Vladimir Verkel stepped forward.

'Hello everybody, and please, do call me Vladimir. And this gentleman is my accountant Viktor Pasternak. And I'm here today because I need to speak to you all. I want to talk to you about your opal ring, and I'd like you to hear me out before we all go off to the auction at Christies. You see, I may have a deal for you that could be advantageous to all of us.

You may not know this, but I am Russian. I am a Russian citizen and for quite a while I've been committed to reinstating Russia's lost artwork. I don't intend to lie to you, I am a great lover and collector of Russian art and all things Russian. As an avid collector, I have a small museum in

St Petersburg where I'm trying to put a together a collection of Russia's finest treasures and I have to tell you, your magnificent opal ring would fit beautifully into my collection. I already have one or two pieces by Vasily Orlof Bratz, he was a truly wonderful craftsman. Did you know that he's buried here in London...No?'

Nilesh and Kalpna just shook their heads.

'Anyway,' Vladimir continued, 'you want to sell the ring and I want to buy it. Now we could go to auction and fight over it, of that there's no doubt, but I may have a better plan. I've spoken to Viktor here and he tells me that the starting price for the ring would probably be around one hundred thousand pounds, and then would be open to offers. But he tells me that there is every chance of the ring selling for more and he has come up with an estimated value of somewhere between two hundred and two hundred and fifty thousand pounds. Am I right?'

'You possibly are right,' said Paul Lancaster. He had been listening to Vladimir Verkel and he felt that at some point he should make his presence known. Later he would also be having words with Peter Giles about this very irregular meeting. Paul Lancaster knew exactly who Vladimir Verkel was, and he knew all about Vladimir Verkel's private museum and his legendary purchase of the Faberge Royal Easter Eggs.

Vladimir Verkel smiled at Paul, he understood.

Then he continued, 'I have spoken to my accountant this morning and we have discussed the matter. Two hundred and fifty thousand pounds is quite a lot of money.'

Paul Lancaster took a sharp intake of breath. Verkel was going to make a cheap offer and Paul was suddenly ready to step in.

'However,' said Vladimir Verkel, 'Viktor and I gave the matter some consideration, and we then came up with a figure of half a million pounds.'

Nilesh and Kalpna went rigid.

Vladimir Verkel turned to his accountant. 'That was the figure wasn't it Viktor?'

Viktor Pasternak was expressionless, he just nodded. But he wasn't impressed at all, because he and his boss had never had any such conversation.

Paul Lancaster wasn't impressed either, but for different reasons. He wasn't entirely happy with this sudden show of good will.

'You are aware that there are other interested buyers Mr Verkel,' he said, 'we know that there are other interested parties who could quite possibly equal your offer.'

Vladimir Verkel smiled. 'You are quite right Mr Lancaster and that is why I am here. I have no intentions of getting into a bidding war unless I have to. This morning Viktor came up with a figure of half a million pounds. That was his figure. However it wasn't mine,'

Victor Pasternak's head suddenly shot up. What on earth was Vladimir doing?

Vladimir Verkel looked at them all.

'So this is the deal I am going to offer you. It's a onetime only deal, so you must take it or leave it. I am prepared to pay you one million pounds for the opal ring. That is one million pounds to Mr and Mrs Chandry in total. Along with that I will pay Mr Lancaster's commission and also Mr Giles's commission. I will also pay any expenses incurred at Christies.'

Viktor Pasternak coughed and coughed loudly enough to catch his boss's attention.

'Can I have a quick word Vladimir?' he said in a low voice.

'No you may not, old friend" replied Vladimir Verkel, in a tone that told his accountant that he may be overstepping his mark.

'One million pounds" said Vladimir Verkel "That's my offer. Either that or we go to auction, and at auction you must take your chances. The ring may make over half a million pounds, but then again it may not. It may only sell for two hundred thousand pounds, who knows? But I wonder if anyone will actually bid a million pounds. Again, who knows? However, I do think my offer is very fair, and I think it's more than you expected. So, the decision is yours.'

Paul Lancaster glanced over at his father. Harry Lancaster then gave the slightest of nods. He was nobody's fool.

Paul then turned to Nilesh and Kalpna and saw the look in their eyes. It was unmistakable.

'I think we have a deal Mr Verkel,' and he reached out and shook Vladimir Verkel's hand.

The tension broke, and suddenly everyone was talking at once. As an act of goodwill Vladimir Verkel decided to order some champagne for his guests.

It wouldn't be a problem. After all, he did own the hotel.

Viktor Pasternak sighed and stood there in silence. He never would understand his boss.

As his guests drank their champagne, Vladimir Verkel asked Viktor Pasternak for the chequebook. He then wrote out a cheque for one million pounds and handed it over to a still shocked and incredulous Nilesh Chandry. Nilesh and Kalpna couldn't help but grin with happy smiles of excitement.

Vladimir Verkel then asked Peter Giles to ring Christies and tell them to withdraw the ring from auction, and to also advise them that he would be sending someone down there immediately to collect the ring.

Verkel then turned to his accountant and spoke something in Russian.

'Viktor, go to Christies and pick up the ring, and also call in at the auction room before the biding starts. Stay there for a while. I want to know who's there.'

Viktor Pasternak nodded and went off to do his boss's bidding.

After another ten minutes of pleasant banter, Vladimir Verkel once again shook hands with everyone and then he went to leave.

As he left he asked both Paul Lancaster and Peter Giles send their respective bills to him at Verkel Industries head office, and he gave them both his business card.

Not that Peter Giles needed one.

Once Verkel had gone Peter Giles turned to Paul Lancaster.

'I really need to apologise to you Paul,' he lied, 'Mr Verkel rang me early this morning and said he needed to meet us all. He wouldn't talk over the phone but he picked me up in his limo and he discussed his plans on the way here. It's all been very much out of the blue,' Peter Giles lied again.

Paul Lancaster just shrugged, 'Not to worry Peter, it all seems to have been a success. Though I must admit, I was really looking forward to the auction.'

After another ten minutes Peter Giles also left. He went downstairs and through the foyer and then got into a black cab. As he set off through Westminster's busy traffic, Peter Giles smiled to himself. He was a happy man. Six months ago, when Paul Lancaster had phoned him and told him about Vasily Orlof Bratz's opal ring, Peter Giles had immediately contacted Vladimir Verkel. He'd worked for Vladimir Verkel on previous occasions, when he'd assisted Mr Verkel in procuring two or three very important Russian artefacts. And Vladimir Verkel had in turn been very generous.

Peter Giles had organised the sale of the opal ring at Christies. But there had never been any intention of going to auction, none at all. It had been planned from the very start that Mr Verkel would buy the ring by private arrangement.

Yes, Peter Giles was a happy man. In an envelope in his inside pocket was a cheque for thirty thousand pounds. Thank you very much Mr Verkel.

It was Peter who got Christies to send Vladimir Verkel the notification in the first place. And then some months ago Peter Giles had spoken to him all about Vasily Orlof Bratz's spectacular opal ring, and that he'd come up with a plan. Vladimir Verkel had listened and agreed. He also promised Peter the money on the successful completion of sale

Vladimir Verkel sat comfortably in the back of his limousine as he was being driven back to The Savoy Hotel. It had been a success, a total success.

Peter Giles had managed to acquire a list of the people who were attending the auction. There were several contenders, one of whom was Khalid Singh of the Singh Diamond Company. Vladimir Verkel had problems with Singh in the past but estimated that Khalid Singh would run out of steam at around the million pound mark. It was Hassan bin Siad who was going to be the real problem. Hassan bin Siad was the enemy. Vladimir Verkel had publicly humiliated Hassan bin Siad and quite rightly too. The man was an arrogant pig. However, Hassan bin Siad had the family money behind him, which was estimated to be over five hundred billion pounds.

Oil had been very kind to the Siad Family.

Vladimir Verkel knew that Hassan bin Siad would be at the auction for one reason, and one reason only, and that would be to try and exact his revenge. And in that frame of mind, Hassan bin Siad may have gone to five million, even ten million pounds, because he just wouldn't care. However, there would have been one definite outcome. The opal ring would have cost Vladimir Verkel a whole lot more.

The added touch in all of this was that he had sent Viktor Pasternak to the auction, and that would have convinced those main buyers that Vladimir Verkel would also be present, somewhere.

Nilesh and Kalpna Chandry returned home, along with Paul and Harry Lancaster.

For Nilesh and Kalpna it would mean a new start and a new future.

In the end they would buy five terraced houses at roughly one hundred thousand pounds each. After having them tidied up and painted and decorated the houses were all rented out for decent money. The Chandry's also extended and finished off their own house and then immediately put it up for sale. They were suddenly in the property market and were on to a better and brighter future.

Three months after the purchase of the opal ring Vladimir Verkel and Viktor Pasternak were in Verkel's private museum in St Petersburg, Russia.

They both stood looking at a large free-standing glass display case, which was full of jewellery dedicated solely to the work of Vasily Orlof Bratz. Amongst the glittering pieces was a stunning blue sapphire ring. The sapphire had been cut into an oval shape and was encased within a large piece of blue lapis lazuli gemstone. The stones had been set onto a pure silver mount and decorated with Greek scrolls. There too was the famous Flower ring, with its dozen small glowing opals. The opals sparkled under the bright lights, illuminated by the mix of equally small bright diamonds. Also in the display was the most exquisite brooch, made from a fabulous pear shaped ruby. The blood red stone was set into a twisted platinum and white gold mount surrounded by five 'brilliant' cut diamonds and on the narrow 'stalk' end of the ruby was an exquisite square cut green emerald. The contrast in colour and shape was ingenious.

In the absolute centre of the glass display case and holding pride of place was the beautiful opal and diamond ring. The ring that Vasily Orlof Bratz had created for his lost Princess. The bright lights in the display cabinet shone down onto the ring and the diamonds threw their light into the centre of that most fabulous opal and made it shine as though it had a life of its own.

Long ago, Pavel Bratz's true gift to his son Vasily Orlof, was the inherited skill and artistry to create a masterpiece, something that was so extraordinarily beautiful, it was almost priceless.

Viktor Pasternak looked across at his boss and was slightly bemused. Vladimir Verkel was just staring at the jewelled ring, it was as though he was spellbound.

After a while Vladimir Verkel turned to his long suffering accountant.

'What do you thing Viktor. Is it not the most beautiful thing you've ever seen?'

Viktor Pasternak just shook his head, he didn't understand.

'Yes Vladimir, it is beautiful. But at a million pounds, was it really worth it?'

Vladimir Verkel turned back to look at the ring. It was a work of art. He stared at the opal and he smiled. He knew that Viktor Pasternak would never understand the importance of the ring, or for that matter, any of the other pieces of exquisite jewellery that glittered and sparkled within the brightly lit display case. In truth, Vladimir Verkel had always known that his accountant regarded the museum as a complete folly and a waste time and money, because where was the profit in it all? The artefacts in the museum would never be sold, never in Vladimir Verkel's lifetime anyway. And even after that, it was Verkel's intention to pass on the museum and the whole of its contents over to the State for the benefit of the Russian people. Vladimir Verkel had become the curator of his own private museum, his and his alone.

Verkel acknowledged his own weakness, if it was a weakness. His desire to attain and to acquire the historic art of Russia had consumed him, and it still consumed him. Within the walls of his museum was so much history, and so many incredible objects, which had brought immense pleasure to some and untold suffering to others.

It was a legacy, a legacy that he would leave to others, with the simple hope that he might be remembered. Money was not important anymore, not to Vladimir Verkel.

He had done all of this because of his dedication and devotion to the only thing he had possibly ever loved, and the only thing he had ever really cared about.

All and everything, for Mother Russia.

Adieu.

Lightning Source UK Ltd.
Milton Keynes UK
UKHW012308200921
390912UK00002B/478

9 781911 596394